RISE OF THE DRAGONSLAYERS

EVAN OLIVER

BOOKS & BARBELLS PRESS

Contents

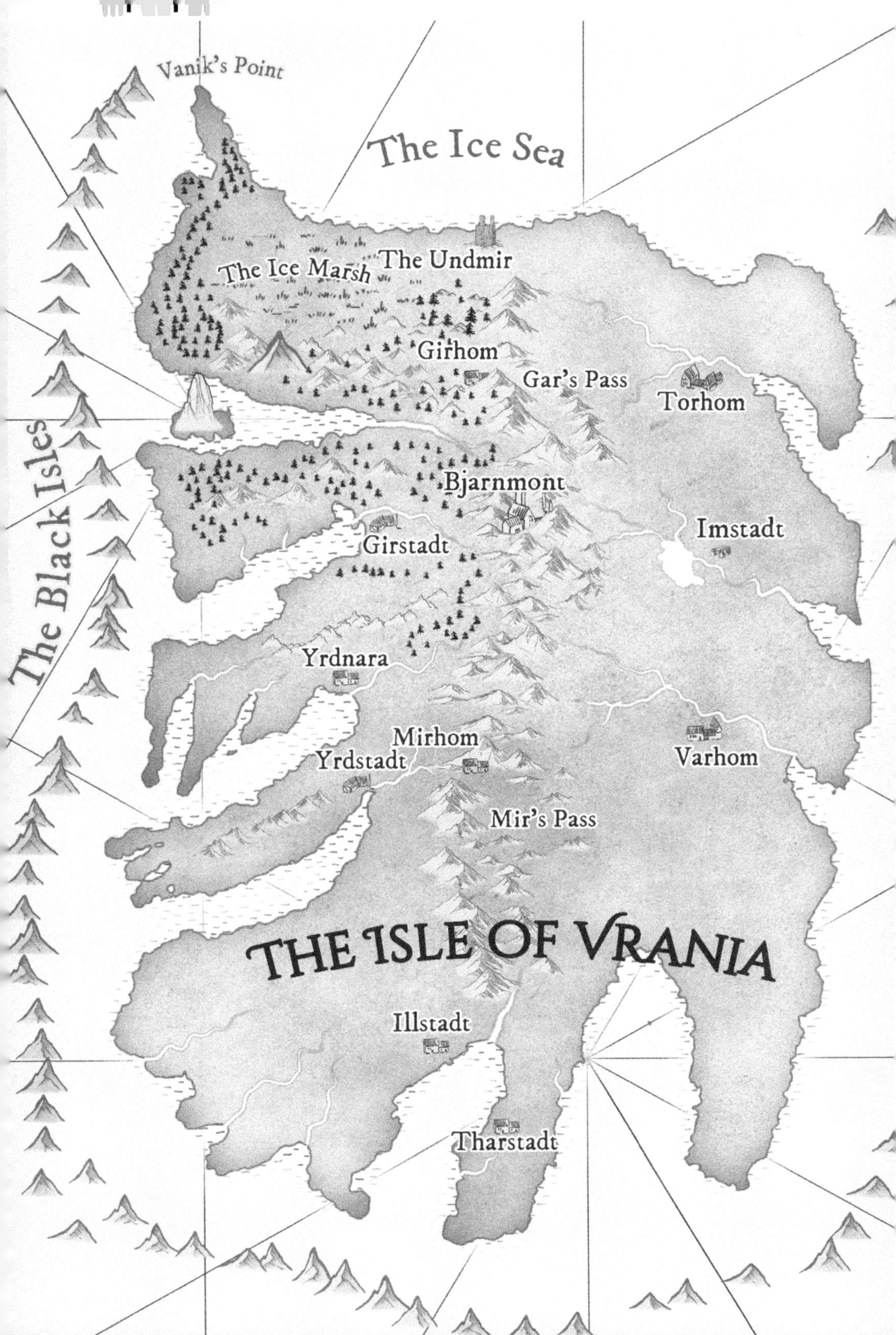

Vanik's Point
The Ice Sea
The Ice Marsh
The Undmir
Girhom
Gar's Pass
Torhom
The Black Isles
Bjarnmont
Imstadt
Girstadt
Yrdnara
Mirhom
Varhom
Yrdstadt
Mir's Pass
THE ISLE OF VRANIA
Illstadt
Tharstadt

KARIK'S FIRST BATTLE

BOOK I

PROLOGUE

The wind and snow were howling outside, but within the hall a fire was blazing. Many years before, they had built the hearth first, laying the long stones end to end, before raising the beams around it. Now, although the edges of the hall disappeared into the shadows, the great fire burned hot and bright in its centre.

At the benches, wives and husbands polished off the last of the evening's meal, and the scent of roasted meat and fresh bread mingled with the smell of smoke in the air. More than one cheek was flushed, as cups of sweet mead and dark beer were supped by those who had worked all spring, summer and harvest to prepare for the winter. Now that the snow had come, it was time to enjoy their labours. Down by the fire, the children played games of bones, or busied themselves with the puppies and hounds which lolled about, as close to the fire as they dared.

As conversation slowed, the lord seated at the high table leaned forward, peering through the gloom. "It is time, I think, for a tale."

From the corner, an old man rose slowly and moved toward the fire, a long deerskin cloak hanging from his shoulders. "So, then..." his rough voice was deep and soft, yet still clearly heard throughout the hall, "what tale should be told this night, hmm?" He looked over the children, who were clustering around him.

"Of Throlf Dragonsbane, perhaps?"

He glanced from one child to the next, his gaze settling on one young boy who still toyed with a dark, speckled puppy. "Many know how he slew the great dragon, but few still tell of how he fought the nine fey folk, on the Hill of Karkarost."

The young boy now looked up, and the bard smiled. "Or, perhaps you would hear tell of Alheim the Ancient, and his battles against the demons of the north?"

"We have heard Faerie stories enough," one of the older men said, with a chuckle. "Let us hear another story – one the children do not already know by heart."

The bard's eyebrows dipped low, as he scanned the upper benches for whomever had spoken. "Very well; no Faerie stories." He cleared his throat. "A tale of real men, then. Of heroes and kings; of loves lost and loves won; of sacrifice... and of death."

"Sounds like a fine story," another of the men spoke up, "if it is as you say."

"I shall tell," the bard said, looking about the room, as if gathering himself, "the saga of Karik Haldsson."

The hall suddenly went quiet, and many of the elders set down their cups.

After a moment, as the light from the fire flickered on the bard's face, the lord spoke: "It has been some time since that name was spoken on this side of the sea."

"Even so," the bard said, smiling at the children, who were now looking at him with eyes wide and mouths agape, "the tale is a good one, though some still fear to speak it.

"The place to begin is, of course, at the beginning..."

Untying the deerskin, the bard let it fall, rolled back his shoulders and made ready.

"So. I shall tell first how Karik was driven from his home, and how this led him to a dragon..."

Exile

It is said that the isle of Vrania is named for the trickster Vranr. He was so cunning, the stories say, that the seven kings turned away from their wars against the dragons to imprison him on the distant isle, barring his return with treacherous rocks and storming seas. Whatever the truth of the old stories, the isle of Vrania is harsh beyond measure, its shores surrounded by the tumultuous waters of the great sea, and swept by the frigid winds and storms which come howling down from the icy North Sea. Hard and short are the lives of those who live there, as they strive, year on year, to hoard enough food to last the winter.

In the days when Karik was young, King Viglir ruled the eastern plains of Vrania, from the sea to the first mountains, where his people raised herds of cattle. King Jarhost, from his great hall on Bjarnmont, ruled the eastern portion of the isle, from the mountains to the western coast, where the poorest of Vrania worked in their little fishing villages.

One of these villages was called Yrdnara, and it was here that Hald and Elva made their life, with their sons: Hald Haldsson, the eldest, who bore his father's name; Karik, the second born; and Mirn, who was the youngest.

Like the other villages along the coast in those days, there was often too little food in Yrdnara to last the winter. Some years, the harvest was better and the fishing less sparse, and so it was only the very old and very sick who breathed their last, as the land was buried in snow. But, on other years the harvest was barren, the inlets bare of fish. The cold would come, and in the summer there would be many new graves on the slope, north of the village.

Because of this, in the years when the harvest was at its worst, and the winter looked at its most grim, it was customary to send out the young men most likely to make a way for themselves. Some of these outcasts made their way deep into the mountains, and lived lonely lives among the rocks, surviving off of the meagre provision of the mountains. Others took the path from the sea to Bjarnmont, where their king held court, and launched cattle raids upon the plains of Viglir. This had not taken place for several years when Karik was born, and happened only once when he was a very young child.

The people of Yrdnara were hardworking, and laboured from dusk to dawn, gathering food and preparing their village against the storms which plagued them. In Karik's sixteenth summer, however, the fish dived deep before their time, and the fjord surrendered little to their nets. Then came the winter storms, far earlier than usual, and much of the meagre crop was destroyed. The villagers tightened their belts, and helped each other as best they could, sharing what food they had. Meanwhile, Hald took his sons into the forest, hunting whatever they could find in the snow.

In the evenings, Elva showed her sons how to sing and tell tales, for songs make the cold and hungry nights of winter pass more easily. But, even the mightiest songs cannot hold back death forever, and the god of the underworld was busy that winter.

Karik's uncle, Halric, died of frostbite, as the first icicles formed on the rooves of Yrdnara; Grita, the wise woman of the village, was placed beneath the snow as the winter solstice drew near.

On the longest, darkest night of winter, before the door of every house was built a bonfire, to burn through the night and ward away Dunharvic, the horseman of the dead. But, it was in vain, for of the nearly one hundred souls who lived in Yrdnara, twelve did not wake the next morning. And, when Karik rose from his bed after Dunharvic's Night, he found his brother Mirn sick. It was the cold sickness, born of too much cold and too little food.

Elva tended him as best she could, and Hald took his two sons deep into the forests, to seek out anything they might eat. They hunted as often as they could, by sun or by moon, but the storms often drove them inside, even as their food grew less every day.

Then, Hald grew ill, and Karik hunted only with his older brother, and often alone, as he attempted to cover more ground. Many times, their father had warned them of the treacherous snowdrifts – the deceptive ice packs, where a man could be lost in an instant – but, each time, Karik found his way home through the storms. And, each time he found Mirn sicker than before.

In the end, Karik found that all of his effort was for nothing; as the snows deepened, in the heart of winter, Mirn breathed his last, and Karik helped his father bury his brother, on the northern slope which overlooked their village.

The wind howled outside their small hut, as the snow piled high against its walls. Karik stared into the fire, as he sat there with his mother. His father and brother were asleep, and it was Karik's turn to tend the fire.

"I miss him," Karik said, simply.

He felt his mother look up at him, but his own eyes remained on the fire, watching the small flames gnawing away at a damp log. With a pop, each flame would then go out, winking away into the few glowing coals. Karik felt among the sticks at his feet for some dry wood, which he could use to coax the coals back into flame.

Slowly, his mother rose and came to sit beside him.

"We will meet the dead again," Elva said, quietly. "There will be a day when we are rejoined, in the halls of the All Father."

Karik's fingers were almost numb from the cold, but he found a pair of sticks which felt more dry than wet, and placed them on the coals surrounding the damp log. "Yet, I miss my brother still." He laid the sticks in place and blew on them gently, until a small flame flickered to life. He looked up, to see the glint of a tear on his mother's face, reflected in the fire's light.

"I do as well," she said, softly. "I miss him very much."

Karik stared into the fire, watching the flames rise higher. He thought of how Mirn had coughed, toward the end, his whole body seizing and shivering with cold. He thought about how Mirn had suffered, and how his father had suffered, and how his mother still suffered. A few more sticks set the fire to crackling again, and he saw the log begin to catch, at last.

It suddenly occurred to him that his mother had watched Mirn grow sicker alone. While he had distracted himself by hunting, she had watched his brother every day, as his cough worsened, his shivering grew more violent, and he slipped farther and farther away.

"I am sorry," he said, quietly; "he was your son before he was my brother."

Elva gave a sad smile. "Next year will be worse," her voice shook as she said it. "It may be that they will throw lots for outcasts."

"We will hunt," Karik said, firmly, "and the fishing will be better."

"Even so," Elva shook her head, "a year such as this is hard to recover from."

Karik stared into the fire, and a question which had been burning in him for some time finally came out: "Perhaps I should try to make the passage of the Black Isles."

Elva looked up, sharply. "Do not say such things, on the day when I have already buried one child!"

"We came from the west," Karik persisted, "or so the tales tell. There must be a way."

"Unless the gods have closed it," Elva's voice was suddenly bitter. "Many have been taken by Dunharvic, who thought to cross the Black Isles. There is a curse on them that our people cannot break."

She turned her eyes on him, fixing him with a stare which burned brightly in the fire's glow. "The only thing worse than burying a child is knowing that your child is dead and not being able to bury him. You will not chance the Isles!"

———◇———

Winter turned to spring, but the new season brought little relief to the village. Hald and Hald Haldsson turned to laying out crops, while Karik was sent to hunt and fish.

When he hunted, he went alone, but when he fished, he took out a boat with Igil Tormsson, a young man of his own age. Together, they were very cunning with a boat, able to slide into narrow places, where other fishermen were too careful or too wise to go. Igil shared Karik's curiosity about the Isles, and his mother had told him more about it than had Elva.

"The last ship to try the Isles from Yrdnara went only a few years after we were born," he told Karik. "Apparently, the bow carving washed up on the shore a year later. Although many tried before then, none have tried since."

"I have heard that those up the coast achieved much the same result," Karik said, as he slowly pulled in a net, "as far north as Yrdstadt, at least."

Igil nodded, then the two of them worked in silence for a while, listening to the lapping water against the boat, the cries of the gulls and the moan of the wind, as it came sweeping over the cliffs overlooking the fjord.

"There will not be enough food," Karik said, at length.

Igil looked up, sharply. "Why do you say that?"

Karik gestured at their boat, empty of fish. "My father's crops take slowly, for all the work he and my brother put into them." He shrugged;

"When the fishing is poor and the harvest is weak..." He shrugged again. Igil shook his head.

A heavy gust of wind suddenly blew over the cliffs, howling loudly, and both young men looked quickly to the sky. No dark anvil clouds could be seen over the mountains, nor the long, heavy clouds which often preceded them, so they turned back to their fishing.

"The hunting is nothing to speak of, either," Igil grimaced, and jerked his head to the wooded slopes, where his brother Revik had disappeared on a hunt that morning. "Revik said yesterday that it's been a whole week since he found a fresh deer track. Even the wolves are growing sparse."

Karik nodded but, before he could answer, he felt a pull on the net. Slowly, he worked it in, his heart beating faster, until the whole net rose out of the water, and he saw three fish tangled in it.

Igil grinned at the catch. "I was worried we would go back empty. Perhaps today will be a good one."

Igil's optimism was well-founded, and when they drew their boat back up on the shore, they had enough fish to feed their families for the day.

Still, Karik thought on his conversation with Igil, and he knew that there was little being put aside for the winter.

⊹

Spring dragged into summer, and although the whole village worked from sunrise to sunset – and, at times, beyond – the stores of food for winter grew slow, indeed.

At last, the day came when Jarl Ingbor called them all together, and told them that the village would be sending out exiles.

"We will not have enough food," he said, quietly, "so I have determined that five of our young people will be sent out, to seek a life for themselves elsewhere."

Karik rose slowly, and he heard his mother catch her breath behind him. Igil rose as well. The jarl nodded slowly, in thanks. Lots were then cast to choose three more.

The first lot to fall was that of Umir Malsson; the second that of Wisic Unlisson; and the third was that of Revik Tormsson, Igil's brother.

"You will be given until the last day of summer to prepare yourselves, and give your families whatever aid for the winter you can," Jarl Ingbor told them. "But then, when the sun sets on the last day of summer, you must be gone, not to return for at least one year."

Before the assembly was dismissed, Bori Longbeard, one of the oldest men in the village, suddenly rose to his feet and said that he required a boat.

"I have seen many years in this village, and it has cared long for me," he said, in a voice ancient and cracked. "Now, I would go to the hall of the All Father, having done a great deed: I will attempt to find a passage through the Isles."

"That is not necessary," Jarl Ingbor said, quickly. Pondering this response, Karik remembered that Ingbor was the son of Bori's sister.

"The years lie heavy upon me, my jarl," Bori said, wearily. "It is in my mind that, even in failure, I will do more for my people by going than I would by staying."

At that, another four of the village's elders stood and said that they would go with Bori.

"We have no ship capable of passing the seas," Ingbor protested.

But they would not be deterred. "We have the fishing boats," Bori said. "In the coming days, we will see if we can make one more fitting for the rough seas beyond the fjord."

<hr>

That night, after the last light of the sun had faded from a moonless sky, the five young men gathered around a fire, outside of Igil's and Revik's home.

"It seems that we are to make our way together," Revik said, when they had gathered. Though he had not yet seen his eighteenth winter, he was the largest man in Yrdnara, and although Igil came close to matching him in height, none could match him in strength.

"So it seems," the others agreed.

"It seems to me," Revik continued, "that it would best for us to go to Bjarnmont. King Jarhost is ever in need of warriors, to aid in his cattle raids – it may be that we can win some measure of glory, before our lives are over."

Karik hesitated for a moment, then leaned forward. "Many go to Bjarnmont each year; few make a name for themselves."

He held his hands toward the fire, to capture some of its warmth. "Let us go northward and see what we may find. Perhaps there is land, near Vanik's point, where we could grow food, or find hunting which has not been overtaxed."

Revik shuddered and shook his head; "No. I have no wish to die slowly, trying to grow onions in rocks. In Bjarnmont we will be warm for the winter, we will eat of Jarhost's cattle, and we will die swiftly, on a spear's point."

Karik ground his teeth; "We will do better for our people if we can find a place to grow food."

"Karik makes a good point," Umir pressed, "but, although I dislike Revik's plan of dying, he does as well."

He glanced at the faces around the fire. "Winter will not be far off when we leave; we will not have time to find a promising place in the north, build a home and lay aside stores in time to survive. Our best chance is to find another settlement, where we will be welcome. Along the coast, that will be hard to find, but Bjarnmont may have its doors open to us."

Over this, they argued for some time, until the wind grew too cold and the knowledge of the next day's work drove them to their beds. But, before Revik banked the fire, they agreed that they would make for Bjarnmont together, when the time came.

Karik returned to his bed deep in thought, for it was in his mind that there might be many things in the north of more value than one of King Jarhost's cattle raids. He thought that if they could perhaps gain some small measure of wealth, they might be able to explore the lands in the north with more advantage. With these thoughts in his mind, he lay himself in his bed of furs piled over straw, resigning himself to the service of King Jarhost, and fell asleep.

But, although the matter seemed settled, it did not remain so for long.

Into the Mountains

A week later, the men of King Jarhost came to take their share of the fish and crops back to the hall on Bjarnmont. They brought with them tales of the latest battles against King Viglir, who was ever attempting to slip over the mountains and raid the lands of King Jarhost.

But, they also brought word from the king himself. His crops had been ill, just as all the rest, and although he and his men had raided without cease, to bring some portion of Viglir's herds back to Bjarnmont, it had all been for little gain; he had barely the food to feed his own household, much less newcomers cast out from their homes. He would therefore accept none of those the villages chosen for exile.

"Where, then, does the king think the outcasts should go," Revik asked them, "if the king will not take anyone into his service?"

"Perhaps he will take men next year," one of the taxmen answered. "But, this year you should seek out other villages like your own."

"If we do not have enough to feed ourselves, then surely neither do others," Karik countered.

The taxman shrugged. "I have heard that there are a few in the north, who might accept your help and give you shelter," he replied. "But, do not venture too far north; I have heard that the land there is more dangerous than it is safe."

"Dangerous, how?" Karik asked.

But, the taxman only laughed. "Who knows? Some say there is a monster. Some say the winter cold is too bitter. Some say the land there is cursed.

"But, get going. I have spent too much time in gossip. I came here to collect taxes, not to advise you on your life."

That evening, the five young men gathered by the shore, where Igil had been at work on a fishing boat. Karik and Revik told the others what they had learnt from Jarhost's taxmen.

Revik suggested that they should seek service with Hegli, the jarl who ruled the great fortress of the Undmir, in the far north.

"If he does not accept us," he suggested, "then we should cross the mountains and see if one of the western jarls will take our service. If we are able to make a name for ourselves, then our lives will be much easier, going forward; a hero is rarely turned away from a hearth, when the cold winds come from the north."

But, the others opposed this. "It will take several weeks of hard travel to reach the Undmir," Wisic said, "and if the northlands are as dangerous as we were told, then we may not make it that far. Winter will not be far off when our time comes to depart, and it may catch us on our way, with neither hall nor home in which to shelter."

"Besides," Umir pointed out, "if King Jarhost, the wealthiest of all the kings in Vrania, is too poor to take new swords, then there is little chance that anyone else will."

"When last we spoke," Karik said, slowly, "we determined that between seeking a place in the north and seeking service in Bjarnmont, the latter was the better option. As that way is closed to us, perhaps seeking a place in the north is now the best option available."

Revik grunted and rolled his eyes, but Karik pressed on: "The taxman said that there are small villages in the north which may accept us. And, if there is land in the north too dangerous for our people, perhaps we can make it safe."

"If Bjarnmont is too poor to take us," Revik objected, "then what makes you think these other settlements will?"

"If the northlands are as dangerous as we are told," Karik said, "then perhaps they can use strong hands, and your good ax."

Revik laughed at that, and said that Karik's plan was more likely to leave them freezing in the mountains. when the first snows fell.

"That is a chance, whatever path we take," Igil said.

"Igil is right," Umir nodded, "and I do not wish to think only of myself. If Karik is right, and we can make the northlands safe, it may save many lives in the coming winters. I say we give Karik's plan a try."

Wisic agreed as well. Igil shrugged; "The five of us are not without skill. Even if things do not go as planned, I think we may yet find a way to survive." He looked to Revik; "And, if things do not go as Karik has suggested, in a year or so it may be that Jarhost will take more warriors to his hall."

At last, they agreed to go north. But, Revik just frowned at the glowing coals of the fire, and would not speak to Karik.

———◆———

At last, the summer drew to an end, and they made the final preparations to travel northward.

The night before they left, Karik sat with his father by the fire, and they spoke of many things. Mostly, though, they spoke of Karik's desire to end the famine.

His father shook his head, with a sigh. "We have lived this way for many years," he said. "If there was a way to end it, should we not by now have found it?" He stared into the flames for a long while.

"It may be," he said, heavily, "that we are cursed. Perhaps the All Father does not permit us to leave, and the isles are of his doing."

"Perhaps it is rather because we have not made enough effort to free ourselves," Karik suggested.

His father laughed, bitterly. "There are more men and women of Vrania lying beneath the waves than there are walking the earth," he said. "We have tried, time and time again, yet there is always nothing but death, death and more death."

He looked at Karik, across the fire. "I know that the Isles lay heavy on your mind, but I think you have made the right decision to head north: you may find land there that is good for farming, or for herds. Both are badly needed."

"I will see what I can do," Karik answered, but in his mind he wondered how long a new settlement would be of benefit. It seemed that another settlement might be of use for several years, but eventually it would grow too large, and would bury its starving dead, the same as all the rest.

———◆———

The next morning was the last day of summer, and the sun shone only briefly, before vanishing behind heavy storm clouds. With a nervous eye toward the skies, they prepared to leave.

An offering of beer was poured out for Thor, lord of the sky and the storms, to give the company of Bori and the company of Karik safety from the sudden storms and fierce winds. Then, a young goat was slaughtered and burnt on the rough altar, in the midst of the village. The old priest, Norvi, marked each of them with its blood on their foreheads, and bid them go with the goodwill of all, and the blessing of the All Father.

Then, as Bori and his company went to their boat, Karik and his friends set off on the trail northward.

The trail climbed steeply, slowly working its way up from the fjord, into the hills which encircled it.

It was near to noon when Umir stopped and pointed westward: "The ship."

They all stopped to look. From where they stood, the hills north of the fjord sloped away from them, toward the cliffs and the sea. In the glinting water, they could make out the dark shape of Bori's boat, its sail full as it rushed toward the mouth of the fjord.

"The wind is too strong out of the north," Igil said, quietly. No one answered.

Within the fjord, the waters were somewhat protected from the north winds, but beyond its mouth, the open sea raged, as the north wind howled and screamed over its waves. They watched as the boat rose and fell on the swells, then staggered as it passed through the mouth of the fjord, and was spat into the open sea. For a moment, it disappeared as it slipped into a trough in the waves. Then, it was back again, rising high on another wave crest. Though they all knew how it would end, Karik found himself holding his breath, hoping that the boat would somehow survive.

"They won't even make the Isles," Revik muttered.

"They might have had a chance if there was not a storm coming," Karik shot back.

Wisic snorted at that; "Karik, this is Vrania! The only time a storm isn't coming is when it's already here."

Revik shook his head and turned back to the trail, but Karik's eyes remained on the distant boat. It disappeared again, as the waves rose and fell beneath the black clouds. Twice more it reappeared.

The third time, it did not reappear.

"Come," Igil said, quietly. "They knew what they were doing."

"There must be a way."

"If there is," Igil replied, "we aren't going to find it waiting for that storm to catch us. Come along."

They found a small hollow, as the rain blew in, and made a sort of shelter against the rocks, which was enough to keep off the worst of the storm. But, it did little to keep away the cold, and they were happy to be moving again, when the storm eased.

———◇———

They travelled for several days, passing through the many little settlements and outposts which spread along Vrania's eastern shore. As they hiked over each cliff, Karik would gaze out over the sea and imagine that, in the distance, he could pick out the shapes of the Black Isles.

Most whom they met treated them with kindness, but there were few who would permit them to even rest for the night within their walls. The harvest was nearly all brought in, and each house and hall was calculating how much hunger they would suffer, before the spring came again. But, they were all fair hunters, and most days they were able to share a rabbit or a squirrel between the five of them.

After several days of travel, they came to the village of Girstadt.

A log palisade encompassed the small village, opening onto the cold waters of the fjord, which split the land for miles, until it lapped at Girstadt's doorstep. The jarl, Ingbert Garsson, welcomed them kindly, but warned them that there was no place for them in the village.

"I can offer you little in the way of hospitality," he told them. "You may shelter in my hall tonight, but in the morning you must continue onward."

"We are skilled hunters," Igil said; "is there no way that we might earn our keep?"

"There is little enough game in the mountains here. Though I wish we could take you in, there are many here who will go hungry this winter, and we cannot spare any food."

Karik thanked him for his kindness, and asked if he knew of any other place where they might find refuge for the winter.

"There is still room in the mountains to the north," Ingbert told them, "dangerous though the lands may be. I have heard that some small companies, such as yours, even took to the northern marshes last winter."

"Do they live still?" Usic asked, dryly. Ingbert had to admit that he did not know.

"Why are the mountains so dangerous?" Karik asked.

Ingbert shrugged; "I know little of it, only that there are places where few of the wanderers will go. Of those who have gone north, few have sent back word, and fewer still have returned." He looked them over for a moment, then sighed. "I wish there was a place for you here, but since you must go north, do so with care."

They thanked the jarl for his hospitality, and prepared to stay for the night.

Karik went down to the shore, where the sailors were at work, pulling in some boats for repair, and getting others ready to spend the night fishing. As the sun slowly sank over the gleaming fjord, he lent his hand here and there, seeking out the most experienced sailors, and asking what they had seen of the Isles.

"The currents there are treacherous," they said; "the water there swirls and bends, with no account. The Isles are of bare, black rock, which will cut a ship in half, or scrape her keel clean off. And, once the ship is gone..." the men shook their heads, "no man can survive those waters; if he is not pulled under by the currents, he will be beaten to death upon the rocks."

"Leave it, boy," one wizened old man said to Karik, as they wrapped up the last of their work. "There's naught there but death. Whatever is beyond them is forbidden by the gods."

"But, did we not come from beyond them?" Karik asked. "Did our forefathers not come from across the sea?"

Two of the men smiled again, then laughed; "There is always one who thinks he knows better than the rest of us."

A grey-bearded fisherman raised a bony finger and pointed at Karik; "You're not the first to think of passing the Isles, and I doubt you'll be the last. If you want to go..." he shrugged, "no one will stop you. Some might even say that one mouth fewer is not an ill thing."

He picked up his net and slung it over his shoulder. "But, there are many ways a strong man such as yourself may be of use to the starving. Perhaps you should look for those adventures, rather than seeking your death in the black rocks off our shores."

Karik returned to his companions, wondering now if the Isles were a foolish venture. But, as he walked, the thought came to him that they had never been explored in the east. If they did not encircle all of Vrania, then perhaps there was a way around them.

He stopped and looked to the west. The sun had fallen into the sea, and only a fading glow remained, in the cold wind which was sweeping over the fjord and into the village. There had to be a way through the Isles, or perhaps even around them. The North Sea was full of ice and snow, but perhaps in the winter a way could be found there. And, if not, then perhaps boats could be carried over the ice, before it melted in the spring.

A grin broke over his face. It would take much work, and he would have to see how it was for himself, but it was the beginnings of an idea. If they could find a place to survive the winter, then next year he might be able to begin his search.

Umir met him as he was coming back from the beach. "Nice of you to rejoin us." He was carrying an armload of wood, and he looked skeptically at Karik's empty hands.

"I was talking with some of the old sailors," Karik apologized. "I think there may be something for us in the north."

"Another village?" Umir shifted the wood in his arms.

"Perhaps," Karik shrugged, "or enough game and shelter to get the five of us through the winter."

"I am not sure that I believe you," Umir shook his head.

Wisic appeared from behind one of the long huts, carrying two buckets of water. "I do not, either," Wisic smiled. "It is my belief that we should begin drawing lots over who is to be eaten first."

Karik raised his eyebrows; "Eaten?"

"Eaten," Wisic nodded, cheerfully. "All five of us aren't going to make it through the winter, so by giving up his life, one of us can make the odds a little bit better for the rest." He leaned forward, winking conspiratorially; "My vote is Revik: that beast is large enough to feed us for a month, at least! And, I could use his shin bone to make a good spear."

"Revik would be a tough beast to bring down." Umir shifted the wood in his hands again, turning back to Ingbert's hall.

"That's a point," Wisic muttered, then turned his eyes on Karik, looking him over, critically.

"That's enough of that," Karik laughed. "Let's go get some food in you, before you decide to eat one of us tonight."

They left Girstadt the next morning, just as Ingbert had asked.

The days were growing shorter now, and the cold winds were coming more often out of the north. Though they passed through several more settlements, they found nowhere that they were welcome.

At last, a day came when they found themselves in the far northern mountains. There, they came upon the place where the path split, one side leading northwest and the other east, higher into the mountains, toward Girhom and Gar's Pass. Revik said that Girhom might be worth visiting, but Wisic pointed out that if Bjarnmont did not have a place for them, then Girhom was far less likely.

As they argued over this, Karik thought that he saw a man across the gorge, making his way among the rocky slope. He asked Wisic who he thought the man was.

"Well, given his stride, and that bow, and the fact that I've never been in this area..." Wisic said, as he peered across the gorge, "I have no idea."

"He is likely an exile," Igil said, as he shifted his pack; "one who has taken to living by himself, away from the village, just like us."

Karik nodded; "I would speak with him. As Wisic has said, we are new here, and unfamiliar with the land this far north; perhaps he may be able to tell us why these northlands are considered so dangerous."

They made their way down, across the gorge, and sought out the man they had seen. But he had vanished; no sign of him could be found.

"It is not likely that he would sit here and wait for us," Revik said, "and I doubt that he would be happy at the prospect of sharing his food with strangers."

"You may be right," Karik scanned the trees around them, "but I would still very much like to talk with him. It may be that he knows something of the northlands."

"It may be that he is lying in wait for us," Wisic muttered, frowning into the trees, "looking to rob us!"

"We have little enough to entice robbers," Igil said, dismissively.

Wisic shook his head; "Perhaps, but there is that." He pointed to the great ax Revik carried on his back.

Revik only glared at him. "If he's waiting for that, I'll cut him in half."

Igil was looking about them, searching the rocks and the trees for any sign of the man's passage, when he suddenly broke out in laughter. "What fools we all are," he said, "searching for a man here in the rocks. It would be much easier to find his mark in the sky."

Revik frowned at his brother, for Igil often articulated in a roundabout manner. But, Karik was already looking to the sky.

And, rising from the tops of the gaunt pine trees, a short way ahead, he saw the faint trace of smoke. They made their way toward it.

They soon found themselves on a sparse footpath which led down into a small hollow. A space had been cleared, and a hut had been built among the rocks, in such a way that it was impossible to tell where the house ended and the rocks began. It was covered with earth and rough stones, into which a small wooden door was set. All about the clearing were the bones of animals, and from nearly every tree hides and furs were hanging.

By the door of the hut sat a man, honing his ax with a stone; at his feet sat a great, black hound. The man did not look up as they approached, but the dog watched them with bared teeth, and a growl on the edge of his maw. Karik bade his companions wait, while he advanced toward the man, with Revik close behind.

He introduced himself, and asked if the man was averse to some company, for a short time.

The man answered that his name was Dranri, and if they came in peace, he was willing enough to be a host.

"It is not easy to be cast out from your home," he said. "You cannot stay here for more than a day, but I will give you such help as I am able. We exiles must help each other as best we can, for there are few others who will."

Together, they ate a mountain goat which Dranri had killed the day before, gnawing at it in the setting sun, until nothing was left but a pile of white bones beneath the pine trees. Then, when they had finished, they slept that night in the clearing beside Dranri's house.

Karik did not lie down with the others; he sat by the fire, while the wind blew through the treetops, and the stars shone high above them. And he spoke with Dranri as the night grew cold. The fire burned low while he spoke of his hope to find food for his people.

But Dranri shook his head, and his great beard wagged as he did so. "It does not exist here, on this isle," he said. "Northward there is good fishing, in the little bay that you will find, but there is only a little left over for the people who live there. We trade with them every year, some of the other wanderers and I – our furs for their fish – and the trade is good.

"To the east, in the cattle lands which Jarhost so loves to raid, there is more food and less hunger. But, even if we were all to eat together, we would soon consume it, and be worse off than before."

"What of the lands farther north?" Karik asked.

Dranri shook his head, with a laugh; "Trust me, I have searched. Beyond these mountains lies the icy marsh and, beyond that, the land rises to Vanik's Point. No crop will grow there, and the beasts which make it their home are not numerous enough to sustain a village. There is not enough fodder for goats, until you reach the lands of Jarl Hegli, in the Undmir, and that is already claimed."

Karik watched the fire, and his heart sank as Dranri spoke. So, there would be no new village; no safe place to where he might one day bring his family?

"We have heard that the northern lands are dangerous," he said, when Dranri had finished. "What is this danger?"

Dranri poked at the fire for a moment, and the logs collapsed, letting loose a sprout of flames, which threw off a small shower of sparks. At last, he spoke: "It is said, among some here, that Vranr came ashore in the bay nearby, and that a curse lies heavy on that place. Curses are a danger in and of themselves, but I have also heard rumours of dark and terrible creatures. Men fear to speak of whatever is nearby, and it is a danger I do not care to meet."

He pointed a stick at Karik. "If the village does not take you in tomorrow, then do not linger. They fear starvation, the same as do all the rest of us, and you would do well not to anger them. We all do terrible things when we are afraid."

Karik thought for a moment, wondering what the next day would bring. What would they do if no village would take them in?

"Why does Jarhost not give aid to the villages which he claims to rule?"

"Because he is comfortable in Bjarnmont," Dranri answered. "When I was exiled, I wandered these mountains for two years, before loneliness and hunger overcame me. I served Jarhost for three years, yet he threw me out, when he had to tighten his belt at the table." He spat into the fire. "Above all, Jarhost loves comfort, and as long as he has it, he will not move, no matter the plight of our island."

"If it is not within our island," Karik asked, "then perhaps beyond the Black Isles? What might lie there?"

At this, Dranri chuckled. "One day, we may discover what lies beyond there, indeed." He shrugged, as he poked at the fire. "But, there are troubles enough for us on this isle. The wars between the jarls never end, and the wolves and other beasts prey upon the weak."

He pointed his stick at Karik. "Spend some time in the settlement I shall send you to, then let us talk again. The world is dark and dangerous; those who claim to lead us do little but look out for themselves."

"Then, perhaps we need new leaders," Karik suggested.

"That may be," Dranri acknowledged, "but if every man rises up and claims to be the leader, then are we not worse off? A bad jarl is often better than no jarl at all, for chaos does no one any good. Watch and learn for a while; you will be surprised at what you come to understand."

"Many have watched and learned, while others went hungry and starved." Karik stared into the fire, and it seemed for a moment that he saw Mirn's face within the flames. Dranri grunted in agreement.

The fire crackled between them for a moment, before the man spoke again. "No matter how ill matters may seem," he said, "there is always room for them to get worse.

"I can tell you are not a man to sit idle and quiet, while there are matters which need to be addressed, so I will give you a piece of advice..." he peered at Karik, through the firelight: "whatever you do, others will have their own opinions and thoughts on it. Think on what those might be. Few men view matters the same way, and what seems prudent to one may seem rash to another – you and your friend Revik are a good example of this. Think carefully before you act; like a good sailor – who examines the skies and the waves far from the shore, before launching his boat – think what troubles and ills may lurk in your future."

Karik agreed that this was good advice, and assured that he would consider it in the future.

UNHOST

The next morning, they rose and thanked Dranri for his hospitality, promising to repay it if ever they were in a position to do so.

Dranri dismissed that it was not likely this would be the case, then pointed them in the direction of the village.

"When you arrive, tell them that Dranri the Hunter sent you, and that I will be there soon, for the forests have been generous these months past."

Karik agreed to do as Dranri said, then they made their way onto the path he had pointed out, down the mountainside, toward the sea.

The wind was blowing in from the north, whipping the stubby trees along their path, and high above them dark storm clouds were rolling in.

Revik said that if this village did not take them in, then it might be that they had chosen the worst path, after all.

"That may be," Karik answered, pausing to catch his breath on the steep slope, "but it may also be that we have taken the best path."

"You are a fool!" Revik spat into the trees and pushed past Karik.

In more than one place, the path dropped almost straight down, and they had to take great care to ensure that they did not go tumbling through the pines, which grew along the lower slope.

Soon, the path drew near a stream, which came down out of the mountains and, shortly afterward, they came upon the village Dranri had spoken of.

A rough, rocky strip of land ringed the fjord's beach, dotted by low, stone houses roofed with turf. By their height, Karik guessed that they were dug into the ground, with most of their interior space beneath the surface. He wondered at this, for none of the other villages they had passed through had been built in such a way. Stone pens surrounded many of the houses, and men could be seen tending small gardens about the village. Beyond them, the dark waters of the fjord stretched northward, as the shore rose into low cliffs along it, widening as it went, until reaching the sea.

Karik peered out in surprise, for it seemed to him that, at the mouth of the fjord, there was an island rising into a mountain. It was far in the distance, and clouds hung heavy over the whole fjord, so it was not an easy thing to see. Karik thought it strange that the fishing boats should be here, rather than out near the mountain; fishermen often lived along the fjord, closer to the deeper waters, where they might find bigger fish, yet here it seemed that the mountain was actively avoided. Karik noted this, thinking that it might be a thing worth keeping in mind.

To the west, a wide stream plunged from the mountains, hurrying down toward the fjord. To his surprise, Karik saw several farms on its banks, stretching back into the mountains. Men had said that this far north there was little point in growing wheat, yet here, although the plots were small, thick stalks stood tall and heavy with grain.

Revik grunted; "This place is not very promising."

"It may be there is more here than meets the eye," Karik answered. "They are growing wheat."

"There are also a great number of fishing boats," Wisic pointed out, "yet a relatively small number of houses."

Revik scoffed at this, as they began to make their way into the village. "I am of half a mind not to even bother with this place," he said. "Perhaps we are not as well suited to each other as was first thought."

"Come, brother," Igil replied, "you will not get far before the darkness, and we have not yet seen what this village has to offer."

"It is a desolate settlement on a rocky coast," Revik waved his hand toward the shore; "what more could there possibly be?"

"Revik," Karik took a step toward him, "I know things have not gone your way since we left our homes, but please stay for a little while longer. After this winter, perhaps things will be better. Besides," he gestured toward the houses, "we do not know if they will even take us."

Revik hefted his ax and thought for a moment. "We will see," he said, at last. "But, I will not dawdle forever."

As they came out of the trees and approached the village, they saw but one man, who approached them with a friendly smile. He informed them that he was Unhost, the jarl of the settlement.

"It is not much of a jarldom," Revik muttered, and Igil thumped him to be quiet.

But, Unhost only smiled, and admitted that it was indeed not much. "But, it is ours, and we work hard to make it what it is."

As he looked them over, Karik stepped forward. "Dranri of the mountains sends his greetings." Then, he added, quickly: "He told us that you should look out for him in a week's time."

"That is excellent news," Unhost smiled. "I take it that you are exiles, seeking a home?"

Karik nodded.

"Well, we have much work that needs doing," Unhost told them, "and if you are willing to lend a hand, then it is likely that we will have a place here for you."

He invited them to join him for dinner, if they did not mind helping him to make it. The promise of food was welcome to them, and they agreed, happily. A small basket of onions was washed, in a bucket of cold water, and several fish were cleaned and gutted, before the lot was thrown into an iron kettle to boil. It was short work for the six of them, and soon they all sat about the fire in Unhost's home.

Yet, throughout their work, they saw only a handful of fishermen, returning from their labours and pulling their boats up onto the shore.

Unhost's dwelling was a small building, with a thin roof and walls only a few feet high. The greater part of it had been dug out and lined with rocks and old, thin hides, in order to make it look less like a badger's den. About the upper edges, where the rocks met the roof beams, there were many cracks and holes. Karik thought this a strange thing, for it would be poor shelter in the winter.

While their stew boiled, Unhost asked them many questions about who they were and where they were from. All were answered without too many words. When the stew was done, they set to eating eagerly, careful to pick the fish bones out of the hot broth.

Karik then spoke his thought out loud: "It seems that there are very few people here. We hardly saw anyone but yourself when we arrived."

"There is a reason for that," Unhost replied, "and it is this: there are very few people here."

They laughed at this – Unhost the loudest of all. But, to Karik it seemed that his eyes did not laugh with the rest of him. In fact, he noticed that Unhost's eyes never seemed to stop moving between them all.

"But," the host continued, after a moment, "the few of us there are here must range far and wide, to gather for the winter. Our fishermen are often out in the bay, and our hunters and foragers are often deep in the mountains. Our farmers live a little way from the beach, where the northern storms which sweep in from the sea do not reach them. Our herdsmen are farther still, up in the hills, where they keep our goats.

"Tell me, what kind of skills do you have, and what kind of work are you accustomed to?"

Revik said that he was a great hunter, to which Unhost replied that would be very welcome. Igil said that he was skilled as a fisherman and boat builder; to this, Unhost said that they already had a boat builder, but he would be very grateful for assistance. Wisic said that he was a fisherman, and he knew more than a little about the keeping of nets; Unhost answered that this was a skill which was ever needed. Umir explained that he was a better hunter than fisher, but also had some skill as a forager; Unhost nodded and said that these were also very useful abilities. Karik said that he had some skill as a hunter, but his greatest skill was as a farmer; Unhost said it was late in the year to sow crops, but there were herds to be gathered and cared for.

"There is plenty of room, and there is always work to be done," he said. "The fish are often plentiful, and there are even a few farms along the stream. Several of them could no doubt use help, and would be happy to share."

They talked more as the night grew close, and Wisic asked why the village appeared to be such a poor place, if they could so easily take in five exiles.

Unhost smiled a little at this, his rough beard shifting as he did so. "It is how I like it. If we are too prosperous, King Jarhost will come with his swords and his thanes, and demand that I pay him tribute. As long as we remain a tiny village, barely able to feed ourselves, he leaves us alone. As to why we can take you in, it is because there is so much work to do here."

As the night was drawing in, he showed them to a shed, where they often kept their boats, when the storms came in.

"It is not overly comfortable," he said, "but for one night it will suffice."

It was cold, with only a thin deer-hide hung over the doorway, and the stars could be seen through the branches which had been laid over it, as a roof. But, there was a fire pit in the center, and spare wood set by the door.

When Unhost had left them, they stacked a little wood on the fire, until the flames were crackling happily in the darkness. The hut was a poor thing, but it kept off the wind, and kept in the warmth from the fire.

They gathered around the dancing flames, to decide what they should do. Karik was not surprised that Revik spoke first:

"This is a poor place you've led us to. We should have never listened to you." His eyes glowed amber across the fire, and shadows danced on his furious face. "There is no great danger here, and no glory to be won – only another poor village, trying to scratch a living out of the earth."

"You've done nothing but complain since we left Yrdnara," snapped Karik. "Look around you for a moment. Why are the houses buried in the ground? Does that not seem strange to you? Can you not see that there is something which keeps these people afraid?"

"I cannot," Revik snapped, "and I think it was a waste of our time to come here."

"This is a poor village," Wisic said, quietly, "and though there may be no honour to be won, nor glory to be gained, winter is close; within a few days we will see snow. It would be a bad time to still be searching for shelter, when that happens."

"All villages are poor," Karik said. "And, as for glory or honour to be won here, that remains to be seen. This is where we should stay."

"Who made you our ruler?" Revik asked. "Or, have I forgotten something?"

"We all agreed to come here," Umir said. "Karik and Wisic are right: it is too late in the season to go anywhere else, and hope to be accepted."

"I blame you, Karik!" Revik grumbled. "If we had done what I suggested—"

"We'd be freezing on the slopes of Bjarnmont, or hiking the frozen marshes," Karik interrupted him. "I am only trying to do what is best for us."

"At least we would be moving toward something," Revik snarled, his fingers tightening on his ax hilt. "Instead, we sit here, having left one poor village to settle in another."

"Your desire for glory would have you freezing in the mountains," Karik answered him. "If you would rather be dead, beneath a glorious pile of ice, then go and let us be rid of you."

Igil stood and beckoned Karik to follow him outside.

In the dark night, with only the occasional flicker of firelight coming through the hut's patchy wall, he turned to Karik. With his face like ice, he said: "My brother and I are as one; if you drive him away, then I shall go with him. What right do you have to be so arrogant? You have led us to a tiny village of very few people, all of them so poor that they can barely cover their dwellings with furs."

At this, Karik suddenly stood, as if momentarily struck to stone.

"That's it!" he said, gripping Igil's sleeve. "Did you not feel it, Igil, when we came here: the feeling that something is wrong? Something here is very strange."

"You have lost your wits," Igil sighed.

"Then, where are they?" Karik whispered. "The furs in Unhost's hut cannot be less than two years old. And, if the good furs are not in the jarl's hut, then where else would they be?"

Even with so little light to see, Karik could tell that his words had struck true with Igil. Slowly, his companion nodded.

"Come, we have a few hours of darkness." Karik kept his voice low, even though they could see no one moving among the huts and pens. "Let us wander about and see if I am right. We may find something which explains why this place seems so strange."

⸻❖⸻

Unhost's hut glowed with firelight in the darkness. As they crouched beside it and looked in, they saw Unhost speaking in hushed tones, to three other men they had not seen before.

After a moment, the men left the hut and sat beside the fire in the centre of the village, all of them watching the shack where Karik and the rest were supposed to be sleeping.

"Strange," said Igil, watching the men in the dark.

"Here is something stranger still..." said Karik, his voice thin with nervous wonder, as he brought his face closer to the crack in the wall.

Utterly bemused, Igil pressed him for an explanation. And Karik told exactly what he had seen: Unhost had vanished through the floor of his hut.

"What?" Igil snorted, quietly. "Whatever you think you saw, you must have imagined it. It will take a closer look to learn what manner of mischief is afoot here."

"Come, then," Karik said, preparing to move.

Igil held him back. "Walking through the village is one thing," he whispered, "but, it is another to break into his home. Our host will not take kindly to finding us prying into his business."

"Then, we must not be caught," Karik smiled, in the darkness.

Quietly, they crept inside, crouching over the place where Karik had seen Unhost disappear. Feeling about the floor with his hands, he found only a pile of thin furs, worn with age.

"Perhaps he is a skin-changer," Karik whispered.

"Or, perhaps he crawled through this door," Igil replied, lifting the latch on a small trap door, hidden underneath the furs.

Karik looked down. "Yes, I suppose that is more likely," he conceded.

Slowly, they opened the door and peered down, into a tunnel cut into the rock. They dropped inside.

They felt their way along, taking care to move silently. They had not walked far, when the tunnel began to be lit by a warm glow.

Soon, the sound of eating and drinking was echoing off of the rocks. They peered around each corner, each time apprehensive that it was the last.

Then, peering around the last rock, they saw the true court of Unhost. A rocky cavern had been hollowed out, and furnished like a jarl's hall, proper. A fire blazed at one end, and Unhost sat about it with several others, drinking from horns and speaking in low voices.

Karik and Igil pulled back behind the rock. "We should go," Karik whispered; "I'm not sure our host would be pleased if he found out we've discovered his secret hall."

"I think that is wise," said Igil.

The two of them hurried back up the tunnel, into the village. At the doorway of Unhost's home, they stopped and looked out at the men, still sitting by the fire, watching their shack. Igil said it would be impossible for them to make it back into the hut without being seen.

"I have a plan," Karik said. With that, he crept slowly away from the settlement, to where the brush had not been cleared. When they reached it, he stood with an audible sigh, and began to relieve himself in the bushes.

Igil tried to shush him, but Karik only yawned louder, as he fastened his pants and began to make his way back toward their hut.

"Come," he said, vocally and sleepily, "I am tired." He stumbled and tripped over every branch and rock in his path, as he returned.

The men sat by the fire stood quickly upon seeing them, then quickly sat back down, as Karik muttered an apology. Without question, Karik and Igil entered their hut, where they promptly wrapped themselves up in their furs.

Umir, looked up as they entered, and asked quickly where they had been.

In a hushed voice, Karik told the group what they had seen: that the greater part of the village was below ground, cut out of the rocks. "Clearly, something very strange is afoot here," Karik said.

Revik only yawned. "Or, they live beneath ground to escape the cold, and the snow and the wind." With that, he shrugged his massive shoulders and wrapped his blanket tighter around himself.

Karik inched closer to him. "Do you not find it at all suspicious that a settlement lives underground, in secret?"

"But, they aren't in secret," Revik replied; "they just didn't tell us about it. You went skulking. You are making more of this matter than it warrants."

Karik looked at the others, but Umir only shrugged. Wisic said that if they wanted to live underground, that was their business. Only Igil agreed that the matter seemed strange.

"Perhaps it would be better to see how matters continue for a while, then determine what we should do."

Karik nodded and lay back down on his bed.

But, his mind still rankled with the wrongness of this place. It seemed that the mountain, toward the end of the fjord, where fishing should be good, was being avoided, and now they had learned that the village was mainly underground. It all struck him as very strange. Deep into the night he turned it over in his mind, until at last he fell asleep, to the sound of the wind moaning outside, and the water lapping at the edge of the beach.

YLMI BODVARSDOTTIR

The sun was not yet over the horizon, the next morning, when they heard the sounds of the village stirring to life; boats being brought in and nets repaired at the shoreline.

When Karik stepped out of their hut, a cold wind, blowing in from the sea, struck him in the face. A heavy fog was rolling across the water, and he could see but a short way out; the mountain he had seen the day before was now hidden from him.

He did not have long to look about him, before Unhost appeared out of the grey morning, to greet him and his companions.

Igil he sent to work on the fishing boats, with one named Havar. Although Havar was not an old man, his knowledge of boats was considerable, and Igil learned much from him.

Revik was sent to work with a man named Almir Alsson, who hunted the cold woods to the north, and the two of them set out, with little talk passing between them.

Wisic went out into the inlet, on a small fishing boat, with a man named Torig Ingsson. Torig was an old, shrunken man, but his long fingers were very skillful with a net.

Umir set out with Flovi Grimsson and his wife, to forage in the foothills, rising alongside the stream which poured into the inlet; there were many berries, mushrooms and nuts to be found there.

When his friends had been sent to their work, Karik asked Unhost where he would be most useful. Before Unhost could answer, the bleating of goats was heard, and an older man appeared out of the wooded slopes, driving a crowd of goats before him.

And so, Karik met Bodvar Miriksson...

Bodvar was an older man, and he greeted Karik warmly, saying that he was glad of the help, for their goats were scattered widely in the mountains. Karik replied that, as of yet, he was not overly familiar with these mountains, but Bodvar was happy that he would soon learn.

"Besides," the herder said, "loneliness is my greatest enemy among the mountain pines."

It was the work of several hours to distribute the goats which Bodvar had brought, for they were apportioned out among the village. It seemed that there were many more goats than was appropriate for the small number of people in the village. But, for the time being, Karik kept his thoughts to himself, and simply helped Bodvar work.

When they had finished, for their efforts Unhost saw to it that they received a number of fish which had been salted only recently. With these on their backs, Bodvar bade Karik follow him.

He took Karik to his home, which was set in a cleft of the rocks, not far above the village. Like Dranri's house, it was built among the stones, where it was difficult to see where the house ended and the rock began.

"Where are the pens for the goats?" Karik asked.

"We do not use pens," Bodvar replied, "but caves – there and there." He pointed to where the bushes grew thick, against the rocks. "We cover the entrances with brush. It keeps the animals quiet and hides them from predators."

"Do you have many wolves here?" Karik asked.

"Among other things," Bodvar said, and led him into the house.

Inside, Karik saw that what he had perceived to be a tiny house was in fact little more than its doorway; Bodvar's real home was itself set inside a cave. No wind swept through holes in the walls, and no melting snow fell through cracks in the roof. A fire burned in one corner, the smoke lifting up and vanishing into a hole, which had been cut into the turf.

"It is not much," Bodvar said, "but it is comfortable, and it is mine."

A woman came around the corner and embraced Bodvar, before asking who he had brought with him.

"This is Karik," Bodvar answered. "He is an exile who has come to us. Unhost says that he has experience as a farmer."

"He was exiled?" The woman shook her head. "Are you violent?" she asked Karik. "Did you break some law in your village?"

Karik shook his head, smiling.

The woman nodded. "You men and your silly rules make no sense," she said, before grabbing Karik and dragging him before the fire. "Come, let's have a look at you."

"This is my wife, Siggi," Bodvar laughed, as Karik stumbled across the floor. "Siggi, where is Ylmi?"

"She went hunting," Siggi replied, as she sat beside the fire, pulling Karik down with her. Taking his face in her hands, she peered fixedly into his eyes. "What village did you come from?" she asked.

"Yrdnara."

Siggi looked back at Bodvar. "Is that north or south of Geirstadt?"

"South," Karik answered.

Siggi gave him a withering glare; "I didn't ask you. Husband?"

"He is correct, I believe." Bodvar settled himself in a chair, and began sipping from a wooden mug. "Three, maybe four fjords south of here."

"Ah," Siggi replied, looking Karik up and down. Her eyes lingered on his worn clothes; "It was a long journey, yes?"

"It was."

"And, now I take it that the good Unhost welcomed you into our little settlement?" Siggi peered into his eyes. "He welcomed you warmly, no doubt?"

Karik shrugged. "He welcomed us."

"There are enough of us here already," Siggi replied, then stood again. "It is difficult enough for us to make our living, with that weasel squeezing us for all he can."

"I do not wish to be a burden," Karik replied. "I can work well, and I will make more than I eat."

"We will see if that is so," Siggi muttered, returning to the meal she was preparing.

Karik rose to his feet, and the dogs quickly surrounded him, with wagging tails and warm tongues. He had not been there long, however, when the dogs suddenly leapt up and ran to the door, barking and wagging their tails.

"It seems that Ylmi has returned," Bodvar said, as he set a pair of logs on the fire.

The door creaked open, and Karik immediately leapt to his feet, as a massive wolf shouldered the door, peering at him. It sniffed the air and let out a low growl, as Karik backed up against the wall.

"Easy, now," Siggi called; "he's alright."

"Who's alright?"

With the voice, the door swung all the way open, to reveal a young woman with long, brown hair pulled back into a single braid. She set her bow by the door and glanced around the room.

As her eyes found Karik, her jaw tightened; "Another exile?"

"Indeed," Bodvar nodded, gravely. "This is Karik. He will be staying with us for a while."

He smiled unconvincingly, as the young woman looked at him. "It is not too much of a burden, my daughter. The herd is large indeed this year, and I am sure that Karik is an excellent worker."

Ylmi's gaze snapped back to Karik. "You had best pull your weight. I am weary of feeding slackers."

"I do not intend to be a burden," Karik answered.

This was how Karik met Ylmi Bodvarsdottir.

***

The next morning, Bodvar took Karik with him into the mountains, to look for goats. As they walked, Karik asked many questions about the village and about Unhost. Most of them Bodvar answered, but Karik often found that the answers did little to address the questions.

Finally, he stopped, and said to Bodvar: "I get the feeling that you are hiding things from me. There are many strange things about this village that concern me."

Bodvar replied that life was often concerning. "Besides," he said, "you are young and you have much to learn. Additionally, you are new to our village, so you should not expect to be told everything at once. Trust must be earnt, and so far you have earnt little."

The rest of their day was spent gathering the goats. Karik noted that Bodvar's eyes often turned northward, toward the mountain in the sea.

Later that day, they sat on a ridge and looked down on a small valley, where the goats were grazing peacefully. While they rested, Karik told Bodvar of his hope to find food, to feed his people.

"Not all ills in the world have a remedy," Bodvar replied. "Often, our lot is to struggle. I have struggled for years and, even so, I do not know that we will survive the winter. But," he added, as he smiled at Karik, "I have a warm home and a loving family – to face the winter with them is enough." Karik thought on this as they worked.

The settlement's goats had been let loose into the forests, to forage for themselves during the spring and summer; although Bodvar had done his best to keep track of them, they were now spread over miles of forest and hilly terrain. Each day they managed to bring back a few, penning them up in the caves. Then, when the caves began to grow crowded, Bodvar announced that the next day they would take what they had down to the village.

"We will keep a few," he told Karik, "as payment for our work, but most will be returned to the families that own them."

Karik looked over the herd; it seemed to him that there were many goats, for such few families.

"The winter will be long," Bodvar said, "and there must be enough left over to put out to pasture in the spring."

Karik nodded. But, even so, it seemed unusual to him for so many goats to be brought in.

———◆———

The next day, they made the journey down into the village. It was very slow going with the herd, and nightfall drew near as they completed their work.

Bodvar said that he would spend the night with Unhost, and Karik was welcome to do the same. But, Karik said that he would like to see his companions, and to hear how they were getting on.

Wisic and Umir he found hard at work; though they welcomed him, they said that they did not have time to sit around talking. From them, he learned that Revik and Almir were on a hunting trip, and were not expected back until the following day. With some disappointment, Karik went walking along the shore.

The wind was blowing in, cold and steady from the north, and in the dim light of the setting sun, he could see the dark shape of the mountain, to the west. A storm was approaching on the wind, and the mountain seemed to split the sky, between dim light to the south and darkness to the north.

As the wind howled, a fork of lightning ran the length of the clouds, seemingly snapping on the mountain itself.

"Karik!"

He turned to see Igil coming toward him, out of the gathering darkness, and the two embraced.

"At least it seems that you are happy with how things are here," Karik told him. "Have you discovered anything more about this place?"

"Indeed, I have," said Igil, "and it was for this reason that I came looking for you. Come." With that, Igil led him away from the rising tide.

Just as they reached one of the low houses, the rain came pouring down, soaking them. Igil hurried the last few feet and pulled Karik down, through the doorway.

Inside, they shook off the rain and, with a quick smile, Igil lifted a small door in the floor, not unlike the one they had found in Unhost's dwelling. Karik laughed and they slipped through it, as thunder echoed over the fjord outside. As in Unhost's dwelling, a passage had been carved into the rock, though here the rock had not been smoothed or finished.

At the end of it, a small door was set in the rock; iron pins held it in place. It screeched as Igil pulled it open.

"I have brought him," Igil said, excitedly.

Karik saw that he was speaking to a tall, lean man, who sat beside a small fire.

Thus, did Karik Haldsson meet Havar Ivarsson – and much sorrow would come from that meeting.

Karik looked about him, and saw that a small but comfortable home had been carved from the rock. He asked what manner of place it was.

"A safe one," Havar replied, as he stoked the fire. "The world is not yet safe for us all. When you came down from the hills, did you see the mountain isle, which sits some ways off our shore?"

Excitedly, Karik nodded.

"There is a beast which dwells there," Havar said, slowly: "a dragon of the north."

Karik's eyes widened, and a hundred thoughts went through his mind at once, followed by a flash of understanding.

"This is the reason your homes are buried so deep," Karik said: "you dug your homes from the rock to protect yourselves from the dragon."

"It is so," Havar replied. "At least, that is how matters began. There are hot springs deep under the ground, and that is the reason why our crops grow so well. The first men who came here dug deep to escape the beast and to find warmth... but, they found more than that."

With that, he reached under his cloak and pulled a small, leather bag from his breast. Weighing it in his hand for a moment, he tossed it to Karik. Loosening the drawstring, Karik slid his fingers inside the leather, and drew out three small lumps of cold, yellow metal.

"Gold?" Then, he shrugged; "What use is gold to those who are starving?"

"Little and more. This gold has worth beyond what others may think. For, Unhost has dealings with the dragon."

He smiled at the shock on Karik's face, then continued: "Yes, indeed. Each year we present him a measure of the gold we have found, along with a number of sheep and goats, and thus he allows us to flourish, in sight of his mountain."

Karik thought on these things for a moment, enjoying the warmth of the fire. Above them, the storm could be heard faintly, as it thundered over the bay.

"Why is Unhost so secretive on this matter?" he asked, after a while.

"Because dragons attract all manner of attention," Havar replied. "And, for all of the beast's greed, Unhost has prospered, here in its shadow. Tell me, Karik, if the king of Bjarnmont heard that one of his coastal villages had found gold, but that it was all paid to a dragon which lived nearby, how long do you think that village would remain prosperous?"

"The king would try to take the gold for himself," Igil answered, simply.

"So," Karik eyed Havar, carefully, "why have you told us this?"

"Because," Havar answered, quietly, "the gold is beginning to run out." He looked between the two of them. "Unhost has been sending more and more of us to dig in the mine shafts, but the veins are running out, and less gold is being found every week."

He shook his head, slowly; "When it is all gone..."

"Your use to the dragon will be at an end," Karik muttered.

"So I suspect," Havar replied. "Dragons are not known for keeping oaths, yet Unhost will not allow an attack on the dragon for fear of what failure might mean. We are prosperous now, but when Unhost can take him no more gold, the dragon may decide that a tiny bay at the edge of our isle is not enough; he will seek out other conquests, and then we will be destroyed, however deep are our hovels. How long can we live without crops? Without hunting?"

He spread his hands in vain; "Unhost does not want us to attempt ridding ourselves of the beast. But, we are the sons of Vranr! I have long plotted a way to destroy the dragon. Alone, I do not think I would have a good chance... But, if you would join me..."

Their eyes widened, and Havar smiled. "It is known that the gods love those who are cunning enough to care for themselves. But, if a man is greedy, the fates may take all away."

"This might be true," said Karik, "but if you mean to slay this dragon, it will take more than a few men to accomplish the task."

"It is as you say. But, there are many in the village who agree with Unhost, that the dragon is best left alone. If word gets out about our intentions, Unhost will not deal gently with us. Your companions, and no one else, must be enough to challenge the dragon."

Karik thought on this for a moment, watching the flames of Havar's fire wrap around a piece of driftwood.

"Let us see if they are willing," he said, at last. "If so, we will try to think of a plan that will work. A dragon is no small foe."

The next morning, Karik told Bodvar that there were matters he needed to resolve with his old companions, and that he would follow him up the mountain, shortly. With warning not to wait too long, lest he be caught on the path after dark, Bodvar left him. Karik went to look for Revik.

The village began to come alive as the sun rose. Yet, even with more people than Karik had ever seen there before, it still seemed a lonely place. A pair of fishing boats pushed out into the morning light, and here and there a few men and women came to separate out the goats; two were butchered and hung to be cleaned, in the centre of the town.

It did not take long for Revik to appear, bearing a thin, scrawny buck over his shoulders.

"You again," he said, when Karik came to greet him. "Should you not be in the mountains, chasing goats?"

Karik replied that he had caught many goats, then added that he had come to tell Revik something which he might find interesting.

"Is it about a really big goat?" Revik mocked.

Karik looked about him, curiously; "Where is your companion, Almir?"

Revik shook his head, as he hung the deer. "The man is clumsy and a poor hunter. He fell on the mountain and injured his arm, so now his hunting is left to me."

With a heave of his shoulder and massive arms, Revik pulled the deer's hide halfway down its back, in one movement. Then, he looked back at Karik; "You said you had something interesting to say?"

Looking about carefully, to ensure that Unhost was nowhere nearby, Karik leaned forward. As they worked together, to strip the deer, he told Revik of the dragon.

Revik nodded as he talked, while cleaning the deer's carcass, removing the hide, then cutting out the thin strips of meat which hung from its bones. When Karik had finished, a wide smile split Revik's face.

"I will go." Revik could barely contain his excitement. "When do we leave?"

"In a few days. We must think of a plan first, to ensure our success, then we will go."

Revik said that he would be ready. Karik thanked him, before gathering his spear and beginning the climb back up the mountain.

He had not gone far, when he paused for a moment and looked back. From his small ridge, he could see, between two pine trees, the settlement spread out before him, going about its business. Smoke was rising from some of the houses, and he could see Havar and Igil at work on one of the boats. A pair of children ran along the stream and vanished out of sight in the bushes, a puppy bounding along happily after them.

If they failed in their task – if they attacked the dragon and it survived – it would burn everything he could now see. It would have no need to defeat them; it could simply rise into the air, fly across the bay and rain fire from the sky.

As his fingers worked the wood of his spear shaft, Karik wondered if it was not a vain decision to try their hand against the dragon. He heard the children shouting from the bushes, but in his mind they were screaming, as they burned in dragon-fire.

Shaking off the vision, he turned and continued up the mountainside, his thoughts turning and tumbling over each other.

The Watching Stones

The day after they came back from the village, Ylmi returned early from her hunting. "I have found the tracks of a boar," she said, as she greeted the hounds, "and tomorrow I mean to go after it. Father, will you come with me?"

"I cannot," Bodvar answered, "several of the goats are sick and need careful attention. Perhaps Karik can carry a spear and help you when the beast is dead."

Ylmi looked sideways at Karik, and asked if he had any experience with boars.

"I have killed one before, but I carried the bow," he answered. "Though, I think I can carry the spear well enough."

"As long as your nerve doesn't fail you," Ylmi said, with a shrug.

They set out just as the first light of dawn was beginning to break over the eastern mountains. High they climbed, through a low pass and into one of the tiny valleys which are so frequent in that region.

"The hunting here is very good," Karik observed, as they climbed; Ylmi grunted in agreement. "In all the villages I have passed on my journey, I have not seen better," he continued.

"Those villages are older," Ylmi answered, "and since they have more people and have hunted their lands more, I do not know why you are surprised by this."

Karik stopped and leant on his spear. "How many of your people died of hunger this past winter?"

"Only Sava, but she was old and in poor health, anyway. Why do you ask?"

"We buried nearly two score in Yrdnara, when here you had plenty."

"Plenty for us," Ylmi answered. "If there had been forty more mouths to feed..." she shrugged, "we might not have had enough."

She set off again, moving easily up the steep slope.

It began to rain, the wind moaning overhead as it passed through the mountains.

Karik reckoned himself strong, but Ylmi was well used to these mountains. And, as he began to grow weary, she seemed to him utterly tireless.

After they had covered many miles, or so it seemed, Ylmi raised her hand.

"Fresh rootings." She pointed to the torn ground, where the boar had been hunting for food. "Have your spear ready."

They moved more carefully through the pines, over the rising and falling mountain slope. It was not long before Karik heard a grunting in the trees and the rough, ripping sound of a boar rooting through the earth.

He was a massive beast, with yellow tusks lifting his mouth in a savage snarl. Karik ran his hand swiftly over the spear shaft, muttering a swift prayer to Vingir, god of the hunt, that the wood was sound.

Ylmi nocked an arrow and released it in one fluid motion; there was a sharp thok as the arrow found its mark.

With a grunt, the boar shook its head and turned toward them, even as another arrow buried itself in his chest. He grunted again, looking back and forth for the source of this assault.

A third arrow Ylmi let loose, but by now the boar had seen them. Lowering his head, he charged, and the arrow rebounded off of his skull. With a roar, he barreled toward them, crashing through the low brush which stood between them, as Karik raised his spear. Out of the corner of his eye, he saw Ylmi dart off into the trees.

He dropped low and braced the spear, even as the boar lunged. Karik felt the spear shudder, as the boar drove itself onto its point; with a sickening crunch, the spear shaft cracked under the weight of the huge beast.

Frantically, Karik threw himself to the side, as the boar charged past him, one of its tusks grazing his thigh. He leapt to his feet, his breath coming in great gasps, as he still held the broken spear shaft in one hand; in the other he drew his knife. The boar eyed him angrily, huffing as Karik's spear blade still dangled from its chest. Karik took a step to the side, setting a tree between them, so that the boar would not be able to charge.

He glanced around for Ylmi. Before he could spot her, there was another thok, and a third arrow sprouted from the boar's side. The boar's breathing grew labored, and it staggered.

Karik smiled, but it was too soon; with a sudden grunt, the great boar charged again. Rounding the tree, it swung its tusks, as Karik leapt sideways and buried his knife swiftly in the beast's neck.

The blow was needless, though; with its last strength spent, the boar stumbled forward a few more steps and slumped down into the leaves, a pink froth forming around its mouth.

Karik dropped the spear shaft, his hand shaking and his breath coming unsteadily.

"Were you surprised to encounter a boar on our boar hunt?"

Ylmi looked down from where she knelt, on a large boulder. She cocked her head to one side, looking him over; her face was flushed, her shoulders rising and falling with her own breathing.

"The suddenness was not expected," Karik answered. "And, he got very close."

"That's generally what happens when you try to kill a boar." Ylmi knelt down by the carcass. "Especially when you are using a spear."

Karik gave a shaky laugh. "Fair enough."

Ylmi stared at him a moment longer, with narrowed eyes, then shrugged. "This is why I needed someone to help," she turned her gaze to the boar: "he is very large."

"Your arrows did most of the work."

"Oh, I didn't need help killing him," Ylmi corrected, rolling her eyes; "I need help taking him down the mountain."

They set to work, removing the entrails and cutting away anything they would not need, to make the return journey a little easier. Still, when they lifted it onto their shoulders, the carcass was no light burden.

They moved more slowly now. Karik made sure to mark the paths they took and the direction they travelled.

As he marked the mountains, he saw through the rain what looked like great rocks, set upon a ridge, high above the valley. He pointed at it; "What is that?"

Ylmi looked up. "The Watching Stones," she answered. "It is said that Vranr and his sons built that place, and others like it, throughout the isle, when first they came here. The way is treacherous and steep, even for these mountains, and the winds at its summit are terrible. It is said that wisdom will come to those who survive the climb... but, I have heard of little to be found there."

They shifted the boar, then continued their descent.

For a few minutes, there was nothing but the sound of the wind in the trees, and the rain falling on the path about them. The boar was heavy and the path steep but, as Karik picked his way down the mountainside, he determined to think more on the Watching Stones.

Two days later, Karik returned with Bodvar from gathering goats, to find Revik skinning a pair of rabbits with Ylmi, by the house. They ate and drank together, as the night set in.

After the meal, Revik asked Karik if they could speak outside. He followed Karik to the sheep pens, where they might speak privately.

"So," Revik started, "have you given any more thought to dragon slaying? The days are not growing any longer, Karik."

"I have thought of little else," Karik said, pushing away one of the goats, which was nuzzling at him. "But, the matter is not an easy one; I see new difficulties whichever way I consider it. Killing a beast that large is no easy matter, and even more difficult when it can fly. How are we to pin it down without being burnt alive? How are we to get close enough to land a killing blow? And, even if we do get close enough, it will have to be a mighty spear indeed that can reach its heart."

"It is as I thought," Revik said, with a sneer: "you have little stomach for this matter. I will take on the dragon myself! You are welcome to come along, but I will not wait forever."

"Revik, if you fail the dragon will awaken and burn the coast for miles, in vengeance – nor will Igil or I ever see you again. Have but a little patience, and you will earn renown beyond your imagining. Otherwise, you will achieve little but to throw away your life for nothing."

"We all die sooner or later, Karik. I would prefer that I die challenging a dragon rather than starving to death in the winter."

"A week," Karik told him; "give me a week, and together we will make a decision."

Revik thought on this for a moment, then sighed. "A week is not overly long, I will wait until then. But know this Karik, in a week, my patience with you and your waiting will be at an end."

He lifted his spear and horn bow from beside the hut, and nodded to Ylmi as she stepped outside. Then, with long, steady steps, he disappeared into the darkness beyond the clearing.

"Did I miss a fight?" Ylmi asked, as Karik came away from the sheep pens. "Does your friend not know that it is dangerous to go down the mountain during the night?"

"The night does not frighten Revik Tormsson," Karik told her.

"It should."

Ylmi glanced out toward the sea, and Karik followed her gaze.

"Many things should," Karik added.

"Tell me," she said, turning to face him, as she wrapped a deerskin around her shoulders, against the wind, "what do you speak of, that secrecy is so important?"

Karik asked her what she meant. She replied that there was little reason to stand in sheep shit when talking, unless he wished their bleating to cover the conversation.

Karik was silent at this. He then took a moment, to carefully choose and craft his words. "Unhost has been gracious to us," he said, at last, "but we seek more than simply scraping and gnawing at life."

"Unhost is gracious to himself and no one else," Ylmi retorted. "What are you considering, that calls for so much secrecy?"

Karik pointed silently westward, and Ylmi's eyes followed his finger. Through a gap in the dark pines, the moonlight fell on the dark shape of the mountain, far out in the fjord.

Ylmi starred out at it for a moment, then nodded her head. "Such a deed would be good for our village, if success was achieved. But, that is a very large 'if'!"

Karik nodded, solemnly.

"Do you have a plan?" Ylmi asked. He shook his head.

Then, he stepped away from the goat pens, and stood at the edge of their small clearing. "I am thinking of the Watching Stones."

Ylmi looked up the mountains. Somewhere to the east, in the clouds and darkness, high above them, the Stones were looking down at them.

"Has anyone ever sought them out?" Karik asked.

Ylmi shrugged; "A few."

Karik glanced eastward. "Did they make it?"

Ylmi shook her head.

"How many?"

"How many made it, or how many didn't?"

"How many made it?"

Ylmi was silent for a moment; in the distance an owl hooted. She glanced toward the mountain, then gave a sigh. "As far as I know... one."

Karik looked at her in surprise; "You?"

She nodded; "Two years ago, I made the climb." She shrugged. "There was nothing there but stones: no answers; no advice... Although, I did find one thing..." she looked at him, with a defiant grin: "bones."

Karik was silent. Again, the owl hooted, somewhere between them and the village. Ylmi glanced westward, toward the darkness, where the dragon lay beneath his mountain.

"We should go inside," she said, finally.

Karik nodded, but he did not move. "I will go up the mountain tomorrow... if you will tell me the way."

Ylmi chuckled at that. "Sometimes, I think you are more brave than you are smart. I could no more tell you my skill with a bow." She clapped him on the shoulder and turned toward the house. "I will come with you."

———◈———

They rose while Bodvar and Siggi were still asleep, and set out.

They spoke little in the dim light of the early morning, as they climbed up through the pines, from rolling slopes to rocky ridges, which rose ever higher. The clouds hung low and heavy as they climbed, and the day did not seem to grow brighter as time passed.

At last, Ylmi stopped and seated herself beside a spindly pine tree. "We are here." She pointed upward.

Before them rose a towering, rocky slope, almost bare of trees and shrubs. It towered before them in slopes and cliffs, its heights disappearing in the clouds which hung heavy in the sky.

"Where is the path?"

Ylmi grinned, darkly. "There is no path, Karik Haldsson," she said. "It may be that we will die today."

"I'll not die on a rocky slope," he said, shaking his head. "If I am to die, it will be in dragon-fire, or the sea's dark embrace."

Ylmi laughed. "How poetic. I'll remind you of that when we're both tumbling to our deaths."

They drank from a small mountain spring nearby, then began to climb. Ylmi led the way, with Karik a short distance behind her.

A short slope led them to a cliff face almost twenty feet high. Ylmi began to climb. A moment later, Karik followed, the slimy moss wet beneath his fingers, squelching into the rough rock, as he tried to pull himself up the cliff face.

One cliff followed another, rising ever higher into the clouds. An arctic wind rose; the air grew so cold that Karik's fingers grew numb.

"How much farther?" he asked Ylmi, when they reached the top of yet another steep slope.

She pointed north. "A little farther there is a long ridge which runs upward – it will take us along the edge of the fjord, until we are not too far from the mountain." She took a deep breath and pulled her cloak tight. "After that, the final climb. It is the most dangerous part."

Karik nodded.

He noticed that her hair, which had been pulled back in a braid, was coming undone, the wind pulling at it as they climbed.

There came a flash of light and the crack of thunder. They both flinched. The wind had been gathering, and it now came with a great howl, out of the north. Flecks of rain were on the wind. Karik felt a sudden sense of dread. "Perhaps it would be wise to turn back."

He glanced around them. Clouds hung heavy, above and below them, the whole world caught in writhing tendrils of the mist, driven by the wind. Ahead, where their path lay, the clouds were darker – harbingers of a great storm.

But, Ylmi only gave a dark smile, her green eyes flashing. "The way to the Stones does not lie through sunlit paths or mountain meadows. Vranr was a dark trickster, or so the tales tell; his Stones are not easily reached."

Karik wiped the rain from his face. "I thought you found nothing when you came here?"

Ylmi shook her head; "I found no answers. I did not say I found nothing."

At this, Karik was seized by a burning curiosity; a hunger to know what lay atop the mountain, among the Watching Stones. "Then let us go."

They continued to climb, ever higher, past the last trees. Karik saw snowdrifts, unmelted from the past winter and still bitterly cold. By Karik's reckoning, it was more than a little way, but at last they came to the ridge of which Ylmi had spoken. It ran northwest, nearly into the teeth of the wind, slowly rising upward.

Karik's legs and arms ached, and at first he was glad to not be scaling cliffs. But, as they struggled into the cold wind, he soon began to yearn for the protection of a cliff face. The flecks of rain soon turned into heavy drops, beating down upon them, and the lightning grew more frequent. Karik questioned more than once if he was a fool; the mountains are no place to be, when the clouds do battle.

Still, Ylmi went onward, never stopping and never slowing, even as the rain grew heavier. Karik was soon soaked through to the bone, the wet clothes rubbing like ice on his skin, the wind sucking any hint of warmth from his bones. At last, they reached the end of the ridge.

Ylmi pointed wordlessly at a narrow path, which wound up a rocky cliff face. Through the rain and gloom, Karik peered upward, following the path as it wound in and out of sight.

"It's not going to get any easier," he muttered, and was rewarded by a dark grin from Ylmi.

Together, they began to climb the path, placing their feet carefully with each step, attempting to avoid the rotten stone and slick surfaces which were so prevalent. More than once, one of them slipped, only to be caught and steadied by the other. Karik's arms throbbed from gripping the rocks, and the wind burned his face, as it whipped over the path.

Once, with his shoulder pressed against the cliff, he glanced down. The path was barely wide enough for two feet together, then fell, in a steep cliff, for almost a hundred feet, onto another ledge. Below that, through the ragged clouds, he thought he could see the ridge which had brought them to the cliff face.

What, he wondered, had possessed Vranr to climb this high and place the Stones here – if it had even been Vranr in the first place? And, how had he done it? Vranr was more legend than ancestor – at least, from the tales he had heard.

"It will be a fine thing if we climb all the way up and find nothing" he muttered to himself. But, the words were snatched away by the wind, as a mighty gust came hurtling down from the clouds, high above them, and whipped about the cliffside. A thunderous crack of lightning exploded the air in front of them, sending rock and mud splintering through the air, as they pressed themselves to the cliff face. Karik reached out, grasping the hood of Ylmi's cloak, as the roar of the thunder deafened them.

But, with a smile on her face, Ylmi turned and beckoned him onward. After a few more steps, they climbed over a small ledge, where they felt the full force of the north wind.

And, so they came to the Watching Stones of Vranr...

DVENGRHAL

Thunder boomed over the mountain top, and the clouds rolled and writhed about them, in the howling wind. Four great stones were set upright, each the height of two men, and wide enough that Karik could shelter from the wind behind one. One faced north, one south, one east and one west, and there were strange symbols and designs carved into them. Above them all, in the center of the Stones, a seat had been carved into the peak of the mountain, facing southwest.

Karik reached out his fingers to touch the runes, then quickly jerked his hand away; although nothing had moved, he felt as though the Stone had reached back.

Lightning flashed over them with an earsplitting crack, and Karik could taste the burning of it on his tongue. With a wince, he felt the air suddenly grow heavy, humming as if he was within a thunderclap.

Ylmi stood still, as one who had been struck to stone; her eyes were fixed on the great stone seat above them. Karik followed her gaze. His eyes widened as a great, black raven dropped, with flapping wings, onto one of the arms. Heedless of the storm, it folded its wings and cocked one eye, first at Ylmi, then at Karik.

A heavy voice cut through the wind, behind them: "It has been many years since a son of Vranr visited this place."

Karik turned to see a bent figure, leaning against one of the Stones. Cold eyes gleamed blue from beneath its hood, darting from Karik to Ylmi, where they lingered. "Even longer still since any came a second time."

Karik glanced at Ylmi and saw her struck dumb. Her jaw worked, but her face was twisted in surprise.

"Nonetheless, you come late," the figure snarled, "Oh, Karik Haldsson." He eased himself down, to sit against the great stone.

"Who are you?" Karik asked. "How do you know my name?"

The figure groaned. "You may call me Dvengrhal. The gods have seen fit to make me their messenger to you."

Karik felt his heart stop in his chest, and he sank to one knee, before the emissary of the gods.

"Oh, stand up!" Dvengrhal snapped. "I am but a messenger, not the gods themselves!" His eyes flicked up to the raven, which still sat on the throne, then came back to Karik. "I was told you were a great man, so stand on your feet and act like one."

Slowly, Karik pulled himself to his feet, wary of every movement. Was all of this a test from the gods? Should he have brought a sacrifice?

"Are you going to stand there, until you both freeze and my bones turn to dust?" Dvengrhal interrupted his thoughts. "Or, do you have questions you would ask?"

"It is in my mind to slay the dragon," Karik said, through the wind. "But, the slaying of a dragon is no small matter."

"'Slaying a dragon is no small matter'," Dvengrhal mocked. "All Father, have mercy! Is this what the children of Vranr have become? If you have already discovered this for yourself, oh wise Karik, then for what purpose have you come all this way?"

"I seek wisdom," Karik answered, "and guidance. I would not seek danger unneeded."

Dvengrhal snorted. "And, what danger is that, Karik Haldsson? Do you fear death?"

"I do not..." Karik answered, "but for others. If I fail in my attack on the dragon, and I am bested, the dragon will take a terrible revenge—"

"Either death is to be feared by all, or by none," the hooded figure interrupted him. "So, which is it? Should death be feared or welcomed?" The rain was now pouring heavily upon all of them.

Karik stared at the figure before him for a moment. "A man should welcome death for himself, but fear it for those he is charged to protect."

"That is a double answer!" Dvengrhal spat. "Tell me, do you fear to cause death to these people?"

Karik nodded.

"Do you fear that the dragon will burn their land, kill their goats and destroy their crops?" Dvengrhal's eyes glowed from beneath the hood, as Karik concurred.

"Tell me, how many of their crops and goats go to the dragon every year? Enough for ten people? Twenty? Forty?"

Karik was silent, and for a moment all that could be heard was the storm. He staggered as a gust caught him, and he hurriedly slid down, to sit on the southern side of the stone chair.

"How many have died because of the food the dragon has consumed, just last year alone?" Dvengrhal asked. "Or, do they not count those the dragon killed by starvation, instead of fire?"

"Very well, then," Karik said, after a moment. "If I slay the dragon – if I succeed – what actions will Unhost take? He has served the dragon for some years, and the arrangement has not been a bad one for him. What of King Unhost?"

"So, if you fail you will be answerable for the actions of the dragon? And, if you succeed, you will be answerable for the actions of your jarl and your king? I was told that you were a wise man, Karik Haldsson, but perhaps this was a jest played upon me?

"Go back to your village and scratch more grain out of the sand. The other villages will bury many children this winter, but it will be the dragon's fault, not yours. And, when your little village grows beyond its means, and the graves are dug into the mountainside, it will be Unhost's fault, not yours."

"And, if the dragon burns the coastline?" Karik asked.

The blue of Dvengrhal's eyes narrowed, and his hood shook for an instant. "If the dragon burns the coast because you had a poor plan of attack..." he rose to his feet, "then that will be your fault.

"I grow weary of discussing whose fault this will be or that will be; go do, Karik Haldsson, and let lesser men worry about whether it will be their fault or someone else's."

"Wait," Ylmi stepped forward, her voice tense. "I too have questions I must ask, questions for which I have scaled the path to the Stones not once, but twice."

"I know your questions," Dvengrhal said, harshly, "and I give you an answer: go! And, take!"

Ylmi stared. "That is all? Where was this answer when I climbed the first time, when I yet braved the heights and the storms?"

Dvengrhal shook his head. "There was no answer then; this answer has only come now." He looked again to the sky. "The world is changing, and the pieces being brought together will shape the lives and fates of many."

Ylmi's breathing was coming quicker now, and Karik realized suddenly that she was furious.

"And, what of the lives and fates of those, two years ago?" Her voice was a snarl – rage, hurt and fury all wrapped together. "Two years!"

But, Dvengrhal only laughed. His voice was heavy; "The threads of the world move without regard to your desires. The gods do not remove the doom of a man because he is evil; the price must still be paid. But, the accounts will be settled; all debts will be paid in the end."

He turned to leave, then stopped suddenly. He turned back to them, the wind whipping at his cloak, and Karik saw a few grey strands of hair slip from beneath his hood, to dance in the wind.

"You have said, oh Karik Haldsson, that you will not die on a rocky slope," Dvengrhal proclaimed, "yet, though you may sail to the end of the Earth, or climb to the highest mountain, still I tell you that your body will lie, broken and lifeless, on the rocky slopes of this land."

"What of me?" Ylmi asked, savagely.

Dvengrhal looked at her for a moment. When he spoke, it was in a voice both bitter and sorrowful: "You will receive what you desire most. And, when it is taken away, you shall be given what you hope for."

And, with that, he was gone.

Ylmi stared at where he had stood, the grey mist ragged among the black stones.

"Once again, I risk death to climb to these stones," she muttered, "and this time I am given nonsense, instead of nothing. Truly, the gods hate me, and Vranr remains the most senseless of men."

⋄

Two days later, a heavy storm blew in from the north. The rain was heavy and cold, and ice formed at the entrance of Bodvar's home, and on the brambles which hid the sheep caves. But, inside, Bodvar and his family stayed warm by the fire.

Karik sat in silence, his mind turning over everything that had passed since they had come to the village.

On the evening of the second night, Siggi made a stew of goat, onions and peas. While it boiled over the fire, they all sat together to keep warm.

"So, tell me, Karik," Bodvar said, "why it is that you came north?"

Karik said that he had already told them: it was because of the hunger in Yrdnara.

"That I know," Bodvar answered, "but why did you come north? Surely there are other places where you might have found refuge?"

"Fewer than you might think," said Karik; "though it seems that this place fared well enough, most of the other villages on this island suffered a great famine, this past year."

Siggi confirmed that they had heard this.

"Bjarnmont has no place for outcasts," Karik continued, "and, in the south, the western jarls are still able to raid, out of reach of King Jarhost in his hall."

"Surely they could use such well-built men as yourself," Ylmi suggested. "And, if your companions are as strong as you say they are..."

"They have no use for warriors," Karik replied, "especially those who come in the autumn, when the work of harvest is nearly done, and the lean months are close at hand."

"So, you came north," Siggi nodded, "because there is nowhere else to go?"

Karik shrugged. He made to speak, but the words escaped him and he fell silent.

The fire crackled, and the stew began to hiss as the water boiled. After a few moments, Bodvar's keen eyes glinted in the firelight, and Karik saw that he was staring.

"There was another reason that drove you," Siggi stated. Her voice was soft.

Karik found himself pouring out his thoughts; he spoke hurriedly, his voice trying to keep up: "Our people came here from the west, so there must be lands to the west which have food and riches... lands where the people do not need to scratch a living out of the rocks, or cower in fear when the bitter cold comes. It must be out there.

"And, if it is there, there must be a way to get back. The Black Isles are impassible, as far as we have found, but they must have an end; surely they cannot encircle the whole island. To the south, no one has ever found their end, but to the north..." he raised his hands, "I have never heard that this is the case. There must be an edge, somewhere."

"Why?" Bodvar's soft voice was barely audible, over the crackling of the fire.

"Why what?"

"Why must there be an edge?" Bodvar continued. "Why must there be a way to reach the lands to the west?"

"If we came from there, then..."

"That was many years ago," Bodvar pointed out. "Many storms, tides and waves have passed since then; the way may be closed now. The Isles may go as far north as the ice sea. Tell me, have you ever spoken with one who has sailed in the waters north of Undmir?"

Karik admitted that he had not.

"There are a few tiny fishing outposts there," Bodvar told him, "and they have sailed along the coast, as far as their boats will take them. Do you know what they have found?"

Karik shook his head.

"Ice, storms and little else."

Bodvar studied the fire. "The storms there are sudden and terrible. They come howling out of the north and churn the sea into waves greater than Bjarnmont itself. The fishermen do not stray out of sight of land or their homes, for if they are caught in those storms... well, they have not yet built a boat that can withstand them. They are crushed on the rocks or swallowed by the waves."

Siggi stood and stirred the stew, which was bubbling happily, and the smell filled their dwelling; Karik felt his stomach turn with hunger.

Bodvar leaned to look around Siggi, who stood between them as she stirred the stew. "I do not say that there is not a way, only that there may not be one, and even just looking to find it is more dangerous than you know."

"You speak as though you know the North Sea well," Karik said.

"My brother sailed it for several years," Bodvar replied, "until he strayed too far from the shore; the mast from his ship was washed ashore several days after the storm."

"That is enough talk from the two of you." Siggi brandished her ladle. "A passage there may or may not be, but there is a bit of land, just north of the sheep pens, which would do nicely to grow peas and onions, or even a cabbage patch, if you would dig out a few trees. So, plan your way through that." She smiled as she filled their wooden bowls with the steaming stew. The conversation turned to the prospective cabbage patch.

But, Karik took Bodvar's words to heart and, that night, as he wrapped himself in a bear fur and lay in the darkness, he turned them over in his mind. Outside, the storm raged and the winds whipped through the trees, as the fire burned to embers inside their cave. Karik watched the red light glowing within the ashes, and his mind turned from the storm-swept Black Isles to the dragon.

Winter was hard upon them, and the next storm they saw would carry heavy snow.

When this storm broke, it would be time to challenge the dragon.

DRAGON FIRE

When at last the storm broke, it left behind a bitter cold which did not relinquish its grip, even in the light of the noon sun. There was much work to be done, for winter was now at hand, and Bodvar said that the heavy snows would soon be upon them. Ylmi ranged far afield each day, seeking any game that she could find, but the forests were swiftly growing empty, as every bird and beast sought shelter against the cold, in nests and dens.

While Siggi saw to it that the last vegetables were harvested, Bodvar said that the goat herd must be parted. "I do not doubt that there are still some still wandering the hills, that we have not found. But, let us take what we can down to the village, that they may have all they need for the winter. We will survive on what is left, and any others that we find in the coming weeks will be a bonus. But, I do not wish to wait and find myself in the village with Unhost, while the snow covers my path home."

⚬

So it was that Karik again made the trek to Unhost's village.

The going was slow. When they arrived, the village had still the look of a place deserted. A heavy mist which was almost rain hung over the village, so that the slopes which rose inland disappeared into greyness, and the bay seemed to vanish into dim cloud.

When the goats were separated, the day was almost at its end. Unhost agreed to let them rest in his hut for the night, before starting back up to Bodvar's home in the hills. But, Karik took his leave of Bodvar and sought out Igil.

As he suspected, his friend was at work with Havar, laying boards on the keel of a new boat. As he approached, Karik paused and watched them.

They were focused deeply on their task, with Havar explaining to Igil some shaping of the boards, which made Igil laugh.

Crossing the sand, Karik greeted them; Igil embraced him with great joy.

"Havar has been showing me how he makes these boats, to go shallow in the water," he said. "On the edges of the bay, the rocks are deep and sharp, but there also are many fish." He pointed about them: "These boats draw so little water that we can sail right up over them."

Karik replied that this was indeed thrilling, then asked Igil if they could speak together, for a few moments.

The two of them sat together, a little way from the boats, and looked out over the sea. The mist still lay heavy on the water, but Karik thought that he could see the dark outline of the mountain in the distance.

"Have you thought on the dragon?" Karik asked, after a few moments.

"I have thought on little else," Igil replied. "I have spoken with Wisic and Umir, and they are with us. But, even so... Havar says that the beast is twice the size of Unhost's hall, with wings just as long, at least! Something that large will not be easy to kill, even with six of us."

"I have my sword and Revik has his ax," Karik said; "and, all of us have our spears."

"But, they are bear spears," Igil pointed out; "the cross-piece will prevent us from piercing the beast, deep enough to kill it."

"Then, we must beat down the cross-pieces," Karik replied. Easier said than done, Igil's expression seemed to say.

"And, we must determine how to fight a beast that can fly."

Igil nodded slowly, his fingers running over the beginnings of a beard, which barely covered his chin. "It seems to me that fighting a dragon in the open is the way to a quick death. We must face it in its lair, or not at all."

"We do not know what manner of cave it dwells in," Karik pointed out.

"That does not matter," Igil replied. "If we face it on the mountain, it can simply leap into the air and burn us alive, or make for this village and turn it to ash, while we sit helpless on its mountain."

They discussed the problem among themselves for some time, until the grey light began to fade into darkness.

———◆———

The next day, Karik told Bodvar that he had matters to attend to in the village, and would need a few days to see that they were resolved.

"Do what you must," Bodvar told him, "but do not stay too long: the path up the mountains is more than treacherous when the snows come."

Karik promised not to wait longer than he had to, then set to work with the others.

Umir took time away from Flovi and his wife Greta, while Wisic took his leave from Torig, to help them. During the day, they laboured to prepare themselves for the great undertaking and, after darkness had fallen on the settlement, they sat together in Havar's dark cavern, discussing how best to go about the attack. Ever they came back to the matter of the beast's flight, and the difficulty in landing a killing blow.

"How far must we thrust a spear, before it reaches the heart or a lung?" Wisic asked. "And, how are we to do it, unless he determines to stand still?"

"It must be confused," Karik replied, "and wearied by many blows."

"You want us to confuse it?" Umir asked. "How will that be accomplished, oh Karik the Wise?"

Havar spoke up: "By the number of us." He looked around at their faces, lit by the flickering light of his fire. "If we all keep moving, attacking from different sides, and never let it rest—"

"You do know that we are talking of a dragon," Wisic pointed out, "not a large ox?"

———◆———

On the third day, Ylmi arrived at Havar's house, accompanied by a tall, lean woman of their own age, who carried a spear with the longest spearhead Karik had ever seen.

"This is Thora," Ylmi told them; "she is a friend to me, and no friend of Unhost. Even better, she is more skilled with a spear than any other person in the village – which may be of some small use in the killing of a dragon."

"You told others?" Havar asked Karik. "I thought it was agreed that it would be best for a small company: me and your friends. Our company may grow too large for this task."

"I am no sage or ancient wise man," Wisic said, "but I fail to see how the key to slaying a dragon is to bring fewer spears; I confess myself baffled."

"Havar has a point, though," Revik paused running a stone over his ax; "too many people may cause confusion."

"Confusion is our only hope!" Karik spoke firmly: "Not only is the dragon more familiar with the lay of his own mountain, he is far stronger, even, than all of us together. I have not seen him but, if legends are true, then we might as well be fighting a whole company of snow bears. We must confuse the beast, turn him to and fro, and never give him time to chase one of us down."

"Still..." Havar eyed the two women skeptically.

Karik pointed to Ylmi: "She is one of the best archers in this settlement."

"The best," Ylmi corrected.

"The best," Karik nodded. "Without her, our chances drop significantly. And, if Thora is as good with a spear as she says, then all the better."

"What good will her little arrows do, against a beast as massive as the dragon?" Havar grimaced. "Don't you agree, Revik?"

Revik shook his head; "I have seen her shoot enough to know that she is no weakling. But, I still think it important to have a small company."

"Revik," Karik turned on him, "do I have to explain every single detail to you, or will you listen to me for once?!" He glanced between Havar and Revik; "I have listened to you both debate and argue, and it seems to me that your best plan is to charge headfirst at the thing, and let him eat you one by one, as he pleases."

Havar glared at him, but the others said nothing.

Karik took a deep breath. "The chances that all of us are going to finish this fight are slim to none." He looked around the room, taking in all of their faces, in the flickering firelight. "Even if we are not killed outright, we may be laid out and need time to recover.

"Now, with Thora, we are eight; that's two from each direction. With that number, I think my plan will work! But, for my plan I need you all. And, I especially need Ylmi!"

He looked again to Havar, and saw that he was now wavering. "Trust me, Havar, I can see the dragon dead and this village freed of him. How many others in Vrania will be able to say that they are dragon slayers?"

At last, Havar nodded, and agreed that he would go along with Karik's plan.

<hr>

When night fell, they slipped quietly down to the boats, each with his own weapons. Each of them carried a pair of long spears, the crossbars bent down or broken off. Across his back, Revik had slung his great two-handed ax; his brother carried on his belt a seax: a short blade with one edge, honed finer than any sword. Karik and the others carried spears, as well as small axes stuck in their belts, or slung over their backs. Over her shoulder, Ylmi carried her longbow and a quiver of arrows. For a moment they stood there, looking out over the stillness.

"Well," Wisic muttered, "if we're all agreed that we're going to die in dragon's fire, then let's get it over with." A few of them chuckled at that.

Ylmi and Thora stared darkly toward the mountain, then stepped toward the water.

They slid Havar's boat into the waves, rippling black under a cloudy sky. The moon's light shone through the clouds, giving off a faint glow, in the bitter cold of the early night. Carefully, Umir and Revik slid their oars into the water and began to row, as quietly as they could.

Over the lapping waves, the only sound was that of the wind moaning, over the cliffs on either side of the bay. Karik felt his heart beginning to race. Once they were a little way out, Havar raised the sail.

They glided smoothly along, rising and falling with the gentle waves, which caressed those northern fjords between storms. The moon was well overhead, when the dark shape of the mountain appeared out of the gloom before them.

Igil and Thora stood in the bow of the ship, holding oars wrapped in rags, which they used to push off from the rocks which rose out of the water. More than once the sharp rocks scraped against the side of the boat, and Karik feared that they would sink before they reached the island.

But, they reached it safe enough.

Together, they pulled the boat ashore, that the falling tide would not take it out to sea, and they took up their weapons.

As they prepared to move forward, Karik noticed snowflakes falling in the moonlight, and a shiver went down his spine. The ground was steep and rocky, and they had great difficulty moving any distance in the darkness. Havar said that, as best as they could tell, the entrance to the dragon's lair was on the western side of the mountain – so, that was where they went.

They had not gone far, when Karik, who was leading the way, discovered – to his great surprise – a path cut into the rock. This astonished him. Havar said that he had no knowledge of where it might have come from.

Their first sign of the dragon was a huge mound of broken rocks and stone – it was piled like rubble, as if thrown from the mountain.

Igil and Karik confirmed that this place would work well enough for their plan, so all set to work.

When they were ready, Karik took Revik and Havar with him, into the mountain.

The moon had set, and it was the dark, cold hour before dawn as they crept into the tunnel. Karik carefully led the way, feeling along the walls. But, as he did so, he noticed that the rock was smooth, as if it had been carved by hands, rather than simply a fractured cave. Down they crept, through the wide passage, which turned and twisted as it descended, taking them ever farther from the entrance.

Of a sudden, an orange glow began to light the tunnel, and they could see doors and passageways cut into the mountain around them. Karik wondered more and more on this; the thought began to come to him that they had not counted on the dragon having allies with him in the mountain.

They felt their way along smooth pathways, until they saw the first light of dawn, pouring in from the east. Thinking they had passed right through the mountain, Revik said that it was far smaller than he had thought. But, Karik raised his hand for silence, and crept a little farther in.

The path led them to a ledge, from where the glow seemed to rise. Approaching it carefully, Karik looked over the edge.

Below them, the dragon lay upon a gleaming mound, his sides rising and falling as he breathed. The fire within him glowed with an angry hue, which bathed the walls of the cavern in a red glow.

In its light, Karik marveled to see where they stood. This was not a cavern hollowed out for the dragon's resting place; staircases and balconies rose up along the walls, and walkways were carved deeper into the mountain, beyond these. This was a fortress, built within the mountain. But it was broken and blackened by dragon-fire; the stairways were shattered in a dozen places. Karik gazed in amazement around him, wondering what manner of place they had stumbled upon.

"You come uninvited into my home?!"

The dragon's voice echoed like distant thunder, and it seemed to Karik that all suddenly stood still.

"But then, you are guests even in your own home, it would seem."

The great beast stirred, and the rattle of armor and metal on stone filled the hall.

"Once, it was warriors who challenged me; who fought me like men. Now, it is..." he paused, to take a deep breath, "...children." He ground out the words like the shifting of rock on a mountain. "Younglings now slink through my halls unannounced, like thieves, their greed knowing no bounds." His head slowly rose from the gold underneath him, and he turned his glinting eyes to the balcony where Karik hid.

"Tell me – for I am curious – who it is who slips so carelessly into my home? Or, have you not even manners enough for that?"

Karik determined that it would not be a wise choice to speak, so he remained silent and stepped back.

But, the dragon rose, with a speed that Karik did not expect from a creature so large. "As I expected," he snarled.

The mountain shook, as the creature stretched to his full height. His head rose up, then back down, as he peered down at the balcony where they stood.

"Go on..." the dragon nodded toward the exit: "run! I like to see your fear." He smiled, and the flames flicked over his fangs. "Run away, Karik Haldsson."

Karik shook at that, and found his voice: "How do you know my name?"

"It speaks!" the dragon hissed. "Oh, come now, Haldsson. I am not a badger, to hide in my burrow, while the world passes by outside. Do you imagine that I would be blind to knowing what passes, in the village on my doorstep?"

A heavy, clawed foot struck the ground, as the dragon took a step forward. "I am here to rest – to recover my strength, after years of war. The doings of your petty village amuse me, but I care little for the scrapings of your little rock, you mannerless starling."

"All the same," Karik replied, "we little like one who eats what he did not grow, and feasts on what he did not kill."

"Oh?" The dragon's voice then sank low, and to Karik it seemed that he chuckled: "Have no fear, Karik Haldsson, I shall remedy that at once."

With that, he reared back his massive head, and Karik leapt behind one of the great pillars, as a thundering torrent of fire hurled down on the balcony.

VIII

When the fire abated, Karik dashed for the passage, Havar hard on his heels. But, once they reached it, they slowed: Revik was not with them. When Karik peered out of the passage, he could not see him on the balcony.

The dragon laughed, a great rumbling noise which filled the cavern and echoed off of the rocks. "I take it you have never fought a dragon before."

He composed himself. "Dragon fire is... quite terrifying – or, so I've been told." He shook himself. "Still, I do not feel like fighting today; there was a particularly large whale yesterday, which still sits heavy in my stomach."

He arched his neck, until his great head hung but a few feet from the floor, and peered into the passage where Karik had taken refuge with Havar.

"Hmm..." He sniffed at the rock. "Perhaps we could come to an agreement; I could use a servant as capable as yourself."

"You think to flatter me?" Karik asked, in surprise.

"Well," the dragon chuckled, "you did come with more than one companion – which is more than I can say for your unfortunate predecessors. I think you might make a fine jarl – perhaps, in time, a king, if— Ah!"

He snarled, for Revik had suddenly made a deep cut upon his wing, with his ax.

"Cease!" With a growl, the dragon hurled another gout of fire, driving Revik back into another passage.

And, while his head was turned, Karik and Havar leapt forward with their spears, thrusting at his great neck. But, his scales grew heavy and closed densely together; their spears did little.

An instant later, the beast again bathed the balcony in fire. Again, they darted back into the passage, but the dragon's fire had caught Karik's shoulder.

"You have the manners of a fire drake!" the dragon snapped.

Havar tore off his cloak and wrapped it swiftly around the flames, as Karik writhed in pain.

"Am I a snow bear," the dragon asked, "to be needled to death by your little pinpricks? Is that your plan? STOP!" He suddenly whirled around, just as Revik stepped out of the tunnel. Revik slowly lowered his ax and backed away.

Karik took a deep breath, as the pain began to subside, but his shoulder was raw to the touch, and the leather jerkin he wore was burnt away where the fire had touched it.

"A dragon is not an ill friend." The dragon's voice was calm again, though when Karik glanced out, he saw that its eyes did not stray far from Revik. "With me as your ally, you could be a jarl. If you serve me well enough, perhaps I would even make you king of this little island. It does not matter to me."

His large eyes glowed in the gloom, as he peered down at where Karik was hiding. "And, if it seems that little settlement beside the sea is too little for you, it would be but a small thing for me to seat you in Bjarnmont, after a time." His giant head leaned toward the passage, which Karik felt growing hot, as his breath passed over them. "What say you, Karik Haldsson?"

Revik saw his chance and leapt forward unseen, dealing a mighty blow to the dragon's wing with his ax, hewing at the beast with all of his strength. The dragon's roar filled the cavern, deafening Karik and Havar, until blood trickled from their ears, and they nearly collapsed with the pain.

Swiftly, Karik roused himself and staggered forward, leaping from the cavern to slide down the dragon's body, seeking purchase for his spear. Havar quickly followed, shouting as he lunged. The dragon twisted and turned, for as soon as he drove one of them off, the other two attacked. Yet, for all of their efforts, their weapons were pitiful against him, better suited for hunting wild animals than piercing the scaled armour of this ancient terror. But, his wings were not so armored, and it was these that they attacked.

Soon, he grew weary of the matter, and determined that better sport would be had in the open air. Raising his great bulk, he lifted himself onto the balcony and made for the mountainside.

Staggering through the smoke, Igil and Revik followed him, as Karik struggled to his feet. The dragon heard them follow and laughed to himself, thinking that he had not enjoyed such sport since his first arrival at the mountain. With a laugh, he lunged from the mountain.

But, he found himself foiled...

For, over the great entrance, Igil and the others had hung a great net of rope, stone and chain, which fell in thick folds about him. In a moment of fear, he thrashed this way and that, in an attempt to extricate himself, but found that this tangled it ever thicker.

Karik rushed out after him and stood there with the others, wondering how best to attack the beast, for he writhed and turned so violently that it seemed there was no way they could approach him. On his left, Thora gripped her spear and took a slow step forward while, behind him, Revik came climbing from the cavern, his great ax hanging in his hand. There was a twang from overhead, and Karik looked up to see Ylmi standing above the cave's entrance, drawing another arrow.

But, the sound which came from the dragon sent them all to their knees; in all of his battles thereafter, Karik never heard a sound so full of rage, pain and malice as the screaming roar the dragon let loose, there on the mountain.

It turned toward them, hobbling through the net as best it could, and Karik saw an arrow protruding from one eye. He smiled. Still, the dragon had one good eye, and its gaze lit on Ylmi, drawing another arrow in her bow. Tangled in the net though he was, the dragon drove toward her, heedless of the blows that Revik and the others laid upon him as he passed. Fire ripped through the air and black blood splattered the rocks, as the dragon hurled himself at Ylmi.

"Get him! Get him!" Karik shouted, leaping toward the dragon.

As the beast lunged, the net was beginning to be pulled away.

Karik struck at the twisted membrane of the wing, his ax opening a gaping hole which dripped with hot blood. From somewhere nearby, Umir was shouting and Revik was howling,

Yet for all their attacks, the dragon paid them no mind, lunging up the cliff face after Ylmi, who was now climbing up the mountain, as fast as her legs would carry her. Even bound, however, the dragon was swifter, tearing up the mountain after her, raining rocks and dirt upon Karik and the others, as they gave chase.

Then, the dragon raised his head and released a torrent of fire, which bathed the mountainside in white and blue flames. To Karik's horror, Ylmi came tumbling through them, her hair and clothes on fire as she fell, tumbling over the rocks. She crashed into a rock, where she lay dazed. Karik climbed hurriedly toward her.

The dragon raised himself up and, with a roar, broke the chains that had bound him. With a snarl, his jaws caught Umir and bit him in half, hurling his body into the sea. His tail whipped through the air, catching Havar in the chest and hurling him down the mountain. Then, with a triumphant roar, he spread his great wings out over the mountainside, blocking out the light of the rising sun, and leapt into the air. Karik's heart fell into his stomach.

But, as the dragon made to beat his wings, cut and nicked in a dozen places, they folded, and the great beast went hurtling down, crashing into the mountainside below them. Swiftly, they rushed toward him.

He quickly righted himself and turned his one remaining eye on Karik, glowing red with hate and rage. He spoke in a voice dark and deep:

"Karik! I curse you and your sons, and your sons' sons! Death and fire will cling to you like a cloak. Your every victory will turn to defeat, your triumphs to tragedies, your conquests to calamities. Never shall you have rest. Never shall a home provide you comfort. I doom you to this, oh Karik. Now, despair... and die!"

And with that, the great beast, dripping with blood from his many wounds, charged. The last fire he could summon raged over the mountain, blinding Karik and all the rest with its heat and smoke.

The mountain shook and, up in his mountain hut, Dranri saw smoke and fire rising in the morning sky; he wondered what these things meant.

Even farther north, King Jarhost was woken from his slumber, with the word of a dragon's rumour in the sky.

So they fought, and this was the first great battle that Karik waged. The dragon was weakened, but even so he was a terrible beast, and the fey death strength was upon him. Never before had he been so challenged, and there have been few such battles since. For, though the dragon was mighty, he was outnumbered, and those who attacked him were no mean warriors.

Here and there Igil darted, his seax biting deep – first on this side, then on that, with cunning and crafty strokes. Thora wielded her spear like a blacksmith's hammer, striking again and again, seeking wherever she might do the most damage. Karik and Wisic also attacked as swiftly as they could, seeking to slip their spears between the beast's scales and draw a trickle of blood. But, none could match the strength of Revik, who wielded his two-handed ax to the dragon's great discomfort. Beset on all sides, the dragon knew not where to turn: if he attacked to the right, Karik and Wisic came upon his left; if he struck to his left, Igil and Revik, with his deadly ax, attacked from the right. One eye he had already lost to Ylmi's bow, and Thora seemed to be ever just out of sight and reach.

There was another twang, and Karik saw an arrow strike the scales on the dragon's head, careening away. With a snarl, the beast's head snapped in the direction from which the arrow had come, and his lone eye found Ylmi, leaning against a rock, as she set another arrow to her bow. Like a thunderbolt he leapt, shattering rocks and raising a cloud of dust as he landed, narrowly missing Ylmi, as she darted away again. In frustration, the dragon roared then whirled around, as Thora thrust her spear deep into his haunch. An instant later Revik's ax sliced deep into the dragon's tail. In a fury, the dragon reached up the mountainside and tore down a boulder, sending a landslide tumbling onto both of them.

But, as he turned back to Ylmi, she loosened her arrow at point-blank range. This time, he did not scream, emitting only a low growl, as he swept his tail over the mountainside and sent her tumbling down among the rocks.

Karik's breath was coming in great gasps now, as he climbed again toward the dragon. Even without its wings, the beast moved over the mountain with incredible speed, bounding from ledge to ledge as it fought. Karik lunged again, thrusting his spear at a chink in the dragon's scales, but the dragon turned, snapping the spear and sending Karik flying, with a great blow to his chest.

Wisic and Igil came close upon the dragon, and Igil's seax slipped beneath the dragon's scales, piercing deeper than any cut yet. The dragon roared and turned again, tearing rock from the mountainside, to fall in an avalanche upon Igil and Wisic. A rock struck Igil in the shoulder, so that he could not move his right arm. Wisic bled from the nose and mouth, as he struggled to his feet.

Yet, with that blow, the dragon wrought his own doom.

Karik struggled to pull himself to his feet, as the fight raged. His ears rang, and it seemed to him that the mountain moved back and forth. Shaking his head only made the mountain move more, and with a convulsion he vomited into the dirt, drawing deep breaths, as the dragon pulled down a second avalanche upon Revik. Karik looked about him for his spear.

Then, a gleam caught his eye.

The morning sun was just beginning to peek over the horizon, and its rays shone off of a blade, buried in the rocks.

The blade was Farndrang, which for years had lain on the mountainside, buried in a past battle and now dislodged from its resting place, by the dragon's strike on Igil. Karik lunged for it, hurriedly pulling away the debris.

Revik had dodged the better part of the dragon's avalanche and, looking about him, saw his brother bloody, Wisic staggering and Karik doubled up on his hands and knees. He roared his defiance and the dragon roared back, as the two came up against each other. Revik's great ax hammered at the dragon's scales, and the dragon struck left and right with his talons.

Then, the dragon screamed – a cry of pain, anger and disbelief. For Karik had taken up the gleaming sword and pierced the dragon's side. Longer than a man's arm was Farndrang, and Karik had buried it to the hilt.

The dragon turned, reaching for Karik, but the work of the warriors was now beginning to show. Slower the great beast moved, for the mountainside was now spattered with his black blood, in a hundred places. And, the wound Karik had dealt was not a small one.

"You should have taken my offer," the beast snarled, as he set his eyes on Karik. "Warriors such as yourselves would have been kings of this land in short time, with my help."

"We may be still," Karik replied. His breath came in gasps, and the sword felt heavy in his hand.

The dragon laughed at that, but it turned into a choking cough. "The kings of this land are all cursed, and my curse will lay heavy on you as well, if you ever try to wear that crown."

But, even as the dragon glared at Karik, Revik swung his ax; the black blade, dented and notched by the dragon's scales, finally cracked through and bit deep into the dragon's neck. The dragon roared with pain. As the beast drew in another breath, Karik heard a twang, and an arrow flashed between the dragon's teeth. With every bit of strength he had left, Karik lunged, driving his sword up through the dragon's open mouth, into his brain.

With a choking cough, the dragon twisted, but there was no strength left in his limbs. As Karik pulled his sword free, the beast collapsed before them, sprawled out on the mountainside.

THE BEGINNING

Karik looked about him and surveyed the mountain, in the grey light of the dawn. Smoke rose from a dozen places, where the dragon's fire still licked at the mountainside, and broken rock surrounded them, creating the danger of a landslide if they moved too carelessly.

By the dragon's head, Revik sat on a large stone, his ax still buried in the monster's neck. His clothes were torn and his left arm was red and blistered, where the dragon's fire had touched him.

Thora held her spear, its long head black and smoking, though whether from dragon's fire or dragon's blood, Karik could not tell. Both of her arms bore the marks of dragon-fire, and her sleeves hung from her shoulders, her bare arms exposed to the harsh wind.

Not far away, Igil and Wisic lay on their backs, resting as they breathed. They too had been marked by the dragon's fire: Igil on his right hand and Wisic along the right side of his body. He had cut off the greater part of his shirt, and now his body sat exposed to the cold wind, red and blistering.

Ylmi sat above them on a broken rock, her legs dangling over the edge, as she stared at the dragon. Karik saw, with a pang of guilt, that she had been burnt as well, along the side of her face; the hair on the left side of her head had also been burnt away.

A little while later they found Havar, a short way down the mountain. He, alone of them all, remained unmarked by the dragon's fire – in later days some would say that this was no small feat. But, although he was unburnt, he was covered in cuts, bruises and blood. Not one of them looked better than any other.

Exhausted and weary, they made their way back into the dragon's lair. As Karik had noticed, it was a great cavern, hollowed out and made into a fortress, and not a cave, as they had expected. At the base of the great hollow, where the dragon had rested, they found a small pile of gold. It was a pitiful thing, unworked and filthy; given to the dragon by Unhost. The small horde had not improved by the dragon's keeping.

"It seems to me that the dragon took this place from someone who was here before him," Karik said. The others had no idea who it might have been, or where they had gone to.

Karik kept the great sword he had found. Although he did not know its name, he knew that it was no work of any smith in Vrania.

They crept down into the rubble, where broken stone and dust mixed with the gleaming gold. All about the edges of the cavern were the broken remains of ancient passageways: doors and arches, which had been broken and blocked by the dragon's wrath.

"What was this place?" Havar wondered, his voice echoing in the cavern. He stooped down and picked up the hilt of a broken sword, glancing from it to the blade which Karik now held. "No smith we know made these weapons."

"The old tales say that Vranr was exiled." Karik ran his gaze over the broken staircase, which ran over the wall. "Perhaps those tales were more than legend. Perhaps his exilers set a watch on him."

Ylmi began to speak, but her voice was gone, and she had to cough twice to recover it. "The tales tell that they did, and that Vranr watched them in turn, and called upon them something dark and terrible."

"Something like a dragon?" Karik asked. Ylmi nodded, the effort to speak eluding her.

"Let's go!" Revik's voice boomed, from above. Karik looked up, to see him peering over the ledge at them. "We are all weary, and we have still to reckon with Unhost on this matter."

"Also, I am hungry," Havar tossed the sword-hilt to the ground, where it fell ringing on the rocks, "and a cup of mead would go far in easing my pain." There was much agreement to this, for where the dragon's fire had burnt them, the pain was beginning to grow. Slowly, stiffly, they began to make their way back to the mountainside.

Karik paused at one of the doorways and peered down a narrow corridor. Several rooms were set off from it, their shapes shifting in the flickering light of his torch. Alone, he slipped inside, stepping over the fallen stone, which had once been carefully carved. Within the corridor, the stone had escaped the dragon's talons, but not its fire. Black soot covered the blistered rock; remnants of a long-forgotten battle.

The far room still had a door: old, dry wood bound with iron and anchored into the rock – it groaned and creaked as Karik pulled the handle.

Inside, there was nothing but a barren room, with only wraps of hide and leather, set on a shelf cut into the rock. Karik waved the torch around the room, but nothing else could he see. Carefully, he reached out his hand and lifted the bundle from its shelf. It was bound with a leather thong.

Karik dropped to his knees. Propping the torch on the uneven floor, he undid the leather and unrolled the hides.

They revealed parchments covered in dark lines. Some were straight and stretched the length of the paper; others wound their way among them. What they were, Karik could not begin to tell, in the flickering light of his torch.

From the cavern, Revik's voice echoed again, with a call for Karik to hurry. Swiftly, Karik rolled the hides back up and thrust them inside his shirt. Snatching up his torch, he hurried back to them.

Outside, Ylmi looked out over the fjord, where snow had begun to fall in earnest. She looked up as Karik came out of the cavern; he marked that there were tears streaking her cheeks.

A cold wind blew from the north and sank its teeth into the burns of dragon-fire. Covering themselves as best they could, they began the hike back to their boat. Ylmi did not move, waiting until the others had passed, then grabbed Karik by his arm. He winced sharply, the burn on his shoulder screaming in pain. Then, she dropped the arm; "Karik…"

The word caught in her throat for a moment, and Karik thought in a panic that she might be dying. She took a shaky breath and steadied herself. With an effort, she straightened and looked him in the eye. "Did you find any bones?" The words tumbled out of her in a rush.

Karik shook his head, then stopped as his shoulder screamed again. "No," he took a deep breath, "no bones."

She nodded and her shoulders fell. In an instant, she turned and began hiking back down toward the boat. Karik stood for a moment, wondering if there was something he could say or do, but she did not walk slowly.

The path felt far longer than it had seemed in the darkness, and they were all stumbling with weariness, as they pushed the boat back into the water, with cold fingers and shivering limbs.

A grey light hung over the fjord, but they could see the shapes of the settlement in the distance; the smudge of dark smoke could be seen rising into the sky, in a dozen places.

"I don't know how Unhost will respond," Igil said, quietly, "but he will surely respond, somehow."

"Unhost can rot with the dragon." Ylmi ran her hands over her bow.

"Unhost is not the only one," Karik winced, as the wind gusted, catching the burn on his face unprotected; "the other jarls will be more than a little interested in a dragon horde, so close. And King Jarhost will not remain silent."

He sighed, deeply: "This matter is only beginning."

EPILOGUE

The light of the fire had dimmed to a dull, red glow, the gloom creeping out from under the eaves of the hall, toward the tables. The bard sat still for a moment, his face glowing red in the firelight. Then, he reached for his cup and sipped the sweet honey mead within.

"The rest of the story," he said, as he surveyed the children's wide-eyed faces, staring back at him, "will keep until next time."

Several of the parents began to rise, slowly at first, then more joined in, as they gathered their children together and made their way through the falling snow, back to their own warm homes.

"If Karik had spoken more with Unhost," one of the older men said, "matters might have gone better for him later on. Well-spoken words may avoid well-placed blows later."

"You have been over long at the mead," one of the other men replied. "How is it Karik's fault that Unhost kept too many secrets? You cannot blame the young man for his lord's failings."

"If Unhost had been less of a weasel," someone muttered into their cup, "a great many things might have been avoided."

"There are many weasels in this world," the first man replied. "We need to find how best to work around them, not simply resort to doing whatever we think is best."

"Hmm," another man chimed in, "but perhaps the old man – what was his name? Dengerhil? – was right: we can only be responsible for our own actions, and not those of others."

The bard smiled to himself and pulled the deerskin close. He would sleep here tonight, by the warm fire, and drift off to the older men arguing over his story. As he closed his eyes, he noticed the lord's children – a boy and a girl – listening closely to their elders. He hoped that they would learn something.

The fire was warm, the story had been long, and the mead from the mountain bees was very good. He closed his eyes and let sleep take him.

YLMI'S SAGA

Book II

PROLOGUE

It was a quiet evening in the lord's hall. The winter storms were growing worse here in the mountains, and most of the townspeople were huddled in their own homes, around their own fires.

But, in the lord's hall, the lord's family were not the only ones; though no crowd filled the hall with their shouting, the lord had more than enough close friends present, who relied on him for shelter.

So, now they ate, the meal quieter, if just as cheerful as the loud feast of several nights before. Below the dais, the bard feasted happily. One of the serving girls had noticed his appreciation of the mead, and she was making sure that his cup did not run empty. He made sure to thank her on each turn, and he closed his eyes as the sweet, cool liquid washed over his tongue, as delicious now as it had been the first time he tasted it.

At the head of the hall, the lord pushed back his chair from the table and sighed in satisfaction, the plate before him empty. One of his dogs padded up to him, looking for a morsel, but the lord pushed him away with a smile, and beckoned to his young children. The boy and girl could each not be more than eight years of age, and they were similar enough to be twins. They came to him and he gathered them into his arms, settling them on his lap.

"Oh, bard," the lord said, his voice relaxed in the quiet hall, "you told us the beginning of a mighty tale, three nights back."

The bard nodded gravely. "And, you are ready to hear what came after?"

"Hmmm," the lord said, thoughtfully, "I believe you have told but half the tale, for in the tales I have heard, it was not Karik alone who did great deeds, and it was not Karik who was the first to scale the Watching Stones."

"Ylmi One-Eye," the bard nodded, sagely. "It is of her you would hear."

"Even so," the lord nodded, "if you have not drunk too much of our mead to remember the story."

The old bard's eyes narrowed, and he pulled his bushy brows close together, staring at the lord from beneath them. "If you did not brew such excellent mead," he said, slowly, "I would take your words as an insult."

The lord laughed, and the children bounced on his knees from the force of it. "I see your tongue is still as sharp as ever! So, tell us a tale."

The bard pulled his chair close to the fire and cleared his throat. "Then, I shall tell you the saga of Ylmi One-Eye: how she helped to slay the dragon, how she came to sail the Undersea, and how she became the mightiest woman in Vrania since Alena the Vicious."

PART I: THE MOUNTAINS

Ylmi

The tale of Ylmi One-Eye begins as many do in Vrania: with famine. Driven by hunger and a shortage of food, Wiltha, along with her husband Torin and her brother Unhost, set out to find a place where the hunting was more plentiful.

After much hardship and suffering, they came to the northernmost fjord in Vrania, and were surprised to find the hunting there was good, and the vegetation growing thick and plentiful. Warm springs they found beneath the ground, and with the help of those wanderers who joined them, they dug down into the earth, to get better access to the springs.

Then one day, as he dug beneath the earth, Unhost struck a vein of gold.

He told no one of it, and kept it to himself.

But it was not long before Torin found another vein, and gathered gold as well. When he told Wiltha, the three of them agreed it was best to keep the gold a secret.

"Wealth brings many robbers," Wiltha said, "and it would be better for us to keep what we find, instead of giving half our work to a king." To this they agreed, and the secret they kept even from the others who joined them, telling only a few at a time, so that they might keep the matter hidden.

But, gold was not the only thing lurking in that fjord.

Within the mountain in the midst of the fjord, a dragon rested, rebuilding his strength, and the labour and tumult of the growing settlement roused him from his slumber.

For a time, he contented himself with occasionally carrying off a portion of their herd, or even any of them who wandered outside after dark.

Torin decided that something had to be done, and together with Wiltha and a few others, he made ready to attack the dragon. But, Unhost pointed out that they were few in number, and though by now there were almost a dozen people living in the village, even all together they were not skilled warriors, nor mighty champions. Nonetheless, Torin led a company against the dragon, in an attempt to end its deprivations.

The battle they waged was short. The dragon's fire burned Torin blind in both eyes, while Wiltha lost the use of her arm, and ever after walked with a limp. Two others died on the mountain.

When it was over, the mighty beast rose into the air and drifted over the tiny settlement. With barely a wisp of effort, he bathed the place in flames and burned every building to a smoking pile of ash.

Then, even as his sister was still screaming in agony from the wounds dealt her by the dragon, Unhost knelt before it. He offered the dragon gold and the pick of their herds, if it would spare the village.

"What village?" the dragon laughed. "There is nothing here but ash and bones."

"I can rebuild," Unhost begged, quickly. "I will bring in others and, with your protection, we can build a prosperous settlement – one that will keep you fed and wealthy for years to come."

"And, how," the dragon asked, "will you rebuild when every wanderer fears to live in my shadow? Who will you bring here that does not fear me?"

"I can keep it a secret," Unhost pleaded. "Spare my life and I will bring exiles, the hungry and the desperate here, to work the land and grow our herds. When they have a life here, if they find out that you live nearby, they will be reluctant to leave the safety of what they have built."

At this, the dragon's flames quietened somewhat, and he considered. After a moment, he struck the earth with one claw, shattering the rock and sending a spray of dirt and stone into the air.

"Done," he said. "Rebuild your village and I will not burn it, as long as you fulfil your end of the bargain."

And, that was how Unhost came to offer service to the dragon who blinded his brother-in-law and maimed his sister.

So he began to rebuild, leaving Torin and Wiltha to care for each other.

Little by little, wanderers and outcasts drifting through the mountains came to settle with Unhost, and help him build.

The hunter Almir Alsson and Torig Ingsson were the two first, but close behind them came Bodvar Oliksson and his wife Siggi Worviksdottir. They came from one of the little fishing settlements which dotted the northern coast of Vrania, travelling south to find food and escape the terrible storms which so often drove terrible seas upon the coastline.

They were hard workers, and became well-liked within the village as it grew. And, though they were not pleased when they learned of the dragon,

Bodvar helped Unhost to dig deep beneath the ground, and in that way made dwellings protected from dragon-fire.

Despite the presence of the dragon, they made for themselves a life more comfortable than most in Vrania. The mountains gave them shelter from the worst of the storms, there was food and shelter enough for their small number, and it was not long before Siggi gave birth to a boy, whom they called Lanvir, and soon after to a daughter, whom they called Ylmi.

The two children were little alike; whereas Lanvir was energetic and talkative, Ylmi preferred quiet and stillness; whereas Lanvir was curious, Ylmi was cautious; and whereas Lanvir often found himself in trouble, Ylmi was often found close to her mother, watching and listening.

So they grew together, until the day that they went gathering in the forest, and Lanvir stopped with an enormous smile on his face.

"Father told me the most incredible thing last night," he whispered: "there is a dragon here, living in the bay."

"Why are you excited?" Ylmi asked, with a frown. "That sounds like a bad thing."

"It is not like that," Lanvir assured her. "Unhost has a bargain with it: the dragon will leave us alone, as long as we give him a portion of the gold and sheep which we get for ourselves."

"In the stories," Ylmi pointed out, "little good ever comes from bargains with dragons."

"Perhaps," Lanvir agreed. "But, still... a dragon!"

In the days which followed, the thought of the dragon never left Lanvir's mind, and Ylmi saw him now every day looking out toward the fjord. At night, if there was a full moon, he would slip to the door and look out, until Bodvar told him to come back inside.

Often, he would ask anyone who would listen to tell him of the dragon. Sometimes, he would bring the stories back to Ylmi: tales that Unhost was paying the dragon with gold they dug out of the ground, or with naughty children who didn't obey their parents.

When she heard this, Siggi thumped him and said he should not tell such ridiculous tales.

"Children are not given to the dragon," she said, "disobedient or otherwise. They are spanked by their parents." She gave them both a look. "Your father and I would never give you to a dragon. All the same, it is not prudent to be out after dark."

"Because the dragon might eat us?" Ylmi asked, with eyes as large as chicken eggs.

"A dragon or a wolf or a bear," Siggi told her. "Vrania is dangerous at all times, and more so after nightfall."

After this, Lanvir told her fewer stories, but Ylmi did not think that her brother was any less obsessed with the dragon.

Not long after, Ylmi returned from her gathering in the forest to find that Lanvir had not returned from his fishing, along the northern edge of the bay. The sun was drawing low, and Bodvar was hard at work, deep underground, carving tunnels into the rock with several other members from the village.

Siggi was called away to help a woman named Sutri, who had fallen ill, and she told Ylmi to watch the boiling stew and to eat with Lanvir when he returned.

So Ylmi waited, but though the sun set over the sea, and the moon rose high over the mountains, her brother did not return. For a while, Ylmi waited, growing more fearful and nervous with each passing moment.

At last, despite her parents' warnings to stay inside after nightfall, she slipped out of their hut and made her way northward, hoping that her brother had not come to trouble.

The waters of the fjord were rough, with a harsh wind blowing in from the sea, and far in the north thunder rumbled amid distant clouds. The moon was waning, but still shed enough dim light for Ylmi's young eyes to follow the faint trail they often used to fish, on the northern edge of the fjord.

It curved around the northern lip of the fjord, and ran beneath the rising cliffs for a long way – so long that Ylmi began to grow weary with the distance. She called to her brother, but the wind tossed away her cries, even as she shouted as loud as her young voice would allow.

At last, she came upon Lanvir's fishing rod, set upon a rock with the rest of his fishing gear, lying with the basket he was to carry the fish back in. His shirt was folded neatly beside them and Ylmi was filled with a sudden fear.

The great mountain, where the dragon was said to live, loomed before her, not far out into the fjord, and Ylmi guessed that her brother had swum out to it.

For a brief, terrible moment, she hesitated, debating whether she should follow, or return to the village to get help.

But, she was still a young girl, and she knew a dragon was beyond her. She turned and ran back down the path toward the settlement. High overhead, the thunder boomed as the storm drew closer, and she rushed down the path as fast as her legs would take her, gasping for breath as she ran. Twice she fell, but each time she rose and hurried on, desperate to reach the village.

Rain had begun to fall when she finally saw the glow of the little fires and warm huts, and she dashed to find Sutri's house, where her mother was tending the sick woman. Ylmi's chest was burning, and she could barely speak for gasping for air, so fast had she run.

As soon as her mother understood, she told Ylmi to stay there and rushed away. There was much tumult that night in the village, and Ylmi understood little that happened.

In the following day's light, she was taken by old Olga to the shore, where her parents were being shouted at by Unhost. There was a great deal of yelling, much of it by people she was unfamiliar with, and little of it done by her parents. By the end, Unhost made it clear that they were no longer welcome along the shoreline, with the rest of the settlers.

"The dragon has agreed not to burn us all, though the price was a high one," Unhost said. "I have been forced to promise him more gold, what we have now and more besides. As for you," he turned on Bodvar, "go up into the mountains; there is no home for you here in this village. If you are able, manage the sheep and goats. Otherwise, do not trouble the rest of us, who are trying to make a living."

"But," Bodvar said, pointing to their house, "I have built my home here. Winter is only a few months away!"

"You built it on land I gave you," Unhost retorted. "With the help of others, you have endangered us all with your recklessness, by angering a dragon. Go, before I change my mind and cast you out completely."

Ylmi was quiet as they climbed up into the hills. When they stopped to rest in a small clearing, she broke down in sobs.

"I'm sorry," she said, through her tears, "I should have stopped him. I should have..."

Bodvar reached over and lifted her in his arms, to pull her close. "My daughter, it was not you who were at fault." He held her there for a moment, as she sobbed.

"But, if I had stopped him," she said, "then he would be here with us, and we would not be without a home."

"If." Bodvar wrapped her in another giant hug. "If is a silly word. Lanvir knew what he was doing, and that should not rest on you. As for a home," he looked around them, "we will make one in these hills. There will be plenty of room for you to climb trees, to plant a garden with your mother..." He looked over Ylmi's head at Siggi.

"But," he added, bending down and taking Ylmi's head in his hands, "you must know that we love you. Always. And none of this is your fault."

So Bodvar talked with his daughter, then and in the days to come.

They found a place where caves had been hollowed out of the mountainside, and around the largest they built their home, laying sod and earth around it, so it was as warm and sheltered as the dugout houses by the shore had been.

But, though they made the house warm, there was little time to gather and store food for the winter. Siggi planted the best garden she could, but they had few seeds saved and the rocky soil was poor, even in the best places. She watered it from the nearby mountain stream, and said it was a blessing that water was so much closer at hand.

When he was not at work on their home, Bodvar went into the forest and hunted. Often, he brought Ylmi, and she learned quickly how to move silently through the trees. She held the squirrels her father shot, while he scanned the tree branches for others. She marked how he moved, and how he looked for leaves which moved without the wind.

When the first snow came, they shut the door to their hut and watched it pile up outside. Siggi said that things were not as bad as they could be and, perhaps with a full year, next winter they might have more food than now.

As they sat by the small fire, Bodvar stood. Sending Ylmi for his large knife, he took from one corner a thin bundle of tightly wrapped hides and drew out a long stick, a little larger than Ylmi's wrist.

"This winter will be long, cold and hungry," he said, as they settled again by the fire, "and it will do none of us good to deny it. But, when there is cold and hunger, the best course is to keep idle hands busy." He took the knife, as Ylmi handed it to him, and lifted the stick. "This..." he waved it before her, "...will be your first bow."

So, while the snow fell, the three of them worked on the bow. Sometimes they talked, taking turns telling stories to each other as they worked. Bodvar's tales were of the conversations between animals in the forest: the wolf was forever trying to catch the fox, so the stories went, but the fox was always able to outsmart the wolf and escape.

But Siggi's stories were older, darker, and Ylmi soon found that she preferred her mother's tales. In the darkness and the cold, Siggi spoke of old Vranr, exiled from the west, to the isle where they now lived. She told of his tricks, and how he fooled and cheated kings and lords of the faraway western lands, from the great northern wastes to the blazing plains of the south. He grew ever bolder, until he met the daughter of a powerful king, who bested him at his own tricks, and the two fell deeply in love.

But, for all the stories, Ylmi noticed that their food grew ever less, as the snow grew deeper on the mountain around them. She noticed when her father ladled an empty spoon into his bowl, thinking he had deceived them both. She did not believe her mother when she said she was full, and poured the rest of her stew into Ylmi's bowl.

And, each night, she saw the empty space where Lanvir should have slept, and should have whispered to her as they fell asleep.

They huddled together, as the days grew shorter and the cold deepened, until winter reached its peak.

———◆———

On the shortest day of the year, they cleared the snow from before their door and gathered uncut wood, to build a bonfire in the clearing.

As night began to set, Siggi lit the fire with a burning brand from their housefire. As the dark of Dunharvic's Night fell swiftly around them, the clearing blazed with a warm light, reflected back by the glimmering snow.

"What if he comes anyway?" Ylmi asked, as she watched the flames rising.

Bodvar chuckled: "Oh, he will come, but the fire will keep him at a distance."

"But the white goddess will warm herself by it," Siggi added. "Skathi, the winter huntress, will warm her hands by the flames, and send Dunharvic on his way, for there are no dead here tonight."

Ylmi listened, as she watched the flames rising into the sky, and wondered.

———◆———

Slowly, the winter whiled by.

Ylmi grew used to the pangs of hunger, even as she watched her bow take shape. The limbs were smoothed and rubbed with deer fat, over the fire, by far Ylmi's favourite part of the bow making. The warmth from the fire felt good in her hands, and as excess fat fell into the fire, it hissed and crackled and smelled like roasted meat.

When the snows slackened, Bodvar would go out into the forest, to see if he could find anything to add to their store. Occasionally he found a snow rabbit, but more often than not he returned with empty hands, and a weariness that did not seem to leave, even after a full night's sleep. As the winter went on, he spent more time resting by the fire, and it seemed to take more effort for him to move.

He showed Ylmi how to make arrows, carving nocks in the butt end and fire-hardening the sharpened points. "One day," he told her, with a deep breath, "when your bow is stronger, you'll need iron tips for big animals." He took another moment to catch his breath. "But this will do well enough for rabbits and squirrels."

As the winter dragged on, Ylmi noticed that her father now rarely ladled an empty spoon into his bowl, and her mother pressed him on more than one occasion to eat more.

But, even so, the food dwindled, and they spent more days wrapped tightly in the fur blankets, not rising to eat but only telling stories. Ylmi would peer through the flickering orange light at her mother's face, poking out of a large bear hide, as she told of how Vranr and the princess he loved had escaped her father, and went on one adventure after another, climbing the high, white mountains, or delving deep beneath them to seek the dwellings of the mountain folk, who had passed far, far underground.

Slowly, the cold lessened, until one day it began to thaw.

Ylmi was the first awake – the first to hear the dripping of melting ice – and she slipped out of the house before her parents woke. She was eager to try her new bow, and she thought that fresh meat would do her parents good.

She returned soon with a pair of squirrels, much to her parents' delight, and they laughed as they ate, the warmth and strength returning to their bodies, as the winter slowly receded.

From then on, whenever Bodvar did not need her help with the goat herd, she ventured into the forest to hunt. While her mother laid a new garden and her father gathered goats, she ranged farther and farther into the mountains, learning the paths and trails of the animals.

One day, when Ylmi returned from a long hunt, she found her father waiting for her, in the small clearing by their home. He had cut down a few trees, giving them a small space useful for planting, working and herding the goat herd, which was beginning to grow.

"Come, daughter," he said when she had come down through the trees, "it is time that we talked."

Ylmi nodded, laying out the rabbit and squirrel she had taken. Bodvar produced his knife and started to work on the squirrel.

"Your mother and I are worried about you." His fingers moved swiftly over the carcass, stripping away the hide carefully and keeping the meat clean. "You talk little, and always you are hunting or working. You are a child, and though life here is hard, it is good from time to time to rest among the mountain flowers and watch the birds in their play." He took a deep breath and smiled at her. "We want you to know that we do not blame you for your brother's death."

"If I had stopped him," Ylmi said, quietly, "then he would be alive and we would not be stranded on the mountainside." She looked at her father, and saw that his face was no longer as gaunt and haggard as it had been at the end of winter; he moved easier now, needing less rest. Perhaps they could make it better through the winter if she hunted more...

"If I had taught him better..." her father said, quietly. "I was his father; it is I who should have stopped him, Ylmi. You were his younger sister – the youngest member of our family – and you do not bear the burden of being warden to your elders. No," he took a deep breath, "you bear no blame. Do you hear me? None."

Ylmi nodded, silent for a moment. "Father, how long can we last up here?"

Bodvar gave a shaky laugh. "We made it through one winter, with less time to prepare." He shrugged. "I do not think we will have such a hard time again."

Ylmi drew in a breath, but something broke in her throat and she bent over, sobbing into her hands.

Swiftly, with long arms, Bodvar drew her close and held her against his chest, his beard tickling her neck. "I love you, little one," he said. "None of this is your fault." He held her until the tears subsided, then lifted her up.

"All is not as bad as it could be," he said, with a forced smile: "we have a warm dwelling, the goat herd is growing, and perhaps Unhost will leave us alone here, in the mountains."

She smiled and wiped her tears, but she did not forget his words. It was Unhost who had sent them away, thrown them out when her brother was missing. Unhost had allowed a dragon to take shelter near their village, and now her brother was dead. Instead of seeking to be free of the beast, Unhost had given it shelter, brought it gold and food, all to ensure that no one would ever question him, and would do all that he said without complaint.

Siggi cooked the rabbits that night, in a pot of onions and peas, but Ylmi barely tasted her food, her mind turning to Unhost and the dragon. Which of them was more at fault for the death of her brother and the suffering of her parents, she was not sure. But while Unhost was sitting warm in his hall, they were cold and alone on the mountain, and that did not seem right to Ylmi.

Home in the Mountains

So Ylmi grew, spending each day in the forest, hunting the trails around her home.

The next winter, she and her father made another bow, stronger than before, and when the snow melted, she ranged farther than she had the year before. To the north, the mountains rose in rocky cliffs and dangerous precipices, but to the west and south, the mountains kept their trees and were home to many creatures.

As she ranged far and wide, she often met other hunters and joined them on their hunts. From the ice marshes in the north to the mountains in the east, she roamed in search of game. It was with Oscar Kolsson that she first hunted a black bear, and that hunt was a long one, for it was while they hunted it that King Viglir made his first great assault on Girhom.

The eastern king had grown tired of the raids and squabbles between Jarhost and himself, and tried to force passage through Gar's Pass. The fighting lasted several days, and by the end of it the woods were so full of scouts and spies that Oscar said they were more likely to be hunted themselves, than to find a bear. So, they returned west.

The fighting in the pass took a great toll, and there was no trade with Girhom that year, and little in the year after.

The following year, she slew her first wolf with Leiban Longspear, and gave the pelt to her mother to wear as a cloak.

But, of all the hunters she accompanied, it was from Dranri Longbeard that she learned the most.

She met him high in the mountains overlooking the coast, south of Unhost's village, while she was tracking a herd of deer. He said that she was a very young girl to be so deep in the mountains, but she replied that young girls were hungry, the same as anyone else. He laughed at that, and together they tracked the deer into a small valley.

From then on, the two often hunted together, and Dranri showed her many things in the forest: he showed her how to follow a trail, how to move soundlessly through the trees, and how to lay snares to catch rabbits and squirrels. Together they hunted the rare black boars which made their homes in the high mountain glens, and once, when an ice bear wandered south from the cold lands around Vanik's Point, Dranri took her with him to hunt it down.

As they followed the trail, Ylmi looked at his long, heavy spear. "Would that be better for a bear than a bow?" she asked.

"It is best to have both," Dranri answered. Besides his spear, he also had a bow of black wood, tipped with bone and backed with goat horn. "One arrow may not always finish the job, and if a bear or boar charges, it is more comforting to have a spear than naught but a bow."

The bear's trail wound up into the mountains, and when they stopped to drink from a stream, Ylmi picked up Dranri's spear.

"Have you used a spear before?" Dranri asked her, and she shook her head.

"Hold it lower on the haft," he told her. "The chief advantage of a spear is its length. Hold it just below halfway... like so." He nodded as she shifted her hands. "Now move your left foot forward... Good."

He stepped up to her and took hold of the spearhead, wrapping his hand around it, just below the blade. "If I push here..." He gave a slight shove, and grinned as Ylmi teetered off balance. "Even so, get down on your right knee, and drop your right hand as far back as is comfortable..." He nodded as she did as he said, even as he held the spearhead. "Now, push down with your right hand and press the butt into the ground."

When she had done so, Dranri shoved the spear again, but Ylmi barely moved. She felt the steadiness of her position, even as he shoved again, even harder.

"Even a little twig like you can hold off a boar like this," he told her. "Let the ground take the brunt of the attack, and you're immovable."

She nodded, thinking on what he had said.

So they climbed northward, into the mountains.

The next time they stopped, Ylmi pointed off into the distance. On a lonely peak in the north, high above them, she could see through waving pine needles what looked like three tall stones, all standing in a circle, and she asked Dranri if he knew what it was.

"Those are said to be the Watching Stones of Vranr," he told her. "But, no one that I know of has found the way up to them, in many years."

"Not even you?" Ylmi asked.

Dranri chuckled. "I looked, for a time." He took a deep breath and shrugged. "But I was hungry, so I left to do other things."

Ylmi looked back through the wind-tossed tree branches. "Why are they called the Watching Stones?"

Dranri shrugged. "I have heard it is because Vranr would watch for ships from the west, though none ever came. I have heard it is where he looked for the gods, and I have heard it is where he performed his dark magic and wove his wyrd."

"People speak of wyrd," Ylmi said, "but I fail to see how it is different from fate."

Dranri looked thoughtful for a moment, and stared up at the Stones. "Fate is the path the gods lay for us," he said, after a moment; "wyrd is how we shape it with our own steps." He paused for a moment, thinking a little more, and Ylmi suppressed a laugh at how his beard twisted over his face.

"Think of it this way," he said, quickly: "your father has set your home on a mountain. You did not choose the place of it, nor the paths which lead to it, yet, if you set out northward and fall into the waters of the ice marsh, is it your fault or your father's that you have a long, cold journey home?"

Ylmi thought immediately that the answer to that was Unhost, who had forced them to live far from the settlement.

"So, whose wyrd caused my father to live alone on the mountainside?" she asked. "Or caused the death of my brother?"

Dranri looked uncomfortable at that. "If I had the answer to that, I would be a wise man," he said. "Our wyrd is rarely untangled from that of others; all our decisions are woven together with those of others. That is what Vranr fought against: the wyrd that others wove for him." He pointed up at the Stones; "I think, in some way, that is what the Stones were for."

"I have heard that he spoke with the gods from time to time." Ylmi gazed up at the distant peak, as clouds rolled in about it.

"Perhaps that is where he did it," Dranri shrugged. "Perhaps it is where they gave him guidance, depending on what tales you believe."

The clouds had hidden the peak by then, and Ylmi tore her gaze away, to follow Dranri up the rough slope.

They hunted down the bear, and as night was falling, Dranri's black bow twanged. The struggle that followed was vicious, and left none of them unhurt, until at last the bear was dead. They took a great deal of meat from the bear, and when it was over Dranri gave Ylmi the pelt.

Through her hunting, she also became friends with Ethna, who worked with her husband Ymr in the settlement's tiny forge. From time to time, Ylmi came down into the settlement, sometimes bartering meat or hides for items which she did not make herself. To Ethna she gave soft rabbit fur and strong deer hide, and in return she received arrowheads and a long knife, of which Ylmi was particularly proud.

She traded also with old Torig and with Havar, from them gaining fish in return for deer bones, which were made into fishhooks. With Olga, she traded for vegetables and sometimes leather, for none in the village were better than Olga at turning hides into leather.

The third winter they spent in the mountains began better than the first two. Bodvar had brought many goats down into the village, and in return had brought back salted fish and beer. Siggi's garden had grown strong and bountiful, so there were onions and peas, potatoes and garlic, and many other vegetables with which to fill their stews. And, for her part, Ylmi had brought in much game and hides, so they were all warm both inside and outside.

But, at the height of winter, when the cold was deepest, Siggi began to cough and was seized with the shakes. Though they wrapped her in every fur they had, and set her near to the fire, she could not get warm.

Whenever the storms abated enough to venture outside, Bodvar went out to bring in more firewood, to warm her, but every day she seemed weaker than before, until she could not rise from the bed. Ylmi tended to her as best she could, urging her to sip broth whenever she woke, but it seemed to do little good.

To make matters worse, Bodvar's time in the cold did little good for him. Each day, he spent more time outside in the wind and snow, and in the evenings he shivered by the fire, trying to return warmth to his bones.

Until, one day, he could not rise from his bed, either.

Ylmi looked upon them, shivering despite the warmth in their cottage, and for a moment she despaired. There was no one to help her care for them. And, if she herself fell ill, the three of them would freeze alone.

She took a moment to consider the situation. Her father had piled almost a week's worth of firewood inside the door, and for that she was thankful. She would do what she could for them, and prepare a stew which would last several days. She would spend only a few minutes in the cold each day, to add a little to their store of firewood. She hoped it would be enough.

For three days it went as well as could be hoped. Her mother even ate a little on her own, and her father was able to sit up. But, on the fourth day, Ylmi woke with a wracking cough. Each cough rattled her body, and when they all came together it was enough to bring her to her knees. By the end of the day, she crawled onto her pile of furs and wrapped them around her as she shook. She slept fitfully through the night, often waking to violent coughing, which seemed determined to pull her body inside out.

When morning came, she awoke with a start. The air was cold, and she saw her breath hanging in the air before her face. The fire had gone out.

Coughing against the pain in her chest, she crawled through the darkness, seeking the warm ring of stones which marked their firepit. But, when she found them, they were cold. She moved her hands over the space before them, her hands finding a small patch of warmth. She dug it out with a spare stick, hunting for the coals beneath them, and when her stick brushed against something rough, she hurriedly fed it bits of straw and twigs she found in the piled wood.

She coughed as she worked, and her parents stirred in the darkness, asking what had happened.

"The fire is gone out," she said simply, and went back to work.

Outside, she could hear the wind howling and the storm battered at their door, rattling it like a hungry bear. Soon, all three of them were huddled around the firepit, trying to gently coax the flames back to life, without smothering them in kindling. When at last the flames sprang to life, and licked at the sticks and twigs they had prepared, Ylmi could not feel her fingers and her feet were numb.

"Go lie down," her father told her. "I can tend the fire for a while."

Ylmi nodded, and sank gratefully into the furs which were her bed. As her aching body fell into sleep, she saw the flames of the young fire flickering happily in the darkness.

She did not rise from her bed for several days, as the cough worked its way through her. But, though her body did not move, her mind ran wild. In the settlement, neighbours checked on each other through the winter, ensuring that when a fire went out it was swiftly rekindled. When someone became sick, there were two others to lend a hand and see that the cold and hunger were driven away. But, here on the mountainside, Ylmi knew there was no one; they only had each other, and it was not an uncommon thing for three people in one house to grow sick.

Late one night, she dreamt that she saw her parents standing by a bonfire before the house, piling wood onto the flames. In the darkness, she heard a horseman riding slowly through the snow.

She felt a cold wind pass, and a woman's voice spoke from beyond the dark trees: "Go. There is nothing for you here."

When she woke, she found her parents huddled around the fire. They still shivered, but it seemed that the worst of their illness had passed.

"We're glad you are awake," Bodvar, said with a weary smile. "You have slept for a long time."

"I was tired," Ylmi replied, simply.

Bodvar nodded. "You have taken good care of us in every way that can be thought of."

"I will accept payment in stories," Ylmi said. A stew was boiling, and the smell of it set her stomach to growling.

"That is fair enough," Bodvar laughed. "What manner of story will you accept? Do you wish to hear the further adventures of the fox? Or shall your mother tell you more of Vranr's antics?"

Ylmi looked at her mother. "Do any of the stories tell of Vranr's Watching Stones?"

Siggi looked up from the fire, the flames dancing in her eyes. "They do. Why do you ask?"

"Because I have seen them, and I am curious what the stories concerning them are."

Bodvar shifted and wrapped his hide blanket closer over his shoulders, as Siggi moved closer to the fire. Outside, Ylmi could hear the wind howling and moaning, as it came rushing over the mountains from the north, while close beside her the fire crackled and popped, as it gnawed at the wood they had laid on it.

"When at last Vranr was cast out of his homeland, separated from his wife Princess Sol, and exiled to this island," Siggi began, "he was filled with a terrible rage. Within a week, he had fashioned a raft and set sail for the mainland, but they watched for him and returned him here. So, he built a ship and slipped by their watchers, landing on the mainland. When they caught him, they brought him here again, taking from him any tool that he might use to live or build." Siggi shook her head; "But, Vranr was a clever man, who ever loved to escape.

"For a year, nothing was heard from him, and many thought that he had at last died and they were rid of him." A smile crept over Siggi's face, in the firelight. "But, one day, when the guards went to bring food to Sol, they found her gone, the door broken open from the outside.

"The chase Vranr led them on that day is a tale all of its own, but in the end even the two of them together could not escape the might of three kings. Sol was taken and imprisoned again in a secret place, and Vranr was returned to this isle. Then, calling on the black magic of ancient demons, the three kings raised the Black Isles all about Vrania, creating treacherous seas which no man could traverse. And they set a watch on Vranr, and told him that if ever he began to build a ship, they would remove his fingers one by one.

"Vranr did not listen, of course, but for all his cunning he could not evade the Watcher, and they took his little finger on his left hand. Twice more Vranr sought to build a ship in secret, but each time the Watcher discovered him, and removed a finger. After the third time, Vranr realized he could not escape. In despair and anger, he called on the gods to give him vengeance, crying out day and night.

"So, the Allfather sent Skathi, who walks the storms and knows the hunger of vengeance. She came to Vranr and told him that, if he wished to have his revenge, he would need a place to call it. So, atop the highest peak on the coast, Vranr built his Watching Stones. It is said that they are carved with his fingerbones and anointed with his blood. From there, Vranr watched The Watcher.

"In the storms Vranr cursed him, and in the calm Vranr prayed against him. The gods visited him upon the Stones; their footprints on the mountain made the way treacherous and deadly, and Vranr further wove the path with doom and danger, lest The Watcher attempt to reach him atop it. When it was finished, and his curses had been made against The Watcher, Vranr went down from the Stones, and set to work on this isle as best he could."

Siggi finished the story and shrugged; "At least, that is the tale as I was told it."

Bodvar reached an arm out from under his cloak and wrapped it around her. "You know all the best stories."

"Is it true, though?" Ylmi asked. "Did Vranr really set the Stones there?"

"The Stones are there," Siggi answered. "As to whether it was Vranr or another, I do not know. As to the curses, and The Watcher, who can say?"

"Dranri said that guidance comes to those who reach the Stones," Ylmi pressed. "Mother, is there guidance to be found at the Stones?"

"You should not believe everything that Dranri tells you," Bodvar chuckled. "He has lived too long by himself, and his beard has grown long, while his mind has grown in rings around itself."

"Oh, hush," Siggi smiled, "that is not what she asked." She stared at the fire for a moment, then looked at Ylmi. "I do not know what is there, on that mountain top. Dark words were spoken there, by all accounts, and guidance is only as good as the giver."

She was silent for a moment, then added: "I have found that it is better to think long and carefully on a matter, then bring it before others – others you trust. Then, you will find guidance, and there will be none of that treacherous climbing that the Watching Stones require." She smiled at her daughter and Ylmi smiled back, but the smile was painful.

———◆———

The spring came at last, and Ylmi returned to her hunting. But, whenever the hunting was good, she often turned her path toward the north, to the mountain where she was sure a path lay to the Watching Stones. At first, she often lost her way among the cliffs and ravines, but with long days spent climbing about the mountainside, she slowly untangled the maze which lay about the mountain.

Even then, she still lost her way from time to time, but she was careful, and knew by the position of the sun and other mountain peaks how to find her way out again.

One day, as she hunted with Dranri, she told him she thought she might be near to finding a way to the Watching Stones, and he looked at her in amazement.

"You should be careful," he told her; "there are those who have died seeking the Stones. I did not mean for you to go looking for them yourself."

But Ylmi only laughed, and said that she was more than capable of looking out for herself. "Besides," she told him, "I have searched for almost four months now, and no harm has befallen me."

"Ylmi, I know your parents love you," Dranri said to her, "and, for my part, I enjoy the company you bring when we hunt together. Do not pursue this further, for the closer you get to the Stones, the more dangerous the path will become."

"If that is the case," Ylmi observed, "then the more true the stories sound, and the more likely it is that I will try to reach the Stones!"

Dranri laughed at this, and said that Ylmi had the better argument. "Still," he said, "be careful, and do not attempt what you cannot achieve."

They hunted on, but in her mind she laughed. How could one know what could and could not be achieved unless they tried?

"Be wary as you hunt," Dranri warned her that evening, when they parted: "the trails lead further into the mountains than they used to, and two days ago I came across a hunter from Garhom. Not all hunters are like me, and some consider those who hunt the same game their enemies." He patted her on the shoulder. "I like you, Ylmi, and I would not see you come to harm."

———◆◆◆———

It was at this time that she also became fast friends with Thora, the huntress, who was as skilled with fishing nets as she was with a boar spear.

Thora was the daughter of Torin and Wiltha, Unhost's sister, who had come with him to found the village. Thora had been born after they were wounded by the dragon, but Unhost had done little to help them, even though they were so injured. When Thora was still young, Torin died in a "phantom", as they called the silent storms which came out of the north, and Wiltha had died a short time after.

After Wiltha's death, when Unhost thought to expel Thora, there were many who objected. Both Olga and Almir, though they had no great liking for each other, took in Thora who, though she grew into a skilled huntress at an early age, kept often to herself. So, it was difficult for Unhost to find a reason to cast her out.

She and Ylmi hunted together often, and became fast friends.

———◆◆◆———

Now, it happened that one day, when Ylmi returned from hunting, she found it was not only her family who waited in the clearing by their home, but Unhost as well.

"Greetings, Ylmi," he said to her, as she came through the trees. "I trust your hunting went well?"

"It went as ever it does in these mountains," she answered, unsure of why he had come.

Unhost barely heard her. "I have heard that you have found a way to the Watching Stones of Vranr, and I would very much like to be shown the way."

Ylmi laughed at this, thinking that if she had found a way, she was not likely to show it to Unhost. But, to him, she only said that he had heard wrong. "I have looked," she admitted, "but all I have discovered is that the way is long and treacherous, and the path more dangerous than even the stories tell."

Unhost chuckled at that, and tossed aside the stick he had been toying with. "It is said that the Watching Stones are where Vranr built his throne and buried his golden hoard." His eyes suddenly narrowed and he stepped toward her. "You would be very foolish to keep that for yourselves."

"Unhost, what are you talking about?" Bodvar said. He stepped forward to put his arm around Ylmi. "Vranr's throne? A golden hoard? What use do you think we have for it?"

All the pleasantness suddenly fell from Unhost's face, and his mouth twisted into a snarl. "I know you are seeking Vranr's treasure," he hissed, "either to try to buy the dragon's loyalty or to gain favour with King Jarhost. You live here by my good grace—"

"Why would our daughter lie?" Bodvar asked, taking a step toward Unhost. "She is not yet fifteen years of age. Why would she try to deceive our jarl?"

"Because she is of your family," Unhost replied, "and, like the rest of you, ever a thorn in my side."

He pointed at Ylmi; "You will show me the way up the mountains, or you and your family will feel my wrath."

Bodvar stepped between them and looked down on Unhost. "I do not think you should stay long on this mountain; you have a long journey back to your home before nightfall."

"I am safe enough," Unhost snarled at him. "And, perhaps you should be more careful how you talk to one who has the ear of a dragon."

"Much good it has done your people," Siggi said, quietly.

Unhost turned on her and began to shout, but before he could say more than a few words, Bodvar picked him up by the back of his shirt and carried him to the edge of the clearing. They shared a few words, before Unhost turned and took the trail back down to the settlement.

"I am surprised that he left so quietly," Siggi said.

"He will require more goats than last year to smooth this over," Bodvar replied. "I wish that matters were different. I am sorry, Ylmi, for his harsh words."

"Perhaps it is time that someone put an arrow through his heart," Ylmi replied, but Bodvar shook his head.

"Matters would only grow worse from there," he warned her, "though, I would not be sad if he tripped and suffered a terrible accident, on his way back down the mountain."

When Ylmi made to follow Unhost down the path, Bodvar's eyes widened; "By the nine realms, Ylmi! I did not mean to send you off after him! Are you so ready to take his life?"

Ylmi shrugged and set down her bow. "As you said, it would not be a terrible thing if he were to die."

But Bodvar watched her closely, and wondered that one so young would be so ready to offer death.

A Bad Jarl

The next day dawned grey and dim, and as Ylmi made her way down the mountains, the mist turned to a fine rain.

She picked her way carefully over the path, for in places the stones were slick, and even a small slip could send one tumbling far down the mountainside. As she came down from the mountains, she stood upon a small ledge which looked down into the village.

It had grown little over the years; there were still less than a score of little huts dotting the rough land beside the fjord. A few small pens had been built from rock, to hold the goats her father brought down from the mountain, and here and there the ground had been worked into gardens and tiny fields. It was back-breaking work, and not for the first time Ylmi was glad that her role was hunting and herding. She was quite happy with her sore feet and aching legs, in place of clawing rocks from the mud.

The rain was thickening, and she hurried down the path toward the smithy, where she could hear Ymr pounding away on his anvil.

The small forge was under a lean roof, so the coals were out of the rain, but Ymr was drenched when she arrived. Ethna was little better, her hair pulled back into a rough braid, leaving her free to work the bellows.

Ylmi stood just beneath the lean roof, enough to avoid most of the rain, and waited for them to reach a stopping point. She looked toward Unhost's hall, where several children were playing in the mud. She chuckled at that; they'd grow cold in a few minutes and learn why that was a bad idea.

An instant later, she jumped as Ymr's hammer slammed down on the anvil, and she turned quickly to see Ethan laughing at her. "Surprised to hear a hammer in a smithy?" she asked.

Ylmi rubbed her ear. "Surprised to hear a hammer at all. It gets quiet in the mountains."

"Less so of late," Ethna shook her head; "we heard that King Viglir is making another attempt on Girhom."

Ylmi glanced toward the mountains to the northwest, and winced. Fighting in the mountains was never good.

"They are fighting again in the pass?" she asked.

"I heard that they made it as far as Girhom itself," Ethna shook her head, "though you never know with these rumours. Still, perhaps it would be best to give Gar's Pass a wide berth."

Ylmi nodded, her jaw tightening. Perhaps it was time she hunted through the ice marsh; it was dangerous, but there might be some food worth finding there.

"But, how can I help you?" Ethna grinned. "I do not think you came only to hear the rumours of what may or may not be happening." Her eyes went to the handful of pelts Ylmi held.

"Even so," Ylmi replied, "I am in need of arrowheads, and perhaps a new knife."

"If it's a new knife you're after," came a voice from behind her, "make it long and sharp."

Ylmi turned to see Thora leaning on her spear, a wide grin on her face.

"Look what tumbled down from the mountains." Thora stepped forward and clapped Ylmi on the back.

"You're in a fine mood," Ethna laughed. "What has cheered up the thundercloud of the northern fjord?"

"A bear has moved into the old cave upriver," Thora's solemn face twisted into a rare grin, "and I'm looking for a couple of hunters who are as hungry as I am."

"You've come to the right place," Ylmi replied; "I'm looking for some good hunting at the moment."

"I was just coming to see if you could sharpen my spear," Thora told Ethna; "there's a dent from the last boar that I can't get out."

"If we can get some of the meat," Ethna said, quickly, "we'll keep your spear sharp for the rest of the year. You too, Ylmi."

"Bones."

They all looked at Ymr, who almost seemed as startled as they did at the sound of his voice.

"Bear bones." He gestured at the pile of glowing coals in his forge. "Makes for strong spears."

Thora nodded. "I'll bring some of the bones, then." She turned to Ylmi; "Almir already said he'd come, and you make three – seems enough to me."

She stiffened suddenly, and Ylmi looked around her to see Unhost walking up from the beach.

"Greetings, all," he smiled. "I hope your days have been profitable thus far!"

"Productive enough," Thora said shortly, but Unhost's smile didn't flicker.

"Ethna," he said, speaking past them, "I am in need of a good spear. Orli tells me there is a bear moved into the upriver cave, and we are going to take it tomorrow."

"It is mine!" Thora blurted out. "Orli only knows about it because he overheard me tell Almir. We are going to hunt it tomorrow."

"Don't be ridiculous," Unhost laughed; "you're children! And, let us be honest, Almir is missing more than little of his mind."

"He's still the best hunter in the village," Ylmi replied, quietly.

"Only because he does not know how to care for his own safety," Unhost chuckled, "and, thus, he is not the kind of person two young girls such as yourselves should go bear-baiting with. Fornik and I will go, along with a few others."

Ylmi and Thora stood there for a moment. The rain had weakened back into a cold mist, and Ylmi pulled back a strand of hair, plastered to her face.

"As you say." Thora's voice was flat and empty, as she turned to walk away.

Ylmi took a deep breath, partly to wash away the heavy pit in her stomach, and turned back to Ethna. "Do you have any arrowheads at hand?"

"A few," Ethna nodded, and lifted a small basket, woven of green pine twigs and dried by the fire. It held four iron heads, the black metal sharpened to a shining white on the edges.

"I have a deer pelt," Ylmi said, quickly. "It is already treated and has no holes."

Ethna took it in her hands and ran it through her fingers. Ylmi saw her hesitate and her eyes flick to Unhost, who leant on his spear.

"Hurry," Unhost said, "the bear will not keep forever."

"Two arrowheads," Ethna said, quietly, "but come back and we will discuss the knife later."

Ylmi nodded. She was down to only five tipped arrows, and she did not like the idea of running into a wolf pack with so few. But, if her luck held for a while... she might make it a little longer.

At least, that's what she told herself, as she stepped back into the frigid wind. Ymr's forge was warm, if nothing else. The river rushing down from the hills to the south was loud – a sure sign that a storm was blowing in from the mountains – and Ylmi grimaced.

But, before she could begin the climb back home, she saw Thora standing by the old tree, just past Olga's rough garden. Thora jerked her head for Ylmi to follow, and turned to walk away. Ylmi followed her through the thickening mud, past a few houses and abandoned goat pens, to where Thora had built her own rough hut, nearly at the village, in the shadow of two great pine trees. Thora held open the door and Ylmi followed her inside.

"I should have been more careful," Thora muttered, as the door shut behind her. She lifted a handful of twigs and leaves from by the door, and blew on the smouldering ashes which lay in the centre fireplace. She tossed the twigs onto them, carelessly. "Unhost always seeks to take away what I have."

"I do not think he is a friend to either of us," Ylmi muttered. "I could have used a portion of that bear."

"Perhaps he will give me a little." Thora held her hair back, as she leant down to blow on the smouldering sticks, and a tiny yellow flame burst to life. "I did find the thing."

Ylmi huffed. Her fingers felt a little warmer when she had dried them, and now she listened with relief as the storm poured down outside.

"Thank you for sparing me that storm," she said, as Thora built up the fire.

"You are welcome," Thora nodded, "but I did it in part because I could use your help."

Ylmi looked up at her, through the dimness of the hut. Thora's face was lit by the dancing light of the warm flames, as she slowly piled larger sticks onto the blaze.

"I needed that bear." Thora looked into the fire. "I've had a bad run of late, and I could use another hunter to help."

Ylmi nodded; "It is often easier to hunt with another. Shall we go when the storm ends?"

Thora nodded and Ylmi lay back, closing her eyes as the fire grew, and the warmth washed over her.

The storm lasted late into the night, and Ylmi woke to hear thunder rumbling away down the mountains, as the dark clouds headed south. She sat up, noting her breath hanging white in the air, as she rubbed her eyes.

The fire had burned low, though it still glowed red, and a gnawing hunger had taken seed, deep in her belly.

Seeing her stir, Thora shifted slightly, and took a dark loaf wrapped in a heavy skin; she broke it in half and handed one portion to Ylmi. "Sorry," she muttered, quietly, "it's all I have left."

Ylmi took it, slowly. "It is that bad?"

Thora only nodded.

"Surely there are others who could help?"

But Thora shook her head; "Everyone is trying to save up for winter. I've got a barrel of salted fish that I'm trying to fill, but things will have to get better over the next couple months... or I'll be eating my blankets, just to make it to next spring."

"Surely Unhost won't let you starve," Ylmi said.

"He wouldn't mind." Thora shifted ashes to cover the glowing coals. She snorted as a new thought entered her mind: "If I don't start bringing in something soon, he might try to exile me. Only reason he hasn't done it already is because I'm a good hunter."

She stood and stretched, careful to avoid the low rafters, and stepped toward the door. "Should be good now. You ready?"

In answer, Ylmi stood and took up her bow. Her quiver held three iron-tipped arrows, and ten with only fire-hardened tips, best for smaller animals.

They set off southward, following the bank of the cold river which rushed down from the mountains.

An owl hooted, somewhere off in the early morning mist, and Ylmi shivered.

"Unhost was wrong to take the bear," she said, as they walked. "I am sorry for that."

"It is what he does," Thora shrugged.

"A good jarl should not behave so."

Thora snorted at that and shook her head. "Well, it is what we must learn to bear."

Ylmi ducked under a low branch, holding the quiver at her belt, so it did not spill her arrows into the river. She shivered as the branch dripped down her hood and onto her back.

"Must we, though?" she asked. "Why does Unhost get to treat you and I as he does, when another would do better?"

"I have thought on this, more than once," Thora muttered. "If anyone challenges him, he will simply exile them. Vrania is a harsh place for those with no friends, and even those like Dranri and Oscar depend on a trade with our village. Even with Unhost, life is better in the village."

"He could not exile anyone if he was no longer jarl," Ylmi said.

"He has too many friends who benefit from his behaviour," Thora shrugged. "Besides, who is going to take his place? I, for one, do not want to deal with a dragon, and I doubt there are any in the village who do."

"The dragon is another matter which I do not think should stay the same."

Thora turned and clapped her on the back. "Well, until the gods come down and give you Skathi's bow, and I her spear, there is not much we can do..." she nodded and looked up into the mountains, "...except hunt."

So, together they picked their way through the trees and along the mountainside, for most of the day.

Ylmi found that she was glad of Thora's company – especially when they finally found the tracks of a lone deer. While Thora tracked it, Ylmi looped around north, where it eventually appeared with Thora close behind. Ylmi dropped it with one shot, and was more than a little relieved when she found the iron arrowhead was undamaged.

They skinned and cleaned it, before turning to hike back down to the village, in the warm light of late afternoon. Ylmi was feeling the soreness in her legs when she reached the settlement.

As they came down out of the trees, Thora stopped, suddenly. "There are strangers in the village," she said.

Ylmi followed her pointing finger, to where four men, heavily armed, were arguing with Unhost. "They do not seem friendly," Ylmi muttered. "Not at all."

KING VIGLIR

Ylmi and Thora slipped quietly into Thora's hut, though the sound of the armed men shouting outside could still be heard.

"Have you seen any of them before?" Thora asked. Ylmi shook her head.

Together, the two of them crept out, careful not to draw the attention of Unhost or his guests. When one of the men turned to spit, Ylmi saw the shield hanging from his back, painted with the red and green of King Viglir.

"We are a poor settlement," Unhost was complaining. "We have little enough to simply scrape through the winter."

"There is a bear hanging right there," the leader of the men snarled. "If you can kill one, you can kill another."

"It's not like herding cattle," Fornik spoke up; "we can't just go find another."

"Then, perhaps you're not very good hunters," the leader said. He had a short, dark beard and an ax hung from his belt. "Now," he waved his spear in a wide motion, "you go get enough food to fill our packs and we'll be on our way. Or..." he held up a finger as Unhost opened his mouth, "we start burning your little huts until we get what we want. They aren't that much to lose; I'm sure you could rebuild them easily."

"What good will it do Viglir to take this land," Fornik asked, "if all its people die of starvation and hunger?"

"He will have fresh land to give to those who actually can hunt," the leader smiled and shrugged, tossing his pack at Unhost's feet.

In the end, most of the bear was given to Viglir's men, along with fish and cheese which Unhost had been setting aside for the winter.

"Your reluctance has been noted," their leader said. "When Viglir has taken the pass and Garhom bends the knee, I will return to see that you have learned better."

The village was quiet as they turned and hurried away, back into the mountains, to where Viglir's army was gathered.

"That was a great deal of food," Olga said, when they were gone. She was an older woman, but her garden grew fuller than that of any other in the village.

"And, yet, no blood was shed," Unhost replied in a loud voice. "And, if King Viglir wins through the pass, he will not come looking to burn our settlement."

Havar, the young boatbuilder, had come up, with a net over his shoulder, and he shook his head. "There were only four, Unhost; we could have killed them and thrown their bodies in the fjord, if you were worried about Viglir's vengeance."

Unhost turned on him. "Does anyone here have a sword," he asked, "or a shield? Did I miss something? Have you been building weapons while you were supposed to be repairing fishing boats?"

"There are a dozen spears within shouting distance," Havar snapped back, gesturing toward Ylmi and Thora, "and more than a few bows, as well. If you were not so quick to give up what we work so hard to gather—"

"We all see matters differently," Fornik was the one who spoke now, his smooth voice cutting through the growing chaos. "And, though we have lost some food," he nodded to Havar, "no lives have been lost. You are right, Havar, we might have killed them, but you might also have been killed, or even Unhost. So, we must gather more food, and go hungry for a few nights now. That burden is easier to bear than having to dig graves and bury our boatbuilder."

"I thank you for your wise words." Unhost clapped Fornik on the back. "There is less of the bear than we had hoped, but enough perhaps for you to make a stew. Havar, I believe you have the last goat in the village? We will slaughter it and share it with everyone."

"I am saving it—" Havar began, but Unhost shook his head.

"We must all pull together if we are to make the best of this." He turned to Ylmi: "You, hurry up into the mountains; tell your father to gather more goats and bring them down. We will need to be fed if we are to work."

Ylmi's stomach growled, the hunger growing in her with each passing moment. "Darkness is approaching," she objected; "perhaps it would be best if I waited until morning—"

"If you would deprive us all of food for another day..." Unhost spread his hands, "...do what you think best."

Ylmi saw Olga turn to look at her, and at the same time felt the eyes of everyone else turn to her, as well. She hated Unhost in that moment – a burning, starving hatred, which was quickly swallowed by the void in her stomach.

"I will go," she said, quietly.

"And, for that we are all thankful," Unhost smiled.

"What will we do when they return?" Ylmi asked.

There was a sudden moment of stillness, and all eyes turned back to Unhost.

"You are only a child," Unhost shook his head, "though you seem to have a little skill in hunting. Do you worry about your work, and leave me to mine."

"She's right, though," the old voice of Torig grated on their ears, like a ship dragged on rocks. The old man waved his crooked fingers at Unhost; "You'd best have a plan, youngling."

"What do you suggest?" Unhost challenged. "If you have a plan, please share it with us."

Torig gave a wheezing laugh, and his wispy beard bobbed back and forth as he chuckled. "No, no, no," he waved a finger; "my job is fishing. Plans and whatnot are yours."

"We could apply to the king," Havar suggested, and Unhost almost winced at the suggestion.

"You want the king here, coming down to our settlement?" Unhost shook his head; "No, he will take all our gold and half our food."

"That is better than Viglir's men taking all our food."

Almir appeared from behind one of the huts, several rabbits hanging from his belt. "You are all fools and children," he muttered, but loud enough for them all to hear.

"Who do you call children?" Torig barked.

"Them," Almir gestured, widely; "you are a fool."

"Dunharvic came for you long ago," Torig replied; "he took your mind, but the Allfather bade him leave your body, as he did not wish something so grotesque in his hall."

"These are yours." Almir handed two rabbits to Unhost. "If you want to do something about Viglir, you join Jarhost's army and help him retake the pass."

He turned back to Torig; "Look at that: this empty head came up with a better idea than your full one, old fishbones."

The two of them continued to insult each other, but Fornik nodded at Unhost. "If a few of us go to fight with the king, we may be able to help turn back Viglir."

"If you say that you are wanderers..." Unhost nodded, thoughtfully.

"Six of us," Fornik suggested, "perhaps more?"

Ylmi shook her head and turned back, Thora following her. "If he had stood up to them, none of this would have happened."

Thora nodded. "He is a bad jarl, forever putting off doing what is difficult."

The trail into the mountains was not an easy one, and more than once Ylmi had to stop to make sure of her way in the dark. She reached home just as another storm began to blow in, and her parents looked up in surprise when she shut the door behind her.

"You are out very late," Siggi said. "We thought you were staying in the village, or hunting with Dranri."

"I was," Ylmi answered, "but other things have happened."

She told them of what had occurred in the settlement. They listened quietly, but Bodvar's face fell as she told of Unhost's demand for more goats.

"The herd is larger than it has been in two years," he said, quietly, "but this year has been hard on it already. If he keeps making demands, there will be little enough for us in the winter, and it will be hard to regrow the herd next year."

He sighed and rose to his feet. "I will start tomorrow, to gather what I can. Perhaps I can convince him to take fewer later this year, or fewer for the dragon."

The next day, Ylmi went looking for Dranri. She found him checking snares by the stream, not far from his house. He smiled when he saw her.

"I am glad to see you here," he said. "The northern slopes are full of scouts and spies at the moment."

"King Viglir's men," Ylmi nodded. "I heard."

"Viglir's, Jarhost's, Hegli's..." Dranri retrieved a squirrel from one of the snares, and set to replacing it, "they're all crawling all over the slopes, and driving any creatures far away. Viglir is making another push for the pass, Jarhost is trying to stop him, and Hegli is hanging upon the borders, as usual, to see if he can gain an advantage."

"Unhost is sending some men to go fight," Ylmi said, "to help Jarhost hold the pass."

"A wise decision," Dranri muttered. "Unhost can always be trusted to do the right thing – as long as it's also the selfish thing." He finished with the snare and stood, looking Ylmi up and down.

"Have you come here to bring me news," he asked, "or are you in the mood to hunt something large and dangerous?"

"Both," Ylmi said, quickly. "The village is in need of food, and more work will not get done with so many going to war."

"Unhost should take in more exiles." Dranri glanced back at the snare, making sure it was set properly. "The settlement is still too small, and for even a few to go is no small thing."

"Dranri," she said, quickly, "there was another thing."

He had been preparing to go back to his hut, but he stopped and looked back, his bushy eyebrows raised.

She spoke quietly: "You have told me that you fought in Jarhost's hall for two years, before you came to the mountains."

"Yes...?" His eyebrows suddenly dropped in suspicion.

Ylmi took a deep breath and nodded. "You have shown me how to use a spear against bear and boar. Show me how to use it against a man."

"You are hardly even fifteen years old," Dranri protested; "you should not—"

"Scouts and spies," Ylmi repeated, "and robbers, too. What good is my hunting, if it is taken away by any who happen upon me?"

Dranri thought for a moment, his eyes heavy on her, as the wind blew cold through the pine trees. At last, he took a deep breath. "I will teach you," he said, "on one condition: that you swear not to go hunting Unhost, or try to murder anyone in the village. I know you have little care for them, and some you hate."

She chewed her lip, thinking over his words. "I will swear not to murder anyone in the village, unless it is in defence," she replied. It was similar, but it left her plenty of room to find her way out of the oath, if needed.

But Dranri looked doubtful. "If you shed innocent blood, and it is I who trained you, that blood is somewhat on my hands."

Ylmi only shrugged. "I have no desire to stir up trouble," she said, "but I would not be caught defenceless."

Dranri snorted at that and rolled his eyes. "Ylmi, you are among the least defenceless people I have met."

He thought for another moment, before at last nodding; "You raise a good point, so I shall teach you. But, seek always a way beyond battle."

And, with that, he took up his spear and taught her.

A HUNGRY SETTLEMENT

In the days which followed, Ylmi noted that Unhost travelled often to the mountain where the Watching Stones were set. Once, she even followed him, watching from the trees as he attempted the climb. But Unhost was not a brave man, and was reluctant to truly pursue a path said to be deadly and dangerous.

For her part, Ylmi had little time for the Stones. Orli had gone up into the mountains with several other men, to fight with Jarhost, and they left behind much work to be done: there were houses which needed patching, gardens and livestock to be tended, and the constant work of laying aside food for the winter. Additionally, they left behind families who badly needed their help. Darros's wife, Nanna, was left to look after a small child, with another on the way. So, Ylmi spent more and more of her time in the village, helping with the work which had to be done, and the fruits of her hunting were split between her family and those who had need.

From dawn until dusk, she hunted and worked, 'til her bones ached and her limbs were sore. And, all the while, the fighting in the pass went on, as Viglir and Jarhost tried to gain the upper hand, one over the other.

One day, as she brought Ethna a pair of wolf hides, Ylmi noted that she had not seen Unhost in the village for several days.

"He is utterly obsessed with the Watching Stones," Ethna said, as Ymr hammered on the anvil behind her. "He has been searching for the way to them for some time, and has even offered gold to anyone who will find the path."

"And, has anyone tried?"

Ethna shook her head with a laugh. "We have little enough time for our own work. Although, two exiles from another village arrived here yesterday evening," she pointed; "that is their boat there, on the sand. Unhost has offered gold and a place in his hall to either of them who will show him the way."

Ylmi looked at her in shock. "We have all been working ourselves to the bone, to make up for those who left to fight," she said, "and Unhost sends them to look for stones?"

Ethna nodded; "Trust me, you are not alone in this. But, the families of those who went to fight will not stand up to him, lest he hold back the aid he has been giving them. And, Olga will say nothing; she is too old to be sent into the wilderness alone."

Ylmi sighed. Ethna was right: even if one of them did stand up to Unhost, who would replace him?

Her eyes turned northward, to where the Watching Stones were. She could not see them from the settlement, but she knew where they were. Perhaps the gods would have an answer to her questions. "I do not think they will find them," Ylmi said.

"The Stones?" Ethna asked. "There must be a path, and if it is there, can it not be found?"

Ylmi stared at the boat for a moment, and thought of her mother's stories. "I see no reason why there must be a path," she said, at last: "even if one was carved there some time ago, there are storms and avalanches in these mountains every year, and they may have wiped out any path which might be found."

But Ethna's words gnawed at Ylmi, as she made the climb back up to her father's house.

━━━◆━━━

The next morning, she bent her path northward. There were rock squirrels in the northern mountains, and she told herself that she might even find a deer on the heights.

Yet, her eyes did not look for deer, but rather for the young men whom Unhost had hired to find the Stones for him. It was almost midday when she found them, climbing up a cliff face. It was one she had scaled before, and she found an overhanging rock she could sit underneath and follow their progress.

It did not surprise her when, after a short time, it began to rain. The storm worsened the higher they climbed, 'til she could barely see them in the pouring rain. They stopped when they reached the top of the cliff, and Ylmi guessed they were debating how best to proceed. There were two paths from where they were, and Ylmi had yet to discover which one led higher.

But, while they discussed, they suddenly began to fight. One shoved the other who, to keep his balance, grasped at the one who had shoved him. In a blink, they were falling – falling from the cliff it had taken them hours to scale.

Ylmi took a short time to reach them, and found them lying a small distance from each other. Their bodies were horribly broken by the fall, and one of them still had his eyes open, staring blankly up at the sky. Ylmi wondered what they had been fighting about, before it occurred to her that Unhost had doubtless told them that only one would receive the reward.

The waste made her angry; they had brought a boat, and might have been good fishermen. There was always more work that could be done, and if Unhost was going to simply throw lives away, then why did the gods still allow him to be jarl?

Ylmi thought on it, as she stared at the bodies. She thought on it when she returned home, and she thought on it as she lay down to sleep that night.

Two days later, she was sitting by one of the deer trails which ran northward over the mountains, toward the ice marshes, when she saw Thora picking her way through the trees. A west wind was blowing steadily through the trees, and moaning over the mountain heights. Far off, she could hear a flock of ravens screaming.

Thora turned toward her, approaching slowly up the mountainside.

"The fighting is over," she said quietly, as she took a seat next to Ylmi. "Viglir has abandoned his push through the pass and returned to his hall at Torhom."

Ylmi nodded, but her friend's tone was not a happy one. "You sound as though you have come bearing ill news."

"Visrik is dead, as is Darros," Thora replied. "Bogli is missing an arm and walks with a limp now. Orli and Flovi have a few wounds, but nothing serious." She picked up a stick from the ground and began to idly break it into pieces. "Nanna will have her child in the next few days. The winter will be hard for them."

Ylmi said nothing, but only looked through the pine trees, down the rocky slope. Her eyes slid easily over the land, watching for movement. How much more she could do, she was not sure.

"How are you?" she asked, at last. "Have you been able to set aside a little more for the winter?"

Thora shrugged. "More than I had, less than I'd like. Almir and I found a boar two days ago... I gave half my portion to Nanna."

"And Unhost took a third for himself?"

Thora spat. "He gave it to Orli and Flovi, in thanks for their fighting, though Nanna stood by. It is no wonder those two are glad to have him as jarl."

"Between them and Fornik, it is no wonder he is never held to account." Ylmi pushed a crick out of her back, as she picked up her spear. "They are as much to blame for his foolishness as anyone else."

Thora spat again. "The gods will have them pay a heavy price. Of that I am sure."

— ◇ —

Three more exiles Unhost sent to find the Watching Stones. One slipped and fell while climbing the cliff face. The second made it past the cliff, but fell when he tried to jump over a ravine – Ylmi had no idea how he thought he could make it, and was surprised that he had come close. The third saw the three skeletons at the base of the cliff, and hesitated for a short time. But, he scaled the cliff and made it to the ravine. Then, when he peered down and saw the body of the last to try, he shook his head. After a moment's consideration, he turned around, climbed down the cliff, picked up his bow and pack from the base of the cliff, where he had left them, and hiked off northeast. Doubtless, he decided that whatever Unhost had promised him was not worth what seemed to amount to certain death. Ylmi did not blame him. The bodies were piling up on the way to the Watching Stones, and it was looking less and less appealing. As winter approached once again, and the winds turned colder, Ylmi saw but few more exiles from the village attempt the climb.

At last, she saw Orli the Tall, one of Unhost's hang-abouts, scale the mountain. He made it up the cliff and looked about for some time, peering around the cliff, and exploring the other pathways which led from the clifftop. But, by now there were many bones about the mountain, and Orli seemed to determine that his life might be better spent in the village; he climbed back down.

When Ylmi was next in the village, she asked Ethna if any more exiles would be sent in search of the Stones.

The smith shook her head. "It seems Unhost has given up on the Watching Stones," Ethna told her. "He seems now more concerned with the gold which is dug up from the ground."

"It is a waste," Ylmi told her; "we cannot eat gold, nor will it keep us warm."

"Fair enough." Ethna answered; "it would be better if we worried less about gold and more about fishing. But, the gold does have its uses." She showed Ylmi a spearhead, freshly forged by her husband. "Unhost is able to get good iron from the west with it, though he cautions us that we cannot use too much in one place, lest the king in Bjarnmont hear of it."

Ylmi acknowledged that this made sense, but privately thought that gold they were not allowed to spend was the most ridiculous thing Unhost had yet concocted.

Unhost was increasingly less than capable as a jarl, it seemed to her, and she thought that perhaps another would do a better job than he was doing.

Ylmi bartered for a few more arrowheads, and as Ymr beat them out of iron ore, Ethna told Ylmi of the ongoing raids between King Jarhost and King Viglir: "After the summer, they are back to picking at each other here and there."

"It is a waste," Ylmi said; "they would be much better off building together."

"Even so," Ethna agreed, "one will not yield to the other, and so the fighting goes on."

"At least this time their fighting does not reach us," Ylmi shook her head.

"For now," Ethna replied. "For now."

The Watching Stones

She thought on Unhost and his decisions, as she made the climb back up the mountain. There was an entire village of hunters and fishers, men and women, who were more than comfortable with the spear, bow or ax. If Unhost led them all against the dragon, would they not have a good chance of success? If they were free of the dragon, would that not be a good thing? They could spend more time gathering food for the winter and building better homes, instead of grubbing for extra gold.

A storm approached as she walked, and she hurried on her way as the thunder rolled in. If there was another jarl, her family might be able to move back to the village. Then, if their fire went out, or they fell ill, there would be someone to help them. Otherwise, what would happen when her father was too old to track down the goats? What if he broke a leg now? They were surviving the winters by a hair's breadth, and if one or two things more went wrong...

She did not want to watch her parents sicken and starve. And, as long as Unhost was the jarl, that was always only one injury, one misfortune away.

She was quiet that evening, as she sat by the fire. Her father was pleased: one of the goats had just given birth to twins and, the way matters were going, the herd would be in very good shape this year.

But Siggi was less sure. "I have heard wolves howling these past four days. If the wolves get among the lambs..."

"That is why there are rams," Bodvar replied, but after a moment his shoulders fell and he sighed. "I am sure the wolves will take some, but they do every year. That is why two lambs are better than one."

But he was silent for the rest of the evening, and Ylmi lost herself in her thoughts, as she fastened the arrowheads she had bought from Ethna onto new arrows.

Ylmi rose early the next morning and set out, but she did not go south to the tree-lined slopes, where Dranri preferred to hunt. Nor did she guide her steps westward, to the mountainous forest which led upward, into the great mountains where the black bears made their home. Instead, she marched northwest, toward the Watching Stones.

She climbed up through the mountains, into the twisting, fog-filled valleys and cliffs which lay beneath the Watching Stones. She picked her way carefully, following small markers she had left as her path went higher and higher, until she reached the first cliff face.

By the time she had scaled it, the fog had filled with rain, and she could see the dim glow of lightning to the north. She followed the eastern path, for though it led away and down from the mountain top, she thought it made sense. If Vranr was climbing to spy on the Watcher, whatever it had been, perhaps the old trickster would have preferred to remain hidden until he was near the summit.

But, the eastern path led to yet another cliff, this one covered in moss and lichen, rendering the stone slick and treacherous. Ylmi rubbed her fingers in the gritty mud, and began to climb.

Twice she almost fell, and survived by ramming her fingers into crevices in the cliff face. By the time she reached the top, her face was covered in dirt and rain, and blood was running down to her elbows. A small ledge provided a brief respite, but there was no way forward, except up another cliff. Shaking her head, she began to climb.

The thunder was upon her now, lightning flashing overhead, before letting out an ear-cracking boom which reverberated through her chest. She was wet through, and she realized suddenly that it was making her heavier. She chuckled madly at that, and eyed her bleeding hands. The rain was pouring down her arms as she climbed, mixing with the blood and dying her deerskin shirt red.

The top of the cliff revealed a steep slope of broken rock, transfixed by little rivers and rivulets which poured down it. She was approaching the clouds now, and the rocky slope led northwest, rising steeply until it disappeared in thick clouds, some way above her.

Her arms ached and there was a cramp in one hand, but her blood was up and a thrill ran through her. If anyone had made it this far up the mountain, it had not been for many years. And, if Vranr had actually built the Stones, then perhaps she was walking in his footsteps. She smiled; she had been right about the eastern path, after all.

She climbed higher into the clouds. The clouds were heavy and the wind seemed to grow harsher within them, though Ylmi suspected that was only because she was climbing higher. She must have been above most mountains this side of Bjarnmont!

When she reached the top of the rocky slope, her whole body was burning. Her arms and shoulders ached, and her legs felt as though they would seize up at any moment. Out of the north, the wind came howling down now, driving the clouds and rain before it, so Ylmi could barely look northward at all.

But, northward the next path led, up through boulders and broken rocks, many still surrounded by snowdrifts, still frozen from the past winter. Slowly Ylmi went, picking her way forward as best she could, but now unsure if the Watching Stones were in front of her or behind, as the clouds rolled thick and heavy about her. Up she climbed, over further slopes, feeling her way upward as she went, guessing that, had Vranr climbed this mountain, he would have had to climb upward as best as he was able. Where he had gone, Ylmi guessed that perhaps she could go.

Still she climbed, until the wind blew a gap in the dark clouds. In an instant, she saw she was on a long ridge, the land sloping down around her, the ridge running due north. And, along the ridge, she saw a cairn.

Old stones had been piled waist-high, set one on top of another, and Ylmi almost shouted for joy when she saw it. She was close, she felt sure of it, and the cairn was a sign she was on the right path.

Shaking rain from her face, she pushed on, climbing up the rising ridge, growing more excited with each step, until she reached the end of the ridge. It rose up and up, until it ended at the foot of another cliff.

The sheer rock face rose up before her, disappearing into the clouds above her. Her shoulders sank at the sight of it, and she wondered if she had the strength to scale it. She did not know how long she had been climbing, and the descent would take some time.

She had come farther than any other she knew of. She knew a great deal more of the way than she had before, so doubtless if she returned on another day, she could make it yet farther.

The wind howled and the rain lashed down upon her, but Ylmi glared at the rock before her and snarled. Vranr was not the only one who had lost loved ones. He had climbed this mountain to gain something, and now she would, too.

Her hands were red, still covered in their own blood, and she set them into the rock and began to pull herself up.

She had made it perhaps ten feet, when her hand settled onto a ledge. Pulling herself onto it, she was shocked to discover that it was not a ledge, but a path, narrowly cut into the rock and almost invisible from below. Carefully, she followed it, winding upward into the cloudy gloom. It was old but unworn, as though it had been used only a few times before.

As she climbed, the lightning came closer and the thunder boomed, as the rain lashed against the cliff, driven by the north wind, which whipped and snapped at her. Once, it caught her cloak and almost yanked her from the cliff face, but she pressed herself against the rock, and wrapped her cloak tight within her belt. It did no good to her now, anyway; the rain had found its way through all her clothes, and she was as soaked as if she had leapt into the sea. She gave herself over to the misery, letting the weariness wash through her, as she took one more step.

There was no way back and no way forward; she lived on the cliff now. In her exhaustion, she felt as though she could not remember the warmth of a fire, or the fullness of a good meal. She lived on a cliff, and she put one foot in front of the other. Her legs burned, her back ached and her shoulders cramped almost constantly. So, she put one foot in front of the other. Until the path came to a small ledge.

Ylmi pulled herself over it, looking for the next cliff.

But there was none, for Ylmi Bodvarsdottir had come to the Watching Stones of Vranr.

They rose before her, two… three times as tall as she was, runes carved into them from tip to root. And, in the midst of them all was a high, stone seat, cut into the very peak of the mountain. The wind howled and screamed, but in the midst of the Stones Ylmi felt it kept at bay. It whistled about the massive stones, pushed at them, but within the Stones it could barely lift the wet hair from her face.

Ylmi turned round and round, gazing in wonder, then in yearning.

"I have come," she said, almost quietly. "I seek wisdom… guidance."

Around her, the wind howled and moaned.

"Why do you allow Unhost to rule?" she asked, looking from stone to stone, wondering what form of guidance they offered. "A dragon rests upon our doorstep, and he does nothing. What am I to do?"

Lightning flashed in the sky overhead and, an instant later, thunder boomed across the sky.

"I was told that the gods would make their will known." She glanced around, her voice rising: "I seek only to know what I should do."

The rain came down in sheets, splattering on the Stones.

"Or, perhaps it is the ghost of Vranr who speaks here?"

She looked around, but there was no answer, only the storm raging above and around her – and below her, she realized. Here on the mountain-top, she was within the storm itself.

"You are said to be a trickster," her voice was a shout now; "I did not think you extended that to your own children."

There was no response, but the moaning of the wind.

"Answer me!" she shouted, turning from one Stone to the other. "Or, am I meant to hunt until I die on a mountainside with a broken leg, or sicken and starve in a half-built cave?"

She was furious now. Furious that the climb had been in vain. Furious that the stories were all fake – all wrong. The Stones were here; they were real; someone had carved them, cutting a path into this mountain, even if it was not Vranr.

"If you would have me die, then say so," she snarled, "and I will leave this mountain swifter than I came."

For an instant the wind howled. Then the world exploded.

A flash of lightning split the air before her, in a blinding boom which left her blind and deaf, staggering to her knees. The taste of burning air filled her mouth, and her ears rang as the lightning subsided. For a time, she blinked, her vision coming slowly back to her, as she knelt in the rain.

And then the storm broke.

The wind still howled, and the rain still fell, perhaps even heavier than before. But the thunder was gone.

The Coming of Karik

VII

The Coming of Karik

Siggi and Bodvar were more than a little concerned when their daughter staggered out of the forest, covered in dirt and blood, and soaked through. But Ylmi said nothing, and only stared with hollow eyes at the fire, as she ate.

At last, when Siggi seemed close to tears, Ylmi looked up, as one who had woken from a dream. She said that she had climbed a great deal that day and was deeply tired. Bodvar said this gave him more questions, not fewer, but Siggi pulled him away, and said that the matter was probably best left alone for now.

⊷◆⊶

It was still very dark when Ylmi was woken by the howls of a wolf, off in the woods. She lay in the darkness for only a moment, before rising silently from her bed. If Vranr would not give her the guidance she asked, or the gods would not tell her if she should go against Unhost, then at least there would be one less wolf to prey upon her father's goats.

She slipped out into the predawn gloom, a long knife at her hip, and her bow held lightly in her torn hands. The forest was lit by the faint glow of the cloud-covered moon, gently filtering down through pine branches, swaying in the morning breeze. She followed the wolf's howling, guessing the ridges it would make for, and slipping among the trees like a ghost.

As the sun peeked over the eastern mountains, she found a set of tracks. Uneven and bloodstained, the paw marks led deep into the hills, and Ylmi hurried along the trail.

At last, she came upon the den. Set deep in a tiny dell, the wolf den was almost invisible under the low hanging rocks and bushes, cloaked in the shadows cast by the mountains in the morning sun.

An arrow on her bow, Ylmi stepped forward quietly. A wolf head appeared at the cave entrance, and the two of them locked eyes.

The wolf was old, scars covering its face. The grey fur was shredded with white and black. With a limp, it stepped forward to face Ylmi and bared its fangs. Ylmi's eyes took in its limp, the rear leg held just off the ground, as though it was in pain.

Behind it, a wolf cub climbed out of the den and stared at them, its eyes wide and dark within its soft fur. For a moment, Ylmi's eyes softened. With a broken leg, it was only a matter of time before the old wolf, the she-wolf, died. It would not be a quick death, either; long and slow by starvation. And the pup would follow soon after – if the mother was not driven to eat her cub first, by hunger.

Ylmi raised a hand and spoke quietly to the she-wolf. "I will end your suffering," she said, "quick and as painless as I can. And I will raise your pup. She will live through winter, and eat with me."

She sighed. "But you will not let that happen while you live."

The two locked eyes, and the old she-wolf stared back. Then, she bared her fangs.

Ylmi loosed an arrow and the wolf half turned in mid-air, but still struck Ylmi in her leap. One hand went to her knife, and the other buried itself in the wolf's coarse fur. The two rolled about in the mud, striking and wrestling to gain the advantage, one over the other.

When it was over, Ylmi pushed herself into a sitting position. Her left hand was covered in blood as far as the elbow – dark, gleaming blood which had poured from a dozen cuts. Most of it was wolf blood, she was sure. When she moved her right arm, a lancing pain went through her shoulder, and bone grated on bone.

For an instant, a sick feeling went through her stomach. A broken shoulder rarely healed properly, and it would make wielding a bow next to impossible. She would not hunt. They would starve...

But, she stopped and took a deep breath. Twice more she breathed in through her nose and out through her mouth, calming her nerves as the pain began to register – not just in her shoulder, but other places as well. Her back ached where she had landed on it, there was a hot itch developing on her forehead, and she was sure she had hit her elbow on a rock.

Dropping the knife, she ran her fingers over her shoulder. It felt weird – out of place – and then she laughed. The laughter hurt a lot, which ended it quickly, but Ylmi still smiled with relief: her shoulder was dislocated, not broken. With an angry grunt, she yanked it back into the joint, and gasped at the pain. Nausea filled her stomach, and for an instant she thought she would retch.

Slowly, she came back to herself, the pain finding its place, and her breathing returning to normal.

Beside her, the old she-wolf lay dead, with open eyes staring up at the sky. Ylmi pushed herself to her feet and slowly limped to the cave. Under the outcropping, the baby wolf pup blinked up at her with giant eyes, whining as she came closer.

"It's you and me now." Ylmi reached out a hand, and the pup looked from it to her, then shrank back. With a grunt, Ylmi leaned in farther, grabbing it by the scruff of its neck and lifting it into her arms.

"It's going to rain soon. Let's get home."

Siggi was tending her garden when she heard her daughter returning. The late afternoon sun was blotted out by heavy storm clouds, and Siggi was glad that, for once, Ylmi would not try to hunt until the storm hit. She looked up to see a red figure, blood-soaked and dripping, standing at the edge of the clearing. With an oath, she reached for the ax nearby, before realizing that it was indeed her daughter.

"By the nine realms, Ylmi!" she swore, as she rose. "What madness—"

"I have a pup." Ylmi raised the whimpering ball of fur in her arms. "Her name is Ulfr."

That night, Ylmi slept with Ulfr curled up in the blankets next to her. The little pup whined, but Ylmi held her, and soon Ulfr was snuggled up against her, snoring deeply.

In the morning, when Ylmi rose, she found her mother waiting for her by the fire.

"Sit, daughter," Siggi ordered, and Ylmi did so. Ulfr squirmed in her arms until she let her go, and the little pup scampered around their dwelling, exploring and smelling everything it could find.

"Twice now," Siggi said, "you have left in the dark of the morning and returned covered in blood and bruises. Each winter you grow more grim, and you speak less with every passing day. Tell me, what is in your mind, daughter?"

For a moment, Ylmi said nothing, letting the fire between them fill her eyes. The flames were low, gnawing at the broken branches Siggi had fed to them. "It is in my mind," she said, without lifting her eyes, "that we are one mistake away from death, here on this mountain."

"So are many in this land," Siggi replied. "Is it the nearness of death that so troubles you?"

Ylmi bit back a bitter laugh, as she felt the anger rising within her chest. "Death would not watch so close if Unhost had not beckoned him."

"You fear the dragon?"

Ylmi chuckled at that. "Why should we fear the dragon, when Unhost has so carefully bought his loyalty?" She spat into the fire and glanced to Ulfr, who was sniffing at the door. She took a breath and noticed with a quick grin that her hands were shaking.

"Unhost has made peace with a dragon he should have challenged. He has exiled us to this mountain where we can barely survive in the winter." She looked into her mother's eyes. "What if I break my leg? What if we all get sick at once? We are alone on the mountainside, my brother is dead and it is all Unhost's fault. It seems that every decision he makes is the wrong one, and creates more work for others."

Siggi listened, letting her daughter speak.

After a moment, Ylmi continued: "I would kill him and leave his body for his precious dragon, but if I do we will be outlaws forever and no one will take us in – so, we will be worse off than before. And, that does not even consider the matter of the dragon."

"Is that why you have been hunting so?" Siggi asked. "You want to see if you can kill a dragon?"

"I am angry," Ylmi answered, "not foolish." She sighed and looked down at her hands, which were still bloody and torn from climbing the cliffs. "I scaled the mountain and went to the Watching Stones."

A gasp escaped Siggi and her hands went to her mouth.

"Oh, hush," Ylmi snapped at her. "It was all for naught. There was no answer there, no guidance, no council to be found from Vranr's rocks."

"You are indeed a wonder of a daughter," Siggi said, after a moment, "and I am blessed that you are mine." She paused for a moment, gathering her words, and thinking how best to answer the young woman who sat before her.

"Our situation is not what would be hoped," she said, at last, "and if we were back in the settlement, things might indeed be easier. Yet, your father has done well here in the mountains, and the goat herd he has tended is now larger than Unhost thought he could gather."

"Because Unhost thought we would die on the mountain," Ylmi interrupted.

Siggi nodded; "Even so. But still there are many on this isle who would be more than happy to trade places with us. We have survived the winter alone well enough—"

"We have almost died each winter!" Ylmi corrected.

"Almost," Siggi said, with a small smile, "but not quite. In no small part because of your hunting, I might add."

"So, that is it?" Ylmi challenged her. "Hunt on the mountainside and hope nothing bad happens? Hope that Unhost finds an exile he can marry me off to? Already I must hunt farther than before, and our hunger does not grow less."

She closed her eyes for a moment. "Unhost drives us closer to death every year, and under him the settlement has weakened. There was no need for Darros and Visrik to die, and for Bogli to be lamed. There are several bodies lying beneath the Watching Stones that could have helped us, but Unhost threw away their lives."

"Running a settlement takes more work than it seems," Siggi said, with a small smile. "Your father has his hands full with his goats, and a village is more headstrong than a goat herd." She shook her head. "Though, I do not disagree with you that Unhost does his duty poorly."

"Then, what am I to do?" Ylmi looked up in frustration. "The gods will not answer me, the ghost of Vranr is a tricky spite, and the only advice I seem to get is to do nothing."

"No," Siggi corrected her, and Ylmi looked up quickly, "I do not say do nothing; I say wait. You are still young, you are still growing and you are learning. Because the winds of fate blow one way today does not mean that they will blow that way forever. They may change, and when they do, you will not wish you had done less while you waited."

So Ylmi waited, though it was bitter in her mouth and galled her stomach.

For several years she hunted and explored the mountains, 'til there were few in the village who hunted as well as she.

But, most often, she hunted with Dranri. She learned much from him, who told her of the battles he had fought for King Jarhost in Bjarnmont, against Jarl Hegli and King Viglir in the west.

"Viglir was an honourable man," Dranri told her once, as they looked over a small mountain valley, "but I have no liking for Hegli."

When she asked him why he had left Jarhost's service to live alone in the mountains, he stared into the distance for a moment, before answering.

"There were many reasons," he said, at last. "I was one of those chosen to escort his sister to Hegli, and that was an ill thing. Hegli treated her very poorly, and after she gave him a son, Tanvir, he treated her worse." He spat into the snowbank. which hid in the shade of a pine tree. "Jarhost should have done something about it, but he did not. The powerful too often shirk their duty to protect those who have less."

She brooded on these matters often, even as she hunted the hills and forests which surrounded her home. Her hunts grew longer and longer, as she searched for animals which grew increasingly scarce.

The scarcity of the animals concerned her, and it was on this that she had set her mind one day, late in the year, when she came down out of the mountains into the clearing. Ulfr, trotting beside her, paused to sniff the air, but Ylmi called her on.

"Father has only brought down more sheep," she told her. "You know what they smell like."

But then, Ulfr's ears pricked forward, and she stepped quickly into the house with a growl.

Siggi called out a greeting from inside, and Ylmi entered to see a young man speaking with her father.

"This is Karik Haldsson," her father said, "an exile who will be staying with us for the winter."

"There is not overly much food as it is," Ylmi told him, "so I hope you are a good worker."

Karik looked down at Ulfr, who was smelling at him suspiciously. He reached out to touch the wolf but she backed away, baring her teeth in a low growl. He chuckled and looked back to Ylmi. "I can work as well as any, and better than most."

"We'll be the judge of that," Ylmi muttered.

The next day, Karik left with her father to seek out sheep in the forest, at first light.

As the door shut behind him, Ylmi turned to her mother. "This seems to me the latest burden," she said, "in Unhost's attempt to kill us."

"What do you mean?" Siggi asked, her eyes fixed on the hide she was picking clean.

"Another mouth to feed," Ylmi asked, "with winter only a few weeks away? How on Earth are we to feed all four of us?"

"He will do his share of the work," Siggi assured her, "and the goat herd is larger than it has ever been. If he works hard, I do not think we will have a more difficult time than usual. Besides, with him helping your father, there is more time for you to hunt."

Ylmi acknowledged this was true, but she still suspected Unhost of foul play, as she took her bow and quiver, and set off into the woods.

She hunted hard that day, ranging far north to the edge of the ice marsh, to see what she could find. But there were few tracks and fewer animals, so she was in a foul mood when she returned that evening.

Yet her father seemed very cheerful, and Ylmi noted that he seemed to enjoy Karik's company.

Several days later, Ylmi was hunting through the southern forest, when she came upon Thora.

"It is good to see you," she said, as they embraced. "How fares the hunting?"

Ylmi shrugged; "Well enough. And yours?"

Thora shrugged with a grin, the boar spear on her back, glinting the light cast by a clouded sky. "I heard your father was saddled with one of the exiles," she said. "I was sorry to hear it."

"He seems to enjoy his company," Ylmi replied, "so I am not overly saddened by it. How many others were with him?" She eased down on a fallen tree, and Thora joined her, both of them letting their legs swing. They felt the miles fall from their feet as they talked.

"Four others," Thora said, shaking her head. "I have met a couple. Revik is very loud and I am not fond of him; he speaks only of winning glory in Jarhost's hall. His brother Igil, however, is very quiet, but he is at work with Havar the boatbuilder."

Ylmi grimaced, for Havar was a strange one, who loved only his boats. "I dislike living with someone I know so little of," she said, after a moment, "especially with winter drawing near."

"I have a plan," Thora suggested, "if you wish to hear it."

"Go on..."

Thora grinned at Ylmi's doubtful expression and forged ahead. "Next time you find a bear or boar trail, take him with you."

"No," Ylmi shook her head, "I enjoy the quiet of my hunts. I do not wish a chattering oaf to scare away my prey."

"It is but one hunt," Thora said. "Come on, Ylmi, one hunt. Worst case: you find nothing, and you learn if he can keep his mouth shut and move through the woods without complaining. Or, perhaps you find your bear; if he's a good fighter, and brave, you'll have someone to help you carry it down the mountain. If he's not..." she shrugged, "...the bear gets a last meal before you shoot it."

Ylmi looked at Thora with wide eyes. "You've done this before?"

Thora threw up her hands and glanced up toward the mountains. "Unhost wanted to marry me to one of the exiles who came in, two years ago. I told him I would marry him gladly, if he came hunting with me. He was shit, so I let the bear eat him."

"I am surprised you have not invited Unhost hunting with you," Ylmi muttered.

Thora laughed. "Oh, I have. He's too cowardly to even do that. He knows I seek out the bear haunts and the boar rootings. Even if he trusted me with his life, he would not go hunting with me after that game, not without half the spears in the village between him and the beast."

"Fair point," Ylmi agreed.

The treetops were stirring, and dark grey clouds were beginning to appear over the mountains: sure signs that another storm was on its way.

"Look in the northwestern hills," Thora suggested, rising to her feet; "I've seen a few trails heading that way in the last few weeks. If you have good hunting, let me know, and I may check them myself."

Ylmi thanked her and thought on her words, as she retraced her path up through the trees and hills, arriving back at their home soon after the rain began to fall.

⸻ ◆ ⸻

With Karik helping her father, she was free to hunt, and it was the work of only a few days to find an appropriate quarry. With winter drawing near, the boars were rooting about for their last food before the snow fell, and she found where one had made his home.

As she hurried back south, the thought came to her that her parents might not feel altogether happy if she invited the new man out to hunt, then came back without him. Her mother, she was sure, would suspect something, so she determined the matter was best handled in a roundabout way: she asked her father for help, and when he declined and offered to send Karik in his stead, she looked appropriately annoyed. But Bodvar encouraged them both, and Ylmi found herself hoping that Karik would prove himself well.

The next morning, they set out as the sun was rising. They followed the little game trails up into the mountains, and Karik moved quietly behind her. The path she led him on was not an easy one, but he made no complaint, even as she pushed the pace.

They spoke a little, and for all her early distrust, she began to understand why her father enjoyed his company.

When they found the boar, it was nearly noon. He was larger than Ylmi had expected, and her first arrow struck true, as did her second. The boar grunted angrily, but stared stupidly in the wrong direction, so Ylmi let her third arrow bounce off his skull.

That drew his attention, and she quickly slipped to the side, as he sighted Karik and charged.

She nodded as Karik braced and caught the boar on his spear. But, the next moment, a ragged crack ripped through the trees, as his spear shaft broke.

In an instant, Ylmi had another arrow on her string, and she felt it bite into her fingers as she drew. But the boar had pushed Karik behind another tree, and she had no clear shot. She could only watch as the boar lunged and Karik tumbled to the side.

In an instant, he was back on his feet, and she expected that he would run, or take refuge in one of the trees. Instead, he drew his knife, spread his feet and awaited the boar. But, as it rushed, the boar passed the tree.

Ylmi's bow twanged a fourth time, sending an arrow slicing deep behind the boar's shoulder and piercing its heart.

She took a deep breath, as Karik looked up from the boar and smiled at her. He had acquitted himself well, she decided. The matter had been closer than she would have liked it – she had not expected his spear to break – but when the cold came, she did not think he would shirk his work.

The following day, as Karik left to help her father, and Siggi set to harvesting the last of their garden, Ylmi set off southward, to seek out Thora.

But, instead of her friend, she found the largest man she had ever seen, following the trail of a small herd of deer. He greeted her courteously enough, and introduced himself as Revik, one of the exiles who had recently come to their settlement. At his invitation, she joined him on his hunt, as was customary.

But the trail ran out, and for all their searching they could not recover it. They were both more than a little frustrated at this.

As they headed back, Revik asked if she knew where he might find Karik. "There is a matter I would like to discuss with him," he said, "and he seems ever to be where I am not."

"My house is nearby," Ylmi said, "and your friend Karik is there, if you wish to see him."

Revik thanked her and followed her back to the small house built into the mountainside, surrounded by a garden, where Bodvar herded his goats as best he could.

They ate together, and Ylmi noted that Revik seemed little interested in Bodvar's talk of goats or Siggi's garden, but glared often at Karik.

When they were done eating, Revik and Karik stepped outside to talk, and Siggi heaved a sigh of relief.

"I am not overly fond of that man," she said.

Bodvar shrugged. "He is as most of the exiles: dreaming of battle and glory, while the world around him starves."

Ylmi noted this was not the way Karik seemed to her, and she went outside. By the sheep pens, Revik was snapping at Karik, and though his voice did not carry over the sound of the sheep, Ylmi could see the anger in his movements. Yet Karik simply looked on, calmly.

After a few more minutes of talk, Revik turned and made his way back down the mountain. He seemed angrier than before, but she did not stop him. She went to Karik, who still stood among the sheep, arms folded over his chest as he stared into the trees, a frown on his face. He appeared deep in thought.

She startled him, and asked what made him so thoughtful. "Perhaps you should stand where there are less sheep," she recommended; "I find they do not help thoughts to find their way."

Karik said that some matters were best kept secret, and that he did not wish to offend Unhost.

Ylmi replied that Unhost was a man who should be offended, and often. "He has been less than kind to me and my family."

So, Karik pointed northwest, toward where the dragon's mountain lay in the midst of the fjord, dark in the moonlight.

Ylmi's breath caught in her throat, and a fire went pouring through her veins. She didn't know what she had expected: a bolt of lightning? A great trumpet? Not just a simple pointed finger to tell her that, at last, the time to take on the dragon was here. And, from this lean, wiry man, who was hardly more than a boy.

She looked at him again, his jaw working as he stared at her, his fingers returning unconsciously to the knife at his belt, his green eyes boring a hole in her head. Yes, he might be able to do it.

But, she controlled her eagerness and glanced back toward the mountain. "Such a thing would be a great deed, truly, if success was achieved. But, that is no easy thing."

"I know," Karik sighed. "Failure does not frighten Revik Baglirsson, but that is only because he does not think of what will come after."

Ylmi nodded and agreed this was the truth. "Do you have a plan?"

Karik shook his head and, stepping away from the sheep pens, looked northward, toward the Watching Stones. Ylmi saw in his eyes the same hunger that she had felt.

She was not sure if the Stones were useless. When she thought back on it, it was the climb that had taught her, had hardened her. After that climb, she had known that it was not her frailty that kept her from removing Unhost's head and setting it on a stake; it was that she knew what would follow. But now, if Karik would help with the dragon...

Her thoughts were interrupted, as Karik asked if the way to the Stones was known.

"Not by many," Ylmi answered; "most do not survive the climb."

"Most?" Karik asked.

"Die," Ylmi answered; "most die."

Karik replied that someone must have made it to the top, otherwise she would have said "none", rather than "most".

With a hidden smile, Ylmi replied that she was the only one who had made the climb.

Karik seemed surprised, but not overly so. He looked again toward the Stones and nodded to himself. "I will go to the mountain, if you will tell me the way."

At that, Ylmi laughed. Ulfr looked up from where she lay by the house, and stared at them. "Your bravery is not outpaced by your brains, oh Karik Haldsson," she said. "I could no more tell you my skill with a bow. I will show you the way."

He looked at her in surprise. "You would do that?"

She nodded her head; "It is time I went back."

Later that night, as Ulfr curled up next to her, Ylmi wondered what she expected to find atop the mountain. She could still hear the wind moaning over the rocks, the word "wait" hanging heavy upon them.

Had she imagined it? Would she hear the same thing as before?

Or, did the gods still walk among the Stones that Vranr had built, so long ago?

The Dragon

The next morning they rose early, and Ylmi led the way toward the mountain, with Ulfr padding along the trail ahead of her. There was a pit in her stomach as she walked – a burning, blazing pit, which welcomed the coming climb as much as it dreaded it.

"Is it true," Karik asked as they climbed, "what they say of the Stones?"

"You will see soon enough for yourself," Ylmi replied without slowing.

She smiled to herself as the first cliff came into view, and a cold wind blew down from the north.

She bade Ulfr wait and, with a nod to Karik, she began to climb. The first cliff was easier than she remembered, but when she reached the top, Karik still struggled behind her, just barely halfway up. She waited for him, and gave him a hand up when he was close.

"That is not a small cliff," Karik said, glancing back down it.

Ylmi laughed. "We have only just begun," she smiled, "so do not count it too much."

It had not yet begun to rain, but the wind was blowing out of the north, howling over the heights like a pack of snow wolves. She and Karik could barely hear each other, and the cold began to numb her fingers and her face.

With a sinking feeling, she realized that the coming rain would only make the cold worse. Far, far worse. It had been the spring when last she climbed, or so she remembered. Karik, for all his strength, was not so great a climber as she, so more than once she stopped to wait for him, and to allow him to regain his breath.

As they climbed higher, the wind turned into a storm, with thunder and lightning hammering away within the clouds. Higher still they climbed, past the last twisted trees, into the dark clouds which whirled thick and heavy about the mountain.

Then came the rain. It was cold and bitter, edged with ice and hail, so they walked bent almost double to withstand it. Ylmi wondered if Karik would be angry that she brought him through this all, only to find silent stones and an empty chair.

But, it was not empty stones that they found, and Ylmi stared in astonishment and fury. For, flying as though the wind did not touch it was a great black raven, fluttering down to perch upon the high throne, gleaming black in the dim light. A fear seized her, its cold fingers gripping her heart, as the thunder blasted through the sky above them.

"It has been many years," a harsh voice said between thunderclaps, "since a son of Vranr visited this place."

She turned to see a bent figure, leaning as if in weariness against the southern stone, and the fear suddenly evaporated, burnt away by a rage which erupted at the sight. She had climbed these stones before, covered in her own blood from head to toe, and received no answer.

The figure looked to Ylmi, the glint of eyes beneath his hood meeting her wrathful stare. "Even longer," he said, "since any came a second time."

There was so much, so many things – an avalanche of accusations – that she wanted to say, she nearly choked. She took in a deep breath.

Then she heard what seemed to be her mother's voice, as if beside her ear, saying: "It is an ill thing to demand an answer from the gods."

"Who are you," Karik asked the figure, "and how do you know our names?"

"You may call me Dvengrhal," the figure groaned. "The gods have seen fit to make me their messenger to you."

Karik sank to one knee, even as Dvengrhal protested, but Ylmi only glared at him. The name Dvengrhal stuck in her mind, but she could not place where she had heard it.

"Will you stand there, the both of you," Dvengrhal asked, "until you freeze and I pass into the wind? Or, do you have questions you would ask?"

So, Karik told him of the dragon, and his fears to kill it, and the old one challenged him to make his decision.

But Ylmi did not listen. The blood was pounding in her ears as she looked around the Stones. It seemed to her now that there were faces carved in the top portion of the Stones, all looking inward. Their eyes seemed to find her, to grin at her, to laugh at her.

Beyond the Stones, beyond the ring they guarded, the clouds pressed close – a tumbling, whirling mass of mist and gloom. There were voices, too, close but far away. She tried to hear them but they slipped away, caught up by the wind that continued to blow.

What was this place? When last she had come it had seemed simpler, though she had imagined voices coming from the Stones. Or, had they been real? Was this place nothing more than one of Vranr's tricks? Something which had answers, but held them just out of reach? Who was Dvengrhal? Was he truly a messenger or a trickster? The voices grew stronger, then fell away again, and she looked up at the leering faces. The burning rage welled up within her, and she turned to the seer.

"You have answered Karik's questions," she said, "but I too have questions, which I have twice borne up the height of this mountain."

"I know your questions," the old one turned his eyes on her, "and I give you your answer: go! Take!"

Ylmi stared at him. That was it? "This is all you have for me? For the first to ascend to Vranr's Watching Stones in a hundred years? Where were you when I first scaled the black cliffs of this mountain? When I pulled myself up the mountainside, through all the fury of a northern storm, wearing a cloak of my own blood to find this place?"

The old one only shrugged. "You did receive an answer then. It is not the fault of the gods or of Vranr that you did not listen, or did not like it." He pulled himself to his feet. "Tell me, daughter of Siggi, is it day or night?"

"Day," Ylmi spat back.

"But, if I ask you the same question when the moon is high," the old one pressed, "will you not give me a different answer?"

Ylmi stared at him, enraged.

"The world is changing, and the fate of Vranr's children will be shaped by fire and blood in the days to come. There is a terrible fate upon the both of you, and the pieces being now brought together will shape the lives and fates of many."

Ylmi's breathing came quick and hard, her chest on fire, as though she would tear the seer to pieces with her bare hands. "Two years. What of the lives and fates of the last two years?"

"The threads of the world move without regard to your desires." The old one's voice was suddenly heavy and tired. "The gods do not remove the doom of a man because he is evil, but the accounts will be settled, and all debts paid in the end."

He turned to go, but mid-stride he was seized by the mind of the Allfather, and he turned back to them, his eyes white, as he saw with the Allfather's sight.

"Whatever words you have said, oh Karik Haldsson, though you may sail to the ends of the Earth, or climb the highest mountain, still I tell you that your body will lie broken and lifeless on the rocky slopes of this land. As for you, Ylmi Bodvarsdottir, you will receive what you desire most. And, when it is taken away, you shall be given what you hope for."

A stray bit of cloud blew through the Stones, and when it had passed the old one was gone. Ylmi glared at the spot where he had stood.

"Once again, I risk death to climb to these Stones," she muttered, "and this time I am given nonsense in place of nothing. Truly, the gods hate me, and Vranr remains the most senseless of men."

⸻◇⸻

Ylmi did not tell her parents of their climb to the mountain, nor of Karik's desire to challenge the dragon. It was her burden to bear, she decided, and telling them would only take away from the limited time they had to prepare. Winter was close at hand, and on the chance that they failed, she did not wish her family to go hungry.

She hunted from first light 'til the moon vanished. Bodvar was surprised at the urgency she showed, but she told him that she was nervous, with winter so close and an extra mouth to feed. Bodvar agreed this made good sense, and said no more on the matter.

But, after only two days, a storm blew in. Heavy and dark, it was the herald of the winter storms to come, and it drove them inside with a fury of wind and sleet. While the rain fell, Ylmi stewed within their hut, thinking on the dragon and wondering what plan Karik might have.

For his part, Karik sat silent, at times without moving, just staring into the flames of their small fire. When Bodvar and Siggi were otherwise engaged, he told her of his four friends, the brothers Revik and Igil, as well as Wisic and Umir. He also said that Havar the boatbuilder had thrown in with them, as well. Ylmi said that she knew another in the village who would be useful and eager to hunt the dragon, and Karik agreed they would need all the help they could get.

The storm raged for days, but when it lifted Ylmi and Karik went down to the village, telling Siggi they would be gone for several days. Karik said that he had matters with his friends to deal with, and Ylmi said that she wished to get the supplies to make a new bow, over the winter.

In the village, Karik gathered his friends, and Ylmi went in search of Thora.

When Ylmi told her what they had planned, Thora said that it was high time such action was taken, whether they succeeded or not. "We are the children of Vranr," she said, "and it is not fitting that we live under a dragon."

But Havar was not pleased when the two of them arrived at his house, and he said that their company was growing too large. There was some discussion at this, for Revik said that he could see how too many people might cause confusion in a battle with the dragon.

Karik laughed at this, and said that confusion was their only hope. "If the dragon is able to turn to one of us, then we will all die. We must keep him turning, threatened in two directions at once, at all times."

They argued on the matter in the hollowed-out rock of Havar's home, until Wisic said that he himself was little better than a fool, but he failed to see how the secret to success against a dragon was to bring fewer people. Thora said this made sense to her, and they had better discuss more how they intended to kill the dragon, instead of bickering over their number.

Karik and Igil explained their plan. They were fashioning a large net of anything they could find: ropes, chains, logs – anything which they could use to restrain the beast.

"Above all else," Karik said, "he must not be allowed to fly. If he flies, then we all die and the village dies; he can drop out of the air and hunt us like an owl hunts rabbits."

"How long do you think you can restrain him in this net?" Thora asked. "It is mostly rope and he breathes fire."

"Not long," Igil replied, "but hopefully long enough to damage his wings. So, when the fight starts, forget about his neck, his maw or anything else; cut his wings."

"That will have the added advantage of bleeding him out," Karik replied. "I do not think this will be a quick fight. We must be like a wolfpack wearing down an elk: one blow at a time 'til he wearies." He looked to Revik; "There will be a time for a killing blow, but do not go hunting it in the beginning."

Revik nodded, his massive arms folded over his chest as he listened. Ylmi thought he seemed very different from the brash, frustrated man she had encountered in the woods before.

"There is one exception," Karik said, and looked to Ylmi: "take out his eyes – your arrows will do more damage there than to his wings."

"But, be ready to move," Igil put in; "I do not think he will enjoy that!"

"You'll get maybe four shots while he's in the net," Karik said, "and once he's out, my guess is that he'll come for you first." He looked around at the others, gathered about him. "That means we all have to be very, very annoying."

"Get the angry dragon's attention," Wisic nodded, gravely; "be more annoying than the person trying to shoot him in the eye. Yes, I am thrilled with this plan! Does anyone want to guess how many of us get killed in this?"

"Are you scared?" Ylmi asked him.

"Oh, no," Wisic grinned, "not at all. The way I see it, if I get burned alive, then I don't have to starve to death this winter." He spread his hands wide, with a smile; "Win-win."

———◇———

Ylmi almost did not notice the weight of the boat as they pushed off the shore, nor the icy water as they waded out. She wondered how far Lanvir had gotten that night, so long ago. It had been six years, and she wondered if he could see her now. He had not wanted to harm the dragon, nor to cause any trouble; he had only been curious, as young children often are. And he had died for it.

The water rippled gently as they rowed across it, the darkness hanging heavy over them, as the clouds covered the moon. She wondered what would happen if they failed. Would the dragon burn the village? Most of it was deep underground, so she wasn't sure how much damage it would do. Did the dragon know that her parents were up on the mountainside? She doubted it. If they failed, the dragon would burn much of the shoreline, her father would keep the rest of his goats, and they would make it through the winter.

She rolled her shoulders and gripped her bow tightly. She did not intend to fail. Even if it killed her, she would do her part in killing the dragon. Lanvir would be avenged, and Unhost would be revealed as the cowardly piece of dung that he was. If they, all less than twenty years of age, could bring down the dragon, then what did that say about Unhost, when he had claimed the task was too dangerous to be attempted?

They reached the mountain, and Ylmi looked upon it with a strange sense of foreboding. Every ripple, every footstep, sent chills through her spine, and she imagined more than once that a dark shape was crawling over the mountain-top and down toward them.

The net Havar and Igil had made was heavy and awkward to carry. They all helped to lift it from the boat as quietly as they could, and walked slowly up the mountain, searching for the entrance to the dragon's lair.

They soon realized they were on a path – an actual path, carved from the mountainside – and Ylmi's mind went to her mother's stories of Vranr, and the Watcher set to guard him. A very different chill went down her spine: a sudden fear that there might be more here than just a dragon. Had the dragon been sent to watch Vranr? That made no sense; what need did a dragon have of such a path? And, besides, the path was barely large enough for them to walk, much less a massive dragon.

It was Karik who found the entrance, and they stood there only a moment, while Havar and Igil decided how best to lay their trap. It was short work to lay the net over the entrance and, as soon as it was done, Karik, Havar and Revik slipped inside. The rest of them took up places around the entrance, ready for the dragon to break out. Ylmi and Thora climbed to the ridge which overlooked the entrance and made ready.

"Do you think it will work?" Thora asked, quietly.

Ylmi nodded. "We have numbers, and if Karik is like any of his friends, then we are in good company."

"You have fought with Karik before?" Thora asked, with a small smile.

"I have climbed to the Watching Stones with him," Ylmi replied. "It is not an easy climb, but he did well."

Thora looked at her with admiration. But Ylmi could not share a strange feeling from the back of her neck; it was as if she was being glared at, and she could almost feel the heat of anger and rage beating down on her. She turned and looked up.

Far above, beyond the mountain's peak, the moon had broken through the clouds, and now the moonlight fell in the distance, upon the Watching Stones of Vranr. In the pale light, the stones seemed to glow, though they stood small and distant. They gazed down on her, and she felt their malice in the dawn's early gloom. Whatever others might say, there was a power in those stones, and Ylmi wondered again at how they had come to be made.

They waited in the calm, as the current from the sea pushed into the fjord and lapped against the mountain. There was no sound from the cavern, and Ylmi wondered after a time if Karik and the others had gotten lost.

Then came a thunderous roar, echoing from the cavern's entrance. Ylmi fixed her grip on her bow, flexing her fingers. She drew her breaths slowly, willing herself to be calm. In and out, she told herself, in and out.

Then the mountain shook. With a roar, the dragon launched himself out of his den, crashing headlong into their net, and for a moment all they could see was a mass of writhing scales, twisting limbs, and dust being thrown up into the air.

Ylmi rose, her hand on the string, an arrow tight.

When the dragon turned to them, she drew and let loose in one motion. His eye was the size of her hand, red and gleaming, with an iris like a black diamond. The arrow sank home with a wet, snicking sound, and the dragon screamed with pain, writhing like a man on fire, as gouts of flame blasted from his mouth.

Thora jumped down, her spear held ready, as Karik and the others burst from the cave mouth. For an instant, they hesitated, trying to decide how to get close to the writhing dragon.

But, with a terrible suddenness, the dragon stopped, his head bent down, even as Ylmi searched for a shot at his other eye. "I will burn every last one of you!" His snarl was slow and deliberate, and as the last growl passed his forked tongue, he uncoiled. He struck the rocks above the cave entrance, narrowly missing Ylmi and shattering the shelf of rock she stood on. Only by leaping aside did she survive, and she scrambled higher on the mountain.

But the dragon was focused on her, and it was after her that he came. Violently, he tore up the mountain after her, and Ylmi realized suddenly that she was running away from Karik and the others. She doubled back, looping around a boulder, and diving through the storm of fire which suddenly appeared before her. Ylmi screamed as she passed through the flames and crashed down the mountainside, tumbling over the rocks and dirt. The heat of the flames was beyond anything she had ever felt; they seemed not to just burn her skin, but to reach down inside her body, stabbing at every bone and muscle. She rolled to a stop not far from the cavern entrance, her whole left side arcing with pain. Flames licked at the sleeve of her shirt, ignoring her frantic efforts to put it out. In desperation, she drew her knife and cut off her whole sleeve.

Karik and the others were swarming the dragon, who was now turning back and forth, to find who was the biggest threat.

Ylmi took a deep breath. Her throat was sore from her scream, and the whole left side of her face burned, as though the fire still licked at her face; it was red and puffy, but no flames still gnawed at her skin. Worst of all, her left eye was quickly swelling shut. She blinked several times, trying to push it back, but the pain remained and, if anything, her vision grew worse.

Above her on the mountainside, the dragon was raging, but Ylmi saw blood dripping from him in a dozen places, and his wings hung in bloody rags, useless at his sides. She struggled to her feet, checking her bow quickly, and nocking another arrow.

The dragon snarled, roaring his wrath at his attackers, and Ylmi saw someone go tumbling down the mountainside, as if struck by a thunderbolt. Ylmi spat the blood out of her mouth and began climbing toward the dragon. She heard Karik and Igil shouting, and Revik howling like a madman.

There was a scream, and suddenly the dragon was holding someone in its giant maw, fangs crushing bones and ripping flesh; Ylmi froze in horror. With a savage snarl, the dragon whipped his head and hurled the body off the mountain, sending it falling into the cold waters, far below. Then, he turned back and snarled at his attackers.

Ylmi loosened her arrow. With one eye swollen shut, it was not as accurate as it might have been, and it careened off the dragon's forehead. He roared in fury and charged her. She leapt over the stones on the mountain, dodging his snapping fangs and the thunderous blows of his tail.

Suddenly, the dragon roared in pain. Ylmi turned to see Revik pulling his ax from the dragon's tail, before the beast swung a bloody wing in a giant arc, and sent Revik tumbling down a slope.

The dragon turned to find her again, and Ylmi let loose again. She was close this time – far closer than she had been on the other shots, and the arrow flew straight and true. It sank deep into the dragon's eye, and the beast staggered back.

But, only for a moment. In the next instant, Ylmi was hurtling through the air, struck full in the chest by the dragon's sweeping tail. She struck a rock and continued falling, tumbling down the slope and slamming into one stone after another, as she desperately gasped for breath. When she came to rest, her lungs screamed for air. As she gasped for breath, she realized she could not see. Panic set in, and for a moment she knew she would die.

But then air entered her lungs; her chest rose as the cool, early-morning air filled her. She spat out a glob of blood. Her face was covered in blood and dirt, and when she wiped it away, she could see out of her right eye again.

Breathing slowly, she looked upward. Hidden from her by a ridge, the dragon still fought on, but she could feel the mountain shaking beneath her, and a plume of smoke and dust rose high in the sky.

Most of her arrows were broken, snapped into pieces when she'd tumbled down the mountain. But her bow was whole, lying in the rocks a short distance away. She crawled to it, and stood slowly on shaking legs.

Slowly she climbed, hearing the battle above her rage on. Twice the mountain shook, and she had to duck her head as rocks slid down from the heights, bringing with them little avalanches and rockslides.

When she crested the ridge, the dragon was snarling at Karik, blood pouring from him in a dozen places. Igil and Wisic lay sprawled on the mountainside, covered in blood, and a short distance away Thora was reaching for a broken spear, with her left arm.

Then she saw Revik, rising behind the dragon with his ax. The dragon was weary, all its focus on Karik, who stood before it with a strange sword. Revik raised his ax and brought it down into the dragon's neck. The dragon roared.

Ylmi's bow twanged. An arrow disappeared down the dragon's maw, and Karik drove his sword up through the back of the dragon's mouth. The beast twitched for a moment, then collapsed.

The air was silent, all of them gasping for breath. Wisic pushed a rock off his chest and coughed, spitting blood.

"It's over?" Thora asked. "We did it?"

"We did it." Karik nodded, trying to catch his own breath. "We are the dragonslayers."

He looked swiftly over the mountainside. "Who is still with us?"

One by one they spoke up, and Ylmi was glad to see Thora still standing, though she too wore the marks of dragon-fire on her face and arm. Ylmi could feel her skin blistering as she tried to stand, and she watched as Karik took count of everyone's injuries. All had been marked by the dragon-fire, and forever after they would count themselves closer than siblings because of it.

WINTER

As they made the short journey by boat back to shore, to Ylmi it seemed that her wounds grew more painful, not less. The boat was silent as they let the wind blow them back to shore. Umir now rested at the bottom of the fjord, and there was not one of them who did not feel most painfully the wounds of the dragon.

The shoreline was covered with onlookers when they returned and, to Ylmi's surprise, Unhost welcomed them with open arms.

"You have delivered us from a great evil," he said, and blessed them all.

But, Wisic had begun retching every few minutes, and the rest of them were little better themselves. So, Unhost said it was best that they all return to their homes and receive the care they needed. Ethna and Ymr offered to take Ylmi and Karik back up the mountain, and they accepted gratefully, for they were both deep in weariness and pain.

They walked in silence up the path, each small knoll feeling like a mountain unto itself, and Ylmi felt the pain growing on her with every step. Her world shrunk to her, to the next step she must take and the burning pain on her left side.

Suddenly, she looked up to find her father staring into her face, his eyes filled with shock and fear.

Ylmi forced a painful smile over her cracked lips, and peered at him with her one good eye. "The dragon..." she said, slowly, "...is dead."

Then the darkness took her.

━━◈━━

There was a fog of fever, hunger, thirst and pain. Ylmi did not know how time passed, only that she heard Karik muttering in her dreams, and from time to time the face of her father or mother would appear out of the murk in front of her.

She dreamed of the dragon-fire – dreams as real as life itself; ten times, twenty, a hundred... she passed through the fire, again and again. She drank, she froze, she slept, she burned...

When at last she woke, she could hear the wind moaning outside, and the gentle cracking of a small fire, settling through the night. Slowly, she pushed herself into a sitting position and felt a small smile on her face, as Ulfr rose from the shadows beside her, to sniff at her face.

"Easy," Ylmi shushed her, but the words felt rough and painful in her mouth.

Siggi sat by the fire, and she looked up at Ylmi when she heard the noise. A look of relief passed over her face, and she smiled at her daughter. "I did not know," she whispered, as she came to Ylmi's side, "that I had given birth to the war goddess. Are you hungry?"

Ylmi nodded, her jaw and tongue too stiff to move. She blinked again at the gloom, something feeling off, but she was unable to find it. Siggi handed her a bowl, warm from the fire. But, when Ylmi's fingers touched it, she jerked them away, as if she had been burned.

"Too hot," she managed to say, and Siggi nodded and rose. A moment later she returned, a handful of snow slowly melting in the warm soup. Siggi set the bowl beside her, and Ylmi used her right hand to slowly raise a spoonful to her mouth. The effort left her almost too weary to chew and swallow but, when it was done, she felt a welcome strength beginning to return to her.

"How long?" She glanced about the room, the hides of her many kills hanging from the ceiling, to give some measure of privacy in the small home.

Siggi smiled at her. "Almost three weeks. The snows have come."

"I should hunt tomorrow." Ylmi bent to take another bite.

"You most certainly will not," Siggi smiled, but there was iron in her voice which Ylmi knew better than to argue with.

Ylmi took another spoonful and looked around again, 'til her eyes lit on Karik. He lay closer to the fire, a deerskin blanket pulled up under his bare shoulders. His arms lay atop it, and almost the whole of his right arm was an angry, molten red. Ylmi's eyes widened, and her fingers went suddenly to her own face.

"Stop." Siggi caught her hand. "You should not touch it yet; it is still healing... we think. Dragon-fire is a foul and deadly thing, and all of you, it seems, were determined to bathe in it."

Ylmi jerked her hand away, but the effort left her suddenly exhausted and weary. The stew in the bowl looked horribly far away, and Ylmi eased herself back down to the furs, and fell asleep.

When she woke again, the air was bitterly cold. The fire had burned low, the coal glowing several feet away from her.

But, as she looked at them, something seemed strange. The ache in her eye was lessened, but not gone. Slowly, she closed her right eye: the coals were almost invisible. Her right eye snapped open. For a moment, she could only breathe. If she could not see, could she still hunt? Could she still shoot? If she could not hunt... would her family be able to support itself? Or, would she be only a burden, like an ancient grandparent rotting by the fire. There was one way to find out.

She covered her right eye again, with the same results, and her hand dropped back down. Ulfr's head rose from by her feet, the wolf's eyes glowing in the faint light of the coals.

She glanced around the room, to see who else was awake. By the moan of the winds, and the way the fire had burned down, she guessed it was late at night. In the gloom, she could see the red light of the fire reflected off of Karik's burnt shoulder. On the opposite side of the room, the deerskin curtains had been pulled to hide her parents' bed, and Ylmi guessed them to still be asleep.

Quietly, she crept toward the door. The room seemed strange and unfamiliar as she picked her way through it, and there was a dryness in her mouth which she couldn't seem to swallow away. Her bow was by the door, where she always kept it, but only two arrows were in her quiver, and she guessed it was a miracle that there were any at all. She took them up and stepped outside.

The cold pierced her like a spear, and she gasped as the wind struck her. The snow was knee-high, and before she could take more than a few steps, her feet were numb. The moon was behind clouds, but they were thin, and the result was a soft, dim light which cast black shadows across the clearing. Glancing around for a target, her eye found a stump, its broken crown protruding from the snow.

Carefully, she nocked an arrow, with fingers growing numb from the cold. The wind was blowing steadily – no gusts or swirls, just a steady current of cold. She shivered, feeling as if an icy hand had grabbed each shoulder and shook her. Her arm burned as she drew, and her right hand would not stop trembling. Her fingers brushed her cheek and the arrow loosened.

The string hummed, striking her forearm like a red-hot brand. She dropped the bow and fell to her knees with a choking cry. The skin on her arm was cracked, and a bloody pus was oozing from where the string had struck her. Her whole arm was rough to the touch, like a hard scab. In the darkness she had not noticed it, but now it was all she could see or feel. She was deep in the snow now, all thought of the arrow gone from her mind, the cold and wet numbing her legs and arms, as the wind blew her hair over her face.

Tears dripped from her eyes, and froze on her cheeks as she sobbed. She had lost the use of her eye, and perhaps her arm as well. And yet, things were no better than they had been before. Unhost had cheered from the shore as if they had done him a favour, and now her family would starve, because she had slept through the first few weeks of winter.

A sudden warmth on her shoulder made her look up, and to her surprise she saw Karik bending over her.

"It is too cold for us to be out," he said, quietly. Then, his eyes went to the bow, and the arrow that had fallen nearby. "Come." His voice was gentle, and Ylmi hid her face, ashamed and angry at all that had happened.

"What is the point?" she asked. "I have lost an eye, we will not survive the winter, and Unhost sits still in his warm hall, counting his gold."

"We will not starve," Karik responded. "And, after the winter, many things will change. We are the dragonslayers, and much will happen that was previously unthinkable."

She leant on him as she struggled to her feet, a task made more difficult since she could feel little below her knees. She bent to catch up her bow, and looked for the arrow she had shot.

"I don't know if I can hunt." She forced the words through her teeth, looking in vain for the dark fletching, by the stump or in the snow. "My eye... If I can't shoot straight..."

Karik followed her gaze, then wrapped an arm around her, to guide her back to the house. "Ylmi, it is freezing, with a strong wind, and you still have dragon venom running in your veins. When we are healed, then it will be time to test ourselves again."

She looked once more after the arrow. Then, with sagging shoulders, she let Karik guide her back inside, where she collapsed into her bed. Slowly, the feeling worked its way back into her legs, and her fingers tingled as the blood returned. Karik laid several sticks onto the fire, rebuilding it to provide a bit more heat. As the warmth came over her, so did sleep, and her eyelids fell lower and lower.

But, her last view was of Karik, sitting with a deerskin wrapped around him, as he stared into the fire.

As the days passed, their strength returned. Winter was in full swing, the cold and snow burying them inside their home, but this time they did not tell stories.

They heard from Bodvar how Unhost had taken several boats and gathered the gold from the dragon's lair, to take it as his own. Karik was greatly displeased at this, but the others said it was what should be expected from Unhost and there was little they could do about it. Ylmi, however, was just as displeased as Karik, when Siggi told them there had been no reward given to any of the dragonslayers or their families.

"Unhost claims that since he never asked for the deed to be done, then there is no reason anyone should be rewarded for having done it," Siggi explained. She also said that the others who had been burnt by the dragon-fire had suffered the same sickness as Karik and Ylmi. "We have heard nothing since the snow came. But, as you two were the ones who were burned the worst, and have recovered as well as you have, I see no reason to fear for the others."

"Do the people of this settlement just allow Unhost to do whatever he wants?" Karik asked. "He did nothing with the dragon, yet gains all its riches for himself!"

"There are some in the village he is very good to," Bodvar responded, heavily, "and with their support, there is little he is not allowed to do. Or else you'll end up thrown out."

Then, it was time for Ylmi to tell her story. She told her parents how they had planned the dragon's killing, and the way they had gone about it. Karik was silent as she talked, and she wondered if he brooded that others received the credit.

But, after she had told the tale of the dragon's killing, and answered her parents' questions several times over, they at last turned to Karik, to see if there was anything he would add.

"Unhost may have the gold," he said, quietly, "but I have the greatest treasure yet found in that mountain." He drew out the long leather wrapping he had taken from the dragon's hoard. Within were wrapped charts, maps and calendars, all tools of navigation. They gazed at it curiously, unsure of what Karik found so enthralling.

"I have found a way through the Black Isles."

"You can read these?" Bodvar asked.

Karik shrugged. "Not the words, but I can tell a map when I see it. And I know how to tell where there are islands, and where there are not. These lines here, they must be currents; they bend around any land they meet. And here, where there are lines and arrows, they must mark a passage."

"You have indeed come upon a great treasure," Bodvar agreed, "but the sea is ever-changing, and paths that were once open may be closed after only a few years. These maps have lain unused for generations, and the seas may have shifted in that time."

They discussed this matter through the winter, while Ylmi and Karik regained much of their strength.

⋯⟡⋯

Ylmi's eye, however, though it ceased to pain her, did not regain its former sight, and this troubled her greatly. Even so, she fashioned a new bow, stronger still than the one she had used before. The tips were capped with deer horn, the handle was wrapped in deer leather, and wool from the goats was woven into the string, to quiet its twang. She also fashioned new arrows, some with bone tips, others with the few iron tips she still had.

One day, as the cold was beginning to lessen, Ylmi returned to cutting wood. Her muscles were stiff with disuse, and the dragon-sickness was slow to leave her body. But, as the ax swung, she began to feel some of her old strength returning. Her breath went up in great clouds as she worked, while Ulfr ran through the snow, happy to be out of the cramped hut.

Out of the corner of her eye she saw movement in the trees, and turned to see a large figure coming through the snow-heavy pines. For a moment, she thought a bear had woken early from its sleep.

But it was no bear – only Revik, wrapped in many furs against the cold.

"It is early and cold for you to have come so far," she said, when he had made himself known. "The paths are still very treacherous."

"I am hungry," he said, in his deep voice, "and besides, I am weary of huddling by a fire like a child." He nodded to Ulfr, who had run to stand by Ylmi, then looked her over critically. "It seems you have come out of the dragon-fire well enough."

"He wounded my eye," Ylmi answered. "But, seeing as I took both of his, I do not count it an evil trade."

Revik laughed at that, his whole body shaking as his laughter formed clouds in the cold. "Fair enough. I have come to speak with Karik, if he is still here."

"Is there somewhere else I should be?" Karik said, as he came out of one of the goat pens, where he had been checking on the young lambs. "You should not have made the trip."

Revik shrugged. "We have grown bored in the snow," he said, "and more than a few of us wondered if both of you had survived." His eyes went between them, lingering on their scars. "The dragon's fire marked you most of all."

"Well, as you can see," Ylmi replied, "we are alive."

"Even so..." Revik eyed her carefully, before turning to Karik. "It is in my mind that perhaps we should go to Jarhost's hall, when the spring clears the path to Bjarnmont. To me, it seems better to arrive in the spring, to put in a year of work, rather than in the winter with our hands held out."

Ylmi felt a flash of anger and her eyes narrowed. "As you arrived here? With your hands out?"

"We did our work as best we could," Revik answered her, "and if you have not noticed, there is a dead dragon which we had something to do with."

"The death of the dragon does little to fill our bellies," Ylmi retorted. "The dragon is but one danger among many."

"Enough!" Karik's voice was firm, as he looked Revik in the eye. "The fact that we slew a dragon has not put food in their stores, nor has it made the winter shorter." He looked between them. "But I have a plan which might."

Ylmi folded her arms as Revik shifted his cloak, careful to keep his eyes off of her. "What plan?"

"I have charts which will allow us to sail the Black Isles," Karik said, quickly. "They were in the dragon's hoard, in a chamber where they must have lain since the first exiles came here."

"You think they are reliable?" Revik asked, more than a little disbelief in his voice.

"I am sure of it," Karik replied. "Ask Igil and Havar to begin planning a boat which could make the passage. When I come in the summer, I will convince Unhost to give us enough gold for the building of it."

Revik thought for a moment, before saying: "I am inclined to listen to you, but we should all have a voice in this. All of us," he said, and nodded to Ylmi, "should talk on the matter. If you can convince us that it is a good plan, and my brother Igil thinks that it is possible, then I will wait to go to Jarhost's hall, and throw my lot in with you."

Then, promising to speak with Igil and Havar about the matter, he bade them goodbye, and soon disappeared into the snow-covered trees.

"If you can convince Unhost to give up a handful of that gold," Ylmi said, as she picked up the ax to continue chopping wood, "then you have a gilt tongue to rival Vranr, if even the most fanciful stories are true."

Karik laughed at that. "We would need more than a handful, but not more than a quarter of what was in the dragon's hoard."

"Unhost has doubtless added it to his hoard, and glories in being the richest jarl on the coast," Ylmi grumbled. She checked the edge of the ax, before she spoke again: "After the death of the dragon, I do not doubt that he is trying to determine how to turn all this to his own advantage. And, if he can injure me or my family in the doing, he will not hesitate."

"Once we have a boat," Karik assured her, "there will be little he can do to harm us. We are the dragonslayers, after all, and I do not think that counts for nothing.

Ylmi only grunted, swinging the ax to snap a branch in half. Revik had brought back her foul humour, though, as she reflected, it was the word of Unhost that had been more galling to her than anything Revik had said.

It also came to her mind that, with the dragon dead, it was Unhost who now bore the remaining blame for Lanvir's death and her family's suffering. Yet, with the dragon dead, Unhost had simply taken his precious gold, and was not more satisfied and powerful than before.

She swung the ax savagely, and imagined that the branch was their faithless jarl.

Dragon's Hoard

It was another week before they deemed it safe and necessary to make a trip to the village. Ylmi had more than a few furs, which she would trade with the villagers, and Karik had several of his own, which he intended to trade for an ax from the blacksmith. Ulfr padded quietly along with them, sniffing along the trail as they went.

When they reached the low ridge which looked out over the village, Karik remarked that it was livelier than he had ever seen it. "Perhaps the slaying of the dragon has made it easier for everyone to do their work above ground."

But Ylmi's eyes narrowed, for she saw many men she was not familiar with, and they all were armed so that the village seemed to bristle with spears.

"Many of them are not from here," she said. "As they are armed, and yet the village does not appear to be under attack, I would guess that Jarhost has come sooner than we expected him to."

Karik's face went still and she saw his jaw tighten. "We should find Igil and Havar."

Igil and Havar were together on the shore, scouring the underside of a fishing boat, and they looked up quickly when they heard Karik and Ylmi's feet on the sand. It was a joyful meeting, as they embraced and greeted each other after the long winter.

But Ylmi cut their greetings short: "What is the meaning of all these men?"

"The king is here," Havar said, his voice suddenly dark. "He is taking the gold that was found within the dragon's den. He claims it is rightfully his."

Karik shook his head. "We guessed he would do something along these lines. Has he given any of you a hunter's portion?"

Igil leaned on the boat and spat into the sand. "He is taking all of it. He claims that he should have been told when it was first found, and that Unhost has cheated him of taxes for a long time."

Ylmi and Karik stared at him. "All?"

Igil nodded and Karik glanced skyward, thinking.

"Karik, we can't build a boat to attempt the crossing without the gold." Igil kept his voice low, but Ylmi heard the frustration in it.

Karik winced. "Not even a small one?"

"Without any gold to buy settings, rope or wool?" Igil thought for a moment, then shook his head. "The biggest we could build would be fair enough for coastal sailing, but it would be dangerous to try to cross the sea in it."

If they were truly to try to cross the Black Isles, Ylmi did not want to do it in a boat that was dangerous enough even without treacherous currents and howling winds.

Karik scratched the side of his head. "I'll see what I can do."

Igil nodded and Havar went back to scraping the bottom of the boat. They stood there for a moment, the bustling of the village behind them fading into the sound of the waves gently falling on the beach. At last, Karik said this did not seem right, seeing as they had killed a dragon and were now receiving nothing for their troubles.

But, before he could say more, a group of men carrying spears and axes approached them from the village, and said the king wished to speak with the dragonslayers.

<hr>

And so they all were gathered before Unhost's hut, before which sat a large man, tall and broad, with a gold-hilted sword hanging from his hip. His black beard was woven into a braid, clasped with a ring of gold at the end, and a black-iron crown rested on his head. His eyes took them in, as the dragonslayers were brought before him, his gaze lingering on Revik, before passing quickly over Thora and Ylmi, then lingering again on Havar. Though she had never seen him before, Ylmi knew him to be Jarhost, the king of Bjarnmont and ruler of the western portion of the isle.

"How is it that you bear no scars?" he asked, in a deep voice. "Did you go into battle with the others, or hold the boat for their return?"

"I bear scars," Havar replied, "though I was swift enough to avoid dragon-fire. The beast fought with more than flames."

The king shrugged. "It is dead now, and I am thankful to you all for your work in keeping the coastlands safe. As a reward," he waved forward one of his men, who stood behind him, "I give you these rings. Though they are of copper, they mark you as those who are always welcome in my hall."

The man who held the rings was thin, with a scar over his right eye, but his left seemed to bore into each, as he handed them a twisted ring of copper which barely fitted over their wrists. Ylmi turned it over in her fingers, frowning as she did so. It was a small thing to earn for the slaying of a dragon.

"Moreover," the king continued, as they eyed their small rewards, "I will offer to any of you the right of service in my household guard."

"For that we thank you, Lord," Karik said, quickly, "but the deprivations of the dragon were heavy, and we must rebuild." He stepped forward. "Lord, if we could have but a little gold with which to build, this settlement would quickly become a prosperous outpost of your lands."

"The gold is not mine to give away," Jarhost sighed; "I have jarls and warriors who guard your coastland from eastern raiders. Your jarl—" he pointed at Unhost, who stood with his arms folded sullenly over his chest, some way away, "—has kept from me what is my due, and stolen my protection without payment. But, if you come to my hall, there will be cattle raids in the summer months, and you will earn all the wealth and glory you could wish."

Ylmi followed Karik's eyes as he looked over Jarhost's followers, and saw that though they wore fine clothes, they wore few arm rings, and most of those were of copper. Ylmi suppressed a heavy sigh as the realization hit her: the king wished to hoard the gold for himself, even as Unhost had. She wasn't sure what else she had expected, but perhaps a little of her had hoped that Unhost had lied about the king as well. She felt the corner of her mouth turn up slightly, twisting the burnt skin in a bitter smile. Of course, the one area where Unhost could be trusted was in the greed of others.

For a moment, Karik seemed deep in thought, then bowed low before the king.

"I thank you for your gracious offer," he said, tightly, "but I have made this land my home, and there is much work for me to do here."

As he stepped back, Ylmi stepped forward. "My father and mother have great need of me, so I must decline your kind offer." With great effort, she bit back the torrent of words and accusations which boiled up in her throat, and stepped back. One after another, each of the dragonslayers stepped forward and declined service with the king.

Jarhost's face grew dark and he glared at Karik, as Revik went last, rejecting the king's offer and declaring his intent to stay in the settlement.

"As you wish," Jarhost's voice was grim, "but if your stomachs grow empty and the work of these fishermen grows tiresome, come swiftly to Bjarnmont, or you may find the doors closed against you when the cold comes."

Ylmi glanced at the copper ring around her wrist, and wondered if the king's earlier words had been meaningless.

With that, the king signalled to his men and began the long march back to Bjarnmont. As she watched them go, Ylmi took some small joy in the fact that the march up the mountains would not go easy, with the weight of gold in their packs.

The village seemed to hold still as the king's company slowly walked away, and Ylmi felt the ocean breeze blowing gently out of the west. Somewhere, a gull screamed.

Ylmi turned to see Unhost glaring at Karik.

"Are you happy now, you ungrateful swine?" his voice bit out, harsh and savage. "You had to go hunting a name for yourself, and now the king has marked us as thieves and skinflints."

"That he marked you as one I do not doubt," Karik said, simply. "Whether he thought the rest of us such, I do not know."

"If that is what you think," Unhost said, his voice rising, "then perhaps this settlement is not the best place for you."

Ylmi stepped forward. "Is that how matters are to be handled, Unhost? You will simply exile anyone who points out your greed?"

Unhost turned on her like a serpent turns on a mouse, but Fornik Lievsson stepped forward quickly and raised his hands. "I am sure that my friend Jarl Unhost does not mean to exile the slayers of the dragon." He looked meaningfully at Unhost. "But this is a heated matter, and we must all agree that it is as our jarl said in the beginning: once the king pays attention to our village, we suffer."

"We suffered under the dragon, as well," Ylmi said, turning a bitter glare on Fornik.

Havar pushed past Igil and pointed at Unhost. "Unhost took more than his share before the king ever lifted a hand to us," he said, looking around at the villagers gathering around them. "Why should we then be surprised that the king in turn took more than his share from him?"

Unhost spat into one of the unmelted snow drifts, which clung to a spot shaded by his hall. "You are as ungrateful as you are ugly." He turned and pointed at Ylmi; "When your brother disturbed the dragon's rest, and broke the careful peace I had built, I saw to it that he did not burn half the village in retribution. And, you!" he said, pointing a shaking finger at Havar. "You who do little but fiddle with boats, from dawn to dusk, what claim do you have to the gold that I found, that was dug from my land? It was mine! And now it is stolen, because none of you would do as you were told!"

There was a murmur from the crowd, and Ylmi knew that unless she spoke Unhost would spend the coming days and weeks ensuring that everyone here knew it was the fault of Karik Haldsson and Ylmi Bodvarsdottir, that the king had come and robbed them blind.

"And yet the dragon is dead." Her voice was louder than she had meant, but the heads of everyone there turned to her. "The dragon is dead and we are safe. Our herds and harvests will not be halved by a dragon's tax each year. We need not fear that the darkness will bear a hungry beast upon its wings. Things are not as they could be, but they might be a deal worse." She paused for a moment and looked around at the small crowd. "I for one will take comfort in that."

She did not wait to see what else they had to say, but turned quickly and made for the blacksmith's hut.

There was no one there when she reached it, but Ethna was close behind her and took the furs she had brought. "Arrowheads?"

Ylmi nodded, anger and fury coursing through her, as she attempted to still her legs. She longed to turn and drive an arrow through Unhost, and watch him bleed into the sand.

"You speak well," Ethna said, as she gathered a handful of arrowheads and laid them on the little counter for Ylmi to examine, "and the people listen to a dragonslayer."

Ylmi shrugged. "For now. Unhost and Fornik will have them calling for our heads soon enough."

"People like what is safe – what is comfortable," Ethna said. "When Unhost was the one who dealt with the dragon and kept it from burning the village, there were more than a few who were willing to put up with him. Now that it is not the case..." she looked Ylmi in the eye, "...it may be time for a new leader."

Karik stepped up behind her and raised his bundle of furs, for Ethna to see. "Do you have an ax?"

Ethna stepped back and lifted a thick ax head from a box. "It won't do much for fighting, but you can clear trees with it well enough."

"All I need it for," Karik said.

Ylmi watched him hand over the furs, then turned back to Ethna. "I need a new spearhead."

Ethna nodded. "Boar spear?"

"Longspear," Ylmi answered, and both Karik and Ethna glanced up at her, for a longspear had little use in hunting. Without the crosspiece below the head, a longspear would allow a boar or bear to charge right up the shaft and reach the user. But, in battle, the longspear could slide around a shield, or slip through a small hole in an enemy's guard.

Ethna stood and laid out a leather-wrapped spearhead for her. When Ylmi undid it, she smiled. The whole piece was as long as her forearm, with a lengthy socket, which would seat well on whatever wooden shaft Ylmi could cut. She glanced from the spear and arrowheads to the bundle of furs on the counter. "Is it enough?"

Ethna only smiled at her. "For a dragonslayer, perhaps; for an old friend, more than enough. Now, be gone with you; it is a long trail back to your house, and I would not have you making the climb in the darkness."

As they made their way out of the village and up the mountainside, Ylmi thought on Unhost, and what Ethna had said. There were the words of the seer to consider as well.

When they reached the ridge that overlooked the village, Karik stopped and looked back. His hands worried at the ax head he carried, and his jaw worked as he looked down.

"That gold would have done much good for all of us," Karik said. Ylmi's eyes went to his hands, working over the iron ax head, as he stared down into the village. "Now it will rot in Jarhost's hall, and we will be left to fend for ourselves once again."

"So it ever goes with these men," Ylmi said. She tightened her fingers around the spearhead and thought of where she would find a sapling to use for the haft. "They are comfortable, so little will change as long as they decide how matters will be settled."

"And scores more will starve in other villages." Karik spat into the snow.

Here on the mountainside the wind was colder, and there was more shade from the trees, so the sun had melted far less here than it had in the village. "If we are to change this, if we are to prosper, we must find a way off this isle," he said, as his voice slowly rose, "and we cannot do it without gold!" He finished in a shout, and with one more glare back at the village, he turned and continued back up the mountain.

Ylmi looked down at the village, the small scattering of just over a dozen buildings, and wondered what they all thought of Unhost. What would they do if she walked down there, right now, and gutted him in the doorway of his own home? Thora would approve, of that she was sure. Havar and Igil would not have a problem with it, and Revik would likely help her, if she asked. But Ethna would disapprove of the murder, and there were many in the village who were friendly with Unhost...

And Unhost was not the end. Even if all her dreams were to come true, and the village was freed of his greed and laziness, there would still be King Jarhost, coming down to take what he did not earn.

Ylmi gripped the spearhead again and glanced back up the mountain toward Karik. Her time for Unhost was not yet ripe, and even with the death of the dragon she could not challenge him.

If they could cross the Isles, she could take her family away from Vrania. That might be the answer – if she could find a place safe from the cold of winter and the greed of Vrania's kings and jarls.

But, all that depended on passing the Isles, and for that they needed gold. Gold which Unhost had confiscated for himself, and in turn had been confiscated by King Jarhost. They had faced dragon-fire, she had lost her eye, and yet they could simply decide that it was theirs. If this was all that it led to, then what had been the point?

She glanced down at the spearhead in her hand, and resisted the urge to hurl it down the mountainside. Unhost was doubtless whispering about the reckless dragonslayers, telling anyone who would listen that, if only the king hadn't been drawn to their village, things would be better.

Perhaps he was right. Perhaps Jarhost was as bad or even worse than Unhost.

She spat toward the village and continued her climb. Their situation was hopeless, and nothing they did made any difference.

PART II: THE UNDER SEA

SKATHI

She slept little that night, rage and anger turning within her, so that she often found herself staring up at the rock of the cave where they had built their home.

At last, when morning was drawing near, Ylmi rose and, taking her bow, set off with U

lfr at her side. The wind was out of the northeast, and Ylmi took a path which led her in that direction, that the wind would carry her scent away from her prey.

They loped along together, pushing away from the village, skirting the edge of the ridges which Oscar Kolsson hunted, and farther toward the spine of the mountains which ran toward the sea. Ylmi saw little but sparrows as she went, the snow unmarked by anything but bird feet.

The mountains were crisscrossed with little paths and passes, and Ylmi found herself in one of these, still with no sign of anything worth hunting. Behind her, the forest stretched back, rolling and rising over the foothills. Before her, the land sloped away, the trees growing fewer and fewer as the land flattened, giving way to the great ice marsh.

She stopped there to rest and to think, as the wind moaned out of the north.

Unhost had confiscated their gold, then had it confiscated in turn by Jarhost – there was always a bigger fish, it seemed. She chuckled at that, but her mind turned to how matters now lay.

The dragon was gone, and that was not an ill thing. But if Karik was right, it was only a matter of time until the village grew too large and hunger came clawing back. In a few winters, they would be starving as surely as every other village on the coast.

Her eyes ran over the ice marsh before her, the small, twisted trees bending in the wind, little black shapes against the white snow.

There were few places left to go in Vrania. The hunting was already growing thin, and if hunters from Girhom were already coming this far west, it was a bad sign indeed.

So, what then to do?

They needed to get off the isle. That, or kill enough people like Unhost and Jarhost to see that there was enough food for another generation. But, even that pushed matters back only for a time. They needed to find a way across the Isles, and soon, or she would watch her parents starve.

They had barely survived the winter when the goat herd was plentiful; what would happen when the goat herd was thin? She spat in the snow and hissed, the thought of Jarhost taking more goats in taxes enraging her. They had gone from paying tribute to a dragon to paying taxes to a greedy king. She was not sure which would do them more damage.

Ulfr nuzzled up under her hand, sensing her frustration, and Ylmi allowed a small smile, as her fingers ran through her thick fur.

"Come," she said, "we'll find something yet."

The hunger in her stomach was annoying now, so she picked her way down the slope toward the marsh, looking for tracks in the snow or gnawed branches – anything which might indicate an animal she could hunt.

The wind was stronger here. In the mountains, it twisted and turned over peaks and valleys, but there were no such impediments on the marsh; here, it howled over the landscape, rushing through the squat trees and little bushes which dotted the marsh.

Ylmi pulled her cloak tighter about her shoulders, still searching – until suddenly she wasn't. Ulfr's ears pricked up and she froze. The wind howled again, but this time there was something else howling, as well.

She was good with her bow, but there were predators on the marsh and in the mountains, which were at least her match. She did not doubt that they were hungry as well.

"Come," she beckoned Ulfr, and began to run at an easy pace back toward the pass. Even if she was imagining it on the wind, it would be better to be headed home in any case, as it was already midday, and she had much ground to cover. But then the wind lulled for a moment, and the howl came again.

A mountain wolf.

Ylmi winced. Where there was one, there would soon be more, and they were downwind of her. With the hunger of a long winter in their bellies, they were on the hunt, and if they were on her trail, that was not a good thing.

She picked up her pace, Ulfr padding next to her, her ears pinned back as she sniffed the wind nervously.

The howl came again, and this time it was answered by another, and another. Three, then, Ylmi guessed, perhaps four. Not quite a pack, but still enough to be dangerous.

She slowed for a moment, trying to guess if they were already at the pass. Her breath came in clouds which hung white before her face, and she shook her head.

Then came two more howls, much closer. Ylmi turned on her heel and ran in earnest.

This was a pack, hunting with the hunger of late winter, and they were following her trail. They were over the pass by now, or close to it, and she would have to find another way back over the mountains. She thought as she ran, trying to remember exactly where she was, and where she would find another way.

There were plenty of passes over the mountain, ways which she could follow back into the forest. She did not want to be caught on the ice marsh by a pack of wolves; in the forest, she could find a place to make a stand, or at least put her back against a tree.

Suddenly, she came upon one of the many little paths left by the deer and other animals, and she followed it, her heart pounding and her breath coming quick and heavy as she ran. The long winters left her body unused to long exertion, with little strength to spare, and she was feeling it now.

As she had hoped, the track rose higher, and Ylmi smiled as she crested the first ridge, for she was sure it would lead her over the low hills and back into the forest. But the wolves were howling again, close on her tail, and she looked back to see where they were.

And her heart stopped.

On the horizon, as far as her eye could see, heavy, black clouds were piled one upon another, bearing down swiftly upon her.

Very rarely, in the last gasp of winter, the phantom storms would come out of the north. Great, black clouds heavy with snow were pushed southward by terrible winds. Ahead of the storm, everything would appear calm, barely more than a light breeze in the air, until it struck.

Men had been known to die in the phantoms, wandering in circles only a few feet from their door, blinded by the wind and snow.

Ulfr's ears were back now as he smelled the wolves on the wind, and Ylmi breathed deep. If she ran hard, she might make it back to her home.

Her feet pounded the trail as she took off, scrambling upward. Where she could, she left the path and climbed. Within a few minutes she was sweating, and she had to force herself to slow down. It would do her no good to dash a mile or two more, then collapse in exhaustion.

On she ran, until she crested a ridge and saw the forest laid out before her. She took a quick glance over her shoulder and saw the dark clouds were approaching the edge of the marsh. She felt a sick feeling in her gut.

"I'll be faster the rest of the way," she told herself, but even as she said the words she did not believe them.

She threw herself down the slope, leaping from tree to tree as she hurtled down into the woods. Ulfr padded along behind her and, as she ran, she heard him growl.

"Come, Ulfr!" she shouted. They had no time for the wolves now. No time for anything.

A light breeze had begun to blow, rustling the trees around her and warming the air. It was the first trick of the phantoms, to push all the warmth before them, leaving only the hard, hungry cold beneath their clouds.

The wolves howled again, almost on top of them, and Ylmi gripped her bow, and wished that she had her spear.

Another howl echoed through the trees ahead of them, and Ylmi swore. "Allfather," she muttered between gasping breaths, "unless your time for me has come, send me aid."

A dark shape flashed through the woods on her left, and she realized the pack had caught her.

They were running alongside her now, waiting for her to tire. Waiting for her to stumble. Well, she wasn't going to. She had no spear, but there were eight arrows in her quiver, and a long knife which had tasted wolf blood before.

So she ran, the wolf pack around her, calling back and forth, coming closer and closer.

Then, one leapt through the trees and lunged for her heel, only to be caught by Ulfr. The wolf gave a pitiful whine as Ulfr's teeth sank into its neck and suddenly the forest seemed to explode with wolves.

She skidded to a stop, turning to see Ulfr snarling as she stood her ground. Ylmi had an arrow on her bow in an instant and loosed it, striking the lead wolf in the chest. It fell with a whining growl and the other wolves hesitated.

Ulfr growled again, backing toward Ylmi, her ears back and her teeth bared. Ylmi was breathing heavily as she let loose a second arrow, wounding another wolf.

But the pack was hungry, and they had hunted humans before. They quickly encircled them, even as Ylmi let loose another arrow. She counted eight wolves, but before she could finish, three lunged at Ulfr, snapping at her legs and neck, even as Ylmi saw the rest of the pack push at her.

The wolves were trying to split them up, to take them one by one, and Ylmi would not have it. She let loose another arrow and drew her long knife. With a shout, she lunged toward Ulfr, throwing one wolf off her and slashing at another.

They retreated, but Ulfr's dark coat was wet with blood, and she was favouring one leg. Ylmi wiped the sweat from her eyes and moved toward a tree. The wolves could smell the blood and circled them, patiently. Thrusting her knife into the tree, Ylmi drew another arrow and let it fly, but the sweat dripped into her eye even as she loosed, and the arrow only grazed the wolf she was after.

They snarled and drew closer as a pack. One more arrow Ylmi was able to let fly, before they charged. Ylmi snatched her knife from the tree and buried it in the chest of the first wolf which lunged at her throat. But, even as its weight threw her against the tree, she felt teeth close around her leg and she was pulled to the ground.

Ulfr was snarling and snapping, and Ylmi slashed with her knife as the world shrank to a stinking, steaming darkness of fur and fangs. She kicked out, feeling her feet shove off a wolf, even as she felt the fangs of another sink into her shoulder. She screamed as she felt the teeth grate on bone, and the wolf shook her. She stabbed and slashed frantically, her mouth full of fur as she struggled until, with a snarl, the fangs released her. She shoved a dead wolf off of her and pushed back against the tree, spitting bloody fur from her mouth and sucking in the cold air.

Four wolves lay dead around them, and two more were limping in the trees. Ulfr was still breathing, her ears flat against her head as she watched what remained of the wolf pack, a snarl on her lips.

Ylmi pushed herself up, her left shoulder aching as the blood ran down from it. She was bleeding from her legs as well, and from both forearms.

A swirl of snowflakes drifted down through the trees.

The wolves eyed them again, determining if this prey was worth the continuing fight. Ylmi summoned her strength and shouted, stepping forward as she brandished her knife. One wolf backed away and Ylmi shouted again. The rest of the pack suddenly turned and trotted off into the woods, determined to seek easier prey.

But Ylmi felt her shoulders sag, as a cold wind blew through the trees, carrying another flurry of snow.

"Come on, Ulfr," Ylmi muttered. "It won't get better if we stay here."

Ulfr wagged her tail and limped toward Ylmi, licking at her wounded leg and gazing at Ylmi with large, dark eyes, wincing a little as the wind moaned through the trees.

Ylmi choked back a sob, knowing that Ulfr trusted her with her life, and she would likely be frozen stiff before long. The excitement from the fight with the pack was over, and weariness hung on her limbs like a heavy blanket.

The snow was falling steadily now, and the wind was picking up. There was no more running now, even if both of them hadn't been wounded. The falling snow swiftly obscured the ground, and one false step would be enough to cripple her.

She kept her eyes open for a cave or crevasse where she might take shelter, but even if she found one, she wasn't sure how much it would help. The phantoms could last for days, with the cold as deep as in the height of winter.

The wind was blowing steadily now, howling down from the north and bringing with it the cold. Ylmi felt the chill at first on her face, as the wind chilled the sweat on her face, but then she noticed her fingers going numb, even as she walked.

She was not sure exactly where they were, and with the snow falling she could not see the mountain peaks by which she would find her way.

"One foot in front of the other," she told Ulfr, and the wolf looked up at her with a sympathetic expression, as if in agreement.

But they were both limping, and Ylmi's shoulder was growing more painful as the cold bit deeper. It was a throbbing ache now, where the wolves had bitten her, and it felt as if her veins were turning to ice, as the cold flowed in from the wound.

She could see less than ten paces now, the wind-driven snow falling thick and fast, swirling and gusting so that Ylmi felt as though the world moved about her, even as she walked. The snow was piling up, treacherous snow traps forming as the fresh snow fell on the old, frozen drifts.

Ylmi pushed on, forcing herself to take one step at a time. The phantom was fully on her now, the swirling snow and heavy clouds shrinking her world to a few gloomy paces, filled with snow and cold. Her breath hung before her in a cloud, as she picked her way through the snow-laden branches of trees hidden in the gloom.

Her face went numb and she slung her bow over her shoulder, so she could keep both hands tucked under her arms. It was hard to walk now, and she realized that the snow was getting deeper, her path a ragged trail ripped through the new-fallen snow, only to disappear as she watched the falling snow erase the evidence of her path.

Numbly, she looked down at Ulfr. The wolf's dark coat was speckled with snow. Ylmi watched as Ulfr leaned down to lick at her paw, stupidly realizing that she had stopped.

She was tired, and she had no idea where she was. If she sat down for a moment, just to rest, perhaps she could continue in better spirits. Perhaps even a nap...

She growled at herself, a guttural fury which sputtered as it passed her frozen lips. To rest here was death, and she would not die now, not when Ulfr depended on her. Not when she had come this close to achieving what she desired. Not when the seer had said she would live.

She had not achieved all she desired, and nothing could be taken away from a dead woman, so she would survive this. Let come what would: frostbite, hunger, pain, so be it – she would not die.

With a deep breath, she started forward again, pushing through the snow which had built up as she stood still. Suddenly she was falling, her feet stuck behind her. The snow made for a soft, if chilling fall, and Ylmi looked down to see the dark wood of a broken stump peeking out of the snow. She laughed. It was a harsh, bitter sound, filled with despair that Ylmi would not admit to herself.

Suddenly the air seemed to press down upon he, and there was a pain in her ears, as if she had suddenly dived deep into the fjord. She winced as the pressure grew, closing her eyes against it, as it rose higher and higher.

"You seem to have fallen."

It was a woman's voice, quite close, cutting through the sound of the wind, and the pressure on her ears seemed to lessen.

"Nothing escapes your keen understanding," Ylmi muttered. Her eyes opened, and she shook her head to throw off the snow and the ringing in her ears.

"No," the woman replied, and Ylmi saw a dim shape coming through the snow. She was wrapped in pale leather, edged with the white fur of an ice bear, and her white hair danced in the wind. She leant on her spear as she looked down at Ylmi. "You will not last long in the snow."

"I am aware," Ylmi said, as she tried to get her feet. "But it is proving difficult to get up."

The woman watched her for a moment, as Ylmi struggled to force her numb limbs to obey her. After a moment, Ylmi looked up at her. "Will you help me?"

By way of answer, the woman extended her hand, grasping Ylmi by the front of her cloak and pulling her to her feet.

Something surged through Ylmi, and she looked up at the woman who towered over her. The falling snow stung as she stood, and she spat frozen blood from her mouth.

"Where are you from, that you are out in this weather?" Ylmi asked, squinting against the wind as she spoke.

"Tell me, first, why you hunt so far from home," the woman asked, "when there are matters so much more pressing."

Ylmi looked at her, askance. "What is more pressing than hunger?"

As she looked, she saw the spear the woman carried, its white-steel blade frosting in the cold, with a blue gemstone set in the haft. Her eye widened.

"Skathi..."

"The wind is cold, and you have been in it a long time." The woman took Ylmi under the arm and began to walk. The snow was blinding now, falling thick, even as the wind whipped it into gusts and clouds, and Ylmi could see little but the tall, white figure who walked next to her.

"You were told to wait," Skathi said, holding Ylmi's uninjured arm in her hand, as they walked. "And, when a god speaks, it is right that a mortal listen."

"I did," Ylmi answered; "I waited, and now I wait again."

"Even so," Skathi replied, "you were told to wait. I tell you now, wait no longer."

"I thought that Karik was the great man," Ylmi said; "I am the woman who goes unanswered. I climbed the Stones twice and did not receive an answer."

"Ylmi..." There was a warning edge to the woman's voice, and Ylmi suddenly felt fear rising up within her, filling her throat and screaming at her to run. But, the goddess held her firm by the arm, and spoke in a voice firm and clear: "The gods do not answer to you, or any other mortal. Vranr's little pebbles may be heavy with our footsteps, but we are bound by no one." She turned Ylmi to face her, and Ylmi saw that one eye burned a clear blue, the other a deep red, like an old coal left aside from the fire.

"I have come to you not because you earned my presence, but because I wished it. The Allfather ordered you to wait, and wait you have. But, the time for waiting and watching is over, and the time of great deeds is at hand."

She turned and continued walking, pulling Ylmi with her through the gloom and wind of the storm. "Vengeance will have its place, and the law will be fulfilled. You have three paths before you, Ylmi – three which lead always to three more. You may choose to wait, to bide your time, and watch as the world about you starves and fails. This path is the easiest.

"You may choose blood – to pour out that of yours and your enemies, in a river which will bring pain and fire upon all you despise, and upon those you love. That path is the simplest.

"Or you may choose neither, to defend those about you, to give justice where you may, and to avert some of the evil that the years may bring. That path is the most difficult."

Ylmi shivered as she listened, wondering what was the point of all of these words, if she would be frozen in a few hours. "What am I to do with all this?" she asked. "I cannot even deal with Unhost, or gain the rightful profit of our battle with the dragon. What hope have I of accomplishing aught else?"

"Simply because there is a path the gods will you to take," Skathi's voice cut through the wind, "does not mean that we will flatten your path before you, and smooth out every obstacle – then you would be little better than a boulder, which tumbles down the path which is easiest for it. We would have you become more, and thus you must seek out the best path and the best way forward."

"What, then, would you have me do?" Ylmi's feet were numb in the snow as she walked, and it felt as though even her bones were turning to ice. "Storm Bjarnmont and demand back our gold? Lift Unhost's head on a spear and rid our settlement of him?" The words had not left her mouth before the pressure in the air rose, and Ylmi felt again the sudden pang of fear.

"I have told you before not to demand answers of the gods." Skathi replied, and a flicker of lightning danced about the head of her spear. "Know that for every path downward there is one upward, if only you will take the time to look for it."

Ylmi staggered suddenly, her foot striking a stone beneath the snow, and she stumbled forward. The wind struck her cold like a wave, and when she looked up Skathi was gone.

For a moment, Ylmi sat there, wondering if it had been a dream. The snow and blood in her mouth was cold, and she spat it out.

Then she laughed. Throwing her head back, she laughed into the storm, shaking with cold.

She had risked death more than once, and come close to it again and again, seeking word from the gods, and she had gone unanswered. And now, when she was near to death, trudging through a storm, that was when the gods chose to appear. Her laugh turned into a choking cough as the cold air burned her lungs, and she shook with the heaving pain of it, before she could rise again.

Nearby, Ulfr shook herself, tossing the snow off her back and into the air. After a moment, the wolf sniffed the snow, then lifted her head and howled into the wind.

Ylmi shook her head and glanced around them. She could see the shapes of a few trees, but the gloom was turning into darkness, and she knew night was approaching.

"Well," she said to Ulfr, "I guess we'll see if this dragon mark provides any protection against cold."

Ulfr only howled again, and Ylmi forced herself to rise, though every muscle in her body screamed against it.

"Come on," Ylmi muttered and pushed into the woods, doing the only thing she could think of: moving forward.

Ulfr howled again, and in answer Ylmi heard a shout carried upon the wind. What it said, Ylmi could not begin to guess, but a voice meant companionship, which might keep them alive.

"Here!" she shouted into the snow, and pushed through the trees.

Ulfr bounded past her in the snow, her tail wagging and ears up, as she paused and looked back. Ylmi laughed, the despair in her chest suddenly turning to hope, and she pushed though the hip-deep snow as fast as she could. Again Ulfr howled, and again the voice called in answer. Ulfr barked happily, and Ylmi saw a shape pushing through the trees ahead of her.

"Ylmi?" Karik called.

"Here!" she called again, but her voice was cracked, and wind blew away her words. But Karik had seen her, and a moment later he was there, his arm around her.

"Where have you been?" he shouted through the storm. "We thought you were lost."

"Me, too," she answered. "Where is the clearing?"

"That way," Karik gestured, vaguely. "Hold onto me."

He had tied a rope around his waist, and now he pulled it in, Ylmi holding his shoulder, until he found the tree he had tied it to. A branch had been peeled there, pointing the way, and he followed it to another tree, and on again.

Soon, the door of her house appeared out of the shadows, and Karik pulled it open, both of them staggering inside.

Siggi rushed to hold her and, after a quick embrace, pulled off her outer clothes. "Careful! Slowly... slowly..." she crooned; "if we're too fast you'll get frostbite. Slowly, though it will not be pleasant."

"I'll find Bodvar," Karik said quickly, and disappeared back into the snow.

"Father?" Ylmi croaked.

"He went looking for you as well," Siggi answered. "Karik has a horn to call him back."

Ylmi winced as her mother led her to the small fire, and began gently rubbing the feeling back into her limbs. Ylmi looked down and ground her teeth together; she knew the pain that was coming.

By the time Karik and her father returned, she had stopped screaming, and the worst of the pain had passed, so she was able to give her father a quick smile when she saw his worried face.

"I'm near unkillable," she said, with a tired smile: "a dragon, a phantom, the Watching Stones..."

"I would prefer you not to put that to the test," Bodvar answered her. "What happened?"

Ylmi shifted against the wall, easing the ache in her shoulder for a moment, before it returned. "I was chased by a wolf pack, then caught in the marsh when I saw the phantom coming in."

"I am glad you are safe," Bodvar said, quietly. "Now sleep – the gods know you need it."

Her bones aching with weariness, Ylmi let her mother draw the wool blanket over her. As the warmth settled over her, she wondered if it had all been a dream. There was no way the White Huntress would have visited her...

A tiny prick of something cool in her hand made her open her eyes. When she looked down, she saw in her hand three tiny stones: one red, one white and one green.

Many Paths

Ylmi was pulled from sleep by a burning pain in her legs. Desperately, she heaved the piled furs and blankets off her and stared at her feet. In the light from the fire they gleamed, as if covered in wax, and her toes were bright red.

Ylmi groaned as she looked and fell back to her bed. She had hoped to avoid frostbite, but she supposed that surviving a phantom with relatively mild frostbite was as good as she could hope for.

Siggi appeared from behind her and held out a cup.

"Drink this, foolish girl," she said with a smile, and pressed it into Ylmi's hand.

Ylmi propped herself up on her elbow, wincing as her feet dragged over the blanket. "I am injured, mother. You should not scold me so." Her shoulder ached, but it had been bandaged and the pain was less than she had known in the past.

Siggi shook her head. "How did you come to get caught by a phantom?"

Ylmi drank deeply at the cup. It was mead, and the sweet liquid felt warm as it filled her stomach. "My bad eye was to the north," she answered between sips; "I can't watch both ways at once."

"It is not like you to be so caught," Siggi shook her head, "though I am glad to see you in a good humour."

"I escaped a wolf pack and a phantom," Ylmi shook her head, "and it seems that my wounds are slight indeed." She glanced around the hut, seeing the faint glimmer of daylight at the door, but the longsword Karik had taken from the dragon was gone. "Where are the others?"

"Your father is pushing the goat herds out for the spring," Siggi replied. "And, Karik... has gone to Bjarnmont."

Ylmi sighed for a moment, and drained the last of the mead. "He is seeking a way to get the gold back."

"What need have we for gold?" Siggi straightened the covers over her. "My daughter has been returned to me, safe again. The winter is nearly over, with us safely through."

"But the winter will come again," Ylmi said. She stared at the fire, thinking of all the lonely nights she had spent waking to see that it did not go out, and the terror that had possessed her the few times that it had. "Winter will come again and again and again. Our village will grow, the herd will shrink, and we will face starvation like that which drove Karik and his friends out of their village and into ours." She looked up at her mother. "But there is nowhere else to go – not on this island."

Siggi set down the bowl she was holding and turned back to her daughter. "You are thinking of attempting the Isles?"

"I am," Ylmi answered, "and I think that we can do it, if only we have the gold to build a big enough ship."

"Many have died in their attempts to cross the Isles," Siggi said quietly, her eyes fixed on the fire, "and I would be sad indeed if you never returned to me."

"I have faced death more than once and returned to you." Ylmi gestured at her feet and her face: "I bear the scars of more challenges than one."

"I am aware of your accomplishments," Siggi said, dryly; "it is I who wrestle you back from Dvengrhost's grasp, each time you go pounding on his door."

She settled down beside Ylmi and took her daughter's hands gently in her own. "I think that it is for you to accomplish many great things. I warned you from the Watching Stones, but you conquered them; we cautioned you for many years concerning the dragon, but you survived him; and now you come walking out of the snow, a phantom raging about you, with a trail of dead wolves in your wake." She was silent for a moment, then fixed Ylmi's one eye with her own. "I will not caution you against this. Not now."

She kissed Ylmi softly on the forehead, and pressed her back down. "But, before you sail, you must sleep. Few schemes are well made on a sleepless mind."

Ylmi smiled as her mother drew her covers over her head. The mead was doing its work, the pain in her feet and hands slowly ebbing away, as a pleasant warmth was falling over her, like a blanket of sunshine on a warm summer day.

It was a few days before Ylmi's feet were well enough for her to walk. While she waited, she took a small bit of squirrel skin and sewed it with leather, to form a tiny bag. This she hung about her neck, and within it set the three stones she had been given.

By the fourth day she could walk without help, but it still brought her more than a little pain. Even so, she was restless and eager to be useful, so the next morning Bodvar took her a short distance into the forest, to where the cold mountain stream bent around fallen logs.

In the pools there, the shadows of small fish darted about, and the two of them began to fish. They spoke little, but enjoyed the light of the sun filtering through the trees, and the beginnings of spring.

Ylmi thought on Skathi and the three stones, red, white and green. There was not always a way, she reflected, but if Skathi was urging her forward, then there must be one. And if there was a way forward, she would find it.

They returned to their house, walking slowly to ease the pain in Ylmi's feet.

Bodvar said little, but as they approached the clearing, he stopped and pulled her into a massive hug. He did not speak, but planted a kiss on her forehead.

Ylmi smiled as she took the fish, and limped to the log where they would clean them. If Skathi was leading her, then she knew that she would find a way to care for her parents. The day would come when the winter found them, safely entrenched against its cold and hunger.

Laying down the fish, she stepped inside to retrieve the knife used for preparing them, but paused as she made to leave. Beside the door, Karik's longsword rested in its usual place, the blue stone in its hilt flickering with the light of the fire.

"Karik is back?" she asked Siggi.

"He did his work this morning," she pointed to a pile of freshly-chopped wood by the house, "then took his ax and left. Said that he wanted to see to that clearing we mentioned in the winter."

Ylmi shrugged and set to cleaning her catch, tossing them into the black iron pot.

But, even after the stew was set to boiling, Karik did not return, nor did he appear as the darkness settled over the mountains, and Bodvar shut in the goats for the night.

The next morning, Ylmi took her bow and limped slowly along the mountain stream, following it north toward the clearing. As she approached it, she heard the rhythmic sound of chopping, and smelled the scent of smoke and ash upon the wind.

Overlooking the clearing, there was a rise in the ground, before it sloped evenly toward the base of a cliff. From the rise, the little clearing stretched out with a scattering of trees, which led down to a gurgling brook, running down from the melting snow, high in the mountains. The brook ran beside the little knoll, rushing happily and noisily down toward the sea.

Along the edge of the clearing, Karik had felled several trees into the snow, and close by was the smoking wreck of a bonfire, which had clearly been burning through the night. Though there was a small breeze in the clearing, Karik had removed his shirt, and Ylmi could see the burned scars of the dragon-fire rippling over the muscles in his shoulder. In a couple of places the burns had cracked open again, letting out thin streaks of blood, which mixed with his sweat.

There was a loud crack, and the tree before Karik shivered and fell, falling gracefully out of the sky, to land in the clearing with a crash. Briefly, Karik checked his ax head, to make sure it was still seated firmly on the handle he had made for it, then he turned to trimming the branches from the trunk, wielding his ax smoothly through one cut after another. After a few moments he paused, as if catching his breath.

"Are just going to stand there?" he asked, without turning.

Ylmi stepped into the clearing, around a pile of stripped branches, and sat by the fire, easing off her feet. "You were here all night?"

Karik lifted the ax again. "I will start building a house here soon. Waiting will gain me nothing."

"The cold is not yet gone," Ylmi said, glancing northward. Over the pines, the mountain peaks were still white with snow, and above them the clouds were dark and heavy, warning of more storms to come. "It may gain you sickness, if you are intent on such work without taking rest." She looked around the tiny clearing, before adding: "Why build here? Is there no space in the village?"

"There is room for farming here," Karik replied. "And, if I am nearby, perhaps there will be less danger from the winter." He kicked aside the cut branches and sucked in a deep breath. He was silent for a moment then, with a crunch, the ax fell into the snow and Karik's shoulders sagged.

"So, Jarhost has taken the gold we won," Ylmi said, quietly. "Will you sulk until he returns it?"

Karik turned to face her, stepping off the fallen tree and stumbling momentarily, as his boots slid into the snow.

"If it were just the gold," he said, pulling his feet from the drift, "I would move on. But it is not just the gold; it is Umir..." He pointed at her face: "It is your eye. It is the wounds that we still carry." He flexed his arm and winced at the pain, as another bead of blood squeezed between the cracked skin. "And all of it was for nothing."

He raised his hand as she opened her mouth. "And I know that the dragon is gone, and the village will now prosper – for a time. But soon the village will grow; others will hear of us, and come seeking refuge in the winter. Before long, we will face the same hunger and starvation that the rest of Vrania faces every year."

Ylmi noticed that he was beginning to shiver, so she picked up his shirt and tossed it to him. "Put your clothes on."

He glared at her, but she returned his stare until a cold breeze came down through the trees, and Karik shivered so that his shoulders shook.

"We have slain a dragon and survived the winter," she said, as he pulled it slowly over his shoulders. "A new year now presents itself, and there are many paths open to us. But, first," she raised her bow, "we must do what is necessary to ensure we do not starve. I am off to do my part, and while I hunt I will think."

She glanced around the clearing. "You are a clever man, and I think you will come up with your own plans while you work. But, do so in a way that you do not become a burden to others; if I have to carry your sick and coughing body back to our hut because you didn't rest, I will see that your head thumps into every tree between here and the sheep pens."

She left him there and went on with her hunting.

When she returned to her parents' home that night, Karik was there. He helped her clean the thin buck she had tracked down.

* * *

The next day, Ylmi returned from her hunt to find her father emptying the sheep pens. It was hard work, cleaning out the leavings of the herd from the winter, but Siggi used it in her garden, which had grown much larger since they had first come up the mountain.

"Have you given thought to returning to the village?" Ylmi asked, almost before she thought it.

Bodvar paused in his work and rested on his shovel. There was a streak of grey in his beard, Ylmi realized, and he stroked it as he thought.

"Now that the dragon is dead," Ylmi continued, "I do not know on what grounds Unhost would keep you exiled here." Ulfr nuzzled at her hand, then began making his rounds about the little steading.

"Possibly on the grounds that he does not like us," Bodvar chuckled. "Though, for my part, I like him little as well."

Ylmi watched as he set back to work, then set aside her bow and quiver, before taking the rake from where Bodvar had left it. "But, surely he would not forbid us from returning – not after I have killed the dragon."

"Perhaps not," Bodvar agreed, "but he could make things very unpleasant for us, if he wished. Here," he waved his hand about the clearing, "we raise our goats, your mother tends her garden and you hunt. All things considered, it is better than many others on this isle."

"And yet we are alone." Ylmi set to work with her rake. "If things go poorly with us—"

"Then matters can be difficult indeed," Bodvar answered. "But, being alone has its advantages: Unhost pays us less attention than he otherwise might, and he demands less from us than he might if we lived and worked in the village. Besides, if Karik builds his home, that will be one neighbour nearby."

Bodvar paused in his work, and his hands tightened for a moment on the rough wood of the shovel. "I have not forgotten that Unhost thought to kill us by sending us here, and I am not eager to live again under his thumb. Here, far from his home, we have some measure of peace."

Ylmi thought on his words as they continued their work. It seemed to her that her father would not return to the village while Unhost still ruled there, and if matters continued as they were, that would be for a very long time.

But, there were many in the settlement who enjoyed Unhost's rule, and it would take more than a dragon-slaying to sway them.

——◆——

As winter receded and the cold lessened, Ylmi returned to her hunting and Karik continued the work on his homestead. Occasionally, Ylmi would visit him at his work, as did Igil for a short time. Before the last snow had melted in the clearing, a small, long house stood warm and solid at one end, and Karik began setting aside food for the winter.

Ylmi often did not see him for days at a time, for he was hard at work on his farm, and her hunting often led her far into the mountains, as she sought out game which was growing ever more scarce.

And as the deer grew more scarce, they grew more wary; Ylmi found that, in scouring the forest floor for their passing, she found little. So, she took to sitting upon the ridges and cliffs which overlooked the land, watching for where they moved. She watched the birds, to see where the wolves hunted, and she looked for the circling ravens which hung above carrion, a place that deer and boar would avoid.

And, while she watched, she thought, turning over in her mind what Skathi had said. She thought on the stories her parents had told her, and she pondered Dranri's tales of his service to Jarhost.

Things carried on in this way for some time, until a day came when she visited Karik, finding him hard at work on his house, with Igil. It was not a great, long house, but it was snug and well-built, and Ylmi thought it would stand up well to the winter.

"Since you are here," she said, "I take it you are not planning to rob Jarhost?"

"Not at the moment," Karik replied.

Igil chuckled: "I could do it, though Karik doubts me." He tossed down the hammer he had been working with. "The issue is that if that gold goes missing, then we will be the first suspected of taking it. Even if we escape, it will appear very suspicious when we build a great boat."

"You are not deterred by the walls and guards of Bjarnmont?" Ylmi asked him.

Igil shrugged in response. "It is the same as building a ship; if you wish one part of the ship to do one thing, you must build another part a certain way. Robbing Jarhost would be no different."

"That does not make sense," Ylmi said, as she stared at him.

"Nonetheless," Karik shook his head as he climbed down from the roof, where he had been fastening sod, "robbing Bjarnmont is out of the question. Also, the mines beneath our settlement are dry, and Unhost has no more gold, courtesy of Jarhost's taxes."

"Then, perhaps we should pay Jarl Birin a visit in Mirhom," Ylmi suggested. "I have heard he is wealthy."

"His wealth is in cattle and warriors," Karik replied, "and above even the king I would not anger Birin. He is said to be a vengeful man, and he has the men to scour the island for whoever stole from him."

Ylmi thought for a moment, then it was as if the answer suddenly revealed itself to her: "Hegli."

"What?"

"Jarl Hegli." A smile spread across her face. "He has gold in the fortress of the Undmir. He is wealthy and powerful, but only because no one can breach his fortress. He will not announce the loss of his gold for fear that Viglir and Jarhost will think him weak. And, even Jarhost's lazy self will not sit idle if Hegli sends a company of soldiers scouring his lands."

Karik looked thoughtful, but Igil shook his head. "How on Earth will we get gold out of the Undmir? The walls are stone, and taller than three men."

"Taller than four," Ylmi corrected him, "but I thought you just said robbing a jarl was the same as building a ship."

"I said robbing Bjarnmont was that easy," Igil said, quickly raising his hand; "I never said—"

"We don't have to go over the walls," Karik interrupted.

"What?"

"The charts," Karik looked up, with a grin, "they map the coastline of all Vrania. We can go through the Undersea."

Igil looked at him as if he was mad, but Ylmi smiled broadly. She felt the burnt skin behind her ear crack, but it only egged her on. This was what the goddess had spoken of – what she had been looking for.

"An unsailable sea," Ylmi said. "Hegli keeps his gold in the mines which border the Undersea. We can sail in, take it and be gone before he knows we are there."

"We will need a boat," Karik said, deep in thought; "something bigger than the fishing boats."

Igil laughed: "And, once again we find ourselves at the issue of not having a boat."

But Karik shook his head; "A ship to sail the Isles must be large and strong – able to carry a large crew and many goods. But a ship to sail the Undersea will have to be small. It will need only a small crew, and we need it to carry only a small amount of gold. It must be larger than the fishing boats only so that it may withstand the storms and waves of the Ice Sea."

Igil considered that, and Ylmi felt the excitement rising in her chest. This was the next step, and now that she had found it, she was burning to begin. "How soon could you build the ship?"

"There is a fair bit of wood set aside," Igil said, "and I do not think it would be difficult to convince Havar to use much of it for a boat. Unhost may ask questions, however."

Ylmi laughed: "Let Unhost ask. Tell him that it is a new ship for better fishing, and the fool will eat it up. He knows nothing of how his village is run."

Igil shrugged. "That fits well enough with what I have seen, but we will have to be careful, nonetheless."

"We will need to get the others to agree," Ylmi said. "This plan is the best we have, and I think will lead us to success. But it is not without danger, and the sooner they are told what we intend, the better."

Karik nodded. "Besides, it is time that the dragonslayers gather again and drink together. The winter is over, our wounds are somewhat healed, and also we never celebrated our deed, nor poured out a drink for Umir."

A New Boat

It was agreed, and three days later Ylmi sat with Ulfr by the mountain trail, watching as the other dragonslayers came hiking up from the village.

Revik led the way, the dragon's burns visible on the edge of his neck. Behind him, Thora kept up with his long strides easily, her spear over her shoulder, the dragon burns on her cheek and fingers bright red in the afternoon sun.

Wisic followed after them, a small barrel on his left shoulder. He seemed unburnt at first glance, but after Ylmi and Karik he had suffered the most, for the dragon-fire had scorched him from shoulder to thigh on his right side, and Ylmi could see the red, cracked skin on his hand, beneath his sleeve.

Farther behind them followed Igil and Havar. Igil's burns were small, only his hand having been scarred by the dragon's flames, and Havar had avoided the dragon-fire altogether.

Ylmi stood and greeted them when they reached her, Ulfr sniffing cautiously as they came close.

"Why," Wisic breathed heavily, "did Karik not build his home a little farther down the mountain?"

"There is no place for it," Ylmi replied, and Wisic rolled his eyes.

They followed her along the path, 'til they smelled the smoke and the scent of roasting meat. Karik sat in the clearing before his small home, a goat roasting over a firepit outside the door. It was a fine evening in early spring, and a soft wind was blowing out of the south, rustling through the pine trees as it made its way northward.

"Greetings, friends!" Karik stood when he saw them and welcomed each one. "It is good for us all to be together again."

"Indeed," Wisic responded, with a sidelong glance at the goat. "It was a long climb and we are famished," he said, as he handed the barrel to Karik. "I trust there is more than one small goat for the lot of us."

"There is bread, as well," Karik promised him, "but I am no king, to feast you all as you deserve."

"No," Wisic agreed, "if that were the case you would give us a tiny ring before, all in one breath, inviting us and then barring us from your hall."

They all laughed at that, and Karik said it was a good thing they all had so much humour. The barrel Wisic had brought was filled with mead, and they drank as the goat finished cooking.

A small portion of the mead was poured into the fire for Umir, and before they ate they threw in a small portion of the goat and a piece of the heavy, brown bread, which Karik had got from Siggi. The smell of meat and bread mingled with the smell of smoke and the pine trees, and Ylmi thought, as she slipped a piece of charred meat to Ulfr, that this was not a bad way to spend an evening. They talked and laughed, and when more than a little mead had been drunk, it was discovered that Wisic could perform an excellent imitation of Unhost's nasal voice.

The sun had disappeared over the western trees, leaving behind only a warm, red glow, when Karik stood up and raised his hand.

"As joyous as this merriment has been," he said, with a grin, "it is not the only reason I called you here tonight."

He looked over their faces, and Ylmi felt a tremor go through her. She had seen that look before, the night he had told her he wanted to reach the Watching Stones.

"I have told you all that I have found what may be a way through the Black Isles," Karik's voice was grim, and everyone nodded slowly, "and we are all aware of how the gold we took from the dragon was distributed."

More grim nods.

"Igil and Havar have told me that, without it, we could build but a small boat – one which would be better for little beyond sailing the coastlines." He glanced at Havar. "Is that correct?"

Havar nodded.

"Then, if we are to try the passage, we must have gold." Karik paused, and one of the sticks in the fire popped, sending sparks into the air. "And, I believe I know where we can get it."

"Karik..." Wisic's voice was a warning, "...we have discussed this."

But Karik only smiled. "I have no intention of trying to rob Bjarnmont." His smile faded for a moment. "I went there to speak with Jarhost and ask for gold, and it did not go well: Jarhost will not let go of the gold, and Bjarnmont is not easily robbed. Besides, he would suspect us at the first. No, I say we rob the Undmir."

Ylmi smiled as she looked at the shocked faces around the fire. None spoke for a moment, only the sound of the fire crackling, and the soft wind blowing through the pines.

Then Wisic shifted on his seat. "Karik, I would say that you've lost your mind. But then, the last two times I've thought that you had a plan, so..." he leant back against a log, "...spit it out."

"Jarl Hegli rules the fortress of Undmir," Karik spoke quickly, biting off his words in his excitement. "Beneath the fortress, the Undersea runs for miles, and it is rumoured that, within it, Hegli mines for gold. We can sail in, load a few ingots and sail out, with no one the wiser."

"There are so many things wrong with what you just said," Thora said, with her eyes closed, "that I cannot tell where to begin."

"We could start with the fact that Undmir is impenetrable," Wisic said, looking around the circle. "That seems a good place to start."

"Why not rob from King Viglir?" Revik asked. "Torhom is not much farther, and if he pursues us we could fight him in the mountains."

"The wealth of Viglir is in cattle, not gold," Havar answered, "and they would be more difficult to move than gold. Besides, Viglir's army is larger even than Jarhost's."

Revik shrugged; "If we have to fight, I would rather face the warriors of Torhom in the open than fight through Hegli's fortress. My ax doesn't like stone, but it can cleave men well enough."

"We won't go through the fortress," Karik answered; "you're right: it is impenetrable. We'll sail through the Undersea."

Thora rolled her eyes. "The Undersea is part of Undmir. No one has ever sailed in or out. Ever."

"We have the charts," Ylmi spoke up, and in the firelight they all turned to look at her. "They show the path in and out. We can be halfway back home before Hegli even realizes we've been there. Once we are gone, the lord of the impenetrable Undmir will not make it widely known that he has been robbed. And, if he were to send armed men into the countryside seeking us, Jarhost would declare war on him before they came south of Girhom."

Karik nodded.

"How much do these charts show?" Havar asked.

Ylmi shifted her leg, which was falling asleep under her, and turned so she could see him with her good eye. "Most of the isle. There is little it does not cover."

"We still do not know how reliable these charts are," Havar said, thoughtfully. "Even if they are perfect, I worry that, in the years since they were made, the sea may have changed."

Karik nodded. "That is why it is a challenge."

Wisic upended his cup into his mouth and glared into it. "Karik, all your challenges seem to end with us staring death in the face. I'm not sure I like that."

"Little comes to those who do not dare," Karik said, and from the other side of the fire Revik nodded. Ylmi lifted an eyebrow when she saw it; Revik seemed more in favour of Karik since the dragon.

"Hegli stands apart from both King Viglir and King Jarhost," Ylmi explained. "He trusts the Undmir to protect him from both kings, and he will be reluctant to pursue us for a tiny amount of his gold, lest he provoke war with Jarhost. We will take only a small bit of gold; the loss to him will be minimal."

"These charts aside," Thora asked, "how are we going to get there? The Ice Sea is treacherous in the best of times, and I doubt any of our boats could sail it, even if they did round Vanik's Point."

Karik nodded; "You are right: none of the boats we have could make the journey." His eyes locked with Havar. "You said that you could build a boat without the gold, just not one big enough to cross the open waves. Can you build one that can sail the Ice Sea?"

Havar looked into the fire, and in the quiet Ylmi heard an owl calling from somewhere off in the forest, lower down the mountain.

"Perhaps," Havar said, at last, "but I will need help." He looked around the clearing, most of it now nearly invisible in the gathering dark of dusk. "There is some timber in the village for building a new boat, though Unhost will likely wonder why we are building one so large."

"We could tell him it's for fishing farther out, past the mountain," Thora suggested. "With the dragon gone, there's good fishing there which we should make use of anyway."

"It would work, and the fishing should not be ignored," Ylmi nodded. "Though, it will be important to keep the gold out of reach of Unhost when we return."

"Even so," Karik said with a nod, "it will all work together. We can each take time to lend Havar a hand in building the ship, and in a short time."

"Do you think that we will be enough to do it?" Thora asked, glancing around the circle. "Mighty as we all are, we are only seven. That is a small number to sail an impassable sea and rob from an impenetrable fortress."

"The plan relies on secrecy," Karik answered; "the more who know, the more likely that Jarl Hegli will learn of our coming. And, if we arrive and find his warriors arrayed against us, I do not think it will go well."

The fire cracked and popped, as overhead the stars began to appear. Ylmi glanced down at Ulfr, who had raised her head and was listening intently. Somewhere up in the mountains, a wolf was howling at the young moon.

"I am shocked," Wisic muttered after a moment: "Karik Haldsson finally finds odds he does not like."

A grin split Karik's face in the firelight. "The plan is to not find them, Wisic. If all goes as planned, we will be gone with a hull full of gold before Hegli even knows that we've been there."

"Karik," Thora spoke up, "do you really think we can sail the Undersea?" She paused as they all looked at her. "Even the fishermen on the northern coast stay away from its waters. I've heard that the currents there are as treacherous as anything in the Black Isles, and there are even whirlpools, which will suck a ship down to the bottom without a moment's notice."

"It is dangerous," Ylmi said, sitting forward, "and even if everything goes well, there may be dangers we do not anticipate. But, before long there will come another winter, as long and dark as the one which came two years ago. Our settlement will be a village by then, and we will be older – perhaps much older." She took a deep breath. "When that winter comes – when starvation comes knocking – I do not wish to watch my parents freeze to death and think: If only I had risked more to pass the Black Isles. Beyond those dark rocks lies our only hope, and the Undersea lies between us and attempting that passage. It is what we must do."

"I'll go with you," Revik said. "Even if you don't like the odds of Hegli's guard, I'll wager my ax can buy us a little time. And, if you run into a storm in the Ice Sea..." he stretched his long arms over his head before folding them back down, "...you'll need someone with some strength to pull you from its frozen waters."

"I appreciate your words," Karik grinned again, but Thora snorted.

"Do you think you can solve every problem with your ax?" she said, looking sideways at Revik.

He shrugged. "Most of them."

As the fire burned low, they rose, one by one, to rest in the shelter of Karik's rough hut.

When Revik unfolded his massive bulk and stood, Ylmi rose as well, and followed him away from the fire, before pulling him aside.

"Revik, I have a question to ask you," she said, quietly. "When we first met, you had little good to say about Karik; you seemed to argue with everything that he said. But now, you defer to him and agree with what he says."

Revik nodded. "This is true," he admitted. "What is your question?"

"Why? Why the change?"

Revik thought for a moment, then glanced back toward the fire, where Karik was talking earnestly with Igil.

"My brother has always loved him, though I did not agree with his decisions," Revik answered. "I do not think I will live overly long in Vrania – it is a harsh place, full of ways to die – and I do not wish to disappear or be forgotten." He grinned. "Karik bade me trust him, and now I am Revik Dragonslayer; I will not be forgotten for a long, long time."

Ylmi looked at him in surprise. "You are very open," she said, "though you and I are not the closest of friends."

Revik grinned at that and raised his hand, marked with the scars of dragon-fire. "We are the burned ones; brother and sister through fire. And now it seems we will attempt yet another legendary feat." His grin widened. "If we are successful in this, there will be few who will forget us, Ylmi, for we are doing things no one thought possible."

They slept that night in Karik's home, cramped together on the packed dirt floor, wrapped in the few furs which Karik had not traded away for tools. Ylmi fell asleep with Ulfr curled up against her, and slept warm and deeply through the night.

In the morning, they went their separate ways.

Igil and Havar returned to the settlement to plan the construction of their boat, while Revik, Karik and Wisic began felling trees and shaping planks, which could be used for the ship's construction.

Ylmi returned to her hunting, and Thora asked if she would care for company. "I have my spear, and if we find anything larger than a rabbit, perhaps you will be glad to have me along."

Ylmi agreed, and the two set off into the mountains, seeking the trails which the great bears often make, as they emerge from hibernation and seek out food.

"This Karik," Thora said, when they had gone a little way, "he is full of great plans."

Ylmi ducked under the low branches of an old pine. "So far, that does seem to be the truth."

They walked a little farther, then Thora spoke again: "The slaying of the dragon was a great deed, and one that I am glad was done, despite the scars we all bear. But, how much more does Karik think is necessary?"

Ylmi slowed and looked back at her. Here in the trees, the wind was less noticeable, but she could still hear it in the tops of the pines, high overhead. "What do you mean?"

"When the dragon died, it meant we were safe." Thora leant against her spear and looked around. "It meant half of our herds weren't taken by the dragon, as payment to keep him from eating us; we are safer and we have more food. If we sail the Undersea, what will that do for us? Will the gold allow us to buy more food from the traders who never come? I think it more likely that the opposite will be true. Gold breeds greed," she said, with a shake of her head.

Ylmi nodded as she listened. "I hear what you have said, and if matters had gone differently when we returned from the dragon, I might still agree with you." She took a deep breath, feeling the weight of the stones in their pouch, hanging from her neck. "Whatever extra we have now, Unhost will take. And, whatever extra we have beyond that, Jarhost will take. The dragon may be dead, but we are not safer; when Jarhost's taxmen come in the harvest, do you think they will be more generous than the dragon?" She laughed: "Even the dragon allowed Unhost to keep a handful of gold, but the king took every speck of dust that had a shine to it. Mark my words, Thora, Jarhost will bleed us drier than the dragon ever did."

"Then, perhaps the dragon was best left alive," Thora muttered.

Ylmi turned on her, fighting down the urge to strike her. "Never speak those words again." Her eyes narrowed, and for a moment Thora's jaw worked, as the two glared at each other beneath the trees.

At last, Thora looked down the mountains. "I spoke wrongly, and for that I apologize."

Ylmi nodded and laid a hand on Ulfr, who had sensed the tension, and come to stand pressed against her leg. "Because a second robber follows the first, it does not mean the first should have been left."

Thora chuckled at that. "You think Jarhost the same as the dragon?"

Ylmi shrugged. "I will not speak those words today. But Vrania is a harsh place, with hunger and cold reaching every hut and hamlet from the Undmir to Tharstadt. I have survived several winters in the mountains with my parents, and each time we have heard the sound of Dunharvic's footsteps, hard upon us. It will not get better, until we escape the prison that was built to hold Vranr."

"I wonder often how much of those stories is true," Thora said; "I think them truer with every passing day."

They returned to the trails, and Ylmi's mind turned to what would happen if they found a passage. The vision of her parents sitting by a warm fire in their old age passed before her eyes and she pressed on, clenching her jaw as she thought of the hunger they had endured for the last several years.

Thora said little else as they hunted, but as the sun descended, she thanked Ylmi for letting her hunt with her, adding that it was a thing they should do more often. Then, she started down the mountain.

She paused and turned back to Ylmi. "You will sail with him?"

Ylmi nodded, simply.

Thora toyed with the haft of her spear for a moment, then nodded: "If you go, then so will I. And, if we are successful, perhaps it will mean less power for Unhost." Then, with those words spoken, she shouldered her speak and set off down the mountain, disappearing swiftly through the trees.

Ylmi thought on what she had said, as she made her way back home. So engrossed in her thoughts was she that Ulfr's unease, as they approached the clearing, went unnoticed.

She stepped out of the woods...

...and found Unhost waiting there, with her father.

Bodvar was splitting wood, a little more menacingly than usual, while Unhost sat nearby on a rock, picking his fingernails with a small knife.

"Ah, the mighty huntress returns!" Unhost exclaimed when he saw her. "I trust your hunting was productive?"

"It was not," Ylmi said, as she unstrung her bow. "Though now I know why."

Unhost's face reddened at the insult, but he swallowed his anger and instead put on a smile, as he stood up. "I was hoping to speak to you and your father about—"

"You may keep hoping," Ylmi answered, and made for the house.

"It is time you were married," Unhost continued, "and I believe we have found one who will be of benefit to us all."

Ylmi stopped in her tracks, and Ulfr padded onward for a few steps, before turning back to look at her.

She heard Unhost step forward. "Your renown as one of the dragonslayers has already spread beyond our little village," Unhost spoke quickly, "as have rumours of your beauty."

Ylmi's grip on her bow tightened and she turned. Bodvar had stopped chopping wood and was glaring at Unhost.

"This is what you came here to talk about?" her father growled. "You wanted to..."

Unhost's face suddenly went white. "I only thought that the girl should hear what I have to say, as well." He was positively sprinting through his words now. "I knew that, as a father, you would be reluctant, but she should have a choice."

"Excellent." Ylmi fixed him with her good eye and smiled. "My choice is no. Now go, before I weary of restraining Ulfr."

Unhost's eyes went to the big wolf at Ylmi's side, and his white face turned green. "But, it is the son of a great warrior..."

Ylmi widened her eye. "I don't care."

"The Jarl of Mirhom has offered to marry you to the son of one of his warriors," Unhost spat out. "Will you just consider it? It would do much good for our settlement... for your parents..."

"If you do not leave now," Bodvar said, quietly, "I will not raise a finger when her wolf rips out your throat." There was a tremor in the ax he was holding, and Ylmi realized he was shaking with rage.

Unhost took one more look at both of them, then bolted down the path.

"Good riddance to bad rubbish," Ylmi muttered.

But her father sighed and shook his head. "As long as he is the village jarl, we can only push him so far, and I fear we may approach that point." A long breath escaped him. "But, gods, I want to open his head with this ax!"

Ylmi giggled, more than a little nervous energy seeping through her from the encounter. "I am glad to know that we both think the same."

Her father laughed. Stepping over the pile of chopped wood, he gathered her into his arms and pulled her close, whispering in his deep voice: "I am so proud of you, dragonslayer."

She giggled again and pushed him away. "Please tell me that you will not start calling me that, too?"

"No chance," her father smiled.

Laughing, she returned her spear to the house, and thought no more of Unhost that day.

KALBORG

It was not many days later that Ylmi made her way down to the village, carrying a pack of hides and meat, which she took to Olga's small hut. The old woman was sitting outside in the sun, watching her garden as she worked a deer hide back and forth, curing it into leather.

"Ylmi Dragonslayer," she said, when she saw Ylmi, "you are a welcome sight for these old eyes. It has been a while since you graced my door. I am glad to see that you survived both the dragon and the winter."

"I am glad as well," Ylmi said, and felt the burnt skin tighten over her face as she grinned. "I have brought you a little food, and work as well." She set down her pack and produced the hides she had brought, and a long cut of a deer.

"I have nothing with which to barter at the moment." Olga pointed toward her garden with her wooden stick: "The peas have just been planted, and little else is ready to be harvested."

"Then, take the meat as a gift," Ylmi smiled, "and work the hides for me. I will ask for peas when I have need."

"You are a kind girl," Olga nodded.

But, Ylmi's eyes were suddenly drawn past her. Unhost was walking through the village, and Orli walked behind him, carrying a longspear. He stopped to talk with Fornik, who was tending his own garden, and Olga saw where Ylmi's eyes had gone.

"Yes, our fearless jarl," she muttered. "Someone has annoyed him, so now he goes about with a bodyguard."

"Has Orli nothing better to do?" Ylmi asked. "Are all the nets mended? All the boats cleaned?"

"Orli is one who Unhost favours," Olga answered, as though it was obvious, "so he does as Unhost commands. But, those who Unhost favours grow few."

Ylmi turned to look back at her. "What do you mean?"

"A good jarl provides for their people." Olga folded the deer hide and began to work it again. "A good jarl protects their people and leads their people. Unhost provides for fewer than he used to, and I think Bogli, and the families of several others, would have more than a little to say about the protection he provides. As for his leadership...." she shrugged, "...that is a hard thing, but a fool makes it harder."

"Then, perhaps the village should choose a new jarl," Ylmi muttered. She was surprised when Olga nodded.

"Perhaps they should."

"Who?" Ylmi asked. "Fornik or Orli would be little better, and though Torig and Almir are old, they seem to have little interest in the rest of the village." She glanced past the old shed to where Torig sat, bent over a net as he worked.

"Even so," Olga smiled, "even so. But, there are others who might do a great deal... like yourself."

Ylmi's eyes snapped to the old woman, who smiled at her, then turned back to her work. "I am very young..."

"And a dragonslayer," Olga nodded. "There are not many who can say that, and it is no small thing. It is also very heroic. People like to follow heroes."

She smiled to herself again, then looked back at Ylmi. "Will you stand there all day, bothering an old woman? Go! I am sure you have work to do," she chuckled.

Ylmi gave her a smile before leaving, but in her mind she was considering what Olga had said.

She visited Havar and Igil, hard at work on the ship, but she hardly heard what they told her. Would she make a better jarl than Unhost?

As she climbed back up the mountain, she took the stones from their pouch and ran her fingers over them. The white stone was easy; the red stone was simple... would the gods smile on her challenging Unhost to a duel? She didn't doubt she could best him, but wouldn't that be the simplest choice?

A cool wind was blowing out of the north, rustling the boughs of the pine trees as it passed southward, and Ylmi stopped.

She raised her hand, examining the stones. To do nothing was the white stone; to kill Unhost now was the red. Surely this was the situation Skathi had considered, when she gave her the stones. So, what was the green stone?

She considered them a moment longer, the wind pulling at her hair, 'til she tucked it behind her ear.

The green stone...

She sighed and thrust the stones back into her pouch. It had seemed simple when Skathi explained it to her, but it seemed less so now.

As spring gradually crept in, the settlement set to work, hunting, fishing and laying in crops. Ylmi and the others did their share and more, and took it in turns to help Igil and Havar.

Slowly, their boat took shape. Twice as long as the other fishing boats, Havar built it just as narrow and with a wide keel, which would let it skim over the waves.

As Karik had warned, Unhost quickly took an interest in the boat, and though Havar told him it was only for fishing in the deeper waters, the jarl took to stopping by every day to see its progress, Flovi and Orli following him each time he did so.

Torig would also visit from time to time, running his crooked fingers over the planks and making suggestions. Havar grated at these attempts, but Igil learned a great deal from Torig, and promised that they would fish together when the boat-building was done.

So matters continued, as winter gave way to spring, and the heavy snowstorms gave way to thunder and rain.

Ylmi spoke to none of her conversation with Olga, but she made more trips to the village than before. To Bogli she brought fresh meat, and wood for a new crutch, and to Ymr and Ethna she brought bones whenever she could spare them. To Nanni she brought rabbits and furs, with which she could warm her children. Her eldest was now six years of age, and Ylmi taught him how to use a bow, and fished with him in the river which ran out to the fjord.

There were few in the village that Ylmi did not help in some way, even more than she had before, and they did not forget it.

Spring was drawing to a close as their ship took shape, even as did Karik's small homestead upon the mountain. In the clearing about his small house, he burned out several stumps and cleared space for planting. With seeds he got from Olga, he laid a small garden of peas, onions and other vegetables, and watered them from the mountain stream.

"It is not a great deal," he told Ylmi, when she stopped by the clearing one day, "but it is a start, and perhaps I will have the chance to lay in more, as the year goes on."

"You have been very busy," Ylmi nodded, "but the ship is not yet ready..."

"Igil and I will return to Yrdnara," Karik said. "I do not think they will allow us to stay long, but we should tell Umir's mother that he is dead, and the others in the village will be glad to know that a few of us are still alive."

"Wisic will not go?"

Karik grimaced. "Wisic and his father are... not fond of each other." A wind was blowing out of the north again, and Ylmi could hear it howling over the craggy cliffs above them, even as the stream a little way off filled the air with its rushing and crashing, as it made its way down toward the fjord.

"Do not tarry too long," she said, after a moment; "you will be missed here."

"I will not." He turned to look at her, and there was a warm light in his eyes. "I will miss this place, too."

———◦———

It was nine days later, at the end of a long day of hunting, when Ulfr's ears pricked up as they approached their home. Ylmi saw that Siggi's tools were lying by the garden, and there was more than a little smoke rising from the chimney. Telling Ulfr to wait, she hurried inside with a smile, to find Karik and a sturdily-built woman talking with her mother.

"Mother, this is Ylmi, of whom I told you," Karik said quickly, looking from the woman beside him to Ylmi.

The older woman looked her over, and Ylmi was suddenly very conscious of the tightness of the scar over the side of her face, and the blood on her hands from her hunt.

"I have heard many good things of you," Karik's mother said slowly, her eyes taking in everything about Ylmi's appearance; "many good things. I am glad my son has friends such as you."

"He has proven himself a good friend as well," Ylmi said, grasping for what words would be appropriate. "I take it you have come to live with your son?"

"Even so," she answered. "Karik tells me there is a small hut in the forest, and a garden which could use the touch of an experienced gardener."

They left soon after, and Ylmi thought it strange that Karik's mother had come to live with him, but he had made no mention of his father or brother.

That night, she followed the path through the trees, which led to the clearing where Karik had built his home. But she did not go to the house, instead turning to climb the small rise which overlooked the mountain stream nearby.

She was not surprised to find Karik there, sitting in the gloom cast by a pine tree in the moonlight. She said nothing as she approached, but when she was close, she kicked a small rock down toward the stream. Karik glanced over his shoulder but said nothing. The clearing he had made was considerable, and Ylmi could see it from where they stood. His hut gave off a warm glow from underneath the door, and she guessed that his mother was there still. The stream rushed down from the mountain, its gurgling and splashing filling her ears as she waited.

"It is only your mother that comes with you?" she asked, slowly. He nodded silently.

The water rushed on, splashing over the rocks, and over the sound of the rushing water, Ylmi could hear the wind brushing the tops of the trees. Farther down the mountain, an owl hooted.

"My father broke his arm on the ice." Karik's voice was slow and broken, but he took a deep breath and wiped something from his face. "My brother went hunting after the snows came, as we often did together, but never came back. They found his bones in the spring, buried in a snowdrift, both legs broken." Karik took a deep breath and shrugged.

"My father's arm became infected, and they had to cut it off. He did not recover."

Ylmi waited, as the water rushed by. Karik was silent. "I am sorry," was all she could think to say, though it felt useless.

"Yrdnara is in a bad way," Karik's hand went to his face again, and Ylmi looked away, "as are many of the other settlements. Today it is my father, next year it might be me who breaks an arm and cannot hunt."

He hurled a rock into the stream. "If we cannot find a way past the Black Isles, then it is a matter of when, not if..." He stared into the gloom, where the water was rushing loudly over the rocks.

"I left because I thought it would help, but if I had been there—"

"If you had been there, you all would have had to hunt more," Ylmi interrupted him, sharply, "and the dragon would yet live... eating our food and depleting our herd."

Karik said nothing for a moment, then tossed another rock toward the stream. "Tira did not take word of Umir's death well." He took another deep breath, but it seemed to catch in his throat for a moment. "When she saw me and Igil, she smiled... until we spoke."

Ylmi took a step forward and sat down beside him. She was unsure of what to say, though she remembered how it had felt when Lanvir was gone... when the pain was still fresh.

"Death lies heavy on Vrania," Karik said, after a moment, and a bitter edge crept into his voice. "It seems that any choice I make leaves those close to me dead." He was silent for a moment, and she knew that he was thinking of the dragon's curse.

"We can only go forward," Ylmi said, quietly, "or the dead are for nothing."

"We must get off this island," Karik muttered, "or we will die like starving wolves, all gnawing at each other, until the cold takes us."

"The boat is near complete," Ylmi answered. "We will gain the gold we need and pass the Black Isles."

She stood. "The time for half measures is passed, Karik. We are the dragonslayers, and it is for us to escape this isle – this prison of Vranr. Together we have slain a dragon, and together we will force a way through the Black Isles. You and me, Karik... together we will end the misery that besets us."

She saw Karik's eyes gleam in the moonlight, and a weak smile crossed his face. "I thank you for that, Ylmi Bodvarsdottir."

"You are not the only one who has parents," she said, grimly. "The boat is almost done, and soon it will be time to sail. You should rest while you can."

He nodded silently, but his gaze went back to the stream rushing by. "I will be here but a moment longer. It is difficult to say goodbye when they are already gone."

Ylmi nodded. "I know."

⬦

The most difficult portion of the boat was the sail, for such a large piece of wool sheet was neither cheap nor easy to find. At length, Igil was forced to trade all the copper rings they had received from Jarhost, along with several furs, for two square sails, which they sewed together. The thick material was difficult to work, and they all had bloody fingers by the time it was done.

But, at last, the boat was floated into the water, and Havar named her Kalborg. She bobbed and danced on the waves, as she sat empty on the incoming tide.

Unhost clapped his hands with glee when he saw her. "You have outdone yourself this time, Havar! Tomorrow, let us take her out for a test."

The following morning, with Unhost on board, Igil and Havar sailed her around the mountain where the dragon had dwelt.

When they had finished, they sent Wisic into the mountains, to bring word to Ylmi and Karik.

"Igil says she sails as smooth as could be asked," Wisic told them, "and steady enough to take the waves just off the coast."

"As long as we avoid storms," Ylmi said grimly, and Karik nodded.

He glanced over the small field of his farm and then looked back to Ylmi. "Is there anything that needs to be done before we sail?"

Ylmi shook her head; "I am ready when you are."

Three nights later, they gathered under the cover of darkness and made ready to sail.

Karik was the first to meet with Igil and Havar, who were making final preparations on Kalborg, and setting in six days of provisions, for they guessed that the trip would not be a short one.

Ylmi and Thora arrived next, their faces grim in the moonlight. They greeted Karik, laid their weapons in the boat and sat by the fire, to wait for the tide.

Wisic arrived next, his boar spear hung over his shoulder. "I will not lie to you, Karik," he said, slowly, "I have many misgivings about this undertaking, but I will trust you."

As she sat by the fire, thinking on Wisic's words, Ylmi kept an eye toward the mountain path which led down from the hills, until she saw a familiar shape approaching out of the gloom.

"Dranri?" Karik rose to greet him in an embrace. "What brings you so far from your mountains this night?"

"Well..." Dranri shrugged, "Ylmi promised me a dangerous voyage, and stealing from Jarl Hegli." He smiled at Ylmi through his beard. "It seemed too good an opportunity to pass up."

"It would be good to have a..." Ylmi paused for a moment, "...more seasoned mind on our journey."

Dranri chuckled and nodded. "I have missed the sea, and I have little love for Hegli."

Karik patted him on the arm. "I am glad to have you with us."

"As am I," Ylmi said. "Thank you for coming."

Behind them, Revik came striding down from the hut he shared with Almir Alsson.

"The old man will not stop telling stories," he grumbled. "Are we ready?"

"Almost." Havar's low voice carried over the beach. "The tide is almost ready to go out; we will ride with it as it goes."

So they waited on the sand. The wind was blowing out of the east, its moaning the only sound, other than the waves lapping at the beach. Gradually the waves slowed, coming at almost the same place for a moment. Then they all watched as the next wave came in, a little lower, then the next, then the next... The tide had turned.

"It's time." Karik stood. "Wisic, give me a hand with the boat."

With all their gear stowed in the boat, they pushed it to the edge of the water, and one by one they climbed in, while Karik and Wisic held it steady. Setting their shoulders against the planks, they eased Kalborg into the water, and she floated easily on the waves. Karik and Wisic pulled themselves onboard, and with Havar at the rudder, the rest of them began to row out into the fjord.

They did not go far before the wind caught their sail, and Kalborg skimmed easily over the waves. She was faster than any fishing ship Ylmi had been on, and their speed took her breath away, as the ship rose and fell over the waves, shooting spray up over the prow when it came down.

"It is as if the gods will us forward," Karik said to Ylmi, as they stowed their oars. "It is a good beginning."

But Ylmi thought that the wind just as often drove ships onto rocks, as it did to their destination.

The night was cool, but they were all too excited to sleep. Instead, they watched the fjord pass by in the moonlight, and spoke in quiet tones about one thing or another.

Thora alone sat silent, watching the cliffs slide past, and Ylmi wondered if she was regretting her decision to join them.

They sailed around the great mountain, and Dranri looked up in wonder when Ylmi pointed out the dragon bones, which could be seen gleaming white in the moonlight. "I knew you were a talented huntress when I met you, several years ago," he told her, "but I did not think that I had met a dragonslayer."

He looked again at the great bones, rising pale against the dark stone of the mountain. "Wyrd favoured you all on that night, and you seized your opportunity. Perhaps the fate of our isle is changing."

"Wyrd did not favour Umir," Karik said from the rudder, "for all it smiled upon the rest of us... as we laid on death's door all winter."

"You came alive from battling a dragon." Dranri shook his head. "Do not wish for too much."

Thora barked a laugh from where she sat by the prow. "Fate is a grindstone, slowly pressing us all into dust. I will not dance for joy because there was a space between its weight. The death of the dragon has led us to this voyage, which seems an ill thing enough. And there is yet another, worse voyage waiting if we are successful here."

From the rowing bench across from her, Wisic nodded. "I like you, Thora; you are very straightforward. No honeyed words from this one; no sweetening of the truth," he nodded again, "just a good, heavy reminder of the truly terrible situation in which we find ourselves."

Thora glared at him, and even Karik had the sense to leave the conversation where it was.

Dawn found them nearing the mouth of the fjord, where the waves and wind grew stronger and more unpredictable.

"Everyone to the oars," Igil commanded from the stern, where he was taking his turn on the rudder. "There is a current which may try to pull us into the Black Isles."

He did not have to say it twice; a moment later they were all at their oars, save for Havar, who manned the ropes holding the sail. The land slipped by them, rising in giant cliffs and headlands as it met the open sea. Ylmi stared up at the cliffs in wonder and watched as, with a great gust of wind, they fell behind her, and Kalborg was thrust into the open sea.

Only on the Watching Stones had Ylmi ever felt such a wind; it came howling from every direction, filling the sail one moment and leaving it flapping uselessly the next. The ship lurched beneath her, and she understood suddenly what old sailors meant when they spoke of being in the grip of the sea. She was a speck to it, and the waves cared nothing for her, nor for their tiny boat.

"Oars out," Igil called, "and row!" He leant on the rudder and the ship shuddered, as it turned northward. Ylmi felt the pull of the current in her oar, and struggled to keep it in rhythm, as Havar called out the beats. They rowed steadily, but for a few moments they did not seem to move. Her arms began to grow tired and her hand sore, as she pulled at the oak oar.

There was a spot on the handle which had not been fully smoothed out, and it soon became very noticeable. She just closed her eyes and pulled.

Her shoulders were aching when she felt the change: her oar slid through the water with less resistance, and Kalborg felt as though it was under less strain. Glancing over the side, she saw the fjord's mouth falling away behind them, and the wind was growing steady again.

"The sea does not like people sailing out of the fjords!" Dranri laughed over the wind, and Ylmi grinned.

Karik's voice cut back: "The sea will have to learn to like it."

"Oars in!" Igil called out. "But be ready, in case there is need for them again."

Ylmi laid her oar in the boat, but made sure it was on top of their provisions. "You think that can become a regular passage?"

"It will need to be if we are to pass the Isles," Karik said with a shrug. He glanced back at Igil; "The passage did not test you too much?"

Igil shook his head, and glanced back at where the fjord was disappearing behind them. "Once we have done it a time or two more, it may become easy enough."

Dranri glanced up at them both. His long hair and beard were whipped all about by the sea wind, and Ylmi thought he seemed even wilder than he did in the forests. "You made it in a clear sky without a storm oncoming," the old man said. "When the seas are rough and a storm lingers, then see if the passage may become easy."

"No sailing is ever easy in a storm," Havar countered. He had looped the ropes from the sail in place, and now leant against the stern, next to Igil. "But, a good sailor may make passage where a lesser one fears to attempt it."

Or die upon the rocks, Ylmi thought.

"Far different from our fishing boats," Thora muttered, next to her. Ylmi nodded, her eyes following the birds swooping and diving over the cliffs. Thora glanced westward and Ylmi turned to see her shake her head.

"If it is so difficult simply sailing here," Thora's voice was quiet, "I am more concerned than ever about sailing the Black Isles – it is no wonder that so many have died upon them. Dranri speaks of wyrd, but I begin to think wyrd may bind us here, as it has bound those who came before us. Wyrd or something else."

The waves splashed against the boat, as Ylmi thought of Vranr's stones, and her mother's tales of the Watcher.

"They did not have the charts," she said, after a moment.

Thora grunted; "Yes, the charts." Her eyes went back to the turbulent water around them. "If they are accurate."

In the distance, thunder rumbled, and Ylmi thought she saw a flash of light in the north, as if lightning had passed through the clouds. But, nothing followed, and she turned back to her oar.

THE ICE SEA

They followed the coastline northward, keeping close enough to the shore that they could take shelter if needed, but not so close as to be in danger of the waves.

As the sun rose overhead, there was little to do but watch the land go by, and weariness settled over them. The excitement of the ship faded behind weariness from a sleepless night and the hard labour of rowing. The sun's light was warm, and Ylmi dozed as she leant against the side of their ship.

She found her dreams going back to her mother's stories of Vranr, and his attempts to escape the island. In her dream, she saw Vranr – a dark shape in the gloom – guiding a small ship through the waves, beneath a sky full of black clouds. The wind pulled at his cloak and hair, so they streamed out behind him as his ship rolled on the waves.

Go back, came a whispered voice, go back.

No, Vranr snarled in answer, no.

A chill passed over her and Ylmi sat up suddenly. The sun was now overhead, she had slept for several hours, but the cold of the dream did not dissipate, and she pushed herself upright to pull her cloak tighter.

There was a quiet thump outside the ship, and Ylmi snapped her gaze over the side. A small piece of ice was slowly spinning away from where it had bumped into the boat.

Ylmi looked out over the water and her jaw tightened. The water no longer looked the clear blue that it had in the fjord, or even when they had first reached the sea. It was black, and spotting it far into the horizon were bits of white ice.

"Nothing too big, so far," Karik said.

Ylmi glanced behind her. He was sitting up on the low rowing bench, looking out at the sea. The wind was pulling his hair back from his face, and the fur of his cloak was flapping about in the wind.

"You think it will get better?" Igil asked. On the opposite side of the boat, Thora was asleep, and behind him Revik and Dranri were snoring.

Ylmi shrugged in answer; "Ice this far south could mean that the ice around Vanik's Point is broken up, and we are seeing the pieces coming south." She spat over the side. "Or... we may have come too early in the year, and the ice floe is still packed, which means we are seeing the beginnings of an ice pack which will make sailing very dangerous."

"How dangerous?" Igil asked, sharply.

Again, Karik shrugged; "It depends on the ice."

Karik took a turn on the rudder next, and Igil lay down to sleep, but not before they both agreed that the ice was getting thicker.

Ylmi felt a sick feeling nestling in her stomach, and she wondered what it would feel like to slip into the black water. She shivered again and decided she did not want to know.

She gnawed on a piece of dried meat and some goat cheese, and watched the sea. But her eyes no longer watched the shore pass by. Instead, she watched the ice, comparing each piece as it floated past. She dozed a few more times, waking once to see that Thora was watching the ice as well. Her face was drawn, and there was a tic in her jaw, as if she had bitten into something bitter. But, she only nodded at Ylmi, before looking back to the ice.

The sun was falling low in the sky when Karik said they should look for a good place to spend the night. The ice was thickening and Ylmi was beginning to grow concerned. They found a tiny inlet, barely big enough for their ship, and Karik leant against the tiller, pointing the prow landward, 'til they ran up on the shoreline.

The forest grew down almost to the waterline, but the trees were small and bent, punished year-long by harsh, northern winds, which came howling across the freezing cold of the Ice Sea.

While the others gathered wood for a fire, Karik took up his spear. "I am going to go along the coast and see if the ice gets any better farther up."

Dranri nodded as he bent over the kindling, but Ylmi caught up her bow. "I will come as well. Perhaps there will be something worth eating."

Karik nodded and the two began hiking up the rocky shore. The wind was screaming in their ears, whistling over the rocks and waves, now blowing hard out of the north, and Ylmi wondered how many had sailed this way before. They hiked through the small trees and upward as the shoreline rose, and before too long they found themselves atop a cliff, looking down at the sea far below.

"Well," Karik said with a sigh, "that is unfortunate."

Below them, the ice moved sluggishly, packed tightly together, and farther off in the distance it merged together.

"We cannot sail it," Ylmi said, quietly.

Karik stared at it, his jaw clenching as he looked. After a moment he agreed: "We cannot."

After they returned, they all ate around a small fire of driftwood, silent at first, as each of them thought on what Karik and Ylmi had discovered.

When he had eaten, Dranri set aside his bowl and spoke: "It is no foolish thing to turn back when the way is blocked. Though we have not been successful, we have sailed farther than anyone I am aware of. We have shown that this boat is capable of handling the seas as well as we could have hoped."

"As you were not with us in our first endeavour," Revik said, calmly, "I do not see why you should tell us what to do now."

"Because I invited him," Ylmi replied, "and because I value his wisdom."

Revik only shrugged, but Havar grumbled at that, glaring at his bowl as he did so.

"Could we wait here for a time?" Thora suggested. "The ice may clear any day, and I would hate to turn back now, only to have the way open up as soon as we have determined the matter hopeless."

"I do not think so," Ylmi said, but then she shrugged. "I may be wrong, but I do not think the ice will break in the next couple of days. And, the longer we wait here, the more noticeable our absence will be; Unhost will quickly find who is missing from the village, and matters will only grow more complicated from there."

Karik nodded. "We have not only to worry about Unhost; Jarl Hegli is friends with many exiles – hunters like Dranri. If they discover a boat lurking this far north, he may guess that we intend to raid his fishing villages. I do not wish to find Hegli's warships arrayed against us, once we round Vanik's Point."

"Then you think we should turn back?" Wisic asked.

For a moment, Karik hesitated, and to Ylmi it seemed that he was trying to find an answer he did not have. The fire crackled as they stared at him, the smoke dancing around them as it rose, the wind pulling it in a dozen directions at once. At last, Karik shook his head: "We cannot sail back tonight, so let us rest here. In the morning we will be rested, and we will see if things appear in a different light."

They all agreed to this and, as darkness was already falling, they lay together in the shelter of Kalborg, and wrapped themselves as warmly as they could against the wind.

But, as Ylmi prepared to settle in next to Thora, she saw Karik walking the beach. For a moment she watched him, then laid her blanket down, going to join him.

The cold wind had not grown less with nightfall, and the sound of the sea crashing upon the shore filled the air. In the east, she could see the stars beginning to appear over the trees, and she could make out the dark shape of the mountains to the southeast.

"You do not want to go back?" she said, when she had drawn close to Karik.

He turned to her. "No." The wind was pulling at their hair, and Ylmi pulled an errant strand behind her ear, so she could see.

"Is it your pride?" Ylmi asked him. She saw his crooked smile in the moonlight, as he tried to respond.

"I don't think so?" Karik struggled through the words. "There is definitely a part of me that doesn't ever want to fail. But, I think the other reasons I have are what guide me."

"What reasons?" Ylmi pulled her cloak tighter over her shoulders, as the wind picked up. It pulled at Karik's hair as he squinted northward.

"Unhost has little liking for any of us, and he is suspicious of us. If we return, all in the new boat that he is already suspicious about, I do not think that Havar and Igil will long be in possession of the boat."

"He will take it," Ylmi agreed. She knew that Unhost would relish the opportunity to show his authority over the dragonslayers, and remind everyone that he was still their jarl.

Karik nodded again. "But they are right: we cannot sail through the ice."

Both shivered as a blast of frozen wind struck them. It was blowing out of the northwest, sweeping southward over the ice floes, which were packed as far as they could see. Ylmi felt it pulling at her cloak, cutting through her clothes and scraping against her skin.

What was it the seer had promised her? "You will receive what you desire most, and when it is taken away you shall be given what you hope for." Whatever that meant, she did not think it meant submitting to Unhost.

"There is a way," she said, suddenly sure of it. "I do not know what it is, but there is one here. I do not think we should turn back." If the loss of several fingers had not stopped Vranr, then she did not think an ice floe would have, either. Her hand went to the small bag at her neck, feeling the three stones which hung there. Skathi's words echoed faintly in her mind, and she set her face against the wind. They would not turn back.

The rocks crunched behind them, and she turned to see Igil stumping toward them, leaning forward as he pushed against the wind.

"This looks like plotting," he said, when he reached them, "and I am very good at plotting. What have you discussed?"

Karik chuckled. "We cannot sail over the ice. If we wait, Hegli and Unhost are likely to learn of our purpose, and our journey will have been in vain. If we go back, Unhost may seize our boat, and we will not receive another opportunity like this."

Igil rubbed his hands together. "A delightful puzzle."

"They do not think so," Karik said, jerking his head toward where the rest of the company lay under the boat, Revik feeding small sticks onto the fire.

"It was not their plan," Igil shrugged, "and I do not think they will be overly upset to go back to their former lives."

He shook his head. "You two love the wind too much," he muttered, and went to crouch in the shelter of a large boulder, which lay on the beach.

Ylmi grinned at Karik. "The wind is pleasant."

Karik smiled back at her, but went to sit with Igil, and Ylmi followed.

"So," Igil picked up a handful of gravel and let it run through his fingers, "what is our plan?"

Ylmi closed her eyes, looking with her mind's eye at the chart Karik had showed her, of the northern edge of Vrania. "How far would you say it is from here to the other side of Vanik's Point?"

"A couple of miles," Karik shrugged. "It may—" He stopped, as he saw where her mind was going.

"How heavy is Kalborg?" Ylmi asked Igil.

"It needs almost two feet of water..." he looked back and forth between the two of them.

"Can we haul it?" Karik cut him off.

Igil stared at the two of them. "You want to..." he cleared his throat, "...you want to haul Kalborg across Vanik's Point?"

Karik smiled. "It's an idea."

"It's a shit idea," Igil responded. "Kalborg isn't light, and if it gets dropped, it could open holes in the calking. We'd have to walk home."

"What if we were careful?" Ylmi asked.

"'What if we were careful'?" Igil mocked, then glared at her. "It's a boat, Ylmi! You're carrying a boat! If they can even lift it it'll be minor miracle. It doesn't have any handles... It's not meant to be carried." He looked from Karik to Ylmi. "It. Is. A. Boat!"

"We will think on it tonight," Karik said, "and if we cannot find a way to make it work, then we'll see if anyone else has any bright ideas." He stood. "I am going to get some sleep."

Ylmi glanced out to the sea and watched the water washing up onto the shore, bits of ice riding the waves onto the beach. When she looked back, Igil was staring at her.

"The two of you terrify me," he said, after a moment. "He was ambitious before, but the two of you together...! I think the two of you will attempt anything."

Ylmi looked back to the sea. "A frozen death is coming for us all," she told him. "We can lie down and wait for it, or fight. Few odds are too high when compared to certain death."

Igil was silent for a moment, staring at her as though seeing her for the first time. At last, he spoke slowly: "I do not know what you and Karik saw upon the Watching Stones, and I am not sure that I want to." He paused for an instant, before saying: "I thought I knew my friend well, but now I see the two of you are closer than I knew, and you terrify me."

Tucking his hands back into his cloak, he stood and went back to the boat, and Ylmi could hear him muttering in the wind:

"Carry a boat... Nonsense."

—◆—

The next morning, Ylmi woke to the sound of rain on Kalborg's hull. It was a light rain, nothing fierce, but when she stuck her head out from under the ship's shelter, the cold of it made her wince and suck in a breath. The sun was rising somewhere behind the clouds in the east, and a dim, grey light was spreading over the beach.

Leaving her bow where the string would stay dry, she wrapped herself in her hooded cloak, took her long spear and stepped into the rain. The pine trees faded into the thick mist, and the land sloped gently upward, away from the beach. She stepped out, making her way under the rain-heavy branches, and began hiking east.

The slope was not difficult and the ground not too treacherous; she thought it might not be an overly difficult thing to move the boat over land.

For most of the morning she hiked, slowly making her way eastward, seeking the other side of Vanik's Point. Mostly, the land sloped gently upward, and though there were a few rocky points, she suspected it would not be difficult to manoeuvre a ship over. On the whole, the land did not seem too difficult.

She had hiked several miles when she reached a low ridge. It ran from the northwest, where she guessed it ended on Vanik's Point, to the southeast. Eastward, she could see the glittering waters of the Ice Sea; the land sloped down toward it. Ylmi guessed that if they had some way to lift Kalborg, the passage was at least possible.

She retraced her steps, and arrived back at their camp as the sun was nearing midday.

The others were gathered around the fire, arguing with Karik and Igil, and Ylmi guessed that Karik had just explained his plan.

"Do we know if the path is even possible to pass?" Havar was asking. "For all we know, there are cliffs and mountains between us and the other side."

"It is possible," Ylmi said, loudly. They stopped talking and turned to her, as she emerged from the pine trees. "The land slopes up to a ridge, then back down to the sea. It will be hard work carrying a boat, but it can be done."

Havar grimaced. "Have you ever carried a boat before?" he asked.

"I have not."

"Then," Havar said, with a frustrated smile, "how do you know that it is possible?"

"Because I have an imagination," Ylmi replied, "and I know what it means to carry heavy loads in the mountains. Those slopes," she pointed east, "are passable."

"If you say so," Havar grumbled, and Ylmi repressed the urge to stick him with her spear.

Wisic cleared his throat. "Not to be a glutton," he began, "but how long do you think it would take us to cross over?"

Karik looked to Ylmi, and she thought for a moment before answering. "If things go well, and the boat doesn't need much patching when we are done... I guess four, maybe five days."

Wisic grimaced. "Ah, we brought provisions for six days!" He counted on his fingers: "One day we've already eaten, plus five days hauling a boat," he looked around, as if to emphasize how ridiculous he still found the idea, "which sounds like very hungry work, and we're out of food before

Kalborg is back in the water, never mind before we get to our journey's destination. And we are still not counting the return journey."

"We can make the food last a little longer," Karik replied, "but we will have to tighten our belts."

"I saw some game trails on the ridge," Ylmi said; "Dranri and I can doubtless find a little game."

"Enough to feed us for twice our journey's intended length?" Revik asked. "I find that unlikely."

"Then you have never seen those two hunt," Thora muttered.

Ylmi rolled her eyes as she turned toward him. "I did not say that – only that we could add to our stores. Besides, we will not die of hunger in five days."

"It will be cold," Havar pointed out. "We will be hauling a boat, and after that we have to sail an underground sea, that no one has ever navigated successfully."

"Someone has," Karik said, simply. They turned to him and he shrugged: "Someone had to make the maps."

"My confidence in these maps slips every day," Havar grumbled.

Revik shook his head. "I am weary of listening to you all talk. Will we carry Kalborg or not?"

All eyes went to Karik.

"I say we carry it," he said, slowly. "But, if most of you wish to return," he took a deep breath, "I will not force you onward."

"I will," Ylmi said, quickly, and they turned on her in surprise. "I did not come this far to fail because there was hard work to be done."

"So, you will—" Havar opened his mouth, but Ylmi cut him off.

"Yes!" she snapped. "What happens when we return, and Unhost seizes the ship? I will not spend the rest of my life serving him."

"None of us have any love for Unhost," Thora snapped. "I do not see Fornik or Orli anywhere on this trip. But there is a difference between foolishness and boldness."

"Of that I am well aware," Ylmi said, "but we have slain a dragon, and done what many said was impossible. What we speak of now... it is merely hard work."

She set her jaw and fixed them with her one eye. "We will find a way off Vrania and through the Black Isles – that I know."

She thought of Skathi's words on the mountainside, and felt the stones cold against her skin as she spoke: "But it will demand sacrifice and boldness, such as few in Vrania have known. We must be as determined and cunning as Vranr himself, if we are to succeed. But it can be done."

"Nothing great is ever easy," Dranri said, slowly. "So, I will agree with you."

"I as well," Revik nodded. "That is four. Who else?"

Igil agreed, as did Thora. With a reluctant sigh, Havar joined them.

Wisic stared at Kalborg, lying on the beach, then back at the rest of them. "The boat looks heavy, and our provisions look light. But I will not hold you all back with grumbling." He narrowed his eyes at Karik; "But, if we get stranded up here and begin to starve, I'm going to suggest we eat you first."

Ylmi looked at him in horror, but Igil and Revik only laughed.

"Wisic," Karik said, with a smile, "you are far too fond of that threat, and one day I am worried you will not mean it in jest."

So, with little more talk, they began the task of hauling Kalborg over the land of Vanik's Point.

All the gear and ballast stones were taken out, and the canvas sail taken down and rolled up. Igil used the rope from the sails to fasten loops around the benches, and they thrust the oars through these so they could lift the weight of the ship onto their shoulders. Three on each side, they were able to move forward, slowly and carefully.

But, even so, the weight of the ship was considerable, and it was exhausting work, even though they took turns.

By nightfall, they had covered a little less than a mile, and every one of them was exhausted and sore.

"I thought we would cover more ground," Igil admitted to Ylmi, as she checked her arrows. The others were gathered around the fire. Wisic already dozing.

"It was the first day," Ylmi pointed out, "and we were still figuring out how best to carry the ship. And, we did not start until after midday. Tomorrow we will cover more ground."

Igil looked doubtfully at the others lying by the fire. "I am not so sure about that."

The Dark of the Undersea

The next morning, Ylmi and Dranri took their bows and set off, looking for any trace of game they might add to their stores.

"It is in my mind," Dranri said, as they stepped away from the boat and into the wind-tossed trees, "that the hunting here may be good, so far from anyone else."

But Ylmi spat southward, and the north wind carried it a long way before it hit the ground with a crack. "It is in my mind," she answered, "that it is too cold and windy here for much of anything to make a home."

Dranri chuckled at that, and Ylmi laughed as well, their breath rising in little clouds in the frigid air.

Ylmi rubbed her chin, nodding to his: "It keeps you warm?"

Dranri stroked the tangled hairs fondly. "Very."

They hunted for the better part of the day, the gnawing in their bellies driving them on. Twice they came across the remains of small hunting camps, where exiles and hunters had rested for a short time before moving on. Firewood was stacked beside stone rings, and in one a small bothy had been tucked between two trees.

"Unused for a week or more," Dranri guessed, when he peered into it. "Unlikely they will be back soon."

"There is no way to tell." Ylmi glanced around the woods. "We should be careful."

They came at last across the trail of several deer. They split up, looping around so that Dranri drove the herd toward Ylmi. When it was all over, they had a fine buck, and Ylmi acknowledged that the hunting was at least passable here.

"Your friend Karik is a very tenacious person," Dranri said as they cleaned the deer, and made ready to carry it back. "Risks and dangers do not seem to faze him as much as they do others."

Ylmi shrugged.

"He reminds me of someone else that I know," Dranri grinned at her.

"I do not know what you mean." Ylmi lifted the deer's stomach out of the carcass and gently set it to the side.

Dranri chuckled again. "How many times were you told not to go climbing for the Watching Stones?"

Ylmi rolled her eyes at him; "If the stories were true, then there was a way."

"Do you think they are?" Dranri asked. "True, I mean? You have not spoken of what you found there."

For a moment Ylmi paused, her hands warm with the deer's blood, and she thought on what she had seen at the Watching Stones, about the stories her mother had told her and the vision of Skathi, walking through the snow. She shrugged.

"Perhaps," she said slowly, "perhaps there is truth there, if one is willing to pick it out of the old stories. Perhaps one day we will know the full truth of how Vranr came to this isle. A mighty trickster he may have been, but I do not think he made sons for himself from three bear cubs, as I once heard. The Stones are there, and the climb to reach them is unlike any I have ever attempted. And the peak... it is..." She searched for the words. Dvengrhal was not a god, of that she was sure, nor had he been a ghost. But she was equally sure he was not a mortal man. "It is a strange place, perhaps best left alone. How much truth there is to the other stories, I do not know. I am sure they have been embellished many times over many fires, to make storytellers a better welcome or longer stay. Who can tell?"

Dranri nodded. "If you and your friend Karik continue this way, it may be that we will find out."

They retraced their steps, slower this time, as they carried the buck carcass with them. They found Kalborg farther up the slope, and Ylmi reckoned that they would crest the hill the next day, with ease.

Thora was the first to see them, and waved happily when she saw the deer. The boat had been set down, and Revik came down to help them with the deer, along with Igil and Havar.

"You moved far today," Ylmi noted, as they took the deer. "It went well?"

"Well enough," Revik shrugged, "though Karik might not think so."

Dranri laughed. "If you had moved it all the way in one day, Karik would wish it had been done in half."

Revik chuckled at that, but shook his head; "That is not what I meant, though it is true. No, our friend suffered a small injury."

"What happened?"

"The boat came down wrong when we set it down earlier," Havar said, "and caught his hand against a rock. It could have been worse; the only injury was to one of his fingers."

Ylmi left them to the boat and went up to where they had made a campsite, where she found Wisic and Karik sitting together by the fire. Karik was sitting against a tree, his skin white as ash, save for the burn marks on his neck, which now took on a brownish tinge.

"What happened?" Havar had made it sound as if it were not so bad, but she had not seen Karik look this weak, even from the dragon's poison.

He looked up when he heard her, and a weak grin came to his face. "They said the boat was rather light, but my finger disagrees."

"They set the boat on his little finger," Wisic said, curtly, "and crushed the bone."

He looked up at her. "Revik was going to have to do this, but he's gone and you're here," he pointed at her. "Put the bow down and get over here."

A knife blade lay on the fire's coals, Wisic's ax was out, and Ylmi decided that she did not like where this was going. "What are you doing?"

Wisic took a deep breath. "The bone is shattered – I can't set it – and his finger has been bleeding for almost an hour now. I am trying to make sure he neither bleeds out nor gets infected. Now, get over here and hold his shoulders. Karik, give me your hand and look at her."

Karik gave her an apologetic smile. "Is it better if I say I'll try to be still?"

She dropped her bow and stepped around the fire. Wordlessly, she gripped his shoulders, feeling the muscles tensing beneath her fingers, as she pressed him back against the tree.

He looked up into her eyes, and she saw his jaw clench and a shiver pass through him, as Wisic took his left hand and laid it on a log.

"Ylmi, I don't know how this is going to go," Karik babbled, the words tumbling over each other. "I just hope it doesn't—"

There was a thump as the ax blade sank into the tree, but Ylmi still heard the sickening crunch of it slicing through bone. Karik's eyes fluttered, rolling into the back of his head, but with an effort he pulled himself together.

"I imagined," he said, shakily, "that it would be worse."

But his eyes had been on Ylmi, and he had not noticed Wisic reach for the knife in the fire. There was a hiss and Karik yelled out, arching away from the tree with a curse and an oath. Ylmi shoved him back against the tree, until she saw that Wisic was done.

"By the nine realms, Wisic!" Karik snarled. "Tell me next time you're going to torture me and I'll tell you whatever you want to know!"

"Excellent," Igil chuckled, as he came up to the fire, holding several strips of meat: "you're still alive!"

"I hope you fall in the fire," Karik snarled. He slumped back against the tree and stared at his left hand, the little finger now ending in a red nub, just above his knuckle.

Dranri looked at it and shook his head. "Now, that is deeply unsettling."

"Oh, go jump in a glacier," Karik growled at him. But Ylmi saw that the colour was fading again from his face, and a moment later he leant his head back against the rough bark, the strength draining out of him.

She sat down next to him, careful to sit on his right side. "You did make good progress today."

Karik took a shaky breath and looked around, nodding. "We did. And you brought back meat."

"A buck."

Karik smiled weakly at that. "Should keep them quiet about food for a day or two." He looked at her beside him. "Do you think you'll be able to find more?"

She nodded.

"Here," Igil stopped before them and handed Karik a cup. "I should have thought of this earlier, but better late than never. It's some of the beer we brought."

Karik sniffed it and took a sip, before making a face.

"That bad?" Ylmi chuckled.

"It's weak and bitter." Karik stuck out his tongue. "But, I have lost a lot of blood." He lifted the cup again and swallowed it all in one gulp.

"Carrying the ship back will not be easy," Ylmi said, quietly. "Especially if we have gold."

Karik nodded slowly. "There's a chance the ice will open up while we are in the Undersea, but if not..." he burped and looked reproachfully at the cup, "we'll have to do this again. I do not look forward to it."

"Will you rest tomorrow?"

Karik shrugged. "It's my plan and our boat. As long as I stay on the left side and keep my hand protected, I should be fine." He closed his eyes and leant back on the log. "I very much hope that this voyage is successful."

It took three more days to get Kalborg to the water on the opposite side of Vanik's Point. Karik's hand swelled up, but no infection set in, and Wisic remained very proud of his medical skills. On the second day a storm swept in, and they navigated the eastern slope in a torrent of wind and biting rain, which soaked them to the skin.

When they reached the shoreline, it was already late in the day, so they built a fire and sheltered under Kalborg, drying themselves as best as they were able.

"That went as well as could be hoped," Dranri said, as they sheltered: "a little over four days, and with the hunting we are not overly short of food."

"You are all fortunate that I was here," Revik said, picking meat off one of the roasted deer bones. "I told you that my strength would be needed."

"Don't overstate your importance, brother," Igil chuckled; "it was Ylmi who had the idea to carry the boat."

Wisic looked up, his eyes narrowed in mock anger. "Yes, and do not think I have forgotten it."

"Things will be different if the ice does not clear," Havar muttered. "I do not look forward to hauling this boat up that ridge."

Ylmi agreed with him. Hunting had not taken all her time, and she had spent two days under the boat. It felt to her as if there was a permanent dent where the poles had rested on her shoulder.

The storm broke in the night, and the next morning they faced only a stiff west wind as they reset the mast in Kalborg's hull, rehung the sail and slipped into the water.

"Once again," Wisic said, as he sat down at his oar, "the boat carries me, and all is right with the world."

"Save my finger," Karik muttered.

Wisic looked at him, sideways. "All is right with my world; your finger is no longer my concern." He ducked as Karik whipped a piece of rope at him, and they all laughed, happy to at least be done with carrying the boat for a moment.

But, they were hardly in the water for more than a few minutes before Karik stood up from his bench and stepped back to the rudder. He muttered a few words to Igil and wiggled his maimed finger. Igil shrugged and moved forward, to take Karik's place on the oar.

The wind blew them along at a steady pace, the sail and ropes creaking and groaning as the wind pulled at them relentlessly. Northward, in the distance, they could see the ice cliffs and moving snow mountains, which marked the edges of the Ice Sea. More than once, Karik was forced to lean against the rudder and guide them around floating mounds of ice, slowly washing their way toward the ragged coast.

When darkness fell, they slid ashore on a rocky beach, pulling Kalborg out of reach of the incoming tide.

In the morning, they rose and slid their ship back into the sea. Ylmi noticed that they all had dark circles growing about their eyes, and the gaunt look of hunger was setting in. She found herself measuring their food over and over in her mind, wondering if a little extra here or there would leave them enough for the return journey, but she knew better. As hungry as she was now, it would be worse heading back.

As they made their way east, the coastline rose. Cliffs and dark rocks rose out of the sea, only occasionally sloping down again to meet the water. Where this happened, they saw signs of fishing villages and tiny settlements, sometimes only three or four buildings. At each of these Karik was careful to guide Kalborg out to sea, hoping to avoid being seen.

"We are getting close," he told them, as the sun reached its peak. He had not rowed since Vanik's Point, and Ylmi realized suddenly that it must be difficult to row with the wound on his hand so fresh. She glanced at it, and saw that the hand was not as red and swollen as it had been. Perhaps the cold was good for it.

It was late in the afternoon, and most were dozing as best they could in the cold wind, when Karik straightened at the rudder and grinned. "There it is!"

They had reached the Undersea.

Ahead of them, where the cliffs were at their highest, a vast cavern gaped open, like a maw in the sea. Jagged stone hung from the opening, and on either side the sea foamed around hidden rocks, as the current twisted and turned, some flowing in, some flowing out.

"Are we sure about this?" Thora asked, quietly.

But Karik only grinned. "Too late to turn back now." His eyes were fixed on the cavernous opening, and his cheeks were flushed. "Get to the oars. Havar, get the lantern."

He was excited, Ylmi realized, and suddenly she was, too. No one else had sailed the Undersea, and when they came out, they would be hearing the stories for years about the mysterious crew who had done the impossible, and sailed the unsailable sea. She gripped the oar in her hands, barely noticing the icy water which ran from its head down to her hand, when she dipped it in the water.

Kalborg shuddered as Karik turned it southward, directly toward the Undersea. The ship rolled gently with each wave, slipping sideways ever so slightly, as the wind and current continued to push it eastward.

When Karik gave the command, she slid her oar into the water and pulled. The current pulled back, pushing and pulling at the oar as she rowed. The water here was cunning, twisting and winding in on itself, unlike the calm, steady waters of the fjord. More than once her oar clattered against Igil's, behind her, but she was not the only one; the others struggled to control their oars, until Havar called out a slow, steady beat, allowing each one to wrestle with the current which gripped their oar, and bring their strokes into time with the rest.

She did not think she had been rowing for more than a few moments, when a shadow fell over the boat. She looked up to see the gaping mouth of the cavern wide before them, the sun blotted out by the towering cliffs, high above.

"No need to wait for morning," Havar chuckled; "no light where we're going, anyway."

A moment later, the sky was behind them, only stone above and darkness ahead.

Karik and Havar huddled around the lantern Havar held, their eyes glued to the map Karik had brought. At first, Karik guided the ship close to the rock on the right, following it when it turned to the right, then slipping into a much narrower passage, shortly thereafter.

Within the passage, the sunlight was gone, their only light coming from the tiny lamp which swung from Havar's hand, and a second that Igil quickly hung from the prow. The darkness was suffocating.

As the water calmed, Wisic suggested they take shifts on the oars.

Whether time passed quickly or slowly, Ylmi could not tell. There was only darkness, the occasional swirling of the water, where an oar dipped in, and Karik's hushed voice, as he watched the map with Havar. From time to time they heard tapping, or the sounds of mining, but where the sounds came from or where they went, Ylmi could not begin to tell. At times they were in narrow passages, the rocks close at hand reflecting the light back into the boat, but more often they were in great caverns, Karik guiding the boat along one side, as close to the rocky walls as he dared.

Once, the boat lurched as it slid out of a passage, a sudden current gripping it and shoving it sideways. Igil slammed into the rudder, leaning his whole body into keeping Kalborg on the right heading, even as the current tried to spin it in circles. As everyone jerked awake, there was a splash and a muffled shout, as Havar was pulled under the water.

A second splash followed the first, and Ylmi felt something sliding past her ankle as she turned. She jerked her feet back, but in the dim light saw it was only rope, being pulled quickly over the side.

"Everyone be still," Igil's voice snapped. "If you all go to one side, we'll tip over." The rope continued to slide overboard, and the sound of frantic splashing could be heard in the darkness. But, strain her eyes as she could, Ylmi saw nothing.

In the darkness, she felt fear settle next to her, one cold hand in her stomach, another on her neck. There were a dozen ways to die here, she realized. They could not see Karik to seek him, and if Igil did not know the way out...

She stopped and looked around, the light of the lanterns flickering around them, save for the passage they had just slipped out of. They were not moving quickly – the gentle rocking of the boat was sign enough of that. She fixed her eyes on the passage as the boat floated under her, and forced herself to breathe.

"Dranri," Igil's voice was tense, "draw in the rope."

She heard Dranri's grunts as he pulled on the rope, felt the boat shake as the slack was taken out, and Dranri pulled in whatever was on the other end of the rope. She blinked and the passage moved. She fixed it again with her eyes, and felt the boat being pulled away from the passage. The shine on the rocks dimmed, and she realized with a sinking feeling that it would soon be out of sight.

Overhead, she could see rocks hanging like teeth from the ceiling, and she felt about the bottom of the boat. On the other side, the splashing was getting louder, and Dranri was talking to whoever it was. She sighed as her fingers brushed the haft of her longspear, and she lifted it just as the passage disappeared. The point scraped along the hanging rocks, showering the water with dust and bits of loosened rock.

Behind her, she heard the splashing grow suddenly still, and the boat lunged as someone grabbed hold of it.

"Easy now," Dranri said, and Ylmi turned to see Havar being pulled into the boat. He was soaking wet, and as he hit the bottom of the boat he rolled onto his back, gasping for air.

Karik's voice was breathless as he urged: "Push away. Push away." There was a grinding sound, as Thora set her oar against a rock and pushed. Kalborg shuddered, and Ylmi realized suddenly that a current was gripping at them. Thora's oar kept them steady for a moment, but Ylmi felt the boat shift again. There was no one behind her to row, but she slid her oar into the water and pulled in sharp, strong strokes, toward where she could still see faintly her mark on the ceiling.

Karik was pulled into the boat, dripping wet, a rope knotted quickly around his torso.

"Where is the passage?" he asked quickly, and Igil gasped.

"It's lost," Thora said, quietly.

"That way," Ylmi pointed.

Karik squinted through the darkness. "Are you sure?"

"I marked the rocks in the ceiling." She pointed to the white line in the rocks. "It is that way."

A relieved grin broke across Karik's wet face in the lantern light. "Ylmi, you are a gift."

It was a moment more before the tightness in her stomach subsided, and she felt she could breathe again.

"I do not like this place," Revik said, quietly.

From the bottom of the boat, Havar took a deep breath. "Try getting sucked under water you can't see!" he gasped. "It's even worse."

"The fact that I'm here," Wisic replied, "where that happens, is why I don't like it."

"What was it?" Thora asked. "I've seen Havar swim through tide and waves alike... Could you not see the lanterns?"

"I couldn't get to the surface," Havar answered.

Karik pushed some of the water off his hair. "There was a current there – something strong. It pulled me down the moment I touched the water."

"I agree with Revik," Ylmi said: "I do not like this place."

The momentary heart-stopping fury of Havar and Karik going overboard quickly gave way to the silent darkness of the Undersea, and once again time seemed to lose all meaning.

They ate and drank as little as they could bear, but even that seemed to have no effect on the passage of time, as they hung suspended between the two lanterns on Kalborg, with only the lapping of the water to break the silence.

⸻◦⸻

She was drifting off to sleep when she heard it: not just a tapping, but a rhythmic banging and cracking, which seemed strangely familiar to her ears.

"Miners," Havar whispered.

The boat was immediately alert, each of them attempting to breathe as quietly as possible. Ylmi shook her head; anyone nearby would see their lanterns, long before they heard their boat.

In the distance, they saw the warm glow of a torch on the water, then it was gone, swallowed up again by the darkness.

"Havar, Igil," Karik's voice was tense, from the stern, where he was once again on the rudder, "keep to the passage. Don't follow the lights."

They were close now, and Ylmi felt a sudden surge of elation. They had done it: they had passed through the Undersea.

But, the thrill was gone as suddenly as it had come, for she realized now that its whole dark distance now lay between them and the sun. They were barely halfway.

The lights and noises became more frequent, and once Ylmi saw the shadow of someone flickering against the wall in the torchlight. These were the miners of Jarl Hegli, or so she guessed.

Slowly, they inched along through the darkness, careful to keep their oars from bumping on the rocks.

Suddenly, the darkness to their left disappeared, as they passed into a great cavern, and they saw a line of dim figures at work on a distant shore, lit by lanterns and torches set in the ground, or hanging in the air.

"Lantern!" Karik hissed, and as he pulled the cover over the stern lantern, Ylmi lunged forward and did the same to the prow lantern. "Hold water."

Thora eased her oar into the water, and a moment later it struck the bottom. They floated there, motionless in the gloom.

On the distant shore, one of the workers had stopped and pointed toward them, gesturing at one of the other miners. They looked out over the water, squinting toward where Kalborg floated in silence.

"Hallo there!" one of them shouted, and Ylmi felt her stomach drop out of her chest. "Who goes!"

"Not a word," Karik's whisper was tense, and Ylmi felt everyone in the boat holding their breath.

After a moment, the other miner waved his hand in disgust, and a ripple of laughter went along the line. The first man peered toward them again, then shook his head before returning to work.

"Back," Karik whispered.

They slowly eased Kalborg backward, punting her against the bottom like Thora, until they had slipped back behind whatever barrier it was that had blocked the miners from view.

"That was close," Havar muttered, but Karik shook his head.

"Our voices carry," Karik said, his voice so low as to be almost inaudible.

Ylmi shook her head. More waiting – just what she wanted.

The darkness felt oppressive, weighing down on her as they waited for the miners to finish their work for the day and return home. Ylmi tried to count the strikes of their tools on the rocks, but that did not help the time pass, so she dozed again.

⸻ ◆ ⸻

She awoke to the sound of a great door being shut; the boom followed by the clanking of a large lock being turned. The lanterns were uncovered, and in the yellow light she saw Karik grinning, as he looked ahead.

They went carefully, using their oars to punt along the bottom, instead of rowing. The light from the miners' torches were gone, leaving only a dim orange light ahead of them. Slowly they pole-shunted along, keeping close to the rocks on their right.

Suddenly, two torches came into view.

Ylmi looked at them curiously, wondering why such torches were left alight with no one nearby. They were set into the rock on either side of two heavy doors, and before them a shelf of stone reached out into the water, before splitting off into half a dozen walkways and paths, which led off into the darkness.

But, on the rock shelf beside the torches, the ground gleamed with gold.

There were several beaten bars of the gleaming metal, and more piles of gold ore, with bits of stone still hanging out of it, where miners had picked it from the walls.

"Don't be greedy," Karik said quietly, as they reached the shelf; "take some for yourselves and enough for a boat. I do not wish to swamp our boat carrying out a treasury."

Ylmi shivered at the thought of being pulled under by the current, but she was the first one out of the boat, the cold water splashing around her boots as she pulled Kalborg up. The rest of them were out in a flash, grabbing what gold they could carry. When Karik had taken his piece, he took several of the ballast stones out of the boat and replaced them with gold. Ylmi handed him a lump of gold ore as big as her fist, and he smiled widely at her. "The charts work."

She nodded, then realized what he meant: if they were accurate here, in the Undersea, then they would be accurate in the Black Isles.

"That's enough," Karik whispered, as Havar dumped a handful of nuggets into the boat, and turned to grab more. Havar glared at him but said nothing, only lunging back to grab a piece of ore, which he stuffed into his pocket.

"For me," he muttered.

Slowly, they pushed off from the shore, and Kalborg slipped back into the darkness.

Sailing Homeward

They returned the same way they had come, Karik and Igil now guiding Kalborg close by the rocks to their left, as they retraced their path. Ylmi's hand went to the rough pieces of gold in the hull, hoping that the added weight would not cause problems. They had left half their ballast when they took on the gold, hoping that the weight would remain at least close to being the same. The orange light of Jarl Hegli's treasury now disappeared behind them, and they fell again into the gloomy darkness.

Their food was low – enough for only another day or two, if she guessed right. As the gnawing sensation in her stomach grew stronger, Ylmi found herself thinking that perhaps hauling the boat over Vanik's Point wouldn't be so bad, as long as she was able to bring down another deer when they landed.

The current pulled at them more on the way out, slow and gentle whenever they were in a cavern, swifter and more treacherous as they approached one passage or another, and more than once they had to use their oars to push off against the rocky wall.

Ylmi dozed often, feeling the boredom and darkness seeping into her bones and draining her strength.

"I hate this place," she whispered to Thora, at one point.

Thora shook herself, the long braid she wore whipping back and forth. "I just want to feel the wind again."

Behind them, Dranri let out a sigh. "Oh, to feel the wind on my face."

"Shut up," Ylmi muttered. "You have so much beard you haven't felt the wind on your face in years."

There was a moment's silence, then Wisic's laughter shook the boat and Dranri chuckled. "You have grown a sharp tongue, Bodvarsdottir."

"Quiet," Karik whispered, but Ylmi could hear the smile he spoke through. "We are not out yet, and echoes travel far."

Ylmi slept again, woke to gnaw on a strip of deer meat, then went back to sleep.

She awoke with a start, staring into the darkness. The lantern at the prow was waving back and forth, and the ship was shaking.

"We've hit the out current," Karik said, with tension in his voice. "Everyone to the oars. Ylmi, Thora, be ready to push away at the bow."

"Push away at what?" Thora muttered, peering into the darkness, but Ylmi gripped her oar tightly.

Aside from the danger of getting lost and wandering the darkness 'til they starved, this was the most dangerous part of the voyage. She and Karik had looked it over on the charts for many long nights: the place where the Undersea spat itself back into the open waters. Coming in, a steady current would carry a boat inside easily enough, but it was almost impossible to sail out against the current, with only six oars on a small boat. Instead, they had to split away from where they had come in, and approach the entrance from the opposite side. Here, the path twisted and turned, the current bending around on itself, as it made its way back to the sea.

The first rock appeared out of the darkness with no warning, and Ylmi felt it jar her shoulder as she caught it on her oar, guiding Kalborg around it and back on course. Then, an eddy caught them and the ship twisted, shuddering as Karik leant on the rudder, shoving the ship against the current. They pushed off the rocks and reached the other side of the eddy, sliding sideways as Kalborg was spat forward.

Ahead of them, faint light could be seen, and Ylmi's eyes widened as saw the waves thundering and crashing about the gaping maw of the Undersea. Beyond, she could see daylight and the cold waters of the Ice Sea.

The current grew stronger now, rushing them forward, even as Ylmi and Thora pushed off the rocks and tried to slow their momentum.

They came around a corner, and the grey light of the afternoon sun appeared in a blinding flash. Ylmi winced, her eyes more used to the darkness, and as she winced the ship lunged upward. Caught on a wave, it rose then plunged down, soaking them all in the ice-cold water.

"Steady!" Karik called, for now the wind could be heard howling over the entrance, as the waves crashed against the rock. "Only a little farther."

They were approaching the opening on its eastern side, whereas they had entered on the western side, and the waters here thrashed and boiled, as the Undersea emptied itself into the icy currents of the Ice Sea. Kalborg shuddered, jerking to one side before violently spinning in the other. There was a thumping crash as Kalborg's stern was slammed against the rock wall.

"Row!" Karik screamed, and in an instant every oar was in the water, pulling steadily for the open sea. Behind her, Ylmi heard Karik cursing, and with an oath he called Havar to take the rudder.

They pulled hard, and Ylmi felt the rough spots on her hands burn, even as the frigid water wetted the wood of her oar. Her breath was coming in ragged gasps, the cold air burning her lungs as she pulled. Behind her, Havar was gasping as well, but with a last, shuddering twist, they shot out of the cavern and into the Ice Sea.

The wind howled over them and Ylmi closed her eyes to enjoy the feeling: the wind in her hair, the rise and fall of the ship, and the taste of fresh, cool air in her mouth.

Her joy faded as she heard Karik behind her, swearing in a breathless voice.

"What the hell?!" Wisic said, as she turned. "Karik, can you not keep your fingers all together?"

In the stern, just in front of the rudder, Karik was slumped over, holding his left hand cradled tight against his chest. Ylmi's eyes widened in horror, as she saw the blood dripping down onto the deck.

"What happened?" she snapped.

"He tried to push us off the wall," Havar answered, with a shake of his head, "and he caught his hand between the stern and rock."

Karik pushed himself back to lean against the side of the ship and closed his eyes, taking deep, slow breaths, as the blood continued to drip over his shirt.

"It is not..." he said quietly, "...my whole hand." His teeth clenched for a moment, as he breathed through them. "Just a finger..." He closed his eyes again.

Ylmi stepped over the gold in the bottom of the boat to reach him. "Let me see it." She steadied herself as the waves rolled them forward, and gently lifted Karik's right hand off his chest. The colour was gone from his face as he tried to steady himself, and she winced as she saw the finger.

"Well, we can't all watch," Havar muttered. "Get the sail up; I'd like not to be here when Hegli realizes what's happened."

Ylmi gently brushed away some of the blood from Karik's hand, and he winced as she did so. "I'll be careful," she assured him, and he simply nodded, closing his eyes again.

It was soon clear enough where the wound was: his fourth finger was not simply covered in blood; it was a mangled mess. Ylmi looked at it a moment, trying to figure out how to set it, but the bone was in several pieces, and she saw flakes of it in the blood that continued to well up. She paused, and Karik saw her face.

"It's shattered, isn't it?" he asked.

She nodded.

"At this rate, I'll lose all my fingers by the time we get back," he said, with a forced smile. He took a deep breath. "Alright, let's just get this over with."

"Someone heat up a knife in one of the lanterns," Ylmi said, "and give me an ax!"

In the end, it took them three tries to cauterize the finger. Lanterns, it turned out, were not especially good at heating up knives. When they were finished, Karik was barely able to chew a few mouthfuls of old meat before passing out in the hull. They tried to lay him on cloaks, as best they could, but there were few ways to lie comfortably on gold ore and ballast stones.

But, even as Ylmi tried to give Karik a little comfort, Igil gave a shout and pointed to the north. Ylmi looked over the side of the ship, into the depths of the Ice Sea. Great, frozen packs of ice rose and fell upon the waves in the distance, but above them black clouds were piling up high, into the sky.

"Prepare yourselves," Revik chuckled, "if you are not all too weary."

Havar shook his head, and Igil winced as they all turned to their oars, and began to steadily pull.

"It seems as if we are to learn just how sound a ship you have built," Dranri said, as he stared at the coming storm.

"I'd rather we didn't," Wisic muttered.

The sea began to roll, each swell rising higher and falling farther, as the wind turned cold and began to moan. While Havar manned the rudder, Igil worked the sails and Kalborg quickly picked up speed.

Where at first the narrow ship had risen and fallen, rolling over the waves as it reached them, now its narrow prow cut through the waves, sending spray and foam into the air, much of it falling directly onto Ylmi and Thora. At first it annoyed her, but as she rowed Ylmi became glad of the cold spray, which drenched her hair and cooled her burning ears. Behind her, the ropes creaked and groaned, as the wind picked up and pushed Kalborg forward, with ever-increasing speed.

Thunder boomed over the sea, and in the dim light of storm-shadowed day, she saw the faint blink of lightning, reflected off the dark waters before her. Though she pulled on the oar as fast as she could, it met less resistance as it went, until Havar finally called them to bring in the oars.

"We can't go any faster with them now," he shouted over the wind.

Ylmi turned to see him, feet splayed out on the deck, both hands on the rudder, the wind whipping his hair and cloak about him. There was a smile on his face, even as his shoulder rose and fell with weariness, and a joy that seemed to warm him, even as the cold waters soaked his boots.

Ylmi pushed her wet hair out of her face and looked north. The black clouds were almost on top of them now, and she could see the wall of rain hanging beneath it, like a dim curtain. Kalborg shuddered as it slammed through a swell, and they all tumbled to the deck – save for Havar, who clung desperately to the rudder.

"The swells are getting too big!" Igil shouted, as he pulled himself to his feet. "You have to take them head-on!"

"I'm trying to!" Havar shouted back. Ylmi shook her head; both of them were red-eyed and exhausted, and she could see the anger boiling in both.

The wind was louder now, and thunder boomed again from the storm. Rain began to fall as Ylmi made her way through the ship to the stern, holding onto the rigging to keep her feet. As she passed the mast, Kalborg rose up into the air – higher, higher... – and then fell. Ylmi's stomach lurched, as she felt the deck suddenly drop beneath her; her hands stung as they locked onto the rough ropes with a death grip. Kalborg slammed into the water with a crash, spray rising high over their heads, and Ylmi saw the swell rolling away behind them, almost as high as the ship's prow.

"Havar," Ylmi took another step, "it will be a long night outrunning the storm. We should take shifts."

"I can steer my own ship, as long as there is breath in my lungs!" Havar shouted back.

But Igil nodded at Ylmi. "She's right, Havar!" he shouted. "Stop being proud!"

Ylmi threw him a look and turned back to Havar, who had fixed his face in a scowl.

"Havar, when night comes this is all going to be worse, and your skill will be needed more then. You've brought us through the Undersea; don't wear yourself out trying to ride a few swells."

Havar hesitated and Ylmi saw she had won. Slowly he nodded, and Ylmi stepped up to take the rudder.

She climbed up, braced her back against the stern post, and set her feet against the raised boards Igil had laid for traction. The wind struck the side of her face, annoying her good eye, and she felt her hair being pulled with the wind. She took the rudder from Havar.

On the deck, Kalborg moved like the sea: rising and falling with the swell; running upon the wind. But the rudder in her hands felt as though she held a boar by the ears. It was like a living thing, fighting and pulling as it battled the sea, the wind and even her.

A great swell rose up before them, and Ylmi pressed to the right, to line up the prow with the wave. Kalborg leapt to her command, the prow turning smoothly to slip up along the wall of dark water, and rise swiftly up its face – even as the sea fought to tug the rudder from her grasp. Up she rose, higher and higher, as the swell seemed to rise even more; they climbed and climbed it until, for one terrible moment, they hung upon its crest. The rain was falling heavily now, and Ylmi could see all about her the rising swells, and off in the distance the faint, far gloom of land.

Lightning flashed overhead with an ear-splitting boom, then they were plunging – down, down into the trough of the wave. Ylmi began to understand why men feared the Ice Sea.

"We can't outrun the storm!" Wisic called to Havar. "We have to put into shore and wait it out."

Havar shook his head: "We can make it."

"Can we?" Thora shouted back. "Havar, there is no point in dying for this gold."

The wind was howling now, and the waves were growing stronger. Without warning, Kalborg suddenly dropped, falling from the crest of a swell, and slipping into a trough between the waves. Just as they all lunged for a hand hold, another wave caught them and lifted them back up.

"Ylmi!" Thora shouted. "Make for land!"

"There's a fair chance we'll break the boat!" Dranri shouted. "Trying to land on strange shores in this storm is madness."

All of them began shouting at once, until Ylmi snatched the ram's horn, which hung from the stern, and blew a loud blast on it, which rivalled even the thunder. Thora winced and glared at her, and Dranri rubbed at his ears, but they all stopped shouting. Ylmi dropped the horn and grabbed at the rudder, even as another wave rose above them.

"Igil," Ylmi snapped, sending her voice cutting through the wind, "can Kalborg ride out this storm?"

Igil shrugged, holding tightly to one of the ropes, as they rose higher on the wave.

Ylmi shouted back: "Yes or no! You built her; you tell me right now if we can weather the storm."

They all braced as they crested the wave, hanging for a moment high above the sea, before crashing back down in a spray of freezing water.

Igil glanced back at her. "We can make it," he answered.

"Are we more likely to die in this storm, or trying to land on a beach we don't know?" Ylmi asked again, shouting as loud as she could.

"With these waves..." Igil shouted back, "...we'd shatter on the smoothest beach in Vrania."

Ylmi glared at them all, raking the boat with her one eye. "The matter is settled: we can ride out the storm, or beach; we're more likely to die if we beach. And, if Hegli's men catch us, we die anyway! So, we ride out the storm."

She looked to Thora, for if any of them would try to fight her, it would be the woman she had known longer than any of them. But, Thora only glared at her for a heartbeat, then grabbed one bucket and bailed out the mixture of spray and rainwater, which had begun to collect above the ballast stones.

The wind drove them on, slowly shifting until it blew out of the west, hurling them onward with a speed that shocked Ylmi, as she held tightly to the rudder. But the swells did not grow larger and, as they watched, the worst of the storm eventually passed behind them, to crash upon the Undmir and its villages.

When Ylmi was weary, Igil took his turn on the rudder, guiding Kalborg back and forth through the waves, as the wind carried them away from the Undersea, far faster than they had come.

Though the storm faded, the wind and waves lessened only a little. But, as she rested in the bow, Ylmi gazed over the water and finally saw the grey cliffs of Vanik's Point. Ylmi stared. They were farther north than they had intended, yet the ice floes were still off in the distance. She called Havar and pointed to the cliffs.

"Am I mistaken, or is that Vanik's Point?"

Havar stared through the pouring rain, sheltering his eyes. "By the nine, it is." A smile split his face. "I did it, Ylmi! I sailed the Undersea!" He clapped her on the back, a smile spreading over his face. "My boat! Igil!" He threw his arms in the air with an exhausted shrug, and slumped down to one of the benches.

"The passage is clear?" Dranri asked. He was sitting on his own rowing bench, slumped against the ship, his heavy beard thick with salt and spray.

Ylmi nodded. "Perhaps the storm broke up the ice. Perhaps it drifted north."

"Perhaps the gods opened the way." Dranri kept his voice low, as he commonly did when they hunted together. "This voyage has been very strange, and there are many things I do not understand."

"It has," Ylmi nodded, her thoughts turning to the legends of Vranr and his seven fingers, before she looked at where Karik lay, his own bandaged hand held close to his chest. "Things are bound to be strange."

As she looked, Karik pushed himself into a sitting position. He was soaked and his hair hung wet over his face. Beneath it, he was very pale.

"We are through?" he asked, hoarsely.

Wisic nodded and patted him gently on the back. "We're rounding Vanik's Point now."

Karik looked confused; "But the ice..." He looked around and shivered.

"The ice is broken up," Ylmi told him. "Rest."

Had they been dry, the wind would not have bothered them overly much, but they had been drenched by the rain, the spray and the waves. Ylmi was soaked from the roots of her hair to the toes of her boots, and the wind made her clothes and hair feel as if they were made of ice. The only good thing about the wind, she decided, was that it was moving them faster than they could have rowed.

The storm passed as the night settled in, and though they furled the sail so it caught less wind, enough light from the moon filtered down through the clouds, that they could continue to sail. They saw the sharp rocks of the Black Isles rising out of the sea.

The night was cold and long. The wind blew steadily and Ylmi longed for the stillness of the Undersea. The last of their food was eaten around the lanterns, each of them trying to get a little warmth from the flickering flames inside, but it was a futile effort.

Slowly, Ylmi watched the moon make its way across the sky, trying to guess how much higher it would move before she could bear to look at it again. She had lost feeling in her hands and her feet, when she finally felt drowsy, but something in her mind screamed at her not to close her eyes.

"Igil." She forced herself to sit up, almost toppling over the bench, as her legs refused to move. "Igil, we have to row." The words felt thick in her mouth, and her jaw seemed almost frozen shut, but she forced the words out and fumbled with her oar. "We have to row or we'll freeze."

There were a few mutterings here and there, but the sound of oars thumping and bumping along the ship filled the night air, and a moment later so too did the sloshing of the sea, as they pulled at the oars.

After a moment, Ylmi was struck with a cold so deep and so paralyzing that she thought she would die. It felt as if someone had poured ice water through her veins, and she shivered uncontrollably.

"Igil!" she gasped. "We have to get to shore."

Igil only grunted, but she felt the boat shifting in the sea, and turning toward the dark shape of the shore they could see in the distance. Slowly, the shakes subsided as she rowed, and Ylmi even felt a tingling in her feet, as she braced against the hull and pulled.

The waves were calmer than before, and the spray that the prow threw up rarely made it as far as her bench. But Ylmi still winced at every drop of the ice-cold water that landed on her face.

She glanced skyward and saw the moon was just reaching its peak. The night was halfway over and they were half dead. The thought struck her as humorous, and she began to laugh.

"What is wrong with you?" Thora grunted from beside her.

"Nothing." Ylmi was too tired, too cold to explain, and she wasn't sure if she could.

The gloom of the shoreline slowly grew closer, and as it did, the sound of waves breaking on stone grew louder.

"We can't land here," Havar said, loudly, and Ylmi thought it sounded as if speaking hurt him as much as it hurt her.

"No, no," Wisic snapped, "I was just thinking that breaking ourselves on the rocks was the perfect way to end this voyage!" His voice rose: "Of course we can't land on the rocks!"

"Keep rowing," Ylmi shouted, before anyone else could speak up. "Igil, just get us to land as soon as is safe."

"I," Igil slurred, slowly. "Am. Trying."

Ylmi forgot to look at the moon. She forgot what time was, lost in simply rowing and breathing, feeling the blood coming back into her feet and feeling her toes again.

But it struck her that Karik was not rowing. Karik was asleep. She glanced back, but all she could see was the mound of furs and cloaks they had wrapped him in. She took a deep breath as she pulled on her oar. With any luck, maybe it wasn't all soaked through.

She thought for a moment of what her life would be without Karik. If he died, would his mother stay in the hut he had built in the mountain clearing? She would not see his smile again, or the gleam in his eyes when he had a plan.

He had a hunger which matched her own: a hunger to push through danger, chasing the faint hope that they could save themselves from Vrania's dangers. She felt the small, wet pouch hanging from her neck, the stones cold within it.

Her mind went to Skathi's words, and three paths that lay always before her. She had chosen the third to go on this voyage. That path is the hardest.

She gritted her teeth and pulled deeper on the oar.

"Steady oars!" Igil's voice was barely more than a hoarse whisper as he leant against the rudder, and Ylmi felt Kalborg turning landward. They all waited, motionless, their oars out of the water, as they waited for the ship's speed to slow.

"We can't run up on the beach," Havar muttered; "someone needs to guide us in."

"So kind of you to volunteer," Wisic said.

"I can't feel my legs." Havar's head snapped up. "So, unless you want to jump in after me and pull in to shore..."

"I'll go," Ylmi said, stepping toward the prow.

The land was coming closer now, and in the moonlight she could see the thin, white lines of small waves breaking on the shore.

"Revik, you're strong." She turned and flashed him a smile. "Help me bring her in."

Revik grunted. "We won't get any warmer sitting here," he said, pulling himself to his feet and slowly making his way to the prow.

"I don't want to get too much closer," Igil said, his voice barely carrying over the sound of waves on the shore. "I have no idea what we're going into."

"Grab a rope," Ylmi said, and took a deep breath. Now that there was a task, she felt better than she had sitting in the boat and freezing. If she could push toward something, it was a hundred times better than waiting for a dawn she could not bring closer.

She pulled herself to her feet, kicking them against the bench, to knock the numbness from them. Without thinking, she jumped over the side.

The water engulfed her and she could not breathe, all air driven out of her, as her whole body seized. Every muscle screamed in protest. But, when the splash was gone, the waves only came to her chest. They fell to her waist then struck her chest again, rhythmically freezing her. Her breath came in short, shallow gasps, but she pushed her feet against the bottom and stumbled forward, the rope grasped tightly in her hands. The water rose and fell as the waves rolled into the beach, and soon the rope was taut in her hands, as she struggled forward. She gave a pull and felt the rope burn in her hands, even as Kalborg sluggishly responded.

Her next step sent her sprawling in the water, her foot caught on a rock beneath the surface. There was an instant of panic as the water closed over her head, but the water was very shallow and she pushed herself up, her head breaking the surface as she sucked in the frozen air.

She climbed over the rock and shouted to Revik to move away, so the ship would avoid the rock. A moment later, her feet splashed through the shallows and stepped onto the slick rocks, beaten smooth by the waves. Revik was close behind. The two of them set their feet in the rocks and pulled. Slowly, Kalborg slid onto the beach, the prow grinding over the rocks.

In an instant, the others bailed out, and the heavy task of lifting Kalborg out of reach of the tide began. Igil lifted Karik over the side and lowered him against the side of the ship, letting Ylmi catch him as he almost fell. Karik shivered violently in her arms, and in the moonlight she could see his face was pale, his lips turning a dark blue.

"We'll have a fire going in a moment," she told him. She leant him against a rock, out of reach of the waves. "Just sit here and try to get warm."

Everything was wet and cold, and moving the ship in that condition was no easy thing. But, at last Kalborg lay propped on its side, safely out of reach of the tide.

"Dranri, you start work on the fire," Ylmi said, the minute Kalborg was still. "Igil, try to figure out some way to keep this rain off of us. Everyone else collect firewood."

"Who put you in charge?" Havar asked. "I don't remember voting."

Ylmi turned to him: "I'm just trying to get us warmed up. If you have a better plan, speak up."

He glared at her for a moment, before turning back to the boat.

A little driftwood was scattered over the beach, and by the time Ylmi dumped an armload of it beside Dranri, he already had a small flame licking at a handful of twigs.

"We'll need a lot," he said, "though I fear we may simply be creating a beacon for anyone seeking trouble."

Ylmi shook her head. "From the sea they will see nothing," she said, pointing to the ship. It lay with its keel pointed to the sea, so now their fire, lit on the opposite side, was hidden from the waves. "And the little ridge there will prevent anyone from seeing the fire from land. Even if Leiban comes walking a hundred paces away, he will not know we are here."

Dranri looked impressed; "You have a mind for this."

Ylmi shivered as she looked at the tiny flames. "Just get us warm."

The moon was halfway toward the horizon when the fire was blazing and Ylmi finally felt warm. They laid out their soaked clothes as best they could to dry, and even Karik got some colour back in his face. One after the other, exhausted after their ordeal, they dozed off.

The next morning Ylmi woke to find Dranri roasting a pair of squirrels over the fire, the smell of them reminding her just how hungry she was. The rain was gone, and on the other side of Kalborg she could hear the sea rolling onto the beach. No one else was stirring, content to rest under the shelter of Kalborg.

All save for Karik: he was still wrapped in blankets from the night before, now staring at his left hand, where the two missing fingers had been. Slowly he worked it back and forth, his eyes fixed on the stumps, which twitched when the other three fingers moved.

"At least it's your left hand," she said.

He looked up at her and blinked, his gaze going to her left eye. "Even so..." He twisted the fingers again and winced. "At least there's no dragon poison from this injury."

"Wyrd draws a heavy cost from you, Karik," Dranri said, from by the fire. He glanced at Karik's hand, now both scarred from the dragon-fire as well as missing fingers. "Some men would take that as a warning – perhaps a sign not to overreach. It is one thing to seize what is offered, but another to grasp at what is withheld."

Karik groaned as he pulled off his blankets and struggled to his feet. "Nothing worthwhile was ever free," he said, then almost stumbled as he took a step.

"You," Dranri said, pointing a stick at him, "need to rest."

"I need to move." Karik twisted, working the stiffness from his muscles, but Ylmi saw that his face was still as white as fresh snow.

"You need to eat," she told him.

Karik only gave a weak laugh at that. "We all do. Besides, from what I hear, you are the one who got us here, while I was asleep in the boat." He smiled and made to step away from the boat, but a moment later he dropped to the ground in a heap.

Ylmi was out of her blanket and crouching by him in a flash, every muscle screaming at the sudden movement. Karik was laughing weakly. "I'm just lightheaded," he told her. "I'm fine."

When he deemed them ready, Dranri pulled the squirrels from over the fire and they all ate, ravenously. Ylmi burned her fingers and mouth, even as she tried to eat slowly, but the hollow pain in her stomach forced her to hurry. After a while the eating slowed, and one by one they pushed themselves back, double-checking the bones for even a small scrap of meat which had been missed.

"So," Havar said, with a rising grin, "I suppose this means we won?"

Slowly, Karik nodded. "We'll hide the gold in the inlet just within the fjord," he explained, "then begin building a new ship. As long as we don't flaunt a new hoard, we should be able to spend a little here and there without rousing suspicion."

Igil chuckled and shook his head. "Never satisfied, Karik."

"There's still a fair chance of starvation this coming winter," Karik answered, with a shrug. "Until that danger is gone..."

Dranri grunted as he set the remains of two ribs by the fire. "As long as the north wind blows," he said, "and the sea rises and falls, that danger will always be there. It is the fate of Vranr's children."

"Then, I will make a new wyrd," Karik replied, darkly, "for myself and my kin, though it may cost me every finger I own."

Ylmi's eyes were fixed on the fire, and she heard her voice speaking almost before she knew it: "Wyrd has little to do with the death of many, when kings and jarls take what they did not earn, and waste what would otherwise make better the lives of others."

"The two of you are full of dark words," Dranri said. "It is my mind that wisdom will be more sure when we have not spent so many days in a boat."

But Karik only spat into the fire. "I'll not sit back and let wyrd determine the life of me and mine." He rose unsteadily to his feet. "We should make ready."

⸺◇⸺

The sailing was smooth and quiet, as they slid out of the open sea and back into the fjord. Ylmi thought it strange that she should find the dragon's mountain a comforting sight, but she felt safer seeing it before her.

As Karik had suggested, they hid most of the gold in the little inlet just inside the fjord. It would be close enough for them to reach it when needed, and they would not have to explain to Unhost a boat full of gold when they landed.

When the gold was hidden, Dranri, Revik and Wisic set off for the village, to give less of the impression that they had been on a raid.

"If Unhost sees Dranri sailing back in with us," Ylmi pointed out, "he will have many questions indeed. The five of us will give less cause for suspicion."

"Unhost will be suspicious, nonetheless," Thora muttered.

"True," Ylmi agreed, "but as long as it is not obvious to the rest of the village, he will be slow to do anything."

Even so, Ylmi felt a tightness in her chest as they approached the beach by their village.

Unhost was hurrying down to the waterline, along with a company of four men behind him, who carried spears and shields.

"I do not like the look of that," she muttered, and Thora agreed.

Karik rose from the centre of the boat and, pulling himself up against the mast, he peered over the water to where Unhost was waiting.

"We could land a way away," Igil said quietly, from the rudder; "make him walk."

Karik shook his head: "No need to go hunting for more trouble."

"Trouble has found us," Dranri muttered.

When they were close, Karik leapt over the side and waded into the shore. Ylmi noticed that he kept his left hand close to his chest as he did so.

"Greetings, Jarl Unhost," Karik said. "What brings you to greet us returning?"

"You have been gone many days." Unhost looked them over, taking in their exhausted and bedraggled appearance, and the condition of their ship, as Havar tossed a stone overboard to serve as an anchor.

"We thought to test her seaworthiness," Karik said, apologetically, "but a storm caught us outside the fjord, and it was some time before we could get her back under control."

"Is that so?" Unhost's eyes were narrowed. "I do not believe you, Karik, and I think you are lying to me. But, unfortunately, this will have to wait for another time."

"And why is that?" Ylmi asked, as she waded through the water, up to the beach.

Unhost's eyes turned on her. "Because you all have been summoned to war." There was an unpleasant gleam in his eyes. "Jarl Hegli of the

Undmir has challenged King Jarhost to war, and the king has called the dragonslayers to his banner."

All of them exchanged glances and Karik let out a sigh.

"You can't fight wyrd," Wisic muttered to Karik.

PART III: YLMI ONE-EYE

TANGLED WYRD

The path to her parents' house was almost free of snow as she began to climb into the mountains, but Ylmi barely noticed. She had gone only a little way when she met Dranri, hiking back up toward his mountain home.

"I thought it best to avoid the settlement," he said, when he saw her.

His smile faded when she told him of Hegli's march to war.

"What did you mean," she asked, "when you spoke of the wyrd that binds Vranr's children? It is not wyrd that drives us to battle, but Hegli and Jarhost."

"The twisted thoughts of men are often the tools of wyrd," Dranri said. "Every action weaves another strand, until we bind ourselves and others in the wyrd we have woven."

"It seems to me that the weaving of jarls is of more consequence than our own," Ylmi muttered. "Are we doomed forever to waste ourselves in the bickering of Unhost and whatever jarl he's offended most recently?"

Dranri sighed heavily through his beard. "I have often wondered."

Ylmi stepped around a trickle of water leaking from one of the remaining snowbanks, and spat. "I have now risked life and limb twice," she said, bitterly, "and each time I return to find the hooks of a worthless jarl and a greedy king as deep in me as ever."

She looked up sharply as a branch rustled, and a moment later she had an arrow on the string. "Dranri," she said quietly, "step forward ten paces, if you would."

Dranri did so, a smile on his face, and Ylmi's bow twanged as the squirrel appeared over the branch. She snatched it up from where it fell.

"I am glad to have food," she said, "but I would rather I was loosing arrows at Unhost."

She paused as she reached the ridge which overlooked the village. Kalborg had been drawn up on the beach, and she could see the figures of Igil and Havar at work, cleaning her hull and refitting her. A little way up, past the old shed and Torig's hut, she saw Unhost standing with Fornik and Orli, watching the work.

"Perhaps Jarhost should face Hegli without us," she muttered, quietly. The settlement was not overly large, and with a little work they could erect a palisade about the place, which even Jarhost would find troublesome. She could gut Unhost, turn their settlement into a fortress... and then they would all starve to death in the winter. She gripped her spear tightly in frustration.

"As much as it pains me," Dranri said, slowly, "I think that all of the blame does not fall on Jarhost and Hegli, though they carry the boar's share in this matter."

"Speak plainly," Ylmi gripped her spear, tightly; "I have no patience to unwind your words."

"It may be that Hegli marches to war now because his mighty fortress seems mighty no longer."

Ylmi was silent for a moment, in her mind's eye seeing Hegli, confident in the strength of his fortress, opening the doors of his treasury only to find that his perfect fortress had been raided. How must he have felt to find that there was a hole in his defences – one he could neither understand nor explain?

By the time Dranri bade her farewell and followed the path to his own house, she was sick to her stomach and burning with a helpless rage. If their path did not lie through Hegli, then why had Skathi urged her on so? Unless it was not Skathi who had spoken to her.

As she climbed, the wind turned cool and she saw the beginnings of a storm creeping down from the mountains. She had not thought to return to the village tonight but, by the size of the clouds, she guessed she might not return the next day, either.

A yelp echoed through the trees, and Ylmi looked up in time to see a dark blur shooting through them, as Ulfr came bounding down to greet her. Even in her foul mood, the wolf brought a smile to her face, her great tail throwing leaves and dirt as it wagged back and forth.

"You missed me?" Ylmi grinned. "I missed you, too. It would have been nice to hold you, more than once; it was very cold."

Ulfr looked up at her, smiling through her fangs, and Ylmi laughed. "You, at least, cause me no harm."

Siggi and Bodvar, for their part, were as happy to see her, but when they asked where she had been, Ylmi answered that it was a long story, best told beside a fire.

"Well, there is a storm coming," Bodvar chuckled, "and I have a good store of wood set aside."

"And I have a squirrel," Ylmi lifted it from her belt, "so perhaps we will have a fine time of it while the storm rages."

So, as the rain poured down and the wind howled, Ylmi ate with her parents, and told them how they had sailed the Undersea. It was a long tale in the telling, and it was late when she had finished. The fire had gnawed deep into the thick log Siggi had laid upon it, and Ulfr lay with her head in Ylmi's lap.

"I am honoured to have such a daughter," Bodvar said, as he looked at her in the firelight, "though I confess that I sometimes wish you did not tempt death so often."

"Living in Vrania is to tempt death," Siggi's voice was low, and her eyes were fixed on the fire. Ylmi thought of Lanvir and her jaw tightened.

Bodvar was silent for a moment, staring into the fire, as the flames licked at the charred edges of the log. "Even so."

"So, now Jarhost summons you to war," Siggi said, "to do battle with Hegli."

Ylmi nodded, silently. "Unless I can discover a way to avoid it." She did not touch them, but she felt the weight of the three stones, hanging from the pouch at her neck. It would not be a terrible thing, she thought, if both Hegli and Jarhost perished in the coming battle.

"You are thinking to persuade Jarhost against an attack?" Siggi said, raising an eyebrow.

Ylmi laughed; "I might as well try to persuade the winter to be less cold." She shook her head; "No, it is Hegli I am thinking of."

<hr>

Two days later, Ylmi pushed open the door of Havar's hut to find Karik resting by the fire. He cracked an eye open and smiled when he saw her.

"How is your hand?" she asked.

He wiggled his fingers and winced. "They aren't growing back, but the pain is less." He set his hand gently back into his lap. "How are your parents?"

Ylmi grunted as she set her bow by the door, and took a seat by the fire. "They are beginning to wonder just how many dangers their daughter is going to go running into."

Karik grinned at that. "Did you tell them we are going into battle?"

She nodded and he closed his eyes again. "Flovi says we are to leave in three days. Hegli's army is gathering south of the Undmir."

"All this over a little gold," Karik muttered, pushing himself upright, wincing as his left hand touched the ground.

"I have been thinking on this, and I do not believe it is about the gold." Ylmi took a deep breath. "Jarl Hegli and King Jarhost have long hated each other, for Jarhost is not happy that one of the mountain jarls rules alone and answers to no one. And yet, he can do nothing because the Undmir is an impregnable fortress. So, if the Undmir is no longer impregnable..."

"Then Hegli is no longer secure," Karik nodded, and pinched the bridge of his nose in frustration. "I should have considered this. We have robbed Hegli of his shield, and now he strikes out before another attack can come."

"It will be a long, difficult fight if we are to take the Undmir." She considered for a moment. "Do you think we will need to sail the Undersea again, to crack the fortress?"

Karik shook his head. "Sailing Kalborg in to retrieve a little of his gold is one thing; storming the fortress with Kalborg's tiny crew is another."

Without him seeming to notice, his right hand went to his left, touching the fingers that were still there. "I have the beginnings of a plan."

Ylmi settled herself by the fire. "Go on, then."

"Hegli is going to war because he fears the Undmir is no longer impregnable," Karik explained. "So, what if we offered to help him?"

Ylmi thought for a moment, then saw where Karik's mind had gone. "We offer to show him how we got in, if he promises not to go to war?"

Karik nodded.

"Assuming he doesn't just kill us..."

"We aren't the only ones who know," Karik grinned; "if he touches us, Igil and Havar will tell Jarhost how to sail the Undersea."

"It won't work," Ylmi shook her head; "Hegli is stubborn, and once he has called his men to battle, he will not send them home without a fight."

"That is ridiculous," Karik objected. "Even if he wins, he'll lose half his men, just to spite Jarhost. He doesn't have the men to take Garhom, much less the throne in Bjarnmont."

Ylmi shrugged. The idiocy of the matter made it no less likely. She had heard enough of the jarl from Dranri to know that he was not a reasonable man. Just like Jarhost, and just like Unhost.

She straightened, suddenly. Just like Unhost.

A bad jarl always had disgruntled followers, and Hegli was no exception. Her mind went back to conversations with Dranri, about Hegli and the sister of Jarhost. She had heard rumours, from Dranri and other hunters, of Hegli's son...

"Have you heard of Hegli's son, Tanvir?" she asked. When Karik shook his head, she continued: "According to rumours, Hegli treated his mother very poorly, and Tanvir resents him still. But, Hegli has been careful to keep his son at arm's length; far enough to be safe, but close enough that he does not enter the service of Viglir or Jarhost, and betray the Undmir. If we made the offer to him..."

"Help him seize the jarldom..." Karik's eyes widened, suddenly.

Ylmi smiled. "Even so. He will know what warriors can be trusted, and how best to ensure matters are resolved."

"Speaking with him will not be easy," Karik said, and stared into the fire for a moment, thinking.

"We need to move quickly if we are to avoid war." Ylmi settled back against her pack. "First thing in the morning, we must go. We will come up with our plan as we walk."

⎯⎯◈⎯⎯

The next morning, Karik and Ylmi rose while it was still dark. The waves were washing onto the beach, and Karik sighed at the sound.

"You are reluctant?" Ylmi asked him, hefting her pack over her shoulder.

Karik shook his head. "I would rather we were building a boat, or setting out toward the sea." He rubbed his eyes for a moment. "I would even rather be there..." He pointed to a small boat, fishing in the moonlight.

"Trust me," Ylmi shook her head, "you do not wish to be throwing nets with Torig Ingsson; his tongue is sharper than any hook. But, yes, soon we will be at sea, and all of this behind us."

Karik chuckled at that and shook himself. "Let us get this over with and come back. There is much work to be done in this place."

Ylmi nodded, and she thought that Karik did not know the half of it.

They hiked north, taking the trail which led toward her parents' house. The whole way, Karik was silent.

Around noon, they turned their path more to the west, and followed the mountain slopes downward, away from Girhom and toward the cold marshes which lay between their settlement and the Undmir.

"I am sorry for your fingers," she said to him, at last.

He continued to wind his way down the slope, picking his way between the trees. "I am sorry for your eye. They were both of my own doing."

Ylmi did not know what she thought of that, so she simply settled her long spear on her other shoulder and continued onward.

THE STUBBORNNESS OF JARL HEGLI

Two nights later, Jarl Hegli sat in his camp, awaiting the last gatherings of his army. Before the door of his tent, a large fire burned brightly in the night, a pot of small fish in a thin broth boiling beside the flames.

He could call far fewer men than King Jarhost, so he could not afford to hurry forward without the use of a single spear. Besides, the king would come to him and, if his plan worked, Jarhost's numbers would only work to his own detriment.

"This is our chance to crush Jarhost," he said to the messenger, who stood in the door of his tent. "And tell your king that I can delay only a little longer; if he does not make haste, the opportunity will pass." He waved his hand, and the messenger took up his spear and set off through the darkness. Hegli felt a twist of hunger in his stomach, as the smell of the stew flitted into his tent, carried by the cool night breeze.

He was pondering if he could wait another week, when one of his guardsmen entered the tent, holding a young man by the arm.

"He came to us and said he has news for you." The guard gave the young man a shove forward, and Hegli examined him in the torchlight.

He was young, barely more than a boy with a hint of a beard, but he had strange burn markings on his neck and on his right hand, while two fingers from his left hand were missing. He was soaked from the rain, but there was a strange calm in his eyes which Hegli found unnerving. The old jarl cleared his throat and spoke: "What is it you have to say?"

"I know why you are marching to war," the young man spoke softly, his eyes flicking over the tent, "and I know who stole your gold."

"Is this so?" Hegli's hands tightened on the sword at his belt, and he felt the familiar tightness in his neck as he tried to control his fury. "Speak!"

But the young man shook his head. "I am only a messenger. He said that he wishes to speak with you, to settle this matter in a way which is more advantageous to you. If you will go to the clearing by the tall oak tree, where the stream splits, at dawn tomorrow, he will tell you everything you wish to know."

"Why would he do this?" Hegli sensed a trap, but he was desperate to know how his fortress had been breached. Whoever had stolen his gold had done so in such a way that not one guard in his fortress had seen or heard them before slipping onto a ship. He badly wanted to know how it had been done, lest he wake one morning with Jarhost's thanes storming his hall.

The young man shrugged. "I do not know; I only bring his message."

"And, what if I beat it out of you?" Hegli glared at him. "Or gut you here and now, then hang you in the morning for the ravens?"

"If you lay a finger on me," the young man warned, "then you will not see him tomorrow, and in a week's time every jarl and wanderer from the ice marshes to the pastures of Varhom will know how to enter your fortress."

Hegli considered for a moment, then nodded.

"See him fed," he told the guard, "then send him on his way." He turned back to the young man, who was staring blankly at the dark corner of the tent. "Go and tell your master I will hear what he has to say. But I promise no more than that."

⸻ ◆ ⸻

There was a soft rain starting to fall as Ylmi watched the guard take Karik, and she wondered how well anyone knew of the dragonslayers in the Undmir.

With her hood pulled up over her face, she slipped through the shadows, her spear held in one hand. When she reached the first tent, she straightened. Passing beside the campfires, she saw men and women huddled against the coming rain, seeking to draw in some of the warmth from the flames.

She did not know Tanvir's face, but she guessed she could discover him well enough. At the centre of the camp was Hegli's tent, and she saw Karik taken inside to speak with a lean man wearing a short, stubbly beard. The closest tents to Hegli housed older men, many of them cleaning weapons or armour, and Ylmi guessed that they were Hegli's bodyguard. There was a small tent just beyond them, in which a figure was asleep on a pile of twigs and furs; a sword hung from the tent pole. No one else seemed to have their own tent, and the hanging sword seemed the final proof. With a quick glance around to see that no one was watching her, she strode quickly to the tent and stepped inside, dropping the flaps as she did so.

The figure on the bed sat up, revealing a young man little older than Karik. His eyes widened as Ylmi dropped her hood, and his mouth fell open.

"You are Tanvir Heglisson?" she asked.

"I am," he answered. "And you are...?"

"One who walked into the bowels of the Undmir, took what gold I pleased and left unseen. Your father is marching to a war that he cannot win, and will leave many dead."

Tanvir continued to stare at her, but there was a sharpness in his eyes which made Ylmi suspect he was not as confused and stunned as he pretended. "Wars often leave many dead. That is commonly why they are waged."

"If your father has his way, half the Undmir will lie dead in a fortnight." Ylmi took a step forward. "The Undmir will be besieged as winter sets in, and by summer there will be barely enough left alive to crew a fishing boat."

"Are you threatening me?" Tanvir asked, and his eye flicked from Ylmi's spear to his sword.

"I have come to offer you a bargain," Ylmi said, "the same one as is being offered to your father this moment: call off the battle, return to your fortress – save the lives of your people – and we will show you how we are able to come and go so freely through your fortress."

"I am not the jarl," Tanvir answered, with a twisted smile; "the people are not mine to command."

"And that is why I will also offer you this," Ylmi replied, "which we have not offered your father: help us in this, and we will help you become jarl."

"You would have me kill my father?" Tanvir's question was not an accusation, as Ylmi had half-expected. Instead, his shoulders sagged as he asked, and she thought she saw fear in his eyes.

"Perhaps it would be better if one of the dragonslayers did the deed," she offered. "It is an ill thing to have the blood of a parent on one's hands."

Tanvir nodded slowly: "Even so." He thought for a moment.

Ylmi's heart quickened as she heard footsteps outside. But they passed by the tent, and she looked back to see Tanvir working his hands in the flickering light of the candle.

It was a moment before he spoke again, and when he did, his voice was quiet but hurried: "I cannot defeat my father here, before the battle; there are too many who are loyal to him. His bodyguard would have me dead before the sun set, and I would be of no use to anyone; the battle would continue and the people of the Undmir would be leaderless, and fodder for Jarhost to burn."

He then looked up at her. "But, when the battle comes, there will be many challenges for single combat, and some of my father's most loyal men will die. Then, when the battle is joined, you and your friends can make for the jarl. Half of his bodyguard is old men, well-seasoned and proven; the others are young, and many have more love for me than for him. These I will draw away, and you may do what you wish with Jarl Hegli. I will pull back the warriors of the Undmir, and you will have your peace."

Ylmi raised an eyebrow; "You are willing to let a number of your elders die thus?"

Tanvir looked back at her, the muscle in his neck working a moment before he spoke. "What power does one man have over another, if others do not help him? You are not ignorant of how my mother was treated, or you would not approach me for this." His eyes fell for a moment, then he stood, looking Ylmi in her one good eye. "Whoever you do not kill, I will. So, yes, I am willing to let them die."

"You think you can break off the battle?" Ylmi asked, doubtfully. "If Hegli falls in battle, Jarhost will seek to press his advantage."

"Jarhost will think he has won a victory and defeated an important rival," Tanvir's words were spilling out faster now, "but I am not a fool, nor unused to battle; I will find a way."

He turned away from her, head bowed in thought. "I will send him gifts to placate him. And, you," his eyes snapped back to Ylmi, "will show me how to secure the Undmir. All will be saved."

He shrugged. "It will be a short battle to avoid a longer war, and many lives will be spared."

Ylmi thought for a moment. It was not perfect; any number of things might happen once the battle was joined. But, the death of a jarl was usually enough to break up the fighting. Besides, she reflected, with Revik, Igil and Thora, she liked their chances against any group of bodyguards, no matter how seasoned.

"It is done," Ylmi told him. "But know this: if you hesitate to draw your people back, or press the attack on, by the end of the year, every soul in Vrania who draws breath will know the way into the Undmir."

Tanvir nodded, solemnly; "It is agreed."

Ylmi was the first back to their hidden camp. Ulfr was waiting under the little bothy of branches they had built, and leapt up happily when Ylmi appeared.

"I have left you alone much these few days past," Ylmi muttered, but the wolf only rolled over and looked at her, tongue lolling out of the side of her mouth.

"We are surrounded by fools," Ylmi told her, "and those who are willing to let others die that they may keep their glory."

It was not long before Ulfr's ears snapped up, and Ylmi heard Karik coming in the darkness, the sound of him splashing through the stream shallows faint over the noise of the stream itself. Here, it gurgled and splashed over small stones and small brush, as it emptied into the icy marshes, but Karik's splashing was easy to hear. He climbed over the small rise and slid down beside the fire.

"You spoke to Hegli?" she asked. When he nodded, she turned back to the fire and added another stick. "How did it go?"

He grinned, smiling at her as he wiggled his maimed left hand. "No one takes you seriously when you're missing fingers, apparently." He pulled off his wet boots and stretched his cold feet toward the flames. "He said he'd come. Now we just have to hope that he listens." His stomach growled loudly, and he pulled a piece of hard bread from his bag.

"Will he?"

"I don't think so," Karik answered. "What of Tanvir?"

Ylmi explained Tanvir's plan and Karik sighed.

"If the dragonslayers make first for Hegli, I do not think it is beyond us to kill him swiftly," she said, "and it will give Revik a chance to swing his precious ax."

Karik stared into the flicking flames, as they wrapped about the small sticks Ylmi had stacked. "There are many opportunities for it to go wrong. Even if all goes right, there will be many dead."

"Then, Hegli should take our offered deal," Ylmi muttered. She had not thought she would plan the murder of another jarl while Unhost lived, yet here she was. And it galled her.

She looked into the fire, wishing she had found a rabbit or squirrel; the bread was almost four days old, and meat would have been welcome. Sighing, she pulled her cloak tight over herself and lay down, as Karik took his turn tending the fire.

A few of the marsh birds could be heard singing in the trees, when the sun rose the next morning. Karik belted on the longsword he had taken from the dragon, and pulled on the dark, leather vest he wore as armour. Ethna had sewn iron rings into it, over the shoulders, so it was better than nothing, and Ylmi thought he looked very fierce in it. For her part, she wore a similar vest of boiled leather, but instead of iron rings, she had sewn the bones of her kills into the shoulders. There were fewer gaps than with the rings, but neither would stop an ax blow.

They did not have to wait long.

Hegli, accompanied by seven other men, appeared at the edge of the clearing before them, looking across the stream to where Ylmi and Ulfr sat with Karik, on the bank. Hegli's eyes passed over them and fastened on Karik. "Where is your master?"

"I confess, I was less than honest with you last night," Karik said, as they both rose to their feet. "I am the one you seek. It was I and my friends who stole your gold."

"I do not believe you," Hegli snarled, "and I have little patience for any other lies you may have to tell me."

"I am Karik Haldsson, one of the slayers of the dragon," Karik's voice carried across the clearing, and stilled Hegli as he turned, "and this is Ylmi Bodvarsdottir, who also slew the dragon. We sailed the length of the Undersea to steal your gold."

Behind Hegli, Ylmi saw Tanvir listening quietly, his arms folded over the sword which hung from his belt. Only one other man wore a sword: an older man, who seemed tired and annoyed at being roused so early.

Hegli regarded them for a moment, before shrugging. "And why should I not kill you both now?" He gave a flick of his hand and three of his men raised their bows.

"Because we did not sail alone," Karik replied. "If we do not return alive, then my companions will tell King Jarhost how to navigate the Undersea, as well as any other jarl or king who asks."

Hegli paused and Karik continued: "If you will agree to end this war and go back to your fortress, Jarhost will abandon the fight as well, for he still thinks the Undmir to be impenetrable. And I will show you how we passed through the Undersea, and how to secure yourself against it."

Hegli seemed to consider for a moment, but then shook his head. "You are both very young, and even if I did believe that you were capable of doing what you say you have, I am not interested in trying to come to an agreement with you, because I do not think you are important enough."

"You do not think the dragonslayers are worth dealing with?" Ylmi asked. She saw several of the men shifting uneasily, but Hegli did not seem convinced. Instead, he spat toward them.

"If it was two such as you, then the dragon must have been a small thing, or sick."

Ylmi watched, and saw Tanvir eyeing his father. Hegli was the problem; Hegli was the one keeping them from coming to an agreement. If he was removed...

"I challenge you, here and now." She hefted her spear and pointed toward them. "If I win, you accept the bargain; if I lose, we tell you right now how we reached your secret treasury."

She clenched her jaw as Hegli only laughed at her. "I do not fear Jarhost and I do not fear you. If you are determined to throw away your life, then so be it."

Karik grabbed her arm. "Ylmi, you don't have to do this." She snatched it away.

"I have fought bears and boars stronger and swifter than any of them," she muttered. "If Hegli dies on this mountain, then many will live who would otherwise have died."

"You against me, then," she said to Hegli, "and you might avoid the death of many of your people." Ulfr's ears were back, and there was a low growl in the back of her throat.

But Hegli only laughed again. "I am a jarl, while you two are nothing but little children from the coast. I will not sully my sword with your blood." He turned and pointed at the older man, who stood behind him: "You, bring me her head."

The man stepped forward with a deep breath. There was a streak of grey on one side of his beard, but he drew a fine sword from his belt. It hummed as he swung it through the air.

"I am Lasvik Horsson," he said, as he raised his shield and drew his sword. "I have killed twelve men in single combat, but you will be the first dragonslayer."

"There is no need for this," Karik said, but Ylmi simply handed him her bow and quiver. "He's not a dragon."

She was angry now. Angry that Hegli was no better a jarl than Unhost was. Angry that Hegli, like Unhost, relied on others to do his dirty work. Everywhere it was the same: foul men surrounded themselves with others to keep them safe.

"I will peel his supporters from him like bark from a tree," Ylmi hissed to herself. "Stay!" she commanded Ulfr, and splashed across the creek, before pulling herself up on the other bank.

"Well then, Lasvik Horsson," she said, "let us not dawdle."

And, with that she lunged, her long spear flashing out, but Lasvik stepped quickly back. He eyed her warily, then stepped forward, catching her spear on his shield as he moved forward.

She danced back, thrusting with the spear high, then low, forcing Lasvik to work his shield, until finally she scored a hit, slicing through his leg just below the knee. He stepped back with a curse, the dark cloth of his pants already growing slick with blood.

"Oh, for Heaven's sake, Lasvik," Hegli shook his head in frustration. "She's not a child. Kill her!"

Lasvik gathered himself and rolled his shoulders. Whatever thoughts he had carried of an easy victory were now gone, and he was settling down to the business of the fight. He rushed her like a boar, and she only just avoided his sword, but his shield caught her in the face and sent her hurling to the ground. Swiftly, she rolled to her feet, blood running from her nose.

For a few moments, they struggled. She avoided his sword, but he caught her with his shield. He avoided the head of her spear, but she struck him more than once with the iron-tipped butt.

Then, he raised his sword, and her spear blade slid over the top of his shield and sank deep in his throat. Lasvik's eyes widened, blood bubbling from his mouth, and his sword fell from his hand.

With a jerk, she withdrew her spear and he fell to his knees, reaching for the sword, but his hand was already failing. He fell sideways, his arm splayed out.

Ylmi stepped forward, as Hegli and his men looked on, and set Lasvik's sword in his hand. She was breathing heavily, and her nose felt as if it would burst. "May the Allfather forgive you your choice of jarl," she muttered, "and grant you a seat in his war hall."

Lasvik's eyes met hers and fell empty.

She stood there a moment. Then, when she was sure his soul had passed, she lifted the sword from his fingers. Her face felt strange, and a dull throb was building at the base of her teeth.

"I have defeated your champion." Ylmi wiped her hands on the damp grass and rose to face Hegli. "Accept our bargain, or face me here and now, and let us have this matter settled." She blew some of the blood out of her mouth and winced at the pain.

He said nothing.

"Jarl Hegli," she took a deep breath and pointed to Lasvik's corpse, "his death is on your hands." Still breathing heavily, she sloshed back across the creek, where Karik stood with his arms folded and his jaw tight.

He glared at her for a moment, then turned back to Jarl Hegli, adding: "I will show you how to secure the Undmir, and I will see that no others learn of the passage I have discovered." His voice carried over the water to where Hegli and his men were still transfixed by Lasvik's corpse. "You can save the lives of your men, and avoid the bloodshed that will come with a needless battle."

But Hegli only sighed heavily, before gesturing toward them with one hand. "I weary of this," he said; "kill them."

"What?" Karik started, but two of the men were already raising their bows. Ylmi saw Tanvir rolling his eyes as she turned, and an instant later she was off the knoll and dashing into the trees. Ulfr was beside her, lopping along as cheerfully as if they were going on a hunt.

She glanced back to see Karik following, his sword in one hand as he ran, ducking as an arrow passed over their heads.

"Are they chasing us?" she asked.

"Three are," he answered, and the two of them sprinted up the slope, pulling themselves through the trees and up over another small rise. They ran 'til Ylmi's breath was coming heavily, and she felt the sweat running down near her good eye. She wiped it away and turned to look back.

They had crossed several small ravines, and were beginning to rise into the mountains again, so that the forest spread out, sloping gently away from them.

"We should have just gutted Hegli in his sleep," Ylmi said, softly. Her eyes went from tree to tree, watching for movement in the underbrush. "Your desire to avoid bloodshed is admirable, but sometimes killing is the swiftest way to peace."

"It was worth a chance," Karik muttered. "Do you see anyone?"

Ylmi took a deep breath, slowing her breathing as best she could. The wind was blowing, gently shaking the green leaves and grey branches of the undergrowth, but she saw no other movement.

"I doubt any of them run as swiftly as us," she grinned at him. "That's what comes of sitting in their fortress all the time."

"We should keep moving," Karik glanced around; "they may have tried to circle and cut us off."

Quietly, they turned and made their way uphill, rounding the great rocks which rose here and there from the rough ground.

Karik took a deep breath but, before he could speak, there was a sudden grunt, and he disappeared behind the stones.

Ylmi leapt forward just as steel rang out, and she rounded the stone to see Karik struggling with one of Hegli's men, Karik with his sword drawn and Hegli's warrior struggling to bring his ax to bear. Ylmi lifted her spear, but before she could drive it forward, Karik twisted around in a sudden pull, and buried his sword in the man's stomach. He choked but, before he could cry out, Karik snatched his knife from his belt and slit the man's throat.

Ylmi watched as Karik pulled his sword free, and the two of them scanned the trees and rocks yet again.

"Still think we should have given Hegli that chance?" she asked.

"You're right," he muttered. "Let's go before the others come to him."

They ran for most of the morning, slowing to walk up the steeper slopes, but keeping their pace up until they were back in the mountains, far from Hegli's camp. They stopped, at last, beside one of the small streams which flowed from the snow-covered peaks, to fill the ice marsh.

"So much for Hegli, Wise Jarl of the Undmir," Ylmi said. "What a useless shit." She bent and drank deeply from the ice-cold water, and sighed.

When she looked up, Karik was glaring at her. "Why did you do that?" he asked. "There was no reason for you to challenge him."

She rose and poked him with the butt of her spear. "You're worried about me," she teased, but he caught the spear in his right hand and yanked it away. A growl erupted from Ulfr, and in an instant the wolf had stepped between them. Karik stepped slowly back, but his eyes remained locked on Ylmi.

"Of course, I am!" His jaw was tight, and there was an anger in him she hadn't seen before. "Going up against the dragon we had all agreed, and knew what we were getting into; it wasn't going away and facing it was the safest thing we could do. But, sailing the Undersea? I almost got all of you killed – and, if this battle doesn't go how I hope, I may still get you all killed, anyway."

He stared at the sky and sucked in a deep breath. "Ylmi, I told you the plan; you knew it. You knew we didn't need Hegli to agree."

"Karik, I have my own reasons," she kept her voice level. "Besides, I thought there was a chance, a small one, that this could all be resolved without a battle." She had hoped that Hegli would be baited into taking the challenge himself, and things would have been resolved then and there, but the old jarl was too clever – or too cowardly – to fall for it.

Karik sighed and his shoulders slumped. He glanced at Ulfr then, handing her the spear back, bent and drank from the stream. "We're all a hair's breadth away from death," he said, as he wiped the dripping water from his chin; "there's no need for us to chase it."

Ylmi shook her head; "Why are the jarls such incompetent fools?"

"Because everyone is too hungry and tired to challenge them," Karik answered.

They continued hiking southward through the trees.

With every step, Ylmi's annoyance grew. Karik was not her jarl, and it was no business of his who she chose to fight. Did he think he was the only one who had the right to risk his skin? If he was going to snap at her every time she made her own decisions...

She was mid-thought when she realized that Karik had stopped.

"Ylmi," he said, with a sigh, "forgive me. It is not my place to command you. Thank you for your help." He looked down and flexed his hand. "I want to protect you, but you're more than capable of doing that yourself."

"Keep yourself, Karik Haldsson," she smiled at him, coldly; "I have done well enough for many years. I am not some child you must keep watch over."

Jarhost's Folly

They found Jarhost's camp a little way west of Girhom: a collection of tents and cooking fires which sprawled along one of the mountain streams, winding through the pine trees. Leiban Longspear was keeping watch, and he recognized Ylmi with a smile.

"You come late, dragon killer," he chuckled, "though it is good to see that you have a proper spear for warfighting."

Ylmi flipped him a rude gesture as they went past. "Better late than never."

Orli was less pleased when they found him. He began some lengthy lecture about how they were rebelling against authority and were useless as soldiers, but Ylmi was tired. Her feet were sore from the long trek south, and the hunger pangs had been growing worse all day. She accepted the bowl of stew Thora offered her, and settled gratefully by the fire.

"Was your trip a success?" Thora asked.

Ylmi shrugged as she chewed. "Could have been worse; could have been better."

Thora's eyes went to the sword Ylmi wore at her belt: "That is new."

"I fought a man in single combat," Ylmi shrugged. "I won."

Thora's eyes took in the gold wire beaten into the pommel and hilt. "That is no mean sword, and I do not think it was carried by a simple man."

"It was not," Karik took the bowl Thora offered him; "it was carried by Lasvik Horsson."

Igil lowered his spoon and looked over the flames at Ylmi. "Isn't he one of Hegli's bodyguard?"

"His champion," Thora nodded.

"Not sure why you're all surprised," Karik said; "she killed a dragon, and she made much shorter work of Lasvik."

Ylmi looked up at the rest of them and raised a corner of her mouth in a mock snarl. Thora laughed.

"The odds are well in our favour for this battle," Revik said. "I wonder what it will be like to be on the side that has the upper hand."

Igil threw a stick at him. "Thank you for tempting the gods, brother," he muttered, and shook his head. "Hegli has not fought off Jarhost for so long by being a poor leader. He knows he cannot win a straight-up fight; he will have some kind of trickery up his sleeve."

Her spoon stopped partway to her mouth, and Ylmi felt a cold shiver go down her spine. For their plan to work, they needed to at least have a chance of winning the battle.

"We have our orders from Unhost," Orli said, as he and Flovi sat down beside the fire with them: "we are to only fight as needed. Jarhost has plenty of men here; he does not need us risking our lives."

"You say 'we'," Wisic muttered, from where he lay against a small tree, "yet as far as I can tell, Unhost sent only you and Flovi; the dragonslayers were ordered to come by the king."

Orli glared at him. "You all think you are so special and important, but it is Unhost who is jarl, and it is his decisions we will listen to."

Wisic returned his glare with a laugh, but it was Thora who spoke: "We have slain a dragon, and proven ourselves useful to the settlement many times over – Ylmi, Havar and I have done so for many years. What has Unhost done?"

Orli spluttered, but Thora rose and walked into the trees.

"You should be more careful with your words," Havar told Orli. "Like it or not, the dragonslayers are of more worth than your jarl."

That night, as darkness approached, they were visited by Gorli, one of Jarhost's sworn men, who was very happy to see that Karik and Ylmi had joined them.

"Tomorrow we march," he said. "We have heard that Hegli is moving toward a small valley, some ways north of here, and there we will meet him in battle."

Ylmi straightened. "A valley where two hills meet, one on either side?" she asked. "A small stream running toward the marshes on its northern end?"

Gorli shrugged; "It may be. I have not seen it myself. Either way, we will meet him there and crush him. Our scouts have told us that he has only half our numbers."

He then bade them goodnight and returned to the king.

"Jarhost did not like our decision to stay away from his hall," Wisic muttered, "or he would have greeted us himself."

"He does not like having men so important as ourselves challenging his fame on this isle," Havar grinned. "If we grow much more famous, he may determine to outlaw us." He did not seem overly upset by the idea, but Ylmi only frowned and glared at the fire.

"How many men do we have?" Karik asked Orli.

The man shrugged, sullenly. "Two hundred, perhaps."

Karik turned to Ylmi: "You know the place he mentioned?"

She nodded; "It is an excellent place for a trap."

"If you were Hegli," Karik directed his question to her and Igil, "how would you use the land?"

<hr>

The next morning dawned cool and cloudy. Small fires about the valley flickered, as the warriors and farmers warmed themselves and armed for the fight.

Before the sun was all the way over the mountains, the calls came to march. As Jarhost ordered his men, Ylmi fell in at the rear, with Karik and the other men of the sea villages. Orli and Flovi tried to give them orders of where to stand, but Ylmi and Revik laughed at them, and Karik only shook his head at their attempts to assert control.

In the fore marched Jarhost and his son Jarvik, with their bodyguard and sworn men, all in mail and bearing shining spears; more than a few wore swords. They were the wealthiest and best-armed men of Jarhost's army, and had proven themselves more than once in battle, against King Viglir and the warriors in the west.

Behind them marched Jarl Olvik of Garhom, with his sworn warriors. Of all Jarhost's domain, Garhom lay the nearest to the Undmir, and it was they who had most often fought against Jarl Hegli and the warriors of that place.

Behind these marched Jarl Birin of Mirhom, with his company of warriors. Though Mirhom lay farthest to the south, Jarl Birin was reckoned the wealthiest man on the eastern side of the mountains, after King Jarhost, and his company of warriors numbered almost as many as those of the king.

Last of all marched the men of the coast, a ragtag collection of men and women from Yrdnara, Yrdstadt and Illstadt. Few wore armour, and even fewer had more than a spear. Their jarls had stayed behind, because there was more important work for them to do than to fight in Jarhost's battle, and they had spared only a few men from each village to come fight.

But, despite the small number, Ylmi soon noticed the stares and disturbance among them, as she and the others stepped up to the column; whispers of "dragonslayers" were less than subtle. Thora grinned at her, as one man behind them said, in a voice meant to be quiet: "Look at the scars!"

Ylmi turned and grinned at him, and felt a burst of joy in her chest when he blanched at the sight of her burned eye and cracked skin.

As Gorli had said, they did not have far to march, but Ylmi was surprised when she saw no scouts being sent out. It was barely noon when they reached the head of the valley, the ground sloping down, northward to where Hegli's men were drawn up in a shield wall.

It did seem as if Hegli had struggled to raise an army: less than a hundred men stood in the old jarl's shield wall, but they had chosen a good position. At the back of the valley, their flanks were protected by steep slopes covered in trees which grew thick together, and the stream which ran down behind them was so shallow as to pose no obstacle of escape, if needed.

But, as the back end of Jarhost's army came over the low ridge, Ylmi stared into the valley, and saw far fewer warriors than she expected. Karik was staring into the valley as well, his face tight and drawn.

"He had more men in his camp," Karik muttered, "and I see none of the women who were filling many of his tents."

"It's a trap," Ylmi hissed, and Karik took off at a run. Ylmi lifted her spear from her shoulder and followed him, jogging past the men of Girhom and Mirhom, to draw up near the king.

"My king!" Karik called. "My king!"

Jarhost looked around for the voice, and frowned when his eyes fell on Karik. "What brings you shouting so?"

"My king, I believe Hegli has laid a trap," Karik said quickly, and more than a few faces turned toward him at those words.

"I have hunted far north," Ylmi said, as she joined them, "and this valley is not strange to me. Jarl Hegli doubtless has more men than the pitiful force before us, and I do not doubt he has brought many of his women to battle as well. The ridges on either side of the valley," she pointed right and left, "are excellent places for small companies to lie hid, or to hide an attack that comes only after the shield walls are met."

Jarhost chuckled and looked toward Hegli's troops, then back around the valley. "The pups think one great deed makes them masters of war!" he said to his men, and most joined in his laughter, but Ylmi did not miss that more than a few eyed the tree-covered slopes on either side of the valley.

"Perhaps it would be best to let a few go check the hills," Gorli appeared beside Jarhost, "just for the ease of men's minds."

Jarhost considered for a moment, then shook his head; "I will not be ordered about by children. There is a place for cunning and trickery, but we have the stronger force and will shatter Hegli in a matter of moments."

He looked over the valley and pointed ahead of him: "The dragonslayers will fight here, in the centre, where their bravery may inspire the whole army." He smiled at them, but Ylmi saw a challenge in his eyes, and she felt the familiar twist of hatred rising in her chest.

"As the king commands," Karik said tightly, and the two of them turned back. Ylmi felt her face tighten with rage, and she felt her hand wringing the wooden haft of her spear.

"Why do we serve such fools?" she hissed, as they trudged back along the line.

"An excellent question," Karik replied. "A most excellent question, indeed."

By the time they reached their friends, the column was forming itself into a shield wall, and already the clattering of spears on shields was echoing over the valley.

"Wisic, Revik, Thora, Havar!" Ylmi shouted, and waved her spear over her head. "We're fighting in the front."

Thora grinned and hefted her own spear, but Orli shouted angrily: "No! Get in line!"

"Orders of the king," Ylmi shrugged with a grin, and almost laughed as Thora shouldered past Orli, who still protested.

"I don't care what the king said," Orli's voice was petulant; "I am the leader sent by your jarl, and you will—"

"Shut up," Ylmi snapped, as she lifted her spear toward him. She would be dead on the spot if she killed Jarhost, and she had not yet been given the opportunity to kill Unhost, but if Orli tried to restrain her...

Her eyes settled on Ulfr, who was lurking among the trees, not far off. The wolf was unsure of so many people in one place, and her ears were low against her head. Reluctantly Ylmi decided there was no place for her in a shield wall. "Go!" she ordered her wolf. "Go hunt!"

Ulfr looked up at her curiously for a moment, then padded off, stopping to look back once, before vanishing into the trees.

With Ulfr safely away, Ylmi turned back to the army, now forming into a shield wall. She wondered what Jarhost expected them to do with no shields. Whatever it was, he was likely to be surprised by what was about to happen.

Halfway to the king, Karik stopped and pulled them all together. "Hegli is planning a trap, and it is plain as day something is off," he said, "but Jarhost will do nothing."

"I am stunned," Thora rolled her eyes, wryly.

"We have to kill Hegli," Karik said, "and fast."

"How fast?" Revik asked.

"How fast can you move?" Ylmi asked. "I say we get behind the big one," she jerked her thumb at Revik, "and try to punch a hole in their shield wall."

Revik straightened and looked over Jarhost's men, forming across the valley from where Hegli's shield wall was already formed. "I can punch through that easily enough."

"Excellent," Karik nodded. "It is decided. If any of us fall, push on; we have to kill Hegli as quickly as possible, or his trap will spring and we'll all be dead."

"You think his trap is that big?" Igil asked.

Ylmi snorted. "Half his army isn't here. Yes, it's big."

They took their place in the back of the shield wall, but the order to attack did not come. Instead, several men stepped forward from Hegli's army and issued challenges. They shouted and screamed and scoffed at Jarhost's army, until one of Jarhost's bodyguards stepped out of the shield wall. He met one challenger halfway between the two armies, but after a short fight, Hegli's man won, and Jarhost's bodyguard numbered one fewer.

Hegli's warrior stepped forward and raised his sword to the air, shouting: "Jarhost! False king! Come and fight me! You are a coward and a weakling!"

Ylmi shook her head, but suddenly Karik was pushing forward, and an instant later he had gone through the shield wall.

"I am Karik Haldsson," he shouted, "and I fear no man!" The long sword he had taken from the dragon was in his hands, but he carried no shield. Ylmi wondered if he was insane.

But, Hegli's warrior only laughed and beckoned him on. The two approached each other swiftly, shouts rising from both sides. As they drew close, Karik swung his sword in a great arc, which flashed down toward Hegli's warrior.

He raised his own sword up to meet it, but Karik's gleaming blade cut through the sword like wood. There was a crack and, an instant later, Karik pulled his sword from the man's heart.

"Hegli! I know you are there!" Karik shouted. "I know you are sitting back and hoping other men will win your victory for you. I know you pray that you will never have to raise a blade in your own defence. The Allfather turns away from your cowardice, and his ravens hide their eyes from your disgrace."

Suddenly, Ylmi realized what he was doing. If Hegli died here, before battle was joined, he would have no chance to spring his trap, and Tanvir could take command. She pushed forward, shouldering her way through the shield wall, and pointed her spear at one of the other champions, who was beginning to make for Karik.

"I am Ylmi One-Eye!" she shouted. "I have slain a dragon and I have slain Lasvik Horsson. Face me if you are not afraid!"

The warrior laughed and ran at her. Ylmi grinned and ran as well, and as they came closer, she leapt.

The old man brought up his shield, but all her weight was behind the spear, and his block had little effect, the spearhead screaming as it scraped over the iron rim of his shield, before she buried it in his face.

He fell backward, his feet flying into the air as she landed on hers, the spear passing through his head and pinning him to the ground. She jerked the short seax from his twitching hand, even as he went still and raised it in the air.

"Face me, Hegli!" she shouted. "Or will you wait for me to kill more of your warriors?" The blood was pounding in her ears, and it felt good to shout through the valley. Not far away, Karik grinned at her, his face covered in blood, and she grinned back.

Turning to the dead man behind her, she set her foot on his neck and pulled out her spear. His chainmail was old, but seemed in good condition, and about the right size. Carefully, she pulled it off of him, then over her head, letting the mail fall over her and hang heavy from her shoulders. The weight felt good, and she grinned at Karik's envious glance.

Revik met another challenger, as did Thora, all of them calling for Hegli. But he did not come. Instead, five more champions came to face them, and each one spilt their lifeblood on the ground between the shield walls.

While they waited for Thora to finish off the fifth, Karik stepped toward Ylmi. "Tanvir is urging them on." He kept his voice low, but between the shield walls there were few to hear.

Ylmi looked and saw the lanky form of Tanvir speaking with several older men and pointing at them. "He's using us to remove those who will challenge him, and who are loyal to his father," she said in realization. It was a cunning move, and Tanvir was certainly making the most of the situation.

"How long will you hide behind the wooden skirts of the shield wall?" she shouted, and pointed her spear at the group of men Tanvir was urging on. "Or, did you come only to watch other men fight?"

She thrust her spear butt into the damp ground and drew her sword, a savage smile on her face as she held it aloft. "I have the sword of Lasvik!" she shouted at them. "Is there anyone brave enough to take it from me?"

That was enough to draw out another: an older man with a grey beard. He moved slowly toward her, holding his shield close as he drew his own sword. It was not gilt, and had none of the decoration of Ylmi's sword, but he held it as one who knew its use.

"I am Ymvor of the Red Hand," he said, when he was closer, "and I will kill you slowly."

Ylmi only smiled as she watched him with one eye, and raised the sword.

Ymvor moved slowly to her left, trying to hide in the place her missing eye should have been watching. Ylmi took one step back and he lunged. She swung her sword but it met nothing, and she felt a sharp sting on her thigh as Ymvor stepped back. She glanced down and looked up to see him smiling back at her. "I said it would be slow."

She charged, raining down blows on his raised shield, until the iron rim cracked and her blade sank into the wood. With a swift twist, Ymvor spun the shield and ripped the sword from her hands.

She staggered forward, then rolled past Ymvor as his sword passed over her. He dropped his shield as he turned, ready for the finishing blow.

But Ylmi had reached her spear, snatching it from the ground and lunging in one movement. It caught Ymvor in the shoulder and he staggered at the unexpected blow. Still, the iron rings held beneath his tunic, and he pushed it away with his sword.

"You know a spear better than a sword," he grinned. "Now perhaps we will have a real fight."

Both of them were breathing hard, and Ylmi could hear shouting on both sides as they circled each other, warily. He was older, so she might outlast him, but he seemed as quick as she was, and if she waited for him to attack, it would not go as well as it might. So, she advanced, her spear flicking out high and low, forcing him to work his sword in defence. Twice he tried to grab the spear by its haft, but she moved too swiftly for him. The third time, she feigned too slow and his hands caught it just beneath the spearhead. With a grin, he jerked at the spear, seeking to pull her forward and off-balance. But Ylmi lunged with the spear and, as Ymvor staggered backward, she pushed the spear free and caught him with its butt in the head, as she went past him.

He tumbled over backward, and as he rose Ylmi thrust three times: the first he parried away from his face, the second he parried away from his thigh, and as he raised his sword to parry the third, the spear slipped past his blade and buried itself in his leg.

He gave a sharp cry and fell to the ground, bright-red blood gushing from the wound.

"I thought you said it would be slow," Ylmi laughed, as she caught her breath. "Are you quitting on our battle, Ymvor?"

The old man looked up at her with hate in his eyes, and she laughed. She laughed because he had been better with a sword than her, and he still lay bleeding on the ground. In her mind she heard Tanvir's words: "What power does one man have over another, if there are not others to help him?" She laughed because he had doubtless thought himself safe, and now he lay bleeding at her feet. She laughed because it was men like him who kept the fools like Hegli secure on their thrones, and now even Hegli could not save him.

"You do not deserve that sword," Ymvor hissed between his teeth.

"And yet," Ylmi chuckled, "I've beaten Lasvik and I've beaten you."

"I am not beaten yet," Ymvor snapped, and he pulled himself to his feet, gripping his sword in blood-red hands. He swung at her, but she had only to lean back as the blade passed over her. Then, as she whipped back upright, her spear flashed out and caught him in the throat, just above the iron rings of his mail shirt.

For an instant, his eyes bulged in shock, then the light went out of them and he slumped backward, falling to the ground.

Ylmi looked around and saw Lasvik's sword on the ground. Picking it up, she slid it back into its sheath and looked to her left.

Karik was pulling his sword out of another man, and it looked as if no one had been foolish enough to answer Revik's second challenge.

Just then, a horn sounded from Hegli's army, and the shield wall thundered as a hundred axes and spears pounded upon the iron-edged planks.

"Back!" Thora called, and with a final laugh and wave to Hegli, Ylmi turned and followed Karik and the others back to the shield wall. Her heart was pounding, and she felt a great warmth blooming over her chest, filling her with strength. When she had faced the dragon, she had felt fear wrap itself around her heart, but there was none of that now. The dragon had done his worst and she still lived. What more could these men do to her?

"I thought he had you there, for a moment," Karik chuckled, as they hurried back. He was breathing heavily, and he seemed to be covered in blood. "Shows how little I know."

"I'm not great with this sword," Ylmi muttered back, "but I haven't met anyone who can best my spear."

"Thank the Allfather for that," Karik breathed.

Then they were slipping between the shields of Jarhost's shield wall, and gathering with Igil, Wisic and Havar in the rear.

"Well, you four sure got things going," Wisic shook his head. "Though I confess I did not expect Thora to kill the most."

Ylmi glanced at her in surprise, and Thora shrugged. "How many?" she asked.

Thora held up four fingers. "When you're not seven feet tall, don't have face scars that make you look like the Allfather, and have a long spear instead of a massive sword... more people think they can beat you."

"She also cut them down like she was spearing fish." Wisic shook his head. "Are you alright?" His last question was directed at Karik, who was pressing his hand to his side.

"I'm fine," Karik answered. "The last one just nicked me a bit."

Ylmi saw him wince and hefted her spear. "We are enough to reach Hegli," she told him. "You stay here and recover."

Karik laughed at that, but cut it off after a moment: "Not a chance, One-Eye." He looked behind them and saw that Jarhost's men had begun to move forward. "Let's go, before the king sends someone to order us elsewhere."

Ylmi nodded, tightening her grip on her spear, and the group moved down toward the shield wall.

"When they meet," Karik said, "Ylmi and I will clear a path to the front line across from Hegli's banner then, Revik, you hit the hole hard.

Don't worry about behind you; we've got it covered. Just get to Hegli's bodyguard."

Revik nodded, tossing his great axe between his hands.

"You clear a path," Igil echoed; "I'll do the killing."

"You have not seen the day when you could kill more than me," Revik shot back.

Ylmi shook her head at them, but as she did so she noticed Karik wince. He pressed his hand to his side and bent over for a moment.

"It's more than a scratch," she said, laying a hand on his shoulder, but he straightened quickly.

"It only stings," he muttered. "For a moment, I really thought we'd be able to get Hegli to come out and fight..." He shook his head; "This better not go on much longer."

A flurry of javelins and axes flew between the two lines as they drew close, then the shield walls came together with a shout and a crash.

Above the mayhem the grey banner of Hegli hung, and they took their position across from it. Jarhost and his son were shouting encouragement to the line, but Ylmi paid them no heed. The shield wall here was four men deep, and once they began to open a path for Revik, it would begin to bend. She grabbed one man by the back of his shirt.

"Stand aside!" she shouted over the clamour. He looked back at her in surprise, but jumped out of the way when he saw her dead eye peering out of the burnt scars.

Karik pulled away the next, and she reached in to grab the man holding his shield against Hegli's men. "When I say, push!"

Behind her, she heard Revik's deafening voice booming over the din: "Hegli! Hegli! Prepare the way! Dragonsbane is coming!"

"Push!" she roared into the man's ear, and dug her feet into the rocky ground. They shoved hard, pushing at Hegli's shield wall, enough to give just a hair's breadth of space.

Then, with a savage shout, Revik charged.

His ax flashed through the air above her head as he charged, and brought it down on the first man in Hegli's shield wall. There was a crunch, as the heavy iron bit through shield and helm and brains, and Revik was through the shield wall.

Igil was behind him, pushing his brother forward, as his seax flashed and carved in the tightly-packed formation. Beside Igil, Havar was wielding his smaller ax to deadly effect, and Thora's spear was flashing over them all. Then Ylmi and Karik followed, with Wisic in their rear, all pushing desperately forward.

Twice her feet slipped as she pushed, and she caught herself on Igil's belt. She did not know how many she killed, only that her hands were slick with blood and an ache was beginning in her lungs.

As they pushed forward, Ylmi saw Tanvir out of the corner of her eye. He was behind the shield wall and he barked a sharp command. Suddenly, they were not pushing any more, and she saw a man in fine armour with a bright sword go skidding across the ground, his chest laid wide open by Revik's ax.

"I warned you, Hegli," she heard Karik shout. Then, they were fighting Hegli's bodyguards. There were only five now, while Karik was raining blows from his sword upon Hegli himself.

Hegli's remaining guards tried to rally, and Ylmi found herself fighting shoulder to shoulder with Wisic, to keep them back. She speared a short-bearded warrior with an ax, then dropped to her knee as a pair of spears were thrust toward her.

When she came up, she had a shield in her left hand, and caught the next spear thrust against it, before lunging forward herself. Wisic fell beside her, then was up again, swinging his boar spear in great arcs, which cleared the space before them.

There was a guttural cry behind them, and Ylmi glanced back to see Karik lift the head of Hegli in the air, by its hair.

"Your jarl is dead!" Karik shouted, as he raised the head aloft.

"Hegli is dead!" they took up the shout.

Then Ylmi saw Tanvir with his companions, taking their stand farther back.

"To me!" Tanvir shouted. "To me, men of the Undmir!"

Ylmi leant on her spear, her breath coming in great, burning gasps. Her fingers had been bashed more than once, and several of her knuckles were bleeding, but she seemed otherwise unharmed. Beside her, Wisic tossed aside a broken spearhead, and pressed his fingers to his side.

"Are you hurt?" Ylmi asked.

Wisic shook his head. "The dragon did worse," he smiled at her.

Ahead of them, Tanvir was pulling his army back, a new shield wall forming in the narrow northern part of the valley.

"Peace, Jarhost!" he called. "Let us have peace!"

"Kill them all!" Jarhost shouted. "I will have the Undmir this day!"

"Oh, by the Allfather!" Karik muttered, and Ylmi turned to see he was sitting wearily beside Hegli's body. "Jarhost is a fool."

"He has his victory," Revik spat, "which we earned. What more does he want?"

Ylmi shook her head. "He wants the Undmir. With that fortress, he can threaten Viglir without having to squeeze his army through the passes."

"Well, he's going to get a lot of his men killed doing it," Thora muttered.

Ylmi followed her gaze and shook her head. Tanvir's shield wall now stood in the narrowest part of the valley, its flanks protected by towering cliffs. Only a score of men wide, it was at least five men deep – perhaps more. "Good luck with that," Ylmi muttered.

But, Jarhost's shield wall was advancing, as the king and jarls urged on their men. Ylmi let the shield wall pass them by, finally catching her breath.

"Peace, Jarhost!" Tanvir called out again. "You have been victorious this day. Let me bury my father and return home!"

"Press on!" Jarhost shouted to his men, as he strode up and stopped next to Wisic, his son Jarvik close behind him. "What are you all resting for? The battle is not yet over!"

"You've won!" Karik snapped. "And Tanvir's position is a strong one; we cannot break it. Take your victory and let Tanvir bury his father."

Jarhost hefted his sword. "The young pup will learn to fear me as his father did not, if I have to chase him all the way back to his fortress."

But, Ylmi's eyes were fixed on the east. "Birds," she pointed. "Birds are flying in from the east."

"Don't birds usually come to battlefields?" Wisic asked.

"Ravens do," Thora answered, following Ylmi's gaze, "but those aren't carrion birds."

"Stop worrying about birds," Jarvik snapped from behind his father, "and get back to the fight."

Ylmi fixed him with her one eye and wiped her bloody hand over her face. "Your hands seem clean, young one," she said, softly. "Perhaps it is you who should get back to the fight."

"The birds are fleeing the men Hegli set to ambush us on the flanks." Jarhost shook his head. "The craven coward. But get up; the battle is almost won."

"Let them go," Karik said, rising slowly to his feet. "The Undmir has lost good men today, and their jarl."

"And I mean to see them lose more," Jarhost snapped. "Now, cease arguing with your king and get back in the fight!"

But Ylmi's eyes widened, for upon the eastern ridge a line of men was forming. And, as they raised their shields, the sun shone red and green upon them: the colours of King Viglir.

HEGLI'S SURPRISE

Ylmi gazed in horror as the line of men on the ridge grew longer and longer, spears and banners waving three or four deep.

"King Viglir!" she shouted, as loud as she could. "Viglir is come!"

Jarhost looked at her in astonishment. "What do you mean, Viglir is come?" His voice dripped contempt, and Ylmi felt the urge to spit him on her spear.

"His men are coming up to that ridge," she snapped, as she pointed behind him, "and there are not a few of them."

Jarhost began to respond, but the words died on his lips as he looked eastward. Row upon row of Viglir's warriors marched through the trees, and began coming down the slope on the eastern side of the valley. Jarhost began shouting and stormed down the battlefield, to turn his shield wall to meet this new threat.

Ylmi turned to see Revik helping Igil tie a bandage over his arm, as Karik leant on his sword.

"So," Karik said, wearily, "Viglir is come." Slowly, he pulled himself to his feet, his leather vest soaked in blood. "Tanvir said nothing of this?"

Ylmi shook her head. "I would like to think it was a thing he did not know of."

"I don't know what you are talking about," Havar snapped, "but maybe we should get out of here."

"I fear the raiding of Viglir will be worse than the ruling of Jarhost," Ylmi answered him. "Besides, it is an ill thing to run from a battle."

"There is no getting out of this," Karik said, "so let us do what we can."

"What we can..." Igil was looking up at the slope. "My brother is less an immovable object, more an unstoppable force, and the rest of us with him. I do not think we will do much in the shield wall."

"We also do not have shields," Havar pointed out.

Ylmi followed Igil's gaze, and shook her head in disbelief. Viglir's men were now arrayed in full above the valley, forming a strong shield wall, even as Jarhost and his jarls struggled to reform their men in line, to face this new threat. But, Jarhost's battle line was thinner than Viglir's, and both sides knew it. Shouts and taunts were now being thrown back and forth, but Viglir's men seemed far more enthusiastic.

"Can everyone still fight?" Ylmi asked. Karik was breathing heavily and seemed weary beyond reason, while Wisic was bleeding from a cut above his hip and a gash in his arm. But, they all nodded.

"Put me to the right of someone," Thora said, "and I'll be fine; my left arm isn't working wonderfully at the moment." Ylmi nodded, seeing the broken arrow which protruded just above her elbow.

Igil was looking thoughtfully at the sides of the valley, and Ylmi saw a plan forming behind his eyes. "What are you thinking?" she asked him, quickly.

Igil pointed off into the trees: "Our friends from the coast appear to be making themselves scarce. I am thinking that perhaps if we follow suit..."

"If we run now," Ylmi shook her head, "we'll be defending our homes against Viglir's army by ourselves in a week's time."

But Igil waved her words away, wearily; "If we appear to follow suit, we may fall upon their flank as the shield walls come together. Even a few of us might be enough to turn the tide and send Viglir scurrying back to the lowlands."

Ylmi nodded, and found the rest of the group was doing so as well. She turned to look at Karik. "Are you able to come with us?"

"I am," he said, grimly. "I started this mess, and I'll see it through to the end."

"Don't be ridiculous," Ylmi snapped. Then, she cast her eye over the group. "Follow me."

As the shouting between the shield walls built to a crescendo, they slipped off into the trees, Ylmi easily finding a looping path which hid them from prying eyes.

But, none of them noticed Flovi and Orli following after them.

Ylmi took her bow in one hand and her spear in the other. When it came time to attack, she would try to give the others cover with her arrows – all the more useful if Viglir had more men following behind.

A shout went up from the valley, a challenging roar, then the sound of two hundred shields clattering together, and Ylmi guessed that Viglir's men were charging down the slope. She picked up her pace, seeing in her mind's eye all of Jarhost's men fleeing, his shield wall shattered in one violent push by Viglir's men. Much good they would do then: one more little party, all on their own against the might of Viglir's army.

They came over the spur of the ridge, near where they had first entered the valley that morning, and Ylmi looked down on the battlefield. The two shield walls had collided, and Viglir's army was pressing Jarhost's force back, step by step.

"No time to waste," Revik said calmly, and raised his ax. With a deep breath, he raised the great ax and roared: "Dragonsbane!"

The rest took up the cry and ran, as Ylmi thrust her spear into the dirt. Drawing her bow, she loosed an arrow into the unprotected side of the nearest enemy. He was wearing leather armour, but he crumpled as her arrow took him under the arm and sank deep into his chest. She let loose another arrow, cutting down another man, even as he turned to look for the danger.

Then, Revik and the rest struck the end of the shield wall, and it crumpled. Revik's ax rose and fell, and Karik's sword flashed in the sunlight. Behind them, the other dragonslayers were wielding their spears with deadly efficiency, against men who could not turn their shields.

Ylmi heard a twig snap behind her and she whirled, arrow on the string, to find Flovi and Orli standing behind her. "Don't just stand there," she snapped; "help!"

They looked at her for an instant, with something in their eyes that she did not like, then Flovi spoke: "It is a better thing for us to see first that Viglir does not come from this victorious." Orli nodded, and the two of them made their way down to the battle.

Ylmi loosened the rest of her arrows, picking her targets carefully, but in her mind she wondered what Flovi had meant by "first". When her last arrow was gone, she took up her spear and advanced into the battle.

By now, Revik's charge had slowed. Instead of shattering, Viglir's line had reformed and bent back on itself, so it now stood like a distorted half circle at the base of the slope.

These were warriors who had stormed Gar's Pass, and fought more than few times against Jarhost and his army, and they were not easily routed. The grinding of the shield walls as both sides pushed against each other filled the air, joined by the continued shouts and taunts, still hurled back and forth.

Picking up a shield which lay on the ground near one man she had killed, Ylmi advanced next to Revik, and found herself beside Wisic. He grinned when he saw her.

"Welcome, One-Eye!" he laughed, and she grinned in answer. Together they thrust their spears over the men in front, probing and pushing at the enemy's shield wall.

But, Viglir had more men, and though his shield wall had been beaten back, it was still stronger. And now, after fighting Hegli's men and facing the first attack of Viglir's army, Jarhost's men were tired.

In unison, Viglir's men pushed forward, step by step. In front of Ylmi Jarhost's line was pushed back, again and again, until Viglir's line had unbent itself. Ylmi and Wisic pressed against the men in front of them, but here on the edges Viglir's shield wall was three men deep, and they were pushing forward with ease.

Suddenly, there was a plucking at her shoulder, and she turned to see Karik, covered in blood, his mouth wide as he gasped for breath. "We have," he said, "to punch through." He pointed to where Revik was trying to swing his ax over the top of the shield wall. "Grab him."

Wisic joined them, sucking in air in great gulps, his leather jerkin slick with blood. Though he still smiled, there was a limp in his step, and his left arm hung at his side.

"Get to the rear," Ylmi told him, but he only laughed.

"I can still swing an ax with the best of them," he said, but then his eyes went to Revik, and he shrugged. "Well, maybe not the best, but with most. We'll need to fight together if we're going to win this one."

Ylmi couldn't argue with that, so she reached forward, grabbed Revik's shirt and pulled him steadily back from the press. He quickly realized what was happening and, with one more great blow from his ax, he backed out of the line and came to talk with Karik. Behind them, the shield wall was sagging again, and Karik was up against them, setting his hand on the shoulder of the men in the press.

"Hold a little longer!" he shouted. "Just a little longer."

"You're going to use me as a ram again?" Revik was covered in blood but smiling grimly, as Igil and Havar followed him up.

"Yes, come on." Karik turned and they hurried down the battle line.

Jarl Birin was shouting at his men to hold firm, and when he saw Karik and the rest of them hurrying toward him, he pointed with his short sword: "Right there!"

Ylmi looked and saw that, here, Viglir's line was only two men deep. She lifted her spear.

"Right, Revik in front," Karik ordered, "and everyone else press close."

Revik laughed, raised his ax overhead and, with a roar, they charged forward. Revik's ax bit down through the first man's head and hurled him back into his companion. Ylmi thrust her spear low, taking another man in the leg, so that he fell. Wisic finished him off and they were through.

Ylmi felt Igil's hand on her shoulder, holding her so they did not go too far, lest Viglir's line reform behind them and cut them off. Thora was next to her, fighting to push back Viglir's men, who pressed in on them. Ylmi saw someone hack Thora's spear in two, but an instant later Thora lashed out with a small ax and the man fell back, blood streaming from under his helmet.

It was a small gap but they held it, pushing hard as Viglir's men tried to close it. A spear snaked in and Ylmi dodged it. When it came in again, she heard Wisic grunt, and felt him leaning into her, as the press of the fighting held them together. She thrust with her own spear in response, catching flesh she could not see, through all the shields and shouting.

"Push!" Jarl Birin was shouting. "Push!"

There was a staggering crack as someone struck her shield, and Ylmi felt the wood split. The gleam of a spear blade appeared over her arm and she twisted to pull at it.

Then a horn sounded, and Viglir's men began to give back.

Again and again the horn blew, and the space before them cleared, as the two shield walls drew apart.

"Peace!" someone ahead shouted, and the warriors before her began to draw back. Wisic fell back behind her, but she stepped forward, noticing Havar on her left, as she kept her eyes on the man directly across from her, a dirty smile leering over a battered shield, as he stepped back.

"Peace!" came the shout again, and the shield walls fell farther apart.

Looking around, Ylmi saw Revik with his ax, with Igil close beside him, and the shield wall falling apart, as everyone eyed each other.

"Let us have peace," a short man shouted, waving a gold-hilted sword in the air, a green and red shield in his other hand. "Jarhost! We have all fought well today and acquitted ourselves as men." His voice echoed over the sudden stillness which settled across the valley.

But, as she looked, Ylmi felt something pinch in the small of her back, as she was shoved forward. Stumbling a few feet, she turned quickly to find Flovi staring at her in confusion, a chipped knife in his hand. Ylmi's eyes widened as she watched him suddenly trying to hide the knife. Havar turned to see what had happened.

"Did you just try to stab me?" Ylmi was incredulous. But suddenly she saw Unhost's smile in her mind, and how close Flovi had become with the jarl, and she saw the truth.

"I was not..." Flovi began, but Ylmi stepped quickly forward, raising her spear. Yet even as she did so she checked, for she saw Karik, his eyes on the ground, as Orli lunged with a knife.

In a swift movement, Ylmi reversed her hand on her spear and hurled it, narrowly missing Flovi as he leapt aside, and striking Orli in the ribs, just as he thrust the knife into Karik's side. Karik twisted as Orli was thrown past him, and slumped backward, his knees giving way as he reached for the knife.

Behind her, the kings and jarls were coming to some kind of an agreement, but all Ylmi felt was rage, her vision tinged with red.

Flovi should have run or protested his innocence, but he must have known either course would have been fruitless, so he pulled his ax from his belt and lunged.

Ylmi's hands were slick with blood as she reached for her sword.

Suddenly, a dark blur erupted from the trees and struck Flovi, hurling from his feet. By the time they landed, Ulfr had him by the neck and Flovi was screaming. His ax had fallen a short distance away, and his hands grasped at empty air.

Ylmi drew the short seax from her belt and stepped forward, calling softly to Ulfr. The wolf rolled her eyes up at Ylmi, her jaws still tight on Flovi's neck, and Ylmi slowly reached out her hand.

"I've got it," she said, softly. "Good girl."

Ulfr looked at her for a moment then, with a last shake, let go. Ylmi knelt beside Flovi. "Unhost sent you, didn't he?"

He nodded, choking on the blood streaming from his neck.

"In a few moments," she told him softly, "you will stand before the Allfather, and he will ask you how you died." She held his eyes with hers, watching the fear and horror filling them. "And you will answer truthfully, for none can stand before him and lie in that judgement: you will tell him you died as you attempted to murder a young woman of your own village, after she had fought to save it." She smiled down at him. "I look forward to seeing your reward."

Grasping him by the shoulder, she jerked him up, thrusting the seax deep into his heart. His eyes rolled back and he fell limp, his body falling off the short blade with a wet, sucking sound.

All around her, Ylmi felt eyes on her and she rose, facing them with a feral smile. "Anyone else want to try to kill me?"

Her eyes went to Karik, slumped on his knees with his back to her. She stepped around Igil, who was pulling the knife from his side, and saw why Karik was so motionless.

Before him lay Wisic's corpse, a dozen wounds slowly leaking blood, even as pink foam was drying on his lips. The eyes that had so often laughed and winked now stared, cold and sightless, into the sky.

"It was not my intention for him to die," Karik said, slowly.

A cold rain began to fall, slow and light, the drops falling noisily onto the bodies, weapons and debris which covered the field. Slowly, the armies drew apart, Viglir's men retreating up the ridge and Jarhost's army falling back, to the centre of the valley.

Revik set down his ax and knelt by Wisic's body, cradling his head in his hands, as he stared into the sightless eyes. Without looking up, he said: "Tanvir got away in the confusion, along with most of the men of the Undmir."

They were alone now, the dragonslayers among the dead, sitting at the base of the eastern slope.

Karik staggered to a tree and, with a sigh, sat back against it, closing his eyes wearily.

"The ones who fought will be the ones loyal to Hegli," Ylmi said. "With them dead, Tanvir will take his father's jarldom unopposed."

All save for Karik looked at her in surprise. "You planned this?" Thora asked.

"Well..." Ylmi wiped at the blood which covered her face, and looked at her hand, "... not this part. Nor Viglir's arrival – that, I confess, I did not expect."

"I'm not sure many did," Karik said, quietly. His hand was pressed to his side, but his leather jerkin had a wet gleam to it.

"You've been stabbed," Ylmi said, as she narrowed her eyes.

"At least twice," Karik slurred his words and blinked his eyes open. "No hot knives this time?" he smiled, then slumped over.

Ylmi was the first at his side, ripping off the leather he wore, now so mangled as to be useless, and found more than a few wounds. "Don't just stand there!" she snapped at Revik. "Find something I can use to stop this bleeding. And someone see to Thora, as well."

"I'm fine," Thora protested, but Ylmi glared at her. She had snapped off most of the arrow, so that now only a small wooden stick protruded from her arm.

Ylmi snapped at her: "You are not. Get that out and cleaned before it becomes infected."

She turned her attention back to Karik. None of the cuts were life-threatening, she hoped, but the bleeding had gone on for so long that half of Karik's clothes were soaked red and sticky.

Revik returned a moment later with a long cloak he had found, and they cut it into strips. Some Ylmi used to bandage Karik, the rest were used to bandage their other wounds.

Igil pushed the arrow out of Thora's arm, and she swore more violently than Ylmi had thought possible. Havar had also received a long gash along his right arm, but he insisted it was more gruesome than bothersome.

By the time they were finished, Viglir's army had taken their dead and wounded and withdrawn, agreeing with Jarhost to be beyond Gar's Pass by nightfall the next day. The eastern king had come to help Hegli and to win an easy victory over his rival, but he had arrived too late.

Jarhost's army gathered their own dead, and built twenty-six funeral pyres. Wisic was laid upon the last, together with his spear.

"He should have been burned with a piece of the dragon's gold," Thora said quietly, as the flames rose.

They said nothing, only watched the fire lick at the green wood, as others of Jarhost's army celebrated their victory over Hegli and their repulsion of Viglir's attack, which they were calling a vile trick.

They stood there together for a while longer, as the flames roared, and Wisic Immelsson – who had passed through dragon-fire and lived – was consumed by fire, and sent to feast in the war halls of the Allfather.

One by one they stepped away, and Ylmi's mind turned to Flovi and Orli, and to Unhost, whom she knew had sent them.

When she stepped away from the crumbling blaze, she saw Karik sitting by a tree, on the edge of the valley. He was covered in blood, his face upturned to the sky, with his eyes closed against the light, cool rain. She crossed the field and took a seat opposite him.

"Our plan worked well enough," she said, looking him over, "all things considered." His bandages were stained red, but the blood did not appear to be flowing. With his shirt cut away, the scars of the dragon-fire stood out, dark and cracked, over his arm and shoulder. He shivered in the cool evening wind, and Ylmi tore her eyes away from him.

"Here," she said, and tossed him her cloak. "We'll get you something to wear later."

Karik nodded and wrapped the cloak around himself, gratefully.

They sat quietly for a moment, the sounds of nightfall around them, as Havar built a fire. The wind was rustling through the trees on the slope above them, and in the distance the stream was gurgling down from the valley, northward to the marshes.

Thora and Revik disappeared into the woods for a time, and returned with two rabbits and a few roots they had dug up, from near a stream. As the meat cooked over the fire, Havar stared at Karik, and Ylmi thought he seemed deep within his own mind. Ulfr vanished to hunt for a time, but returned to lie at Ylmi's side. It felt good to rest her hand in the wolf's fur, and the weight of her felt safe.

"Ylmi," Thora spoke at last, her eyes on Ylmi and Karik, "the two of you planned all this?"

Ylmi nodded. "We went to speak with Hegli first, and offered him a way out." She nodded to Karik; "He thought that Hegli would turn it down, so offered the same thing to his son." She shrugged; "Tanvir took the deal."

"What was the deal?" Havar asked. "Please tell me you did not offer to return the gold."

Karik coughed, then winced at the pain. "That we did not. Only that I would show them how we passed through the Undersea, and how to secure themselves against anyone else who would learn the way."

Havar swore. "Wonderful! Well done, Karik." He spat into the fire, angrily. "That was not your decision to make."

"Havar, we will soon be sailing and raiding coasts far richer and far wealthier than a hole in the ground with yellow rocks," Karik explained, patiently. "And, I do not want to make a habit of robbing our brethren. The little gold we took harmed Hegli's pride more than his people."

"If," Havar leant forward, "the Isles are passable. If our boat can make it. We have few paths to fame and fortune Karik, and you have closed off one of them."

Karik closed his eyes. "If we gather fame and fortune at the expense of our starving brethren, we are no better than King Jarhost, or Unhost, for that matter. If any of you think differently, let me know now."

Revik hesitated, staring into the fire. "Not everyone will feel the same way about us," he said, "and I am not sure that we should be so kind to those who think to rob and raid us in our turn."

"Until they prove themselves our friends," Havar nodded, "then they are fair game."

"I did not say that," Revik said quickly, with a look to Karik; "only that we should not be quick to claim peace."

Karik leant back on his tree again and closed his eyes. "War hurts. I will always vote peace, when possible."

"You lost your fingers in peace," Havar muttered, and Karik grinned.

"True, but right now it hurts more where I was stabbed."

A ripple of laughter went around the fire at that.

As the night deepened, they ate and drank to the memory of Wisic.

YLMI ONE-EYE

The next morning, they set out for home in a gentle rain. Jarhost disbanded his army when it was clear that Viglir had retreated, and little bands scattered through the hills and mountains, all of them smaller than they had been only a day before.

Ylmi set an easy pace, stopping often to rest. Both Thora and Karik insisted they were fine, but Karik's protest vanished quickly, and Thora cradled her arm, quietly, whenever they stopped.

It was almost dark on the night of the third day, when Ylmi saw the animal skulls which marked the path near Dranri's house. She led the others down the trail to it, and was comforted to hear the sound of Dranri splitting wood. His big dog, Gar, came running up to greet her and Ulfr, and smelled suspiciously at the others.

"I hear you won a great victory," Dranri said, when he saw them. He set his ax on the stump. "But you have come to the wrong place if you are in search of a victory feast."

"No victory feast," Ylmi shook her head, "but we would be thankful for a place to spend the night."

"That I can provide," Dranri said, his eyes taking in their wounds, then looking for the one who was not there. "Wisic...?"

"Dines with the Allfather tonight," Karik said quietly, and sank down to lean against a tree, his face as white as snow.

Revik came up last, tossing a goat onto the ground before Dranri. "You have a fire we can cook this on?"

"My father will not miss one goat for the feeding of his daughter and the other dragonslayers," Ylmi told him. "At least, I hope not."

But, Dranri already had his hands on the goat and was lifting it up. "You are welcome guests, who come with such a gift." Gar sniffed at the goat, but Dranri pushed him back and began to clean it.

While Igil looked to Thora and Karik's wounds, Ylmi followed Dranri.

"I am glad you are back safe," he said to her. "I imagine your parents will be pleased, as well."

"There are some who may be less pleased," Ylmi said, her thoughts going to Unhost.

He glanced at her, and his eyes lit for the first time on her sword. His hands stilled on the goat and his eyes widened. "How came you by that?" he asked.

Ylmi glanced down at the gold-inlaid hilt. "I took it from Lasvik Horsson, after I slew him in single combat."

Dranri was very still for a moment, then asked in a tight voice: "Did he hold it as he died?"

"He held its hilt as he passed," Ylmi answered, suddenly wondering; "why do you ask?"

"He was my friend," Dranri said, simply, "before Hegli separated us. I am sorry to hear that he is dead."

Ylmi searched for something to say, and decided anything would be better than an awkward silence. "I am sorry. He fought well and died well."

"He should have picked a better jarl to serve," Dranri's voice was flat. He said little more until he had prepared the carcass and set it on a long stick.

Havar and Revik had a fire going, though Dranri narrowed his eyes when he saw it. "You have made yourselves very free with my wood," he told them.

But Revik only gave a small smile. "You are about to make yourself very free with our goat."

"Her goat," Dranri pointed to Ylmi.

"As you wish," Revik shrugged. "I will work your ax until the goat is ready." With a weary sigh, he turned to the pile of wood and began to chop.

It seemed to Ylmi that the goat took forever to cook, and when it was done the smell which filled the clearing around Dranri's house made her stomach growl, noisily. As they ate, they told Dranri of all that had passed since they returned from sailing the Undersea. He nodded as Karik told him of their agreement with Tanvir, and how the men of Undmir had fallen back from Hegli, toward the end.

"Hegli was not loved by many of his own people," Dranri said. "He was less than loved by his sons, for the way he treated their mother."

Ylmi nodded at this. "I remember what you told me, Dranri. I am not so weary as to have forgotten."

"I am saying it for the benefit of those who were not here." Dranri glared at her from under bushy eyebrows, but Ylmi only shrugged.

"I am surprised that Viglir turned back when he did," Thora said, as she laid down a bone she had gnawed clean. "If he had pulled back and regrouped, he might have still won a victory."

Dranri leant forward to toss a stick on the fire. "A costly one. Viglir is not interested in wasting men if he will not gain much from it." He waved a stick at them. "If you had not slain Hegli, then Viglir's army would have fallen upon the flank of Jarhost's shield wall, while it was engaged with Hegli. There would have been a great slaughter, Jarhost would have been slain, and Viglir would gain the high kingship he desperately desires." He shrugged. "As it was, he found a shield wall arrayed against him, and a monster with an ax." His eyes went to Revik. "Even if he had won, it would not have been a total victory, and he would have lost many men for nothing."

"If it is true that we won." Karik stared at the fire as he spoke. "I keep hearing that we did, but what did we win? Many are dead, including Wisic, who was dear to me, and it seems that nothing has changed."

"We won gold, a chance to cross the Isles," Havar muttered, "and no small measure of glory for ourselves." Karik's eyes rose from the glowing coals of the fire to glare at him in the darkness, and Ylmi felt a small shiver go down her spine, as the red firelight glinted in Karik's eyes.

"You kept chaos at bay, for a time," Dranri said, quietly. "Sometimes, you must pay dearly to simply preserve things as they are. The cost to improve them is very high indeed."

Karik grunted, but Ylmi saw him flex his hand and the stumps of his missing fingers.

They were silent for a few moments, the sounds of the mountains at night heavy in the air. The wind was blowing from the south, gently brushing through the tree branches, and nearby a stream gurgled, as it made its way down from snow-covered mountain peaks. To the west, an owl hooted. Suddenly, Dranri tore his eyes away from the fire and pointed at the sword Ylmi had set beside her.

"Did anyone tell you the name of that sword?" he asked.

Ylmi shook her head; "Hegli was less than talkative—"

"Hegli was a fool and is well dead," Dranri cut her off. "That blade was forged by the smith Kol Kolsson, and was first wielded by Winmir One-Eye, who slew forty men in single combat. For that reason alone, Ylmi, it is fitting that it should come to you. When Winmir died, he gave the sword into the keeping of his sister Alena the Vicious, who forged the iron crown and made herself the Wolf-Queen. With it, she slew her husband, who had wronged her, and she made her son king in Bjarnmont. It was she who named it Raethbur: the blade of wrath. From her, the sword was given to her son's daughter, where it rested for a generation, then her son's daughter gave it to her son, Bauglir the Outlaw. With it, he is said to have slain five jarls in single combat, until he was finally defeated by King Ingor of Bjarnmont, who set it in his treasury. His son, King Jarhost, gave it to Lasvik Horsson." He sighed and glanced toward Ylmi. "The blade is yours, so you should know its history."

Ylmi stared at him, wondering more at how he and Lasvik had known each other.

"If Lasvik was given the sword by Jarhost," Karik asked, slowly, "how did Lasvik come to be champion for Hegli?"

"That is another story," said Dranri, "and one that I will not tell tonight."

The goat was soon reduced to a pile of bones by the fire, and Dranri hung the hide by his hut. As the moon rose over the treetops, they lay down and slept beneath the stars – all save for Ylmi, who followed Dranri into his house and spoke with him there in the darkness, for many hours.

The next morning they rose, and were surprised to find Dranri making ready to come with them. "I have business in your settlement," he said, when Havar asked. Then, Ylmi told them all that she and Dranri had discussed the night before.

They set out down the pine-covered slopes, and Ylmi noted that the weather was the finest she had seen in many days. The south wind still blew gently, pushing the gloomy clouds and rain ever northward, and leaving a brilliant blue sky, which looked down brightly on them. Their journey was not a long one, even with Karik and Thora's injuries, and soon Ylmi was looking down from the mountain slope above the settlement.

"Well," she muttered, "there is no point in waiting."

Dranri nodded and lifted a small hunting horn to his lips, blowing a long note, which echoed down toward the fjord. A few goats bleated from the small pens, and Ylmi was suddenly glad her parents were not here. She could only imagine what they would think if they watched their only daughter risking death, again.

As they came, the people of the settlement appeared in a crowd, climbing out of their low homes, to see the return of the warriors who had fought with Jarhost.

The crowd parted as they approached, for in his right hand Karik carried his sword, the long blade naked and dark in the grey light. Revik unslung his ax and the others all carried their weapons, as warriors going into battle, rather than returning home. Ylmi left her sword sheathed. She was happier with her spear, and she wanted to be sure of the outcome.

In the centre of the crowd, Unhost spread his hands. "Welcome home, victorious warriors!"

But Karik spat in the dirt. "Save your words, oh worthless bit of cow dung!"

"What manner of—" Unhost began, before Karik pulled off his shirt to show the blood-soaked bandages which wrapped his body.

"This is how Unhost treats his friends!" Karik held his arms wide, and Ylmi saw the shocked looks on many faces.

Unhost did not seem surprised, only setting his hand to the dagger at his belt. Karik continued:

"In the battle, when my attention was on the shield wall, as I fought against our enemies, I was attacked." He pointed to Unhost; "Flovi Grimsson struck at Ylmi and Orli Marinsson stabbed me in the back. Tried to cut me down, with treachery and cowardice. And, they did it on your orders! I, Karik Haldsson, dragonslayer, name you faithless, a coward and unfit to be jarl."

Unhost sneered, but before he could speak Havar stepped forward. "I have laboured for you for many years, and you have always shorted me what I was due. When I and the others slew the dragon, you took our rightful prize, and hoarded it for yourself, because our injuries prevented us from opposing you. I, Havar Hariksson, dragonslayer, declare you ungenerous, greedy and unfit to be jarl."

"Enough of this!" Unhost snarled, all trace of his good humour gone. "You ungrateful swine."

Thora stood forward next, and Unhost faltered. "I have lived here in your village for most of my life," she said, in a cold voice. "You refused aid to your sister when she hungered, and you have treated me, her daughter, with nothing but contempt and disgust. I, Thora Wilthasdottir, declare you an oath breaker, a traitor to your own and unfit to be jarl."

Unhost's face was turning purple, contorted by rage, but Ylmi's face was hard as stone as she stepped forward.

"While a fearsome danger lurked at our doorstep, you conspired with it. You fed it our food for the winter, and you protected it when it killed our loved ones. While we struggled here, working to find food for the winter, you gathered gold and courted a dragon for your own gain. Without you, this village would be much better off. I, Ylmi One-Eye, dragonslayer, declare you a thief, a murderer and a coward, unfit to be jarl."

Fornik Lievsson stepped forward quickly, standing between Karik and Unhost. "Terrible words have been spoken today," he looked from Karik to Unhost, "and it is better that this matter not go further, lest it lead to bloodshed."

"It has already led to bloodshed." Ylmi gestured with her spear to Karik's wounds; "He sent Flovi and Orli to kill Karik and myself. He allowed my brother to die because he wanted to remain on good terms with a dragon which leeched off of our village. He sent my parents into the mountain, hoping they would die of hunger." She pointed to Thora; "Did you not hear her speak? Her mother died because of Unhost's greed."

"You speak of things you neither know nor understand," Unhost snarled. "Be silent and go home, and I will attempt to forget the vile words you have spat like poison among us."

"Often, a poison is best cut out," Ylmi said, allowing a dark smile to spread over her face. She fixed Unhost with her one good eye and spoke carefully: "I challenge you, here and now, to settle this matter between us. I say you are unfit to lead. Either kill me here and now, or be gone from this settlement and never return."

Unhost stared at her, then threw off his cloak. "Give me a spear."

Ylmi grinned, her teeth showing as she laughed at him and unslung her shield. Her long spear felt good in her hands, and she laughed again when Unhost snatched up a spear from Almir and turned on her, with a snarl.

They came together in a clatter, the shafts of their spears rattling as they each pushed and struggled, 'til Ylmi leapt back, dragging her spear blade over Unhost's calf. The leg of his pants parted and a red stain began to pour down it.

"I will not make this quick," Ylmi warned him.

Unhost only snarled, lunging forward in a violent rush, but Ylmi easily dodged the blow and dropped the butt of her spear, tripping him as they passed each other. He was far slower than a boar, she reflected, and Lasvik's blows had carried more strength.

He glared at her from the dirt, coming slowly up off the ground, the spear gripped in one hand. He threw with the other, and she could only flinch as the handful of dirt struck her in her good eye. She cried out and instinctively dropped, wary of Unhost's attack. A piercing pain scraped over her head and she felt the crusted scar of the dragon-fire, pulling and tearing, as Unhost's spear sliced over the side of her face. She rolled to the side and jumped to her feet, furiously trying to rub the dirt and blood out of her vision.

She could not hold her eye open – there was still something in it – but she could blink enough to see Unhost laughing at her, as he approached again. His attack was lazy, his confidence making him sloppy, and she caught his spear as he lunged. Blinking, she saw the surprised look on his face and grinned. She would not die today – that she knew. She pulled on his spear and, as he tried to jerk it back, she kicked him in the chest.

A gasp came from the crowd as he tumbled head over heels, and Ylmi wiped away the dirt in her eye. There were still tears, but she blinked them away quickly and now could see. There was a throbbing pain in her head, and she could feel the blood and dirt smeared on her face. But the seer on Vranr's Stones had told her to go and take. So, she smiled at Unhost and went.

He tried to scramble to his feet, but Ylmi's spear pierced his right hand, as he reached for his spear. He cried out, falling onto his back and begging for mercy. But, Ylmi did not miss his left hand disappearing behind his back, and turned her face quickly to the side, as he hurled another handful of dirt. It struck the side of her face harmlessly, mingling with the blood, and Ylmi laughed: "Pathetic to the last." Then she stabbed him.

The spear went through his heart, and she drove it deeper, 'til she felt the point strike a rock in the ground.

Unhost stared at the spear in his chest, his eye bulging, then slowly looked up at her. She smiled at him, then ripped the spear from his body. The blood gushed from the wound for an instant, and Ylmi watched as the light vanished from his eyes. Then, with a choking cry, he died.

The crowd was silent, though Karik was looking at her with a mix of admiration and... something else she was not sure she recognized – but she knew that she liked it. Her heart was pounding, she felt fire flowing through her veins, and she wondered for a moment if this was what it felt like to be a god. She took a deep breath and smiled.

"My friends!" She raised her spear. "You know me. You know how I have conducted myself since my birth; how I have given aid and help, as the long winters laid heavy on us. You know that I slew the dragon, and know that I have now fought many times over to keep this place safe. Unhost tried to keep us hidden, to keep us poor, that he might hoard his gold, and look where it left us: beholden to a dragon! 'Til I helped kill it. Then, with our gold taken by a king who cares little if we feast or starve.

"It is time for us to become more than a collection of hovels, shivering through the winter on dried bark and gnawing on bones. If you will have me as your leader, I will bring you prosperity, I will bring you safety and, together, we will weather storms and winters as they come. Who will stand with me?"

Dranri made to lift his ax, but Karik was the first to step forward. "I have hunted with you in the mountains. I have sailed with you through storms. And I have fought with you in the shield wall." His voice echoed over the shore, and he nodded at her as he spoke. "And now, more than once, I have seen you take up arms and bleed for your people. I will gladly follow you." He stepped forward and stood beside her.

The other dragonslayers swiftly followed, though Havar was the last to speak.

Others came to her as well: Ethna and Ymr, the blacksmith, Dranri, and some in the village she did not know, as well. Even old Almir Alsson stood behind her, saying that she could be no worse than Unhost had been.

"I do not like this," Fornik Lievsson said, but looking around he saw that most of the crowd had joined Ylmi, and shook his head. "Unhost was kind to most of us, and gave us food when we needed it."

"Did he give of his own stores," Ylmi asked, "or did he take from one to give to another? That is not generosity, my friend, only theft and bribes."

Fornik paused a moment, considering, then stepped forward. "You are young, Ylmi, and while I do not deny the great deeds you have done," he raised his hands, "you do not yet have the wisdom that comes with years."

He turned to address the rest of the village: "Ruling as jarl is not simply a matter of prowess in battle, but of making good decisions, of understanding how to rule. Would you have one so young, so unproven, as Ylmi Bodvarsdottir? I have lived here since before she was born, and laboured in the fields..."

But a harsh rasping laugh cut him off, and he turned to see Almir Alsson laughing. "The wisdom that comes with years must have passed you by," Almir chuckled, through his broken teeth.

"You have not baited a hook or spent one full day in any field," Torig Ingsson spoke up, "unless it was to see that we gave up a share of what was ours to Unhost."

There was a great deal of nodding at this, and Ylmi took her chance.

"We have had a jarl with age and 'wisdom' on his side," she said, "and it seems that a great many of his problems were solved by others. And you have made even Almir and Torig agree on a matter, which has not been done in some years."

"And will not happen again," Torig muttered.

"It seems the matter is decided without me," Fornik spat. Seeing how the matter lay, he took a deep breath; "I am no fool to swim against a current: hail Jarl Ylmi!"

They took up the shout, and Ylmi smiled through the blood and filth, as Dranri's booming voice led the cry: "Hail Jarl Ylmi!"

The sun was setting beyond the fjord, when Ylmi stood at last before what had been Unhost's hall. The roof was low, cracking in many places, and the door was near to falling off its hinges. The setting sun cast a red light off the clouds rolling in from the north, and the wind was unusually soft.

Her hand tightened around her spear, as she pushed open the door and stepped inside. The fur-lined walls seemed to press inward, and the stone-lined fireplace in the centre of the room glowed through the ashes. The opening in the roof for the smoke moaned in the wind, even as a wisp of smoke rose up to vanish. Ulfr padded in behind her, sniffing warily.

Ylmi looked around, then bent to take a handful of sticks from a pile by the door. Tapping the ashes with the butt of her spear, she found where the coals were hottest and tossed the wood onto it. Smoke began to rise almost instantly, and soon bright flames leapt up, casting a warm, dancing light over the tiny hall.

At its head, on a slightly raised platform of stones, was Unhost's wooden throne. It was laid with furs – doubtless a few taken by Ylmi herself. She walked toward it and wondered idly if anything on it had been made by Unhost himself. She considered it for a moment as she stood before it. Then, with the fire crackling and the wind howling overhead, she sat upon it.

The fire caught at the wood she had piled onto it, casting its warm light over the wooden walls. Ulfr sniffed at the furs around the throne, then laid down by Ylmi's feet. Her spear rested against her shoulder as she leant forward, her elbows on her knees as she stared at the fire.

It was hers, all of it.

You will receive what you desire most, and when it is taken away you will receive what you hope for.

It was hers, and now she had to protect it.

Thus, Ylmi One-Eye became jarl of Dragonsrest...

EPILOGUE

The bard paused to drink from his cup and take a breath. But, before he could begin again, the lord spoke.

"You tell the tale well," he said, "but it is overly late, and I fear there is much more of the story to be told."

The bard nodded, and noticed that the children were beginning to doze, their eyes still fixed on him, but their eyelids slowly falling shut.

"You must continue the story another time," the lord said quietly, and rose from the table, a child in each arm. As he rose, so did everyone else, careful to move their chairs quietly.

The lord paused for a moment, before he left the table. "Tell me, bard, are these tales recorded here, in books, as the historians of the empire do?"

"They are not, lord."

The lord considered for a moment. "That is an ill thing, and something which I have a mind to change. It is important that we remember well our history." He turned, deep in thought, with his children in his arms, and stepped away from the table.

As the lord disappeared into the darkness behind the dais, the bard and several of the other guests made their bed by the fire, their rest warmed by the red glowing coals, which blinked from underneath the great log.

Vranr's Curse

Book III

PROLOGUE

The cold of winter was near to breaking, but the last throes of the winter storms still raged outside the king's hall. Within, however, the fire was roaring, and the mead was flowing freely.

The old bard ate happily, but his eyes did not miss the comings and goings within the hall. He was a storyteller, and one never knew when the beginnings of another tale would present themselves.

In the hall's midst, a great company of the king's closest companions, shield brothers, and old warriors were making merry about the great roaring fire. They laughed and sang, rejoicing in the break from the winter's monotony and reveling in the warmth of the great fire.

But on the dais, the king's smile did not often reach his eyes, and the bard marked that it never lasted for long. His mind was not on the feast, and his eyes often left the tables and gazed sightlessly into the fire, as if searching for an answer to some question or gazing through the flames to see something on the other side.

The fire's warmth and light were the greatest they had been all winter, so it was easy for the bard to see how messengers came and went, passing swiftly through the shadows along the hall's eaves till they whispered in the king's ear, then leaving just as swiftly when he had given his response.

The king's children sat beside him, and their eyes wandered often to the bard. They enjoyed his stories thus far, and the bard guessed he might be fortunate enough to win from the king an offer of hospitality.

But to do that, he would have to spin a wonderful tale this night, and the tale of Karik was swiftly moving into... more difficult territory. His mind played over the events of the tale he was to tell and the king's request for how it should end, and he turned his glance again at the king. Something was afoot, and he had a feeling that the tale he was to tell was more than simply entertainment for that night.

He drank of the mead, and blessed again the mountain bee keeper who had brewed it, and turned back to the food before him. It was not long before the laughter and the chatter in the hall grew quiet, and the bard looked up to see the king was looking to him.

"Come bard," the king said in his deep voice. "You have told us how Karik won his first battle and you have told us of how Ylmi came to be called 'One-eye.' But they are remembered for other things, are they not?"

"Indeed, they are," the bard said, rising to his feet.

"Then," the king said, "now that you have reminded us all of how Karik and Ylmi came to be heroes, you may tell us how they came to land upon our shores."

With a deep breath, the bard put aside his foreboding and spoke.

Jarl Tanvir

Many great and terrible deeds were accomplished by Karik and the Dragonslayers, but none were greater than their passage of the Black Isles. Toward this they had thought and labored, setting themselves ever toward that goal.

But even after Unhost was dead and Jarhost satisfied for a time, much still remained between the dragonslayers and their purpose.

For her part, Ylmi turned her focus to the work of the village. Now that she was jarl, it fell to her to prepare the king's yearly tax for the first time and to lay aside for the building of a ship. For his part, Karik was eager to start on the ship. But, before he could lay his hands to it, there was the matter of his bargain with Tanvir, now jarl in the Undmir.

"I do not want to keep him waiting," he told Igil, "nor do I think it a good idea that it should be widely known I have aided one of Jarhost's foes."

"Go," Igil told him, "Havar and I will begin planning our ship."

But as Karik made to leave the settlement, he found Dranri waiting for him.

"You are making for the north?" the old hunter asked.

Karik glanced around to see that no one else was listening, then nodded. "The sooner I fulfill my bargain with Jarl Tanvir, the sooner that matter may be put behind us and our focus turned to ship building."

Dranri nodded as he ran his fingers through his beard. "Would you care for company? I would see how the Undmir has changed since I was last there and learn if those I knew are the same as they were."

"I would enjoy your company," Karik agreed, and they set off through the hills, following the path that would lead them past the battlefield where Karik had just fought and to the Undmir beyond.

"Who do you know in the Undmir?" Karik asked. "And what was your time there like?"

"One who I have not spoken to in many years," Dranri answered. "Whether they will speak with me, I do not know. But certain things have come to pass, and I feel that I should at least visit them."

"You are very mysterious," Karik chuckled. "Would any of this have to do with the death of Hegli?"

Dranri shrugged. "Hegli and I were not on good terms. I was sent to escort Jarhost's sister, Wynthri, to be married to him, and I did not like how he treated her. But there were few who would listen to her or to me, and in the end I was thrown out of the Undmir. I have few fond memories of that place."

They traveled for five days, up over the mountains and around the ice marsh as the rain fell more often than the sun shone. On the afternoon of the fourth day, they climbed up the slope which led out of the marsh and saw the great stone walls of the Undmir rising into the sky before them.

This was the greatest fortress in Vrania, and some said that Vanik had built it with his own two hands. Untaken even by Alena the Vicious, it had stood impregnable until Karik had sailed unseen into its depths.

Now, with the rain falling out of a dark and cloudy sky, Karik grinned at the memory. As he looked on the stone walls, he wondered if he would ever need to find a way through them as well.

From above a heavy gate of ironbound oak, a guard glared down at them through the rain.

"What brings you to the Undmir?" he shouted. "I know neither of you and have not been told to watch for any comers."

"I come on a private matter with your jarl," Karik replied, "one on which he and I have spoken previously."

The guard did not seem overly convinced, but taking Karik's spear and knife, he allowed him within the walls. Meanwhile, Dranri waited outside and asked only that a message be given to someone within. What the message was, Karik did not learn, but he found himself escorted with very little gentleness down a narrow street cut deep into the earth.

The whole of the Undmir was cut into the stone, stairs of rock rising to doorways and windows that led deeper into the mountainside. No wonder, Karik thought, that it was deemed impregnable, for there was nothing on which to catch fire, no crack in the walls to attack, and at regular intervals, there had been set towers that watched and guarded the whole of the fortress.

The sound of hammering and woodworking filled the air, but Karik saw hardly a soul as he was hurried down the street and brought before a small, unremarkable wooden door.

The guard knocked. A moment later, an old man bearing a silver spear appeared, and Karik repeated his speech. The old man glared from under white bushy brows, then disappeared back inside without a word.

A few more moments passed before the door was pulled open and Karik was tossed inside.

Tanvir sat at a table, glaring at another old man across from him.

"Olgvin," Tanvir said through gritted teeth, "leave."

Olgvin glared at Tanvir, then at Karik.

"This matter is not settled, boy!" he hissed, turning to go.

"That will be all, uncle." Tanvir addressed the white-haired man beside Karik, and the man bowed before turning and disappearing through a small door in the back of the room.

"Your rule is off to a rough beginning so far?" Karik asked.

Tanvir looked at him, his fingers running over the beginnings of his beard, as if it was still new to him.

"So, Karik Haldsson," he intoned. "You are the one I have to thank for the mess in which I now find myself."

Karik shrugged. "You are jarl... we did not force it on you."

With a laugh, Tanvir stood. "That is true enough, though I wish you had not begun it by stealing from my predecessor."

"Your father?"

Tanvir shook his head. "He was no father to me. But come, there is more to deal with than my parents. You will show me how you sailed into the Undersea?"

"As you wish," Karik replied. "And I will show you how we came to your treasury."

"I will have a boat prepared," Tanvir said. "Tomorrow, you will sail with me from a fishing hamlet a little way north and show me how you entered the Undersea."

"That," Karik grimaced, "is not a good idea. The waters are treacherous, and they will be difficult, if not impossible, to manage without a crew. It would be much easier to take a small boat from the treasury and sail from there into the Undersea."

"A crew?" Tanvir's eyes widened. "How many did you bring when you robbed us?"

Karik only shrugged. A small smile came over Tanvir's face as he shook his head. "You will give me nothing, will you?"

"I will uphold our bargain," Karik replied. "Nothing more."

"How many know that you sailed the Undersea?"

"In my village, only those of us who did so," Karik replied. "We have told no others."

"It is a secret of many here as well," Tanvir replied. "And I would like to keep it that way." He glanced toward the door with a sigh. "There is little love for outsiders within the fortress, less so after the recent battle."

"Viglir's arrival was a surprise," Karik said, "one unlooked for by us."

"And by most of us, as well," Tanvir replied. "Yet he came too late, as if he were waiting for us all to be weakened. An ill friend is loved less than an enemy... Come, there is a small room in my hall where you shall sleep, and I will see you are brought food. Do not leave it, for I would not like many to know you are here."

Karik nodded, though it had the feeling of a prison, and he spent the night with restless dreams, waking often in the darkness. He missed the sound of the sea and wind, for neither could be heard within the fastness of the Undmir.

The next morning, Tanvir reappeared, escorting Karik through the early morning gloom down to the treasure halls of the Undmir. Stairs cut into the rock zigzagged down deep through the darkness till they reached a narrow path.

"There are few in the Undmir who have come this deep," Tanvir said as they walked. "And fewer still who know there was a theft. I would keep it that way."

"I have no objection to that," Karik replied. He took a deep breath. "It is a long way from the fortress to the Undersea," Karik commented.

Tanvir seemed to nod in the flickering torchlight. "It is deep, very deep. There is safety in the depths."

"Less than you thought..." Karik muttered.

With a sharp breath, Tanvir stopped, and Karik wondered if he had spoken too far.

"This may be a joke to you," the young jarl said through his teeth, "but this concerns the lives of my people." He turned to Karik, the flames of the pine knot torch hissing as a bit of sap spilled out. "I will make it safe again, or I will march my army to your little village and burn you all."

Karik looked him in the eye. "There is an ice marsh and many mountains between here and there," he said, his voice quiet. "And all over Vrania, something is growing. It is stronger than any man, and quieter than any current. No wall can keep it out, no roof can keep it off. It has wrapped the coastlands tight in its grip, Tanvir, and it is coming for you -and your people."

"What?" Tanvir's voice was tense, but Karik thought he could sense an undercurrent of fear. Tanvir was young, and he knew it. He was drowning in dangers, desperately trying to keep them at bay.

"How have your harvests been?" Karik asked. "And your fishing boats... they return empty more often than not?"

Tanvir snorted a laugh, but his hand tightened on the torch. "Food has ever been scarce here in the north, harder than for you on the coasts."

"So you buy what else you need with your gold," Karik replied. "Only the gold buys less and less each year... hasn't it?"

For a moment, beneath the rock and surrounded by darkness, the only sound came from the flaming torch popping as it burned.

Finally, Tanvir shifted a little, the torch slipping lower. "How did you know?"

"Every hunter from Girstadt to Mirhom is running into each other," Karik answered. "There is little for you to buy if they have little to sell, and they have very little."

Tanvir stared at him out of the gloom. "So you can read the signs," he said. "What of it?"

"I sailed the Undersea," Karik replied. "I can sail the Isles."

Tanvir did not laugh but simply asked: "How?"

"There is a passage near our village... we will attempt it soon."

Now, Tanvir chuckled. "And that is why you needed my gold."

"It was your father's gold when we took it," Karik replied.

"Are you asking me to help you in this venture?" Some of the tension had gone out of Tanvir's voice.

"Our future is beyond the isles," Karik answered, "or starving here. I am offering you a way to keep your people safe."

Tanvir laughed at that, the sound echoing through the dark tunnels. "My people will be safer, Karik Haldsson, when the Undersea is once again impassable to outsiders. After that, you still owe me for the gold which you stole." So saying, he turned and continued on his way.

They reached the great oak doors a little while later and, after Tanvir undid several locks, he and Karik lifted three heavy beams set into the doors to prevent their opening from outside. When they pushed the doors open, the waters of the Undersea stretched out before them, dark and cold.

Karik had not thought he would miss the sound of the Undersea, but after a day within the still, silent confines of the Undmir, the quiet ripples of water brushing against rock were music to his ears.

"Show me," Tanvir said, pointing to a small rowboat tied to a tiny dock.

For three days, they paddled around the Undersea, careful not to stray too far from the docks. Karik explained everything he could remember from the charts about the Undersea, but other things they discovered together.

At the end of the third day, as they rowed back to shore, Tanvir gestured at Karik's hand. "You lost your finger sailing in here?"

Karik nodded, then straightened up. "How did you know?"

Tanvir chuckled. "The legend is that Vanik lost a hand when he assaulted the Undmir... it is good to know we still have some protection."

Karik rowed in silence, his mind pondering the old legends of Vanik and Vranr, his father.

They reached the shore and made the climb back through the rock to the Undmir. It was already night, but Tanvir did not lead Karik back to his room, instead making for the massive gate.

"You should leave now," he said. "Rumors of my work have passed through my thanes, and some wonder who you are and what you are doing here. If they know I harbored Karik Haldsson under my roof... I am not sure that I could vouch for your safety."

"I thought you were the jarl," Karik replied. He was tired, and the prospect of making camp on the Ice Marsh that night did not seem appealing.

"I sit in my father's seat," he said, "and wear the arm-ring of the ruler of the Undmir, but there are many who still suspect that I had something to do with my father's death."

"Would you like me to kill them, too?" Karik asked.

Tanvir laughed at that and clapped him on the shoulder. "I thank you for your help, Karik Haldsson, and hope that we may aid each other more in the future. There is much work for me to do here in the Undmir, and that work is best done by me. I thank you for your help, but now I alone must prove myself to the people here. You are not well liked among the families of the men you slew."

Karik nodded. "That is not a small number of people. So, I will wish you good luck and leave you to your business. If you see my friend Dranri, tell him I have gone and look forward to seeing him when he finishes his business here."

Tanvir chuckled at that as one laughs at a secret, then nodded. "I will do as you ask. Now, go- before we are seen being too friendly with one another."

Jarl Ylmi

Ylmi saw little of Karik in the days after she became jarl. The fight with
Unhost was hardly over before he disappeared northward to fulfill their
bargain with Tanvir, and she did not see him for over a week.

Fornik, on the other hand, never left her alone. Although few in the
village wished to have him as jarl, he was always at hand to point out every
shortcoming in Ylmi's decisions. When she ordered Torig to share his rich
haul of fish with the widow Nanni and her two children, Fornik was nearby
to say that such a thing was as close to theft as a jarl could come.

When she tried to hear a dispute between Almir and Bogli over a litter of
hound pups, Fornik was there to interrupt and make a nuisance of himself.

"Have you nothing better to do?" she asked him. "Or are you so well
prepared for winter that you have no need to gather against it?"

"I will go without," he answered innocently, "if I may be of some help
to our new jarl and give you a bit of the wisdom I have gathered over the
years, seeing as you are so young."

"Wisdom is not what you are giving me," Ylmi said, and she fixed him
with her one eye. "Make yourself useful, or you may find little help offered
to you when the cold comes."

"I do not mean to need help," Fornik answered. He gave her a stiff smile
as he departed, leaving Ylmi to deal with Almir and Bogli.

When she was not mediating disputes between her old friends, Ylmi
found there was more work to be done in the village than she could have
ever imagined. Goat pens needed mending, fish traps to be built and laid,
houses that needed repair, not to mention the work to be done on Jarhost's
tiny hall.

One morning, as the village was waking, there was a low grumble
from underground, as one of the mines, long ago dug in search of gold,
collapsed. For over a week, they argued about whether to build supports

into the rock or use the timber to repair their homes above ground. Fornik, of course, said that the mines should be repaired and reworked.

"We do not know what we may find there," he said, "and if we can find gold, it will go a long way to increasing the prosperity of our village. Besides, Jarhost will doubtless expect more gold in taxes, and if we have it ready, perhaps he will leave us alone."

But there were few who agreed with him, and in the end, most of the mines were left to rot.

The matter was settled when Ylmi turned back to her hall, but she heard her name called and turned to see Havar approaching. His breeches were soaked up to the waist, and there were bits of bark and moss rubbed into his clothes.

"You have been preparing wood for ship building," she commented with a weary smile. "I am glad you are so ready to return to it after *Kalborg*. She is a good ship."

"That she is," Havar nodded. He glanced quickly around, "Could we speak... in private?"

"Of course." Ylmi led the way to her hall, and held the deer hide away from the door so he could enter.

"It is good to be out of the wind." Havar grinned as he sat beside the small fire. "I hope Fornik does not give you much trouble?"

"He does as he has always done," Ylmi replied, "argued with anyone doing work. Yet now, Unhost is not behind him to give his complaints weight. He is like a dog that has lost its master and now harries everything it sees out of confusion."

Havar laughed quickly, then forged ahead. "I think the time has come when we must decide."

"Always there is something which we must decide," Ylmi groaned. "Which do you speak of?"

"How to use our ship and our charts," Havar replied. "I know Karik intends to sail west, and thinks that with the charts, we can cross the Isles. But does he intend to go with one ship? We could build a fleet of two- or even three - ships, if we work right. With those charts, we can sail around Vrania, and with *Kalborg*, there are few who could catch us."

"Are you suggesting we turn to sea raiding?" Ylmi asked. "All I hear is that the coastlands are as poor as we are - or worse."

"Along this coast, yes," Havar admitted. "And I would not expect Karik and Igil to go raiding into their old homes. But in the east..."

"Are you suggesting we raid Viglir?" Ylmi asked.

"His men killed Wisic," Havar shrugged. "I am sure Karik and Igil would see no reason not to extract a blood price. We could raid from Torhom to Varhom, and perhaps even Illstadt. They have more wealth than us, and men always flock to wealth and plenty."

"It would be risky," Ylmi replied. "And it would mean we would not sail through the Isles for another year or more."

"But we would sail with a fleet!" Havar pressed. "With raiders who are battle hardened and proven."

"I will be frank with you Havar," she said, after a moment. "I dislike the idea. It bears too much risk for my liking. And I dislike the idea of both King Viglir and King Jarhost having reason to hate us."

"The mountains will protect us," Havar grinned. "They always have. And whatever hatred Jarhost may have for us, he will not allow Viglir through the passes without a fight."

"Perhaps," Ylmi replied. She thought for a moment, recalling the way Jarhost glared at her and Karik as they stood over the dead body of Jarl Hegli.

Dragonsrest was her village to protect. And it was a bad jarl who made new enemies when it was unnecessary.

"We will speak of this when Karik returns," she said at last. "The dragonslayers should keep each other's council. We began together, and we should go forward together." She smiled, but she suspected Karik would agree with her. Thora would back her, certainly. And, if Karik agreed with her, then Igil probably would as well. That left only Revik...

Havar rose with a smile. "We have done great things, and already our names are spoken of all along the coast. Perhaps even in the halls of King Viglir." He clapped her on the shoulder. "We will be feared, One-eye, and our names will last for generations."

"As long as we don't starve to death first," she smiled, patting his back as he turned to leave. As the deer hide fell into place behind him, her smile dropped away as well. For an instant, she could hear the wind howling through the Watching Stones of Vranr, and the voice of the old man:

"You will receive what you desire most. And, when it is taken away, you shall be given what you hope for."

She fingered the small pouch hanging from her neck- the red, white, and green stones tucked safely inside. Something was coming to take away what was hers, and starting a war with a second king only a few days' march away sounded to her like a wonderful way to hasten it.

The next day, Ylmi went looking for Revik, but he was nowhere to be found. Almir was skinning a young deer by his hut, and when Ylmi inquired about Revik, he merely shrugged.

She found Igil with Havar, the two of them climbing all over *Kalborg* as they discussed the design of their next ship.

"It is good to see you, One-eye," Igil said as he dropped from *Kalborg*'s side onto the sand. "I was worried Fornik had annoyed you to death."

"And I was worried you had become one with your boat," Ylmi replied. "You have not strayed far from it for several days."

"I am eager to be at work on the next," Igil grinned, "and a ship such as we must build requires a great deal of planning."

Ylmi nodded, "Even so." She glanced west over the fjord which stretched toward the mountain, and beyond that, to the sea. She shivered as the memory of the Ice Sea washed over her, and she turned back to Igil.

"I am looking for your brother," she said. "Do you know where I might find him?"

"He's gone hunting up into the mountains," Igil replied. "But he's been gone three days. He should return soon. "

"I doubt it."

Ylmi turned to see Thora walking up out of the trees, her spear over her shoulder.,. "Leiban and I saw him heading up into one of the dells west of where your parents live," Thora nodded at Ylmi. "My guess is he's got another day or so before he's back."

Ylmi nodded. "If any of you see him before I do, tell him I wish to speak with him."

"I can go fetch him for you," Thora offered. She glanced sideways at Igil. "Your brother is like a boar, always leaving a trail wide and deep wherever he goes. I could track him blindfolded."

"There is no need for him to be fetched," Ylmi answered. "It will be simple enough to speak with him when he returns."

"As you wish," Thora answered, raising her left hand to hold out a haunch of venison.

"From a young deer?" Ylmi asked, somewhat confused.

"Yes," Thora shook it. "Are you going to take it or do I have to haul it back to your hall, too?"

"Take it?"

"You're the jarl now." Thora shrugged. "It's only your share."

"I don't need you to hunt for me," Ylmi shook her head. "I can..."

"Yes you do," Thora interrupted. "I've seen how busy you are and how little time you have for yourself. Now, take this before I hit you over the head with it."

Ylmi took the meat slowly, but it felt odd... as if she hadn't earned it.

Thora grinned. "You'll settle in as jarl one of these days."

Thora was more right than she'd realized, Ylmi thought the next day. She had not hunted since before their battle with Viglir and Hegli. As she helped take in the fish traps from the river and divide them up among the families, she realized she would need to set to storing food- and soon - if she wanted to do well in the winter.

Thora had also been right about Revik. The big man emerged from the mountains two days later with a small deer slung over his shoulder, grumbling about the terrible hunting.

"I heard you wanted to speak with me," he said when he found Ylmi.

She was helping Bogli reset the thatching on his roof, and her shoulders were sore from it.

"I did," she replied. "I know that you and Karik have had many discussions and that you are happy following him."

Revik shrugged.

"I want to know if you will follow me," Ylmi went on. "I know you have thought before of seeking your fortune with one of the kings, and I would be very sorry if you were to leave this village. There will be much for someone like yourself to do in the coming years, if all goes as planned."

"I was one of those who proclaimed you jarl," Revik answered with a grin. "And, though the hunting here is less than good, I would rather remain with you than in the hall of Viglir... or Jarhost," he nearly spat the last word.

"That is good to hear," Ylmi answered, "because you are a formidable warrior, and I am happy to count you as one of my thanes."

Revik's smile widened, and he clapped her on the shoulder with one massive hand. "And I am happy to serve you, One-eye. As I have said before, we dragonslayers should stick together."

They both laughed at that, and Revik left to see to his deer. When he returned a short time later, the thatching of Bogli's house went much swifter.

Long Roads

Karik made his way around the ice marsh, and back into the mountains that overlooked the coast, his mind heavy with thoughts of Wisic, Umir, and the dragon. Over and over his mind turned to the dragon's words, rumbling heavy over the mountainside as they stood surrounded by fire and blood:

"Death and fire will cling to you like a cloak. Your every victory will turn to defeat, your triumphs to tragedies, your conquests to calamities. Never shall you have rest, never shall a home provide you comfort."

He heard it in his mind, over and over, the quiet of the mountain forest only making it seem louder. With each step, he thought over his actions -what he had done, and how he could have behaved differently. Still, each night he dreamt he was back upon the battlefield with Wisic's bloody body in his arms.

When the dragon lay dead, Umir had fallen as well. And while the joy of sailing the Undersea was still sweet, they had burned the body of Wisic. If he passed the Isles... what would be the calamity to follow from that?

"You cannot escape wyrd." Dranri had said more than once, but it did not seem to Karik an easy thing to surrender to every ill doing and call it wyrd. A curse was one thing, wyrd another, and if it was a curse he worked against, then perhaps it could be beaten... or unmade.

The dim daylight that filtered through the rain and mist was fading when he reached the little house he had built in the mountains. He was soaked through with rain that had been falling since the previous afternoon, and he breathed a sigh of relief when he saw smoke rising from the roof. Dragging his weary limbs the last few steps, he knocked on the door to let his mother know he was there.

"Enter!" she called, and he came through the small door to find her working the stiffness out of a deer hide. "You look soaked."

"It is a long road from the Undmir," Karik replied, "and there is always a storm brewing in Vrania."

Elva looked up at him, the lines about her eyes hardening as she watched him hang his dripping cloak. "What business did you have with the Undmir?"

"I made a bargain with their jarl," Karik replied, "in order to bring a quicker end to the fighting. Jarl Tanvir upheld his end. It was for me to uphold mine."

Elva turned her attention back to the deerskin. "So, you are making bargains with jarls now," she said. "Truly, my son has moved up in the world and has no more need of my wisdom. This is all related to your desire to sail the Isles, is it not?"

Karik sank down by the fire with a long sigh. "It is." He set his hands to his boots but stopped. "You know I have to try…" he looked at her over the flames. "I must try to find a way out of what is happening to our people."

"You say that Jarl Tanvir upheld his end of your bargain," Elva said without looking up. "So tell me: how is Wisic?"

Karik flinched.

"The love of my life is dead," Elva went on, "and my first-born son lies buried in the cliffs above Yrdnara with his brother." She threw down the deerskin. "I do not wish to see my last son sail away upon a faint hope and spend the last years of my life wondering where his body lies."

"You were not the only one who loved them," Karik replied. "And I long for the day when I might once again hunt with my father and brothers in the forests outside the Allfather's mead hall. But I cannot wait for death to strangle those around me."

"Then hunt," Elva replied. "But if you continue to pursue this path, you will either fail and drown beneath the waves or you and all your friends will end as did Wisic."

Karik rose to his feet and took his wet cloak from where it hung. "I wish you a good evening mother," he said quietly, and stepped outside into the rain.

The wind was blowing harder as night drew closer, and the pine trees whipped back and forth in the gray light of the rain and oncoming night.

"Your every victory will turn to defeat, your triumphs to tragedies, your conquests to calamities…"

Clenching his jaw against the chill, Karik set for the path that led down to the village.

He arrived the next morning, having slept for a short time under the shelter of a thick pine tree. His clothes were still soaked from the rain as the stormy night gave way to a cool morning shrouded in fog.

Olga was at work in her garden, and he gave her a weary nod as she smiled at him. He could hear Bogli shouting at his dogs, and it sounded as though there was a great deal of work being done by the river on the other side of the village.

He hesitated a moment, then turned away from Ylmi's hall and headed for the hut which Igil still shared with Havar. *Kalborg* was drawn up on the beach a short ways off, and Karik saw his friend working with Havar, drawing on old hides with bits of charcoal and charred sticks.

"You've been away awhile!" Igil said when he saw him. "And you look terrible. Have you been wandering in the woods all this time?"

"Just last night," Karik replied. "The two of you seem hard at work."

Havar nodded. "Working and planning, for there are many options open to us now that Jarhost no longer rules here."

"Do you think you can finish the ship this year?" Karik asked, "before the storms close the fjord?"

Havar laughed. "I think we could with enough help, and if we had the iron and sail for it." He spread his hands, "but that seems a waste to me. I have already spoken to Ylmi about a second option: I think we should go raiding along the eastern coasts. Prepare for winter that way. We can win wealth, and with wealth comes friends and warriors."

"With wealth also comes enemies," Karik muttered.

"But Karik," Havar pressed on, "we could sail into the west with a fleet! With enough warriors to make a small army."

"The decision is our jarl's to make," Karik replied. His eyes looked over *Kalborg,* and he thought on how the small ship had fared in the ice sea. "I will think on the idea, and perhaps we will speak with her later and see what she decides."

Havar frowned, and he turned back to his drawing. There was a moment of silence, then Karik rose and walked toward the fjord. The waves rolled in, slow and cold. Through the mist, he could hear a boat- probably Torig's- rising and falling on the waves not far off.

Wincing, Karik sat down on the sand, watching the gentle waves rolling in. The wounds from his battle with Hegli were just healing, and they ached with the weariness that came from hiking the long miles between here and the Undmir.

He could still see Wisic's empty eyes staring back at him. The dream of his friend dying in his arms seemed to follow him into the daylight, and though he tried to push it back, it still clung to his mind's eye.

He took a deep breath and gripped the sand with his fingers. The stubs on his left hand burned slightly as he drove them into the rough grains. After a moment, the pain subsided, and he took another breath. It was his fault, as surely as if he had thrust the blades into his friend. He had driven them to that battle, urged them to assault Hegli. And, when Viglir came, he had urged them to attack. The battle had only taken place because he had urged Ylmi to raid the Undmir with him. If they had left Hegli's gold alone... but they needed Hegli's gold to build a ship and pass the Isles.

His eyes suddenly focused, his gaze locking on the great mountain where the dragon had hidden. It all came back to the Isles, to a way to escape Vrania. The dragon had not been the first to that mountain, and Ylmi had told him the tales of the Watcher- how Vranr had striven against him.

He flexed the fingers on his left hand, working out the stiffness that often set in. Who - or what - had this Watcher been? What magic had he wrapped around Vrania?

Behind him, he heard the crunching sound of footsteps on the sand, and he turned to see Igil walking slowly toward him.

"You are not as eager about the ship as you were."

"I am eager," Karik said slowly, "but I do not trust myself. I do not wish to make rash decisions." He hesitated a moment. "I dislike Havar's plan for raiding."

Igil looked out at the sea. "Do you remember why we volunteered to leave Yrdnara?"

"We did it to save the lives of our families," Karik answered. "Much good it did."

For a moment, the only sound between them was the washing of the sea upon the beach and the low moan of the wind blowing in from the sea.

"That may be why all of us went together," Igil answered. "But you and I, we hoped to do more. We wanted to try to save Vrania. That's why we came here. It's why we fought the dragon, sailed the Undersea, and it is why we will build a new ship... why we will attempt to cross the Isles. You've even convinced Revik, in his way. And I think you convinced Wisic, too."

Karik said nothing, looking back to the sea.

"Wisic was my friend, as well," Igil said. "And now, he drinks ale with the Allfather. You should not mourn for him."

Karik sighed. "If we do this - if we cross the Isles..." he paused. "Igil, if we do this, there will be war like none have seen in Vrania. Not since Alena hammered the jarls into submission. I do not think we will find lands uninhabited, and I do not think they will take kindly to the children of Vranr returning."

"Do you speak of war with whoever we find in the west? Or against the jarls here?"

"Either," Karik replied. "Or both. I do not think Jarhost will allow us to grow in peace, however much we may want to be left alone. The only way we avoid war is if we find a place in the west we can live... and I have little hope for that. It is too much to hope that the kings Vranr fought have grown weak or fallen."

Igil eased himself down onto the sand beside Karik. Together, the two of them watched the water rolling in as the tide rose, the water appearing dark in the gray light. The wind was picking up, and Karik thought another storm was likely not far off.

"How much truth do you think there is in those legends, Karik? Do you think we will find five kings arrayed against us when we cross the sea, all of them eager and ready to cast us back upon this Isle with dark magic and sorcery?"

Karik rubbed sand between his fingers as he picked out his words. "By all accounts, Vranr's exile happened many years ago. Even if much of the tale is naught but bard weavings, I do not think we will be welcome."

Igil was silent a moment, watching the small waves roll gently onto the beach as the tide slowly came in. "As you have pointed out, we cannot last much longer on this Isle -I think, in that, you are right. As for what we find across the sea, let us do our best and make do with what we find."

"That is why I am sitting here," Karik answered. "I hope we will find peace and safety, but it seems the only peace we gain is through victory. If we build that ship, we must be ready for war, from wherever it comes. Now is the time to hesitate and think, but if we set out on this path, I will not hesitate again. Cowering will not make our wyrd take a better shape."

Igil laughed quietly. "I like you Karik, if at times your mind runs darker than my own." He tossed a rock toward the cold water, and for a while, the two of them sat together, listening to the sound of the fjord at night.

At last, when Karik's fingers were growing numb, Igil spoke again.

"We know where the path leads if we do nothing," he said in his quiet voice. "Starvation, hunger, cold, and exile. But if there is a path which escapes that doom, then we will have to do something and search very diligently for it. We did not expect the battle to take place, but now Ylmi is our jarl instead of Unhost. Our names are known through much of the coast, which will not be a small thing. It will be harder for Jarhost to revile us now, and we have the beginnings of a friendship with the Undmir." Slowly, he unfolded his long limbs and rose to his feet, towering over Karik to look out toward the sea.

"I think," he said slowly, "it is unreasonable to expect everything to work out better than before. Though things have been hard, and violence is common here, I think we have done well in our endeavors since leaving Yrdnara. A dragon is dead, an ill jarl replaced by one much wiser, and we are ready to build the greatest ship this Isle has ever seen. And that is not to mention the charts you have, which may yet lead us to great things in the future. Consider that, if you must ponder your wyrd so deeply." And with that, he left Karik to his thoughts.

Vranr's Curse

Karik woke with a start, the gloom of evening creeping in through the mist. The wind was soft, blowing in from the sea, and Karik could smell the salt and brine upon it. He thought on what Igil had said, and on what the old legends of Vranr said of the lands across the sea. As he blinked his eyes open, the mist seemed to thin before him, and Karik's eyes fixed on the mountain in the midst of the fjord. Moonlight shone on its summit, and Karik thought on what they had found beneath the mountain's peaks. The water lapped quietly at the shore as he sat still for a moment longer, then rose to his feet.

Havar's hut was a poor place in winter, but in the summer, it was warm enough. Karik did not enter, unlatching the door just enough to take his sword. He had cleaned the long blade of dragon's blood and more than once held it in his hands to test how eight fingers might grip the dark hilt.

It felt good to have such a blade with him. He set it in the hull of a small fishing boat, which he shoved down the sand and into the water. It bobbed lightly as he climbed in and pushed off, slipping through the frigid tide.

He paddled slowly across the water, the moon slowly falling as he moved down the fjord. The mountain drew closer, and the mists seemed to close back in around it.

Lifting a torch from the boat, he lit it with sparks from his knife and swept it around. The path was still there, carved into the rocks of the mountain.

A prickle crawled down his neck - the same one he had felt climbing the Watching Stones. Others had walked this path long before him, and he had the unnerving suspicion they were not as long gone as he would like.

He followed the path to the cavern's entrance, the mist thickening around him with each step. As he approached the gaping hole in the mountain, he passed broken bits of chain, blood-spattered stones, and other remnants of their battle with the dragon.

All they had risked, all they had done, and all the pain they had suffered had been for nothing it seemed. Unhost reaped most of the benefit-Unhost and Jarhost, both.

Karik felt the old rage returning, and his steps grew quicker. By the torchlight, and without the threat of a dragon hurrying him, he could see the entrance to the mountain had been carved smooth. In one corner, a rusted iron hinge still protruded from the cracked rock.

This, then, had been the Watcher's fortress.

The Watcher, he knew of no other name for it, had been sent by the men of the west to keep Vranr in bondage, or so the old stories told. Karik raised the torch, looking at the rusted hinge and pondering who this Watcher had been. A sorcerer or a master of some dark magic? He touched the rock with the three remaining fingers of his left hand and wondered yet again that such injuries should come to him.

He was sure of it now: no Jarl of Vrania would have had the wealth to carve out a mountain, and neither the inclination nor skill to set doors in stone... not of this size.

The entrance to the cavern was damp as water from the mist collected high above on the cold stone, falling to the path with a pattering sound.

Squaring his shoulders, Karik stepped into the cavern. The torch hissed as he passed through the entrance, and the red light of the fire flickered on the dark stone walls. Every step echoed in his ears, and the pressure in the air seemed to grow.

The entrance to the cavern, whatever it had once been, was now little but blackened, broken stone. The dragon had left heavy marks on the rocks, and what must have once been a mighty fortress was now a broken, gutted wreck.

He followed the path into the main cavern and looked down on the leavings of what had been the dragon's bed. The gold was gone. Unhost had scraped up every scrap, but this was not the bottom of the fortress.

On the opposite side, an archway opened onto a narrow corridor that led further down, deeper into the mountain's roots. Here, Revik had taken shelter when they first spoke with the dragon, and Karik ran his fingers over the scarred rock where the dragon had swung at his friend.

Beyond the battle-marked archway, the passage sloped downward, the darkness dipping and dancing away from his torch's light. The fetid smell of the dragon's dwelling did not seem to reach far into the passage, but Karik took the torch in his left hand and held his sword in his right.

Deeper down the passage led, doubling back and forth as it went. Runes were carved into the walls, some that Karik recognized and many of which were strange to him. Those he recognized were of guarding, holding, and protection, but they were few and far between, mingled with others he could not make out.

His curiosity grew as the darkness filled in behind him and the narrow passage led ever downward.

At last, it opened into a small chamber, featureless and empty, save for a strange symbol carved deep into the stone of the far wall. Karik stared at it, wondering what meaning it held. He reached up to touch it.

"He is gone, but his magic still remains," came a heavy voice from behind him.

Karik whirled, sword in hand. But the man who had spoken was sitting against the wall, resting as one beyond weariness.

"Come, sit," he gestured to the broken stone about them, and Karik froze. Only three fingers remained on his left hand and four upon his right.

He saw Karik staring and glanced at his own hands before looking to Karik's.

"As I said," he sighed, "his magic still remains."

"How are you here?" Karik asked slowly.

"That is a long and complicated story," Vranr answered. His voice was deep, but every word seemed weighed down with weariness. "You are trying to decide if you should cross the Isles."

Karik swallowed the dryness in his mouth and took a deep breath to calm his heart. "It is a mighty undertaking, and I do not know what I may find on the other side."

Vranr chuckled again. "You will find men, even as you have here." He rested his hands on his knees and leaned back to look at the stone overhead. It had not been carved smooth, though there were no dragon marks upon it.

"You will find them greedy, grasping, and vicious," Vranr continued. "Do you expect something else?"

"I do not wish to lead my friends into needless danger," Karik said slowly.

"They are in needless danger now," Vranr replied quickly, an edge of bitterness creeping into his voice. "They live upon an island prison in the distant sea, when my children should hunt and plant upon the rich slopes where I was born."

He looked up at Karik and sighed heavily. "I do not have long, Karik son of Hald, so listen closely." He fixed Karik with eyes that were dark as the sea, and Karik felt something within him stir.

"I made many mistakes," Vranr said, "and the greatest was forgetting that the small deeds are often more important than the mighty ones. Do not lose sight of those things which are truly important." He spoke swiftly, hurrying from one word to the next. "All men err, the weak surrender and fall because of their failures. The strong become so because they rise again. I was called Unbreakable, yet I lost more battles than I won. For every time I escaped, I was captured."

"And yet my friends die because of decisions I make," Karik replied.

But Vranr shook his head. "You lost one in the slaying of a dragon and another in battle... you are fortunate you have not lost more." He paused a moment and looked away before taking Karik's eyes once again into his own. "And you will, Karik. You will lose more. I watched my friends and companions die, one by one, until I was the only one left alive. The world is a terrible place, and fate extracts a terrible price from those who seek to change it."

"Then perhaps it is not worth changing," Karik said slowly.

But Vranr gave a bitter laugh and shook his head. "You do not really believe that, Karik. You did not seek to change fate when you left your village, and yet your father and brothers are dead." He stared into the rock as if he could see through it and into the years beyond. "We are all doomed in this life, though if we are blessed, and if we seize the chance with both hands, we may find our doom less heavy than we otherwise might."

"That," Karik said slowly, "is a grim view of things."

Vranr glared at him darkly and flexed his fingers. "I have watched long enough to know it is the right one."

Slowly, he rose to his feet, and Karik was surprised to see how short he seemed even when he stood at his full height.

"If you continue," Vranr said, "and you are able to cross the Isles, I have a request." He spoke slowly now, as if all his strength had been poured into his earlier words, and there was little left for what he had now to say. "These words I have given you at the gods' request: heed them as such. But these next words are from me alone. Reach the west. Burn, kill, destroy. They took my wife, the one most precious to me." His voice cracked. "I could not take my revenge, so do this for me, and make them regret a thousand times what was done to Vranr and Sol."

With these words, the old man pulled himself slowly upright and, with a sigh, melted away into the darkness.

Dranri Returns

It was at the end of a long day of hauling fish traps up the river that Ylmi made her way back to her hall. Making it her own had taken some time, but she had slept in the hall many nights, and her parents had even spoken of moving there with her. It was her hall now, not Unhost's.

A weary smile came to her face when she saw Karik leaning against the doorpost, a pot in his hand.

"You have been scarce of late," she said to him, and he nodded in answer.

"Tanvir was not easily satisfied," he straightened as she approached, "and there were matters I wanted to secure before I brought them to you."

"Matters?" She raised an eyebrow.

He raised the pot in his hand. "Are you ready to eat?"

"The day's work is done," she nodded, "or as much of it as is likely to be done. Come."

The gloom of the hall matched the late gloom of dusk, and Ylmi swiftly poked the fire to life. Ulfr rose from the shadows and yawned, her long tongue curling as her maw stretched wide. She padded to Karik and sniffed curiously at him.

"She has grown," Karik said, eyeing the wolf.

Ylmi sat back on her heels as the flames licked at the dry wood she laid upon the coals. The pot that Karik handed her was filled with water, fish, onions, and various herbs, and Ylmi took a deep smell of it before she set it above the fire to warm.

"Your work as jarl seems unending," Karik said quietly. "Fornik is trying to wear you out?"

"I think he believes he can annoy me into letting him do whatever he wants," Ylmi snorted. "But what are these matters you wished to bring me?"

Karik fiddled with his fingers for a moment before he looked her in the eye. "We are ready to build the ship."

"We have bled enough for it," Ylmi replied. "I would hate to think that trip into the Undersea was for nothing."

"I have come to ask your leave to build it," Karik said.

Ylmi grinned, the dragon fire scar on her cheek cracking as she did so. "You have more than my leave. Build it! Your jarl commands you."

Karik grinned. "I hoped you would still be in favor of it."

"If anything, I am more anxious than ever." Ylmi stuck a spoon into the pot and stirred the stew that was beginning to boil. "We are low on food, and the hunting grows scarce." She sighed as she stared into the pot. "I am dreading Jarhost's tax men. I fear they will demand more than we can pay."

"Should I set aside some of the gold?" Karik asked.

Ylmi thought for a moment. "Do you have more than you need?"

"I don't think so, but perhaps we could manage..."

"Then no." Ylmi shook her head firmly. "If we are to cross the Black Isles, then we will take shortcuts elsewhere, not on our boat."

Karik grinned at her through the steam. "I am glad you see it that way."

Ylmi shrugged. "I do not wish to drown, and if we are right, then perhaps there will be enough to offset Jarhost's greed." She stared into the fire for a moment, relishing the smell of the boiling stew.

"Dranri has not yet returned?"

Karik shook his head. "Not as of yet," he answered. "Though I suspect he will return before long. I do not know what he found so pressing in the Undmir, but he told me it might take some time or no time at all."

Ylmi grunted. "My father once said his mind was as tangled as his beard, and I begin to think him right. Still, I think we should gather for a feast, as we did after the slaying of the dragon." She looked back at Karik. "Havar has spoken with you?"

Karik glanced up at her for a moment. "He has. The idea of a raid appeals to him a great deal."

"Does it appeal to you?" Ylmi asked.

Karik shook his head. "It does not, though the decision rests with you now."

"Perhaps," Ylmi closed her eye for a moment and took a deep breath. "Those of us who sailed the Undersea and fought off Jarl Hegli and King Viglir- we should eat together before we begin our next undertaking, whatever that may be. There is much work ahead of us. The ship will be difficult to build, and when it is complete, there will be yet more to be done. And we should remember Wisic together. He was a good friend."

Karik was silent for an instant before answering. "He was."

"Then we will gather here in three days," Ylmi answered. "The dragonslayers, and Dranri if he returns."

Dranri did return the next day, but he was not alone.

Ylmi was in the river, helping to fix fish traps, when Thora stepped up to the muddy bank.

"Dranri is back," she said.

Ylmi lowered the rock she carried into place, shivering a bit as her arms sank into the freezing water. "No need to sound so disappointed, Thora," she said.

"He's not alone."

Ylmi tested the balance of the stake and looked up at her. "What?"

"I said he's not alone," Thora repeated. "You'd best come and see for yourself."

Ylmi nodded and climbed up out of the river, shaking the water from her arms. "That stake is set," she told Nanni, who was still at work. "One more and the traps should be anchored well enough." She wiped her hands on her shirt and pulled on her boots. Her toes were numb, but the warm fur of the boots would quickly set that to right. Taking up her spear, she brushed her hair out of her good eye and made her way toward her hall.

As Thora had said, Dranri had come, and with him was a tall woman and a young boy. The woman carried herself as straight as a pine tree, and her dark hair was streaked with gray. Her eyes fixed on Ylmi as she approached, measuring her, and Dranri seemed suddenly uneasy.

"Greetings Dranri," Ylmi said as she met them, "it is good to see you returned, though I am curious that you have been away so long."

Dranri smiled nervously and nodded. "I am glad to be back." He cleared his throat. "This is Orlanna and her son, Lasvin. I would take her as my wife, if you will consent to us living among your village."

Ylmi blinked, suddenly realizing that these requests were a part of being the jarl. Dranri, who had taught her so much, was asking her permission to marry...

But before she could think anything else, Orlanna cleared her throat.

"Dranri, alas, leaves a great deal unsaid." Her voice was deep and solemn, but something in her tone made Ylmi suddenly wary. "I was married before, as you may guess by my son. This is Lasvin Lasviksson, for my husband was Lasvik, whom you slew in battle."

Ylmi's eyes narrowed. "I will not apologize for his death, though he died well."

"I do not look for an apology," Orlanna replied. "Lasvik chose his path and whom he would follow, so no one should be surprised at how he ended. He lived by his blade and dealt death to many, and he reaped the rewards of his life." Her eyes met Ylmi's. "As will we all."

"Are you threatening me?" Ylmi asked quietly.

"You slew my husband," Orlanna replied. "Do you expect a blessing? It is no threat to remind you that the path you have begun to walk leads to a certain place... only a warning."

"How am I supposed to welcome you into my village," Ylmi asked, "if I do not know whether you will lie in wait for me or stir up trouble."

"I am no troublemaker," Orlanna replied, "and I will swear before Skathi the White that I do not require vengeance or a blood price. Even in the Undmir, where there is more rock than earth, I could grow any plant I wished, so I do not come looking for charity. But my husband is dead, and it is with Dranri that I wish to spend the rest of my days. One man you have taken from me. Whether it was his fault or no, will you deny me a second?"

Ylmi looked at her a moment in silence, her fingers working on her spear. From behind her, she heard Ulfr padding up through the mud, and a faint growl rumbled through her chest. But her eyes fell to Dranri, and she thought of all he had done for her.

"Orlanna I do not know," she said, "but Dranri I know well. Dragonsrest is young and has its share of troublemakers." She fixed Dranri with her one eye, "Will Orlanna add to them?"

"She will not," Dranri replied quickly, and Ylmi noted that Orlanna inclined her head slightly in agreement.

"Then you are welcome," Ylmi said. She nodded quickly at them and turned to head back to the river.

Thora followed close behind her, and when they had gone out of earshot, she clapped Ylmi on the back. "That, I did not expect."

"Nor I," Ylmi answered. "He said that he knew Lasvik when he saw the sword, but he mentioned nothing of Lasvik's wife."

"Perhaps that is why he and Lasvik had a falling out," Thora guessed. "It is often a woman in the old stories who brings good friends together and splits foul friends apart." She glanced back to where Orlanna and Dranri were talking together. "I would like to know what that tale is."

"I would like to know why Dranri brought her here," Ylmi muttered. "My guess is that Fornik will be plotting to win her to his side before the tide comes in tonight."

"Dranri said she would not be a troublemaker..." Thora began, but Ylmi cut her off.

"I should have said no, at least until I knew more about her." She closed her eyes for a moment, the ache behind her eye growing as she tried to guess what Orlanna's true purpose was.

"Are you alright?" Thora asked, and Ylmi felt a gentle touch on her shoulder.

She opened her eyes to see Thora looking down at her with concern, but Ylmi only shook her head. "I am fine." She sighed and glanced up to the mountains. "How goes your hunting?"

Thora frowned, "That was the other reason I came to speak with you. The deer are growing scarce, and the deer herds I am finding are smaller than they have ever been."

"They have often been scarce," Ylmi nodded. "Another bad year will be difficult."

But Thora shook her head, sighing as she did so. "I have heard you speak more than once of how a goat herd must not lose more goats in a year than it can replace, or the herd will die out swiftly. I have hunted these deer for years, and I fear that we may be hunting down more deer than can be replaced. I have been hunting together with Leiban Longspear all along the mountains, and he says the hunting has gotten even worse over the last few months. Even Leiban said that the trails are not as common as they used to be."

Ylmi took a deep breath of the cold air and looked up into the mountains. For the last few years, the deer had become more scarce with every hunt, even as they hunted further and further from the village. "We will just have to go further..." Ylmi began, but Thora interrupted her.

"Ylmi, I'm saying we can't. Leiban and I started running into hunters from Girhom and Bjarnmont last year, and now, even when we don't see them, we see the signs of their hunting. We're hunting the same herds as two other villages, which means we're hunting the herds three times as hard as we have been..."

Ylmi felt as though she was going to vomit. "So, you're saying we're running out of deer."

Thora's shoulders sagged, and she nodded.

"Then we had best hope that Karik can get us through the isles."

Ylmi had only just climbed back into the river when she was called again, this time by Bogli, who shook his head when Ylmi asked him what happened.

"The king's taxman," he answered. "Truly, I liked Jarhost as little as you did, but he may have had the right idea keeping that leech away from us."

"He kept a much more dangerous leech close at hand," Ylmi replied. "But we will see if the taxes of Jarhost are as burdensome as Unhost claimed."

Bogli led her to where a short man leaned on his spear, a short sword belted to his side and iron rings in his beard.

"Greetings," he said, looking her up and down as he took in her disheveled appearance, "Jarl Ylmi, if the tales are true?"

"They are," Ylmi replied. "I take it that you have come to discuss the king's taxes?"

"Before any such dealings," Gorli smiled slightly, "it is customary to offer food and drink."

Ylmi glanced around and choked back a laugh. "My friend, I have a small bag of onions hanging in my hall and a number of fish sitting quietly in their brine pond. To drink, I have but the water that runs down from the mountain."

Gorli's smile faded and he glanced around. "I believe I saw goats as I came down the mountain..."

Ylmi felt the little patience she had slipping away as she took a deep breath. "We do not have so many that they can be slaughtered on a visitor's whim." She pointed to her hall. "In the name of hospitality, I offer you of my onions and river water, but I cannot offer what I do not have."

"Even so," Gorli glanced around, gnawing a moment on his finger. "In that case, it is perhaps best that we begin immediately. If you are as poor as you say, this matter will go quickly enough. I am here not to collect your taxes, but merely to visit your village and see how matters are progressing. I will tell you what I estimate the king will require of you and leave you to work this summer as you will. When the winter draws close, I will return and make the final decision."

So, Ylmi took him from one end of their settlement to the other. She showed him the fishing boats, the tiny gardens, and the small fields that had been scratched out of the rocks near the river.

Gorli said little the whole time, only asking a few questions here and there as Ylmi explained how their village was ordered. When all was finished, he turned to her with a glint in his eye.

"I understand also that you have mines... where gold is found," he said.

"There is little enough," Ylmi replied. "The mines have run their course, and several have collapsed so that they are unsafe."

"I would like to see them, regardless," Gorli spread his hands. "I must make a report to Jarhost, and he will ask what I have seen."

Ylmi agreed that this was fair enough, and she took him to the home Orli had once lived in. It was abandoned, and even after a short time, it was beginning to show signs of neglect. In the corner, Ylmi opened a small door in the floor and let Gorli into one of Jarhost's mines. It had collapsed a very short way in, dirt and rock piling up in the narrow passage.

"There seems still to be gold," Gorli said, waving a small torch along the narrow walls.

Ylmi shrugged. "There is little, it is true, but it would take a great deal of work to get out the tiny specs, and so little for so much work is an ill bargain when it is food we must have."

Gorli grunted in response, but when they were outside, he demanded to see another mine, and then another, until he had inspected all of them.

When it was done, he stood beside her hall and looked over the land around them.

"I will be honest with you, Ylmi," he said. "You have a village full of strong people who seem to do well for themselves. You yourself are a renowned huntress, and the fjord here seems to be full of fish. There is gold yet in your mines. And though the ground is poor here, it is poor in many other places along the coast as well- yet your crops grow better than most. The king will require a mighty portion from you and from your village."

Ylmi's jaw tightened as he spoke.

"Do you not see the children who are here?" she asked. "Do you not see that it will take all we can to survive the winter?"

"Hunger hangs close upon us all," Gorli responded. "And if your taxes did not keep Bjarnmont full of warriors, then you would have Viglir raiding here instead, and his raids would take more than Jarhost's taxes."

"I doubt that very much," Dranri said. He stood nearby, his arms full of firewood as he spoke. "You never were a good liar Gorli."

"I would answer you," Gorli replied, "but your feelings would be hurt, and you would run away to the forest never to be seen again." He turned back to Ylmi. "Be careful that you do not antagonize the king," his eyes went to Dranri, "nor his messengers. This does not have to be a painful process, but I can make life very difficult here... or I can make it very easy."

"Stop talking like someone who wants to be dragged before the lawgivers," Dranri laughed at him. "Trying to cheat a jarl on their taxes is a bad idea, and you know it."

"Dranri!" Ylmi turned and fixed him with a glare strengthened by all her frustration- at Dranri, for bringing Orlanna; at Gorli, for threatening her; and at her own powerlessness to do anything about it.

Dranri straightened, then with a quick nod, turned away.

"I will deal fairly with you," she said, turning back to Gorli. "And I will expect you to do the same with me."

"I will deal as the king has ordered," Gorli's face broke into another grin. "And though I am come as a taxman, I will offer you this advice for free: do not place over much worth in the words of a man who flees his king and hides in the bushes because life is hard. And with that, my task done. I will wish you a plentiful summer and take my leave."

Ylmi watched him go and wondered how difficult this matter would become. There was also the matter of Dranri and his new wife, whom Ylmi remained uneasy over. From every direction, it seemed that she had dangers and uncertainty to consider.

BUILDING BEGINS

The morning after he spoke with Ylmi, Karik rose before dawn and slipped out of Havar's hut. He rubbed his hands together against the chill and thought regretfully of the little home he had built up in the mountains. His mother still lived there, but he felt it had been a bit of a waste. The thought had come to him that perhaps he should build a home in the village, but the building of this ship was more important. Havar's home had enough room for him, and Igil as well, so there he laid his head at night.

At Havar's request, Ymr and Ethna had sharpened their tools the day before, and all that remained was to begin work. Clouds were gathering in the north, blotting out the stars, but the moon hung in the western sky, shining down over the fjord and glinting off the top of the great mountain in its midst.

'Dragonpeak,' Karik thought he should call it...

His fingers itched to begin work, and the cold breeze blowing out of the mountains made him think of the coming winter. He desperately wanted to finish the ship before the snows came - before the fjord was lined with ice and the storms made sailing far too dangerous.

"You are very eager to begin," Igil spoke from behind him.

Karik grinned. "I am eager to finish the ship."

"We haven't yet begun," Igil laughed. "And it will take a long, long time to complete it."

"I want it done before this winter," Karik said, "I am eager to try the isles."

"As you have said many times," Igil clapped him on the back and stood next to him, staring out at the fjord. "But none of us have built a ship this large before, and it will be completed when it is completed. This is not a ship to take shortcuts on." He glanced down the beach and chuckled.

"It feels a hundred years ago we slept in that little shed... and crept into Unhost's house."

"You didn't want me to," Karik grinned back, "and look how it turned out."

"I'm pretty sure I warned you to stop," Igil replied. Together, they stared out at the fjord. "Do your burns ever... ache?"

"Yes," Karik said simply. "Though now, I have other wounds that ache more often." He flexed his fingers. "I am hoping it does not hold me back too much..."

"Only one way to find out," Igil said. "The dawn is beginning to rise, and it is time we set to work."

So they began the building of their ship.

As the sun rose, Karik, Igil, and Havar began shaping the keel. They hauled the longest tree they had out of the water and set to work with their axes, slowly hacking away wood to form the keel's notched shape. As they drew closer together, Karik stepped aside and, hauling more logs out of the water, began splitting them apart to have them ready for the hull.

Karik's wounds drained his strength swiftly, and more than once he had to stop to catch his breath. Beside him, Igil and Havar vied with each other to see who could work more swiftly, and between the two of them the sound of axes beat like a drum.

All day they worked till the sun was low in the west and their stomachs ached with hunger. Karik felt the pain from his wounds, and the ax felt heavy in his hands, so he took one of the small coracles and pushed it into the water to find fish, while Igil and Havar continued swinging their axes over the keel.

When Karik returned a short time later, with a few small fish, Ymr had banked his smithy's fire and retired to his hut, and the smoke from Torig's fire showed the old man had already gone to sleep. But still Igil and Havar's axes rose and fell.

When Karik had cooked the fish over their fire, they ate together, and Karik saw that Igil's hand was torn and bleeding in a couple places. Even as they ate, they sucked in air between bites as they tried to keep weariness at bay.

They spoke little and turned back to the ship when the fish were gone. They pulled logs out and lined them up, ready to split into boards, and began shaving off the bark that lined them. The night was half over before they halted and threw themselves upon the piled furs where they made their beds.

The next morning, they rose with the dawn, Igil first and Karik soon after, and continued work upon the ship.

--------◦--------

The keel was laid out, notched and ready for the ribs when Thora came down to the beach. She carried her spear over her shoulder and eyed their work critically.

"I have never seen a ship so large," she said as she ran her eyes over the long keel and planks.

"It is almost twice as long as *Kalborg*," Havar said proudly. "And she will be the greatest ship Vrania has ever seen."

Thora's eyes narrowed as she looked over it. "Are you worried it may be too large to maneuver through the isles?"

"I do not think so," Karik said with a shake of his head. "The greatest danger of the isles is the currents, so we must have enough oars to pull against them. The second danger is the storms and the waves which they raise up. Something as small as *Kalborg* would be tossed upon the rocks by the first waves... we need something big enough to withstand them."

Thora nodded. "As you say, though I do not look forward to putting your words to the test." She shook herself. "But I have come to tell you we feast tonight in Ylmi's hall, when the sun is set."

Karik set down his ax and wiped his hands on his shirt. "It would be better if Dranri were here," he said, "I know she enjoys his company and will miss his laughter."

"You have not heard?" Thora asked. "Dranri has returned, and not alone. He has brought Lasvik's wife."

"What?" Karik's head jerked up. "He brought the wife of the man Ylmi killed back to our settlement?"

Thora's eyes were wide. "I thought you knew what he was doing in the Undmir."

"Not at all," Karik replied. "He said nothing to me of this."

Thora shook her head. "Well, as Dranri and Lasvik were old friends, I suspect that ended when they both fell in love with this woman - Orlanna she is called. Well, she picked Lasvik over Dranri. Only now, Lasvik is dead, and Dranri is good friends with the Jarl of Dragonsrest... so, Orlanna has come to live with him."

"Does Ylmi know?" Igil asked. "I am not sure having her here is safe..."

"Dranri came to her first," Thora said. "And Orlanna promised she would not pursue a wergild. Nonetheless, I think she bears watching."

"Agreed," Karik said firmly.

That evening, as dawn settled, Karik went with Igil and Havar to the hall in the center of the village. Ylmi had done more than a little work upon it, and though the roof still leaked in a few places, the cracks had been patched in the walls. Smoke rose from within, and when they stepped inside, they saw the long fireplace in the center alight with a crackling blaze.

"Greetings!" Revik shouted. He sat by the fire, slowly turning a small deer upon a spit with one hand and drinking from a clay cup with the other. "Karik, Ylmi's feasting is far richer than yours - she at least has good drink and plenty of it."

Karik chuckled, but his eyes went to Ylmi, who sat silent and grim in her chair at the end of the hall.

"The deer seems smaller than is your usual game, brother," Igil said as he took a seat. "I trust it was not too difficult for you to bring down."

"It is more than enough to feed a skinny thing like you," Revik retorted. "I would think swinging an ax all day would put some power in those shoulders, yet you stand like a dead pine in the snow... narrow and gnarled."

"There is enough for all," Ylmi said. Her voice was calm, but it cut through their bickering. "Even if Revik eats enough for two, which I have gathered is his want."

"Seeing as I fight for three..." Revik muttered.

Ylmi's fingers rolled her spear back and forth as she sat. "You fight for six, at least. So if you must eat for three, you will hear no complaint from me."

Karik took his place by the fire, glancing up at Ylmi as he did so. Something was gnawing at her, but even as he stared, her eyes fell on him and she smiled suddenly.

"There is no need for a tight hand, not on this night." She tapped her spear on the ground, letting the wood run through her fingers. "Karik, how goes the ship?"

"She takes shape," Karik answered. "The keel is laid, and we have begun to lay the planks for her hull."

"Will she be finished before the winter storms?"

Karik made to answer, but Igil spoke first. "I do not know. If she is, it will be a near miracle. If she is not, then I will not be surprised."

"We need more help," Havar said. "Igil and I built *Kalborg* alone, and she was the greatest ship we have ever seen. It took us almost four months, but this ship is more than twice as big, with more than twice as many oars. If there are others who could lend us aid..."

"All in the village are hard at work," Ylmi said, her voice calm again. But Karik noticed that her knuckles had turned white as she held the spear. "If there are idle hands, I will see you have aid."

"We are the greatest boat builders Vrania has ever produced," Havar said with a smile. "If we cannot finish it in time, then there are none who can."

"Do not tempt the gods," Revik said, pointing at Havar with his cup. "The boat is not yet finished, and the isles remain uncrossed."

"What of the crew?" Thora asked. "You say it is twice as big as *Kalborg*, so it will take a crew of twenty?"

"A crew of twenty-five could sail her," Igil said slowly, "but it would be difficult. She can carry as many as fifty."

"Fifty!" Ylmi looked down at them in surprise. "Igil, there are hardly fifty in our whole village, and more than a few of them are not fit to pull an oar."

"We will need others," Igil admitted, "from other villages..."

"Perhaps we could scrape together twenty five here in this village who could sail," Ylmi closed her eye in thought, as though counting those she could not see.

"The waters in the Isle are strong and treacherous," Karik said quietly. "The more rowers we have, the greater the chance of success."

Thora stepped through the door as he spoke, and behind her came Dranri. Karik watched as Ylmi and Dranri locked eyes for a moment, then Dranri looked away and took his seat next to the fire.

"We are all here then," Ylmi said. "Karik, it is on you to find a crew that we can sail with. If you can gain more from the nearby villages, then they will be welcome."

The smell of the roasting deer filled the hall, as did the warmth from the fire. The shadows danced and played upon the wooden walls, save for where the shadow that was Ulfr remained still as stone beside Ylmi's chair, her eyes glinting in the light from the flames.

"Much has passed since last we gathered for a feast," Ylmi said as they all filled their cups. "We have carried a boat over Vanik's Point, sailed the Undersea, and slain a jarl. We have defeated King Viglir, and killed Jarl Unhost. I have become Jarl of Dragonsrest, and with the fruit of our labors, we have begun the building of a ship - one that will take us at last beyond the Black Isles."

She raised her own cup and stood, the firelight making her scarred face glow in the darkness. "To what has been done, and to what remains, drink with me."

Together they drank, and when it was done, she nodded to Karik.

"As he was your friend..."

Karik cleared his throat and pulled himself slowly to his feet. "Wisic had a quick tongue and a sharp wit. But he was quicker to do what had to be done, and his spear was sharper than his wit. I will not weep for him, but rejoice, for he dines in Valhalla and rests with the Allfather, having been faithful to the end. May we all join him one day." He raised his cup and poured half of what remained into the fire before downing the rest in one gulp.

The others followed suit, and Karik returned to his seat.

Before anyone else could speak, Havar rose to his feet.

"Ylmi, I have spoken with you and with others," he said, "and I think the time is coming when we must decide what path we will take this year." He glanced toward Revik and Thora, who looked up at him curiously.

"I believe we should take advantage of *Kalborg* and the charts we have to raid the eastern coast of Vrania," Havar explained. "We can sail to them unlooked for and be gone before they can summon an army to stop us. In this way, we can gather to ourselves wealth, and where there is wealth, there will always be warriors. In this way, when the time comes to sail into the west, we will sail with a fleet and a host of warriors."

"If we go raiding," Thora asked, "how much longer till we try the Isles? Another year or two?"

"Two, at least," Havar answered. "Perhaps three."

Revik glanced at his brother. "You have thoughts on this?"

"There is great danger either way," Igil shrugged. "But I think there is more to be gained by sailing west as soon as we can."

"If we raid Vrania," Karik said quietly, "then we have taken food out of the mouths of those who are starving as well, and we will survive only until Viglir decides it's worth his time to build ships and raid us here. In this way, we may find ourselves closer to starvation in a few years than we are now, no matter how much we raid."

"I am shocked you oppose this," Revik said. "You are fixed on the Isles..."

"There is no reason to stir up enmity to yourselves," Dranri said quietly, but Revik laughed.

"Don't think you can wiggle your way out of this one, longbeard," he waved a finger at Dranri. "You're part of this village, too. You live here now, remember? And I fear no amount of enmity to ourselves," he glared pointedly at Dranri, "we've beaten Viglir once, we can do it again."

"We beat him with Jarhost and all the jarls of the mountains and the coast arrayed along with us," Karik snapped back. "How do you think we will fare when Jarhost stands back and the seven of us have to face Viglir's army by ourselves?"

"I can take them," Revik smiled easily, but Igil rolled his eyes.

"Take this seriously, brother," he muttered.

"How great an army can Viglir gather if we've burned his farms?" Havar asked. "And when Dragonsrest alone in Vrania has food for all, how long until Dragonsrest has warriors aplenty?"

"Not before Jarhost and Viglir divide our food for themselves," Ylmi replied. "And what you are suggesting is not raiding, it is war. Viglir and Jarhost have raided each other for many years, but if we set fire to Viglir's halls and leave his people to freeze in the winter..."

"When we determined to steal the gold from Hegli," Igil said, his voice cutting through the rest of them, "I agreed because it was the only way to build a ship that would get us across the Isles. We took a small portion of gold ...and unleashed a battle that slew many, including our friend Wisic, who we are supposed to be remembering this evening."

He looked around them all, his eyes lingering on Revik and Havar. "We might gain some small glory in raiding, but it will only sow more hunger and grief among our people, which we will reap sooner or later. If we are to improve our lots and gain fame and fortune, there is no greater fame to be gained than that which will come from sailing the Black Isles. Any fortune in Torhom is a pittance to what we will gain if we can find a way into the lands beyond the Black Isles.

"If there is to be war," he finished with a deep breath, "I will not go. I will build our ship and prepare it for the passage of the Isles."

"I have little to do with the ship," Thora said quietly, "but I will not burn Torhom, either. There is enough death in Vrania without seeking it out or sowing more."

Havar spat into the fire. "There is no guarantee we will find anyone across the Isles..."

"That is my hope," Karik interjected.

"But neither is there a guarantee they will be weaklings," Havar finished. "Or do you think they will meet us with open arms? Perhaps with the offer of an arm ring, then we can trade service from Jarhost to another king just as bad."

"Raiding the west is a different matter," Karik replied. "Though I hope we will find uninhabited lands, that may not be the case. If we must raid to feed ourselves and our Isle, then perhaps in time we may bargain for a land to make our own. I doubt the west has any idea of how to reach us here."

He pointed at Havar. "I know you hunger, as we all do, to make Dragonsrest safe and prosperous. Raiding can accomplish this, and the men of the west will know we are not weaklings, but a force to be taken seriously. But beginning a war, either with Viglir or the west, only ensures that we will find ourselves friendless and destined for a bloody end."

"I have heard enough," Ylmi said. "We will put all our strength into preparing to sail the Isles, and we will leave off raiding Torhom. If matters change, then perhaps this may be debated further, but for now, we will continue to work as one."

Revik shrugged and pulled his knife from his belt, slicing a piece from the deer and biting into the sizzling meat. Quickly the others joined in, and for a while, the hall was filled with the sound of laughter, low talk, and the crackling fire.

Ylmi even cracked a smile where she sat, though Karik noted she did not eat. Rising from his place by the fire, he lifted a strip of meat from the deer and sat down beside her chair.

"How go matters in the settlement?"

The smile vanished from her face in an instant, and Karik felt a sudden guilt. She had doubtless been enjoying an escape from those thoughts, and he had brought them back.

But now everyone was looking up at her, so she took a deep breath.

"We had our first traveler today," Ylmi said slowly. "But she was not an exile. She was a mother with two small children." She stared into the fire, and the crackling of the flames filled the silence.

A mother and two children would bring in less than they ate by far, and they all knew it. It was why such people rarely left their village, and why, when they did, they were often turned away.

"I dislike the idea of turning away anyone in need of help," Thora said quietly. "And as we have survived well enough the past winters and will not have to deal with a dragon this year..."

"We still have to deal with Jarhost's tax collectors," Ylmi said. "Unhost was a foul creature, but he was right that the king takes with a heavy hand." She sighed, rubbing her hand over the dragon scars. It did little to help with the ache behind her eye, but something was better than nothing. "Also, we have lost several hardworking hands. Flovi and Orli may have been Unhost lackies, but their work will not be easily replaced."

Igil was staring into the fire, his hands working over a small piece of wood, his long fingers snapping it over and over. "One more may make the difference between life and death," he said into the quiet, "but if we send her away, there is no doubt that she will die."

"You think I don't know that?" Ylmi snapped. "I know better than any of you the challenges she will face, and she does not have a goat herd to help her as my father and mother did." She closed her eyes and leaned back. "I will decide tomorrow."

"The goat herds are growing…" Karik supplied, but Ylmi cut him off.

"Yes, and likely to be the first thing taxed." She added. "The hunting is growing thin, and we bring in fewer fish than we used to. I know my village, Karik Haldsson. I said I would decide tomorrow, and that is what I will do."

They were all silent for a moment until Karik shifted. "Forgive me," he said quietly, "I spoke out of turn."

Ylmi let her face fall into her hand. "No, you were trying to help. It is I who was wrong."

"Is the hunting that dire?" Dranri asked.

Ylmi's eyes fell on him, and she nodded.

"It is easy to watch the goats and see that we do not eat too many," Thora supplied, "but for those who are not often in the forest, ranging wide, it is easy to take one more deer and not see how it affects us all. When twenty or thirty do so twice a year…" she shrugged.

"I think we should place a limit on how many deer may be killed each year," Igil suggested, "but how many people will obey?"

Ylmi groaned. "And how many will stand by the first time I punish a starving man or woman for trying to feed their family."

"All of them," Revik spoke up. "That is why you keep me around."

Thora froze and dropped the bone she had been gnawing. "That's why she keeps me around," she said with a feral grin. "You're just here for shade."

Ylmi laughed, and her shoulders seemed to relax a bit. "If it were Fornik, then you would be welcome to him. But it is likely that such a matter would play out differently." Her fingers drummed on her chair as she considered for a moment. "It seems all things lead back to your ship," she glanced to Igil and Havar. "Do not dawdle in its building."

"Do not dawdle?" Havar echoed. "Ylmi, I have been at work on that boat before the sun rises and long after it sets. There is no dawdling in my hands."

"That is good to hear," Ylmi laughed. "Nonetheless, I will leave these problems for tomorrow. Tonight, we feast."

But Karik noticed that though Ylmi had escaped her foul mood, Havar now wore his own like a cloak and spoke little the rest of the evening.

The next morning, Karik rose early and slipped out of the hut. A steady wind blew out of the north with a subtle bite of cold as he pushed a small boat into the water. The light of the setting moon was dim over the sea, even as the first hints of the sun's light could be seen on the peaks of the eastern mountains. Tossing a net into a small rowboat, he pushed it into the waves and slid out onto the fjord.

The water was frigid when he tossed out the net, and it felt colder as he pulled it in, empty. Again and again, he threw the net, and each time he thought of Ylmi's words from the night before.

They had left Yrdnara to ensure they would have enough food to make it through winter, but now the same problem was occurring here and all across Vrania.

The net came in empty and he glared at it for a moment before throwing it back. It landed in the water with a soft splash, and Karik let it sink a bit before pulling it in.

Simply crossing the Isles might not be enough. How many raids would it take to feed Dragonsrest all winter? How many raids would it take to feed all the coast?

The net was empty again, and Karik jerked the last few lengths out of the water in frustration. Normally, he would have more patience, but he felt uneasy, as if he needed to jump into the water and swim through the Isles at once.

He sighed and tossed the net back into the bottom of the boat, resigning himself to the hunger that gnawed at his gut. The sun was rising, and it was time to return to work on their ship.

Havar met him as he approached and frowned when he saw the empty boat.

"You are about early this morning," he said. "Though I see it has not been very profitable."

"Even so," Karik answered. He looked over the boat and took a deep breath. "She will be far heavier than *Kalborg*."

"I hope you don't intend to carry her anywhere," Havar replied. "But yes, she will be. Even pulling her off the sand will be something I do not look forward to. It is in my mind that we should build piers."

Karik glanced at the bones of the ship lying on the sand, and his eyes then went to *Kalborg*. She was drawn up on the shore, leaning sideways against her blocks.

"Piers would take a lot of work to build," he said at last. "And we have our hands full with the ship."

"This ship is going to take a lot of work to move," Havar countered. "And they would save the fishing boats a great deal of work, as well."

"I will speak to Ylmi about it," Karik answered, "but I think the matter will be better left until next year, after we have crossed the Isles."

"*If* we cross them, you mean," Havar muttered. "It's not done yet Karik, and I may get sick and die and not be able to finish my boat."

Karik laughed. "That will be a terrible loss, indeed. Though Igil may be able to continue what the two of you have begun." He looked around, "Speaking of Igil, where is he?"

"Marrying that woman who came into town yesterday," Havar answered. "If you see him, tell him to get back here and help. I want to fasten these boards before the next storm rolls in."

Karik's eyes widened. "He's doing what?"

"Marrying the woman who came in yesterday," Havar repeated.

Karik rolled his eyes. "Where?"

Havar set down the board he had picked up. "I don't know. Try the big fir tree south of the village."

Shaking his head, Karik hurried away from the beach. What was Igil thinking? The woman had arrived only the day before. They didn't know who she was, if she was a good worker, or if she was even a decent person. He spat into the cold. Igil didn't have a great deal of food set aside. He had been building the boat and only setting aside enough for himself. Igil was no fool, though, he reminded himself- perhaps he had a plan. Or the woman had some skill he hadn't known of...

He was in such a hurry, he almost ran over Igil and the woman. They were approaching Ylmi's hall, hand in hand, a tight smile on the woman's face.

"You're in a great hurry," Igil said tightly as Karik recovered himself and looked between the two of them.

"I am looking for you, Igil."

"And now you have found me," Igil answered, "what is it you have to say?"

"Have you lost your mind?"

Igil patted the woman on the hand, "Go see to Henla and Torm, I will deal with this," he said to her.

"No." The woman drew herself up and looked Karik in the eye. "I am your wife, and the decision was mine as much as yours."

"So, you are married then," Karik said quietly.

"Fianna and I have promised ourselves to each other," Igil answered. "And we will make a home together..."

"Why?" Karik took a step toward his friend. "There are many responsibilities that come with being a husband..."

"I know this Karik," Igil took Fianna's hand in his own and smiled. "But when have either of us shied away from a little work?"

Karik bit his lip, then turned on Fianna. She did not shrink away, though she took a deep breath when he looked at her.

"Why have you agreed to this?" he asked her. "You do not know Igil..."

But before he could finish, Fianna interrupted him. "I know that he offered help to me and mine," she said quickly. "And I know that I will prove myself a good wife and hard worker, seeing as I have been both before."

"If that is the case, then why are you here?" Karik asked, "and not in Illstadt, where you are well known?"

"You are not the jarl here," Igil said quietly. "And she is not required to answer to you."

"I only want what is best for you," Karik looked at Igil, wondering what had possessed his friend. "We barely know where she is from..."

"I know why she is here," Igil interrupted him, "and I know that she has two small children. I know that if she does not stay with us, they will starve. And," he took Fianna's hand in his own, "I know that she has promised to be a good wife to me as I have promised to be a good husband to her."

Karik looked back and forth between them for a moment, then threw up his hands. "Who else knows?"

"I was going to tell you first," Igil's smile was long gone now. "And then speak with Ylmi."

Karik took a deep breath to calm himself. "Igil, have you thought this through? You will need to take time away from the ship to build the two of you a home. You will need to set aside food for yourself and three other hungry mouths…"

"Karik," Igil asked with a smile that did not reach his eyes, "why are we building a boat?"

"To cross the Isles…"

"So that our people don't starve," Igil interrupted. "That's the point for us. Revik and Havar may be more concerned about the fame, but you and I know what this is really about. It's fine for them, but don't you go that route, too. Do not forget why we started all this."

Karik glared at him but took a deep breath. "You should have spoken with Ylmi first."

"Ylmi has her hands full," Igil answered. "You have been gone, but I have been here and seen what she must deal with. Every day she has to deal with Fornik and everyone else second guessing her and making every decision difficult. Just once, she doesn't have to make this decision." He saw Karik wavering, and his voice softened. "You saw her last night Karik -she's given us a place here and made our lives much easier than they otherwise could have been. Let me do this for her."

Karik hesitated, but Igil's words had found their mark. Their marriage would make the decision easier on Ylmi, and that alone might be enough to make it worthwhile.

He took a deep breath, "Then let me congratulate you both."

Fianna smiled at him. "Thank you Karik, though I know that you are not fully convinced, I will be a good wife to your friend."

"And he will be a good husband to you," Karik replied. "I wish you both great happiness."

Karik watched them go, a tinge of worry in his chest. Their marriage was an insult to Ylmi, having been done without her permission. Whatever Igil said his motive was, it was not likely Ylmi would be pleased with the matter.

When they disappeared around Nanni's hut, Karik looked about the village. Dragonsrest was already larger than it had been when he and Igil had come with the others down from the mountain and met Unhost.

It seemed years ago in another world, almost. They had done many things since then, and Umir and Wisic had passed into the halls of the Allfather. Karik sighed heavily and turned back toward where he could hear Havar at work on the ship.

Change brought danger and the inevitable march of fate. He could no more fix every problem in Dragonsrest than he could swim the Isles by himself, but if he set his hand where there was work to be done, then perhaps he could lessen the blows that wyrd sent their way.

DRAGONSREST

The sun had long set when Ylmi eased herself into her chair and exhaled into the darkness. Her fingers found Ulfr's eager head and slipped among the fur, while below, the embers of the fire glowed with a dull red light that lit nothing. The wind was howling in from the north, rushing over the heights that overlooked the village and moaning over the sod-covered roofs of their little homes.

Her feet ached, her shoulders were sore, and the pain behind her dead eye had been growing worse all day. Slowly, she let her head rest on the back of the chair and sighed, loosening her hold on the spear in her left hand.

Suddenly she wished her parents were there - or Karik, or Dranri, or anyone at all. Well, not anyone. Although, if Fornik were there, alone...

She took Skathi's stones from their small pouch and rolled them about in her hands. The red stone, as always, drew her eye. The killing of Unhost troubled her not at all. Not only had it been payment for attacks on her and Karik, it had been payment well earned by his vile deeds. But she was under no illusion that killing would solve all her problems.

"Only most of them," she muttered to herself.

The white stone was the one that troubled her. It was easy to draw back from bloodshed... killing Fornik would be easy enough, and it would turn half the village against her. But the goddess had been clear: the path of the white stone was as doomed as that of the red.

"I cannot bring back to life one whom I have killed," she muttered. "But I can kill one whom I have left alive too long." A mistake leading toward caution was easier to remedy than one bred from wrath. Although, Fornik was building up wrath for himself...

She blinked away the thought. Dwelling on it only stoked her fury back to life, and she was tired of being angry. Her stomach grumbled, drawing her attention back to the fact that she had not eaten that day at all.

Slowly, she rose to her feet, feeling suddenly stiff as she straightened and stretched her back. Her eyes went to the gloomy shadow where she knew a barrel held fish preserved in brine, sitting beyond the reach of the fire's dim glow.

From the rafters, a few onions hung suspended from a net, but she hungered for something more filling, and her eyes went back to the barrel. She was behind on storing for winter - far behind - and she would need to hunt hard for the next few months if she was to put enough away.

She took a deep breath and stepped toward the onions but paused as she heard a noise at the door - someone pushing inside through the wolf-skin curtain.

"Ylmi?" Karik's voice was quiet, and she relaxed her grip on her spear.

"What brings you here so late?" She turned toward him, though her stomach growled again.

Karik chuckled, his dark form coming into view as he bent next to the dim coals. "I wondered if you were hungry..." He lifted a pot in one hand while he set sticks on the coals with the other.

"It is not your duty to feed me," Ylmi answered.

"I miss your company," Karik replied. "And though Igil is my friend and Havar has been close with us, I weary of them from time to time."

Bright flames slowly licked at the small twigs, and in their light, she could see Karik looking up to smile at her.

"Besides, talk of the ship can only go so far before it begins to go in circles." The flames were rising higher now, and the comforting noise of the fire filled the hall along with a warm light. Karik set the pot over the flames and sat back. There was quiet for a few moments as the two of them watched the fire.

At last, Karik spoke. "Igil came to you?"

"And Fianna," Ylmi replied. There was another lull, and Ulfr rose to stretch, her back arching low and her maw opening in a wide yawn before she padded over and laid down by the fire, across from Karik.

"He should have come to me first," Ylmi said at last. "I am his jarl, and I told him so."

Karik nodded. "As did I. You will let them stay?"

Ylmi's grip on her spear tightened, and she gazed into the fire with her one eye. "Yes."

"He wanted to make the decision easier for you," Karik said quietly. "And he did not wish that she or her children should starve."

"They may still starve," Ylmi responded. "And if they do, it will be my task to see them buried. Hunger will come to Dragonsrest this winter as it has never come before, unless your ship sails." She turned her eye on him, the fire making the wayward strands of her hair glow red as she pushed them back. "How goes the building?"

"It goes," Karik replied. "The keel is complete, and the hull begins to take shape."

"How much longer till it is finished?"

Karik raised his hands to count, and Ylmi watched as he brushed quickly over the stubs on his left hand.

"Two months," he guessed. "Perhaps. If all goes well."

Ylmi let herself back into the chair and watched as the sparks rose over the fire up into the darkness of the roof. The first snows would appear in three months or sooner. The storms would soon grow more frequent and more violent, and the time to sail was running out.

"Perhaps..." she said slowly, and it felt as though something gave in her chest to say the words, "perhaps we should wait."

"Wait?"

"Concentrate on preparing for winter," Ylmi explained, "then plan to sail early next year. The winter will be hard, but we can survive it. You are a capable hunter and fisher, as is Igil... perhaps we have pushed too far too fast."

"If we can sail west," Karik spoke quickly, "then we will provide more than a few extra days of fishing. You have said yourself that the game is running thin, and the fishing is less than it used to be. One trip with our new ship will bring back more than the entire village could gather in weeks."

Ylmi rubbed the back of her neck and grimaced. There was a pain just above her shoulders that wouldn't seem to go away, and the ache behind her eye was growing worse.

"I cannot decide this now," she said, "but we will have to decide at some point... and I do not wish to wait until it is too late."

"In a month's time," Karik replied, "when the bears are fattest before the winter, we will decide. And if we must wait, then Igil and I will bring in enough food to keep us till winter."

Ylmi gave a short bark of weary laughter. "You are full of optimism, Karik Haldsson." She shook herself and groaned before stepping stiffly toward the fire. Its warmth felt good on her face, and the smell of a stew boiling in Karik's pot sent another pang of hunger through her stomach.

"Is that ever going to be done?" she asked.

Karik took a bowl from beside the fire and scooped it full of the steaming stew before handing it to her. "Various vegetables and a trout my mother caught in the mountains," he said. "Your mother had a good eye for a homestead. If there was not much more to do, I think I would be very happy up there, tending the garden and fishing the mountain streams."

Ylmi pulled a spoon from a shelf and took a bite. It burned her tongue but left a good taste in her mouth and warmed her as it went down.

"I should have you cook for me more often," she muttered.

Karik looked up. "Perhaps I will."

Ylmi kicked him as she took another bite, and Karik chuckled as he filled his own bowl.

"Do they still hurt?" Ylmi asked.

Karik looked up, and she nodded to his hands. Glancing down, he paused, as if for a moment he had forgotten that he was missing two fingers.

"They sting from time to time. Does your eye?"

Ylmi shrugged. The ache behind her eye was a little less, but she was trying to ignore it. "Less than it did, more than I'd like."

Karik nodded and lifted a spoon from the bowl. "When was the last time you hunted?"

Ylmi's spoon paused on the way to her mouth. "Why do you ask?"

Karik hummed. "You seem to enjoy it, and it seems to me you have done little of what you enjoy since you became jarl."

"I became jarl because Unhost did too much of what he enjoyed," Ylmi grumbled, but the thought of climbing through the pines with her bow was very appealing. "Though, I would not mind seeing less of Fornik."

"He still causes problems?"

Ylmi felt suddenly tired. The stew was filling her with warmth, and she very much wanted to curl up in her bed with Ulfr and go to sleep. "He never ceases."

Karik suddenly stiffened. "I meant to tell you earlier," he said slowly, "he was having a lengthy conversation with Orlanna this afternoon."

Ylmi dropped her spoon back into her bowl in disgust. "I wondered where he was. It seemed too good to hope he had found some real work to do."

"Do you think the two of them will cause problems?"

"I don't know," Ylmi shook her head and slipped to the floor. "And I don't want to know if Dranri will respect her wishes over mine." She stared into the fire.

"Perhaps you should exile Fornik..." Karik said thoughtfully. "He does little enough in the village, and I doubt he will be missed."

"He would be missed by few," Ylmi replied, "but I do not wish to begin as Unhost did... and there are some who like me little enough as it is," she sighed heavily. "I will hunt tomorrow, and if the village burns down without me, then you may all perish."

"We would deserve it." Karik chuckled. "Go, it will do you good."

Slowly, she stood and took the long stick she used to work the fire, pushing the sticks and embers together into a pile that sparked and flamed up as bits of wood, previously escaped from the flames, were pushed back together. "Goodnight, Karik, and thank you for dinner."

Karik rose and stepped toward the door. "Perhaps I will visit more often," he said slowly, "if you do not mind my company."

"Of all the people in this place," Ylmi answered, "your presence annoys me the least."

Karik grinned and ducked through the heavy wolf's hide curtain, and Ylmi was left alone. She set a heavy log on the fire to burn slowly through the night and made her way to the back of the hall, behind a screen of dried limbs and ruined hides that could keep out nothing but prying eyes. She pulled off the mail shirt she always wore now, and rolled her shoulders free of its weight. She set it to the side with her spear and laid down just as Ulfr padded quietly in. The wolf circled the bed three times before lowering herself onto it and looking up at Ylmi.

Ylmi smiled at her and laid down, the thought of hunting up through the hills to the south filling her with joy. She dozed off, the pain behind her eye forgotten at last.

—◦—

Ylmi rose the next morning and slipped out of the hall as the sun's first light was showing over the mountains. To the north, however, dark clouds were moving in upon a heavy wind and Ylmi guessed her hunt would likely be short.

She set off, Ulfr loping by her side, as behind her the village was coming to life. She could hear Karik and the others working away on the ship, hammering and chopping as they fastened the hull together, and somewhere down by the river she could hear children shouting at each other.

Her long strides took her southwest along the trail that led toward Bjarnmont, till she branched off northward into heavily wooded slopes she hoped had been less hunted of late. The woods were lit with the weird light of the sun beneath the storm, as the rising sun in the east shone its light beneath the storm clouds piling in.

Every swaying of the pine boughs, every movement of the bushes caused the shadows to jump and swing about, but Ylmi's eye was used to such things, and she scanned the trees and the ground looking for sign of an animal's passing or the distinct movement of a squirrel in the trees.

It was not a squirrel that she saw through the trees however, but a man with a long beard and a black bow in his hands.

Her shoulders slumped when she saw him, and she lowered her own bow. "You."

Dranri nodded. "I see we both had the same idea - a hunt before the storm?"

"Much good it did us both," Ylmi replied. "My guess is that we have driven off each other's quarry." She looked up to where the dark clouds were already rolling overhead.

"Perhaps we should have hunted together, like we used to," Dranri suggested.

But Ylmi turned on him, her braided hair whipping with the force of it. "Why?" she demanded. "Why did you bring her here?"

Dranri sighed and looked into the distance.

"You knew the difficulties I would face as a new jarl," she spat the words out. "You warned me of them yourself. So why did you bring her?"

"I love her, Ylmi," Dranri said.

Ylmi snorted. "You have told me that much. Yet it does not change the fact that she has been speaking with Fornik and will likely begin stirring up trouble."

"Fornik came to her..." Dranri began, but Ylmi cut him off.

"What does it matter who came to whom?" she snapped. "Fornik has been a pain in my neck since I was a child, but at least I have been able to keep him contained. He is a fool and rash, but I do not think Orlanna shares his foolishness. What will you do, Dranri, when she makes you choose between me and her?"

Dranri's face had gone suddenly serious. "She will not do that, Ylmi, she has not come to cause trouble."

"I slew her husband," Ylmi rolled her eye. "That is not easily forgotten, whatever she may say." She took a deep breath and glanced skyward. A drop of rain fell on her cheek, below her burned eye, but she felt nothing on the scarred skin. "Do not set yourself against me, Dranri, we have been friends too long for that."

Dranri sighed. "Orlanna and I were friends when I was young," he said with effort. "Lasvik and I went to Bjarnmont together, leaving Tharstadt to make a life for ourselves in the war hall of King Ingor. We gained some fame and glory, for we were both strong and swift. Lasvik was the stronger, but I was the swifter, and we won many battles in the mountains.

"When the time came for us to take the daughter of King Ingor to marry Jarl Hegli, we discovered that we both loved the same woman. Lasvik had the more glory and the sword Ingor gave him," he nodded to Ylmi, "which you have now. He was the greater warrior, so she went with him." He was silent for a moment, staring into the trees.

"Lasvik and I had a falling out over it, and Hegli was not unhappy at the opportunity to add one of Jarhost's best warriors to his own ranks. So, he gave Lasvik an arm ring and threw me out. I think that was when Orlanna regretted her decision, but by then, it was too late. I left Jarhost's hall soon after and moved to the mountains. When you came up the mountainside bearing that sword, I had hope. And, when you told me that Hegli was dead, I soon decided to seek her out and see if she would have me now."

Ylmi sighed and watched Ulfr, who was nosing through the bushes a little ways off. "I understand - a little - why you sought her out," she said at last. "But why? Why did you bring her back here? Could you not have stayed with her in the Undmir?"

Dranri shook his head. "Tanvir is still trying to secure his position on his father's throne, and he is in no position to protect me from those in the Undmir who wish me ill." He looked to Ylmi, "She will not cause trouble, Ylmi, I promise you."

Ylmi turned her bow over in her hands, trying to think. It made more sense to her now why Orlanna had come. She looked out through the trees and took a deep breath.

"You were there when the taxman, Gorli, made his demands," she said slowly without looking at him. "Is he as powerful as he claims?"

"He can make a deal of trouble," Dranri answered. "Though I knew him to be clumsy and unsubtle. Do not take him lightly, but you have a place now in the Thing, and you may come with all the other jarls to lay claims before the lawgivers. If he is unfair, it may be that you can gain relief through them, for even the king must bow to their rulings."

Ylmi sighed, a very little of the tension going out of her and leaving behind a heavy weariness.

"It has been too long since we hunted together, Ylmi," Dranri said after a moment. "The storm is near, and soon everything will be huddled down against its coming. Shall we work together once again?"

Ylmi looked on her old friend with her one eye and tried to remember when the last time had been... before Karik came?

"I would like that," she said, and calling to Ulfr, the three of them moved through the wind-swept forest, hunting as they had in the years before Ylmi lost her eye.

When they finally returned to the settlement, the sun had set and the moon was rising over the mountains. They had each brought down a deer, and Ylmi enjoyed the weight on her shoulders. The storm had been a short one, with violent rain and freezing wind for only a little while. Now, all that remained was a light rain - hardly more than a mist.

It was good to be doing something again, something she knew would make the winter easier, rather than arguing with one person or another. As she bade farewell to Dranri, she heard the sound of axes at work down toward the fjord.

Most of the village had gone inside for the night, many of them doubtless already asleep in preparation for another day of hard work to come. As Ylmi glanced through the huts on her way to the hall, she saw the glow of a fire near Havar's hut. She grinned and shook her head, thinking of when she had first met Karik and wondered if he would shirk his work.

She hung the deer carcass from the pole near her hall, erected for that purpose, and set to work peeling the rest of the meat from its bones.

Ulfr padded up out of the darkness, shoving her damp muzzle up under Ylmi's arm.

"You'll get yours," Ylmi muttered, "but I can't give it to you if you keep bumping me."

The wolf sat back, and Ylmi flipped her a piece of the neck meat. It disappeared in one snap of Ulfr's maw, and Ylmi shook her head as the wolf stared at her expectantly.

"No, no," Ylmi said, waving the knife. "You're not a pup anymore, you can get your own food. You have no need of mine."

It was quick work, Ylmi's fingers guiding the sharp knife through practiced movements until the meat was hung from the rafters in her home

- curing in the smoke rising from the smoldering fire - and a collection of bones were boiling in her pot, the makings of a warm broth that would be filling enough when the scraps of meat too difficult for her knife separated from the bones.

She threw in an onion and a handful of herbs that Olga had given her, then sat down to watch it boil. It was calming, watching the water bubble over the fire as her hall filled with warmth and the appealing scent of cooking meat.

Outside, the sound of the axes continued, faint but persistent.

Briefly, the memory came to her of Karik without his shirt in the snow, chopping trees after Jarhost had taken their gold. She wondered what was driving him now.

She lifted a spoon of the broth, blowing on it before tasting it. For a moment, she considered the broth and the sound of the axes.

Wrapping the handle in a rag, so as not to burn her hand, she lifted it from the fire and stepped back into the night.

The new ship lay like a dragon's carcass in the moonlight, sprawled upon the beach with its prow lit by the long fire Havar was tending and its stern invisible off in the darkness.

"Do you intend to finish the ship tonight?" Ylmi asked, "or will you cease work at some point before dawn?"

They all looked up, Karik pausing mid-stroke with his ax, a breathless smile breaking over his face when he saw her.

"The days do not grow shorter," Havar replied. "And if we are to finish her before winter..." He shrugged and tossed another few branches onto the fire.

Ylmi looked to Karik. "Have you eaten?"

"Half a loaf at mid-day," Karik's eyes went hungrily to the pot, which was still steaming, and she raised it.

"I took your advice," she said, "and the hunt was fruitful, so I have come to repay your generosity from last night."

Igil grinned at Karik, but Havar sniffed the air hungrily. "It smells good," he said. "Have you brought enough for all?"

"I have brought enough to share with those who shared with me," Ylmi replied.

Igil laughed, but the smile dropped from his face when she turned her eye on him. "With Fianna, I meant no disrespect..." he began, but Ylmi cut him off.

"The matter is done, and Fianna is now your wife," she said, suddenly wishing the matter was not one she had to deal with at all. "We spoke of it this morn, there is no reason to pick at it further."

Igil nodded and turned back to the prow with a small smile at Karik again.

"I am hungry," Karik admitted as he stepped away from the boat. "And I am glad of your company."

"As I am of yours," Ylmi replied, and the two of them ate together beside the fjord while the tide rolled in and the new ship took shape behind them.

When Ylmi at last returned to her hall, the moon had risen high above the fjord, its pale light splintered by the clouds that sailed past it in the steady night wind. As she drew close, she saw a pile of firewood beside her door that had not been there when she left. Around the edges of the wolfhide, she could see the light of a fire.

Quietly, she made her way to her door, lifting the hide as slowly as she could.

"I am not a huntress, my jarl," a woman's voice said. "But I know the sound of the wind blowing through a door."

Ylmi stepped cautiously inside, her eyes on the figure of Orlanna, who sat beside her fire.

"You have come as easily into my hall as you came into my village," Ylmi answered, "save that you did not ask to enter my hall."

"There are times when courtesy is defeated by discretion," Orlanna looked up, the flames lighting one side of her face, "and when I do not know how matters lie, I find it is best to maintain discretion."

"Why have you come?" Ylmi set her pot on a stone by the fire and stared at her visitor.

"Because I love Dranri," Orlanna replied, "and he has asked me to speak with you."

Ylmi rolled her eyes. "Go back to your home," she said. "We are not children to be told to make up..."

"That is not what he asked," Orlanna interrupted her. "He said that Gorli Kivsson came and spoke with you on the matter of the king's taxes."

"What of it?"

"You should believe not one word he says, and you should deal as honestly with him as he will with you."

Ylmi was silent a moment as the fire crackled and the wind outside blew over the hall. After a moment, she took a deep breath. "He has seen the village and knows how it is ordered. If the king demands too much, then I will bring my case before the Thing and let the lawgivers decide."

"You are a young jarl," Orlanna spoke quietly but with a firmness in her voice. "One who gained her seat by killing her predecessor. The Thing may not be the refuge you imagine it to be."

Ylmi glared at her for a moment. "Have you come simply to say I should lie to the king? The same as my predecessor?"

"I have said you should treat him as he treats you," Orlanna replied. "For he will take every advantage which you offer him. Hunger has pressed hard on the mountain jarls these past two years. From the Undmir to Mirhom, all have had to tighten their belts. Now, you rise, and your names are spoken of all across our little Isle. King Jarhost will see every opportunity to strengthen himself at your expense."

"He is not the only one," Ylmi said. "I have heard that Fornik has been to speak with you."

Orlanna did not blink, and her face remained calm as she answered. "He spoke with me only once and asked many questions which he had no business asking. I sent him away as quickly as good manners allowed."

Ylmi watched her closely, looking for some sign that she was lying or concealing something, but she could read nothing on Orlanna's face.

"Did he say anything which might hint at what mischief he might cause next?"

"He said nothing, no," Orlanna chuckled. "I think he grows weary of resisting you fruitlessly. You have threatened that he will receive no help this winter?"

Ylmi nodded.

"I think he begins to believe you," Orlanna said quietly.

Ylmi let out a short laugh. "That is the best news I have received today."

Orlanna shook her head. "Men do desperate things when they lose hope, and I think Fornik has lost his hope that he can unseat you."

"Very well, then," Ylmi folded her arms. "What have you seen that others have missed?"

"I have heard that Fornik was a nuisance without cease," Orlanna answered. "That he hounded your steps day and night for many days."

"He did," Ylmi muttered,

"And now," Orlanna continued, "he hunts now, very often, returning with little, though he hunts two days at a time... few others do so."

"He is of little use as a hunter," Ylmi nodded. "So that does not surprise me. But I am glad enough to have him away from me."

"Even so," Orlanna nodded, "you have worn him down or he has discovered some other mischief."

"He is welcome to it if he remains out from under my feet," Ylmi said. "Is that all you have?"

"It is," Orlanna smiled slightly and rose to her feet. "I have spent my life in the halls of kings, of jarls, and of those who fancied themselves both. If ever I may be of assistance, I am at your service."

"I will think on what you have said," Ylmi answered, though she was unsure of what she would do with the older woman's words.

Orlanna paused at the door. "How far is Bjarnmont from here?"

"A day's journey, more or less," Ylmi answered.

"Two days' round trip then," Orlanna said. "It is worth considering."

New Lives

As the winter drew closer, the storms grew more frequent and more violent, so that work on the ship slowed. More than once, Karik sat with Ylmi in her hall and watched the rain pouring down upon the village, the mud too thick and the wind too harsh to allow for any work at all. Also, when the storms let up, Igil took time to rebuild Flovi's old hut with Fianna, but Karik and Havar built their fire high and by its light they shaped logs far into the night.

Even so, there was much work to do in the village, and Havar still had the care of the fishing boats so that, from time to time, Karik was left to shape boards, and work on the ship went slower than any of them would have liked.

When Revik was not hunting, he helped them cut the logs into planks. It was rare that one of them was not swinging an ax, and some in the village complained they could not sleep, for the sound of the axes never ceased.

But they did not slow, Karik and Havar each rising together early in the morning and working till long after the sun had set, for neither was willing that the other should be able to say they did more.

One day, Ethna and Ymr came to see how the work progressed and to be shown what metalwork would be needed for the ship.

"You are building a truly impressive vessel," Ethna said as she looked it over. "And though you have used many nails, I am guessing that you will require more?"

"As many as you have," Karik replied.

Ethna nodded as Ymr ran his fingers over the planks, examining where they had been joined, where the wood curved, and where his nails had been driven deep into the wood.

"We will run short of iron soon," Ethna said, "if you continue to use nails so swiftly."

"The hull is almost done," Havar replied, "and then there will be less need than before. But we will still require more. Also, there are other pieces which it would be best to have made of iron." He pointed to where they had a rough charcoal outline drawn on a cracked log. "The sails will be heavy - heavier than any we've yet made. If it can be held in place with iron rings instead of looped rope..."

"We need more iron," Ethna said decidedly, and Ymr left the ship to come stand by his wife and look over the diagram.

"As well as more rope and more canvas for the sail," Havar replied. "I do not think there is much more to be gained here for those things, and it is for this reason that we have got what gold we could."

Ethna looked at him sidelong for a moment, then shrugged. "If you can get us the iron, we can get you the nails and rings and whatever else your ship will need. But neither of us are dwarrow to pull any metal we choose from rock. You must give us ore to work."

Ymr chuckled at that but nodded. "It is not beyond my skill to craft these things," he said in his rough voice, "if you give me iron."

"Then it is iron you will have," Karik said with a smile. But within him, his stomach sank, for he saw many days spent away from the building of their ship.

"Havar," he said slowly, as they watched Ymr and Ethna make their way back to the smithy, "I am not sure we can finish the ship in time."

Havar laughed. "Do not quit on me now Karik! We have done great deeds before, we will do them again, and it begins with this ship."

"I am not quitting," Karik said, "and I think we still have a chance, but many things must go right in order for us to finish it this year and have time to attempt a crossing of the Black Isles."

⚬

It was not long after this that Leiban Longspear came down from the mountains and staggered into the village. He was bleeding from many wounds and staggered to his knees near to Olga's hut.

The old woman was the first to him, and she called Karik and Havar from their work to help her. They carried him into her hut, where she set about boiling water and gathering herbs while Karik carefully peeled away the old bandages.

Revik arrived soon after, bringing Thora and Ylmi, who looked on Leiban with alarm. "How came you by these wounds?"

The old hunter sucked in a deep breath through his graying beard as he struggled for words. "The outlaw Minri," he gasped, "is making a place for himself in the mountains to the north."

"Who is Minri?" Karik asked.

"He was a hunter, not unlike Leiban or Dranri some years back," Ylmi replied, "until he killed a family and took their home in the winter. He was outlawed several years ago, but few have heard from him since."

When Karik had the last of the old bandages in a bloody clump, Olga began to dress the wounds. "Minri will not attack in the next few hours," she told them, "so let the man rest. You may come back tonight and question him if you like."

Ylmi thanked her, and the rest of them filed out of the tiny hut.

"Is Minri that much of a threat?" Karik asked. "Should we prepare for an attack?"

Ylmi shook her head. "Oh no, I doubt he will come down out of the mountains." She glanced to the north, where the pine trees waved gently in the wind as they rose upon the steep mountains. "But he will not be a help to us, that is true. "

"We should put together a company to track him down," Havar said. "We've killed a dragon, how hard can one outlaw be?"

"We do not have the bodies to throw a dozen into chasing one outlaw," Ylmi snapped, "or have you forgotten that winter is near?" She looked toward the northern mountains, as if trying to guess Minri's purpose.

"Then I will see to it," Revik rolled his shoulders. "I am tired of cutting logs for Karik, and this will be a chance for me to stretch my legs on the mountains again."

"Minri will run circles around you," Thora said. "I will see to him, for I have ever been good friends with Leiban, and I will not be displeased to match my woodcraft against that of Minri."

"I have hunted as long as you have," Revik hefted his ax, "and I wager my ax has a worse bite than your little spear."

"A wager it is then," Thora grinned. "The loser to grant one boon to whomever slays the outlaw Minri."

"One boon," Revik agreed, "setting aside only my ax."

"And my spear," Thora agreed.

Ylmi looked between the two of them. "It would be best if you worked together..."

Revik shook his head, "It is a wager."

"Have no fear," Thora said as she bound up her cloak behind her, "I will be back in a few days, bearing Minri's head tied to my belt."

After Revik and Thora left, Karik turned back to work on the ship. But, as Ethna had warned, iron for the nails began to run short, as well as canvas for the sail.

So, Karik took with him Dranri and Dranri's stepson, Lasvin, and two others and sailed *Kalborg* out of the fjord and southward along the coast. He came first to Girstadt, where he spoke with Jarl Ingbert and told him of his shipbuilding and his need for iron.

"If it is larger than the ship you sail now," Ingbert said, "then it must be impressive indeed. I do not know the wisdom in building such a ship however, even if you think to one day try the Black Isles."

"Not one day," Karik answered. "This year or early in the next. She will need a crew as well, if you have anyone here who is willing to try an adventure."

"There are many who are willing for adventure," Ingbert laughed, "but the Isles are less an adventure and more a death sentence."

Karik nodded at that and looked out to sea. "Many said the same of facing a dragon, and yet here I stand." He turned to Ingbert and looked him in the eye. "I am not sailing blindly into the Isles, hoping to discover a path. I know where to go and how to come safely through to the other side. It will be a good thing to say that you supported this endeavor, if it succeeds." Karik paused for a moment, then continued on. "And if it fails, there will be fewer mouths to feed in the villages that sent sailors."

Ingbert's laughter died away, and he nodded. "That is a good point, though I dislike it." He considered a moment longer, and then nodded again. "Send word when you are ready, and I will make it known that anyone who wishes to sail with you will have my blessing."

Karik thanked him, and they loaded a great deal of iron onto the ship, paying for it with the last of Hegli's gold.

"I hope you are successful," Dranri told Karik as they sailed away from Girstadt, "because even if you survive a failure, I do not think anyone will listen to you again. You are promising many things to those who will attempt to cross the Isles with you, and if they do not come about…"

"We will pass the Isles," Karik said grimly. He held the rudder in his good hand and glanced back at Girhom. "If I achieve that, it will be enough, and we will build on that success." He took a deep breath of the sea air and sighed. "We just need hope, Dranri. If we have hope, then everything will change."

When *Kalborg* slid up onto the beach in Dragonsrest, Karik quickly followed Dranri overboard and, with the help of Igil, they pulled the ship ashore.

"The voyage was profitable?" Igil asked when they were finished.

"I turned gold into iron," Karik replied. "So I would say yes. How goes the ship?"

"We have run out of boards," Igil said and gestured to where Havar was splitting logs not far off. "And since Revik is in the mountains chasing that outlaw, we are unable to keep ahead of the ship."

"We were almost out of nails, in any case," Karik shook his head, "so this may have happened soon, anyway. Hopefully we can keep matters moving forward now."

He found Ylmi working with Nanni upon her hut. Part of the roof had caved in during the last storm, and an old log had rotted through.

Ylmi tossed down an armful of old thatch and nodded at Karik as he approached.

"Your voyage was successful?" she asked.

"More and less," Karik replied. "None of..." he glanced toward where Nanni was sorting sticks with which to patch the roof before lowering his voice, "our gold is left."

Ylmi nodded. There were some in Dragonsrest who had heard rumors of a theft in the Undmir, but so far, none had accused them of it. Karik did not want to find himself in that position.

"Aside from the ship," she said, "there is little use for gold. Even the traders from Mirhom have little they are willing to part with. It seems this winter will be a difficult one, for all we say that each year." She looked back to the roof, and her shoulders sagged. "There is much work that needs doing."

"But it will go easier if we work together," Karik grinned in reply and climbed the small ladder to the top of the roof, where he set to work clearing the rest of the old thatch. So quickly did the three of them work, the task was done far earlier than Ylmi had guessed.

"You are not alone, Ylmi," Karik said to her when all was finished. "All the dragonslayers are at work together, and none are more ready to help you than I."

Ylmi thought much on Karik's words, and they filled her with something akin to joy as she went on her business through the settlement.

The Return of Gorli

But joy does not live long in the cold of Vrania, and though Ylmi looked often for the return of Revik and Thora, it was not her friends who came down out of the mountains several days later.

Instead, it was Jarhost's thane, Gorli, with several others who came down through the trees. They walked the length of the village without coming first to Ylmi, peering into every home as they went, paying special attention to Igil and Havar, hard at work on the ship. When they had finished, he returned to Ylmi and named her taxes owed to be a truly staggering amount of gold, and nearly half their herd of goats.

"We told you that our mines ran dry last year," Ylmi told him. "I have showed it to you! We have less than a quarter of the gold you ask for, and even that has already been spoken for."

Gorli shrugged. "The king has spoken for it," he said smoothly. "And as for the rest, you are building a great ship. Do you expect me to believe that you can afford such a luxury and not afford to pay the king what he requires to keep his warriors in his hall?"

"It is not a luxury," she told him, "but a tool to pass the Black Isles."

At this, Gorli laughed. "Lady, if you wish a boat to float in the fjord while you take your leisure, my king does not begrudge. He asks only that he receive his due. But do not concoct some story about using it to cross the impassible sea to our west."

Ylmi was silent a moment longer, watching him with her one eye. At first, Gorli only smiled confidently back at her. After a moment, his confidence broke. He blinked, a frightened look on his face. "My king expects his due," he repeated, and left.

When he was gone, Ylmi walked the length of the village even as they had, seeing what they had seen and looking to see if there was a way in which she might pay the incredible sum demanded of her.

She watched as Karik and Igil bent a plank into shape over the fire and set it upon the hull. Their ship was growing, large enough now to reveal its power but still far from seaworthy.

She watched Ethna and Ymr at work in their meager forge and counted the racks of drying fish near Torig's hut, watching as the old fisherman mended his nets in the stiff wind.

What did Jarhost think they were? This was no wealthy town. It was hardly more than a dozen hovels together, all of them trying to eke out a way to survive.

Ulfr sat on a small rise beyond Almir's hut gnawing on a bone as she watched all that passed, and Ylmi wished she could speak.

Olga was working in her garden, and Ylmi heard the sound of laughter as she approached. To her surprise, she saw Henla, the young daughter of Fianna, picking weeds with the old woman.

"It has been long since you allowed another into your garden," Ylmi said.

Olga smiled as she came slowly to her feet. "It has been long since my jarl allowed such young children to make their home here." She looked down at the little girl, who had gone suddenly very serious, and ruffled her hair. "Besides, Henla is a good helper and a hard worker."

The girl nodded vigorously, and Ylmi felt a smile tug at one corner of her mouth, but her next words took it away. "How is Leiban?"

Olga bent and pointed to a corner of the garden. "Go pull the weeds from around that bush," she said. "And set the rocks outside like I showed you."

Henla nodded quickly and hurried to the distant corner. Olga sighed, "Oh, to be young again... but I am not unhappy to have traded some years for some little wisdom. Henla learns quickly and has a bit of the green thumb, herself."

"Leiban?" Ylmi pressed.

"Infected," Olga answered. "His wounds fester, and the man can barely remain alive. I do not know for how long... but he will not last."

Ylmi nodded, a sudden tightness in her throat, and she wondered if she had been right to allow Thora and Revik to go after Minri alone. They had been gone several days, and she badly wanted Thora back.

"Do what you can for him," she said. "And if there is anything I can do, you have only to say the word."

She did not wait to listen to Olga's reply but made her way back to her hall. The sun was setting, and the night's cold was not far off. Winter was not far off, and there was still much that needed doing.

There was a door to her hall now, a heavy thing that Karik had built in place of the wolf hide, and she let it swing shut behind her with a satisfying thud. Building up the fire, she sat beside it, drinking in its warmth and trying to guess how best to answer the king's demands.

The door opened slowly, the leather hinges creaking as a bit of the cold wind pushed inside, and Ylmi sighed.

"It has been a long day, Karik," she said.

"He still labors on his boat."

Ylmi was on her feet in an instant, her spear in her hand. Just inside the door, the tall shape of Orlanna could just be made out in the firelight.

"I heard Gorli's demands," she said. "And as you have been so gracious with me and my son, I believe it is time I returned the favor." Slowly, she made her way to the other side of the fire.

"How?" Ylmi's eye did not leave her, though she set her spear back against the wall.

Orlanna sat down and looked over the flames. "I know Jarhost, and I know Rivna, his wife. I have spent my life in the halls of a king and the fortress of a jarl. It may be that I have somewhat more knowledge thereof than yourself."

Ylmi considered a moment, watching the older woman's face as the firelight played over it. No scar or burn disfigured it, and Ylmi wondered what hardships the woman before her had faced.

"So," Ylmi said after a moment, "if you think yourself so wise, tell me how Gorli arrives at so high a figure for our tax?"

Orlanna chuckled at that. "He knew what he would demand before he saw even the smoke from our fires. More."

"More?"

"More than you can afford," Orlanna clarified.

"What does he imagine will happen?" Ylmi asked. "That I will send so much to Bjarnmont that we all starve?"

"Jarhost knows that some upon the coast starve each year," Orlanna said. "And he knows few will blame him for this. But you... you are a new jarl, one who took your throne by killing your predecessor. You are also young, strong, and with growing fame. Over a hundred warriors from all over the Isle saw you slay two men in single combat, and it is no secret that you and the rest of the dragon slayers did more than a little for the winning of that battle. If he allows you to grow rich, then it may be that warriors will come to you who would otherwise serve him."

Ylmi closed her eye. "So, the king wishes to knock me down the mountain a bit, remind me of my place."

Orlanna nodded. "That, and he is also able to make Bjarnmont more comfortable this winter than it would otherwise be."

Ylmi ground her teeth. "Short of killing him..."

"Those are dangerous words," Orlanna interrupted her. "The killing of a minor jarl upon the coast is a far different thing than killing the one who wears the iron crown. However uneasy they may be, most of the jarls understand why Unhost died, and they are not eager to be seen to sympathize with him. That is why no one has attempted to have you outlawed by the lawgivers. But the king..." Orlanna shook her head. "You would have every jarl and warrior seeking your head across all of Vrania."

"What then?" Ylmi asked. "What am I supposed to make of Gorli's ridiculous demands?"

"Treat them as such," Orlanna suggested. "Send messengers to the king, explaining that you cannot pay all he asks, and offer him a way in which he may be king and you may be a jarl."

She leaned forward to Ylmi. "I say this again, One-eye: the king in Bjarnmont is not a jarl for you to kill and move out of the way. You must not challenge him, nor provoke him, or there will be no one to caution him when he rises in anger against you."

Ylmi glared at the fire, a familiar anger rising within her. "So, am I to sit meek and quiet while he attempts to bury my village?"

"By no means," Orlanna replied, her voice calm and even. "Accuse his thanes, blame Gorli for this foolishness, but say nothing against him, and when the lawgivers gather with the other jarls, all will see you to be reasonable, and accusations against you will seem foolish."

"It seems I am once again being cautioned against doing anything," Ylmi said quietly.

But Orlanna shook her head. "Not so, only that where you were cautious with Unhost. Be ten times more so with the king, for there are more swords at Jarhost's command than there are spears in Dragonsrest."

"Ever I am urged to caution," Ylmi muttered. "And I weary of it."

"Caution has served you well so far," Orlanna replied. "Has it not?"

Ylmi's eye rose from the fire to fix on Orlanna. The tall woman stared back across the flames as the wind howled over the mountain tops high above them. "It has...." Ylmi answered after a moment. "But I begin to think that in other matters it has not served me so well... such as in the matter of Fornik."

They were silent a moment before Orlanna took a deep breath, and a little of her bearing seemed to slip away. "You have many good friends, Ylmi, who value you highly, my Dranri among them."

Ylmi looked her in the eye. "Why do you say this?"

Orlanna glanced away with a smile, then looked back. "When I last saw Dranri, many years ago, he was angry and swore he would trust no jarl or king ever again. Yet now... he is more loyal to you than he ever was to Ingor or even Lasvik."

Ylmi was silent a moment. "You gave up your claim to vengeance very easily," she said slowly. "Why?"

"I made an ill choice some years ago," Orlanna said quietly. "Whatever pain you may have caused me, you gave me a chance to make that choice right. That is all I will say on the matter."

The door opened, and Karik stepped inside, setting his ax beside the door. He paused when he saw the two of them by the fire.

"Should I return later?" he asked Ylmi.

Orlanna rose gracefully to her feet. "I have said all I have come to say, does my jarl still require my presence?"

Ylmi looked up at her for a moment, then shook her head. "Go, but we will speak on these matters more in the future."

Orlanna nodded and was out of the hall in a few moments.

"More trouble?" Karik asked quietly.

Ylmi shook her head. "For once, no." She stared into the fire, thinking of whom she should send to Bjarnmont. "Have we heard any word from Revik or Thora?"

Karik shook his head. "I am not worried though, I have known Revik a long time. He is tougher than bear sinew. And it seems to me that Thora is much the same."

"I should have sent more with them," Ylmi muttered. "I do not like having them gone for so long."

Karik came and sat down beside her, his arm over her shoulder. "I heard that Gorli's demands were... extensive."

"Every one of us will starve to death this winter if we pay what he has asked," Ylmi answered. "In addition to the fact that we have almost no gold."

They sat in silence for a while, watching the fire, and Ylmi wondered how many battles still lay in their future. One day, she thought, she would be able to tell the king no. Her mind turned to Tanvir and the

Undmir, impregnable in its strength, defiant of any assault. That was what Dragonsrest needed: a wall.

She laughed to herself. That was just what she needed, another gigantic task to drain her further. Not this year, perhaps not even next year. But, if they made it past the Isles, she would build a wall - a fortress to rival the Undmir.

"What?" Karik asked.

"I am only thinking that we set too many things before ourselves," Ylmi replied. "We take on too many tasks."

"Even so," Karik said slowly. "We spoke some time ago about the ship..." he hesitated. "It has not yet been a month, but I think the time has come that we set ourselves to preparing for the winter and leave the ship for next year."

"I agree, though I was not looking forward to arguing with Havar."

Karik chuckled. "I will speak with him. There will be a little more work that must be done to see that it will sit safely through the winter. But we will turn ourselves to hunting, fishing, and preparing the village against the winter."

Ylmi leaned her head against his shoulder as the two of them stared into the flames. That was one decision she was glad to have behind them, but there was so much that would have to be decided in the next few weeks.

"I do not think I have ever been so eager for the winter to come," she said. "But I will be glad when we can sit by the fire and rest."

"You will be restless and eager to be out within a week," Karik chuckled.

"Perhaps," Ylmi agreed. "But it will be your duty to keep your jarl entertained. I look forward to hearing the stories you were told... I have heard the same ones for many years now."

"That is a good thing to look forward to," Karik said. "Let that keep us going until the winter sets in."

"Only a few more weeks," she said. "Only a few more weeks."

Havar was not pleased with the decision to wait till the following year for the ship. Igil was relieved, however, and in the days that followed, Ylmi saw him almost always with Henla and Torm, Fianna's young children. They fished together and worked with Nanni and her children to harvest the fish traps in the river.

It was Igil whom she sent to Bjarnmont, to beg the king to reconsider the taxes she had to pay. He was gone for five days, but when he returned, the king had not changed his answer.

"I am not surprised that he would say so," Orlanna said when Ylmi told her. "Take it before the Thing when the lawgivers meet with all the jarls in two weeks. It is for this reason that I have urged you to be cautious."

"I would rather that we resolved this before then," Ylmi replied. So the two of them took counsel with Dranri and Olga as to how much they could offer the king in taxes, and yet still have enough to make it through the winter.

It was while they spoke together that Revik and Thora returned.

They were bloody, and Thora walked with a limp, but Revik carried at his belt the severed head of Minri.

"You were gone far longer than I expected," Ylmi said when she greeted them. "I had begun to worry."

"Come Ylmi," Thora grinned, "you know me better than that. Though I will admit, Minri was more of a challenge than we had guessed."

"He was gathering other malcontents to himself," Revik explained. "When we found him, there were almost a dozen of them."

"When *I* found them," Thora replied. "You came late to the party, hence..." she gestured at the bandage wrapped around her upper leg. "Where is Leiban? I would tell him that the injury done to him has been avenged."

Ylmi hesitated, and the smile on Thora's face vanished. "He is still in Olga's hut," Ylmi answered. "But his wounds... he will soon be at rest with the Allfather."

Thora turned without a word and strode toward Olga's hut.

"The two of them were close" Revik said slowly. "She spoke much of him on our way back."

"Her parents were dead soon after she was born," Ylmi replied. "She was raised by the hunters - Almir, Dranri, and Leiban." She glanced down at the head on Revik's belt. "The two of you slew a dozen men?"

Revik shrugged. "They were fools, most of them. Minri was no mean fighter, though if he had brought all his men to face us at once, things might have taken longer."

"It sounds a thrilling tale," Ylmi said, "and perhaps we will hear it in full when the snows have come and we are all stuck indoors."

It was a short time later that Thora emerged from Olga's hut, but when she did so, she carried Leiban's spear. Of all the spears Ylmi had seen,

Leiban's was the mightiest by far, forged of twisted steel and set upon a stave of fire-hardened elm bound with iron bands.

Thora spoke to none as she made her way back to her own tiny hut and slipped inside. After a moment of consideration, Ylmi followed her.

Thora's home had always felt small, and it felt smaller to Ylmi now after spending so much time in the hall. She let the wolfhide curtain fall back in place over the door as she entered, standing there a moment in silence. Thora sat motionless beside the fire, her long braid pulled forward over her shoulder so that it hid her face.

"I am sorry," Ylmi said at last.

"He said he will not need his spear any longer," Thora answered quietly. The two of them stayed that way for awhile. Outside, the sound of the village vanished into the sound of the wind blowing in from the sea.

At last, Thora dried her eyes and said, "I will miss hunting with him."

So saying, she rose and left to hunt.

When Thora returned, she found Leiban gone, and she buried his body on the slopes near the village, beside her parents.

THE THING

The thing was held in the mountains north of Bjarnmont on the peak of a low hill that stood in the shadow of three other mountains. All about the hill, on the ridges and false summits that surrounded it, the jarls from the western portion of Vrania made their camps.

Dranri joined Ylmi and Thora on their journey to the Thing, and the three of them made a small camp beneath the trees not too far from the ring of stones which marked the lawgiver's meeting place.

Ylmi was stomping down the last stake for her small tent when a well-fed man wearing silver rings in his beard came through the trees and bowed low to her. Ulfr rose from where she had been sleeping in the sun and stepped forward to smell at him, but he paid the wolf no heed.

"Jarl Ylmi," he said smoothly, "welcome to the Thing. It does our assembly great honor to have you among us. Allow me to introduce myself - my name is Hathi, and I serve our king. He has sent me to see that you are settling well into your new position."

"I am settling in quite well enough," Ylmi answered, fixing him with her one eye. "And I have come to raise an issue before the lawgivers which concerns your king."

Hathi's eyes widened. "Against King Jarhost? Surely not! What has he done to harm you?"

"Stop it, Hathi." Dranri rose from behind his tent and stepped forward. "You know why we're here, and you've come to intimidate us out of complaining."

Hathi looked at Dranri in surprise. "I thought you said you would take no more masters, Dranri! Though I am glad to see you looking so well. The years in the mountains alone must have been difficult."

Dranri's eyes narrowed, but Hathi had turned back to Ylmi. "Surely any matter you have with the king would be best handled in private?"

"I have attempted to do so," Ylmi answered as she dusted damp moss from her hands. "But I have been ignored and refused an answer. The life of those in my village depends upon the king."

"Ignored?" Hathi said with surprise, and Ylmi thought that this was the most incredulous man she had ever met.

"That is what she said," Thora replied.

Hathi shook his head. "I have heard nothing of this, and it is a grave matter that one of the king's jarls has been put off in such a manner. I will speak more with you to determine who is at fault for this. Rest assured, they will be swiftly dealt with. But come and speak with the king this evening, when the sun is low over the sea. He will be happy to speak with you and determine how best this matter is to be resolved."

Ylmi considered a moment. That Jarhost was unaware her messengers had been turned away from Bjarnmont, she had no doubt, though it was not impossible that this messenger should be so ignorant. But a chance to speak with the king might be preferable to arguing in front of the lawgivers.

"Very well," she said, when she had considered. "I will come."

<hr>

The light of the day was turning red as Ylmi and Ulfr made their way through the camps, the rays of light sifting through the trees and bathing the hillsides in warmth. It was the first pleasant evening in several days, and Ylmi took it as a good omen.

Jarhost's tent was not difficult to discover. Not only was it the largest there, but it bore the four-fingered hand of Vranr sewn into one flap. There were several hounds lying outside it, and they rose, growling at Ulfr as they came close.

"Hush!" called a woman's voice, and the speaker opened the tent flap. She was almost as tall as Ylmi, but her face was soft and filled in, the mark of one who ate well and often.

"Ylmi One-eye," she nodded when she saw her. "Come, enter."

Ylmi looked at her in surprise, but walked past her into the tent, Ulfr following close behind. A pile of furs was laid in one corner, and a large chair sat in the center of the tent.

"My husband was called away suddenly," the woman said, letting the tent flap fall. "I do not know how long it will be, but I thought it best that we talk. I am Rivna, the wife of Jarhost."

Ylmi nodded. "Well met, Rivna. You seem to know well my name."

"It has come up once and again in our hall," Rivna said, taking her seat on the chair. She gestured to one of the stools that stood nearby, and Ylmi slowly sat.

"I understand you come with a complaint about the taxes levied against your home."

Ylmi nodded.

Rivna suppressed a small smile. "Tell me why you think the taxes unfair."

"The king demands more gold than we have," Ylmi answered. "And he demands near-half our herds. If we give him all our gold and the goats he demands, the entire village will be dead this time next year, and we will still not have filled his demands."

"You say you are short on gold," Rivna leaned forward, "yet I have heard that the gold veins beneath your settlement are rich indeed."

"They were," Ylmi replied. "But they began to run dry last year. Now, there are few who even bother to delve, so scarce is it. I have shown this to Gorli, yet it seems he has not given an accurate report."

"But surely you have a great deal set aside," Rivna countered, waving away her comment about Gorli. "Unless you have been dealing with the Undmir and Jarl Tanvir."

"No no," Ylmi shook her head. "But much was taken when the king came down to Jarl Unhost. And much of what was left has been spent on our ship."

"Your ship?"

"We are building a ship to cross the Black Isles," Ylmi answered. "We believe there is a way through."

Rivna sat back in her chair, her fingers tapping the arms of the chair. For a moment, she was silent.

"Gorli mentioned as much," she said thoughtfully, "but Jarhost thought he misunderstood a jest. I do not think you are one to jest so on these matters. "

"Nor am I one to jest on the needs of my people," Ylmi interrupted. "When I say the taxes the king demands will end with us starved, I mean that your next tax collectors will have to dig our bones from the snow."

Rivna nodded. "I believe you, young jarl, but you must also believe me. Your predecessor hid gold for years on end, and there is little reason to believe he acted alone. Many knew of his actions, and many more know of them now. If my husband does not require a heavy price, then what incentive is there for the other settlements to pay their own share? Why should Yrdstadt not withhold its portion, and then, when it is discovered, change its jarl and lay all the wrongdoings at his door?"

"We did not change our jarl," Ylmi snapped. "I killed him, because he tried to kill me, among a great many other matters."

"I am aware of how you handled Unhost," Rivna answered lightly, "but other villages will see an easy way out of paying their taxes and take advantage of what they perceive as a loophole. And when that happens... how do you think it will end?

"The thanes of Bjarnmont now go swiftly through the villages, counting here and there, but for the greater portion, the jarls take responsibility to gather their own taxes. Bjarnmont has never had a large army, and my husband's shield wall will grow thin indeed if the men who are supposed to guard the mountain passes are instead hunting through each village to ensure the honesty of the jarls."

Rivna leaned forward in her chair and fixed Ylmi with her eyes, "I am trying to find a way to help us both," she said softly. "Say you will pay half the gold that was asked and two thirds of the goats. It is enough that my husband can still feed his hall and reward his warriors, and the other villages will see there is no benefit to cheating the crown."

"Even that would be more than a heavy burden," Ylmi answered. She was thinking quickly in her head, trying to guess how quickly the goat herd would grow... if it would grow fast enough to replace the heavy tax...

"A fourth of the gold," Ylmi said, "though there will be none left in our settlement for years to come. And a third of the goats. It will be difficult to survive, but perhaps we will be able to make do."

"Come, Ylmi," Rivna leaned back with a smile, "I know you are young, but even you are not such a fool as to see that is a foul offer."

"I cannot offer what I do not have," Ylmi shook her head. "The deer in the forest are growing few in number, and the hunting has become thin indeed. Our goatherd is all that stands between us and death."

"Death stands close to all in Vrania," Rivna replied. "Have you been told how the jarl in Bjarnmont came to be king? And how he came to rule the mountain passes from Undmir to Tharstadt?"

"I have heard the stories," Ylmi answered, "though I fail to see how it matters here."

"The king rules to prevent chaos," Rivna answered. "Settlements rise and fall, men live and die, but the king remains. It is the king who ensures that Viglir's raiders do not have free reign of the coast. It is the king who ensures that one village does not raid another for food when the harvest is brought in. It is the king who has built the peace that allows you to build your boat, and the protection he provides does not come free."

"I cannot pay what I do not have," Ylmi repeated. "And the starvation of my settlement is not something I am willing to cause."

"A third of the gold," Rivna said, "and half the goats. This is the final offer I will make, and it is offered only because of your service in slaying the dragon."

Ylmi stood, staring coldly at the woman before her. "I slew the dragon and paid dearly for it, while your king sat quiet in his hall. Only when there was gold to be seized, when it was guarded by a spineless coward, only then did the king stir himself. I will speak with the lawgivers tomorrow."

—◆—

The next day, Ylmi was among the first to come before the lawgivers. While the jarls and their followers looked on, she explained the taxes that had been leveled against her settlement.

"The burden laid upon us is far too heavy," she said, "and is beyond what we may reasonably expect to pay. In addition, all the work of improving the settlement, including the killing of the dragon, has been done without his help or aid."

"Have you been attacked by King Viglir or his men?" one of the lawgivers asked. The east wind ruffled his long white beard as he sat beside one of the tall stones. "Or have his raiders come around the mountains?"

"They did," Ylmi said with a small smile, "and I was one there to help push them back, along with Karik Haldsson and Revik Dragonsbane."

"You were alone in this?" the lawgiver pressed. "Only you and the people of your village?"

"No," Ylmi answered slowly. "The king was there."

"And would the battle have been won without the king and the army he led?"

Ylmi felt a cold feeling settling in her stomach. "No."

In the crowd, a little way back, she could see where Jarhost stood with his household guard, a smile on his face. He shook his head a little when she looked at him, and she snapped her eye back to the lawgivers.

"There is also the matter of the taxes which your village has paid in years past," another lawgiver put in. "Will you tell us what that has been? If the king has suddenly demanded more from you than previously, then that might be a matter we could discuss more specifically."

"We did not pay taxes until this year," Ylmi answered, the cold feeling in her stomach growing. There was a small gasp from the crowd, and she felt a prickle on the back of her neck. She was being boxed in, like a deer hunted by a wolf pack, and they were beginning to close the trap.

"You did not pay taxes?"

"Not I, our previous jarl, Unhost," Ylmi answered, "he did not pay taxes to the king out of greed. It is one reason he is no longer jarl."

"Greed is a terrible thing in a jarl," one of the lawgivers said, and all should be careful to see that they do not nurture it in themselves."

For a few moments, the lawgivers turned to each other and conferred among themselves, their long beards wagging as they spoke quietly.

In the midst of the assembly, Ylmi was suddenly conscious of a hundred eyes upon her, and she wished she had her spear in her hand.

Then, the leader of the lawgivers rose and spoke in a loud voice. "This is a matter to be handled with great care, for if the young jarl is to be believed, many lives lay in the balance. We will confer among ourselves and return shortly."

The crowd dispersed, and Ylmi returned to Dranri and Thora.

"That did not go how I expected," she said quietly.

"The king has his hooks in everyone, it seems," Thora muttered, but Dranri shook his head.

"They live in fear of chaos, of every jarl doing whatever they please. There was much death before the king ruled in Bjarnmont, and they seek above all else to prevent that time from returning."

"Many die now because the king refuses to do what is difficult," Ylmi muttered. Ulfr nuzzled up against her, sensing her frustration, but Ylmi's mood had turned foul and she found the wolf's concern annoying.

"Go hunt!" she hissed and gestured toward the forest. "Go!"

Ulfr looked at her a moment, big dark eyes taking her in, then she padded into the trees. She stopped once to look back, but Ylmi sent her on.

"I should have been better prepared for what they would say and do," Ylmi muttered.

Thora spat into a bush. "That," she said, "is goatshit. They clearly planned this out to make you look a fool, which is not how a king is supposed to behave... at all."

Ylmi looked up, a sudden realization taking hold. "That is why Rivna wanted to talk yesterday. She wanted to know what I would say before the lawgivers, and she ensured they had already heard a rebuttal to what I would argue."

"She is cunning," Dranri said, "but I did not think she was this cold."

Ylmi shook her head. "Orlanna warned me that the king would take every advantage against me that he could. I did not think that would include his wife."

"She lives in Bjarnmont and is married to Jarhost," Thora said, "what else should be expected of her?"

Dranri shrugged. "We were friends, once, long ago. She was much younger and happier then."

"She seems happy enough now." Thora pointed through the crowd, and Ylmi looked up to see Rivna walking toward them, a pair of guards at her back.

"My lady," Dranri said as they all rose, but she waved them down.

"Please, sit," she said pleasantly. "I have come on a short matter for your jarl." She looked to Ylmi, "The lawgivers do not find your case convincing," she said quietly. "And soon, they will return and make their ruling. I can offer you the same deal as I did yesterday: a third of the gold and half the goats that you were ordered to pay."

"Why offer now?" Dranri asked. "They will soon rule for the king in any case."

"It is good to see you, Dranri," she smiled at him. "I had heard you were with the dragon slayers, and for your sake I am glad. I offer this deal because we do not wish your settlement to starve, truly, and because we think it best for all. The king would rather resolve matters with his jarls without the lawgivers, and he does not wish to grind you into the dust."

"It's bad," Thora said quietly, so that only Ylmi could hear, "but we could pull through. We'll have to hunt more... but it's better than being on the hook for twice that amount."

Ylmi wanted to draw her sword and run Rivna through right here. Her hands itched to start killing, to kill until the whole mountain was red and the lawgivers lay with Jarhost in a bloody heap.

But she harnessed her anger and drove it down. "If we pay this, we will be gutted," she said, "and it will be some time until our settlement recovers. If I accept, will the king's tax men count lightly next year?"

"For the next two years," Rivna said graciously. "We are not unreasonable."

Ylmi felt sick, and the sudden image of her parents starving in their mountain hut appeared in front of her eyes. This time, it would be her fault. But she saw no other choice.

"Then I accept your offer," she said, and she felt as though she had been punched in the stomach.

"You will make a wonderful jarl," Rivna said quietly. "I understand how difficult this is. I will inform my husband, and the matter will be settled."

She disappeared into the crowd, and Ylmi sank down to sit on a low rock.

"We'll all starve."

Thora was already working her bow. "We will redouble our hunting," she said, "and the fishing will..."

"We have already discussed this," Ylmi muttered. "And nothing has changed since we spoke of it," she looked at Dranri. "Tell me I'm wrong."

Dranri was silent, staring at the dirt. It was all the answer she needed.

"Well," she said, rising to her feet, "let's get this resolved and return home. We have much work to do before winter."

Hathi was speaking with the lawgivers as they returned, and the old men nodded as he spoke. One of them stood and raised his arms for quiet.

"I have been told that the king and Jarl Ylmi have reached an agreement," he said. "Jarl, is this so?"

Ylmi felt as though her face was turned to stone as she nodded. "It is so."

"Then the matter of the taxes is settled," the old man said gravely. "But there is another matter concerning Jarl Ylmi which must be resolved."

Ylmi looked quickly at Thora, wondering what this was concerning. Thora shrugged, but her face hardened as Ylmi looked at her, and she turned to see what had caused this reaction.

Fornik Laviksson had risen from among the men of Girhom, and now he raised his voice. "My good friend, Jarl Unhost, was murdered by Ylmi Bodvarsdottir, and I claim retribution against her for the theft of his title and the taking of his life."

VICTORY TO DEFEAT

Karik sprinted through the darkness, confused and lost, gasping for breath. The air was full of smoke and dust, ash falling from the sky. Something was ahead, something terrible, and though he did not want to find it, something compelled him on.

He couldn't remember why he was here, or what was through the smoke - only that he had to hurry.

Faster, something told him, *now is not the time for care. Faster!*

He stepped through the smoke, and suddenly flames burst to light around him. He was in a settlement, and it was burning. Long houses on either side were wreathed in flames, and by their light, he could see something in the distance.

It was a body, slumped against a tree.

Something within him snapped, and he ran, sprinting between the flames until he stood before the tree.

It was Ylmi, her one eye closed as if she were only asleep. But her face was covered in blood, and as he knelt beside her, he saw she was pierced with many wounds.

Desperately, he tried to close them, but there were too many, and his hands were soaked in her blood.

He woke suddenly, sitting bolt upright as his breath came in great, sudden gasps. What was this? He looked down at his hands, wet with sweat. But there was no blood.

It was not the first nightmare he had dreamed, but this one felt strange. Were the gods sending him messages? Was it a warning?

A sudden chill went through him as he thought of Ylmi at the Thing. Was it a warning that she was in danger? All the jarls swore oaths of peace at the Thing. It was a sacred time to resolve arguments without bloodshed.

But Karik wondered if Jarhost would seek out some way to avoid the oaths...

His mind went to the old tales of Alena the Vicious, Vrania's first queen. In her time, men had driven off their foes from attending the Thing, and Alena herself had attacked her enemies before they reached the protection of the mountain. Jarhost was doubtless as familiar with the stories as any other, and Karik suddenly wondered if the king meant foul play in the mountains.

A few short hours later, Karik slipped out of the bed, shivering as he dressed quickly in the morning cold. The fire had burrowed deep into the oak log he had laid over it the night before, and he built it up with a few pine twigs. Slowly, he fed the flames, till some of the warmth returned to his fingers. When it was blazing well, he laid several oak branches over it and covered them with ashes before grabbing his spear and slipping through the door.

The sun had just begun to rise on the other side of the mountains, and its pale light was beginning to streak across the sky, leaving the winter clouds shades of gray and blue. Down by the shore, Igil was slipping a small fishing boat into the water, and on the edge of the settlement, Bodvar was seeing to the goats.

Karik did not speak to any of them as he walked, slipping quietly through the village and beginning up the path he had traveled many times before.

His legs ate up the distance as he rose higher into the hills, following the path that led to the hut where Ylmi had lived with her parents.

It was almost noon when he stopped to drink from the mountain stream as it ran by the small hut he had built only a few months before. His mother still made it her home, but Karik intended to bring her down to the village when the winter set in. She was at work on the garden that lay before the house, but Karik passed by without a word.

As he left the homestead behind him, he crested a low ridge and glanced up at the dark sky. The sun was hidden by dark clouds rolling in from the north. Black clouds rolled in, and behind them, Karik could see the flicker of lightning.

He set his face against the wind as he saw the storm taking shape, and he continued north.

He had not walked the trail since Ylmi had showed it to him, but the path was not one he would easily forget. Even so, it was late in the afternoon when he stood and stared up at the cliff that led to Vranr's Stones. Sleet was falling, and Karik chuckled. Vranr had been nothing if not thorough in the curses he had woven around the mountain.

Carefully, Karik began to climb. Before he had gone far, he realized the loss of his fingers would make it very difficult, indeed. Slowly, he inched his way upward, gripping each crack and crevice, even as the wind grew stronger.

The wind whipped sleet and ice into his face like arrows as he scaled one cliff after another, and twice he slipped, holding on only by a furious strength as he refused to fall. Once, he did fall, slipping back down a cliff three times, as tall as he was. The rocks cut his face and left his hands scraped and bloody.

But such was the cost of the stones, so he picked a different part of the cliff and climbed again. At the long ridge before the last climb, he paused. His breath was heavy and slow, and he was beginning to shiver. The sleet had soaked him, the wind cut his breath out of his chest with every gust, and he was bleeding from numerous wounds.

He waited only a moment, then pressed on.

The last cliff was the worst. His fingers were so cold he could feel only pain, and the rock bit into them as he struggled to climb. When he pulled himself onto the little ridge, he was shaking so violently he could not stand for what seemed like hours.

With a groan, he pulled himself together and crept slowly up until he reached the stones.

He staggered into their midst and slumped to the ground, leaning against the great stone chair in their midst. For a time, he did not know if he would rise. He shook and shivered, his muscles spasming as he tried to pull some warmth into his body even as the sleet rained down thick and heavy, slowly giving way to a wet snow.

At last, he pulled himself to his feet and reached into his shirt. From a bag around his neck, he lifted a piece of the gold they had taken from Hegli, and he went to lay it on the chair.

But as he stepped toward the stone seat, the wind rose in a violent roar, and he felt as though a great weight was laid upon him. His ears rang, and he felt as though he had been plunged deep beneath the waves, the crushing weight of the sea pressing in upon him.

He staggered, twisting his head as he winced against the pressure.

"An audience with the Allfather cannot be bought with gold," said a deep voice behind him, and he dragged himself about to see two figures staring at him from beside the northern stone.

"And if it could, the price would be beyond your reckoning." The first figure stepped forward and reached out a long arm. Taking the gold from Karik, he tossed it off the mountain as casually as a man throws away the core of an apple when he is finished with it.

"Who are you?" Karik asked, peering through the sleet.

"Two who have come to answer your questions," he first figure answered. He wore a hooded cloak, and Karik imagined that he saw one eye peering back at him. The hood was dark, casting the man's face in shadows, but the glint of a silver beard could be glimpsed as he turned to stand again with his companion.

The second figure looked at him from beneath a similar hood. She, for Karik was sure it was a woman, wore a similar hood, and a long yellow braid trailed down from beneath it, hanging almost to her belt.

She spoke in a voice that was quiet, yet her words reverberated in Karik's chest and echoed among the stones. "You wish to know if your pain is from the gods."

"I would not go against the gods," Karik tried to explain, but the first figure cut him off.

"And yet you offer us the gold of another man?" His voice was that of a lawgiver raised in accusation. "Gold which you stole from one who is your brother? For are you not both descended of Vranr?"

Karik opened his mouth but found no words.

"It is not the gods who have taken your fingers," the woman assured him, "nor was it the gods who left you with the scars you carry."

"The gods forgive," the man said softly. "But you have not come to ask about the past. You ask of the future."

Karik nodded, swallowing the roughness in his throat. "The dragon's curse..."

"Will be fulfilled," there was a hint of sadness in the woman's voice. "The gods will not unmake in this life what mankind has made." She stepped forward and laid her hand on his cheek.

"You have a long path ahead of you, Karik Haldsson," she said softly. "It is dark, and bitter, and full of death."

"Your wyrd is a heavy and terrible thing," the man said. "And there will be much suffering because of you."

Karik shivered as the woman took back her hand, and the wind struck him with renewed force. "What is left to me then to decide, if my wyrd is already set?"

"To decide if you will make it well," the man answered, "or poorly."

—◆—

That night, Karik had the dream again. Again, he held Ylmi's bloody body in his arms, and again he tried desperately to close her many wounds.

He woke in the morning, his thoughts on Ylmi, and it was toward the mountain that he looked when he stepped outside. A cold wind blew out of the north, and Karik glanced up to see dark clouds piling up over the mountains.

It would not be a terrible storm, not yet at least, but it would stop work on the ship. He pulled his cloak tight around him as he pushed through the growing wind and made his way toward where Igil and Havar were hard at work laying out boards for the ship.

"Where were you yesterday?" Havar grumbled when he saw him. "You missed a whole day of work."

Karik grunted and grabbed his ax. "There were things which needed to be seen to."

"What is more important than this boat?" Havar asked.

Igil chuckled to himself. "There are a few things..." he said, and he stopped his work to ruffle the hair of little Torm, who was playing with wood shavings by his feet.

"It is bad enough that we must spend half our time hunting," Havar grumbled. "I wonder at times if we might have finished the boat this year, had you not stopped to be married." He pointed his ax at Igil.

"The boat is only a means to an end," Igil replied. "If we complete the means but lose the end... what profit is there in that?"

With a muttered curse, Havar grabbed a handful of nails and stormed off down toward the far end of the ship.

Igil watched him go with a laugh, but Karik looked up toward the mountains, and Igil paused when he saw the grim look on his friend's face.

"Whatever we do," Karik said, "we seem to increase the dangers we face."

Igil laughed at that, and Karik turned back to look at him in surprise.

"Karik, we killed a dragon," Igil said. "A bigger dragon did not appear. A king, yes, but I'd rather fight a king than test myself against another dragon."

"The king is trying to squeeze us back into starvation." Karik sat down beside Igil and smiled at Torm, who looked up at him with wide eyes as he tasted a stick.

"Don't eat that," Igil told him, and Torm pulled it out of his mouth with an expression of distaste. Igil patted him on the head and looked back at Karik. "Are you going to sit back while that happens?"

Karik shook his head. "No chance."

"And we can't overthrow the king just yet..." Igil grinned. "So, we have to make this village as prosperous as we can... peace and safety cannot be forced... we can only do what is in our power to make their path easier."

"And what if our wyrd is to never have an easy path?" Karik asked. "What if every action we take draws disaster closer?"

Igil took up his draw knife and looked out toward the mountain in the midst of the fjord. "Revik is right about one thing," he said, "we are all going to die one day or another. Now, he may be in more hurry to get there than I am, but we'll all get there in the end. We know storms come in the winter, and with them hunger and starvation. Nothing we do can change that. But is it not better to meet the storm with a good house and as much food as can be stored?"

Karik shook his head. "And when the hunting is thin, the herds few, and the king's taxes heavy?"

"Well, you won't get more food by complaining about it," Igil smiled. "So let us work and make the best of what we have."

Fianna appeared from behind them, a basket in her hands and the smell of warm bread thick in the air around it.

"I thought you might be hungry," she said to Igil with a smile.

Igil rose to his full height, then bent down to kiss her. "I am indeed, though I think Torm is the hungriest one here."

He broke a bit of the loaf off and handed it to Torm, who had climbed quickly to his feet.

"Our noble warrior was trying to eat a stick a moment ago," Igil chuckled. "But I think bread will go down better."

"How come your preparations for the winter?" Karik asked her.

She glanced at Igil, who remained focused on Torm, then looked back to Karik. "Well enough, though it would be good to have more."

"It is always the case," Karik nodded. "And though Dragonsrest has been better prepared for many winters, other villages have had less good fortune in my experience."

"Illstadt is such a place," Fianna replied. "I have never seen as much food stored away for so few people as I have seen here."

Karik nodded. "We are still a small settlement, and Jarl Ylmi has worked long and hard to prepare us for the storms. Also," he frowned, "there is still the king's portion, which I do not think will be over small."

As if to echo him, a boom of thunder cracked over the northern mountains, and the wind which had been blowing all morning began to pick up.

"I must go," Fianna said quickly, "there is work I would have done before the storm hits."

"I will be with you shortly," Igil said, but Karik snatched up his ax.

"Havar and I can see that the ship is made ready," he told Igil. "Go with your wife, I will see to things here."

Igil nodded with a smile. Sweeping Torm up in his long arms, he followed Fianna toward their hut.

Karik watched him go, and it seemed to him that the two of them were happy together. He smiled a moment before turning back to lay aside the tools and cover the ship against the coming storm.

The rain arrived in earnest just as he finished, and as he made his way to Havar's little hut, his mind turned to Ylmi and wished they were sitting together in her hall.

Single Combat

In simple terms, Fornik laid out the murder charges against Ylmi. In his retelling, Ylmi had heckled and harassed the long-suffering Jarl Unhost until, at last, he had accepted her challenge to single combat, whereupon she slew him with a spear, a weapon with which he was unfamiliar.

It was all ridiculous, and Ylmi listened with a growing grin. How Fornik had thought anyone would take him seriously was beyond her.

"There are many among you," Fornik finished, "who will say that, simply because it was in single combat in answer to a challenge, then it is not murder."

There was a dull rumble of assent to this point.

"But shall a jarl be so easily challenged by those he rules?" Fornik pressed. "If a man is caught stealing, then shall he be able to escape judgment simply because he is better with a spear than the one who rules as jarl?" He pointed at Ylmi, "This girl has been nothing but an insubordinate troublemaker for years."

"Funny, I was going to say the same of you," Ylmi muttered under her breath.

Fornik glared at her for a moment as if he had heard, then continued. "She murdered the previous jarl - slaughtered him in a challenge she planned and organized so she could seize control of the village."

Jarl Ingbert of Girstadt stood at this, and the lawgivers bade him speak.

"Unhost, if jarl he was, ruled what was little more than a settlement, hardly a village." He gestured at Ylmi. "Under her leadership, the settlement has prospered and grown, doubtless due, in no small part, to the absence of a certain dragon, for which Jarl Ylmi is in no small way responsible. It seems clear that Unhost mismanaged his settlement quite badly and has paid the price for his foolish decisions."

"And yet," Hathi stood from where he sat near the king, "is it for any random person to challenge their jarl?"

"Yes," Ingbert threw up his hands. "If the jarl is so foolish as to require challenge..."

"But what is foolishness to one may be wisdom to another," Hathi pointed out. "And that is why the jarldom should be settled by the Thing or perhaps by the king."

There was much grumbling at this, and the sound of many voices filled the air so that the lawgivers were forced to raise their hands for quiet.

"In this way, the king would prevent one such as Unhost from ruling so poorly," Hathi pointed out. He turned and looked Ylmi in the eye. "Jarl Ylmi, how long did Unhost rule from his hut beside the fjord?"

"Nigh on twenty years," Ylmi answered.

"Twenty years!" Hathi echoed and spread his hands. "Twenty years or more he ruled there, wasting and mismanaging what is now a prosperous and rich village. For over twenty years, he threw away what could have been great riches but were instead given to a dragon."

"Twenty years he ruled," Fornik responded. "For good or ill I cannot judge, but he was my friend, and Ylmi Bodvarsdottir slew him most cruelly."

"And did Ylmi challenge him before or after he surrendered his gold to the king?" Hathi asked.

Beside her, Ylmi felt Dranri stiffen, and a soft curse fall from his beard.

"After," Fornik answered, and Hathi nodded.

"What we know," Hathi explained to the lawgivers, "is that for nearly twenty years, Unhost ruled the settlement beside the fjord's waters, keeping back the taxes due in payment to the king. And then, after he paid them, Ylmi Bodvarsdottir challenged him to single combat and killed him. And what has been her first act as jarl?" he paused for emphasis. "It has been to pull back on the taxes she is due to the king."

"Ylmi," Dranri's voice was low but full of urgency, "you must claim trial by combat."

"I do not know if this is the case," Fornik said to the lawgivers, "but I believe she was angry that taxes were paid to the king, and she killed Unhost because he obeyed our king and gave him what was owed."

In a moment, Ylmi saw it - what Dranri had seen a moment before. They would claim she was a rebel, had taken the jarldom only to oppose the king, and was a danger to the peace of the coastlands. The king could not make her outlaw for killing Unhost in single combat, but few would argue if he did so because she was a rebel.

Ylmi stepped forward before the lawgivers. "These are lies," she declared loudly. "And Fornik speaks so because he is a sluggard. I slew Unhost because he was a poor jarl and attempted to have me killed on more than one occasion. All this I suffered and stayed my hand. But in the battle against King Viglir, as I and my friends fought for the king, Unhost sent his men to kill me and Karik Haldsson. This is the truth, and I will prove it before you and before the Allfather with my blade."

The lawgivers conferred with themselves for awhile, and when they returned, their leader spoke.

"The slaying of a jarl is a grave matter," he said, "but since the settlement claimed her as his replacement, there is less to be said of it. But if Ylmi Bodvarsdottir is seeking to subvert the rule of the king, that is a matter which bears more weight. Since Alena the Vicious, Bjarnmont has protected our lands from war and kept the peace between the jarls. Life in Vrania is too difficult, too dangerous on its own. We have enough war visited upon us by King Viglir in the east, we do not need more sown among us.

"Therefore, if the king believes that Fornik Laviksson's complaint has merit, let him appoint a champion to meet Jarl Ylmi. If the king has faith in Jarl Ylmi and believes the death of Jarl Unhost was not wrongly done, then let him declare the matter settled."

All eyes turned to the king, who rose from his seat and began to speak. He spoke of many things, but Ylmi grew bored as he spoke, and it seemed to her that he was coating his meaning in many layers. At last, he brought his words to a point.

"In order that there may be no doubt in this matter, I appoint Harvik Bulisson to meet Jarl Ylmi," he said, "to determine once and for all the truth of this matter."

"He could have removed doubt with a word," Dranri muttered.

But the leader of the lawgivers rose, nodding solemnly. "Very well," he said, and Ylmi noted with unease that Hathi was smiling broadly at Dranri.

"Since Ylmi has issued the challenge," the lawgivers continued, "then it is for the king to choose the weapons."

"Let them do battle with sword and shield," Jarhost replied. "For Ylmi bears a noble blade, and it should have a place in this matter."

Ylmi nodded grimly and handed her spear to Dranri. Her last duel with a sword had not gone as well as she would have liked.

Harvik Bulisson was already being brought forward. A younger man with a dark brown beard that he had bound beneath his chin with iron rings, he carried a sword, and Ylmi guessed that he had done good service for Jarhost in order to win it.

A ring of stripped branches was laid out and a shield brought for Ylmi. It was heavy on her arm, but she was happy for its protection. She unbuckled her scabbard from around her ring mail shirt and gave it to Thora. The dark blade of *Raethbur* felt good in her hand, the sharp point gleaming in the cool sunlight.

"Let him hammer away at your shield," Dranri advised her. "And keep it tilted. If he can catch the edge of your shield with his blade, he'll try to split it apart."

"Perhaps you should have taught me more about swords," Ylmi muttered.

"I'm doing my best now," Dranri replied.

Ylmi rolled her eyes and turned to Thora. "And cunning advice from you?"

But Thora only gave her a dark grin. "Kill him, One-eye."

Then began Ylmi's first duel as jarl.

Harvik leaped forward, his feet moving in a blur and striking three times at Ylmi. The first two she caught on her shield, the third she turned away with her sword. But when she struck back, he danced out of reach.

There was little shouting, as all watched closely to see the dragon slayer battle one of the king's thanes.

Harvik attacked again, this time swinging his shield behind a sword strike and catching Ylmi over her good eye. It sent her tumbling, but she rolled to her feet and blinked away the brightness in her eye.

"I wish it had been one of the other dragonslayers," Harvik told her as he drew close. "Killing the one-eyed is less of a boast."

"You must kill me before you boast at all," Ylmi answered.

In answer, Harvik swung and lunged again, this time his sword slipped around her shield and scraped over the ring mail.

Harvik leaped back before she could retaliate, and Ylmi spat in frustration. If she could use her spear, he would not find it so easy to leap out of range.

"Yield," Harvik told her. "You don't have to die for this."

"Who says I'm dying?"

Harvik spread his sword and shield. "I have no doubt you are fearsome with a spear," he said, "but with a sword... I've fought a dozen battles, and know my sword as well as you know your spear."

She advanced on him and swung *Raethbur*, but he caught the first blow on his shield before spinning the second away with a clever parry.

"You, on the other hand..." he grinned.

Ylmi shook her head and began to attack. She worked him high and low, as she would with a spear, thrusting and stabbing instead of wide swings, and Harvik stopped talking.

For a moment, they stood together in the center of the ring, trading blows upon their shields back and forth. Ylmi felt a grin rising within her as she caught his sword on her shield over and over, feeling the rhythm of the fight humming within her.

Then Harvik shifted his wrist midswing, and his sword glanced off her shield to bite into her leg.

Ylmi jerked back, feeling the warm blood flowing down her leg and the sharp sting of the wound. She looked up and saw Harvik grinning, and rage filled her. She lunged forward, swinging *Raethbur* in great arcs so that the air hummed with its passing.

But Harvik caught the sword on his shield with a clang, and Ylmi felt her shield crack as his blade bit deep into its planks.

They drew apart again, and Ylmi looked down. A third of her shield hung useless, split apart by Harvik's strike. She took a deep breath, though the air burned in her lungs, and steadied herself. Harvik was smiling now, and Ylmi saw her victory.

Bleeding and with weariness sinking its claws into her limbs, she stepped forward and swung her sword as before, as if she intended to split Harvik in half with one blow. Again, he stepped forward to meet her attack, and her sword clanged again on his shield. Again, his sword bit deep into her shield.

But Ylmi was ready this time, and with a swift turn, she twisted her shield into Harvik. His blade remained stuck between the boards, and his arm was twisted into his body as she drove into him. Her leg exploded in pain as she pushed off, driving him back, giving him no space to break free.

She drove *Raethbur* up into his chest as she pushed him back, but the blade caught on his chainmail. Back she pushed him, step by step, slamming her sword up into the iron rings as they came up against the edge of the circle.

Harvik braced himself, striking at her with his own shield, and she blinked as the rough wood slammed into her head once, then again. He tried to pull away, but she held him close, his sword locked in her shield, the shield pressed against him as she thrust her sword up yet again.

His shield slammed into her face again, and she staggered back, blinded by the impact, vaguely aware of the pain in her head and face. She could not breathe through her nose, and after an instant, she raised her right hand and wiped away the darkness from her eye. Her face was slick with blood, and she sucked in great breaths as she looked for Harvik.

She found him at last, slumped on the ground with *Raethbur* still protruding from his chest. She had thrust as he raised his shield to strike her, and the final blow had split his chain-mail.

He looked at her, blood trailing from his mouth, his eyes wide in disbelief. Slowly, she limped toward him, though the pain in her leg seemed to grow with every step.

"Boast after you've killed," she said through teeth clenched in pain, "not before, Harvik Bulisson." His eyes went dead as she looked, and when she raised her head, she saw Fornik standing near the king, his face twisted in anger as he looked on her.

⚬

That evening, Jarl Ingbert of Girstadt and Jarl Ingbor of Yrdnara visited Ylmi where she was recovering by a small campfire.

"We wish you health after your victory," Ingbor told her. "It is good to see that not all things go as the king wishes, and we are glad to know that Dragonsrest is in the hands of such a capable jarl."

"How are matters in Dragonsrest?" Ingbert added, "do you run as short of food as the rest of us?"

"I will run shorter now," Ylmi replied. Dranri had set her nose, but she still could not breathe through it, and the side of her head was still throbbing with waves of pain. She took a drink of the cold water they had taken from the mountain stream. "The king's tax will be hard to bear."

"As it ever is," Ingbert agreed. "But if you have excess, we will pay well for it and remember it in the future."

"Dragonsrest is a new village," Ingbor explained. "And along the coast, we try to help each other as best we may, though that may not be much."

"I will keep this in mind," Ylmi replied. "Though I think this year will be the worst we have yet seen."

The two jarls were silent for a moment, then Ingbor nodded. "So it is. Hopefully next year will be kinder, to one of us at least. All our villages will suffer greatly when Dunharvic rides upon the winds this winter and gathers the dead together."

Ingbert shook his head, then asked, "Do you still labor on a ship?"

Ylmi wiped away blood that was trickling down from her nose. "I do."

The two jarls nodded as though it was a matter they had discussed beforehand. "There are few who are still willing to risk the Black Isles," Ingbert said. "But if you are successful, you will have aid from us when the time comes."

"I think you are just saying those words," Ylmi answered. "But I thank you for them all the same."

Ingbor rose to go, but Ingbert hesitated. "I have said those words to others and thought nothing of it. Yet you and Karik do not seem to be the kind of people to pursue folly. I never thought any would pass through the Isles... but I have seen the ship *Kalborg* and heard Karik speak. I am no longer as sure as I once was."

This being said, they left, making their way back to their own encampments.

Thora watched them go, leaning back against the trunk of an ancient tree. "That is a laugh," she said. "You and Karik chase folly all the time."

Ylmi let on a small smile, but small as it was, the pain lanced through her face. She had not thought of it then, but it would have been good if Karik had been there at the fight. She should have brought him with her, but there was plenty of work for him to do in the village.

The next day, Thora left them, saying she wished to do some hunting in the mountains, and though Ylmi later thought that strange, she was too weary and in pain to think much on it.

Her heart was heavy as she walked the path back to Dragonsrest, her mind running through the village over and over as she divided their food in her mind, trying to calculate how much more they could gather and store before the snow came.

A hundred times she glanced to the north, as if the clouds there could tell her when the first great winter storm would come, and each time it was as fruitless as the last.

As they came down into the settlement, Ylmi paused for a moment, and Dranri stopped to look back at her.

"They will understand you did the best you could," he said after a moment. "You have no reason to be ashamed."

Ylmi glanced down at him and rolled her eye. "I do not worry about that," she said. She turned her gaze back to the village and took a deep breath. "I was just thinking that the village has grown a great deal since I was young. It has grown even since I became jarl." She gripped her spear and pounded it into the rock. "We must cross the Isles, or things must change here soon."

Karik was at work on the roof of her hall when Ylmi saw him, and he looked up with a smile to see her. But the smile fell from his face when he saw the limp in her walk and the new wounds on her face.

In an instant, he had leaped from the hall roof and was beside her.

"Who did this to you?" he asked in a quiet voice.

"They are dead," Ylmi assured him. "I fought a trial by combat to prove my killing of Unhost was not murder." In a few words, she told the tale, and by the end of it, Karik's face was white with fury.

"It seems there is no end to those who need killing," he said quietly, and Ylmi saw his left hand flexing back and forth as it often did when he was angry.

"There is nothing to be gained from war with Jarhost," she said wearily. "More than anything, I want to be left alone. The storms are coming soon, and with them we will have some measure of peace."

"I weary of restraining myself," Karik muttered. "It seems that everywhere we turn, someone is attempting to do us harm, and we must turn a blind eye."

"Such is life, apparently," Ylmi said wearily. She was tired, her head ached on every side, and she was hungry. "There will be much work to be done, but I must do it tomorrow. I am weary beyond reason and the sun is setting. We will prepare Jarhost's taxes when the sun next rises."

She glanced toward the roof. "You did not need to spend your time mending my roof."

"Ylmi," Karik gave a faint smile, "you were hard at work seeing that we kept as much as we could from the king... a labor that seems to have been more trouble than it should. It is a small thing for me to mend a hole in your roof."

Ylmi's jaw tightened, his words of praise rough on her ears as she glanced around the village. She had failed, whatever anyone said, and there would be death in Dragonsrest when the winter came. The question was only how many Dunharvic would take when he rode his dark horse.

Silently, she turned and made her way to her hall and shut the door behind her. The fire had gone out, but she did not have the strength to light it. The cold was not so deep that she would freeze. Her head was aching, and if she lost focus for a moment and breathed through her nose, the pain stabbed like a knife into her skull. Somehow, it was more annoying than when the dragon had burned away her eye.

She went past the wooden chair that seemed to always be shrouded in darkness and into the small room behind it. Screens and furs had been set up to shield it from the rest of the hall, and it had often reminded Ylmi of a wolf den.

Now, she sat there in the darkness, trying to will away the pain of her wounds as she tried to prepare herself for the work to come. Collecting the taxes would not be easy, and it would not be easy to watch her village - *her village* - sickening as the winter drew on...

A small sound from the hall drew her attention. A moment later, Ulfr padded into her lap, licking gently at her face.

"How did you get in here?" Ylmi whispered. She stood and stepped out into the main hall.

Karik knelt by the fireplace, laying a few sticks over a small fire that he had clearly just brought from elsewhere. A small pot sat nearby, and as Ylmi watched silently, Karik built the fire.

He glanced up, smiling at her, then hung the pot over the flames before standing and moving toward the door. When he put his hand on the latch, he paused.

"You are not alone, Ylmi," he said as he turned back to her. "There are many here who are ready and eager to help where they may. There are many here who care for you, who love you." He gave a quick, nervous laugh. "We are the dragonslayers after all, as Igil is so quick to remind us."

With that, he shut the door and was gone.

The pot was already steaming when Ylmi stepped down to it. Karik's fire was well built, and the flames danced around the pot, filling the air with the smell of smoke and stew. There was a squirrel in it, along with a few vegetables, and Ylmi's mouth twisted in a small smile. It hurt her nose, but the steam seemed to help a bit, nonetheless.

She ate in the darkness with Ulfr beside her, gnawing at an old bone and snapping up the occasional morsel Ylmi tossed her way. Yet even with the wolf, the hall felt somewhat empty, and Ylmi found part of herself wishing Karik had stayed.

Winter

So it was that Jarl Ylmi gathered the first taxes for the king which had ever been gathered in Dragonsrest, and there was little joy in it.

Almir and Olga contributed their share willingly enough, but the others grumbled that this had not happened under Jarhost.

"Has everyone forgotten that there was a dragon here?" Revik asked loudly after Bogli had made the complaint again.

"Jarhost took the dragon's portion through the year," Thora told him. She was cleaning another deer and hanging it over a fire to cure in the smoke. "And most of it came from Bodvar's goatherd... so people saw less of it."

As dusk blew in with a stiff north wind, Karik and Dranri came out of the mountains, each with a deer that they had slain, and when each had been skinned and cleaned, they gave them out to those in the village as Ylmi directed.

"It is little enough payment," Ylmi told Nanni. "One cut of venison for three goats. But it is the best I can offer."

"That you know the pain we will suffer," Nanni replied, "does not make it less."

They all returned to their homes in the darkness, and even Revik seemed downtrodden by all that had happened.

But Karik went with Ylmi to her hall, and the two of them stood for a moment outside in the darkness, watching the stars peeking through the clouds rolling in from the sea.

"I have never wanted to be jarl less than today," Ylmi said at last.

Karik hesitated a moment, trying to find the right words. "Would you have preferred Fornik to gather the taxes? You know better than most how to distribute the burden evenly."

Ylmi nodded in silence, and the wind blew cold from the west, heavy with the smell of salt and fish.

"Thank you," she said suddenly, "for your help. You have made a hard task less difficult than it could have been."

"I am always ready to help," Karik replied. "It is why I came here and promised to work hard for this settlement," he glanced toward Ylmi, "though I did not expect to meet one I was so eager to help."

"I needed little help before you got here, Karik," Ylmi answered with the beginnings of a smile. "But I am glad you are with me."

Fornik never returned to Dragonsrest, and when Gorli came, with a large smile, to take their taxes to Bjarnmont, Ylmi was surprised that he had not come.

"I would have thought he would have at least come to gloat," she said to Thora as they herded the goats out.

Thora only shook her head. "The less said of him, the better, especially in Gorli's hearing."

Ylmi glanced at her, and thought for a moment on the tale of the man Unhost had tried to make Thora's husband, but she said nothing. But when Gorli and his men were marching up the path out of the village, Ylmi went to Thora, who was sitting in front of her hut, working the stiffness out of a deer hide.

"What do you know of Fornik?"

Thora did not look up from her deerskin, but her voice was clear and soft.

"I have heard his body fell into a ravine not far from the Thing," she answered. "But I expect the wolves have gotten at him by now."

Ylmi shook her head. "Why did you do it?"

Thora looked up quickly. "I did not say I did anything. You asked about Fornik, I answered. How he fell must remain a mystery, perhaps he was careless and slipped. Now go away, This hide has been giving me trouble and I work a hole into it because you distract me, I will demand payment."

When the first snows fell, they secured the ship under as much shelter as they could. It was near finished, and Karik did not wish to see their work ruined by the weather.

Bodvar brought the goats out of the mountains, and the entire herd rested once again within the village. When that was done, he and Siggi moved into the hall, and Ylmi found that her parent's presence brought her a joy she had not expected. For the first winter in her memory, it felt as though their lives did not depend upon her. If she fell sick, there were others nearby who would help them, and death would not hang so close to them all.

Now, though the dusting of snow did not disappear, they continued to prepare for the winter as best they could. Even as the ice in the fjord grew thicker, all turned to fishing from dawn till dusk.

Havar even convinced old Torig to come fishing with them in *Kalborg,* and they sailed to the mouth of the fjord to fish. They brought back the largest fish any in Dragonsrest had yet seen, but Torig said he would not fish on *Kalborg* again.

"She is not a boat for me," he said. "I dislike her bigness... my dingy is enough for me."

Havar shook his head at that, but he took *Kalborg* out as often as he was able. More than once, he came racing back ahead of dark skies and rough seas.

Yet though they prepared, the first storm of winter nearly caught them unaware.

It started, as all winters did, with an icy wind blowing out of the north. For three days, it howled out of the mountains, tossing the fjord into waves and kicking up great gusts of snow and dirt as it whipped through the village.

Still, they fished where they could, though Ylmi's fingers turned blue with cold and she feared more than once that frostbite was too close.

Then, when Ylmi rose one morning, she found Ulfr pacing back and forth before the door. The wolf whined when she saw her, and Ylmi shivered at the sound of the wind outside. When she opened the door, the world was a white, swirling roar of snow and ice. She pushed the door shut and dropped the latch.

Sitting down beside the fireplace, she lifted the log they had set on it the night before and gently coaxed the coals to life. Building up the fire, she pulled her cloak tighter around her shoulders and let out a long sigh. There was little more work to do, for winter had come, and now they had only to endure it.

The first storm lasted only a few days before slacking long enough to let a few hours of gray light into the fjord, and Ylmi took the opportunity to stretch her legs. The wind was still howling, with bits of snow still drifting down even as the dark clouds of a new storm could be seen massing themselves in the north.

Ulfr disappeared into the forest almost as soon as the door was opened, and Ylmi had a moment to enjoy the peace of the snow, free from any worry about the village. There was little she could do now. They had only to survive till spring.

Karik appeared out of the gently falling snow, a long cloak of deerskins pulled close around him, and she smiled as she saw him.

"So, the first storm is over," he said when he was in earshot.

"With many more to come," Ylmi nodded. She glanced to the north again, eyeing the clouds. Karik came to stand next to her, and the two of them stood in the shelter of a pine tree, watching the wind blow down over the fjord, tossing snow as it went.

"It has been a long year," Karik said quietly.

"And we have accomplished much," Ylmi agreed. "If all goes to plan, next year will be busier yet."

"Even so," Karik nodded. He hesitated a moment, then looked Ylmi in the eye. "I have wanted to speak with you... but things seemed always to need doing."

"And now, at last, we can take our comfort by the fire," Ylmi replied. "Yet here I stand in the snow."

"I would marry you," Karik said softly. "If you would have me."

Ylmi blinked.

"We have known each other for nearly a year," Karik continued quickly. "We have hunted together, fought together, and sailed together... I do not think there are many more challenges we must face before we can say that we know the measure of each other."

A smile spread across Ylmi's face as she began to laugh. "I was there, Karik, for all of it, and I will take you if that is what you were asking. And your jarl approves the match."

In an instant, Ylmi found herself enveloped in a great hug, so deep that for a moment even the sound of the wind was cut off.

"I have thought on this for a long time," Karik said as he released her.

"If you are hoping to cleverly get a hand on my jarldom," Ylmi laughed, "then you will be sadly mistaken. I will not surrender it so easily."

"I have fought a dragon," Karik grinned as he held her close. "And I would sooner face it again than meet you on the battlefield."

"Flattering words," she said, eyeing him closely. "But if you are to satisfy your jarl, it will take more than a hug." With that, she pulled him close and kissed him, and for a moment, even the cold of Vrania's winter was forgotten.

⸺◆⸺

They were married together a few days later, quietly, in the forest as the snow fell around them. For awhile, Ylmi forgot that starvation hung over the settlement.

But even Karik's company could not keep it at bay for long, and the grumbling began in earnest before the winter was even a month old.

For her and her family, the winter was the most comfortable they had passed in a long time. The hunger for them was normal, but in the village, they were accustomed to more food, and the grumbling became heavy.

Late one night, they sat by the fire, and Ylmi turned to Karik. "How certain are you we can pass through the Isles?"

He looked up from the flames, startled by the question. "Very sure," he said after a moment. "If there is a way, and I think there is, then we will find it."

She laughed grimly, then dropped her head into her hands. "'If there is a way...' I am fated to never hear a straight answer to my questions."

Karik looked at her as she sat there in the firelight. "I am sorry," he said at last. He tapped his fingers on the rough bench, frustration rising within him.

"Is there danger that some will starve?" His voice felt heavy as he spoke over her silence.

Ylmi stood and went to the jarl's chair that sat at the end of the hall. She stood behind it and rested her arms on its back. She bowed her head for a moment, then threw back her hair and shrugged.

"Perhaps." Her eye fell on the fire, her stare empty. "We face starvation for the first time since I can remember. I allowed too many exiles to come, and Jarhost's taxes took a heavy toll."

Karik turned his own gaze to the fire, thinking of his father and brothers. "If you had not taken them in, then they would be dead already." He kept his voice quiet, speaking slowly. "If you do not feed them now, they may die anyway."

He looked up to see her still staring at the fire. "We will meet next year when it comes. If the Isles are impassable..." he took a deep breath, "perhaps I will take a portion of the village to Vanik's point. The hunting there may allow more of us to live."

"That is a point to discuss next year," Ylmi muttered, rolling her eye. Slipping around the chair, she came back to sit by him on the bench. "Vanik's point is too windy."

The fire crackled and popped before them, and Ylmi at last gave a sigh. "I will not doom some to death now for fear of death next winter." She turned to him and fixed him with one eye. "You will find a passage for me. For me, and for our people."

Karik smiled at her and kissed her forehead. "I will find it," he whispered in the firelight.

"I am counting on you," she said as she rose to her feet. She went to the door. "I am going to tell my father of my decision and to see that more of the herd is distributed." She opened the door and a few light snowflakes drifted in on the wind before she pulled it shut behind her.

Alone in the hall, Karik laid two logs on the fire to keep it burning. They caught slowly, the red and yellow flames gnawing at the wood.

In their light, Karik looked at his hands. His left had healed as well as it could, though the stumps of the last two fingers still ached more often than not. The other three fingers were still strong, but he found himself at times over protective of them, jerking them away from the fire or dropping a nail he was trying to drive.

His right hand still bore the cracked scars of the dragon fire. The wrinkled scarring stretched and flexed like old scabs, and from time to time he still found that it itched or stung.

Your every victory will turn to defeat, your triumphs to tragedies, your conquests to calamities.

He stared into the fire, hearing the words of the dragon's curse once again, as clearly as if the beast lay before him in the hall.

Never shall you have rest, never shall a home provide you comfort.

Karik glared at the flames flickering before him and glanced back at the stubs on his left hand. He had slain a dragon and sailed an unsailable sea, it was true, yet he bore the scars of both conquests on his body, and they would never heal.

From the death of the dragon, Umir was dead and the woman he loved was blind in one eye. Unhost had taken any profit they might have had from the undertaking. The fruit of that victory had been bitter indeed.

The sailing of the Under Sea had cost him two fingers and had led to a slaughter in the mountains. A tragedy of needless bloodshed if ever there was one.

When Ylmi returned, she found him unmoved, the fire burned to coals before him.

"You seem deep in thought." She said when the door was closed. "What troubles you?

"I am thinking," he said slowly, "how best I may serve my jarl."

<hr>

Slowly, they watched the days pass, enduring the cold and distracting themselves from the hunger.

Ylmi had not gathered as much food as she had hoped, but with what her family had gathered, it was no worse than what she was used to, and Karik had gone fishing a few times with Havar, so there was enough to keep starvation at bay.

Still, as Dunharvic's night drew close, more than a few in the village fought off sickness. Olga brewed special broths of her herbs for those who were worst off, but even she suffered from the cold.

So it was that on the longest night of the year, Ylmi stood before the door of her hall, and watched as the fires were lit through the village. Most were little more than faint glows in the darkness, for the snow was falling heavily, and Ylmi felt a coldness on her heart that was not brought by the wind.

The lord of the dead was riding through Vrania that night, and he would pass by her village. *Her village.*

"I know how to keep Jarhost at bay," she said quietly to Karik, "and I know how to keep away those who would rob and steal from us. But I am powerless against the dark horseman. What he will take…"

"There is nothing we can do," Karik assured her. "Only when we have passed the Isles will we escape some of the death that besets us here."

Ylmi stared into the snow and thought of the herd that had been taken by Gorli up to Bjarnmont. How many would feast this night if the king had not taken such a heavy tax?

"Do you think we will find lands uninhabited?" she asked Karik after a moment. "Or will we find land as crowded as Vrania?"

"I hope to find forests thick with game and empty of people," Karik replied. "But I think we will swiftly have to reckon with the descendants of those who cast out Vranr. Perhaps they will be people we can reason with..."

"Or they will be just like Jarhost, grasping and greedy," Ylmi muttered.

"If we must raid..." Karik shrugged. "Such is life... but I would not begin a war if it cannot be helped."

Ylmi breathed out into the cold air, watching her breath rise like smoke up past the edge of her hall's roof.

"I think we will have war in our future," she said, "one way or another. If we cannot find a place across the sea, then for all my dislike of Jarhost I would rather not fight against a king who lives a day's march from my home."

Karik was silent for a moment, watching the wind gusting over the fallen snow, whipping it into clouds only to fall again.

"It is my hope," Karik said quietly, "that on a night not too distant, we may await Dunharvic's ride with plenty of food, a roaring fire, and filled with hope in place of dread."

"We have a long road to walk before that day," Ylmi said. "But I am glad we walk it together."

The next morning, they found the Lord of the Dead had taken a heavy toll. Thora buried Almir Alsson in a cairn of rocks a little ways up the slope, and near to him, Havar and Ymr buried Olga. Nanni's youngest child, Kivli, died the following day, and the young woman wept as she buried her second child with Karik's help.

When it was done, Ylmi brought Nanni a pot of hot stew and a barrel of mead that Bogli had brewed, though the woman spared her little more than a tear-stained glare. But Karik disappeared into the forest. He did not return until night had fallen, covered in snow and with bits of his hair frozen into icicles.

When Ylmi asked where he had gone, he said that he had only been hunting, for all the good it had done.

⎯⎯⎯◆⎯⎯⎯

As the winter deepened and Ylmi's hunger grew, her mind turned to the tales her mother had told her, and she spoke of them with Karik. At times, Siggi would laugh to hear how her stories changed on Ylmi's tongue, but more often she sat by the fire and drank in its warmth.

It was not as cold down by the sea as it was in the mountains, and it seemed to Ylmi that her mother suffered less here in the warm hall beside the roaring fire.

"Your tales are far more numerous than the ones I was told," Karik said one evening. "And they tell of many things I had not known."

"That is because they come from the Undmir," Siggi said quietly. "You are a child of the coastlands, and many there have wandered far from where Vanik, Vranr's first born, founded his first fortress."

"He did not found it," Elva spoke for the first time in many hours, and Karik looked up in surprise at his mother. "Vanik stormed the fortress with his friends and the friends of his father. He slew every soul within and took it for his own."

"Who then was in it?" Karik asked. "For I was told that Vranr and his sons were the first upon the Isle."

"They were not," Elva answered. "For Vranr was not alone in his exile. But Vranr's jailors set guardians upon him in three places -in the north, which was the fortress of the Undmir; in the south where none now know; and in the west, which devoured Vranr."

"Devoured Vranr?" Karik asked.

Elva shrugged. "I do not know what it means, only that it is what the tales tell."

Ylmi set another log on the fire and curled her legs up closer to Ulfr. "If Vranr was not alone, then perhaps you can tell us more of his exile." She looked across the fire and smiled at Elva. "I have told many of my tales, and it would be good to hear more of what may lie across the sea."

The sound of the fire within the hall and the winds without hung heavy upon them for a moment, but at last Elva nodded.

"Someone should hear the tales before I die, and I do not think there are many left who have heard the tale of how Vranr fought the five kings and was banished to this barren rock."

So saying, she sat a little closer to the fire and spoke.

How Vranr Was Banished

After Vranr escaped from Tar-Vinhault with Sol and married her high in the mountains, her father, the third king, called together his brethren and told them what had happened. Never before had any of them been so disrespected, and it was made worse in their eyes because Sol had defied her father willingly.

The first king agreed and, rising before the others, said that Vranr had at last gone too far. "Each of us he has robbed, tricked, and deceived," he said. "But this is the worst thing he has done yet, to turn one of our own blood against us. So let us take counsel together and determine, once and for all, how to deal with this vagabond and rid ourselves of his annoyances."

But the fifth king rose to speak. He was the youngest and saw clearest of all the others. "In the years past, Vranr fought us as a vagabond, as a wanderer, and as a warrior," he told the others. "We could not defeat him because we never know where to find him. But this is the case no more.

"We have two choices before us: we may attempt to make peace with him, knowing that perhaps he grows weary of war and of fleeing. In this way, we may gain a valuable ally and risk very little. Or," and here his eyes turned to the third king, "we may hunt Sol, knowing that wherever she goes, Vranr is sure to follow, and where she is in danger, he will be found."

But the other kings would not hear of peace, for all had suffered mightily at Vranr's hands. So, they were all agreed, and they all swore they would carry out whatever was needed.

But Sol had many friends among her father's court, and Vranr was not an unpopular man, so word soon reached them of what the kings had decided. They only laughed and disappeared from the face of the earth.

For five years, the kings sought them and had much trouble and loss from the looking, but they found neither sign nor sound of them anywhere.

At last, they grew impatient and burned the homes of any who had known Vranr, and they imprisoned those who had been friendly with Sol. When word of this came to them, Vranr and Sol were exceedingly angry, and they came out of their hiding.

Together, they broke the prisons of the five kings, freeing those within. And any company of warriors the kings sent to harass their friends never returned from the mountains.

So many were slain by Vranr and Sol that some said that in their hiding, they had become dragons, and were now wreaking their vengeance.

At last, the kings gathered together in secret, so great had become their fear of Vranr.

For a week and a day, they argued, until the youngest said that if Vranr could outsmart them all, then perhaps they required the aid of one who could match Vranr in cunning.

So, they sought out those who were hidden, those who were cunning, and those who were ancient. Thus the Five Kings sought the counsel of the Fey King. But Vranr suspected they were engaged in a plot to discomfort him, and he took every opportunity to cause them trouble. But at last, through his harassment, they came to the banks of the great river that separated their realm from that of the fey folk.

But as they approached its banks, Vranr loosed a flooding torrent from high in the mountains. It rushed down, gathering strength as it went, until it reached the ford the Five kings were crossing.

A thousand men died in that flood, a thousand and a hundred more. But Vranr had the help of only three men.

So, the five kings despaired to cross the river. Every attempt they made, Vranr foiled, until the youngest again came to their rescue.

Secretly, he sent seven messengers and an eighth to his council in the south.

Seven men Vranr caught, and seven men he killed.

But the eighth slipped through his nets, and for a thousand years, Vranr cursed that night.

For the eighth man arrived in the council of the youngest king, and they went and seized Sol, the wife of Vranr and the rightful heir to the throne of the north.

Then, Vranr left the Five Kings and came to the rescue of his wife. He arrived before the fortress where she was held at dusk and came before the gate.

"Give me back my wife," he called to them, "and this matter will be ended between us. Keep her, and your masters will return to weep over what is done here."

But the commander of the fortress saw an opportunity to gain great fame for himself and rejected Vranr's offer.

"Present yourself here by dawn," the commander said, "wearing only sackcloth, with no weapons, and your hands bound before you, or we will punish your wife for your misdeeds. By the Allfather I swear, if you are not here by dawn, Sol will pay in blood."

Vranr said nothing but turned and strolled out of sight of the fortress.

When the night had fallen, Vranr wrapped himself in the fur of a great black bear, and walking among the shadows, he returned to the fortress.

He climbed the wall in silence and slew the watchmen who had been set.

Going to the prisons, he slew in silence the guards who were there, and he found where Sol was kept, for she had contrived to leave markings that led him to her.

Swiftly, he dressed her wounds and told her to wait for him in the gatehouse. But she would not do it and said that she would not sit by while another took her vengeance for her.

So saying, they went, they two, and slew all who remained, from the bowmen in the watchtowers to the captain in his chambers. And, when this was done, they set the fortress afire and burned it to ashes.

No living thing, save for Vranr and Sol, was left alive in the fortress when the sun rose, and of all their killings, that was the greatest, for the bones that they left there were beyond counting.

But the capture of Sol had served its purpose, for the five kings crossed the river into the fey folk's realm, and when they returned, they carried a promise from the Fey King.

Thus began the hunting of Vranr and Sol, and they were pursued by seven champions, the Five Kings, and all the armies and forces which they could command, and the wreckage of that hunt stretched from sea to sea. There were few who survived unscathed by its violence. But as the war dragged on, Vranr's friends numbered fewer with each passing day, until at last, the third king came upon his daughter Sol in the mountains.

And in the moment that he laid his hand upon her, the promise of the Fey King was fulfilled, and Vranr was cast out and banished to Vrania, along with his sons and three men who were bound to him by many oaths.

Thus was Vranr sent to the Island that now bears his name.

"That tale leaves me with many questions," Karik muttered as they stared at the fire.

"Not all questions have answers," his mother replied. "I was not there, and I have only told you the tale as it was told to me."

"It seems to me..." Ylmi said slowly, "that all these tales have some truth at their root... even if the branches have grown far from it. To focus on the leaves is to miss the point of the tale."

"Your jarl is wise, my son," Elva said. "Vranr was very cunning and gathered friends in many places, yet in the end, it would have been better for him to have remained hidden with Sol. The destruction that came of them leaving their hiding was far greater than what was suffered while he was hid."

"Then what would you say is the point of this tale?" Siggi asked.

"That Vranr was wrongly exiled?" Karik suggested.

Ylmi shrugged. "He came to this Isle, one way or another. And his watching stones are upon the mountain still."

"I had heard they were a myth," Elva said, glancing quickly at Ylmi.

Ylmi did not look away from the fire. "They are not."

Gorli and Regvar

When the snow at last began to melt, Havar and Igil were the first among the village to return to work. They uncovered the frame of their ship and set to work finishing her. She was the largest ship any of them had ever seen, and every day, Karik marveled at what they had constructed.

"How many men does she need?" he asked Havar one gloomy morning.

Havar grinned. "Fifteen men could crew her, but she'll carry almost fifty."

"Fifty?" Karik gasped. "That would be a mighty crew."

"I have built her," Havar shrugged, "it is for you to find the crew."

Karik shook his head with a laugh. "By the nine, Havar, I think you may have set as great a task for me as I have set for you."

When the ice began to melt and the storms slackened, Karik began the work of gathering a crew.

He went first to Girstadt, then to Yrdstadt, then to Yrdnara. He sailed in *Kalborg*, and all marveled at the size of the ship when it arrived. But Karik promised them the ship in which they would cross the Isles was far larger - the greatest ship yet seen in Vrania.

"Even Vranr did not build a ship such as this," Karik told them, "nor did his sons build anything to rival it."

Some said that his great ship would make only a great wreck, and that if it was only a large ship that was needed to pass the Isles, then they would have succeeded long ago.

"You are right," Karik told them, "and if that was all we had, then I would be much slower in coming to you with this offer. But I have something more." Then he would take a copy he had made of the chart showing a path through the Isles and lay it before them.

"I come with more than promises of a ship," he said, "and the offer of a glorious death. I know how to pass the Isles. For the first time, we know how to get through and have a ship capable of doing it. Sail with us, and we will open a way off of Vrania! We will find a way to escape the hunger that plagues us and end the starvation that buries so many of us each winter."

In each village, there were a few who nodded as he spoke and seemed willing to sail. But there were more who shook their heads.

"If there was a way, we would have found it by now," they would say. "Your efforts would be better spent serving King Jarhost or ending Viglir's raiding upon the mountains."

So Karik went from village to village, his small crew riding in *Kalborg*, and Karik saw they were all able to row, to pull an oar as well as could be. But when he turned the prow back northward, there was a tightness in his chest, for he had hoped to gather a somewhat stronger company.

A few young men and women joined him and an old man whose sight had nearly left him but was still strong enough to pull an oar. When at last *Kalborg* was drawn up upon the beach in Dragon's rest, Havar greeted them and looked over the rough company.

"A few wanderers have come in," he told Karik, "and most seem ready enough to sail with us. Together with what you have brought, our crew is at thirty-seven."

"It is more than needed," Igil said as he looked around. "but less than I would like. Sailing through the Isles will not be swift, and it would be good if we could take turns on the oars."

But Karik shook his head. "It is not the rowing that I fear the most, though I do not feel easy about that, either. Weakness invites attack, and I do not know what we will find in the west."

"If we're met by an army," Havar muttered, "one ship will do little, full or not."

"I do not think that will happen," Karik replied. "But a poor host will behave with more kindness when it is a mighty warrior on his doorstep than he would if it were a starving child."

"Then let us hope we find a good host," Igil said. "Or no host at all."

"When has hope ever served us well?" Karik asked, and Igil had no answer for him.

———◇———

The next morning, Karik woke to find Ylmi gone from their bed. Ulfr prowled restlessly in the hall, and the sword *Raethbur* still leaned by the doorway, so Karik guessed she had not gone far. Wrapping his deerskin cloak over his shoulder, he stepped outside.

The sun was rising in the east into a sky heavy with clouds, and the dawn was bathed in a heavy red light. The clouds that hung over the mountains burned like fire, even as an icy wind came blowing down from their peaks to rush out over the fjord.

Ylmi stood on the low rise that looked over the beach, the wind whipping at her hair that she had neglected to tie back. She was pulling her cloak close about her, and she did not move when Karik stood next to her.

"It is a frosty morning to stand alone," Karik said.

She snorted, as if laughing at a hidden joke. "The harvest is almost sown," she said. "And the herds are set out to pasture. Will the ship be ready soon?"

Karik nodded. "With most of the crew here, the final work is beginning. Havar and Igil have the help they need to hand the sail, run the ropes, and complete the final preparations."

"It will be good to cross the Isles," Ylmi said, her voice hardening as she spoke. "Though I wish we had more than one ship. If we find lands uninhabited, it may be that we find life easier in the old lands than here."

"If we pass the Isles," Karik said, "then Igil and Havar will build other ships, and we will find a place where we can be safe. Perhaps we will find rulers like Tanvir, with whom we may come to some agreement..."

Ylmi spat onto the sand. "I find it more likely we will find rulers like Hegli and Jarhost."

"I can only hope," Karik hesitated. "Either way, I think there will be use for more ships."

"Once we are through and the way is known, others will follow, no matter how difficult it may be." She looked out at the fjord and the mountain in the distance before she spoke again.

"We will soon have a child."

Karik blinked. "What?"

She turned to look him in the eye. "Six months, more or less."

Karik felt his face split with a grin as he wrapped her in a giant hug.

"It makes the Isles more important," Ylmi said quietly.

Karik nodded as he took a step back. "You will still sail?"

"Of course I will," Ylmi pulled her cloak tight over her shoulders again and turned back to the sea. "You have seen me face a dragon, kill Lasvik, and scale the watching stones, but these people have not. All they have seen is me facing Unhost, and that was a pathetic fight."

"You looked like Hel when she rides to war," he grinned. "Beautiful and terrifying."

A smile cracked Ylmi's face as he spoke, and she looked at him with her bright blue eye. "You flatter too much, oh Karik Haldsson."

Work continued on the ship, and Havar declared it was time she received a name.

"*Sea Dragon*," Karik said. "She is built with the riches taken from the dragon. She is Vranr's curse called home."

So, the ship was named *Sea Dragon*. Igil slaughtered a goat and poured its blood on the ship's prow, and they asked the Allfather's blessing on the ship's passage, Thor's protection in the storms, and swift passage for all who perished on her from Dunharvic.

It was nearing high summer as the final preparations neared completion, and Karik worked long into the night, that they might sail as soon as possible.

He came one night back to Ylmi's hall and found Elva sitting quietly by the fire. Ylmi sat across from her, but as Karik entered, she rose.

"I will leave you two alone."

She clapped Karik on the shoulder as she passed by him and stepped into the night.

Karik walked slowly to the fire and eased himself down across from his mother. She was looking into the fire, but slowly her gaze rose, the flames flickering in her eyes, till they were fixed on Karik.

"You will attempt to cross the Isles."

Karik nodded.

"I told you once that I did not wish you to do so," Elva's voice was grim in the darkness, and Karik was suddenly reminded of Dvengrhal on the mountain. "I did not think you would succeed where so many others have failed, and I did not wish to lose you."

"Do you still wish that I leave the Isles untested?"

"I do," Elva answered quickly, "but the reason is different."

Karik wasn't sure what to do with his hands, so he picked up a stick and began peeling the bark from it. "Why then do you not wish me to attempt the Isles?"

"Because I think you may succeed."

Karik looked up in surprise and confusion. "You... what?"

"I have not left my mind buried in onions this last year," Elva told him. "Nor have my ears been clogged with mountain mud. For all your cleverness, I know more than you think. I have heard the deeds you have done and seen their fruits, and their fruits are bitter indeed."

Karik looked back on the fire, and it seemed to him for a moment that he saw Umir and Wisic within the flames.

"Where there is poverty and hardship," Elva continued, "there is kindness, and people work together. When there is excess, when there is prosperity, then men turn to greed and grasping." She leaned forward, the fire flickering over the lines of her face, and Karik winced. "Jarhost is not a generous man, nor a wise one. The mountain jarls follow his lead and grasp for themselves every which way. The coastal jarls are little better, for there is little for them to grasp at. Yet they will not stand up to Jarhost, because it is difficult."

The fire cracked and popped between them as the flames ate away at the twisted log Ylmi had set there. Overhead, Karik could hear the wind blowing over the roof, and as he listened, the wind shifted. The gentle south wind fell away and, for a moment, there was almost perfect silence.

Then, the wind came again, rushing out of the north, moaning over the hall roof.

"Shall I tell you, Karik?" Elva asked as the wind howled. "Shall I tell you what will come if you sail the Isles? King Jarhost will take the greater part of what you find, more and more, until you have less than you did before. The mountain jarls will demand their share, and you will be driven to ruin.

"You think you will have allies among the men of the coast because they sail with you, but they will turn on you in an instant if your path seems difficult. And what of those you find across the sea? Will they be friends when you have stolen their herds and their silver? If you pass through the Isles, you will find yourself friendless, alone, against a sea of foes who seek nothing but your misfortune."

"And if I do not?" Karik asked quietly. "If I leave the Isles untried? What then?" He tossed the stick he held onto the fire and threw in the pile of peeled bark after it. "I sit here and watch you freeze to death? Perhaps not this winter, perhaps not even next. But it will happen. I will watch my wife and our children starve until I die and am spared the sight?"

Elva took a deep breath as the fire glowed up through the coals and the north wind howled outside.

"I did not tell you tale of Vranr idly," she spoke again, her voice slow, laying down each word like a stone anchor. "He thought that by great deeds he might be safe, that he might avoid the suffering which pursued him. Yet each success only drew his doom more tightly about him."

Karik felt a chill go down his spine at the echo of the dragon's words.

"Now, you have only the winter and hunger to contend with," Elva went on. "But if you sail, you will raise up for yourself new enemies and new dangers which you cannot hope to overcome."

He stood up and brushed off his pants. "I cannot take a sword to winter or reason with the north wind. If Jarhost wishes to steal from me, he had best do it wisely, or I will do to him what I have done to a dragon. Let the mountain jarls array themselves against me. Let the king in Bjarnmont seek my death. Who can worry about this when Dunharvic rides each year with such deadly purpose?"

And with that, he stepped out into the night.

⸻◆⸻

The work on *Sea Dragon* continued, and all felt the weight of the hundreds of minor tasks that must be done to ensure the success of any great venture.

As they had done with *Kalborg,* Igil and Havar stitched together the sails of smaller ships to craft one large enough for *Sea Dragon,* but Orlanna shook her head when she saw it.

"A canvas so large should not be patched together," she said. "It will last a short time, but the seams will grow more ragged with each repair until you are left with nothing but rags."

"It is the best we have," Havar snapped. "Though if we raided Viglir's hall, then perhaps we might find a canvas more fitting."

"If you found it," Orlanna said softly, "He would hunt you down before you could raise it on a ship. It takes much work and labor to make such a canvas, and they are not lightly lost."

Igil regarded her carefully. "Can you make such a sail?"

Orlanna gave a short laugh. "It is long and hard work for many, hardly a task I could complete myself." Yet she looked over the size of their patchwork sail as the north wind blew over the beach and considered for a moment.

"I could not build one in time for your first voyage," she said at last. "But by the time this one has outlived its use... I might be able to fashion one for you with the help of others."

So it was that while Dranri hunted, Orlanna began to work on a sail for *Sea Dragon*, and Karik noticed that it was not long before Orlanna had a very great deal of help.

Fianna often brought Henla and Torm to help gather wool from the sheep that Bodvar kept in the village, and Nanni would spend her evenings talking with Orlanna as they separated the wool and began to weave it.

Even as Orlanna labored on the sail, so they labored on the ship, and the day of sailing drew near. Igil, Havar, and Karik worked from dawn's first light until the night was heavy upon them, checking the ship and seeing that all things were made ready.

One day, as Karik and Igil were fashioning spare oars, a company of warriors came walking down from the mountains with the sturdy figure of Gorli at their head. They made straight for the boat, not bothering to speak with those they passed by. They ignored the jarl's longhouse, where they should have made themselves known, and stopped only when they had come to the ship.

Karik slid one of the small crafting axes into his belt as he rose, and Igil rested his hand on the seax that hung from his hip.

"Who are you that come so armed into our village?" Karik asked.

Gorli looked them over, noting the scars they bore, and nodded. "I am Gorli, thane of King Jarhost, and he has sent us here to join you." He looked over the boat critically and smiled, "We heard you needed a crew in your passage of the Isles, and Jarhost has sent us, his greatest warriors, to join you in your attempt to cross the Isles."

The company was not a large one, only six men in all. But they all had the look of fighters. The largest was as tall as Revik and broader in the shoulders. There was a mean look in his eye that Karik did not like.

Karik looked them over, a frustrated anger rising in his gut. They had built the boat after the king had refused to help. They had taken the maps from the dragon, which the king had never acknowledged. And now, the king sent his men to steal the glory.

"We have the crew we need," he answered after a moment. "*Sea Dragon* can well be handled by those we now have. King Jarhost is most gracious with his men, but we would not trouble him, not when King Viglir presses so hard upon him."

Many of the villagers and much of the crew were gathering to see what was going on. Gorli looked at them with a brilliant smile.

"But Karik," he said, "you and your companions must know, King Viglir is much less of a threat now after the great defeat he suffered at our hands last year. The eastern king is well in hand, thanks to you and your friends. Indeed, it is in part because of this that our king honors you so, by sending us to sail with you."

"Even so." Karik stood for a moment, trying to see his way out of this before he spoke again. "This is a matter to bring before our jarl..."

"No," Gorli interrupted him with a smile. "You misunderstand our king's generosity. We trust you, Karik, but there are others in your village who have cheated the king of his taxes before. We wish only to aid you where we can and see that our king's interests are upheld."

"Is that so?" Ylmi said as she stepped out behind them. "Tell me then: why does the king so suddenly wish his men to sail on a boat he refused to help build?"

"Ah," Gorli said as he turned to her. "Ylmi."

"I am more commonly called One-Eye," Ylmi answered. "And I am still the jarl of this village, despite the efforts of some."

"As you say," Gorli replied. "But it has been a long journey from Bjarnmont, and we are weary. We should rest and be ready for when the time comes to sail." He turned back to Karik. "How long, do you think, until you are ready?"

"We sail when my jarl allows it," Karik replied coldly.

"And when will that be?"

Igil stepped forward quickly. "Only a few days, three at the most. So you had best prepare yourselves."

Gorli thanked him and led his little party to the long house.

"What was that?" Ylmi asked Igil quietly.

Igil looked from her to Karik tightly. "Do you want to get us outlawed or killed? Because antagonizing the king's men is an excellent way to do that."

Ylmi bit her lip as she looked after Gorli. "I dislike how our property can be seized and the king can walk in on whatever we are doing."

"I don't like it either," Igil answered. "But unfortunately for us, we have neither the might nor the following to gainsay the king."

"One day, perhaps," Ylmi said quietly. "But not today."

"All the more reason this journey must be a success," Karik muttered.

Setting Sail

A storm blew in that evening, lashing the village with cold rain and a fierce wind that drove everyone indoors.

In Ylmi's longhouse, Karik lit a great fire, and the crew of *Sea Dragon* ate and drank together. Gorli and his men kept to themselves, however, mingling little with the rest, save for one. The big man who kept close to Gorli seemed always to have his eye on Revik.

For a while, Revik returned his stare, and Karik wondered more than once if they might come to blows, so unfriendly were their looks.

As they ate from a great cauldron of stew, Revik leaned toward Karik and asked quietly, "Do you know who that is?"

Before Karik could answer, Dranri spat on the floor. "That is Regvar the mighty," he took a long drink from his cup. "I dislike him."

"You know him?" Karik asked in surprise.

Dranri drank again. "He came to Bjarnmont shortly before I left. He is a turd of the highest order, and I hope he falls overboard."

Karik looked again at the men from Bjarnmont. They did not seem an agreeable lot, and there was much trouble they might cause before it was all over.

As the night drew on, Karik and Ylmi left the head table and took Igil and Havar with them, and together they poured over the charts, plotting their course through the Isles.

A thunder storm blew in that night, and they woke the next morning to a steady rain. Ylmi and the rest pulled on their cloaks and set about the work of the day, but Gorli and his men remained in the hall, talking and laughing while they piled wood on the fire.

"I think Dranri is right on this matter," Igil said with a glance toward where Gorli sat laughing with Regvar. "They are turds. Very little good will come of them sailing with us."

"I agree," Karik answered, picking up several oars and laying them against *Sea Dragon*. "But I do not see a way to be rid of them that does not bring Jarhost back to our village."

"I am not eager for that to happen again," Ylmi said as she came through the mud toward them. "He is a greedy man who will take more than is his share. How go things with the ship?"

Igil smiled through the rain. "We are ready." He pointed to the heavy canvas that covered the ship and kept the rain from her hull. "As soon as this rain stops, we'll peel off the canvas and have nothing to do but load her."

Ylmi nodded. "Good." She looked at each of them. "When the storm breaks?"

"When the storm breaks," Karik agreed.

But that was not as soon as they would have liked. For two days, the rain poured down, and there was little that could be done. By the light of a torch, Karik studied the charts he had taken from the mountain, his fingers tracing every line as he committed them to memory. He would not chance their destruction by taking them on the voyage, and within the narrow, twisting passage through the Isles, he would have no time to study them.

"You are nervous?" Igil asked once, as they stared at the charts together.

Karik shrugged. "Of course. They were accurate enough in the Undersea..." he paused a moment and glanced around before lowering his voice. "The waters around the Isles are open and wild as the Undersea is not... if anything is unreliable on the charts, this is it."

"You think the passage may be closed?"

"It could... but even if it is open, I do not think it unreasonable to expect that it has changed somewhat."

Igil stared at the chart, while further down in the hall Gorli and his men were playing a noisy game of dice. "If I give Revik a big enough stick, he might help keep us off the rocks as long as we don't get driven right up on one."

"He can't take the full weight of the ship," Karik snorted. "Your brother isn't that strong."

"No, but he can give us a little more room for error, and we have precious little now." He sighed and rolled his head back to the rafters. "I weary of waiting... we have waited and waited. I am ready to sail."

But still they waited as the rain continued to fall and the storm deepened. Even the fish dove deep and the creatures in the forest hid, so that the food in the long house ran short.

Gorli and his companions complained loudly at this, pointing to the barrels of salted fish and hard baked bread that was piled at one end of the hall.

"This is no way to treat the king's emissaries," Regvar bellowed at one point. "Not when you have so much food sitting ready at hand."

"That is for the voyage," Igil said. He was attempting to carve a small ship for Henla and growing increasingly frustrated with it. At last, he hurled it into the fire and turned to Regvar. "Either we go a little hungry here, or we starve on the sea."

"It is easy enough to bake more bread and catch more fish," Regvar grunted, and there was bitter laughter in the hall at that.

"Regvar," Ylmi called from the other end of the hall. "Shut up."

Gorli rose to his feet at this and made his way to where Karik was dozing against one of the great posts that ran along the center of the hall. "It is not right that the king's men should be spoken to this way," he hissed. "I know Ylmi is your leader, but still..."

"Revgar is behaving like a fool," Karik answered without opening his eyes. "He should not then be surprised to be treated like one." He cracked open one eye and looked up at Gorli. "Listen, you sail on a boat which the king refused to help build after taking every nugget of the gold we rescued from a dragon.

"Building this ship has been a long and difficult process, but we are now ready to sail. We will not now become unready simply to satisfy the stomachs of a few men from Bjarnmont who do not know the meaning of hunger as we do on the coast. Emissaries from the king you may be, but in this matter, you are the crew, and you will do as you are told."

And with that, Karik went back to sleep.

⸺⊸◦⊷⸺

The storm broke shortly after midnight, and Karik was woken by Havar's call. Swiftly, the longhouse came awake, and they began carrying the pile of stores down to the boat.

"Why must we rise while it is so dark?" Gorli asked, "surely the sea will still be there in the morning."

"The tide," Karik answered simply. "It may matter little to you in the mountains, but here on the coast it is no small thing. All of you," he told the king's men, "get your gear together and help carry this down to the ship."

"I am a warrior, not a pack mule," Regvar said with a short laugh. "Carry it yourself."

"If you don't help carry it, you won't help eat it," Karik replied. "So unless you think you can sail through the Isles to whatever is on the other side and back on an empty stomach, be my guest."

Regvar rose to his full height and towered over Karik. "Are you going to stop me, little man?"

Karik smiled, then kicked him between the legs. As Regvar gasped, Karik struck him a heavy blow on the stomach, then a third on his jaw that sent him stumbling backward. "Yes, I am." He looked at Gorli and then at the rest of the king's men. "If anyone else has a problem, say so now."

When even Gorli was silent, Karik guessed he had made his point and returned to work.

Igil, who had been coming up to check on him and had seen it all, clapped him on the shoulder. "Sudden and terrible action," he whispered with a grin. "I was wondering when we'd come to blows with that lout and not sure of the outcome. Be wary of him though, I do not think he will take his beating well."

"He will not," Karik said. "I agree with Dranri, I hope he falls overboard."

It was dark, muddy work to load the ship. The moon was low on the horizon when they finished and the tide was nearing its peak.

They waited, talking only quietly as the waves rolled in, and Karik felt the mingling of excitement and fear in his chest as he looked out over the fjord.

"Go say your farewells," he said to the crew. "But be swift. The tide will turn soon, and if you are not here, you will be left."

Almost half the crew was from outside their village, and so had nowhere to go, but the rest scattered to their homes.

For his part, Karik went back to the hall, where his mother was waiting for him, her eyes set on the fire.

"You will go?" Her voice was quiet, barely strong enough to be heard over the sound of the crackling fire.

The flames were crawling up the logs she had stacked over the coals, slowly biting deeper into the wood and burning off the twigs and bark that sprouted off the old branches.

"I will," Karik answered.

"You have thrown away my counsel," she said, "so I will not waste more on you. But if you are determined to take this path, then there are a few things you should know." She stood and Karik saw she held a narrow bundle as long as his arm. She took a deep breath, glancing at the fire as she did so. The logs were burning fiercely now, the flames leaping into the air as they devoured the wood.

"When Vranr came to this isle, he was not alone, as some tales tell, but his sons and their wives followed him as well, as did three men who were bound to him. Menik, who loved him like a son; Dvengrhal, who betrayed him; and Grenvil, who saved him from his darkest hour."

Karik's eyes sharpened suddenly. "I have not heard much of Dvengrhal."

"There are few who have," Elva answered. "But it is from Grenvil, the third of Vranr's sworn men, that I am descended. This," she held up the bundle, "has been passed from eldest daughter to eldest son for years beyond count. But my eldest son is dead, and I have no daughters, so it is now rightfully yours."

She stepped away from the fire and set the bundle in his hands.

Slowly, Karik unwound the leather strap that held it together, and as the hides fell away, Karik saw it held a sword.

A black iron pommel was set at the base of the hilt, and the grip was of smooth black leather. The scabbard was of dark leather tipped and capped with iron, and when he drew it, Karik saw the blade had been hammered from twisted steel. Whereas his first blade gleamed like silver and shone with a pure light, this sword was dark, as if eating the light that struck it.

"This is a cunning blade," he gasped softly as he felt it in his hand. It was nearly weightless in his hand and hummed deeply as he swung it through the air.

"This was the sword of Grenvil," Elva spoke as one struggling for breath, and Karik looked up from the sword to see a tear falling from her eye. "It was forged in the lands to the west, and with it he did many great deeds."

"Mother," Karik stepped forward, but she held up her hand and wiped away the tear.

"I have wept my last tear," she said. "The Allfather has taken all from me. For if you set sail, you are as lost to me as if you laid in the ground beside your brothers."

"I will return." Karik felt a roughness in his throat as he spoke.

"I think that you likely will." His mother sat back down and stared into the fire, an empty look in her eyes. "But if the way is opened, it will bring such war and destruction that many will say it would be better it had stayed shut. And I will lose you, as I have lost my other children. Go now, I have kept you long enough, and you should not miss the tide."

Karik stood a moment longer, but then turned to the door. As he did so, he heard the fire collapse on itself, sending sparks into the air as the wood collapsed into charred embers that glowed red in the dark hall.

He left the hall, his eyes burning and a rage in his chest. He knew that in some ways, his mother spoke truly. He knew Jarhost would come grasping whatever they gained, but the hunger in his stomach was a constant reminder that they must gain *something* or they'd end the same as his father and brothers. He could not wait and let that happen to others - not now, when he had the chance to push back the hunger for another winter.

But in his mind, he heard the dread voice: *Your victories will turn to defeats, and every triumph will turn to ashes in your mouth.*

He met Ylmi coming back from her parent's hut, and her eye narrowed when she saw him.

"Your mother is still not pleased with our journey?"

"That and other matters," Karik answered. "Let us go."

They climbed aboard *Sea Dragon* in the dark, stumbling over the benches and piles of supplies as they tried to find places to sit. But soon enough, they were ready. Carefully, Karik poured out a horn of mead to Thor to keep them safe and said a prayer for the ship to the Allfather, that he would guide them safely to their destination and back home.

Then, the oars were lowered and they slowly pulled away from the shore, the sail filling gently and pushing them west. The dragon's mountain stood before them, a black pillar against the starry night sky.

"That would have been easier with piers," Karik said to Havar. "If we are successful, I think you are right: they would be an excellent thing to build."

Havar nodded tightly, spitting over the side of the ship as he held the rudder, and Karik stared at him for a moment.

"You are nervous?" he asked quietly.

Havar spat again. "There are many things that may go wrong," he said as he looked down the fjord. "The ship may not be sound, the Isles may prove too much, the lands beyond may be worthless or more dangerous than we know. And I dislike the fact that Gorli and the others are here."

Karik clapped him on the shoulder. "We have done all we can in the matter of the ship and the Isles. Our passage and what comes after is in the hands of the gods. And though I dislike having Gorli here as well, I do not think you should be over worried about him. Not on this journey at least, not when the king has sent him to bring back riches himself." He leaned back and stretched his shoulders. "Gorli will stab us in the back one day, but not today."

Incoming Storms

As they passed the dragon's mountain in the midst of the fjord, the sun began to rise over the mountains in the east. Its rays turned the clouds red, and Igil watched it carefully.

"More than likely there's a storm headed our way," he told Ylmi, "a bad one."

"Can we outrun it?" Karik asked, but Igil only shrugged.

"No way to know until we see it," Havar answered. "Though I don't like the idea of risking it when we're trying to sail the Isles."

Karik nodded, and as the sun rose, they watched the sky. But aside from scattered clouds to the east and north, they could see nothing.

"Perhaps it is not coming," Karik said, but Igil looked at him sideways.

"Remember what Wisic used to say? It's Vrania, there's always a storm coming." Igil looked back up at the sky. "We just can't see it yet."

"If we do, we'll turn back," Karik promised. "But let us see how matters go."

With that, he raised his voice and spoke to the entire ship.

"Family, friends, and men of the king," he called. "We are about to attempt the passage of the Black Isles. Today, you become legends, the men and women who first passed through the bars of our prison. It will not be easy, for few things in this life are, but the rewards of your work will be great indeed.

"The Isles are nearly a mile wide, but the passage we will take is near twice that length. The wind will be treacherous, so you will have to row. It will be hard, it will be exhausting, and you will think we are near death. But," he raised two fingers toward them, "it is only for two miles. Two miles, and we will sail on a calm breeze to the rich lands in the west. Two miles, and you will be remembered as heroes for a hundred years and more. Two miles, and we will rest under calm skies and smooth sailing."

Revik was the first to roar his approval, and the rest of the crew joined in, save for Gorli and his companions, who looked at each other uneasily.

The boat filled with the sound of laughter and jests as Karik settled back on the rudder, watching the cliffs drift by as they approached the open sea. Overhead, the wind was howling, and Havar watched the sky nervously.

"I hope everyone is ready," Igil grinned quietly, and Karik shook his head.

"Hold fast!" he called, "We are approaching the sea!"

The talk died down swiftly at that as every man and woman grabbed hold of their benches, the mast, or the side of the ship, bracing themselves.

Sea Dragon was not a small ship, and she picked up speed as they approached the mouth of the fjord. The wind's grip on her sail grew stronger, pushing her faster and faster until she shot out beyond the cliffs, crashing through the first wave that rose to meet her.

Looking down the length of the ship, Karik saw Gorli stumble and fall across the hull, a rattle of small laughs rolling across the benches as he scrambled back to his place.

Sea Dragon's prow rose as she lifted over a wave, then fell, slicing through the water as the wind drove her on. As the deck rolled under him, Karik tasted the salt spray in the air, and reveled in the wind on his face. This was freedom - a good ship, the rolling waves, and a strong breeze at his back.

Then, Igil raised his hand and pointed north. Dark clouds sat heavy on the horizon, rolling and boiling as the wind drove them down from the Ice Sea in the north.

"By the gods, they are coming fast," Havar marveled, and as he spoke, Karik saw lightning flickering within the storm.

"We should turn back," Igil said quickly. "I know you don't like it, but that is a nasty storm."

Karik nodded, "We can put in at the inlet just inside the fjord." He glanced between the two of them. "That will be enough for the ship?"

Havar nodded. "If we can get her up on the beach, we should not have to worry too much."

More than a little regretfully, Karik leaned on the rudder, and *Sea Dragon* leapt to obey the command. Her prow sliced through the water as it came about.

"Out oars!" Havar called.

A low mutter went through the crew, but Karik saw several pointing north, and there seemed to be not a little relief that they would not have to try the Isles with that storm bearing down on them.

As Karik guided the ship back to the small inlet just inside the fjord, Ylmi's eyes were fixed on Gorli.

She had seen little of Jarhost that would suggest he did things out of the goodness of his heart, and there was no reason to suspect Gorli and his men had been sent only to be of help. They were here to see that Jarhost received his share of whatever they brought back.

What that share was, she was not sure they would agree on. She watched as Gorli sat at his place in the middle of the boat, not one of his men lifting their hands to the oars.

She beckoned Igil, and when he stooped next to her, she jerked her head toward the king's men.

"We should see that they are first on the oars tomorrow," she said quietly. "I do not want to argue with them to pull their weight when we are approaching the Isles tomorrow."

Igil followed her gaze and nodded. "I'll talk to Revik and Thora, we'll make sure it happens."

She watched him go, stopping to speak with his massive brother for a moment, and her hands went to the three stones that hung from her neck.

Tossing Gorli and his men overboard was a tempting prospect. There would be few on the ship who would feel the need to tell Jarhost, and it would be very pleasant to be rid of them. But Jarhost would doubtless pay well to find out the truth of what happened, and she did not know everyone onboard as well as she would have liked. There were many newcomers in Dragonsrest, and if their journey was successful, there were likely to be many more.

She should spend more time walking the settlement when they returned. It was important that she know her village and the mettle of those who lived there.

Her thoughts ran over the shoreline, touching on Gorli, Jarhost, and the settlement. Jarhost would demand more and more each year, unless she made it more costly to him...

She thought of the Undmir, of Hegli, and the mighty fortress that had kept him safe between two kings always at war. Her hall and the settlement were not in as great a position as the Undmir Fortress, but there was much that could be done to fortify it.

If they made it past the Isles, and if they could find riches beyond them, then there was much that might be done.

As *Sea Dragon* slid back into the safety of the fjord, the wind died down a little, and Ylmi thought for a moment of what she would do if the lands to the west were barren. If they brought nothing back, then there would be more matters to deal with.

Sea Dragon rolled up on the beach with a crunch, and a dozen of the crew leaped overboard to pull her up on the shore. Ylmi splashed through the icy water and watched as Karik and his friends directed the crew to secure the ship on the beach. She smiled when he turned to wink at her.

As she watched, Thora strode up to her, glancing northward at the oncoming storm clouds.

"You are not sure Gorli and his men will pull their weight?" she asked quietly.

Ylmi nodded. "They have done little so far that they were not driven to do. I see no reason that will change."

Thora nodded toward the oncoming clouds, "That storm will not be fun."

"We'll survive," Ylmi assured her. "We just need the tents up."

As soon as Karik declared the ship secured, they lifted the canvas tents out of the hold and set them up in the ship's shadow, which provided some shelter from the wind. They were crowded, but they kept off the rain, which was soon pouring down in heavy sheets, soaking anyone who ventured out.

Karik and Ylmi shared their tent with Igil, Havar, Thora, Dranri, and Revik, whose bulk made the already small tent feel smaller.

"Well," Igil muttered as they watched the rain fall, "our voyage is off to a noble start."

"If you'd rather be attempting the Isles in this mess," Karik answered, "feel free to swim."

Havar looked out the tent door at the wind-lashed rain and cocked his head. "I do not think this will be uncommon," he said over the sound of the storm. "It may be that many ships which pass the Isles may need to shelter here for a time. Perhaps we should build here a haven of sorts, a place where ships and their crews may shelter when the winds howl and the sea rages."

Ylmi nodded, "If we return successful, there is much which will need to be built."

Havar glanced at her, then turned back to the rain.

The storm lasted through the night, breaking only a few hours before dawn. Karik woke to find Igil already out, watching the sky and guessing at the clouds against the patches of stars which shone through.

The wind was blowing steadily from the north, the cold waking Karik swiftly even as he slogged through the wet sand and squinted up at the sky above them.

"It promises a clear day," Igil muttered, "though it promised as much yesterday as well."

Karik wrapped his cloak around him a little tighter. "Wisic would ask us what else we expected."

With a chuckle, Igil shook his head. "I wish he were here, but I think he will enjoy drinking with the Allfather over pulling at an oar all day."

"There's still a chance we may all be with him before this day is out," Karik muttered. "There is strange magic around the Isles, and if the passage is real, it will take all our strength to make it."

Igil looked again at the wind and watched the tide rolling out on the beach. "Then we had best get to it."

Sea Dragon was pulled back into the water, and all that had been unloaded, replaced in the hull. More than once, Karik admonished Gorli for dragging his feet, and as they clambered on board, he saw Igil and Thora arguing with Gorli.

"What goes there?" he shouted over the rowing benches and suppressed a sigh when Gorli shouted back.

"Your man thinks to tell us what to do," the king's emissary shouted over the wind. "We are not..."

"He is a captain of this ship," Karik answered. "Do as he says or be left behind."

Gorli made to open his mouth, but one look at the crew made him think better of the idea, and soon, they were rowing back toward the mouth of the fjord.

Ylmi set her hand on his knee and braced herself against the stern timber. "Gorli and his men do not take well to orders."

"They do not," Karik agreed. "And it is a matter that we have let stand longer than we should have."

"They are Jarhost's men," Ylmi said, "and they feel it all too strongly." She fell silent, her eyes fixed on the northern sky.

Karik followed her gaze and felt his heart sink into his stomach. Dark clouds were again piling up on the horizon, riding the wind southward to intercept them as they approached the Isles.

"I do not think those are natural storms," Ylmi said quietly.

"You think they are as those that guard the Watching Stones?"

Ylmi nodded. "Sent by another and of a different magic, but I do not think we will be allowed to pass the Isles unmolested."

Havar, from his post on the prow, had seen the clouds, too, and now came striding past the rowing benches to Karik.

"Storms are coming again," he said when he reached them. "I say we push on. *Sea Dragon* is a strong ship, and if we can cross the Isles in a storm, then we can cross them in the calm."

"We have one chance," Karik said, "and the lives of forty men depend on us." He gritted his teeth. "I hate it, but I do not think the storms will let us pass. I agree with Havar."

He looked to Ylmi and saw her hand go to the small pouch that hung from her neck. Her one eye was fixed on the clouds, and the burned skin that covered the other side of her face twitched.

"We go." She turned to Karik, and he saw her jaw was set, a fire burning in her one eye that brought a smile to his face. There was no one he would rather chance the Isles with, and if they could not cross them here, today, with this crew and this ship, then the Isles truly were impassable.

"At the oars!" Ylmi called. "Stand ready, one and all! Two miles," she raised two fingers in the air as she shouted, "two miles and we will pass the Black Isles. Two miles, and all the world will lie before us. Two miles, and we will be remembered for a thousand years. Two miles, and your names will be spoken with that of Vranr and Vanik, his son!"

"There is a storm coming," Gorli's voice piped up, "surely you cannot mean to attempt the Isles with that storm..."

"What's the matter, mountain boy?" Revik laughed. "Scared of a little wind on the sea?"

"It's Vrania," Igil shouted from beside Karik. "There's always a storm coming."

A ripple of laughter went through the crew, and Gorli jumped up from his oar. But before he had taken a step toward the stern, Ylmi had *Raethbur* in her hand.

"Sit back down," she said quietly.

"Do not threaten me," Gorli snapped, "I am the king's..."

"You are a rower," Ylmi answered. "On this ship, you are a rower, and if you do not follow orders, you will die. Right here."

Gorli stared at her, a half-smile playing on his lips as he studied her, but Ylmi did not blink.

"A rower who does not follow orders," she said, "is more danger to us than the storm. Go back to your oar."

Gorli made to open his mouth, and there was a flash of steel. Ylmi stepped back, and a red line appeared on Gorli's cheek. He touched it and stared at the blood on his hand.

"Argue again, and I'll take your head," Ylmi snarled. "Now, are you going to row, or are you going to die?"

Gorli looked around at the crew, and it suddenly seemed to sink in that he did not have the power he had thought. He turned slowly back to his oar, but *Raethbur* tapped him on the shoulder.

"I asked you a question," Ylmi said. "Are you going to row, or are you going to die?"

"Row," Gorli muttered.

"Good!" Ylmi smiled brightly and slid her sword back into its sheath. "Then row." She pointed to the oar, and as Gorli turned back, she raised her voice.

"You all had your chance to leave two days ago. You've eaten our food, slept in our halls, and even then, we would have let you go with no complaint," her voice cut through the wind as it howled, and she grasped one of the ropes that supported the great mast for balance.

"But now, we approach bars of the prison that have long held us captive. There is no time for the faint of heart, no time for second thoughts. Now, we all sail together, side by side. One misstep, one moment of cowardice could undo us all, and doom to death the one next to you, the one who is straining every muscle and limb to keep you safe.

"So row. Row and remember that we are forging a path many will follow. A path that will bring us wealth and riches beyond our wildest dreams. So damn the winds, and damn the storm - this is our day, and by nightfall, we will look back upon these black rocks and drink to our victory. Onward!"

"Onward!" Karik echoed, and the sound of the crew's shouts rose for a moment, even over the sound of the howling wind.

Karik grinned at Ylmi as she walked by the rowing benches, clapping the shoulders of the men and women even as they set back to their oars.

"If we die today," he said, "it will not be because our jarl was a coward."

"Our king perhaps," Ylmi answered, "but not your jarl."

The wind was roaring now, and the dim light of the sun was fading as the clouds rolled thick across the sky, rising and falling upon the waves. *Sea Dragon* cut through the smaller swells with a splash that was snatched up by the wind, but glided up and down the greater swells.

"You have made a fine ship," Karik shouted over the oncoming storm, but Igil only wiped the spray from his face and shook his head.

"We will see what she is made of truly now," he shouted back, for rising out of the waves before them were the dark, jagged stones of the Black Isles.

CROSSING THE BLACK ISLES

Scattered through the waves, the Isles rose sharp and savage from the water, glistening from the waves that crashed upon them. Some rose high into the air, nearly as tall as *Sea Dragon's* mast, while others appeared as only shadows beneath the waves when a trough opened in the sea. No moss or lichen grew there that Karik could see, only broken rock and raging sea.

But now the test began, as the great currents gripped *Sea Dragon*, and Karik felt their strength as the rudder was jerked almost from his hand and the ship groaned as she was pulled sideways.

Igil and Ylmi were shouting orders, while Revik stood beside Havar in the prow. A long oaken pole was in his hand, bound with iron, while several of the other crew members stood behind him with oars. It would be their task to keep the ship off the rocks as best they could, if Karik's hand should fail him.

The sea roared and a great wave, driven by the northern storm, struck *Sea Dragon* amidships, staggering them all and adding to the growing pool of water in the hull.

In the prow, Havar pointed south, and Karik followed his arm, sighting the split peaks of one jagged rock that marked the entrance to their passage. He pushed rudder, wrestling against the sea, and *Sea Dragon* turned with a groan. But in the next instant, the wind had caught the sail, and they were jerked forward as the sea and the wind together seized the ship in their grasp and made to hurl her upon the rocks.

Faster and faster they sped, crashing through even the greatest waves as Igil and Ylmi struggled to pull down the sail until it clattered to the deck with Igil in tow, even as the current's grip tightened.

"Back oars!" Havar shouted, and with more clattering and scraping of oars upon one another than Karik liked, they did.

The wind in his ears and the first drops of rain mingling with the salt spray falling upon his neck, Karik watched the black rocks rushing closer. With deep breaths and clenched teeth, he tried to guess at their speed and the strength of the current.

"On my command!" he shouted into the roaring sea. "On my command, row forward."

Ylmi heard him, and she passed his word to Igil as he untangled himself from the sail, but how much of the crew had heard him, he could not tell.

"Better soon than late," he muttered to himself and hurled himself against the rudder.

Sea Dragon screamed as she slid sideways in the water, the planks beneath his feet creaking as the ship turned.

"Row!" he roared, and Igil and Ylmi took up his shout. Though her prow was toward the passage, the tide held *Sea Dragon* still in its grasp and continued pushing it toward the rocks.

Then the oars bit into the water, the crew shouting the rhythm together, and she moved forward even as she slid closer and closer to the rocks.

In the bow, Revik braced himself, his pole ready as the jagged rocks drew closer.

Slowly, oh so slowly, *Sea Dragon* picked up speed, easing into the passage and narrowly missing the rocks that bordered the entrance.

Karik let out a breath, but a shout from Havar caught his attention. At the bow, Revik was leaning forward, and Havar was pointing at something in the water.

Karik pulled the rudder, and *Sea Dragon* bit deep into the waves, shuddering as she turned. Revik and several with him were hard at work, pushing off something Karik could not see, their shouts carried away by the roaring wind.

They were amid the Isles now, black rock on all sides, the current swirling through the sharp stones, the wind keening as it blew through the towering cliffs about them. The rain was falling heavily, and Igil was pulling someone to bail water from the hull.

In his mind's eye, Karik could see the charts before him, the tiny lines and dark shapes brought to vivid life before him in the storm.

The passage bent back upon itself soon, and this was Karik's first great guess. For there was no great rock around which he could base his turn. Instead, the waves tossed and turned above rocks hidden beneath the deep. He could not see them, nor the narrow channel that was carved in their midst. He knew only that it was three lengths of *Sea Dragon's* hull past the closest formation of rock.

With a deep breath, Karik pushed the rudder, and the ship came about. A sudden slackness went through his shoulders, and he waited to feel the grinding crack as they struck the rocks.

But it did not come. *Sea Dragon* slipped through the waves, and the second turn was past.

Karik smiled now, for once might be luck, but twice meant the charts were true. Any doubt he had held was gone now, and he began to sing.

The third turn came and went, as did the fourth. Igil began switching out the rowers, for many began to tire, especially Gorli and his men, who were unused to being at sea.

As they approached the fifth turn, the storm turned dark. The gloom had hung heavy on them most of the day, but now the clouds overhead turned black, as though blotting out even the little light that slipped through. Lightning split the sky overhead, deafening them all with a thunderous boom that seemed to split the sky. The ship shuddered as Karik wiped the rain from his eyes.

The waves were growing stronger, rebounding from the rocky Isles back and forth, tossing *Sea Dragon* and jerking the rudder in his hand so that he slipped and slid on the deck trying to hold it steady.

The lightning boomed again, and in the flash of light, Karik saw the rocks ahead of them. His stomach twisted as he realized he had waited too long. He shoved the rudder, and again, *Sea Dragon* shuddered as she turned.

Over the screaming wind, he could hear Revik and Havar shouting, but he was already leaning as hard on the rudder as he could. With agonizing slowness, the ship turned. One rower suddenly turned and vomited, collapsing off his oar.

Igil wrenched him away and threw someone else in his place, but Havar was screaming something. Shouting frantically, he turned and ran to Igil and Ylmi. An instant later, they were pulling the oars in on the left side, shouting at the rowers and grabbing anyone who did not move swiftly enough.

On the bow, Revik braced his feet and lunged. Karik heard the crack of his iron-tipped staff as it met rock and saw Revik's mighty shoulders stark in the light from a bolt of lightning as the big man set himself against sea and stone, and pushed.

And then, *Sea Dragon* shivered. Karik felt it in his feet as her keel met rock, and the full force of the rowing and the wind and the currents pushed her against it.

Lighting flashed overhead, and Karik saw they were hard against a wall of black rock that rose only a little ways out of the water. *Sea Dragon* rose as a wave met her, then fell again, striking the rock with a muffled boom that shook the ship and sent half the crew sprawling from their benches.

Karik pulled at the rudder, but *Sea Dragon's* prow remained still, and though Karik could feel the deck rising beneath his feet, the roll of the ship back and forth ceased with a chilling suddenness.

From the bow, where he stood next to Revik, Havar turned to Karik and shouted over the winds, "We've stuck on the rocks!"

RISING STORMS

"Hold to the rudder!" Igil shouted at Karik, then he was running through the rain, down the slick boards of the ship toward the prow.

"You've run us aground!" Gorli shouted from his bench. "You said you knew a way through!"

Ylmi's voice cut through the wind like the crack of ice when it breaks in the spring. "Hold your tongue! And stand by your oar! Weeping will do nothing for us now."

Karik wiped the rain out of his eyes and looked out over the sea. For a moment, though the current was strong, the waves seemed to be fewer, many of the greater ones breaking upon the black rock of the Isles, wasting their strength upon the stone.

Yet it was only a matter of time, Karik was sure of it. Sooner or later, a wave would rise strong enough to slip through the stones or the wind would drive one up their path and shatter their ship upon the rocks. Only a little crack was all it would take...

"The ship is unbroken!" Igil called out as he turned away from Havar and made his way back toward Karik. "In a moment, we will be at war with the waves once again, so enjoy your reprieve!"

Karik took a deep breath as the deck beneath his feet rose slightly and again wiped away the rain.

"How bad is it?"

"We're stuck," Igil replied quickly. "The swell we were riding dropped us right between two rocks, we missed snapping the keel by only a few feet... we have Revik to thank for that."

"So what now?" Karik asked. "We wait for another swell?"

Igil glanced toward the sea. "That, or the wave that kills us."

"I don't like the sound of that," Ylmi said as she came up.

"When the next swell comes," Igil told them both, "we'll push off and row for our lives."

"The current will take us backwards," Karik muttered and glanced behind them. The black rocks rose out of the sea or appeared only in the trough between waves as the sea roiled behind them. "We have room... but not much."

"We'll see just how well you can manage this ship," Igil grinned. "But once we start forward..."

"Into the turn," Karik nodded. "But we'll need all the speed we can to not be run sideways back into the rocks."

"We'll be ready," Igil nodded, "I may not match my brother in strength, but I am no weakling." So saying, he turned back to the prow, snatching up one of the spare oars as he went and making himself ready.

"If it can be done, we are the ones to do it," Ylmi said. Her eyes were fixed on the sea as the rain poured down her face, her one eye afire as she glared at the storm.

Karik nodded but said nothing. Whatever curse was on him, whatever wyrd had planned for him, he had brought them here, and his battle with the sea was not yet over.

Out of the darkness, over the wind, he heard a great roaring crash and in the gloom, he saw the spray of a mighty wave shattered upon the rocks just off their bow.

"Here it comes!" he shouted, and beneath his feet, he felt the deck begin to rise.

The swell came swift and sudden, and for an instant, he felt *Sea Dragon* leave the grasp of the rocks and rise again in the grip of the sea.

In the prow, he could see the towering figure of Revik, hunched over as he pushed against the rock, attempting to shove the ship back out into the current. Beside him, Igil and Havar pushing in with all their might, their feet braced against *Sea Dragon's* frame as they bent their shoulders against the rock.

Then, with a grinding shudder, the bow slipped sideways, and the current snatched it.

"Push!" Igil roared. "Push!" The oars came out, and as the wave rose again, they pushed off against the rocks and off the stone that had struck them.

Backwards *Sea Dragon* slipped - the wind, the current, the waves all pushing her back toward Vrania.

"Row!" Ylmi shouted, and together with Thora, shouted out the rhythm. "Row! Row!" Through the wind and rain and crashing waves they called as Revik and Igil pushed away at the rocks that slipped by.

Once again, *Sea Dragon* groaned as her crew pulled her free of the sea's grip, and once more, she moved forward.

Again Karik saw the dark shapes rising out of the gloom before him, and again he set himself against the rudder to make the fifth turn. But where before they had gone too fast, now they came too slow.

As the ship turned, the current caught her and thrust her sideways, driving her toward the rocks.

"Row!" Thora shouted. "Pull steady and pull together!"

Ylmi was hurrying down toward the bow, and an instant later, she and Igil were at the side of the ship, catching the sharp cliff that loomed out of the rain to meet them. They pushed even as the crew pulled away at their oars, at Thora's counting.

"Not far now!" Karik called to them, "row but a little longer." And driven by fear, they rowed as few have ever rowed since. *Sea Dragon* rounded the fifth turn, with only two to go.

In the gloom and rain, Karik could not see the damage of the rock, but *Sea Dragon* still responded to his commands, so he sailed on. Havar and Igil were at work near the bow, working at something, but they said nothing to him.

Instead, he looked for the triple peak that marked the sixth turn of the passage. The rain was falling in heavy sheets now, mingling with the wind-tossed spray so that not a one of them was dry.

Through the gloom and the rain and the storm, he could see little but darkness ahead of them.

"Havar!" he shouted, "what is our heading!"

But the roaring wind tore away his words and tossed them into the crashing waves. His fingers slipped on the wet rudder and he gripped it tighter, wishing that - just for this one day - he might have his fingers back. Thunder boomed in the clouds above them, but whatever lightning bolt accompanied it was hidden in the clouds, and Karik shouted again for Havar.

Havar's head jerked up. He was looking, not at Karik, but to the bow. Revik was shouting something, his eyes fixed ahead, and Karik saw suddenly that Revik was bracing.

Frantically, Karik pulled on the rudder, desperately trying to pull her about, for he knew they must be upon the sixth turn and driving straight for the three-headed Isle.

There was a sudden *crack* and *Sea Dragon* jerked, scrapping and skipping over the waves as she turned. Karik looked up and saw the dark shape of Revik in the bow, straining with his ironclad staff against the rocks as the waves and current pressed the ship toward them.

There was the sound of rocks scraping on wood, but it was high and clear, the sound of impact above the water, and not so violent as to break the sturdy beams Igil and Havar had crafted into *Sea Dragon's* hull.

Out of the shadows, the dark shape of black rock came suddenly hurtling closer through the pouring rain. *Sea Dragon* was turning, her stern swinging back to the rocks. Lightning flashed overhead, suddenly illuminating the black stone rising high out of the sea to tower in three jagged pillars far above *Sea Dragon's* mast. There was a crack as the lightning hit the stone high above, and the light was gone as the jagged rocks reached for *Sea Dragon*.

Without thinking, Karik reached out his right hand, desperate to keep the rocks from shattering the rudder. His hand met the wet rock, slick and cold, just as the waves pushed them together. He felt the rudder jerk beside his body, but there was no crack, and he felt the ship pull away.

Just as he let out a sigh, there was a dull thud as a rock, broken from above by the lighting, fell like an ax upon his hand.

In an instant, he jerked his hand back, and the black stone disappeared from view. He glanced down and saw his hand covered in blood, the small finger hanging by only a bit of torn skin.

He stared at it, and then, as the pain throbbed through him, he laughed.

So the Watcher was real or at least here still in some way. And it had taken another finger... as he passed the sixth turn in the prison the Watcher was supposed to guard.

Holding the rudder steady under his left arm, Karik pulled his knife from his belt, chuckling madly as he did so. He set his hand upon the rudder's handle, and with a swift blow from his knife, severed the pulped mass from his hand.

"You want my fingers?" he shouted into the storm, "then you are welcome to them!" And he hurled it back into the storm behind them. Let the Watcher demand payment. If it was only a few fingers to pass the Isles, then let him have his due and have done.

Blood was streaming down his hand now, but Karik did not care. The pain drove all weariness from his body and he felt as though fire and ice burned through his veins. All the ancient forces of the Watcher and the Five Kings and everyone else who had banished Vranr, had fought to keep him stranded upon Vrania, and now he was one turn away from defeating them all.

Ylmi and Igil were rotating the rowers again, and Karik took a deep breath. The worst of his part was almost over, but the rowers were just beginning. Upon the charts, after the seventh turn, it was a straight line to the open sea. But between the dark dots of the Isles, there had been drawn four heavy, dark arrows back into the channel, indicating a heavy, swift current. They would have to row through it, with the wind howling down out of the north.

"Half a mile!" he heard Ylmi shout. "Half a mile and we're legends!"

"Half a mile!" Igil took up the shout, and Karik grinned. They were so close. They could not fail now.

He glanced down as his hand slipped again on the rudder, and he saw it was slick with his blood. Cursing, he wiped it off with his cloak, but his finger continued to bleed.

Igil was the closest to him, and with a shout he called him back. "Bandage my hand, it's getting the rudder slick," he shouted into Igil's ear when he was close.

Igil looked at him in confusion, then with wide eyes as Karik raised his right hand.

"By the nine realms, Karik!" he shouted, but Karik only laughed and cut a piece off his cloak.

"We're close, Igil. We're so close."

Igil's hands were swift. He bound half of Karik's hand tight together, the salt spray mingling with blood so that Karik snarled with the pain. As he tightened the knot, Igil leaned close and gripped him by the shoulder. "Are you good to go on?"

"I am," Karik shouted back through the roaring storm. "This is not the first finger I've lost."

Igil shook his head and turned back. "We are approaching the last turn."

"The Watcher and his curses be damned!" Karik shouted over the howling wind, "we're almost through."

Igil looked at him for a moment, then shook his head.

"Half a mile!" Karik grinned.

"Half a mile!" Igil agreed and returned to the rowers.

A pale light was growing in the east, and by it Karik could see the two low Isles overshadowed by a third that marked the seventh turn and the beginning of the last run.

Carefully, he guided *Sea Dragon* over the waves, around the small bits of jagged rock that poked over the waves, betraying the presence of the invisible ship breakers.

Then, at long last, he pulled on the rudder and *Sea Dragon* turned east, toward the open sea.

The channel opened before them, narrow here but gradually widening as it reached seaward. Black rocks shone damp and jagged on either side, waves rushing in from the open sea to pile up and crash upon them. The ship bucked and jerked as the waves took hold and began trying to push it backwards upon the rocks, and in an instant, all her forward momentum was gone.

"Row!" Igil and Ylmi were shouting, building a chant to keep time as thirty oars rose and fell in the water. Gorli and several others were slumped upon the ballast stones and gear, their mouths hanging open in exhaustion.

Sea Dragon shuddered and groaned, the planks feeling the pull of the current and the push of the rowers as they strained at the oars. For an agonizing second, the ship seemed to stand still.

Then, Revik threw down his pole in the bow and strode to the center of the ship, his arm raised, pointed at Igil.

"Come brother!" he roared over the sound of the wind and waves. "Enough shouting. Let us show these men how to pull at an oar."

He pulled aside one man, who slumped to the deck, and settled at the oar, pulling it in great heaving motions that Karik feared would snap the oak in half. Igil, a dark grin on his face, relieved the rower on the opposite side and pulled, his long arms and legs working the oar in a smooth rhythm.

Holding her balance against the mast, Ylmi raised her voice and called out the rhythm. "Pull! Pull! Pull!"

The rest of the crew - those who had breath - joined in, and soon the ship, the rocks, and the passage echoed with their chant as the oars rose and fell, rose and fell.

For his part, Karik leaned against the rudder, straining to hold *Sea Dragon* steady, for while the current tried to push them back, the wind was howling out of the north to push them sideways. So while the crew battled the current, Karik battled the wind, and slowly they crept eastward.

Behind them, the thunder boomed, lighting splitting the sky as if a battle between storms was raging over the Black Isles.

"Not far now!" Ylmi shouted. "Only a little longer."

Karik winced as the pain in his hand seemed to grow and a cramp pricked him in his leg. The rudder was shaking now, the current wavering as the wind howled and screamed out of the north.

"Pull! Pull! Pull!" The chant echoed over the rocks, and Karik felt *Sea Dragon* picking up speed. Suddenly, he felt her slice through a wave instead of rolling over it, and he looked up as Ylmi shouted in triumph.

"We are through!"

Fire burned through him and, turning back to the Isles, he roared his defiance. They had won! Whatever dark magic the Watcher had woven about the Isles was broken, and they were free.

"Oars in!" Havar cried. "Let her run upon the wind!"

Igil pulled in his oar and leaped up to grasp him for a mighty hug, and the two shipbuilders laughed as their ship rose and fell upon the waves, triumphant over her greatest obstacle.

From bow to stern, the crew laughed and cheered, even as most of them laid on the deck, exhausted from their battle with the sea and wind. They had survived the crossing and had come farther than any of their forefathers. Now before them lay open sea and a good wind.

"The way is found," Revik shouted over the boat, and Karik grinned.

"I told you there was a way!" he shouted back. "Aren't you glad you didn't run to some mountain hall?"

"What are you talking about?" Revik replied. "Not in a hundred years would you have made it through without me!"

There was a roar of laughter as they shouted, and Karik winced at the cramps that stuck in him as he laughed.

"Fair enough," he chuckled, and he clasped Revik in a one-armed hug as the big man embraced him.

"I told you we would find a way through," Karik told Ylmi as she took a seat beside the rudder.

"So you did," she replied with a smile. "Now let us see what we will find in the west."

LANDFALL

To Ylmi's delight, the storm did not last long once they had passed the Isles, and soon they were sailing beneath a clear blue sky with a gentle breeze filling their sail. Karik was so ecstatic that even when Igil seared his finger, he laughed.

"There is something wrong with you," Igil told him.

"Other than that I can't keep my fingers?" Karik grinned.

Igil chuckled but nodded as he finished cleaning the wound. "There is something dark chasing you. Let us hope it is satisfied with your fingers."

"You seem troubled?" Ylmi sat next to him, her fur cloak drying in the sun.

Karik forced a smile and raised his hands. "I match Vranr now," he said, "or at least so much as the tales tell."

"You're deflecting," Ylmi pressed.

Slowly, Karik sighed. "I am worried. My mother warns me of greed and danger that will come from this crossing, and there is the dragon's curse to consider. When the Black Isles stood before me, I knew my challenge and bent myself to meet it. But I do not know from where the next challenge will come."

"I can hazard a guess," Ylmi muttered, her eyes going to where Gorli sat on the rowing benches with Regvar.

Karik followed her eyes and grunted. "I would not care to wager against you there. Let us hope it is an empty land we find, with forests we can hunt and rivers we can fish. We have had enough of bad jarls and greedy kings."

"We will meet the next challenge as we have met the others," Ylmi said with a deep breath, "together. Why else do we gather mighty friends and make ourselves strong, if not to withstand the storms of fate?"

"Even so." Karik sighed and hung his head. For a moment, he did not speak, listening only to the sound of *Sea Dragon* rushing through the water and the feel in his feet as she rose and fell on the waves. "We will do our best, and if the gods do not bless our choices, then we will meet the consequences as they come."

"With good friends and sturdy walls," Ylmi smiled at him.

For two days they sailed thus, watching the stars by night and the sun by day, holding a steady course west by southwest. All eyes strained toward the horizon as the wind filled their sail and *Sea Dragon* rushed over the waves.

As the sun sank low in the west for the third time since they sailed, Havar cried out from the bow where he stood watch.

"Land!"

So sudden was the rush forward that Igil, standing at the rudder, blew a blast upon his horn and ordered everyone to remain at their benches. Slowly, he brought *Sea Dragon* around, and everyone looked out to see a green mass in the distance.

"What is that?" Gorli asked.

"The lands of the west!" Revik laughed. "Our voyage is a success."

"No," Gorli shook his head petulantly, "I meant, what country is that? What people are we to meet?"

"No idea," Karik replied. "That's why we are here."

"How are any of us to have an answer for that?" Revik asked in a loud voice, but he only grinned when Gorli gave him a withering glare.

It was twilight when they sailed into a small inlet and landed on a soft beach that rose into a gentle forest. Karik was the first out of the boat, with Ylmi close behind, and they among Vranr's children were the first to return from Vrania.

Together, they splashed through the surf and onto the shore, where smooth gravel rolled beneath their feet and the sound of birds filled the air.

"We made it," Karik grinned, and Ylmi nodded, a wide smile twisting the dragon scars on her face.

Behind them, half the crew splashed ashore, laughing and marveling as they felt new land beneath their feet.

When the first shock of it was past, *Sea Dragon* was drawn up on the beach, and Ylmi gathered the crew about her.

"Exploration is best left for the morning," she said. "For tonight, let us rest and rejoice in what we have accomplished. All of you have accomplished a great feat, and though there is a great deal of work before us, tonight let us eat, be full, and thank the gods that we have come so far!"

So bonfires were lit along the beach, *Sea Dragon's* rations lifted from the hull, and all ate freely in their light and warmth.

"We are off to a good start," Igil said as he took his seat by Ylmi's fire. "There is not a soul in sight."

"It will be hard to raid if we find no one here," Havar grumbled.

Karik swallowed the dry meat he had been chewing and shook his head. "That is not an ill thing," he said to Havar. "Hunting is safer than raiding. If there is no one here, then we can hunt in peace... *Sea Dragon* can carry a great deal of food back home... and when spring comes, then this may make a good place to build a new home."

"Until we see more of this place," Ylmi said, "we cannot tell what will happen or what will be the best course. In the morning, we will hunt and see what manner of land we have come to."

As the fires burned low and the company fell one by one into a weary sleep, Karik sat with Ylmi and watched the moon rising over the trees.

"I thought you would be happier," Ylmi said. "Since we first met, crossing the Isles has been foremost in your mind."

"I have a bad feeling about this place," Karik admitted, "and the dragon's curse worries me even more... I grow more anxious with every passing moment."

Ylmi chuckled. "I think we are used to things going poorly for us, and it will be good to enjoy success for a moment."

"Even so," Karik said. For a moment he was silent, staring into the fire. "I hope we find no one on this journey."

"I, as well," Ylmi replied. "But even if we do, there is no reason to cower before them as we do before Jarhost. Only one ship has sailed the Black Isles, and it is ours. We will not seek out conflict, but we will not bow before fools to avoid it."

⎯⎯⎯◆⎯⎯⎯

Ylmi woke the next morning before dawn broke. The birds were beginning to sing in the trees, and the sound of the sea rolling into the beach was louder than it had been in the fjord.

Her stomach growled, and she shook the sleep from her eyes. It would be good to eat fresh food before they began exploring the land they'd come to, and dawn was as good a time for hunting as any.

She rose to her feet and, taking her bow, she passed through the camp and set off through the trees. The land rose slowly upward away from the sea. The forest was loud with the sounds of birds and thick with the smell of rain and moss.

In Vrania, the forests were swept by cold winds often on mountain slopes, but here there was little more than a cool breeze meandering through the boughs of trees overhead. Ylmi breathed in again the scent of the forest and smiled.

Karik had seemed to enjoy the ship, but the forest was where Ylmi felt at home, and this was by far the most peaceful forest she had ever seen. Rabbits or some other rodent dashed off through the underbrush, and overhead, a pair of squirrels chased each other through the branches. They were fat - fatter than any squirrel Ylmi had seen - and she shook her head.

A little further on, a faint trail heavy with deer tracks wound through the trees northward. She followed it, marking that the tracks were deep in the soft earth. If the deer were as fat as the squirrels, it might be difficult to carry one all the way back to the shore.

The trail bore the signs of a few human footprints, but they were old - barely visible beneath the markings of deer, wolves, and other animals she did not recognize. The morning light was beginning to filter through the trees, golden beams piercing the canopy of leaves to shine pale light on the forest floor, and Ylmi smiled again.

The deer appeared out of the trees ahead of her, a whole herd of them with the thick, dark coats signifying age, and one held his head high beneath a crown of antlers that dwarfed anything Ylmi had seen in all her years of hunting.

Slowly, she picked her way closer, then raised her bow and loosed an arrow in one fluid motion. The deer exploded, dashing off into the forest in every direction, save one that soon collapsed with Ylmi's arrow protruding from its heart.

When she stood over it, Ylmi could hardly believe her eyes. She had picked the smallest one she saw, thinking of the long walk she had back to the camp, but even still... the deer before her was larger than any she had ever seen in Vrania. She laughed, for all her hopes had been granted.

They had crossed the Isles. They had found the old world, and it was rich. Even if they found no one, they could hunt here for a few days and take back enough food to nearly double what they had stored in Dragonsrest.

She drew her knife and set about gutting the deer, hoping that it would not weigh too much when all was done.

She had not worked long when a sudden shout made her jump.

Five men were coming toward her, armed with bows and spears, with helms on their heads and some form of leather armor.

They gestured at her and the deer, shouting and shaking their heads. Ylmi rose quickly and spread her palms out to show she meant them no harm.

"I have come from over the sea," she said slowly, "I am only gathering food."

One man looked at her strangely, but the others only laughed and pointed their spears at her, slowly spreading out around her.

"I want no trouble," Ylmi said again, but they seemed to understand her as little as she did them. Their leader barked a command at her, but she could only shrug.

They had surrounded her now, and the spear points were getting closer than she liked. Her bow was propped against the deer, and her knife was near to it, but they saw her eyes flick toward it and surged toward her.

She got her hand on one spear and yanked it, sending one man sprawling, but before she could free it from his grasp, the others were on her, beating her down with their spear shafts. She tried to stay upright, but one knee was struck from the back and she slipped, even as she struggled to defend herself. Then, out of the flurry of blows, one caught her on the head and all went dark.

A Strange Land

It was strange for Karik to see the sun coming up over the sea instead of behind mountains, but the joy of the successful crossing filled his chest as he sat on the beach.

The forest behind them seemed to teem with life, and a few of the crew had already gone hunting for their breakfast. The rest were enjoying the warmth of the rising sun and the lack of sudden work that needed doing.

"Well," Igil said from over his shoulder. "You were right. The charts work, and we've found the old lands."

"They are uninhabited so far," Karik nodded. "Let us hope they remain so."

Igil eased down to sit next to him. "Why so? I thought you'd be happy to find people we can trade with."

"Perhaps, but I have little desire to bend the knee to another king." Karik took a deep breath. "I would be happy to find others, once we have land where we can settle. Any we find here will likely be trouble... and I would rather see us safe away from Vrania before we start a war."

"Let us hope, then, that we encounter no one on this voyage," Igil grinned. "Perhaps we can carve out a place for ourselves here."

"That is my hope," Karik replied. "But enough lying about." He stood and slapped his thigh. "Let us see to the ship."

The work went swiftly, and while they worked, a moment did not pass that someone did not return to the camp with a deer or pull a fish out of the water. The air was filled with the smell of roasting meat, and they ate as they worked, laughing and smiling as they tightened *Sea Dragon's* rivets, re-patched the tar that had cracked along the hull, and tightened the seams in the sail that the wind had loosened.

When the sun was full over the sea, Karik walked through the camp, looking to see if Ylmi had returned from her hunting. Finding her nowhere, he stopped Thora as she appeared out of the trees.

"Did you see Ylmi in the forest?" he asked her.

Thora shook her head. "She was gone before I woke," she said. "She should have been back by now."

Karik nodded, glancing into the forest. Ylmi was no fool and would not have allowed herself to wander too far... so why was she not back?

They each took their weapons, and together he and Thora set off into the forest, following the faint trail Ylmi had left behind.

"These forests have more game than I have ever seen," Thora said as they walked. "I saw more tracks in a short walk than I have seen this whole year in Vrania."

"Let us hope the game is the only thing out here," Karik replied. There was a sick feeling growing in his stomach, and he kept imagining he saw the flash of Ylmi's hair in what turned out to be nothing more than waving branches.

They found Ylmi's footprints on a small trail heading north, and for a little ways, Karik breathed easier.

But not for long. They came into a small clearing and found a wide area of trampled grass with blood stains scattered over the grass and pools of blood soaking into the leaves of the forest floor. Karik felt as though a stone had fallen into his stomach.

"We are not alone," Thora said quietly. Her eyes came up, and she looked about through the trees. "There are others in this forest."

"How long ago, do you guess?" Karik gestured at the blood.

"An hour or two," Thora replied. "She killed a deer and started to gut it... they must have come on her then."

"Follow the trail," Karik said as he turned back the way they had come, "but be careful. I will gather our company and return here."

"Be quick," Thora said darkly. "Not all this blood is from a deer."

Karik sprinted back to the beach, ducking around branches as he cursed himself for not waking earlier, for not going with Ylmi. He should have warned everyone to be careful...

They had all been so happy to have crossed the Isles, and he had forgotten to be as careful as he should have. The branches whipped against his face as he dashed through the forest, the warmth gone out of it. Who had taken her, and why? How far would they have to go to find her?

If they waited too long, whoever had taken Ylmi might find their ship. If they damaged it, then there was no way to return home. And how long would the crew wait before determining there was no point in waiting to find her?

He would not leave without her. That was a simple choice. If need be, he would let them sail back to Vrania. He would stay to find Ylmi, and they would meet the ship when it returned.

He took a deep breath. He was letting his mind get ahead of him. The first step was to find her, and Thora had said the trail was easily followed. The next thing they had to discover was who had taken her. Was it a small group of bandits? Or the company of a jarl?

A dozen faces turned toward him as he came running out of the woods.

"Prepare to move!" he shouted and found Havar and Igil speaking by the ship.

"Someone has taken Ylmi," he said as he joined them. "Thora is following the trail, expecting us to follow."

"We should leave some to guard the ship," Igil nodded and turned away.

"I had a bad feeling about this," Havar muttered. "We should have sailed longer along the shore to see better where we were."

"Perhaps," Karik replied. "But it is too late for that now."

Revik appeared next to him, his big ax already out in his hand. "How many are we facing?"

"No idea," Karik replied. "Thora is following their trail. We'll make a plan when we find her."

It felt an eternity to Karik, but it was only a few minutes before Havar and Igil had gathered thirty men and were ready to march. The rest would stay to guard the ship.

"I wish there was a way that we didn't need to bring Gorli and the rest," Karik muttered to Igil, "yet I do not wish to leave them with the ship."

"They've been spoiling for a fight," Igil responded just as quietly. "And perhaps they'll get one. If they all get killed in the fighting... that's not our fault."

When Igil nodded they were ready, Karik plunged back into the forest, following Ylmi's path. Revik walked beside him, the big man's long legs eating up the distance as they went, but Karik still felt that they moved too slowly.

"Calm yourself, Karik," Revik said quietly as they went. "There is nothing to be gained by sprinting hither and thither. You'll only arrive exhausted, and I feel that we have a fight coming on... my burns are itching."

"And my hand hurts," Karik snapped back.

They reached the small clearing, and Karik led them past the blood to where Thora had marked a tree. The path taken by Ylmi's kidnappers was wide and clear, the grass beaten down and branches broken out of the way so that Karik hardly needed Thora's marks to follow it.

They had not gone far before the trees suddenly parted to reveal a narrow track running north and south, with Thora's marks pointing north.

"Now, we run," Karik said grimly. The track was clearly often used, which meant there were more than a few bandits or hunters nearby, and the situation seemed to grow worse with every step they took.

Revik set the pace, his long legs eating up the distance as they loped steadily down the road. All of them, even Gorli and his men, were used to the steep, high mountains of Vrania where the air grew thin and cold. But here, the ground was level and the air thick, so that as they ran, it felt as though they gained strength.

The road led them through the forest, with heavy trees on all sides, and in a few places, it crossed small streams. Deer and squirrels they saw in abundance, but now was not the time for hunting.

The sun was standing high overhead when they reached the edge of the forest. Thora was waiting for them in the trees and quickly urged them off the path.

"Get into the trees," she hissed, "there are lookouts."

The underbrush was so thick that it was not difficult for the entire party to melt into the forest, and a moment later, it was as if they had never been there at all.

"Have you found her?" Karik asked, and Thora nodded grimly.

She pointed out of the forest. "In front of the longhouse with a tower." Beyond the trees, Karik looked out onto enormous fields thick with grain, and past them, the makings of what looked to be a small town. In the center of the buildings rose a stone tower. Beside it was built a longhouse, and in front of that, Karik could see a small figure tied to a pole.

"If we charge in now," Igil said, glancing over his shoulder, "they'll kill her before we can get close or use her as hostage."

Karik glanced back at him. "Who asked you?"

"You were thinking of charging in..." Igil replied quietly. "I just didn't want you getting attached to the idea." He glanced toward Thora. "How many warriors?"

"I've counted at least thirty," Thora replied. "But there could be more. This is a small settlement, but I think someone important lives here, and there have been companies of soldiers patrolling about the whole time."

Gorli stepped up next to them and peered through the trees. "This is far better than hunting. We can carry off more in an hour than we could hunt in a day."

"That may be," Karik said tightly. "But we must first see how best to get our jarl."

New Jarls

Ylmi winced as she adjusted her hands in the ropes again. She was sitting bound to the pole, her hands tied behind her, and her shoulders were aching. And to top it all off, she was being yelled at in a language she didn't understand.

One of the soldiers was questioning her, but her eyes were focused on the man wearing a silver wire on his head. He seemed to be the ruler here, laughing as he glanced her way, and she had the distinct suspicion that he was just Jarhost with a cruel streak.

They were mad at her for killing the deer, that much she had figured out, but she could not imagine why or what she was supposed to do about it now.

"I can't understand," she gasped for the hundredth time, "what you're saying!" She was hungry and so thirsty that her throat hurt with the words, but it was all useless. She was rewarded with a slap that made her ears ring, and she looked up to see the soldier shrug toward his jarl.

The jarl seemed to consider a moment, then nodded. Giving a few quick words, he turned and made his way back into his hall.

Ylmi guessed Karik had noticed her absence by now, and as she didn't see anyone else being brought in from the forest, she found it likely none of them had been captured as well. Thora could easily track her to this village... so she was not completely alone.

It felt that she was, though. A few people who walked by seemed to be sorry for her, but judging by their ragged clothes and dirty appearance, she didn't think they were in any position to help her. Somewhere, a smith was hammering, and she watched as a few horses were brought from a long barn for riders who galloped off northward. She had heard of horses before, but she had never seen them, and for just a moment she marveled at their size.

She was brought back to her situation when one of the soldiers spit on her as he went by. They all seemed to think this was a fun joke, and she was looking forward to seeing their faces when Revik finally appeared.

Suddenly, her heart dropped and her breath froze. Two of the soldiers were busy working on a strange platform that stood before the hall and they had just hung a noose from the top.

They were going to hang her.

It seemed ridiculous, all over a deer? But there was the noose, and here she was, tied up and her ears still ringing from the beating she had taken. Something might have gone wrong with Karik. They might have run into another patrol. She had no way of knowing.

Although... her eyes narrowed. If this was because of Gorli...

She could not count on them to come and save her. She would have to do it herself. The ropes that had bound her hands were less than tight, and as she twisted, burning her wrists, she felt a slick wetness on her fingers and knew she was bleeding.

As the sun drifted down, she worked at the ropes. It burned her wrists as the ropes sawed back and forth, but she could get little purchase on the knots.

The sun sank low and the sound of the smith's hammer stopped as all seemed to come in from their work. A bonfire was being built before the noose now, and Ylmi wondered if she was to be burned as well as hung. What kind of deer had she been hunting?

Suddenly, she was aware of a man crouching next to her, and she flinched back, but he only muttered something soothingly and held up a cup. His beard was short and white, and he had the marks of soot on his face and fingers.

One soldier shouted at him, but the old man shouted back and gestured at the noose. The soldier grunted but stepped back, and the old man held the cup to Ylmi's lips.

She sipped cautiously, and when she tasted the cold water, it was all she could do to not gulp it down at once. The old man reached up to steady her as she drank, and she felt something fall into the dirt beside her hands.

The old man was muttering again, but Ylmi still could not understand him. She shook her head at him and he seemed to grow frustrated but at last just shrugged. He tapped her wrists gently as he rose.

The soldiers snapped at him and jerked their heads as if ordering him away and, with one last look at Ylmi, he obeyed.

She leaned her head back on the post and took a deep breath. The taste of water had reawakened her thirst, and she felt almost crazy with it now. Her tongue was dry and her throat felt like a cracked riverbed that has run dry and baked in the sun.

She shifted and her hands bumped into something in the dirt. Slowly, her fingers felt around behind her and settled on something small and metal. She turned it over in her fingers... and nearly cut herself on the sharp edge of a knife. It was tiny, not much bigger than a finger, but it was enough.

Her eyes went to the old man, walking slowly into one of the rough huts that stood near the hall, and she wondered what he had been trying to accomplish. Was it so common for someone to be tied to this stake that he thought to free her?

She swallowed at the dryness in her mouth and winced at the pain in her throat. Whatever he meant, there was no point in throwing away a chance at escape.

She began sawing through the ropes, then halted.

It would do no good to be free of the ropes if she didn't have a plan. She'd just end up right back here and without a knife.

Attempting to do so without drawing attention, she counted the soldiers she could see... there were fifteen in her view and likely to be more about. She guessed they would converge quickly, and even without the element of surprise they'd had that morning, she doubted she could hold off an entire army by herself.

There were precious few houses around her. The nearest shelter was the forest. She could see it to the south, the trees growing dark with the oncoming dusk, the heavy boughs waving in the gentle wind, and she could almost hear the brook gurgling within it, full of cool, cold water...

She shook her head. She had to focus. They were lighting the fire, and she could see the jarl walking out of his hall to watch. They would hang her when the fire was at its brightest, which would be soon, and if she didn't do something soon, it might be too late.

The road was only a little ways off, and it led straight to the forest. The first trees were perhaps half a mile away... if she could make it, to the trees then she had a chance. She could kill the soldiers as they came after her or hide if they all came together. She doubted there were any here who could match her in the woods.

The sun had sunk behind the longhouse and the shadows were growing long. There seemed to be a celebration of some sort going on, and the jarl was drinking with several soldiers.

Ylmi breathed deeply, filling her lungs with the warm air. Hunger she was used to, but the thirst was new. She swallowed, trying to wet her throat, and silently thanked the old man who had given her a drink. Another deep breath, and she parted the ropes that bound her hands.

A third breath she took, feeling the muscles in her legs and preparing for her chance. The guards nearest her were only a few feet away, but they had been brought drink.

Ylmi only needed a few steps, and she could beat them to the woods. She took another deep breath as the closest soldier lifted his cup...

And then she was on her feet.

She staggered, slipping on the dust, but in an instant she had recovered and was running. Her feet found the smooth ground of the road, and she began to sprint.

Shouts rang out behind her, a few at first, then a clamor. But Ylmi's eyes were fixed on a broad oak at the edge of the forest. It seemed incredibly far and already she was tiring. All day with no food and little water seemed to fill her limbs with stone, making each stride laborious and painful. There was no way she could out run them for long.

But she fixed her eyes on the oak, straining and pushing herself to reach it. If she could just reach the forest, she had a chance. Spread out, she could pick them off one by one... perhaps.

She was sucking in air now, deep breaths that ripped at her parched throat, but her limbs still obeyed, and she felt the ground eaten away beneath her as each stride took her closer to the oak. Something seemed to move in the field next to the road, but Ylmi fixed her eyes on the tree and willed herself onward.

She heard steps behind her, but the oak was close now, and with a silent prayer, she commanded her legs to go faster. They obeyed, and with long strides she sailed past the oak and into the gloom of the forest.

She turned, moving backward into the forest, and saw that nearly ten soldiers had followed her on her sprint. But they were all strung out, the first a few yards away and the others even further.

Ylmi stopped, eyeing the soldier coming toward her. He slowed, but not enough, and in an instant, Ylmi was past his spear and on him, driving the tiny knife up under the cheek piece of his helmet. He fell, pressing his hands to the flow of blood.

But Ylmi had his spear. She killed the next soldier in an instant, but none followed.

Out of the field and through the trees, dark shapes rose as if from the shadows themselves, cutting down the soldiers who had chased her with eerie silence.

One shape came toward her, a long dark sword in its hand, and Ylmi recognized Karik, though his face and hands were covered in soot and mud.

"Took you long enough," she gasped.

"You are hurt," he caught her as she stumbled.

She shook her head. "Thirsty." Someone pressed a water skin into her hand and she drank deeply, heedless of the water spilling around her mouth.

"So it is a jarl like Unhost," Karik said, glancing toward the village. Trumpets were blaring now and the bonfire was full alight. There did not seem to be any urgency to the movements, and as she swallowed the water, Ylmi guessed that they had not seen their comrades cut down.

"It may be a king," she gasped. Her lungs still ached, and each breath felt like a knife to her chest. "I do not know which. He has a number of soldiers with him... but we can match them."

"You want us to storm the village?" Thora asked. She looked fearsome, her face and hair slicked back with mud, and the red light of the distant bonfire glinting off the edge of her spear.

"Storm the village, take what we can, and sail home," Ylmi ordered. "I do not wish to be captured again, and when we come back, we will have to be far more cautious and secretive."

"We could wipe them out..." Gorli already had his sword drawn. "And pick through what they have stored."

Ylmi glanced toward him. "When you raid Viglir, and he raids you...is that how things are done?"

"This is not Vrania," he replied in answer.

"We have no wish to start a war," Karik said, "though I feel less generous toward the men who bound my wife."

Wincing, Ylmi took a sip of the water and felt it begin to soothe her throat. "I did not say we should give them gifts. But neither will we burn everything to the ground."

She drank again and hefted the spear she had taken from the soldier. "There is no point in dawdling. We will take what we can, quickly, and kill as few as we can. There was an old man who gave me aid. Pass the word and make ready."

There was a company of soldiers gathering among the scattered buildings, silhouetted against the firelight, and Ylmi guessed they could see little of what was passing here on the edge of the forest.

As Karik and Igil moved off through the trees, Ylmi grabbed Thora by the arm. "You followed the trail here?"

Thora's teeth flashed in the darkness. "I did."

"Can we make it back to the ship tonight? Or should we perhaps wait here till morning?"

Thora laughed quietly. "Ylmi, I can get us all back to the ship easily enough, even if there were not a full moon."

"I will hold you to that." Ylmi rolled her shoulders again and winced. She had caught her breath, but the adrenaline was draining away, and the ache of hunger seemed to sink into her very spine.

Glancing to her left, she saw Karik waiting in the trees, and on her right, Igil and Revik were watching her.

Raising her spear, she thrust it forward.

They came out of the trees with no cries or shouts, only the glint of iron with the lengthening shadow of the forest. Night was near at hand, the sunlight gone, save for the last few rays that lingered on roofs or on the western side of the village.

The soldiers who had gathered looked out, first laughing to see Ylmi, unpainted as she was, then with widening eyes as they saw the company that approached them. Several stared, dumbstruck, but two turned and ran shouting toward the jarl's longhouse, and a few moments later a horn sounded from atop the tower.

Ylmi began to jog slowly, but her warriors took the signal and, with a roar, charged into the village. She saw Karik, his long sword flashing as he cut through one group of soldiers, and she saw Revik sending others sailing through the air, his great ax swinging back and forth.

Horsemen were galloping away on the road north, and though a few fell to the scattered arrows her company sent after them, most escaped.

It was over in a few moments, and Ylmi looked around the village where she had spent the day tied to a pole. It was small, only a few houses along with the longhouse and tower. Too small for a proper village. There were barely enough houses to hold the people she had seen, and as she glanced again at the tower, she wondered if this was some sort of outpost... but what kind of outpost had such a magnificent hall?

"I posted lookouts on the road north," Karik said as he came up behind her. "And we found a sheep pen."

There was a thok, and Ylmi looked behind her to see an arrow quivering in the ground. "Archers!" she shouted and glanced up at the tower.

Karik grunted, then grabbed her arm and pulled her to stand against one of the stone houses.

"The tower?" Ylmi asked.

"The tower," Karik agreed, snapping an arrow off from his shoulder. "Shall we storm it?"

Ylmi paused for a moment, then shook her head. "We take what we can and go. We do not know if they may have reinforcements nearby, and above all else, we must return home with a full ship."

Karik nodded and sprinted away. A pair of arrows sank into the ground behind him as he ran, and Ylmi peered around the corner up at the tower. She could barely see the glint of helmets high above in the dying light of the bonfire.

A hand on her shoulder made her jump, but when she looked, it was Thora, holding out her bow and quiver.

"Found these for you," she said. "Figured you could use them."

Ylmi smiled as her hand closed around the familiar grip of her bow, and she slung the quiver over her back. "Many thanks," she grinned. "For this, and for bringing an army to my rescue."

Thora nodded. "I do not have so many friends that I can afford to lose them easily." She drew an arrow and looked toward the tower. "Shall we?"

Together, they stepped out. Ylmi's eye locked onto the distant glint of a helmet, and she loosed. Her arms felt stiff, but the arrow disappeared into the darkness and a cry rang out.

"That is for being tied to a post all day," she muttered

The firelight was growing brighter, and suddenly Ylmi noticed flames rising from the hall.

"Who set the hall on fire?" she shouted. Quickly, she set off along one of the paths that cut through the houses. "Karik!"

But it was Gorli she found, with Regvar and the others of the king's company, throwing torches onto the thatch of the hall.

"Enough!" Ylmi snapped.

But Gorli only snarled at her. "We came on this raid as the king's men. And I have had enough of groveling to your whims. We are not aboard your ship, nor are we in battle. This is a raid, where every man must take what seems best to him."

Ylmi lifted her bow. "Drop the torches."

Gorli drew his short sword but faltered suddenly, and Ylmi heard the sound of others behind her.

"Put your sword away," she heard Karik's voice. "Or die."

Ylmi glanced back to see Karik, Thora, and Revik close behind her, and Thora held an arrow drawn on her bow.

"This will be reported to the king," Gorli hissed, but he slid his blade back into its sheath. Regvar took a step forward.

"You and me," he said to Revik. "We have avoided each other long enough. It is time to see who is stronger."

"No," Ylmi said, "it isn't. Any of you who aren't moving back to the ship when I stop talking will die right here... starting with Regvar."

They hesitated an instant, and Ylmi loosed her arrow. There was a twang and a thud as it struck Regvar's ax handle, trembling with the force of the shot.

The big man jerked back and dropped his ax, staring at her wide-eyed.

"Move!" she snapped.

One of the others in the back was the first to move, and as soon as he did, Gorli knew he had lost. A moment later, all of them were moving back toward the forest, though Regvar kept his eyes on them as he slowly walked away.

"We're ready!" Igil ran up behind them. "Sheep are moving down the road. We took more than a little to help us on our journey. These westerners do not lack for food."

"We will follow you close behind," Ylmi said.

Thora moved to stand over her shoulder. "I was just going to kill them."

"It would mean war with Jarhost," Ylmi replied. "And after what has happened here, we cannot afford that."

As they approached the road, Dranri was standing with Havar and several others, ordering them into a tiny shield wall.

"Riders coming from the north," he said when he saw Ylmi. "Only a few. We can hold them off for now, but I do not know how many more may be coming."

"Igil, Thora," Ylmi turned to them, "move back to the ship as fast as you can and prepare to sail. We have pressed our luck further than I like already."

In the light of the rising moon, Ylmi could see the faint white smudge on the road that was the sheep herd and the occasional glint of firelight on the weapons of her crew.

"How many riders did you see?" she asked Dranri.

"Ten, fifteen?" Dranri replied.

"If we hold them off even a little...." Karik muttered

"We can fall back to the forest," Ylmi replied. "I doubt any of them can match us there?"

For a few moments, all Ylmi could hear was the crackling fire as the roof of the hall burned and the shouting of the soldiers who were trying to put it out. But then, she heard a low thunder, rumbling and rolling through the ground.

Twelve horsemen came galloping up the road, pausing by the hall until one of them caught sight of Ylmi and her company. They shouted and turned their horses, preparing to charge, and Ylmi raised her bow.

"Who commands here?" Karik shouted.

The horsemen paused, seemingly confused, and Karik stepped forward.

"I ask, who commands here?" he shouted again. "We have come from across the sea and have been attacked and treated as criminals when we did nothing to endanger anyone."

The horsemen were listening and, when Karik stopped, they seemed to talk for a moment amongst themselves. Then, their leader urged his horse forward and began shouting in return.

Ylmi rolled her eyes. How had no one grasped that they didn't understand each other?

"We speak different languages," she said to Karik.

"Yes, but as long as we are talking, we aren't fighting," Karik answered. "And Igil gets closer to the ships."

The rider had stopped yelling and was staring back, as if expecting an answer, so Ylmi took her turn to reply.

"Do you have no one who can understand us?" she shouted. "Or who can help us to understand you?"

The rider gave an order as she spoke, and the horsemen began to spread out, slowly circling the group.

"No," Ylmi said. She pointed at the horseman. "Stop!" But when he did not reply, she turned to her warriors. "Move back slowly, but be ready to fight."

The leader of the horsemen was shouting again, but Ylmi was focused on the horsemen. They were close enough that she could see their faces clearly, and they were not afraid. They believed they were in command and that it was Ylmi who should be scared. They would not hold off much longer.

"Get ready," she hissed and tightened her grip on her bow.

It was still almost a surprise, one moment they were all staring at each other, and the next, horses were thundering toward them from every direction.

Ylmi loosed an arrow that sent one rider tumbling off the back of his horse, and Revik sent another collapsing into the dirt, but the rest slammed into their group, shattering the shield wall and sending them all sprawling.

Ylmi was struck in the back and thrown to the ground. Her back and legs screamed in protest as she scrambled to her feet, but she caught up her spear and looked for a target.

Revik was still on his feet, facing down a pair of horsemen, a spear in one hand and his ax in the other, while Karik was wrestling with another on the ground.

The rest of her company was scrambling to their feet, and the remaining horsemen were gathering for another charge. Ylmi caught up her bow and loosed an arrow in one movement, sending another horseman tumbling, even as Revik gave a shout and tossed two bodies into the dirt.

Only four horsemen remained, and they seemed suddenly less sure of the situation. Karik climbed to his feet and snatched up his sword as the man he had been wrestling stumbled back to his friends. Revik picked up his ax and roared, as the roof of the longhouse collapsed with a crash and a shower of sparks.

The horsemen took one more look at Ylmi and her company, then fled, snatching up their companions as they went.

"We should go, too," she said as they galloped off. "I do not want to find out if they have more reinforcements."

⁓◦⁓

As they hurried southward along the path they had followed that afternoon, Ylmi felt a sense of unease. Most of them were covered in soot and dirt, but on Karik, the filth had mixed with blood - much of it his own - and there was a strange light in his eyes.

"We should remove the arrowheads before we get back aboard the ship," she muttered to him as they ran. "Unless you want to try burning the wounds shut with a lantern-warmed knife."

Karik laughed at that, moving as easily as if he had not been shot with several arrows. "How is your arm?"

"Well enough," Ylmi said. "It was only a flesh wound, and I will soon be healed."

It was not long before they caught up with Igil, hurrying the sheep down the road before him.

"The gods have seen fit to teach me humility," he grinned at Karik in the darkness. "I have sailed the Black Isles, and now I herd goats, like any man."

"Herd them faster, then," Ylmi said. "Whatever reinforcements these men of the west have, I do not wish to be caught by them."

The moon was high in the sky by the time they heard the waves of the sea and saw the campfire lit beside their ships.

"Load the boat!" Ylmi called. "I do not wish to linger." She grabbed Karik and pointed him at the fire. "Remove those arrows and bandage your wounds."

Karik laughed, and the sound sent a shiver down Ylmi's spine.

"I have suffered much worse than this," he said. "These men of the west have little on dragon fire or even the swords of Viglir."

"Even so," Ylmi pointed again to the fire, "see to your wounds."

The goats were bound to keep them from moving, and set in the ship, along with the odds and ends that had been taken from the rest of the village.

As she helped carry things out to where *Sea Dragon* bobbed in the surf, she noticed Gorli watching intently as each item was loaded into the boat.

"Stop counting your king's portion and help!" she called to him. "There will be time for that when we are back home."

Igil strode by her carrying a large bundle, which he handed up to Revik in the ship. "Set it by the rudder," he said. "It is my portion from the raid and I will not have it damaged."

Revik nodded, lifting the bundle in his arms with ease.

There was a sudden shout from the forest, and Ylmi looked across the moonlit beach to see dark shapes hurrying from the trees and the flashing of steel.

Karik had already drawn his longsword and was moving toward them, but many of the rest were running to the boats.

Her spear was already on board, but Ylmi drew her sword. "Havar, finish loading and prepare to cast off," she shouted. "Revik, Igil, to me!"

Karik was already fighting, and killing, and Ylmi hurried to his side, driving back their attackers. A moment later, Revik arrived, bellowing a war cry as his great ax swung through the night. There was a crunch as the heavy blade crushed a helm and the head within, and Ylmi realized they had some space.

Their attackers paused, hanging back, staring at the ax-wielding giant before them, even as Igil came to stand beside his brother.

A shouted command came from the tree line, and their attackers formed a line.

Seen together, there were not as many as Ylmi had feared, but she did not intend to find out if they had more coming.

"Hurry, Havar!" she shouted over her shoulder.

"Well," Igil said quietly, "what are you waiting for, brother?"

With a roar, Revik charged. In one swing, he shattered three shields into kindling and threw them back. Igil was on his left, cutting and stabbing with his short seax blade, even as Ylmi and Karik followed them.

The charge was short, brutal, and violent, and in an instant, their attackers were fleeing, running back up the beach to the protection of the tree line.

All of them, save Revik, were breathing heavily, and Ylmi shook her head. "I did not expect them to fold that easily."

"I am told that I can be quite terrifying," Revik said.

But Igil only wiped off his blade and looked toward the tree line. "I would run, too, if I were running to that."

Ylmi looked up.

The moon was high in the sky, shining down on the beach and into the first few trees that overlooked the sand. Now, it glinted on steel as a long line of spear wielding soldiers came hurrying down toward them. There were far more than before - at least thirty, Ylmi guessed - and there was no way the four of them were going to hold them off.

"Havar!" she shouted and was rewarded with a horn blast from the ship. "Let's go!" She grabbed Igil and pushed him toward the boat.

But Revik stepped forward, picking up a spear from where it had been dropped in his charge. It was not a javelin but a long spear, with a thick shaft and heavy iron tip. But he held it lightly in his hand, testing it.

Then, with one sudden twist of his shoulders, he whipped his arm forward.

The spear hummed as it flew through the air, striking one of the shields with a splintering crack. The soldier carrying the shield cried out and fell, and the rush of spearmen paused for a moment.

"Revik!" Ylmi shouted, but Karik had already grabbed his friend and was pulling him back to the ship. They sprinted through the sand, stumbling when their feet stuck in it, and then they were splashing through the waves.

Strong hands lifted them up into the ship, even as the oars came out and they began to pull away from the shore. The beach was filling with soldiers now, lit by the moon and the small fire they had left.

"They responded quickly." Ylmi turned to see Karik standing next to her, leaning his forearms on the edge of the ship as he looked out. They were covered in blood, and his face was spattered with it.

"Next time, we will have to be faster," she said. "They will be waiting for us."

Karik was picking at the arrow in his shoulder, his neck twisted at an awkward angle.

"Stop." She batted his hand away and stepped close. He rested one arm on her shoulder as she braced against his chest.

"Did you know that I love you very much?" he whispered.

"If you keep talking," she hissed, "I'll push the arrow in deeper." The scars from the dragon burn had hardened, and now they were stiff as leather around the wound. Carefully, she worked the arrow backwards, easing it around the flesh that tried to grab it.

"There," she held it up. "Karik Dragonslayer is free of arrows once again."

Somewhere behind her, Thora gagged.

Karik chuckled, watching as the land faded away behind them. A breeze was blowing from the south, warm and soft. Ylmi breathed it in deeply and looked back.

"We have proved much on this journey," she said, "but it means only the beginning of work."

"We will need more ships," Havar said, holding the rudder lightly. "Many more."

Karik nodded slowly. "How many can you build by next summer?"

Havar chuckled. "It depends on many things, but I think we will be able to build more than many would expect."

Ylmi cast her eyes over their cargo. One raid, and she had gathered almost half as many goats as her father herded each spring. Even if they did not return this year, it was enough to get them through the winter without too much hardship. She shook her head... so much had changed, and the path Skathi had mentioned had opened before her like a river through snow.

But her eyes suddenly lit on Gorli, his eyes counting everything they had gathered. Things had changed, but much had stayed the same. As Unhost had demanded to reap what he did not sow, now Jarhost would demand a tribute of what they had taken... though he had helped little enough.

And, if she were any judge, Jarhost's demands would grow ever larger. Eventually, she would have to match him in strength if she ever wished to be left alone.

RETURN TO VRANIA

Sea Dragon cut smoothly through the waves as they pushed toward home. The mood of the ship was jubilant, not only had they crossed the Black Isles, but they had also carried out a successful raid with little more than a few bruises and burns.

They sang as they rowed and laughed as the wind caught their sail and drove them through the water. Ylmi noted that Igil never strayed far from the rudder, and he seemed to be shielding his bundle from view. What Igil was up to, she could not guess, but her attention was split between Gorli - who seemed to sit and sulk when he was not forced to the oars - and Karik.

If she did not know him better, she would have guessed that he, too, was sulking, for he sat for long stretches as motionless as stone, staring sightlessly into the planks before him.

There was a great deal to think on. The path through the Isles was open, and the lands beyond were less than friendly. So they faced danger at home and war across the sea...

It was late afternoon when she sat down beside her husband and relaxed into the rise and fall of the ship.

"So, it is a jarl like Unhost," Ylmi said as she eased down next to him.

"Or a king like Jarhost," Karik muttered.

"At least we need not bow to this one." Ylmi pulled her cloak tight against the wind. It was growing colder as they sailed east, colder and stronger.

"Raids on the west might work for a short time, but that is not a sustainable plan," Karik muttered. "Sooner or later, our enemies will catch us before we can make it back onto our boat." He turned to glance at her.

"They raised a small army and found our ship in less than two days..." he shook his head. "Havar thinks we can raid and grow rich, but I am confident that we will all end as carrion fodder if we go that route."

"Havar is too fond of raiding by half," Ylmi agreed.

"If we are to leave Vrania, we need a place to land. A place to make their home, to be safe." Karik shook his head in frustration. "We have little idea of how the land lies, where the settlements stand, and where the best landing places are. There is much we do not know." Karik watched the sail straining against the ropes as the wind blew overhead. "But where there is a king like Jarhost, there are people like us... chafing beneath his misrule. We have only to find them."

"That is easier said than done."

Karik nodded. "We must do more than defeat his soldiers... we need to know what kind of land this is... we need to explore, to find out who lives here, and above all, whom we may befriend. I dislike the idea of making enemies we do not need."

Ylmi leaned her head back against the hull and closed her eyes. "I agree with this. We have enough enemies already."

Karik's eyes went to Gorli, who was speaking quietly with Regvar. "More than enough." He was silent for a moment, and his eyes went to the sea, the waves rolling and slipping by as the wind pushed them homeward.

"I thought many times of this voyage," he said quietly.

"Sailing to the west?" Ylmi asked.

But Karik shook his head with a weak smile. "Sailing home from the west. I thought I'd sail with my brothers... or back to my father." He glanced to where Havar leaned back on the sternpost, the rudder held loose under his arm. "Wisic would have had a great deal to say about our current situation..." he chuckled and shook his head. "But we have come all together through this adventure at least, that is something to be thankful for."

"Your mother will be pleased to see you at least," Ylmi patted him on the arm.

"She's right, though," Karik muttered. "There will be a great deal of trouble from this crossing..."

"There would have been more trouble, had we not made it."

Karik nodded. "I do not say the voyage should not have been made. Only that it is not the end in itself. We must strengthen ourselves and seek to weaken our enemies while we enjoy the advantage of this ship."

Ylmi nodded and sat back against the rowing bench. There was a great deal of work to be done, as there had always been. Yet now she felt, for the first time, that there was hope.

Ylmi woke the next morning as the sun was rising over the sea's edge, its warm light slowly chasing away the worst of the night's chill.

Thora was standing near the stern, looking back to the west, as Igil held the rudder steady.

"The new lands are less hospitable than we thought," Ylmi said to her with a small smile.

Thora turned to her, but there was no laughter in her eyes. "That is one way to put it. I weary of seeing those close to me courting death."

"I did not intend to be captured..." Ylmi began, but Thora cut her off.

"I am not blaming you." She waved her hand. "I am sick of it, that is all. But it seems that is to be our wyrd. That and putting up with vile kings." She glanced to where Gorli and Regvar lay asleep among the crew.

Ylmi was silent a moment, watching the waves tossing in their wake. The pouch that hung from her neck had gotten wet, and now it hung cold and heavy with the weight of Skathi's stones.

"It is easy to avoid needless bloodshed," she said after a moment. "But the difference between wise caution and cowardice is less clear."

Thora snorted. "I worry over many things. The cowardice of Ylmi One-eye is not one of them."

"I do not fear for myself." Ylmi kept her voice low, and Thora leaned in to hear her over the sound of the wind and waves. "But I do fear for my village and those whom I am to protect." She took a deep breath and her hand wandered to the pouch, letting it hang free from her shirt. She had been too cautious, too afraid of bloodshed...

"We have been too gentle with Jarhost," she said after a moment. "Perhaps there are things I should have done differently..." she shook a stray hair out of her blind eye and tucked it behind her ear. "But now that the Isles are open to us, I am less inclined to bear more of Jarhost's greed and foolishness."

Thora nodded and looked back to the sea. "You have mentioned more than once that a wall would be a good thing to have. Now that we have crossed the Isles, we should plan more how it should be built... and how Jarhost should not learn of it until later."

The journey back to the Isles was the most restful Ylmi had felt in what seemed like years. The only clouds they saw were soft white wisps in blue skies, and the currents seemed to run with them so that they came upon the Black Isles after only two days of sailing.

Karik took the rudder and all stood by, but returning through the Isles was far different than leaving them. The current rushed them down the entrance and the rudder drove them smoothly about each turn.

"It is a far easier thing to sail with the current!" Havar laughed as *Sea Dragon* cut through the waves.

The high cliffs of Vrania appeared before them as they passed the last of the Isles, and Ylmi felt a weight lift from her chest. They had passed the Isles twice, and nothing lay between them and home but a few leagues of calm sea.

He felt a smile on his face as *Sea Dragon* slipped past the beach where they had once laid in with *Kalborg,* their hull full of the gold that had given birth to their new ship. Now, *Sea Dragon* rode the same waves, her hull filled with plunder that would build a new fleet.

Ahead, the dragon's mountain rose out of the sea, and Karik raised his hand in salute to the memory of Umir, who's body lay somewhere beneath the waves.

The dragon's bones shone white in the afternoon sun as they sailed past them, and Karik thought again on the dragon's curse. Whatever ashes this victory would bring him, he would deal with them when they came.

But for now, they steered a mighty ship filled with plunder and the knowledge that no one in the settlement would go hungry this winter.

"Set to the oars!" Ylmi called as they passed the mountain, "we are almost home!" As the oar benches were filled and the oars set into the water, Karik lifted the great horn from the stern and blew three mighty blasts upon it.

A moment later, an answering horn came from the village in the distance, and Ylmi grinned.

At Havar's command, the oars moved in unison, and *Sea Dragon* surged through the light waves of the fjord as her crew pulled hard, eager to be home.

As they approached the shore, Ylmi saw a crowd forming at the shoreline, their faces hopeful as the ship drew in close.

"Did you make it?" the calls began to come out over the water, and Karik grinned as Ylmi strode down the center of the ship and, gripping the prow in one hand, stood tall and shouted back.

"We have crossed the Isles and returned!" Her voice echoed over the fjord, clear and loud. "And we bring plunder!"

A roar went up from the shore, and Karik's grin widened. With one last heave at the oars, *Sea Dragon* surged up onto the beach, and her crew leaped ashore.

Ylmi saw her parents standing on the beach, and a fire filled her as she saw them. She had done it, she would give them safety, and she was not even covered in blood.

She pounded her chest with her fist as she stepped forward, a savage smile on her face. "I return whole and unbloody," she grinned. "Your daughter has passed the Isles and returned." She winked at her mother, "And this time, I do not return to you a bloody, fainting mess."

"And yet, there is a bandage upon your shoulder," Bodvar pointed out, but Ylmi only laughed.

"It is a scratch, and a tiny one at that," she said, "nothing for one of the dragon burned."

"Is that what you are calling yourselves now?" Siggi asked, and Ylmi shrugged.

Ylmi took a deep breath, "They are rich lands to the west, very rich."

"I did not think when you were born," Siggi said, "that I had brought into the world one so fearsome as yourself."

"I have good companions," Ylmi smiled, "and my husband is no weakling."

But Ylmi tore herself away from her parents before they could talk more. There was much work to do, and she did not intend to let Gorli get ahead of her.

Those who did not have family at the beach, Ylmi set to work unloading the ship. Igil had disappeared, but Revik was happy to begin unloading, and soon a pile of goods began to take shape on the beach. The goats, Ylmi gave to her father, sending him to see that they were placed as needed.

When the ship was almost empty, she called to Gorli, who had sat down with his men and watched as they unloaded the ship.

"I have set aside gifts for the king," she said loudly, and many turned to listen. None were pleased to watch her, and those who had sailed seemed less pleased than the rest.

But Ylmi did not stint on her gifts, and she gave them a small chest of golden ingots Igil had taken from the smithy, along with three swords of fine, bright steel. To this, she added a large bag of bright silver cups and a handful of other items.

"These are for the king," she said, "in payment of the tax he levies upon us and as a gift to him from the Jarl of Dragonsrest. We thank him for his good rule and the protection he has afforded us."

As she spoke, she saw Dranri leaning against a tree behind Gorli, picking his fingers with his knife. As she spoke of the king's protection, he rolled his eyes until his head fell back and disappeared behind the salt-stained bush of his beard.

Ylmi stifled a smile and gestured to the items. "Take them, and return to Bjarnmont. The king should not be kept waiting, deprived of the fruits of our labor."

Gorli stepped forward, Regvar close behind him, but he stopped quickly. "What of our portion?"

"What of it?" Ylmi asked. "You have not done your work nor pulled your weight. While we unloaded the ship just now, you sat and watched others labor. So you have behaved upon this entire journey. I will not shrink the portion of those who labored long and hard so that you may boast you received a full portion for no work."

"I will not leave empty-handed." Regvar spoke in a quiet voice, and Ylmi nodded at Dranri.

"Of course not," Ylmi smiled. "You are taking the king his portion. You are his men, and it is him you served by coming - not me. Therefore, it is only right that he be the one to reward you. I have spoken."

Gorli was silent now, watching her and Regvar as the large man took another step forward.

"Perhaps you did not hear me, woman," Regvar said coldly. "I said..."

To her left, Ylmi saw Revik stepping forward, his hand on his ax, but she waved him away.

"My name is Ylmi One-eye, boy," she said with a grim smile at Regvar. "I have killed a dragon, sailed uncrossable seas, and slain a dozen champions in single combat. I do not know what you have done."

Regvar's eyes widened, but before he could respond, Ylmi continued.

"I do know, however, that if you take another step toward me, I will count it as an attack, and you will die where you stand."

"You think you can kill me?" Regvar was incredulous.

Ylmi threw up her hands. "Has everyone forgot we killed a dragon?" She shook her head. "Regardless, this time it will not be me. If you move forward, he will shoot you in your neck..." she pointed at Dranri, who now stood with an arrow on the string of his black bow, "and she will shoot you in the heart." She pointed to Thora, who stood with an arrow on her own bow.

For a moment, Regvar stood still. Then, he raised his foot, and two bows creaked as their strings were pulled taught. Regvar's eyes widened, and Gorli set a hand on his arm.

"Take your king's portion and go," Ylmi said. "If you hurry, you will be well back to Bjarnmont by nightfall."

Saying this, she turned and walked away. There was fire in her veins, and she felt sweat on her hands. Had she pushed too far? Or not far enough?

She laughed a little to herself as she walked through the crowd... it did not matter. Jarhost would take it wrong, either way. To him, she was either a rebellious upstart to be crushed or a weak jarl to be used and drained like all the rest. She would no longer lie down and accept what he dealt. If the king wanted conflict... then he would have to move swiftly, for she would not dawdle.

She did not stop walking till she reached her hall. The doors were open, and she stepped inside.

It was warm here, out of the wind. The long fireplace in the center of the hall was smoldering, and the whole place smelled of smoke, comfort, and home.

"Your wolf has whelped," a cold voice said from the shadows.

Ylmi turned, startled. Elva was sitting in the corner, working a deer hide in the dark.

"Where?" was all Ylmi could think to say.

Elva jerked her head. "In the back, near your own bed."

Ylmi took a few steps, then stopped. "Your son has returned," she looked back at the old woman. "You should see him."

Elva said nothing for a moment, but her fingers slowed on the hide. "He is already lost, and the day is coming when the Allfather will take him from me. He has sown blood and fire, and he will reap the same... I have warned and cautioned him. I have no duty to congratulate him as he hurtles toward his own destruction. I have made my peace with it and bid him farewell."

"He's not dead," Ylmi snapped, suddenly angry. "And perhaps he will be soon. Perhaps Jarhost will come down and kill us all. Perhaps the sea will take him when next he leaves these shores, or perhaps the Black Isles will claim him. But for now, he is here, and I, for one, will make the most of what the Allfather has given me." Her face hardened, rage boiling up within her.

"Go. Now," she said. "When I have seen to Ulfr, you will not be in my hall. Go to your son, or go to another house. This home is for me and mine. If you choose to abandon your son, then there is no place for you here."

She turned, striding past the hard wooden throne and into the close, comfortable rooms in the rear.

A warm, wiggling mass was curled up on her bed, and in the gloom she saw the sudden gleam as Ulfr opened her eyes and looked up. Her tail wagged as Ylmi bent down and ran her fingers over the tiny pups that were sleeping quietly.

"You are a mother now," Ylmi smiled. "I expect you will want more food now because of this."

At the mention of food, Ulfr licked her lips and wagged her tail again, and Ylmi laughed. She laughed and ran her hand over her own belly. It was rising, and she could feel the child growing within her.

Hardly more than a year ago, she had lived alone with her parents high in the mountains. Now, she was One-eye - a jarl, a dragonslayer, and soon to be a mother. How things had changed.

Once More

That night, a dozen goats were slaughtered and roasted before Ylmi's hall. All of Dragonsrest sang and drank and feasted as the sun set, and the stars shone through the rolling clouds. Even a drizzling rain did little to dampen the mirth that filled the air as men, women, and children moved between the bonfires that were scattered through the settlement.

As the night deepened, Karik rose from his seat in the great hall. Ylmi smiled at him, and he smiled back, caught for a moment by the way the firelight flickered in her eye.

A moment later, he was picking his way through the settlement as a fine, icy rain drifted in from the northwest. The moon was hidden behind the clouds, but they were thin, and a dim pale glow fell upon the shadows where the firelight did not reach.

He drained the last of his mead and tucked the small horn cup into his shirt. Revik was sitting on a log by one of the bonfires, a pitcher in one hand and a half-eaten leg of goat in the other as he told the tale of their fight before the walls to a crowd of listeners.

"Our fearless captain!" Revik shouted when he saw Karik. "The one who has led us to glory and riches! May he lead us to many more."

Karik grinned. "We have only begun…"

But he was interrupted as half the crowd began begging him to take them on the next voyage. He laughed and held up his hands to calm the crowd.

"If Revik Dragonsbane says you are a good warrior and dependable, then that is good enough for me." He turned to Revik. "I am looking for your brother."

The big man waved the goat's leg toward another bonfire. "Last I saw him, he went that way."

Karik nodded and strode through the mud and thickening rain, but Igil was nowhere to be seen. Instead, he found Fianna and her children eating together, a mass of children picking apart goat bones.

"How may I help you, Karik?" Fianna asked when she saw him.

"I am looking for your husband," he answered. "Do you know where he has gone?"

Fianna shook her head as she handed Torm a piece of bread. "He is busy and has asked that he not be disturbed,"

"I am sure he will not mind a visit from his oldest friend," Karik smiled, "where has he gone?"

"I am glad that you are friends with him," Fianna replied, "and I know he thinks very highly of you. But he asked that he not be disturbed."

"Fianna..." Karik said softly, "do not do this. I have been his friend since..."

"And I am his wife," Fianna smiled. "My husband has asked to be left alone. Have you eaten your fill already?"

"I have," Karik replied. "But I still must speak with Igil, can you tell him..."

But Fianna only laughed. "Karik, your reputation for relentlessness is not unearned. But my husband has asked not to be disturbed. He will come soon enough."

Before Karik could answer, Igil's tall, lanky form appeared out of the gloom. "You push too hard, Karik. My wife asked you to wait."

"We are old friends..." Karik began, but Igil waved him off.

"She is my wife."

Karik looked between them for a moment. He had known that Igil loved her, but he had been unsure of whether Fianna was as concerned with Igil's wellbeing.

"I apologize," Karik bowed his head. " I was wrong."

Fianna nodded with a smile, and Igil wrapped her in a hug. "Thank you, my love," he bent down and planted a kiss on her forehead.

"You were looking for me?" he asked Karik.

"I want to speak on another voyage."

Fianna's eyes widened, and she looked quickly to Igil. "You have only just returned," she said quietly.

Igil smiled. "I have, and I do not think I will sail away so quickly. There is much to be done, and we need more ships." He shrugged and let go of his wife. "Come, I will show you something."

Karik nodded quickly to Fianna as he passed her and followed Igil into the darkness and toward his home. Inside, the fire had burned low, but Karik jumped when he saw movement beyond the coals.

Igil laughed quietly and barred the door behind them. He tossed a handful of wood on the fire, and it quickly caught, blazing up in light that filled the small hut.

A stocky man with a short white beard was curled in the corner, his hands lightly bound and a goat bone lying next to him.

"Who is this?" Karik asked in astonishment.

"One I took from the west," Igil answered. "He is a smith."

The man looked up at them and raised the cup to Igil. "In hagge vasser?"

Igil lifted a pitcher from by the door and looked to the man, who nodded vigorously.

"You can understand him?" Karik asked.

"Bits and pieces," Igil replied. "Their tongue is not so different from ours, and he is very clever." He poured water into the man's cup, and then set the pitcher down next to him.

"This is what you wanted kept a secret..."

"If Jarhost or anyone else gets wind of him," Igil said quickly, "they'll snatch him away. He can tell us much about the west, and if we can learn their tongue... so much the better." He glanced down at the man, slowly sipping from the cup while watching them with narrow eyes.

Igil smiled at him, then turned back to Karik. "Fortunately, Gorli knows us little, and there are enough strange faces among those who sailed with us that I was able to keep him hidden."

"Gorli was too focused on the plunder," Karik muttered. He gestured at the smith, "You think he will help us?"

Igil shrugged. "He seems willing so far. But I will burn that bridge when we come to it," he turned back to Karik. "You are planning another voyage... when?"

"Within the week," Karik answered.

"By the nine," Igil shook his head, "you are so eager to try your luck in the Isles again?"

"Jarhost will demand more and more from us," Karik responded, "and I do not want to have Gorli aboard if I do not have to."

"That is a good point," Igil nodded. "I will begin repairs in the morning... though we came out of that better even than I expected." He stared into the fire a moment, considering. "Can you sail with Havar? I will stay and begin work on a new ship."

"If that is what you wish, then yes." Karik looked again at the smith, reclining now against the wall. "Can you finish more than one ship by next year?"

Igil thought for a moment, then shrugged. "It depends on how much help I can get. I may begin teaching Henla and Torm the craft... if they are interested."

"More will come," Karik said quietly. "And I think we will begin to see wanderers from beyond the coast when word of our crossing spreads. Whatever course we take from here, we must have enough warriors to make it happen."

"More hands make quick labor," Igil said with a smile. "I will build us a fleet such as this Isle has never seen."

Karik nodded and took a deep breath. He could feel the mead in his veins, and he longed for the feel of the rising ship beneath him and his sword in his hand. "Whatever wyrd may have for me, I will not wait it out easily. If I am to fail, as the dragon cursed me, then I will fail because wyrd deems it so, not because I was too slow or too cautious to do what needed to be done."

"Karik," Igil clapped him on the shoulder. "There is no danger of you being too cautious."

⸺◆⸺

As the night reached its peak, and turned toward dawn, the revelry in the village began to quiet. Karik returned to the long hall, where more than a dozen bodies lay upon the floor, snoring and dreaming the mead dreams.

Ylmi was already in their bed, pulling the blankets and furs close around her against the night chill.

"You are already planning another raid," she said with a smile. Karik nodded, sitting down on the bed but reluctant to sleep. He had a feeling he would have the dream again, and he did not want it.

"We need to bring more back to the settlement," he said quietly. "I want Igil to build ships, I want..." he took a deep breath, "I want to be able to feed anyone who comes asking."

He was silent for a moment, then he spoke once more into the darkness. "Next year, I want to go west to make a new home. A place where we can live safely. I want to sail with an army. If wyrd is coming for us, if defeat is always in my future, then I will not have it come one day sooner than it must."

They slept deeply that night, as did all of Dragonsrest, drunk on mead and the thick, heady taste of hope.

But in his hall in Bjarnmont, high in the mountains, Jarhost sat on his throne and listened to Gorli's tale of the raid, and noted that what had once been a tiny settlement was now a village more than double in size. Jarl Ylmi would not grow weaker any time soon, he thought. And Karik Haldsson seemed to perform one troublesome deed after another.

He thought on all this as the night darkened and the fire of his hall burned low.

VORTIMER

Vortimer woke with a start, feeling rather like a drowning man being pulled back to the surface.

"Easy," came a quiet voice, and he looked up to see that he had his hands around Hector's throat. Quickly, he let his hands drop.

His eyes stung, and he rubbed them gently. "Is it morning already?"

Hector shook his head, "It is still night, my king. But there is a message for you." Vortimer saw with a glance that his armor was wet. It was still raining, then. That would not help his knights and horsemen in the morning. He winced as he sat up.

"I assume it cannot wait," he shook his head, blinking himself awake. He looked around, suddenly. "Where is Bedyr?"

As if in answer, a young boy appeared carrying a pitcher.

"You should have woken me," Vortimer told him, "Captain Hector has his own matters to attend to."

"He tried to," Hector said, "but you slept as one of the dead."

"Hmmm," Vortimer rubbed his eyes, trying to force them to stay open. It had been some time since he had gotten a good night's sleep... hell, it had been a week since he had last slept in the same place he woke up.

Bedyr was holding the pitcher, his eyes wide and a look of fear on his face, and when he saw it, Vortimer sighed.

"Next time, pour water on my face," he said, beckoning the young boy over. "Even kings have to wake when duty calls." He took the pitcher, ignoring the cup Bedyr held out, and drank deeply. The cold water tasted good, and he felt his body finally beginning to wake up.

"So, where is the messenger?" he asked, and Bedyr turned to hurry out the door.

"He's still terrified of you," Hector pointed out.

Vortimer winced. "I would be if our positions were reversed. Who isn't afraid of the king who executed their uncle for treason?"

"I still think you should have lifted more heads," Hector muttered. "Baron Easerby was the heart of that conspiracy."

"Callan was right," Vortimer said, suddenly exhausted all over again. "Death breeds death... and I'm supposed to be healing our people."

"Callan's still dead," Hector answered bitterly. "Along with Gillian, Brathus, Drysus..."

"I know their names," Vortimer snapped. He sighed and glanced toward the entrance of the tent. If he listened, he could just hear the sound of the light rain dripping onto the tent. "Hopefully, Bedyr will calm down with the rest of his family when I marry his sister."

"Still think it's a mistake."

"I don't want to marry her, either." Vortimer stretched. "She's as like to stick a knife in my back as smile at me."

"Then lop off her father's head and have done," Hector urged. "Stop trying to smooth things over with people who aided your enemies and help slaughter..."

"We are done discussing it," Vortimer let a bit of the king creep into his voice there, and Hector knew better than to push the matter. Of the six young men who had sworn the vows of knighthood at his side, Hector was the only one left alive. They had been through many battles and fought their way out of many hopeless situations, but at times, he could do without his friend second guessing every decision he made.

They were silent only a moment before the tent flap was thrown open, and a weary looking messenger in wet clothes bowed in the candle light.

"Your majesty," he blurted. "I bring word from Baron Easerby on the coast..." he hesitated and looked Vortimer in the eyes. "Vranr has returned."

"What?" Vortimer looked at him in astonishment. He expected Easerby to be making the most of his absence... a king on the march was less able to control his nobles at home, but this seemed ridiculous.

"Is the king supposed to believe that a myth from children's faerie tales is come back?" Hector's voice was a whip. "You have woken the king the night before battle for this?"

"Let me guess," Vortimer gave a small smile, "the good baron wishes me to give him certain authorities - perhaps the office of marshal - to gather troops and garrison the capitol... all for my own protection, of course?"

But the messenger shook his head. "No your majesty, he begs you to return or send a company to protect him." He looked from Hector to Vortimer. "Your majesty, Vranr landed with one ship several miles south of Balfor. Before we knew he was there, he and his company came out of the forest, painted black as shadows, and slaughtered the Baron's bodyguard. The baron only just escaped with his life. They slew many, including four of his knights, and stole a great deal. They even set fire to the baron's hall."

Vortimer leaned forward in surprise. If Baron Easerby was acknowledging he needed the crown for anything, then this was very unusual.

"Why do you say that it is Vranr who did this?" he asked. "We have long suspected that the empire is putting ships to sea to harry us."

The messenger took a breath to steady himself, then spoke. "I saw him, your majesty, surrounded by fire, laughing as arrows fell from his body. We shot him a dozen times, at least, and we are not mean archers. But he acted as though they were less than bee stings. And when he cursed us, we saw his hands - three fingers upon the left, four upon the right, as all the stories tell."

Vortimer gazed on the man, his own fingers running over his chin as he thought. The man clearly believed what he was saying, and if Easerby was playing a game at this, then it was a very different one than he had played so far.

"Vranr died centuries ago," Hector spoke up. "Whatever stories you have heard, they all agree on that, at least."

But the messenger shook his head. He was afraid, Vortimer saw, and that fear was making him bold enough to forget Hector's rank.

"They agree he died, and they agree he would return," the messenger replied. "The Eldar curse, they called it, that he would return and take revenge on the children of those who wronged him." He looked back to Vortimer, his eyes begging the king to believe him.

"Your majesty," he said, "I know that you must not have an abundance of faith in my baron."

"That's an understatement," Hector muttered, and Vortimer glared at him.

"But I will swear any oath," the messenger continued, "give any pledge to convince you we face a real terror. I was there, my lord. I fought them, and I saw their savagery."

Vortimer looked at the man before him, and a sick, sinking feeling settled in his stomach as he began to believe the man before him.

There was silence in the tent, and Vortimer held back a sigh, pulling tighter the bearing of a king over his face even as he felt unease and anger at the injustice of it all boiling up within him. But a tiny part of him still clung to the hope it was a trick.

"If our coasts are truly under attack," he said slowly, "then for the good of all, the baron should consent for the smith Ninnian to return to the Mondburg..." he paused at the look on the messenger's face.

"Ninnian was among the dead," he said slowly.

Vortimer's mouth hung open for a moment before he could regain his bearing. "Dead?"

"He was in the outhouses beyond the walls," the messenger explained. "They left none alive."

Vortimer looked at Hector, hoping that the captain had heard something different from him, but Hector's face was stricken with shock and rage.

It was true then.

"Baron Easerby will answer to his peers for the loss of the smith," Vortimer said quietly. He thought for a moment, breathing deeply. His reign so far had been a parade of disasters and emergencies, and he had not survived so long by chasing every mishap. As much as he longed to ride back to Balfor and strangle Easerby with his own hands, Antonius and the massive army across the river were the more immediate threat. If Vranr had come and gone, then it would be some time until he returned.

"Tell the barons," he said at last, "that they must see to the security of their own coasts until winter. I will take the matter in hand when I return." He hesitated a moment, then nodded to himself. "When you have given those messages, ride for Kindor, then follow the river west into the mountains. Somewhere there, you will find a man named Kunagos. Inform him that his king has need of him and that he should return to the Mondburg with all haste."

The messenger saluted and turned to go, but Vortimer called him back. "The message can wait till morning. I doubt the barons will leap to action, in any case. Get some rest, eat. Brythas!" he called the captain of his guard, who appeared in the tent, dripping with rain. "See that this man is fed and given a place to sleep for the night."

Callas saluted, and a moment later, Vortimer was alone with Hector.

"Do you think it's really him?" Hector asked quietly.

Vortimer laughed bitterly, the mask of kingship slipping as he let himself sit back on the small cot. "With the way the gods seem to hate me, I would expect nothing less."

He shook his head, rage burning up within him. "We were so close..." he shook his head again. "Even if we win tomorrow, we can't chase them through the mountains. I'll have to pull the army back and redouble the guard on the shore forts."

"It could be a trick..." Hector guessed. "The Cirithulians are a tricky lot, and they set a great store by those old stories. Perhaps they arranged all this."

But Vortimer shook his head. "Even they can't conjure a man who shrugs off arrows... this is something else. That man was terrified."

"We'll find a way," Hector said quietly. "We have always found one so far, and we'll find one through this."

Normally, Vortimer would have found Hector's confidence in him comforting, but right now, it sickened him. He had not even the hint of an answer, and his bag of tricks was empty. He'd gambled everything on the battle tomorrow, and now, even if he won, he would lose.

"Perhaps," he said lightly, "Antonius has a better plan than I do, and the gods shall mercifully allow us all a noble death in battle. Then, I can finally rest, and Antonius can take my kingdom, along with all the problems that come with it, and he can be appointed governor just in time to deal with Vranr returning from the dead!" He chuckled. "Now that, I would love to see."

"Look on the bright side," Hector shrugged, "even if we win tomorrow, there's a decent chance your new bride will murder you on your wedding night."

"Better and better!" Vortimer laughed. "Look at us, solutions everywhere. Now go, I should sleep a little, at least... don't want to make it too easy for Antonius."

Hector laughed and saluted before stepping through the tent flap and into the rain. Vortimer laid back, suddenly wondering if Bedyr had heard them. He should get up and check, he thought, but his body was already falling asleep. They were all likely dead in the morning, anyway...

He fell into a deep sleep, and his dreams were filled with a dark figure, surrounded by flames. Arrows protruded from his body, and his long arms were spread wide, revealing three fingers on his left hand and four on his right.

KVELDMIR
NORVALNIN
Lanae
Balfor
The Heinburg
Cirithulian Empire
Mondburg
Carna
Veldor
MALNIN
Torik
Cirithul
Kindor
River Ousso
Daarven
Sornlos
Mirnlos
Larinor
Vardel
SORNIN
Urhaavn
Vinilos
Telrich
Khoraavn
Forburg
River Rush
Naarvos
Zelkior
0 15 30 45
Miles
Salarios
Neseh
Toranich
Banrich

KARIK WILL RETURN

Karik and the remaining Dragonslayers will return in The Legends of
Karik Book IV,

VORTIMER

THE HUNTING OF THE OUTLAW MINRI

It was late in the year, but before the Thing where Ylmi slew Harvik, that Leiban Longspear came out of the mountains, wounded by the Outlaw Minri. Ylmi and the rest of the village were hard at work preparing for winter, and ship building, so Thora and Revik took it on themselves to see that Minri was dealt with.

Thora disliked leaving Ylmi, but as she snatched up a handful of dried meat from her rafters, she told herself it would be a quick thing to slay Minri and return.

She knew the mountains better than any, save perhaps Osric or Ylmi, Minri would little be able to hide his paths from her.

Catching up two arrows she had finished the night before, Thora shut the door to her tiny hut and stepped out into the pines. As she climbed the slope, and the trees grew thicker, the sounds of the village faded behind her, allowing the soft rhythms of the forest to reach her ears. It was usually calming for her, to walk this path and leave the village behind, but now she was filled with a cold, simmering rage.

The wounds to Leiban would have been enough to urge her onward, but Revik's proud words pricked her even further. These mountains were her home, and Leiban had shown them to her. She would not be outdone in avenging his hurt by a newcomer, however formidable Revik might be in battle.

Her long strides ate up the ground as she walked, taking the path north out of the village to where it branched westward. Leiban said he had been almost half a day's trek from his home, checking on an old bear cave they had once hunted. But Thora did not bother to follow Leiban's trail, Minri was not likely to remain near where he had assaulted the old hunter.

A chill was in the air as the north winds blew down from over the Ice Sea. The autumn season was already drawing close, and the winter followed hard on after that. Picking her way through the trees that overhung the narrow trail, Thora tried to think. It was Leiban who had told her that a good hunter thinks like their prey, so now she tried to think of Minri. He was doubtless seeking somewhere to burrow down and survive the winter, as they all were.

His method of doing so was to kill others until he found what they had made, so Thora set her path to Leiban's dwelling.

It was not near to the settlement, Leiban valued his solitude too much for that, so Thora kept up her pace as the sun sank into the west. Occasionally, when the path was even, she broke into a loping run that ate up the distance even faster, but she was careful not to push herself too much.

"There is no point," Leiban had once told her as they tracked a boar, "in chasing your prey if you arrive too tired to kill it."

By all accounts, Minri was no mean warrior, and Thora had no intention of becoming his next victim. There was a good chance he was settling himself in Leiban's cave, and Thora needed only to stick a few arrows in him. See how great a warrior he was then.

❦

The sun disappeared behind the trees on the mountainside, and the afternoon chill turned colder as Thora approached the hunting grounds of Leiban.

Here and there were the signs of his dwelling and care, a heavy oak he had kept clear so that it would be filled with acorns each year, a pool he had fashioned in the stream to provide an easier place to drink.

The memories flooded back as Thora pushed deeper into the forest that was as familiar to her as her own home. Leiban had disliked Unhost immensely, and Thora suspected that was why she had been welcomed to Leiban's home when so few others even knew which mountain it was on.

He had kept his dwelling secret. No trail of skulls or mounted hides as Dranri or Almir hung about their homes. Only a few stacked rocks here, a faded mark on a tree nearby, were all that marked the place... small pieces that the old hunter had laid out for a young girl who was just learning to hunt, many years ago.

Thora paused a moment, looking at the faded rocks, seeing in her mind's eye how Leiban had set them one atop the other.

"These will show you the way," he had said, only a few days after her mother had died.

Step by step she ate away at the distance, her feet following a path she had traveled more often than she could count.

⸺◆⸺

Leiban's home was set deep in the mountains, and the path led over more than one high, rocky ridge. The rock held no tracks, and it was not a simple thing to find the way.

But as she approached the ridge, Thora turned aside into the pines. If Minri was watching the path, she had no intention of stumbling into him. Her pace slowed as she placed her foot between the fallen twigs and branches on the ground, and her ears listened to the pine boughs sway in the winds, and the calls of the birds as they settled in for the evening.

Atop the ridge, there was small outcropping of rock that looked down on the little dell, and Thora knelt upon it for a moment, hidden against the rock as she looked down on the ridge.

Nothing moved, save the rhythmic rolling of the pines as the wind passed through. All around her, Thora looked about, seeking anything that seemed out of place.

But nothing seemed amiss.

Slowly, she climbed up the rock face, careful to keep low, lest anyone from below should look up and see her silhouette against the night sky. Dusk was not far off, and she wanted a chance to approach Leiban's cave before it became too dark.

The way down was familiar enough that she could follow the path without being on it, and she moved like a shadow through the pines, looking for any sign of Minri.

No smoke rose through the trees, at least none she could see, and Thora wondered if perhaps she would not find Minri there. But if he had not stayed there, then where had he gone? And why would he leave a perfectly good shelter?

At last, Thora stood before Leiban's cave.

The door had been ripped from its place, and Leiban's few belongs were scattered over the ground. Thora stepped carefully through the doorway and looked through the gloom. Nothing had been left undisturbed. Not a single hide was left, and the hooks where Leiban had hung his smoked meat were empty.

Did Minri have a goat he was using as a pack animal? Or had he picked a hideout not far away?

Thora stepped out of the cave and her eyes swept the ground about the cave.

The earth was disturbed, and it seemed Minri had been in a hurry when he ransacked the place. But there was a trail leading away from the cave, and as Thora knelt beside it, she saw the shapes of different feet in the dirt.

Minri was not alone.

How many there were, she was not sure. At least one other outlaw, perhaps two. Her hand went to the arrows in her quiver. She had eleven. If she was careful, and quick, it should still be enough.

The trail led into the pines, northward and down out of the small valley where Leiban made his home, and Thora followed it to the edge of the trees.

Someone had stepped on a patch of grass, and Thora lifted the strands in her fingers. The grass blades had been crushed, and already the wind had dried them out. Thora pondered a moment, considering the wind, the grass, and the fading light.

They must have left a few hours before at least, perhaps before Leiban had even reached them in the village.

She sat down, letting her spear rest against her shoulder as she closed her eyes. In her mind, she swept through the mountains, noting every rise and crevasse of the heights. There was no point in dashing off with half a plan, and less point if she wandered into a trap. That Minri was traveling with others made things more difficult, but it also made Minri more predictable.

There were only a few places they could have camped the night before, and a few more they could have gone to from here, but only if they'd known where to look. She discarded one, as too close, and another because she doubted they could have found it.

That left only one place where she found it likely they would be.

Rising with a sigh, she stepped over to where the door lay on the ground and lifted it with a quick effort. She intended to convince Leiban to remain in the village when he healed, but it still would not do to leave his home open to the wild. Leaning the door back in its place, she propped it there with one of the large rocks nearby.

That done, she turned and headed north, back into the pines.

Rage built within her as she followed the tracks, for it seemed to her that she would be forever tormented by greedy men. Unhost had bullied and fought with her parents, and anyone who disagreed with him, and Thora suspected that Leiban had kept away from the village to avoid Unhost.

Now, Minri arrived from wherever he had been lurking, even more greedy than Unhost. Leiban just wanted to live a simple life, he was no warrior seeking glory. But that, it seemed, was no protection against greed.

Unhost had been greedy, and Thora had been unable to do much more than watch. Jarhost seemed to have a king's share of greed, and there was little Thora could do about that, either.

But Minri did not have Jarhost's army, and Thora was a little girl no more.

She moved quickly, her anger giving her strength as her legs ate up the miles. These trees had seen Leiban teach her more than a little, and she knew them as well as she knew Dragonsrest itself. As she ran, she listened to the wind, to the birds, and for the howl of wolves. It was not winter, but she still had little desire to cross paths with a hungry pack.

Darkness fell, but she pushed on. The night was clear, with the greater number of clouds far in the north, letting the moonlight wash down over the trees. It was a faint light she was well used to, more than once she and Leiban had hunted these woods by only the light of the moon.

The sound of voices filtered through the trees, mixed with the sound of a mountain stream, and Thora slowed her steps. Crouching almost to the ground, she moved slowly from tree to tree, and an instant later saw the warm glow of firelight.

Looking away, she closed her eyes, counting slowly to three. Alvar had taught her that one, to keep her eyes accustomed to the dark lest the firelight make her blind to all else.

She opened her eyes, keeping them in the forest, and crept closer. Twice she stopped and swept her eyes over the small camp, stopping after each time to close her eyes and regain their darksight.

There were four figures around the campfire, eating in the manner of those who have had their fill. She could hear their voices as she crept closer, they spoke in quiet tones and she could not hear their words.

She was about to set an arrow to her bow when something on the edge of the firelight moved, and someone rose slowly from the shadows. Thora looked again and saw there were two, three more people there, sleeping on the edge of Minri's camp.

Seven in Minri's band? And so close to Dragonsrest...

The figure who had risen was a woman, and she went to stand beside the largest figure sitting by the fire.

Whatever she said made an impression, for all the rest of the talking stopped, and the big man, Thora guessed it was Minri, looked up.

An instant later, the woman turned back to her bed, but the men at the fire were no longer talking, their eyes instead turned outward.

Thora glanced back toward the woman's bed, indistinct through the trees and shrouded in darkness. The shape of the blanket was unclear, but Thora was suddenly wary. Had the woman gone back to sleep, or was she slipping into the forest? Had she been discovered?

Thora turned her back to the fire, picking her way through the trees and away from the camp. She moved as carefully as she could, keeping her cloak tight to her shoulders lest the sound of branches scraping across it alert her pursuer.

Slowly, she set her feet down, putting a little more distance between the camp and herself with each step.

Then, as she settled her foot on what she thought was solid ground, she felt and heard a twig snap.

She did not freeze, instead taking three more swift steps to distance herself from the sound. She slipped behind a tree, paused a moment, then took another four steps to round a sprawling bush.

There she crouched down, keeping her eyes low and breathing as softly as she could. For a while, it seemed that nothing followed. An owl hooted somewhere lower down the mountain.

Then, as Thora watched, she thought a shadow moved between her and the camp. Her eyes strained, but she could see nothing.

The wind moved through the pines, carrying with it the smell of smoke, snow, and roasting meat. The owl in the forest below hooted again, and the howl of wolves echoed in a distant pass.

Slowly, the muttered sound of voices returned. Whatever alarm they had taken seemed to have worn away. Minri and his company were back to eating and talking.

For a moment, Thora considered sneaking back through the woods toward them. She was curious why such a large group was working together. Minri was not known as the leader of a warband, and the year was growing late for such a large group to begin from nothing to lay aside their stores for the winter.

But something bothered her. The more she thought on it, the less she felt it, but something in her knew there was danger lurking in the forest about Minri's camp. The night's darkness was deep, the pines thick along the slope keeping at bay the little moonlight that slipped through the clouds.

She would be better off in the morning, when she could see clearly, and there was less chance of someone stumbling upon her unseen by lucky chance.

With a deep, quiet breath, Thora slipped up the slope, deeper into the trees. The glow of the fire slowly diminished as she crept slowly through the dark, the pine boughs reaching out as if to grasp her as she passed through them.

At last, when the camp below was only a tiny speck in the darkness, Thora wrapped herself in her cloak and crept close to the base of a great pine, and laid her head upon the needles. She closed her eyes, but for a while her ears still listened.

The wind blew as it should; the trees moved as they should, and yet the forest seemed still

---

When Thora woke the next morning, the dim light of dawn barely filtered through the pine boughs, and her fingers and feet were almost numb from the cold. She shivered as she crawled out from under the pine and surveyed where she was.

The ridges and rises of the mountainside rose up on either side of her, sloping down toward where she could hear the mountain stream rushing over the rocks, and where Minri had made his camp.

The strip of smoked deer in her pouch was enough to dull the pangs in her stomach as she circled down toward the campsite.

She crept slowly, careful that even if Minri or anyone else were listening for an intruder, they would not hear her.

When she was halfway down, she paused, for the smell of smoke was faint on the wind, and she could hear no sound from the camp.

"Patience is the hunter's greatest weapon," Leiban had taught her. "The hurried hunter often scares off his prey, or rushes in and becomes prey himself."

So she eased herself to the ground, her bow hanging across her back and her spear in her lap, and watched.

Her eyes moved back and forth through the trees, watching the wind move boughs and branches in a gentle swaying motion as it blew in gusts, strong and howling one moment, soft and whispering the next.

Still, she heard nothing, saw nothing, smelled nothing. She was about to rise and continue on when the wind rushed down the mountain again, bending trees and boughs before it as it went by.

When it was passed, the pines returned to their normal position, all save one.

The stillness of the pine caught Thora's attention as the trees all about it moved, but it remained still.

Slowly, she rose and moved down the mountainside. She drifted to the side, so she approached the tree from the west. Her feet made soft crunching sounds as they moved over the fallen pine needles.

A thin strip of rawhide held the pine in tension, disappearing into a pile of pine needles not far off. As Thora looked around, she saw the telltale sign of a deadfall deer trap that a few hunters used from time to time.

It was a nasty thing; when triggered, a loop beneath the pine needles would close around the target's foot, release the rock, and the pine would whip back to full height, pulling the caught animal upside down to hang helpless in the air.

In the mountains, where exiles and hunters used the same trails as the deer, it was frowned upon to use such a trap, and only the most desperate or careless hunters used them outside of the depths of winter.

But Thora had the suspicion it had not been left for a deer. It had been left for her. Carefully, she eased toward the rawhide, and with a quick thrust of her spear, severed the rawhide. It would not do to leave it set, even if it was not on a path.

She crept closer to the campsite, looking out for any similar traps, but she reached the clearing without spotting anymore of the bent trees. It was empty, as she had feared.

The leaves and pine needles had been brushed back over the filled in fire pit, and within a few days, there would be little sign anyone had camped there recently. Minri seemed to know more than a little of woodcraft, which was hardly surprising, as he had been an outlaw for several years.

Thora studied the campsite for only a short time. She knew how many she faced, and she did not like the idea of Minri gathering a group to himself so close to Dragonsrest.

She searched for the trail Minri had taken and soon found it. Three paths lead out of the clearing, but only one had been freshly brushed. Thora set out down, moving quickly, one ear listening for the sound of voices, the other listening to the sounds of the birds in the trees.

As a mist came in from the north, the gray light grew dimmer. The birds chirped and sang their quiet songs as they hopped about the branches overhead and Thora passed beneath, following Minri's trail.

The first moment Thora knew she was not alone was when a bird came to land on a nearby ridge that overlooked the path, then lifted up with two more following closely. The bird that had come down was brightly colored, a male, doubtless seeking a mate, and it launched back skyward with two dully colored female birds close behind.

It was a small thing, but it was wrong, and Thora froze, her eyes locked on the ridge as a shadow moved beneath a tree, and an arrow hummed past, the fletching brushing her cheek as she lurched backwards.

She tucked her feet and rolled again as a second arrow passed nearby, and she lunged for the protection of a nearby pine.

A third arrow followed her in, but the pine branches sent it skittering down to the ground, a shower of needles following it.

Snatching her bow from her back, Thora strung it and pulled an arrow from her belt, her eyes scanning the mountainside for any movement. But nothing moved save the trees swaying slowly in the wind. Overhead, the birds had gone silent or fled and the only sound that could be heard besides the wind was the rushing of a mountain stream far below.

Carefully, Thora steadied her breathing. There was a chance that her attacker had fled, or she might still wait just over the ridge.

But she suspected her attacker was the woman who had pursued her in the night, left the deer trap, and covered the campground, all things that Thora herself would have done.

And had Thora been the one lying in wait on the ridge, only to watch her prey escape and retreat, she would not wait for her prey.

Muttering a quick prayer to Skathi to guide her hunt, Thora lunged out from the pine and sprinted uphill, up the slope that led eventually toward the ridge.

A flash of movement above her showed she had guessed right, and as she darted through the trees, she paused one moment and loosed an arrow, just to keep her attacker wary.

Another arrow came toward her in answer, and as Thora glanced back from around a tree, she saw a dark-haired woman bounding back through the trees toward the ridge.

Thora gave chase, bounding along the slope toward her, leaping from one tree to the next, and swiftly closing the distance.

The woman reached the ridge and vaulted over the edge, dropping to the path below. Thora set an arrow to her string as she put on another burst of speed, and vaulted over the side without hesitation.

But even as her feet left the rock, she saw five outlaws below, waiting for her with weapons drawn.

She landed with a jarring thump, an arrow on her bow string as they eyed each other carefully.

The woman, her bow held to the side as she drew a knife from her belt, stepped forward. "Are you the one they call Ylmi One-Eye?"

Thora looked at the knife the woman held, the blade long and curved with a deer antler for a handle. "Are you the one they call Kassa Longknife?"

"You are alone, and a long way from help," the woman answered. "You will die as quickly as you answer our questions. I do not suggest you draw it out." Her hair was dirty, but tied back in a loose braid, and she had drawn coal over her face in a long dark line.

Thora took a deep breath. She held her bow tightly, but her fingers were itching for her spear. She had only a short skinning knife in her belt, along with a tiny ax better for chopping kindling than bones.

Aside from the woman, who she was sure was Kassa Longknife, three of the outlaws held axes and long knives. But one held a spear.

Thora glanced over her shoulder to where the pine tree she had hidden beneath stood. Somewhere beneath it, she had set her spear, but if Kassa was half as skilled with a bow as Thora had heard, she'd have four arrows in Thora before she made it halfway to the pine.

Kassa glared at her, and Thora glared back. She was acutely aware of her body, the blood pumping through her, the slight tremble of her muscles in eager anticipation of attack. Kassa's bow was the threat she most feared, but Kassa had moved to Thora's right, out of range for a quick shot. But then Kassa raised her knife, and Thora drew and loosed in one movement.

The man holding the spear dropped it and grabbed for his throat. Almost before it hit the ground, Thora snatched it up and thrust toward the closest outlaw, who leaped back out of range as Thora pushed forward, trying to keep the outlaws between her and Kassa's bow.

There was the twang of a bowstring as Thora leaped into the air, and she felt a pinch in her leg as she thrust her spear down, over the guard of another of the outlaws. The spearhead sank deep into his chest, and he dropped the ax as he stumbled to his knees.

But as she stepped back, Thora felt something wet running down her leg, and she looked down to see an arrow protruding from just above her knee.

"Drop your spear," Kassa called, but she had hardly spoken when they heard the distinct thum of a horn bow, and even as Kassa tried to duck, and arrow took her in the side and sent her tumbling off the path.

Thora took advantage of the distraction and with pain lancing through her leg, she lunged at another of the outlaws, swinging her spear in a short arc that left him choking on a slit throat.

The other two outlaws were already running, and Thora launched her spear with all the might she had . She bit back a cry as the pain lanced through her core, and she fell to the ground, her wounded leg held to the side as the spear sailed wide of its mark.

Snarling in disgust, she looked behind her to see Revik walking up the path. Shaking her head, Thora limped toward the edge of the path, where the mountain sloped steeply down to a rushing stream. Far below, the body of Kassa Longknife could be made out on the rocks.

"That doesn't look good," Revik said. He held his bow ready and glanced after the fleeing men.

"I've had worse," Thora snapped. With a deep breath, she looked around at the carnage. Three bodies lay bleeding on the path, the leaves and dirt torn and scattered about as if a boar had been rooting around. Some of her hair had come loose and was hanging in her face, and she shoved it back behind her ear.

With a deep breath, she clenched her teeth and twisted her leg so she could see the damage. Blood soaked her rawhide pants, but she let out a sigh of relief at the sight of the arrow head protruding from the back of her leg. Cutting an arrow out of a leg was a nasty business, and a good way to die. If the blood loss didn't get you, the infection would.

She touched the protruding arrow head gently and winced, the bone tip had not come all the way out. Setting her teeth, she shoved the arrow deeper, till the shaft was visible on the other side of her leg.

"I can take care of that," Revik knelt beside her, but she shoved him away.

"I can handle it," she snapped. "Look out and make sure they don't come running back with help before I can get this cursed thing out of my leg."

Revik nodded and stood as Thora drew her knife and cut a small notch in the arrow shaft. That done, she snapped it in one sudden, painful jerk. Her fingers were slick with blood, but she could still get enough purchase on the shaft to pull the rest of the arrow from her leg.

She tossed the upper part away in disgust, but stuck the iron head in her belt.

"You're going to keep that?" Revik asked.

"Keep watch," Thora answered, "Unless you want to be on the receiving end of the next ambush."

Revik chuckled. "We should move off the path a ways, and make camp ourselves." He nodded toward her leg. "You should stay off that a few days at least."

Thora glared at him. "I've dragged a dead bear over two mountains with a bigger hole in my leg than this. I'm not letting Minri get away just because someone stuck an arrow in me." She moved herself toward the nearest outlaw. "Even if it was Kassa Longknife who shot me."

Most of what he wore was furs, but his shirt had been made of wool, and Thora cut a long, thick strip from it.

"Who is Kassa Longknife?"

Thora wrapped the strip of wool around her leg, keeping it as tight as she could. "The woman you shot when all this started." She glanced up. "You should probably make sure she's dead."

As Revik turned and walked toward the slope, Thora tied off the bandage. It sagged more than she liked, so she pulled herself to her feet and limped toward the nearest pine. She cut a branch that was thick enough and stripped away the bark. Setting it under the top layer of the bandage, she twisted it so it drew the wrapping tight, then tucked the ends under the rest of the bandage to keep it tight.

The pressure felt good, and she took a deep breath.

A few yards away, Revik peered down the slope, to where the body lay on the rocks. "She's dead," he said, before turning back to Thora. "Or at least should be. Arrow took her in the heart, and that is a long fall."

"So," he said slowly. "I think we should discuss what is going on here. Because we came here to hunt Minri, yet I find you fighting someone else… Are these hills just full of outlaws and no one mentioned it to me?"

"They're all working with Minri," Thora said. Walking was less painful, and blood was no longer pouring from her leg. "I tracked them from Leiban's hut, which they ransacked. And I saw Minri last night. I was following them, or trying to, before Kassa ambushed me."

"Kassa is an outlaw, too?"

Thora picked up her bow from where it had fallen and brushed away the dirt. "She killed her mother over some dispute, and King Viglir outlawed her a couple of years ago. I had not heard that she and Minri were working together, but it seems they were."

"Hm." Revik looked up toward the faint path that led uphill and further into the mountains. "You think the one who got away is heading for Minri?"

Thora put her bow under her opposite leg, pausing a moment to think her way through a movement she had done instinctively for years, and unstrung her bow. "That is my guess… though it's possible he's done something different. Kassa was known for her woodcraft, and it nearly fooled me several times today."

"Is she the one who has left those deer traps everywhere?" Revik asked.

Thora nodded.

"Well," Revik looked around, "let's set up camp, then get you back to Dragonsrest."

"No." Thora moved toward the pine where she had left her spear. Her leg hurt, but it was nothing she couldn't work through.

"No?" Revik asked. "Thora, your pants are half red. Let's get you back, get you taken care of."

"And let you claim the glory for killing Minri?" Thora asked. "Not a chance. I haven't forgotten our wager."

Revik laughed. "You are stubborn, but we did not know there were others with Minri when the wager was made, so if you are willing, we will lay it aside. You are injured, and I do not wish…"

"I am not willing." Thora snarled at him. "And you may keep your sympathy to yourself." She snatched up her spear and looked down the path. "Minri means no good for us, and I do not intend to let Minri go on killing about Dragonsrest. The two of us will deal with this matter and report back to Ylmi when it is done."

Revik looked at her out of the side of his eye, but she glared back until he shrugged. "Very well."

They quickly picked over the dead, taking a butt of hardened bread from one, and a pouch of dried meat from another. Thora took up one of the small axes that lay near its fallen owner and stuck it in her belt. It was longer than her small ax and would serve her well enough if she were separated from her spear again.

Kassa had dropped her knife when Revik's arrow had struck her, and her quiver had fallen on the side of the path, spilling arrows as she had fallen. Revik stooped to pick them up, but Thora limped toward him as he did so.

"Give me a few of those," Thora said. "You only got them because she stopped to fight me."

"Fair enough," Revik shrugged. There were eight arrows left in the quiver, three of which had iron heads, the others were of carved bone.

"Five, with one iron?" Revik asked. "Or three with two iron heads."

"Three," Thora snatched the arrows from his hand and glanced up the path. The trees higher up were moving in the wind, and as she slipped the arrows into her own quiver, she muttered a prayer to Skathi to keep the storms at bay long enough for her to kill Minri.

"I was hoping you'd take those," Revik grinned. "I hate making arrows."

"That's cause your fingers are too big," Thora muttered. "And you have no patience."

Revik said nothing, but bent to take the long, curved bladed knife from which Kassa had taken her name.

"She killed her mother?" He asked as he looked at the blade.

Thora checked the bandage on her leg and took a step uphill. "That is what they said. Now come."

They set off down the trail where the remaining outlaw had disappeared, hurrying along a well-marked track of trampled brush and bruised limbs.

They found Minri's most recent campsite as night was falling. It was empty, the firepit still smoking as they came in. The sun had set long ago, and clouds were smothering the few stars that had crept out.

Thora examined the fire as Revik looked over the rest of the tiny clearing. A stiff wind was blowing out of the north, the howling of it mingling with the noise of the icy stream rushing downhill only a few yards away.

"How long ago?" Revik asked her.

Thora shook her head. "It couldn't have been long. The wood is still smoking." She glanced at the pattern of the ashes; the outline of sticks still visible where they had lain undisturbed as the fire ate them. "Perhaps an hour... they seem to have left without putting out the fire."

"They left without more than that," Revik held up a thin cloak. "It seems they left in a hurry."

Thora looked around the clearing. Why would they have fled so suddenly? Were they setting up another ambush?

"Perhaps they think they are being hunted by a war party?" Revik suggested. "When they attacked Leiban, they had to be afraid he would raise an alarm after them, and the one who fled did not stay long enough to see it was only I who was after you."

Thora considered. "Perhaps." She made to rise, but her leg buckled under her, throbbing dully as she tried to move.

"They will not go far," Revik looked up through the pine branches at the dark sky. "Not tonight. They are as likely to get lost or fall to their death as they are to do anything else. And you will be in better condition to fight tomorrow if you get some rest tonight."

Thora took a deep breath, but she was tired, and the wound in her leg was more painful than it had been.

"Fine," she muttered. "But you're getting the firewood."

Revik's only response was to laugh as he lumbered into the woods.

Night had fallen dark and deep when at last they sat beside the fire, and Thora undid her bandage. Blood still seeped out of the hole, and with a sick feeling, Thora knew what she needed to do. Drawing her knife, she set it by the fire.

"You should clean it before you do that," Revik suggested.

"Are you my mother?" Thora snapped. "Because you seem to have nothing useful to add."

Revik shrugged. "It was just a thought. By all means, do as you please. But if you get an infection, I'm not cutting your leg off for you."

Thora glared at him. "Why are you here, anyway?"

"Because chopping logs for that boat is boring, and I thought I might get to chop a few heads."

"It feels as though you're just here to annoy me."

Revik pulled himself to his feet. "I feel like I saved you back there... so perhaps that's why I'm out here."

"I had the situation under control," Thora glanced at the bandage. "I could have taken them. I helped kill that dragon too."

"Sure," Revik grinned, but before she could respond he had disappeared in the darkness.

An instant later he reappeared, dropping his water skin in her lap, filled to the brim with the icy water of the stream.

"Thanks," Thora muttered. Revik went back to gnawing on the little food they had brought with them, and Thora poured the water over her leg, washing away the dried blood.

"I can do that for you if you want," Revik offered, but Thora waved him off.

"It'll be better if I can see where it's going to hurt." She answered. "I dislike being burned still, but I'd prefer if I'm the one doing it."

In a quick motion that left no time for thinking, she took her knife from the coals and pressed it to the wound. There was a hiss, and for an instant she felt nothing.

Then, the pain hit. For a moment she saw white, and the smell of her own burning flesh made her sick. She set the knife down with numb fingers, a sudden relief coming over her.

"How did you find them?" She asked as she leaned back against the tree. Her hands were shaking and she could feel sweat on her forehead despite the cold.

"I climbed to a very high place," Revik answered. "And looked for smoke."

Thora grimaced. "I would have killed them all..."

"I don't doubt that you would have," Revik chuckled. "I saw you fight the dragon... but there is no need to hog all the glory. This is not a small deed, the slaying of Minri and his band, and it is even greater since it is accomplished by only two."

Thora stared into the fire. "I want Minri dead."

"He will be," Revik said quietly. "Soon." He chewed slowly, a habit both of them shared, born of scant food and long hunger. "You seem very intent on killing Minri, but I have never thought of you as one who yearns for glory..."

"You can have your glory," Thora said, picking at the strips of dried venison. She found one small enough she would not feel guilty for eating it, yet big enough she could chew it for a long while. "I want Minri dead for what he did to Leiban."

Revik looked confused. "Is he your uncle?"

Thora glared at him. "No."

"Then why are you so concerned with him?" Revik asked. "He's not even from the village…"

"I care that outlaws do not wound my friends," Thora snapped back at him. "Is that so hard to get through your head? Or does it not come with enough glory for you?"

Revik raised his hands. "Thora Longspear I wish no quarrel with you, now or ever. I am sorry I gave offense." They stared at each other for a moment, then Revik turned back to picking apart his dried meat.

Off in the distance, Thora heard the night birds calling to each other, and their small fire flickered and crackled behind the screen. Thora glanced at the water skin that lay beside her leg, half empty of the water Revik had brought, and sighed.

"I lost my parents when I was very young," Thora began softly. "Leiban was one of those who raised me. Almir took me on my first hunts, but it was Leiban who taught me the most. He gave me my first spear, taught me to hunt boar and bear, showed me how to fend for myself."

She knew she should not stare at the fire, should keep her eyes on the shadows, but there was something in her eye and if she moved, she would have to wipe the tear that was threatening to fall.

"I hoped he might move into the village, now that Unhost is gone… but he said that Ylmi had enough on her to plate without worrying how to feed and house one who was comfortable enough in the mountains."

She took a deep breath of the chilly night air and let it out slowly.

"I will kill Minri for what he did to my friend." Her voice was cold and hard, and she turned her eyes on Revik. "I am a woman of few friends… I have no sister nor brother, and aside from Ylmi there are few in the village who would care if I was gone. Now even Ylmi is drawn away, for the work of a jarl is never done. Almir, Oscar, Leiban, the old hunters of these mountains, they are my friends, the ones who have loved me as their own. I will not lose them before their time."

Revik nodded slowly. "I think I begin to understand you a little more, Thora of the mountains. We will slay Minri. Against the both of us, he stands no chance ."

They took turns sleeping that night and when morning came, they set out.

But Minri had a head start, and he pushed his band hard, twisting and turning through the mountains so Thora and Revik seemed to always been just within a bird's flight of catching them.

Ever Thora pushed onward, though her leg did not grow less painful as they hunted Minri mile after mile.

Neither Thora nor Revik had any problem following his trail. With Kassa gone, it seemed there was no one else with Minri who could match her in woodcraft.

But what he lacked in skill, Minri made up for in speed. Twice, Revik and Thora came within sight of him. Once, as he crossed a ridge, climbing out of the valley, Thora saw the movement above them. She loosed an arrow, even though it was a far shot, with wind blowing strong.

But though she held wide to the left, the wind still took the arrow, and it skittered off a rock a few feet to the right of Minri.

The second time, it was Revik who saw them first, slipping across a mountain stream and over a cliff. His horn bow hummed, and Thora snapped an arrow after them as well, but the distance was still great, and Mirni had seen them.

He and the last of his companions slid over the cliff, and by the time Revik could cross the stream and arrive at the cliff, they had climbed down and disappeared.

But on the morning of the fifth day, Minri turned his path between two ridges, and Thora knew he was trapped.

"There is but one way out," she told Revik. "A narrow pass that leads eventually to Garhom. But this valley twists north before it rises to the pass, and I know a path that will lead us there before him if we head north now."

Revik nodded, considering a moment.

"You go north to the pass. I will chase after Minri." He said. "That way, we may be sure he will not escape us."

"Then be swift." Thora replied.

So they parted, and Thora summoned the last of her strength for one final push. Her leg burned and ached, hunger filled her stomach, and every muscle felt as though it was filled with stones.

The dragon burns along the side of her body had begun to sting in the cold, and along her fingers and neck, where the wind could pick at them, they bothered her most of all. But she pushed on with the renewed hope that the hunt was near its end. Over the slope she ran, dragging her leg when it refused to obey, and gritting her teeth at her body's failing strength.

———◆———

She came to the pass as the first drops of rain fell from the clouds, and she glanced up warily as lightning flashed somewhere in the clouds overhead.

She pressed her tongue to the top of her mouth, tasting it. There was no taste of metal, but Thora's fear did not pass. The top of a mountain pass was no place to be when the lighting was at play, and more than one careless hunter had found themselves blasted by lightning in the pass.

Setting down her spear, Thora bent low over the ground and crept toward edge of a rock, and looked down into the valley.

Below, she could see five men striding wearily up the winding path that led up to the pass. The tallest, she guessed to be Minri, though he walked in the middle of the pack.

"Where are you Revik?" she muttered. Wiping away the rain that dripped down her face, she pulled the hood on her cloak and looked again at where Minri and his band were climbing. They were closer now, just within bowshot, and Thora drew back from the edge of the pass.

Light flashed, and thunder boomed overhead.

She drew all her arrows, only four now, and laid them beside her. Gingerly, she strung her bow, wincing as the rain fell on the string.

"We're almost over," she heard a voice shout. "Not far. We'll head north to Garhom and pick up some friends and have that bitch's village before the first snow falls."

She set an arrow to her bow and rose, her leg screaming in pain as she did so. The first outlaw gasped when he saw her, but her arrow buried itself in his throat before he could move.

Thunder boomed again, and overhead lightning split the sky.

Thora loosed another arrow, striking Minri full in the chest, but the big man only grunted as he snapped off the arrow.

She loosed a third, which struck Minri just below the first.

"Don't just stand there!" Minri roared as he snapped off the second arrow. "Kill her!"

Thora loosed her fourth arrow at another outlaw. He stumbled as the arrow sank into his chest and fell to the ground.

The other two outlaws raised their spears and charged as Thora reached for her knife and ax. She stepped back as they came over the edge of the pass spears held high. But as they roared, Thora tasted metal on her tongue.

She dove away from the pass as the world exploded into noise and fire and blinding, stunning, brilliant light.

How long she laid there, Thora wasn't sure, but her first thought was that Minri still lived.

She had to get up, she had to find him. She blinked and looked around as her vision slowly returned, but all she saw was the rain falling on the pass. Ears ringing, she pulled herself to her feet. The lighting had touched her, but only barely. Its greater force had been spent on the two outlaws who now lay in black and smoldering heaps atop the pass.

Thora pulled herself up, spitting mud and bits of rock from her mouth, and limped over the pass edge.

Below, Revik had arrived.

He stood toe to toe with Minri, each armed with knives as they wrestled back and forth. Revik was larger, only barely, but enough. He gripped Minri in his arms and slowly drove him back, off the path, into the rocks, and then, as Minri's feet caught, Revik slammed him backwards to the ground, driving his knife deep into Minri's chest.

Thora let out a breath as she leaned against a stone, her shoulders slumping in weariness. Her ears were ringing, and her whole body felt as though she had been caught in an avalanche.

She wiped a bit of the blood and grit from her face as it mingled with the rain. Below, Revik rose from the ground and turned back to where his ax had fallen.

But, out of the mud, Minri staggered to his feet, blood dripping from his face and soaking his beard as he rose like a rabid bear from hibernation. His teeth were bared, and he snarled as he lunged toward Revik.

Revik turned, and walking toward him, swung his ax. Even at through the rain, it hummed through the air, and through Minri's neck.

Thora came down slowly, limping more with each step as she picked her way down through the rocks. She paused and stared down at the bloody body of Minri, his head snarling up at the sky.

"He is dead then." She said. "It is good." She let out a deep breath and wiped away the rain from her face. Her muscles ached, and she felt the beginnings of a cramp in their

"If I am not mistaken," Revik said. "Those are your arrows in his chest... it seems we both had a hand in killing him."

"The wager was to deal a death blow." Thora answered. "You are the victor in that, and I have no qualms about it. We have slain Minri and given Leiban his vengeance... and Dragonsrest is safer for it."

Thus Revik Dragonsbane and Thora Longspear slew the Outlaw Minri and his band, which sought to bring harm to Dragonsrest.

Character List

Almir: Old hunter of Ylmi's village and friend of Thora

Birin: Jarl of Mirhom

Bodvar Miriksson: The herdsman of Dragonsrest, and father of Ylmi

Bogli: A herdsman from Ylmi's village, crippled in fighting against Viglir

Darros: A member of Ylmi's village, husband of Nanni, killed in fighting against Viglir.

Dranri: A wandering hunter making his living in the mountains, a friend to Ylmi.

Dunharvik: The Rider of Death, Who comes in the dead of winter to take those who's time has come.

Dvengrhal: A figure who spoke to Ylmi & Karik upon the Watching Stones of Vranr, though they know little else of him.

Elva: Karik's Mother

Ethna: Blacksmith and wife of Ymr

Fianna: An exile who comes to Ylmi's village seeking shelter with her two young children

Flovi Grimsson: A hunter from Ylmi's village and friend of Unhost

Fornik Leivsson: Unhost's closest supporter

Gorli: Tax man and thane of King Jarhost

Hald: Karik's Father

Hald Haldsson: Karik's older brother

Hathi: Thane of Jarhost and skilled swordsman

Harvik Bulisson: A warrior of Bjarnmont and ill-fated champion of Jarhost.

Havar Ivarsson: A skilled boatbuilder who hungered for more.

Hegli: Jarl of the Undmir

Henla: Daughter of Fianna

Igil Tormsson: Younger brother of Revik, and a skilled boat builder

Ingbert: Jarl of Girstadt

Ingbor: Jarl of Yrdnara

Jarhost: King of Western Vrania, ruling from his hall in Bjarnmont

Jarvik Jarhostsson: Oldest son of King Jarhost

Karik Haldsson: The son of Hald, leader of the exiles from Yrdnara

Kivli: Nanni's youngest son.

Lanvir Bodvarsson: Ylmi's older brother, believed to have been killed by the dragon.

Lasvik Horsson: Champion of Jarl Hegli, a skilled and accomplished warrior

Leiban Longspear: A wandering hunter in the mountains, a close friend of Thora and Ylmi

Mirn: Karik's younger brother

Nanni: A gardener in Ylmi's village, and widow of Darros

Orlanna: Former acquaintance of Dranri and wise woman

Olga: Skilled gardener and wise woman in Ylmi's village

Olvik: Jarl of Garhom

Orli the Tall: A fisherman in Ylmi's village, and a close friend of Unhost.

Osric: Wandering hunter in the mountains and a friend of Ylmi.

Regvar the Mighty: A warrior of Jarhost and often companion of Gorli

Revik Tormsson (Also called Revik Dragonsbane): Elder brother of Igil, mightiest of Karik's companions

Rivna: Queen and wife of Jarhost.

Siggi: Wife to Bodvar, Mother of Ylmi, and skilled gardener

Skathi: The Lady of Snow and Ice, Arbiter of Vengeance.

Sol: The wife of Vranr, and according to legend, a princess of a kingdom in the west.

Tanvir Heglisson: Son of Hegli and prince of the Undmir

Thora Wilthasdottir (Also called Thora Longspear): Skilled huntress, and close friend of Ylmi.

Torig Ingsson: Fisherman with fingers almost as sharp as his tongue

Torin: Husband of Wiltha, and with her founded the little settlement in the north.

Torm: Son of Fianna

Ulfr: Ylmi's wolf companion

Umir Malsson: A member of Karik's company, as skilled in the forests as with an ax

Unhost: The Jarl of a little settlement in the north west of Vrania.

Viglir: King of Eastern Vrania, ruling from him hall in Torhom

Vingir: Lord of the Hunt, Watcher of the Forests

Vranr: A half mythical figure, part trickster, part warrior. Ancestor of all who live in Vrania

Wiltha: One of the founders of Ylmi's little settlement. She was also the mother of Thora and sister of Unhost.

Wisic Unlisson: A member of Karik's company, and a skilled fisherman with a quick wit.

Ylmi Siggisdottir (Also called Ylmi One-eye): A skilled huntress in the north, and friend of Thora

THE SHIPS OF VRANIA

Kalborg: The first ship built by Havar and Igil. Longer than the common fishing boats, it was still kept small for ease of maneuvering. It could carry twenty, and be crewed by as few as three. It was in this ship that the Dragonslayers traversed the Undersea and stole from Jarl Hegli.

Sea Dragon: The first great ship built by Havar and Igil for the crossing of the Black Isles. The sail was made by Orlanna and the women of Ylmi's village. This was the first great ship built in Vrania.

Places

The Black Isles: A ring of jagged, black rock that rises out of the sea about Vrania. While some rise high in the air, others lurk just below the waves,

Bjarnmont: The mountain hall where Jarhost rules, high above the coastlands.

Girhom: A mountain village in Gar's Pass. Ruled by Jarl Olvik, it is often under attack by King Viglir

Girstadt: A small fishing village north of Yrdnara

The Ice Marsh: A great marsh in the far north of Vrania, but south west of the Undmir. Full of freezing, icy water it is swept by winds blowing out of the north.

The Ice Sea: The sea north of of Vrania, filled with ice and tossed by storms it is more dangerous than the Black Isles only because of its occasional calm that can lull inexperience sailors to their death.

The Undmir: A fortress of stone built above a great under ground sea that pours in from the north.

The Watching Stones: Ancient stones atop a cliff face, said to have been built by Vranr.

Yrdnara: A small coastal village, and the first home of Karik

ACKNOWLEDGMENTS

One of the best things about writing is the wonderful people I get to discuss my work with and learn from as I go through the writing process. When I first started this journey, I had the beginning of an idea about Karik and his adventures, and as Karik and his friends grow and improve, I feel as though I'm doing a bit of the same as a writer. That process can only happen with the help and insight of others who can give you objective feedback about your writing, characters, and stories.

As always, many thanks to the editors, Clem Flanigan, Susan Barnes, and Leah Cossette for their insight and help in pulling a coherent story out of Karik & Ylmi's adventures. As Vrania has expanded and grown, their help has been invaluable to shaping characters, streamlining ideas, and polishing the world.

Thank you also to the numerous proofreaders, Matt McAvoy and Ebook Launch, and who have worked to pick the errant commas, ellipses and typos out of each of these three stories.

Thank you also to my parents, who filled their home with tales and sagas which fired my young mind, and gave me a hunger for epic tales and wondrous heroes.

As always, any literary work of mine would be incomplete without thanking my grandparents, John and Scherry. They were patient with a young boy over confident in half formed opinions, and have provided love, encouragement, and much appreciated instruction as I've grown. Your continued support, love, and encouragement inspire and motivate me every day, and I can't wait to show you what comes next.

Most of all, I want to thank my wife, who is my biggest encouragement, and Revik's first fan. Her insight, keen eye, and support are why this story exists the way it does. Without her I could not have built it the way I have.

Finally, thank you to all my readers. For an indie author, it is such a thrill to see when people enjoy your story and it is a huge boost, especially when I'm struggling to corral characters and plot points together. A special thanks to those of you who leave reviews or email me, being able to hear what you enjoyed about Karik & Ylmi's world is a real blessing. I'm looking forward to sharing new stories and tales with you going forward!

About the Author

Evan was raised in Texas, graduated from Texas A&M University, and splits his time between old stories, lifting heavy things, and gardening. He is fascinated with the old bards and their stories and now seeks to tell a few tales for modern readers that hark back to the richness and depth of the old masters.

Evan lives in Texas with his incredible wife and hypercuddly dog, and when he's not writing or working, he's trying to get his garden to grow more than one type of plant at a time. He has published the short story series The Blades of Karik and is preparing the fourth installment of The Legends of Karik. To stay up to date on his upcoming books as well as special offers and giveaways, check out his website Evanoliverauthor.com